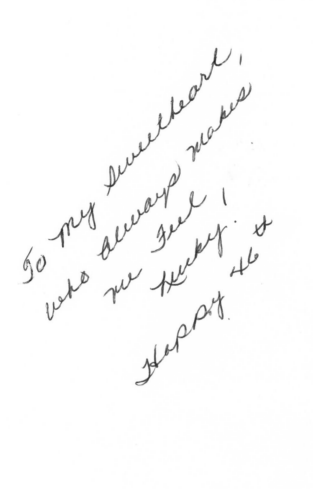

To my sweetheart,
who always makes
me feel
lucky.
Happy 46

HEY, COWBOY, WANNA GET LUCKY?

Other Books by Baxter Black

The Cowboy and His Dog
A Rider, A Roper, and a Heck'uva Windmill Man
On the Edge of Common Sense, The Best So Far
Doc, While Yer Here
Coyote Cowboy Poetry
Buckaroo History
Croutons on a Cow Pie
The Buckskin Mare
Cowboy Standard Time
Croutons on a Cow Pie, Volume II
Dunny and the Duck

Hey, Cowboy, Wanna Get Lucky?

Baxter Black

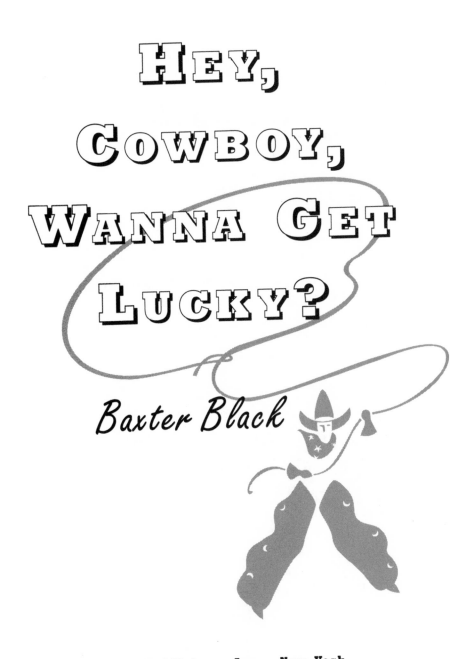

Crown Publishers, Inc. New York

The poems "Legacy of the Rodeo Man" and "Friend Is a Word" are from *Coyote Cowboy Poetry*, copyright © 1986 by Baxter Black. The poem "Junior" is from *Croutons on a Cow Pie, Volume II*, copyright © 1992 by Baxter Black.

Published by Crown Publishers, Inc., 201 East 50th Street, New York, New York 10022. Member of the Crown Publishing Group.

Random House, Inc. New York, Toronto, London, Sydney, Auckland

CROWN is a trademark of Crown Publishers, Inc.

Manufactured in the United States of America

Library of Congress Cataloging-in-Publication Data
Black, Baxter,
    Hey, Cowboy, wanna get lucky? / Baxter Black. — 1st ed.
       p.   cm.
    1. Cowboys—West (U.S.)—Fiction.   2. Rodeos—West (U.S.)—
Fiction.   I. Title.
PS3552.L288H4   1994
813'.54—dc20
                                              93-40603
                                              CIP

ISBN 0-517-59377-7

10   9   8   7   6   5   4   3   2   1

First Edition

*Dedicated to Harley May,
World Champion Steer Wrestler of 1952, 1956 and 1965, and
president of the Rodeo Cowboys Association 1957–1960.
He is the only person in the history of
professional rodeo to have placed in the top fifteen in
all seven events at one time or another.*

*When Baxter asked Harley how today's rodeo
cowboys differed from rodeo cowboys in his day,
Harley replied wistfully,
"Nobody robs a bank anymore."*

LEGACY OF THE RODEO MAN

*There's a hundred years of history and a hundred before
  that*
All gathered in the thinkin' goin' on beneath his hat.
*And back behind his eyeballs and pumpin' through his
  veins*
Is the ghost of every cowboy that ever held the reins.

Every coil in his lasso's been thrown a million times
*His quiet concentration's been distilled through ancient
  minds.*
It's evolution workin' when the silver scratches hide
*And a ghostly cowboy chorus fills his head and says,
  "Let's ride."*

The famous and the rowdy, the savage and the sane
The bluebloods and the hotbloods and the corriente strain
All knew his mother's mothers or was his daddy's kin
'Til he's nearly purely cowboy, born to ride and bred to win.

BLACK

He's got Buffalo Bill Cody and Goodnight's jigger boss
And all the brave blue soldiers that General Custer lost
The ghost of Pancho Villa, Sittin' Bull and Jessie James
All gathered by his campfire keepin' score and takin'
    names.

There's every Royal Mountie that ever got his man
And every day-work cowboy that ever made a hand
Each man that's rode before him, yup, every mother's son
Is in his corner, rootin', when he nods to make his run.

Freckles Brown might pull his bull rope, Casey Tibbs
    might jerk the flank,
Bill Pickett might be hazin' when he starts to turn the
    crank
Plus Remington and Russell lookin' down his buckhorn
    sight
All watchin' through the window of this cowboy's eyes
    tonight.

And standin' in the catch pen or in chute number nine
Is the offspring of a mountain that's come down from
    olden time
A volcano waitin' quiet, 'til they climb upon his back
Rumblin' like the engine of a freight train on the track.

A cross between a she bear and a bad four wheel drive
With the fury of an eagle when it makes a power dive
A snake who's lost its caution or a badger gone berserk
He's a screamin', stompin', clawin', rabid, mad dog piece
    o' work.

From the rollers in his nostrils to the foam upon his lips
From the hooves as hard as granite to the horns with
    dagger tips
From the flat black starin' shark's eye that's the mirror of
    his soul

Shines the challenge to each cowboy like the devil callin' roll.

In the seconds that tick slowly 'til he climbs upon his back
Each rider faces down the fear that makes his mouth go
slack
And cuts his guts to ribbons and gives his tongue a coat
He swallows back the panic gorge that's risin' in his
throat.

The smell of hot blue copper fills the air around his head
Then a single, solid, shiver shakes away the doubt and
dread
The cold flame burns within him 'til his skin's as cold as ice
And the dues he paid to get here are worth every sacrifice

All the miles spent sleepy drivin', all the money down
the drain
All the "if I's" and the "nearly's," all the bandages and pain
All the female tears left dryin', all the fever and the fight
Are just a small downpayment on the ride he makes
tonight.

And his pardner in this madness that the cowboys call
a game
Is a ton of buckin' thunder bent on provin' why he came
But the cowboy never wavers he intends to do his best
And of that widow maker he expects of him no less.

There's a solemn silent moment that every rider knows
When time stops on a heartbeat like the earth itself was
froze
Then all the ancient instinct fills the space between his ears
'Til the whispers of his phantoms are the only thing he
hears

When you get down to the cuttin' and the leather touches
hide

And there's nothin' left to think about, he nods and says,
   "Outside!"
Then frozen for an instant against the open gate
Is hist'ry turned to flesh and blood, a warrior incarnate.

And while they pose like statues in that flicker of an eye
There's somethin' almost sacred, you can see it if you try.
It's guts and love and glory—one mortal's chance at fame
His legacy is rodeo and cowboy is his name.

"Turn 'im out."

HEY,
COWBOY,
WANNA GET
LUCKY?

This is the tale of two rodeo cowboys named Lick and Cody. The story might just as well have been about two baseball players named Duke and Pee Wee, two country singers named George and Tammy, or the pros from Dover. But I, the author, am most familiar with the sport of rodeo and have been to the towns and cities where rodeo cowboys ply their trade.

In their quest to qualify for the National Finals (the Superbowl of rodeo), thus furnishing a plot, Lick and Cody expose themselves to considerable adventure and philosophical examination.

To those of you who follow rodeo: you will recognize the scenery and the characters, both quad- and bi-pedal. If this book is your first trip "back of the chutes," I offer this brief introductory explanation of the sport. Rodeo is divided into timed events (roping, bulldogging and barrel racing) and roughstock events (bareback bronc riding, saddle bronc riding and bull riding).

Our two cowboys compete in the roughstock events, specializing in the bull riding. The bulls and broncs are as varied in their personality and athletic ability as the cowboys who try to ride them. It is also important to remember that as hard as the bull and the rider compete against each other, neither would have a job without the other. It is a weird sort of partnership fraught with mutual antagonism and mutual respect.

Professional rodeo has evolved as a sport. Today the National Finals takes place in Las Vegas, Nevada. The amount of money won by contestants has grown significantly over the years. Although there are still many "characters" competing, the contestants are regarded as professional athletes.

From 1965 to 1984, the National Finals Rodeo was held in Oklahoma City. It was a golden time when rodeo was populated with colorful, flamboyant, hard ridin', hard playin' riders of the purple sage. My story is set near the end of this time period when the contestants, though professionals, were still thought of as cowboys.

As to the telling of this tale, it is the prerogative of an author to interrupt a story's narrative now and then. True, the good authors never exercise this cheesy little device, but they often wish they had. All they need is nerve.

I interrupt when I feel a rescue is necessary. A rescue of you, or Lick and Cody, or myself. I like to think one of us gets a welcome respite this way.

I invite you to ride along with me. I promise you a modest smattering of sex, violence, intrigue and the occasional philosophical observation.

We shall experience, in addition to a walk on the wacko and wild side of rodeo, these universal phenomena:

> The significance of the slow dance
> The misconception that it is easy to be irresponsible
> Equal opportunity highwaymen
> Fear
> The existence of second string guardian angels
> Doubt
> Camels, cowboys, pool players, buckaroos and bigots
> The color purple
> Love
> Interspecies marriage as an option
> And moonlight

The gate blew open like the lid comin' off a boxcar full'a dynamite! Like a lateral from the Bionic Man! Like straddlin' the *Hindenberg* and strikin' a match!

It's hard to believe a creature that weighed eighteen hundred and fifty pounds could duck and dive like a point guard for the Boston Celtics. His feet left tracks the size of a human face and pounded quarter moons into the dirt. As he spun in front of the chute, he kicked so high a freeze-frame showed him standin' on his head! He demanded attention like a runaway truck on a 7 percent grade! He was big and sleek and fast and all business!

Then he faked to the left and set-shot his rider from the three-point line! Cody Wing, bull rider, hit the ground like a bag of loose salt! His lights went out. It was dark inside his brain. Little paramedic neurons groped for the fuse box. Finally tiny pinholes brightened and began to flicker on the backside of his eyelids. Far off a noise tinkled at the edge of his hearing.

His eyelid fluttered, then opened. His pupil slid into sight. The sounds of concern began to piece themselves into recognizable words:

"... ambulance. Good thinking ..."

"Look, he's comin' around!"

"Cody, can you hear me? Are you all right?"

Miming a tropical fish, Cody replied, "Spand ... stpand ... sisspand ..."

"Spam?"

3

"Sisstand ..."

"Stand? What is it, Cody? Talk slow!"

"Yer sisstanding on my hand!"

"Oh! Yeah, sorry. Here, see if you can git up."

Lick gently hefted Cody to his feet. "I think he's okay, boys. I'll take care of him."

"A no-score for Cody Wing! All that cowboy gets is your applause!" The announcer summed up Cody's rodeo career.

The two walked back behind the buckin' chutes. Lick supported his partner as they slogged through the heavy arena dirt. The bull riding continued and the crowd roared on. Lick gathered up the tools of their trade and they headed for the pickup.

"My head hurts," observed Cody, palpating his temples like a ripe avocado.

"No wonder. Looked like he conked you good. You were out for awhile. You okay?"

"Dizzy is all, but I reckon I'll git over it. Did I make the buzzer?"

"Not quite. Close though," answered Lick.

"What now?" asked Cody.

"The dance, I guess."

Cody and Lick were traveling companions, confidants, soul brothers and close as a pair of dice in a crapshooter's hand. They both wrote "rodeo cowboy" under "Occupation" on their tax returns. They made good traveling partners despite their obvious differences. For starters they resembled each other the way a broken gate resembles a bowling ball. Cody was certainly the handsomer of the two. At 6'0", he was tall for a roughstock rider. Had he led a normal life he would have weighed 185. As it was, he was fifteen pounds underweight. He had light brown hair, was clean-cut and clean-shaven. Lick, at 5'9", weighed a solid 160. He wore a size nine boot, had black shaggy hair and a thick black mustache. You only knew he was smiling by his eyes. He carried the coloring of his Spanish grandfather.

They parked outside the Lehi Legion Hall. Smokey and the Orem Ramblers were bangin' through their version of "Good Hearted Woman." The thumping bass carried out into the street.

Cody and Lick milled around in the parking lot for twenty minutes, trying to devise some clever way to sneak into the dance. The lady at the door finally came over and explained to them that if they were contestants, they could get in free. They had to leave their beer outside.

Like two hoot owls, they entered the henhouse.

Cody stood to the side and Lick dove into the fray. Cody waited. A lion on the edge of the savannah. What was not apparent to the King of the Jungle was that the gazelles had already set out their decoys. They watched from their cowboy blind as Cody sniffed the air. It wouldn't take long.

Small town rodeos have small town dances. They are attended by small town girls. Small town girls like to be around chivalrous knights of the rope and the range. Snuff-dippin' dragon fighters engaged in that primitive ritual of impressing the female of the species. The smaller the town, the further a knight can be from the Round Table. Cody was a congressman's salary away from the National Finals!

He circled and stepped up to Kim. Kim was ready. One should never assume that small town girls are naive. They have watched the courtship protocol among dogs, dairy cows and ruffed grouse. They have seen a wrecker back up to a disabled Ford Fairlane. They've been trolling all their lives. They know how to set a hook.

"Like to dance?" asked Cody.

"Umm ..." Kim said, waiting to hear what the next song would be. She knew a fast dance would put her at a disadvantage in employing her powers. A slow one, on the other hand, would allow her to evaluate the prey's potential.

So much depends on the first turn around the floor. It is on this initial exploratory coupling that the evolutionary instincts passed up through eons of amino acid bonding, virus replicating, fish spawning, dinosaur bugling, orangutan flashing, Neanderthal snorting and ragweed pollination all come to a blinding seductive pinnacle ... THE SLOW DANCE!

The Ramblers launched into "Please Release Me."

Kim breathed a sigh of relief. Cody put his right arm around her waist, assuming the Arthur Murray stance. She quickly canceled the three-inch rule. She lay her head on his shoulder.

"Man, you sure . . ." He started to say "smell good" but thought better of it and finished ". . . dance well." Of course she smelled good! She did it on purpose! Her perfume was strong enough to drive a hyena off a bucket of baboon livers! Her perfume was over-powering. It was deliberate, and necessary in the case of cowboys. Delicate fragrances don't hold up well in competition with horse sweat and two-day-old beer.

Cody squeezed her a little tighter. "Good band," he said as he established contact with the positive and negative poles of her estro-gen battery.

"Yes," she replied, and began charging.

They danced three more dances, then walked outside. It was cool after the steamy, rambunctious dance floor.

"So," she asked, "were you up tonight?"

"Yup. Didn't do too well."

"You weren't that guy that got knocked out, were you?"

"That's me, Cody Wing, fall guy."

Cody had started this rodeo season with less enthusiasm than any of the years before. His roots, which went deep, were startin' to pull. He was thinkin' of home more often. He was only twenty-eight, but he'd been on the road nearly ten years and never come close to qualify-ing for the National Finals. This year held no greater promise.

"Where ya go from here?" she asked.

"Blackfoot. I'm up Friday night. Say, would you like a beer?"

"No. Thanks, I don't drink. LDS, ya know, Mormon," she ex-plained. "But I wouldn't mind another dance, though."

They reentered the melee, danced a couple more dances, then walked back outside. Cody kissed her. She kissed him back. They must have found some common ground because they were soon sitting in the front seat of Cody's pickup steaming up the windows.

Just as the heavy petting was about to cross that line between a misdemeanor and a felony, Lick opened the door with a jerk! He jumped in on the passenger side!

"Cody, we gotta go! Howdy, ma'am. I mean right now!" He looked back over his shoulder. "Start the truck! Go!"

Cody cranked the engine and jammed it into gear, whacking Kim's knee! She groaned. "Sorry," he said.

Just as Cody popped the clutch, his door jerked open! A hand reached in and grabbed his collar! Lick reached across Kim and tried to straighten the steering wheel. Not easy, since Cody was holding on to it with a deadman's grip while the attacker was trying to pull him through the open door!

Lick climbed over Kim and got one arm around Cody's waist and the other around his neck. His tug-of-war opponent was now braced against the outside of the door frame with his boots and pulling Cody's arm out of its socket! He leaned back like a crewman on a sloop!

The pickup was chugging through the gravel parking lot in low gear.

"Drive!" commanded Lick to Kim, who now lay under him with one foot on the floor and the other doubled up against the passenger door.

She reached up blindly and grasped the wheel.

"Right! To the right!" he barked.

Kim got her other hand to the wheel and pulled down with all her might. The truck made a slow tow barge correction clockwise. It was enough to miss a horse trailer but she couldn't hold it against the combined weight of Cody and his two-hundred-pound appendage. They jerked it back to the left!

Lick had locked his leg around the gearshift and was trying to stick his thumb in the attacker's eye. Unable to reach it without losing his hold on Cody, he threw a week's accumulation of junk food wrappers he found on the dash at the clinging primate. The pickup continued its slow grind up on the Legion Hall lawn.

They circled the flagpole and headed back toward the building.

Kim felt somethin' roll across the floorboard and hit her foot. She grabbed at it. Clutching it in both hands, she got the top off a plastic quart container of motor oil.

From her vantage point, she could only feel and hear the scuffle. Lick was takin' pokes at the orangutan with his free right hand. Kim jammed the quart of oil up between Lick and Cody and tipped it over the back of Cody's head.

It ran down his neck, his shirt and his close company. Lick got a mouthful. It covered the bad guy's hands and went up his sleeves. His grip slipped. He slid to Cody's elbow. The pickup hit the curb and the antagonist looked briefly as a possum would look just before you hit him with a car. He disappeared like a smoke jumper.

Something that sounded like a full beer can hit the roof of their camper shell.

They got Cody loaded and his door shut. The pickup swerved out of the parking lot and through the quiet neighborhood surrounding it. Five blocks away they pulled over. The cab smelled like a drag race.

They debouched onto the sidewalk a block from Main Street.

Oil covered their faces and hair and shirts. It was wicking itself to every porous nook and cranny.

"Any chance we could clean up at your place?" Lick asked Kim politely.

She studied them. They reminded her of a picture she'd seen in *National Geographic* of two sea gulls washed ashore after an oil spill.

"None," she said, and walked off down the sidewalk.

Cody look at Lick in the glow of a street lamp.

"Jeez," asked Cody, "what happened to your hat?"

"I was tryin' to help this lady tuck in her shirttail when this big bruiser walked up behind me and pulled my hat down over my eyes! 'Bout cut off my ear! I turned around and took a swing at him, 'course I was blind, and hit this woman's arm who was dancin' by an' her hand come out and whacked that big sucker flat across the face. Well, he ducked down, just as I was comin' up pullin' off my hat, and I caught him full fist in the nose! Sounded awful! Sorta like a can bein' crinkled. He was bleedin' all over and blowin' froth . . . by then his sixteen brothers had showed up and—" Lick sighed and wiped a drop of 10W30 off his chin. "Anyway, here I am."

Friday Night, June 25
Blackfoot, Idaho

Cody was up in the bareback riding tonight. Lick was helpin' him set his riggin'. Lick listened as the loudspeaker played the final strains of "Barebackers Get Ready," a.k.a. our national anthem. As the crowd's cheering waned, the announcer took up the baton. "Ladies and gentlemen, thank you and be seated! Those of us here in the booth, behind the chutes and in the arena welcome you to one of America's oldest traditions! The wildest, woolliest, fastest, greatest show on earth! Professional rodeo!

"Sit on the edge of your seats for the next two hours and hang and rattle with the best cowboys! The prettiest cowgirls! And the toughest stock from the purple mountains' majesty to the shores of Tripoli!" (He spoke only in exclamation points!)

"In the spirit of Buffalo Bill Cody, Casey Tibbs and John Wayne ... [not to mention Elmer Gantry, Winston Churchill and P. T. Barnum]!" The announcer paused dramatically. He lowered his voice. "Dear Lord, we ask that you watch over these daring young men and women as they pit themselves in clean competition and reverent sportsmanship against some of your finest workmanship. May their hearts rise to the challenge and may they go home safely. Amen.

"Ladies and gentlemen, little buckaroos and cowgirls, anytime you see anything you like, put your hands together, stomp your feet and yahoo! Speaking of which, how 'bout one more big round of applause for the rodeo board, all the riding clubs, princesses and queens in the grand entry tonight! Weren't they great! Great job, men! My hat's off to you!"

This man was slicker than silk pajamas on a snake! He was rodeo's answer to exploding cake and fluorescent paint! To the ultimate game show host! To the Vatican in party hats! He was young, clever, witty, handsome and smooth. The raspberry-flavored Chap Stick melted off a buckle bunny's lips when she spoke his name . . . Emerald Dune, Rodeo Announcer!

Emerald had style, pizzazz, money, adoration, a long-suffering wife in Santa Fe, a photographic memory and a persistent case of gnawed-to-the-quick fingernails. Emerald was an evangelist. He would have been a superb disc jockey, vacuum cleaner salesman, Baptist preacher, con man, politician or panhandler, but he was a spectacular rodeo announcer!

However, all of Emerald's hypnotic mesmerizing was going over Cody's head. He was in his own small world "psychin' up." He was total concentration, oblivious to the pageantry and preaching.

Emerald would put down the microphone in two hours, three hundred dollars richer. The stock contractor would feed and bed his livestock, then go have a nice combination plate at the Hong Kong Cafe and Bowling Alley. The crowd would drive through the traffic, homeward bound, satisfied that they had spent their eight dollars wisely.

Cody might spend the night in Intensive Care with a concussion or a ruptured spleen. He might wake up tomorrow with a cast on his arm or his back in traction. There was also a fair-to-middlin' chance that due to a lost entry fee, his bankroll would be fifty dollars lighter by ten P.M.!

Inside Cody's body anticipation was stirring the adrenaline. The nerve synapses fire, reload and fire again like the two of clubs clothespinned to a bicycle spoke! The little pili muscles hiding in the follicles have a gang erection and the hairs on the back of his neck snap smartly to attention! Skin prickles, nose tickles, spurs jingle, toes tingle!

Lickity helped Cody down on his bronc. They pounded, mashed and pulled his gloved, rosined left hand through the suitcase handle on the bareback riggin'.

"Out of chute number four, a veteran professional cowboy from Ten Sleep, Wyoming ... Cody Wing, on the Maid Brothers' fine buckin' horse Velvet Try Me! Folks, put your hands together for this top cowboy. You're gonna love ..."

Cody dropped down on Velvet Try Me. She was developing a fine reputation as a pounder of would-be bareback riders. Lick was standing on the decking behind the chute. He had a loose grip on the back of Cody's belt. It was Cody's umbilicus to Earth. A safety line in case the horse did something in the chute that wasn't standard operating procedure. Like tryin' to climb over the top or goin' down on her knees and shakin' like a wet dog! Next to Lick, one of the chute hands was holding the tail of the flank strap.

Cody scooted up on the riggin', raised his boot heels above the mare's shoulders, screwed down his hat and spit out his chew. He went through his mental checklist: Rare back, point yer toes, squeeze the handle. He nodded his head. The gate swung open.

Velvet Try Me rainbowed out of chute number four! Cody marked her out and hung the steel to'er like the push rods on a locomotive! Try Me jumped the track! She slid, slipped and rolled around inside her skin! She punched holes in the arena dirt!

Cody rocked, she fired! She bucked, he pulled! Balance is critical in bareback ridin'. Not much more than a face card worth of contact exists between horse and rider. With your feet up in the air swingin' free, and you rared back so far your head can touch the horse's rump, it's a precarious perch!

It takes balance. Balance and power.

Power is essential in bareback riding. The hand's grip in the riggin'. Only the arm to keep your seat under your hand. The shoulder absorbing the jerk. Meeting a bareback rider is like shaking hands with a marble statue.

Velvet Try Me was testing Cody's salt.

Somewhere in the last two seconds of the eight-second ride, Cody reached his limit. Everything in his firebox ... experience, intuition, talent and training ... were at full throttle and blowin' blue smoke! The enraptured crowd was sitting on Cody's shoulder makin' the ride with him. It was then, over the din of twenty-five hundred rabid fans, that Cody reached down inside himself. He whispered, "Yer mine . . ."

The hair stood up on the crowd's collective neck. The buckin' horse went down!

From the grandstand it looked like Cody's head hit the ground! His legs pistoned! The horse exploded! She climbed outta the hole with Cody stuck to'er like a remora on a shark's back!

Cody was makin' a ride! You couldn't have cut him loose with a laser torch! The whistle blew. The crowd went wild!

Cody quit spurrin' and Try Me broke into a hard gallop. They were racing around the arena counterclockwise. Gallant Fox heading into the stretch.

The pickup men were riding like demons to catch the pair! One finally managed to get close enough to tempt Cody. Cody loosed his grip in the riggin' and leaned to the left to grab the pickup man's waist.

Velvet Try Me still had a trick up her sleeve. At the moment she felt Cody's balance shift, the instant he was committed, she slammed on the brakes and sidestepped to starboard! The pickup man and his horse shot on by. Cody saw the rump glide out from under his nose. He poised for a split second, extended in midair, then flew crablike into the dirt!

He spit dirt and rose to thunderous applause!

Cody tipped his hat, like it was just another day's work. But if you'd touched him at that moment it would have been like layin' your hand on an electric motor. He was hummin'!

Cody had ridden Try Me with all he had left . . . will. Will, want to, grit, gumption, whatever it is that allows housewives to lift cars off babies and Samsons to pull down temples.

The crowd waited nervously for the score to be posted. They were nervous because of a loose brick in the facade of rodeo rules which says: hard-to-ride horses don't always score the highest. Most in the grandstands that night would have been disgruntled but not surprised if Cody's ride had scored out of the money. Style often counts more than difficulty.

But rodeo is not like making a centerpiece out of angel hair and glitter. We're talkin' about a horse that can buck you off and a cowboy that claims she can't. That's how rodeo began and tonight the judges didn't forget it.

Cody had reached the buckin' chutes when Emerald Dune announced the score. Cody and his pardner, Velvet Try Me, scored an 82 . . . good enough for top money that night.

They deserved it.

3

Saturday Night, June 26
Blackfoot, Idaho

The following night, the last performance of the rodeo, our boys' luck continued. Lick drew a good bull and rode him to second place. Cody's score on Try Me had stood up to the competition and split top money. At most rodeos an 82 score would have been enough to win some money, though the roughstock events scoring system is subjective. Vague guidelines in "how they buck": hard, smooth or quick, etc., and "how they rode": spurring action, grace and timing, etc., are used by the two judges. These two judges stand on the arena floor, one on each side of the chute. There are a few nonnegotiable rules, including marking the horse out, not touching the animal with the free hand, proper attire (hat, long-sleeve shirt and boots), and the eight-second time limit. But no one counts the number of spur strokes, bull spins, bucks or yahoos!

These two judges are each allowed to give up to 25 points for the animal's performance and up to 25 points for the cowboy's effort. So it is theoretically possible to get a 100 mark. In real life, however, any score in the 80s is considered very good, but there are rodeos where a 70s score will win.

The score depends on the stock, the cowboys, the competition, the arena, the weather and the judges' dispositions on any given night. However, it would be fair to say that rodeo judges are chintzy with their precious numbers regardless of their mood, as witnessed by the fact that in all the history of professional rodeo, the number of perfect scores could be counted on a cloven hoof.

Lick and Cody, along with a platoon of cowboys, potato pickers and miners, went into town after the show to celebrate.

"By gosh, Lickity, you really done good tonight!" Cody smiled over his third beer. He truly relished his friend's success. "An eighty-five! Terrific!"

"Ya didn't do bad yer ownself," said Lick. "Tough horse. I don't believe the average feller would'a stayed on!" Cody modestly pooh-poohed the compliment, though he was deeply pleased.

"Yeah," Lick continued, lifting his glass of beer and studying the neon reflection in the bubbles. "I got to the inside on the first spin and he jes' kept goin'. Sure was smooth. Pinkeye gave me the book on him and he did just what he said he would."

"Good job, Lick! And you, too, Cody," congratulated LoBall Mc-Kinney. "Lemme buy you cowboys another!"

This waddie bonhommie was takin' place at the Don't Lie to Her, Just Take the Fifth Amendment Bar.

"Lookie there, Lick. Isn't that . . . ?" Cody hesitated. Lick, who was jovially drunk, looked over his shoulder. Headin' toward him like a torpedo in a ten-foot stock tank was what, by any other name, would still be a bombshell!

Whoa! Baxter, here! Baxter Black, author of this careening collection of words. As you can see, we're only into the third chapter and our two heroes are about to tangle with the opposite sex . . . again. Didn't I promise you sex, violence and intrigue? But I hasten to assure you—it is not gratuitous. When you cowboy for a livin' and you're a normal thirty-year-old male, rodeo and women figure heavily in your daily meditation.

Arco Peacock had poured her 130 pounds into a size six dress! It was shiny red and seemed to run out of material three-fourths of the way up! She held a master's degree in plant genetics, but that would not have been your first guess if clothing had been your only guide. Even she conceded she dressed, as songwriter Chris Wall would say, "just a tad on the trashy side"! However, she was without guile and her good nature was genuine.

Lick took in her blond mane, dazzling smile and almost invisible shoulder straps. He swiveled on the bar stool to greet her.

"Bob! It's good to see ya!" She beamed as she brushed by Lick to greet the man at the bar standing behind Cody.

Lick blushed to himself. Cody, embarrassed for his friend, attempted comfort by saying, "Well, you haven't seen her for a while. Maybe she's not wearing her contacts."

As if on cue Arco touched Cody's elbow. "Cody? Is that you? And Lick! You lil' sweetheart! I saw you ride tonight! Great!" Arco slid around to stand beside Lick, unconsciously placing herself center stage for a bar full of admiring cowboys.

I say unconsciously, friends, because I have known people like Arco. Maybe instinctively is an even better choice of words. It may have been simply part of her autonomic nervous system, like postprandial digestion or mydriasis on a dark night. Knowing where to position yourself in a flower bed has a direct bearing on the possibility of pollination. Which is just to say that Arco Peacock innately knew where the spotlight would fall.

Her dress was factory-issue Corvette red. It idled in contrast to her pale white back and legs. She was also the only woman within a quarter mile wearing a dress. She moved, shifted and nickered as naturally as a three-year-old filly with a little pasture exposure!

"Aw, Lick. It's good to see you again."

"You, too, Arco. It's been a while." He remembered her in stocking feet bringing him a glass of OJ. He, sitting at her breakfast table in the morning sun. They were both wonderfully relaxed. It was a Sunday, he remembered, last fall.

"Sorry you couldn't make it to my little party."

"Yeah, well, by the time I picked up my mail, it was too late," he explained.

"Truth is, Lick, I was hopin' you'd made it back this spring. I know you're on the road and all, but I really enjoyed your company."

"Me, too. But I jus' got busy. I think that was the last time I read the funnies out loud. And you made those great big cinnamon rolls. We ate the whole pan! Sure was a great day!"

"Oh, Lick ..." She touched his face with her hand. "I ... it's so good to see you!"

"Would you like a beer? We might go to breakfast later if yer up for it."

"No. No, I can't," she said quickly. "I've made other plans." Their small talk dwindled, and she excused herself, leaving a flickering, palpable electricity in the air.

Cody was talking rodeo with a couple boys at a nearby table. Lick ran his fingers up and down the frosty beer glass and studied the mirror behind the bar. In its reflection he saw Arco reappear from the ladies' room and walk to another table. LoBall came up to Lick. They started visiting and time flew to last call.

At one P.M., Cody, Lick and LoBall stood by the curb in front of The Fifth Amendment. They were feelin' frisky.

"When was the last time you climbed a mountain?"

"Whataya talkin' about, Lick?" asked LoBall.

Lick pointed above the bar. There was a second story. An old sign climbed the vertical face from the bar porch and extended two feet above the roof ledge.

"Gimme a boost," directed Lick as he reached for the porch brace. LoBall lent his shoulders and Lick clambered up. The vertical sign was perpendicular to the brick face and was supported by a rusty angle-iron frame. Lick started his climb as the gathering crowd in the street cheered him on!

"I better help him, LoBall," said Cody, and followed Sir Edmund Screw Loose!

They scaled the roof ledge to tumultuous applause and disappeared. Up on the roof it was peaceful and quiet. The sky was clear and the stars were showering their blessing on the relaxed revelers. They sat, dangling their legs over the edge.

"Arco sure looked good, didn't she, Lick?"

"Boy, I'll say. We had a good visit. I thought we might've hit it off again but she had other plans."

"Too bad. Say, have you heard from Anaconda Kathy lately?"

17

"No. We kinda had it out in March. She said she either wanted something permanent or nothin' at all."

"You were seein' her off and on when we started travelin' together. That's been over two years," observed Cody.

"I know. I don't blame her. I think keepin' me in the cavvy was interferin' with her gettin' involved with anybody else. But anyway . . . it's for the best."

"She loved you, ya know!"

"Yeah, well, I can't help it," Lick said impatiently.

Cody felt a little twinge. Anaconda Kathy was his favorite of all Lick's girlfriends. A good, ranch-raised girl who could ride but wasn't horsey. She and Cody had hit it off. They had had several long talks. Usually about Lick. Cody defended him and tried not to encourage her too much, but she had stars in her eyes. Cody figured she probably had seen the light and decided she couldn't wait any longer. That, and the hurt. He'd seen it in her eyes. The ache of unreturned love.

"Well, she's better off," sighed Cody.

"You can say that about all of 'em!" laughed Lick.

"We sure cut a fat hog this weekend, pardner," mused Cody.

"We had it comin'," said Lick.

"You both come on down!" A voice from below broke their reverie. Two powerful flashlight beams shined up from the narrow alley below them. It separated the bar from Farmer's Feed and Seed warehouse, next door.

Lick stood up on the ledge, did a Tarzan yell, pounded his chest and leaped out into space!

★ ★ ★

The drunk tank is a wretched place. Suffice it to say, our two tarnished Sherpas sobered up instantly as the cell door slid shut with a migraine-splitting bang!

Cody was grody. Lick got sick.

There is one good thing about a drunk tank. It is an excellent place to put a drunk. No one appreciates a drunk as much as another drunk. It's like putting two horse people together at the same table;

no one has to feel guilty about ignoring them as long as they've got each other. In a drunk tank there is no such thing as a fashionable drunk.

Monday Morning, June 28
Bingham County Courthouse

"How do you plead?"
Lick mentally reviewed his options:

1. *Innocent as a newborn babe.*
2. No lo contendre. (*No, wait, he was a Mexican bantamweight from Los Angeles.*)
3. *On my hands and knees.*
4. *Guilty as sin.*
5. *Your Honor, my body was taken over by extraterrestrial beings disguised as Japanese businessmen bearing business cards intent on sabotaging the Farmer's Feed and Seed warehouse.*
6. *I was blinded like Saul, forsook my rabble-rousing ways and took one giant step for mankind.*

"To what?" asked the hyperventilated Lick.
"Disturbing the peace, destruction of private property."
"Uh, Yer Honor, would you explain what happens if I plead guilty or innocent or whatever."
"Sure. Innocent, we appoint you a lawyer and set bail. Guilty, you can be fined and/or sentenced to time in the county jail."
"How much?"
"Time or money?"
"Both."
"Maximum fine, five hundred dollars. Maximum jail, thirty days."
"Guilty, I guess."
"The defendant pleads guilty and is fined two hundred and fifty dollars, plus three days' work at the Farmer's Feed and Seed. Sentence to begin immediately. Pay the clerk. Next case."

"Cody Wing," said the baliff, "charged with disturbing the peace and destruction of private property."

"How do you plead?"

"Well, Yer Honor, I was just tryin' to keep an eye on Lick, there, and I guess I didn't do a real good job."

"Son, I want to ask you a question. Bill, I mean the arresting officer, said you watched your friend jump off the roof of the Fifth Amendment Bar and crash through the greenhouse roof of Farmer's Feed and Seed next door. Not exactly a brilliant move in itself, but then you jumped after him and put a second hole in Harvey Loomis's roof! That doesn't show a whole lot of good sense. What the hell— Strike that! What the hell— Strike it! Aw, hell, what the hell did you do that for?"

"I guess I wanted to make sure he wuddn't hurt."

"Good thinking. How do you plead?"

"Guilty."

"Sentenced to three days working for Farmer's Feed and Seed plus court cost. Next case."

Monday, Tuesday and Wednesday were spent loading feed, restacking pallets, pulling weeds, digging trenches, shoveling elevator pits, sweeping floors, washing windows, and sneezing. Actually, other than for the hard labor, it wasn't so bad. Harvey Loomis thought the whole episode was sort of funny. Insurance covered the cost of the two green sheets of corrugated plastic and replaced the potted Japanese black pine they deboughed on impact. Cody and Lick rebagged the Cow Power fertilizer they'd punctured by landing spurs first. Harvey even took the boys home for supper Wednesday after work.

They left town that Wednesday night, June 30, smelling like Cow Power and fermented grain.

Thursday, July 1

The boys took the scenic route from Blackfoot to Cody, Wyoming. They cruised through the cool pines of four national forests and two national parks. It was an easy day. They were both up tomorrow at the big Cody, Wyoming rodeo.

As they drove north, abreast of the Tetons, Lick finally lost his patience.

"Dang it, Cody! I'm tired of examining my love life! Can't you talk about anythin' else!"

"Well, ya don't hafta git mad! All I said was Anaconda Kathy—"

"Anaconda Kathy, Arco, Chadron, the Women's Army Corps! I'm just tired of it, that's all. Can't we talk about your love life for a change? You've about wore the subject out! I'm just not in the mood to settle down. You want me to git married again? Is that what you want?

"Maybe you already got one picked out! Who? Arco? Wouldn't we be a pair! We'd look like a Snap-On Tool calendar; she'd be the girl with the boom box in her sweater and I'd be the hubcap hammer!"

"I think she's pretty nice, if you ask me," answered Cody indignantly. "She's a lot smarter than she acts like. Hell, she's a college graduate! Got a good job. And I'll bet she'd be as true as a skunk's mate."

"A skunk's mate!" said Lick. "I don't believe it!"

"You know," explained Cody, "when you run over a skunk, the other one hangs around, pining ...."

"I know! I know!" said Lick, "and usually gets run over, too!"

"Ah, Lick, I just think you oughta pay a little more attention. There's a lot of good ol' gals slippin' right through your hands and I don't think you even know it."

"Look, Cody, I'm not interested. Sometimes a feller knows when he's better off and I dang sure know I am. That's the difference 'tween you and me. I never had it so good, and I know it!"

"So what about Chadron?" continued Cody.

"Give it a rest, Cody. I've come a long way to git here and I'm not about to change."

Lick *had* come a long way.

His daddy was a fair-do-well cattle trader, horse trainer, drug salesman, uranium miner and day-work cowboy who could hang Sheetrock. Lick's folks had lived several places while Lick was growing up, mostly in the high plains of Kansas, Texas and New Mexico. Presently they were living in Hereford, Texas, where Papa was cowboying in a feedlot and riding colts for an extra C-note a month.

Lick was the oldest of three brothers: Lick, Clay and Tye. Papa taught the boys how to shoe a horse, sack a colt, doctor a steer, build a tight five-wire fence, plait a set of rawhide reins complete with buttons, spot a sick calf, know the value of steroids when tradin' horses and hang Sheetrock. Everything a man needs to know to spend the rest of his life self-unemployed.

Mama's maiden name was Chavez. Her mother had been a Jannsen who married Elojio Chavez from Las Vegas, New Mexico. Elojio, Lick's grandpa, was proud of the fact that he could trace his family back two hundred years in New Mexico history. Lick had the dark hair and eyes of his Spanish ancestors. Both his brothers were lighter complected and taller than Lick. They had real jobs.

Lick's paternal grandparents had come from Texas and Oklahoma.

During Lick's growing up, his folks never really owned anything. They rented or lived in company houses and always got by. Papa was a hand and never was out of work long. Mama was a genius at keeping a healthy, happy home on an irregular income.

Lick grew up lookin' for a way out. . . .

* * *

As luck would have it, they pulled into the Bronze Boot in Cody, Wyoming, just as the action was starting. The Bronze Boot was packed with cowboys, rodeo fans and wild Wyoming women!

Lick got liquored up by ten, mothered up by eleven, and hustled by twelve! Uva Dell was a snake, in the Adam and Eve sense of the word! She had long black hair, showin' a few lines and wearin' Wrangler leotards! Five foot two and thin as a Nevada mustang, she could fold a dollar bill to the size of a postage stamp with her tongue and slice cheese with her nose!

Son of a scrofulous cad! I knew that woman! Settle down, Bax. Well, it's just that anybody who's ever stuck his hand in a snarling dog's cage to see if he bites can figger out what's comin'! Lick is about to commit a common act of lunacy and even if we were there we would not be able to stop him. It is that indefensible phenomenon that allows a man to climb into a strange car with a strange woman in a strange town and drive off! With no idea as to destination, ETA or return ticket!

"How much further?" asked Lick. "I thought you said it was just outta town."

"It is, cowboy. Just up the road a piece."

Lick looked at her. Her features appeared almost craggy in the green glow of the dash lights. She wasn't a big woman but she certainly looked like she could take care of herself.

"Nice pickup," he remarked.

"Here it is," she said as she wheeled off the highway onto a gravel road. They drove another mile, then Uva Dell pulled into the country equivalent of a cul-de-sac. She switched off the lights. Lick scooted over next to her.

"Let's go for a little walk in the moonlight," she suggested.

They wandered directly to the back of the pickup. She dropped the tailgate and Lick sat on the edge dangling his feet.

"Mighty pretty out here," he said as she rubbed his knees. It was pretty. The Wyoming landscape, the starry night and the overwhelming silence.

He lay back and stared up at the stars. "By gosh, Uva Dell, this sure is nice. Yer place nearby?"

"Close enough, but you're not in a hurry are you?"

"Nope. I'm sure not. I wouldn't mind soakin' up a little of the peaceful."

"Lemme take your boots off," she offered.

He allowed her to pull 'em off. She set them in the pickup bed. Then she desocked him.

"That feel better, cowboy?"

"Just right, Uva Dell."

"Are you still hot?" she asked.

"Humm," he said slyly. "Yeah, I am ... just a bit."

"You get yourself comfortable. I gotta get somethin' outta the front."

Lick did as he was told. Then lay back. He heard her rattle around in the cab, the door shut and she said, "Close your eyes."

He heard her step around to the back of the pickup.

"What is it you do for a livin'?" he asked dreamily.

"I'm a highwayman."

"A what?" asked Lick, eyes still closed.

"A highwayman," she repeated. His brain registered the distinct sound of a revolver being cocked. "And I rob cowboys."

He sat straight up!

"What!"

"Stick 'em up!" Lick was staring down the barrel of the biggest pistol he'd ever seen! If you've ever stuck your head in a well casing, you know how he felt! She held the cannon rock steady. He made a mental note of that fact.

"Slide off that tailgate. I'm serious about those hands. Git 'em high."

Lick scooched to the edge and dropped to the gravel. He winced.

"Now move over a little." He did. She rifled the pockets of his jeans that lay in the bed of the truck. She transferred the bills from his pocket to hers.

"You got a wallet?" she asked pleasantly.

"Uva Dell, this seems like a dumb question to ask, but is this a joke?"

She dropped the barrel of the pistol in the flick of an eye and pulled the trigger! The inside of Lick's bare legs stung from the flying rock and sand! She raised the barrel level to his nose and cocked it.

"I reckon not," he said, his ears ringing like a stuck siren.

"I reckon not," she said, smiling.

"Actually, I do have a wallet but it's in the pickup. My pickup, I mean."

"Oh, well," she said, "I never did do it for the money. I'm gonna have to go now but I can't leave you like this."

"Thank goodness," sighed Lick. He started to reach for his pants.

"Don't move!"

He snapped smartly to his goal post imitation.

"Take off the rest of your clothes."

"Uva Dell, I'm really not in the mood," he complained.

"I believe you misunderstood my intentions," she replied.

"You wouldn't really shoot me, would ya?"

"No. I wouldn't wanna kill you but I'd sure put a bullet through your foot. Only problem is, this pistol is so big it usually takes the ankle with it. 'Least, that's been my experience."

"You mean you've shot people before?" he asked, peeling off his shirt.

"Only in the foot. Off with the shorts, too. Throw 'em in the back of the pickup." She slammed the tailgate up. "All right, walk over there by that hump."

Lick minced across the rocky turnaround.

She started the pickup, backed around and captured him in the brights. "Nice buns!" she shouted, then let out a war whoop, fired her pistol in the air and spewed gravel as the truck fishtailed toward the road!

Lick watched the taillights disappear. The sound of the growling engine eventually faded into the night.

Friends, this might be a safe place for some gentle reflection. Where a man might reevaluate the priorities in his life. A moment to examine the Yin and Yang of the yo-yo of Existence. Where does Homo sapien truly fit on this old mud ball we call Earth? How would he fare were he reduced to his natural state and left alone in the wilderness?

And furthermore, how would Robin Hood deal with Maid Marian turned maniac bandit and foot shooter? It is the ultimate equality. Feminism assimilated to the point where you can't tell the good guys from the bad. Interesting, isn't it, that the instigator of this final solution was not social conscience, divorce lawyers or natural selection. It was Samuel Colt's invention, the revolving cylinder single-action handgun.

Uva Dell's behavior would certainly upset some modern sociologist's chauvinistic preconceptions. Unless, of course, that sociologist was conversant with Wyoming's history of women's suffrage and had spent some time studying Wyoming women in their natural habitat.

As Lick said to himself alone under the stars, "Well pick my nose with a fork-ed stick! That never happened before!"

Dawn found him back on the blacktop. A yard light burned weakly half a mile up the road, kissing the night good-bye. As Lick drew closer to the ranch headquarters, he was able to see the layout of the buildings and corrals in the spreading sunrise. He spotted what appeared to be a chicken house. He circled through the pasture and snuck up on the chicken house. He peered through the chicken wire window. The hens were fast asleep while their bodies were busy accumulating calcium and troweling it into a shell. Lick was looking for a garment to cover his goose-bumped body.

Belfry, cowdog in charge of ranch security, lay by the sheep wire fence in front of the ranch house curled against the morning chill. He opened one eye. He spied a big pink intruder crossing the lane from the chicken house to the horse barn. The hair stood between Belfry's shoulder blades!

Now, dogs take their guarding seriously. However, it does not make great demands on their courage to bark and growl menacingly at the school bus or an occasional molasses salesman. Yet it's part of the job, boring though it may seem to those of us whose jobs include such daily excitements as writing a memo, reading a memo or filing a memo.

Belfry shivered, curled tighter and blinked his eye in the wild hope that the mysterious invader was just a figment of his imagination. No! There it was creeping into the horse barn!

Belfry reviewed his options from the Official Cowdog Ranch Security Handbook:

> 1. *Close his eyes and pretend to be asleep.*
> 2. *Sneak around and get a closer look.*
> 3. *Bark and wake up Wilbur's old lady.*
> 4. *Attack.*

He chose the easy way out: number 3. At the first yap Lick zipped into the tack room and came flying back out wrapped in a turquoise saddle blanket! The high-stepping cowboy cleared the barbwire fence into the pasture and rolled into a ditch! He lay there panting.

"Yap, yap, yap, bark, woof, woof!"

"What is it, Belfry?"

"Yap, yap, bark, bark, bark!"

"Okay, okay. Let me get my glasses."

"Yap, yap, woof, bow wow!"

"What is it, Ethel?"

"Don't know, Wilbur. Prob'ly nothin'."

"Woof, woof, bark and yap!"

"Okay, okay, shut up, Belfry!"

"Bark, bark, woof, woof, woof!"

"Shaddup, you sunuvabitch."

"Yap, yap, yap!"

Wham, wham, whap!

"Whimper, whimper, whine."

Belfry rolled over on his back and grinned ingratiatingly.

"Okay. Good dog. Go back to sleep."

Pat, pat, pat.

"Sigh."

Lick stayed frozen another five minutes, then crept back toward the main road.

It is not easy to thumb a ride at six o'clock in the morning dressed in a turquoise horse blanket. Fortunately, he was stranded in Wyoming, where such behavior is commonplace. He was picked up by an aged ex-prospector who mistook him for a soul brother coming back from a revival in Meeteetse. The ancient 1950 GMC pickup slowed, then stopped. He was taking two small shoats and a week-old Holstein calf to a girlfriend north of Cody. They were crowded in the front seat between a cardboard box of transmission gears and a gunnysack full of aluminum cans. Lick climbed in the back between two bales of hay and a block of salt. There was no room for him in the inn.

On the way through town, Lick unloaded on First Street and walked out to the rodeo grounds. The contestant area was filled with travel trailers. It was 7:30 A.M., not much stirring. He was weaving his way from pickup to camper to horse trailer, looking for Cody's pickup. He was also trying to avoid attracting attention.

"Hey, LoBall, come take a look at this!"

"Who is it?"

"Bill! Wake up!"

"Somebody go git Franco and Charlie!"

"Monty, git yer butt out here! Yer not gonna believe this!"

Somebody started honking his horn. Soon other horns joined in and the entire entourage of rodeo overnighters were piling out of their campers to watch the spectacle.

"Who is it?"

"Dunno. Who is it?"

"Where?"

"Over there."

"I think it's Lick."

"Who?"

"Lick!"

"Hey, Lick, is that you?"

"It is! It's Lick!"

Lick clutched his blanket tighter to his bosom. He led an ever growing number of pie-eyed piperettes through the contestant parking area like a disinterested bitch in heat.

Cody opened the back of the camper to insistent pounding. He looked out at He Who Squats in the Goatheads and then at the throng surrounding his vehicle.

"What the hell! Lick?"

"Let me in."

"Sure, sure."

Lick crawled over the tailgate.

"Look! He's nekkid!"

A woman screamed ... inside the camper! The piercing shriek coursed through Lick's tympanic bullae directly to the microchip in the cerebral cortex labeled EMERGENCY ONLY! Epinephrine was released at the appropriate synapses and his body straightened out like a frog in biology lab! He hit his head on the aluminum camper top! He grabbed his head with his left hand, caught the saddle blanket on a galvanized screw on the tack box, stumbled and braced his fall with his right hand!

The turquoise blanket disappeared as if a magician had jerked a tablecloth out from under an eight-piece table setting!

"This is Sheila. Sheila, this is Lick!"

"Howdy, ma'am."

She screamed again.

5

July 2
Cody, Wyoming

By three o'clock the afternoon following the escapade with Mademoiselle Uva Dell, Cody and Lick were behind the bucking chutes at the Cody, Wyoming rodeo grounds. They were rosining their bull ropes, tying on spurs and distractedly visiting with other riders.

Most of the competitors here today would be up in Livingston, Montana, and again in Red Lodge, Montana, this weekend. This included Lick and Cody, as well. The three towns planned their rodeos to coincide.

Lick was still thickheaded and dry-eyed from lack of sleep, not to mention a little sore from his forced march. The bull he had drawn today was new to him and the other cowboys. Nobody had any information on him. All the stock contractor's pickup man could tell Lick was that he was gentle. He would eat grain out of your hand.

Cody's draw was well known. The "book" on him was that he was a good honest bucker and a money bull if things worked right.

Lick finally threw up and felt a little better. He was able to help Cody get down on his bull, which came in the first chuteload to buck out. Cody got it together and scored a 76, which put him in third place at the time.

Lick's bull came in with the second chuteload. He was a big, beefy yellow Charolais with two floppy horns. He stood quietly in the chute as Cody and Lick set Lick's rope. While Cody was reaching underneath the bull's belly to catch the tail of the bull rope he noticed a familiar brand on the bull's right hip.

"Well I'll be durn!" Cody remarked, "Lick, this ol' bull's got Chubby Duckworth's brand on him. Does he have an underbit on both ears? Sure does! Duckworth's got a gypo deal up south of Sheridan. Runs quite a few cows and never pays over four hundred dollars for a bull. No wonder nobody's seen this bugger before. Chubby's been breedin' cows with him and musta needed some cash so he sold off a herd sire! I don't know nuthin' 'bout him, but if he's anything like Chubby, I wouldn't trust him!"

Great, thought Lick. *Just what I need after spending the night stark naked on the Serengeti of Wyoming.* "Pull it," he said. "I'm next."

Lick was ready by the time the arena director laced his jerk rope through the chute gate. Lick nodded furiously! The gate swung open! Lick could no longer hear the crowd or see anything outside his orbit. The bull's first move was to tense and take a deep breath. The result was a tightening of the rope that bit into Lick's gloved hand! Lick didn't have time to smile, but it felt good. It brought him back to his own reality. The way a familiar hammer feels to a framer. Riding bulls was what he was good at. It was the center of his universe, his bottom line, the caffeine in his primordial coffee.

Most rodeo bulls show little finesse. They rely on quickness and overwhelming power. When you realize they could easily demolish a cinder block building or a five-strand barbwire fence, it is remarkable that every cowboy is not reduced to kindling by the conclusion of each ride!

Big Yellow came out with a respectable first jump. Then he turned back and bucked straight along the chute gates at the end of the arena! Cowboys sitting on the gates and standing in front of them scattered like handbills in a hurricane!

Big Yellow got so close that he was intermittently rubbing Lick's left leg along the boards! Not so obvious that the judges would notice but enough to interfere with Lick's action. Lick was supposed to be concentrating but it was difficult with Big Yellow swooping in and out whacking his knee against the rough-cut two-by-eights.

During the next dive to the outside, Lick picked up his inside leg and drove his spur into the bull's shoulder! The bull swung to the right and bucked straight out toward the center of the arena! The eight-second whistle blew! Lick stopped spurring and the bull stopped bucking. He stood still with Lick sitting astride him. Lick rapidly uncoiled the rope from his hand and waited a moment for Big Yellow to move again, knowing it was safer to bail off a moving bull than a standing one. At least you'd be goin' opposite directions when you hit the ground. The bull continued to stand. The crowd started laughing! Finally Lick slid off and raced a few steps back toward the chutes! Big Yellow stood there a few seconds then quietly followed Lick's exit, sniffing at the ground, looking up at the crowd and good-naturedly appearing to enjoy his part in the show. The crowd loved it! Lick thought it was humorous, too. But the judges had no sense of humor and marked Lick a measly 56.

Cody eventually placed fourth and won a third in Red Lodge. Lick rode all three of his bulls that weekend but was out of the money every time. The boys spent a couple days in Ten Sleep with Cody's folks and Big Yellow was fourteen hundred pounds of hamburger by Tuesday!

6

Wednesday, July 7
Nampa, Idaho

Go west, young man," Horace Greeley said to his incompetent son-in-law in an effort to get him away from the table.

Lick and Cody, well rested and healed after two days of Mama Wing's cooking, also heeded Horace's command. West across Wyoming to Nampa, Idaho.

Idaho. I speak of that great state with the fondness that Willie Shoemaker speaks of Churchill Downs. I spent ten years of my life working for a big cow outfit up there.

Southwestern Idaho, like eastern Oregon and northern Nevada, is cowboy country. Not pickup drivin', CB talkin', team ropin', Marlboro smokin', beboppin' baseball cap cowboys. I mean real cowboys!

I had come up from New Mexico, where I was raised. Cowboys in the Southwest were not flashy. We enjoyed bein' cowboys but we were Spartan in our plumage.

I rode into Idaho and found myself in the Wild West! They reveled in being cowboys! They wallowed in it! Shoot, they call themselves buckaroos!

Ridin' a deep-seat centerfire saddle with a horn like a cedar post! Tapaderos, rommals, rawhide reins, bosals, horsehair McCarties, reatas and big, cover-the-country horses!

Hightop boots tucked in, riding heels, jingle bobs, rowels like spinners on a '58 Olds, chinks, silver buckles, silk scarves and big high-crown black hats. When gazing on one of these sagebrush centaurs you do not confuse him with an insurance salesman from Spokane!

In all fairness, these buckaroos are no better at cowboyin' than my compadres in New Mexico or Texas. But it's possible they enjoy it more. Doesn't a blue jay have more fun bein' a bird than a sparrow does? Dressin' in a Batman suit on Halloween doesn't make you Robin's godfather or entitle you to Superman's home phone number, but if you can do a journeyman's job of ropin' and ridin' and you wanna dress like a Remington painting, more power to ya!

Now, you cannot necessarily assume just 'cause a feller's got on a black hat and he's broke that he's a cowboy! But, as any boondockin' bird-watcher will tell you, if you're lookin' for a certain kind of bird, you've got to look in the right places! These buckaroos do not normally frequent highly populated areas. They are seldom spotted in Baskin-Robbins, a Marriott lobby, or the First Presbyterian Church.

Since cowboyin' is a seven-day-a-week job, you're liable to see them anytime. For those of you who wish to begin "buckaroo watchin'," familiarize yourself with the bars, pool halls and tack shops in places like Grasmere, Mountain City, Denio, Wagon Tire, McDermitt, Three Creek, Tuscarora, Jordan Valley and Reynolds Creek. Just hang out with your binoculars around your neck and your notebook in your hand. You'll know it the minute you see one.

Lick and Cody were in downtown Nampa, at Bits' Saddle and Canvas, swapping war stories with the owners. A few other cowboys were getting tack and riggins resewed or riveted. The brothers who owned the place, Four and Six, always did a healthy business during Snake River Stampede week. They were the best for miles around, and preferred to work on workin' cowboy tack, but backyard horse people and trail ride cowboys contributed their share to the cash register.

"Man!" said Cody. "Twelve hundred dollars for a saddle! How do these buckaroos, drawin' six hundred a month, afford one of these?"

"I don't know, but they do. Sold one yestiddy to a guy cowboyin' on South Mountain fer ol' Tex. Paid cash."

"Are ya up tonight?" Four asked.

"Nope. My pardner is, though. I'm up Friday in the bareback."

"Four Bits! How you doin'?" Four turned to the newcomer.

"Good, Jack. Whatta ya up to?"

"I thought this might be a good place to do an interview with some of the cowboys in town for the rodeo. Sorta get the feel of the show. How about these two?" The radioman turned to Cody.

"Hi, I'm Jack Dale, K2HO Radio." Jack looked like the perennial anchorman. Genial and bright with a modulated voice and hair you could see through. "Maybe you could help us with a little spot to promote the rodeo?" He offered his hand to Cody.

"Sure. Cody Wing." Jack shook his hand warmly.

"How about you?" Jack asked the man behind Cody.

"Be glad to. Do I look okay?"

Cody looked around. It was Ned. Ned? Not Ned!

Nobody liked Ned. It was understandable, of course, so no one gave it much thought. Ned is one of those names that's hard to grow up with. Certainly there are many Neds down through history who have distinguished the name: Ned the Great, Ned the Lion-hearted, Ned the Conqueror, Ned the Red, to name a few. But no modern screen star has chosen the name Ned. There is no Ned Valentino, Ned Gable or Ned Eastwood.

This Ned was a calf roper. His father was a roper turned banker and his mother taught school. They loved him enough to subsidize his roping, for the time being.

But Ned had a way about him that irritated people! It wasn't that he wasn't intelligent, he was; but he wasn't smart. He was intellectual, but not bright; educated, but shallow; literate, but ponderous; enlightened, but not witty; sentimental, but tactless; calculating, but unimaginative. All in all, he was a clod.

He exemplified the difference between risqué and obscene.

His hair was thick and greasy. He had bad breath. He couldn't say "Sasquatch" without spitting on his listener. He cleaned his fingernails, picked his nose, broke wind, or scratched his crotch at indelicate times.

Once he asked Lick why he never had any luck with women.

"Ned," said Lick, "they think you're the kind of person who'd wait under a fire escape for three hours, on the chance you might get to look up their dress!"

"Hum," pondered Ned. "I never thought of that."

✦ ✦ ✦

"What's your name?" asked Jack.

"Ned." Ned had begun to sweat.

"Are you two partners?"

"No! No," answered Cody.

"I just want to turn on this tape recorder and ask you a few questions. Easy, no big deal, and if it's good, we'll run it this week. Okay?"

"Do we have to sign anything? I mean, for royalties and things?" asked Ned.

"Royalties?" Jack almost laughed, until he realized the question was sincere.

"Yes. I've read some AFTRA brochures in my spare time, and often seventy-five dollars is paid for speaking parts. I'm not sure how the FCC looks on radio interviews, but, speaking for myself and my friend"—Ned put his arm around Cody, Cody shrank— "we'd certainly consider it. Wouldn't we, Cody?" He smiled and breathed in Cody's face. Two freckles and a blackhead shriveled like napalmed mushrooms!

"This would just be a sort of man-in-the-street-type interview. Usually no money is paid," explained Jack.

"Certainly, we can see your point, but you must understand that celebrities, movie stars, or rodeo stars have to be careful about allowing visual or auditorial reproductions of themselves or part of themselves to be used by the media to sell advertising space. I'm sure we can—"

"Shut up, Ned," said Cody.

"I'm just tryin'—"

"Shut up!"

"But—"

Cody looked at Ned. Ned shut up.

"Okay, it's on. Just act natural." Jack held up the small cassette recorder. "This is Jack Dale, K2HO Radio, live, down here at Bits' Saddle and Canvas in downtown Nampa. The Treasure Valley has rodeo fever! Several of the contestants entered in the big Snake River Stampede, to be held Tuesday through Saturday, July thirteenth through the seventeenth, are in here picking up supplies. I've been talking to a couple of cowboys, Cody Wing and Ned, uh . . . ?" Jack looked toward Ned for the answer. No answer. Ned was in the ozone. ". . . and Ned.

"Cody, what's your event?"

"Bareback and bulls."

"Ned. Ned, what's your event?"

"I am entered in the calf roping event." Ned enunciated each syllable carefully.

"What would you say is the difference between the riding events and the roping events?"

"Ropers and doggers," explained Cody, "have to haul their horses and it costs more to rodeo. Roughstock riders just haul themselves and their gear. 'Course they get hurt more often."

"There's more colored people and white trash in the bucking events, but we have our share of Mexicans in the roping," added Ned, loosening up a little.

"What?" said the astonished interviewer.

"You know, more Negroid types and riffraff from the lower class," Ned said expansively. "They tend to go into bull riding. Low investment and I've read their skulls are thicker."

There was a pause. Cody turned to Ned. "Did you go to school to learn all this stuff, Ned? Or does it percolate through the sewer pipes in your brain and condense like droplets on your tongue?"

"Well, you're a good example," retorted Ned. "I happen to know you're not a college graduate." He caught Jack's eye to emphasize the point.

Jack, who had earned his high school diploma in the navy, did not acknowledge Ned's evidence. His tape recorder continued to roll along.

Suddenly a big canvas duffle bag popped over Ned's head and

was pulled down to his boot tops! The drawstring jerked tight around his knees and Ned fell over like a limp sausage. Two cowboys nodded to Cody and dragged the package out of the store. It bumped over the doorjamb and disappeared down the sidewalk. Jack and Cody watched it go.

Jack looked at Cody. "Gosh, is he one of you guys?"

Cody sighed. "Did ya ever have a dog that kept messin' on the carpet? He's your dog and you love him, but sometimes you just want to cut out his liver and feed him to the coyotes."

7

Tuesday Night, July 13
Nampa, Idaho

That night, the first performance of the Snake River
Stampede went smoothly. They
were down to the final event, the bull riding. The crowd could sense
the excitement in the announcer's voice:

"Ladies and gentlemen. You are in for a treat tonight! Two-time
world champion bull rider, Manly Ott, from Kit Carson, cool, costly,
colorful Colorado, has drawn bull number ten-twenty, unridden in four
years! He has thrown hundreds of cowboys, never fought a draw, the
pride of Bobby Monday's string, the devil's nightmare, Kamikaze!"

Cody and Lick stood on the chute gate. Every mother lovin' rodeo
cowboy, would-be bull rider, and in-the-know spectator sat in rapt
anticipation. Manly, like Lick, Cody and others of their samurai
persuasion, had tried to ride Kamikaze. Some, several times; all
unsuccessfully.

If Manly conquered ol' 1020, he would more than likely win the
whole shootin' match, but most of the smart money was on the bull!

Manly was a champion. He made a good living riding bulls. He
was short and stocky with an outgoing personality and a baby face.
Not everyone liked Manly's cocky attitude, but they respected him.
He was actually putting something in a savings account!

Bull riders are a strange lot. It takes a man with all his lichens
on the south side to climb on the back of a leather-covered, two-
ton, recoiling artillery field cannon, tie his hand to the breech lock
and have someone push it over a cliff!

They ride without protection. No padding, no helmets, no fifteen-yard penalty protecting them from unnecessary roughness. And no help save the clowns. Rodeo clowns dress in oversize cutoffs, gaudy scarves and painted faces. These clowns are, in fact, bullfighters. They usually work in pairs and it is their job to separate bull rider and beast at the ride's conclusion. Once the rider is down they put themselves in harm's way and divert the revenging behemoth's attention away from the bull rider. Brave? Reckless? A death wish?

Why would anyone become a rodeo clown? That query can be answered only by asking, why do some dogs chase cars?

Most bull riders are young, in their twenties. In their hearts and minds, they are indestructible. By thirty, a man can feel his vulnerability. He can't see the end of the tunnel, but he knows it has one! Ten years of bull riding takes a fearsome physical toll on a man's body. It makes one yearn for a gentler, safer occupation like that of a professional kickoff-return specialist.

And what about that basic lifesaving instinct, fear? It is always there but it is overcome or reckoned with in a million different ways. It is a private emotion. The fear experienced by Peter when the cock crowed the third time; the sinkin' feeling ol' Chris Columbus had after seventeen days of slack-sail calm a thousand miles from Lisbon; the high, faraway voice of panic in the ear of a nineteen-year-old marine pinned down on Tarawa Beach; it's all the same. It makes your bladder loosen, your skin prickle! It puts your heart in your throat and bile on the back of your tongue!

But it is overcome. Threats, love, duty, pride, and Valium. Concentration, will, the power of positive thinking. Lunacy, therapy and partial lobotomy: all methods employed to face our fears.

Manly was ready. But how about Kamikaze? What was he thinking? In all fairness ... whoever named the Dumb Friends League has dang sure punched a few cows! Cows can't think, as in "think tank." Organizing a three-day meeting of Motor Vehicle Department managers would not be their bag. An algebraic equation leaves them cold. A bachelor of science degree is beyond their comprehension. They do things by instinct, like giving milk or growing hair. They learn by repetition the way rainwater hunts a groove in a hillside. Action-Reaction.

They naturally shy away from endeavors that require a specific answer. The most cows could hope to achieve in the modern world would be a master's degree in psychology.

Kamikaze was no different. He knew that cowboys tried to ride him. He knew he didn't like it. If the rider got hurt, it was nothing to him. He didn't comprehend consequences. He was incapable of feeling guilt. He had the attention span of a Bartlett pear. He could associate the bucking chute and the arena with the ride. He could concentrate on disengaging the rider and venting his spleen, but once the conflict was over, he dismissed it.

However, Kamikaze could mull things over in a narrow, bovine sort of way.

He remembered Manly Ott. Kamikaze recognized those cowboys who had tried to ride him. Manly had come back to the pens before the rodeo, leaned over the fence and stared at him for several minutes. Kamikaze had ignored him, although he could feel the cowboy's brain waves boring into his hide. Manly's aura was as recognizable to Kamikaze as his driver's license photo would be to you or me. The more Manly concentrated, the stronger Kamikaze could feel his presence. *Him again,* mused the bull. *Learn slow.*

Manly slipped down over Kamikaze in chute number three. He kept his head well back from the playful two-foot horns that curved up and out like an evangelist's arms during the invitation. Kamikaze was a "chute fighter" to boot. He employed these diversionary tactics to break the concentration of his next victim.

One of the reasons Kamikaze was hard to ride was that he followed no set bucking pattern. Most bulls had a routine that was observed and remembered by the fraternity of bull riders. Whether he spun to the right, spun to the left, bucked straight out or whatever: it was called the bull's "book"—as in "What's the book on this bull?"

Kamikaze's book changed storylines each time, but at least the ending was consistent: buck off the cowboy and try to kill him!

Manly had watched Kamikaze buck many times and tried to ride him three times in the last two years. If anybody could ride 1020, Manly Ott could. He was the best the Professional Rodeo Cowboys of America could put up. Everybody watching knew that. A quiet fell over the tense crowd.

Manly dropped down on the big smooth back, scooted up on his left hand secured behind the hump, and nodded his head. Before the gate was fully opened, Kamikaze exploded through the opening, deliberately cracking Manly's right knee into the post! Sensing Manly's slight imbalance, he wheeled to the left, throwing the rider's leg farther back along his right side and off his rope just slightly. He felt Manly pull himself back into the eye of the hurricane by brute strength! Kamikaze could feel Manly's body and leg coming back into position. When the momentum had just about brought him back, Kamikaze made his next move to the right! Manly's leg carried right on by the ideal spot and slid perceptibly onto the right shoulder. Off balance again, leaning slightly to the right, Manly dropped his head into the range of the lethal horns. Although it couldn't be seen from the fence, Manly felt the huge muscles underneath him flex and move him, against his will, an inch farther into the deadly arc! At the conclusion of the second jump, Kamikaze's front feet hit ground first, hurtling the passenger forward, like the driver in a front-end collision! Reaching back with his big blunt horn, the diameter of a good-sized corral pole, he tapped Manly on the cheek, fracturing his mandible and third right premolar!

Manly's grip released and he came off the right rear quarter. He landed flat on his back. Looking up, he saw one huge cloven hoof, two loosely swinging balls and a final hoof pass over his head, from left to right.

The next thing he knew, the clowns were pushing him up on the fence, out of danger.

Kamikaze ran out of the arena. He stopped long enough to have the flank strap removed and wandered back toward the hay rack.

Two jumps. Not bad, noted the bull. He would spend a peaceful evening under the stars nibbling on Canyon County alfalfa and resting.

Manly Ott would spend four hours on a surgery table under an orthopedist and an oral surgeon at Mercy Hospital.

"Ready?" asked Cody.

"Yup," said Lick.

Normally, Lick would not have paid much attention to the bull riders who went before him. He was concentrating on his own ride. But whenever Kamikaze bucked out, he watched. Everybody watched! The bull Lick had drawn tonight was a pretty good draw. A spinning bull, but not a real whirling dervish. He figured it would take plenty of spinning action to get a very good score.

Now, those of you readers who have never ridden a bull should appreciate that all the action takes place in eight seconds. Eight short seconds. In eight seconds, a man can walk from his Barcalounger to the refrigerator; a car can drive through Patricia, Texas; a 727 can cross the Mississippi River at milepost 204 north of Alton, Illinois; and a solar hiccup can shoot a sunbeam a million three hundred thousand miles into space!

However, it does seem considerably longer if you are a participant! I can vouch for that since I, myself, rode bulls, till my brains came in.

Lick was down in the chute, hand in the rope and nodding his head. Time starts when the bull crosses that invisible line into the arena.

One thousand and one, one thousand and two, one thousand and three, one thousand and four, one thousand and five, one thousand and six, one thousand and seven, one thousand and eight. Whistle! Just that fast.

Lick's mind is on autopilot. Feel, react. The muscles don't even bother to check in with the gray matter. The neurons on the board of directors have already laid out a game plan and unless some new situation arises that demands their attention, they are content to let the muscles handle it. This is natural, of course. That's why a good banjo player can pick out "Lonesome Road Blues" and talk to the bass man at the same time. The mind does the talkin', the fingers do the walkin'. The same applies to bookkeepers on adding machines, jugglers on high wires and radio evangelists quoting Scripture.

The drawback to this useful phenomenon that allows your body to perform a task while your mind is occupied elsewhere is just that! The more accustomed you are to doing something, the less you have to think about doing it. Your brain doesn't have to concentrate and that can be a costly error in the bull riding event. Hence, bull riders and bronc riders in particular make an intense effort to keep their minds on the ride: to concentrate.

Lick concentrated. He rode his bull.

When the whistle blew he released his grip and was tossed six feet in the air. He landed free and clear.

That was the good part.

Unfortunately, he scored a 65, which was out of the money. The bull didn't spin as much as Lick had hoped. Ah, well, the luck of the draw.

Lick had made plans to fly in a private plane with three other cowboys to the rodeo in Salinas, California. He would compete there Wednesday and Thursday, fly back to Nampa on Friday to watch Cody ride.

At 10:45 that night, he and his compadres lifted off the Nampa runway into a starry sky and headed southwest.

Tuesday Night Late, July 13
Nampa, Idaho

Cody had neither the money nor the inclination to join Lick on his trip to Salinas. He would wait in Nampa for Lick's return. While Lick was beginning to doze to the hypnotizing hum of the twin engine Aztec, Cody found himself three miles up Nampa-Caldwell Boulevard in the spidery confines and extraterrestrial neon glow of Pingle's Cowboy Bar. He had danced a few, met and adopted Smila Snees. Smila was a pear-shaped maiden with big brown eyes. She stood by Cody as his quarter stood in line to shoot a little eight ball.

"You need another beer 'fore my game, darlin'?" he asked her.

"No, thank you. How about you?" she countered, carefully choosing her words to avoid her conspicuous lisp.

"Yeah, here's a five. Go git another Velvet and Seven if ya don't mind."

One fourth of the boys in the dance hall were professional rodeo cowboys in town for the show. The rest were local cowboys, ropers, boot salesmen, farmers' sons and would-be truck drivers.

Cody shoved his quarter down the throat of the green-backed turtle with sixteen balls. He racked 'em up. Cody was a marginal speller, a fair guitar picker, an average bull rider and a C+ lover, but that blue chalker could shoot pool! He was even a better snooker player, which made him lethal in rotation, cutthroat and eight ball. When he sighted down a long green shot, it was like a proctologist taking aim on a pachyderm.

That night he played a lot for quarters. The challengers just kept placing them edge to edge along the baize lawn. Tonight he played a little sloppy, deliberately, but never relinquished the table. Finally, one of the local shooters spotted him and offered to play him for five. Cody let him win two out of three, then raised the bet to twenty a game. He won the next three, and was fifty-five dollars to the good.

Smila decided to have a couple glasses of white wine, with ice, which loosened her tongue.

"Thath great, Cody! Thith ith tho ekthyting!"

"I'll play ya, Cody." A bear paw squeezed his shoulder. Cody knew without turning around who was offering the challenge: Big Handy Loon.

They didn't call him Big Handy for nothin'! He was 6'4", 260, wore a 7⅝ Resistol and could palm a forty-pound medicine ball! His reddish blond hair was crew-cut over his cauliflower ears and his unibrow ran from temple to temple. There was no warmth in his smile, no humor in his laughter.

"I wuz jis' quittin', Big Handy."

"Yer luck run out, little feller? Guess he'd rather not play me. Just the local bums." Big Handy addressed Grenadine Sheffliff and winked conspiratorially. Grenadine squeezed his nineteen-inch bicep and smiled. She had long legs, long purple fingernails, long black hair and a long brisket! She wore clothing that diverted an onlooker's gaze from her less desirable characteristics to her assets: designer jeans, knee-high leather boots, five diamond rings, and a sequined, but tasteful, halter top. A two-ounce gold pendant bounced back and forth between her Acapulco cleavage like a one-armed salmon going up a Columbia fish ladder! She attracted considerable attention.

Cody had good reason not to play Big Handy. Big Handy was a compulsive winner. He hated to lose! His temper was legend. Stories of broken windows, tables, bottles and bones were well known to every professional rodeo circuit follower.

"Tell ya what, Cody, ol' son, you and I will play for a measly twenty bucks a game, and the loser buys the ladies a round. How could a fine gentleman like you refuse to buy two such fine-lookin' ladies a drink?"

"I'd rather not," said Cody.

"Ooooh, c'mon, Cody! You can do it! Bethydth, ith tho muth fun wathin' you thoot!"

"Good, lil' darlin'," encouraged Big Handy. "You give 'im a little squeeze for good luck and I'll rack 'em. Don't say good-bye to this quarter, sweet thing, it's just an investment."

Big Handy slipped the coin in the slot.

Cody and Big Handy each played up to their potential. Cody ran the table off the break three games in a row. Big Handy touched the cue ball with his stick five times, sunk two balls and scratched twice. He became increasingly frustrated and his temperature rose one tenth of a degree each time Smila thanked him profusely for the round.

"Oh, thank you, Big Handy. Thith ith tho nith of you. Maybe you'll get to thoot the neckth time.

"Thoot the thripth off 'em, Cody!"

Closing time put an end to Big Handy's financial drain.

"Let's get up a card game," suggested Big Handy with an edge to his voice.

"Jeez, Handy, I'd really rather—"

"You got a hunnerd and twenny dollars of mine, little man." His eyes were glittering.

"Who else wants to play?" He looked at the crowd standing around the table. "Smitty? Bobby? Pork Chop?"

Back at Big Handy's motel room, the boys set up. They spread a blanket over a square table and the five of them played. By three o'clock in the morning, Big Handy was ahead thirty-five dollars, Cody was down fifty, and nobody else was hurtin'. They played dealer's choice, dollar ante, ten-dollar limit and three bumps.

"I'm 'bout ready to call it a night." Cody yawned. Smila squeezed his leg.

"One more hand. Okay?" Big Handy offered. Everybody nodded.

"Jacks or back." Big Handy shuffled and dealt everyone five cards, facedown. "Bobby, can you open? Pork Chop? Cody?"

"Yup, I'll open for ten," answered Cody.

Smitty stayed.

"Your ten and ten." Everybody involuntarily looked at Big Handy.

"Twenny to you, Bobby."

"Fold. See you guys later, I'm hittin' the sack."

"I'm in," proffered Pork Chop.

"Call," said Cody.

Smitty threw his cards into the pot and left the room.

"Cards to the players."

"One," said Pork Chop. He discarded a deuce and was dealt a nine. Five, six, seven, eight, nine: he hit his straight!

"Two." Cody held his openers: bullets, and the jack of hearts. He picked up his first card: ace of hearts. His mind became awake. Three aces. Great! He slid the final card into his hand and fanned it. Impossible! Peeking out from behind the jack, like a hesitant showerer in Phys Ed 101, was the fourth ace!

"Dealer stand pat." Big Handy had dealt himself a full boat, kings and tens. "Bet yer openers," he instructed, feeling expansive.

"Check to the power," Cody fished.

"Ten," bet Big Handy, not wanting to scare anybody out.

"Your ten and ten," upped Pork Chop.

Cody considered the hand. Both Pork Chop and Big Handy figured they could beat his opening pair. He'd held three cards to plant three of a kind in their mind. It didn't plant, or they figured they could beat three of a kind. Pork Chop had drawn one card. Probably holding two pair. Or the makin's of a straight or flush. Whatever he was hoping for in the last draw, he must of hit it. Big Handy was another story. Didn't draw a card. He might be holding a straight or a flush, maybe even a full house. But . . . Cody had four of a kind! His strategy should encourage everyone to stay in the game as long as possible.

"Your ten and ten more," Cody said, and laid his money on the pile.

"Here's your twenty, boys, and twenty more," bumped Big Handy.

"Limit's ten," reminded Pork Chop.

"Anybody got any objections to uppin' the ante, last hand and all?" asked Big Handy.

"Okay by me," said Cody.

Pork Chop studied his hand and looked at the pot. "I guess not. That's the last bump anyway."

"What say we skip the bump rule?" suggested Cody.

"Suits me," said Big Handy.

"Well, I'm gonna save my twenny and let you two high rollers fight it out. Fold." Pork Chop threw his cards on the pile.

"Your twenty and twenty more," said Cody.

"And twenty."

"And twenty."

"And twenty."

"And twenty."

Big Handy dug in his wallet, between his tattered Social Security card and a three-year-old prophylactic, and unfolded a hundred-dollar bill. He laid it on the table.

"I ain't got a hunnert," said Cody. "How 'bout this buckle? It's worth a hunnert."

"That buckle ain't worth a dead horse at the dog track! Tell you what, pipsqueak, I'll take the boots for a hunnert."

"Hell, these are three-hunnert-dollar Leddys!"

"All right, all yer cash and one boot."

Cody counted out thirty-seven dollars, pulled off his boot, and put them in the pot. Then he took off the other boot and set it up on the table.

"Raise you one boot," he said.

Big Handy took off his right boot, then stood up and undid his buckle.

"Call and raise you a buckle."

"Your buckle and a shirt."

"Your shirt plus a watch."

"Your watch and a pocketknife."

"Match yer knife and up you a pair of Wranglers."

"Your Wranglers and . . . and, uh . . ." Cody looked around the room.

"How 'bout my thirt?" volunteered Smila.

Cody had temporarily forgotten sweet Smila. He and Big Handy sat across the table from each other. Each wore his hat, underwear, and socks. Big Handy had on his left boot. Pork Chop sat at the table, guarding the pile of money and clothes.

"Depends on whether he can call in like manner," said Cody, lookin' at Big Handy.

"Hee thtill got hith hat!"

All three poker players looked at her like she'd just stepped off a bus from Neptune! Hats wouldn't go unless the game got serious!

"Grenadine, gimme your shirt."

"Handy, honey, all I got's this halter top."

"Fine. I'll bet your halter top and raise my last boot against the shirt and bra. Call!"

"Oh, goody," said Smila, peeling down.

"Why not," said Grenadine.

The four of them were bareback. Pork Chop sat unnoticed and slobbering on the gathering laundry.

"I called. Let's seem 'em."

Cody rolled over the jack, then the ace of hearts, the ace of clubs, the ace of diamonds.

Big Handy was addin' as fast as his distracted mind would let him. *If he paired jacks, his boat is higher than mine; if he didn't, it's just three of a kind....*

The ace of spades rolled over and snuggled in next to his brothers.

Handy froze. His face became ashen! Pork Chop's mouth fell open. The room was silent.

Blotches began to form on Big Handy's naked chest. The redness crawled up his neck until his cheeks were flaming!

"Pork Chop," Cody said quietly, "see if you can slide the pot into that paper bag there." Cody's eyes never left Big Handy's. Pork Chop gently slid the money and clothes into an Albertson's shopping bag. He picked up the boots and gave Smila the armload. He pointed to the door. She eased out to Cody's pickup.

"I'm gonna be goin' now," said Cody without moving.

Big Handy was undergoing a Vesuvian turmoil inside. His lips were twitching, his hands were quivering and his eyes were glazed over like frost on a windshield! Grenadine slipped out and got in Cody's pickup. Pork Chop followed, but watched through the motel window. From his vantage point, he saw Cody slowly rising, never dropping Big Handy's gaze.

Suddenly the table exploded from the floor and bounced off the ceiling! The air was filled with Bicycle playing cards! Cody flew around the room in his underwear like a turpentined cat! King Kong lunged after him! Big Handy picked up the black-and-white TV set and threw it at the careening figure as it climbed the wall above the picture of the matador painted on black velvet! The television exploded against the wall! Big Handy jumped and fell on the bed! Cody jumped on his back and pulled the covers around the prone body, holding the edges together. An eerie ripping sound accompanied the appearance of two giant paws tearing through the sheets!

Cody skittered to the door. He opened it, slipped through and started to close it behind him. Big Handy crashed into the edge of the door, nose first. He shattered his nasal septum.

The wounded bear screamed in pain and frustration! During Handy's temporary blindness, Cody jumped into the pickup with Pork Chop, Smila and Grenadine. They pulled onto the street and passed the flashing red lights of a City of Nampa patrol car.

"I hope Deputy Dawg has a bazooka," Cody said as he shifted into second gear.

Friday Night, July 16
Nampa, Idaho

L ick sat in the bar in Nampa on the Friday night after his return. He had not done well in Salinas and was not the best company. Cody had left the bar with Smila.

Lick was in a not-too-enthusiastic conversation with a local divorcee. He was also slightly drunk.

"How old are you?" she asked.

"Thirty-two," said Lick.

"How long you been rodeoing, if that's what you call it."

"Hard since ... since I was twenty-five."

"Why?"

"It's what I do."

"Did you go to college?"

"Yeah."

"Graduate?"

"Yeah, even one year toward a master's."

"And you're still ... still playing cowboy?"

"I said, it's what I do."

"Yeah, but you could probably have a good job."

"I did."

"You married?"

"Nope."

"Were you?"

"Yup."

"Kids?"

"No."

"Well, that's good, anyway."

"Maybe, maybe not."

"I don't understand. Does rodeoing pay a lot of money?"

"I broke even one year out of the last six, but this year I'm doin' okay."

"How much can you make? This year, I mean."

"Thirty, thirty-five thousand, if everything goes good."

"That after taxes and travel expenses, et cetera?"

"Nope." Lick took a sip of his gin and tonic and looked into the green eyes of the woman sitting across from him. She was staring at him like he'd just announced his inclusion in the Guinness Book of Stupidity!

"All I learned in college was how to work for somebody else. Drawin' wages. It's kind of a trap. You graduate and make pretty good money the first few years. You feel kind of a moral obligation to use your education. You get married, buy furniture, buy a car, make house payments, join the Rotary. You become responsible. An upstandin' member of the community. Then later, when you realize what's happened to you and you want to make a change, you can't. You can't afford to take any chances that would jeopardize that regular paycheck. All those people are countin' on you.

"You say to the wife, 'I want to rodeo full-time, before I'm too old to compete.' She says, 'You'll be gone all the time, who'll make the house payments? What about my bowling league, I'm president next year.' You say, 'We'll sell the house, you come with me, give your bowling ball to your sister.' She says, 'What about the dog, our vacation to Yellowstone.' You say, 'We'll take the dog and see a lot more of the country than Old Faithful.'

"But she can't see it. Can't understand it. 'Give up all this security? You must be crazy!' And you can't even discuss it with your folks or the guys at work! They're in the same trap, and the occasional person who thinks your idea is great usually turns out to be crazy, too! It's not something you can talk to people about. Eventually, though, you work it out on your own, and if you're willing to give up everything you've accumulated in life, you just do it and damn the consequences."

"Man," she said, "you are something else. What do you want most? I mean, do you have any specific goals?"

"Yeah. I'd like to make the National Finals."

"The National Finals?"

"Kind of the Superbowl of rodeo. The top fifteen contestants in the year compete at the National Finals in Oklahoma City in December. It's determined by the amount of money you win throughout the year."

"You mean the best rodeo riders in the world only make thirty thousand?"

"No. Some guys make more. Fifty, a hundred thousand. Not many make a hundred thousand, though. Plus they gotta pay expenses."

"Are you going to? Make the finals, I mean?"

"Ma'am, I don't know. I gotta good chance this year, for the first time in my life, and if I ride good, get lucky and don't get hurt, I'm gonna give the big boys a run for their money."

The lights in the dimly lit bar came up. It was one o'clock in the morning.

"Can I take you home?" Lick asked.

"Do you have a car?"

"Nope."

She looked at him for a long moment. He crackled into a slow grin. It was the twinkle in his eye that finally won her over.

"Okay," she said slowly. "I think I'd like to get to know you better."

The digital, phosphorescent clock radio was just posting 2:16 A.M. when Lick closed his eyes and drifted into sleep, folded up against the lady's backside. It was only under these conditions, or when he was sufficiently drunk, that he could go to sleep immediately.

He woke at 7:00 the next morning with the delicious feeling of a soft hand rubbing his neck. What an exquisite feeling to wake up that way. He kept his eyes closed, savoring, and groaned. There is nothing more flattering than the attention of an interesting woman.

"Hey, big boy, what would you like for breakfast?"

"Umm, how 'bout a little more of you!"

This lady looked good in the morning!

Ah, friends, there are time-outs in life. People are allotted more than they use. They should be taken when there are roses to be sniffed. For instance, this lady who looked good in the morning. That is something that never ceases to amaze. There are some women who don't even have bad breath in the morning! It's true! And their shape, the softness of their skin. The hollow spot where their clavicles collide, ankles, fingernails, the undercurve of a breast, an earlobe, a ringlet: all designed to take your breath away. Sigh.

"Will I see you again?" she asked, dropping him off at the contestants parking area where Cody was waiting.

"Do you want to?"

"Yes . . . yes, I do."

"Then you will, but I can't say just when."

"Good-bye, cowboy."

"Bye, darlin'."

Standing there on the grassy roadside in the early morning sun, Lick reflected a moment.

Another good one. I mean a good one! Maybe someday.

He leaped into the pickup. Cody was asleep in the back.

"That you, Lick?"

"Yup. Go back to sleep. I'll drive for awhile."

He switched on the radio. Willie was rippin' through "On the Road Again."

That's right, Willie, Lick thought to himself. *On the road again. Like a goose headin' south, like leaves on the Amazon, like a prisoner who just climbed the wall. Movin' just to feel the wind on yer face.*

He sighed. *Suck it up, cowboy, it's time to go.*

Lick smiled and put the truck in gear.

10

It was in Kansas City that Cody was struck by lightning. The thunderbolt hit him right between the eyes, drove the current down his spine and crackled off the end of his lightning rod! He was dumbstruck; he fell in love!

Not puppy love, or "a walk in the park" love. No gentle tendrils of morning mist, no lingering sunset love. No! This was love right out of the bowels of Mount Saint Helens!

Lilac was twenty-eight, had a smooth forehead and wore a size nine Buster Brown!

After the Wednesday night rodeo, Lick and Cody followed the mob to one of Kansas City's finest urban cowboy dance halls. A little place called Jerry's Sandbox on Main. Cody, who had learned his footwork at community dances as a boy, watched this lovely figure dancing the swing with two or three local boys.

"Save my place," he said to Lick. He made his way to her table, where she sat with two other girls.

"Pardon me, ma'am," he said. "Would you care to dance?"

She looked up at him. She had long brown hair, stood 5'10¾", had limpid pools and lips that fit a Popsicle. The band was on the third line of "Help Me Make It Through the Night." Lilac subtly sized him up and, concluding that he was at least six feet tall, said, "I'd love to."

She stood up and looked at him at eye level. She was long and graceful. More like an impala than a cheetah. More prey than predator.

"How are ya tonight?"

"Fine," she said.

"Man, you are gorgeous!" he said, and he meant it. "You can dance, too!"

"Thank you. You're not so bad yourself." Which he wasn't.

She was a city girl gone urban cowperson. She hadn't grown up learning the mating nuances of the slow dance that is natural to small town girls. However, current began to flow.

She backed up so she could look at his face as they danced.

"What do you do?" she asked.

"Ride broncs and bulls."

"What!" She stopped and looked at him.

"Ride broncs."

"You mean horses?"

"Yup."

"For a living?"

"Well, it's not a real good livin' right now."

"What do you mean? You have a stable or something?"

"No, I rodeo."

"Oh, that's why you're here! Kansas City, I mean. For the Shriners' Rodeo?"

"Yes, ma'am."

"You're kidding. Are you sure you don't sell insurance or work in a bank or something?"

"Nope, I rodeo. Have you been?"

"No. Not ever."

"How would you like to?"

"When?"

"I'm up tomorrow."

"What!" She looked at him long. "You're not kidding, are you?"

"No, of course not. My pardner's back there if you need a reference."

"No, no. I just have to think about it a minute."

They said no more until the dance ended. Cody took her back to her group and walked back to his table in a daze. It wasn't her obvious interest in his uncommon occupation that dazed him. He was always flattered when that happened. It was her. Something about her. Though he couldn't put a finger on the feeling, she had just shot a steel-jacketed, fifty-caliber round through his galvanized aluminum status quo!

How do you describe it? Your chest, maybe your heart, gets light. You can feel your pulse beating in your neck. The sounds around you become muffled. A 747 could land on the dance floor and you wouldn't even turn around! A door opens in the recesses of your brain and the only word that comes to the front is **wonderfantastakemarvelous!**

Cody sat down completely unaware of his cronies at the table.

"Well, I'll be a certified hellgramite! What a good-lookin' dolly!" LoBall McKinney said, and slapped Cody on the back. "Maybe I'll take 'er fer a spin myself."

"No!" exclaimed Cody. Then, surprised at himself. "Oh, sure, LoBall, whatever."

"Well, if you got 'er all lined up, it don't matter to me."

"No, no. Go ahead. I didn't mean nothin'."

LoBall traveled with two other roughstock riders. Both Cody and Lick liked LoBall, even though he seldom won and wasn't very ambitious. They'd known the blond Kansas bull rider for several years. He was about Lick's height, with blue eyes and a prominent nose. He was of average build, with an inordinate amount of hair in his ears. There were rookies who assumed his name came as a result of some anatomical anomaly. That was not the case. One night, in Garden City, Kansas, he had won $120 in a hand of jacks or back. No one could open; there were six in the game. The worst hand in the game was a nine high. LoBall won it after putting up his bull rope and Buck knife as collateral. He had a little wheel: ace, deuce, trey, four, and five.

LoBall stood up in time to see some big fellow, with feathers in his hat and designer jeans, take Lilac out on the dance floor. For three minutes he put her through the most intricate series of twirls and spins, loops, dips and catches, he had ever seen. She followed effortlessly. Cody noticed, too. His spirits sank slightly.

The band took a break and a jukebox filled in the void. People relaxed.

Cody made his way to her table.

"Can I buy you ladies a drink?"

"Sure, cowboy. Sit down. I'm Lilac, this is Rita and Maribeth. What's your name?"

"Cody."

He was staring at her.

"One white wine, a Michelob light, a gin and tonic, and ..." she said. He didn't respond. "Cody?"

"What!"

The cocktail waitress appeared at his shoulder. Lilac gave her the order.

"Anything for you?"

"Yes, ma'am. A Velvet ditch. Sorry."

"Are you all right?"

"Yes. Oh, yes. I'm fine. 'Scuze me, I was ... I was ... so, you've never been to a rodeo. If yer willin', I'll take you tomorrow. They got good seats for contestants' wives, I mean friends or ... whatever. You know what I mean."

"What are you doing tomorrow?" she asked.

"Nothin' till tomorrow night." He brightened.

"I mean tomorrow night."

"I'm up in the bull ridin'."

"Are those fellas with you in the rodeo, too?" she asked.

"Those three at the table? Would you like to meet them? All of you?" He turned to Rita and Maribeth.

"Sure, why not."

Cody waved his partners over. They drew up chairs and surrounded the three girls.

"This is Lilac." Cody scooted closer to her, a display of territoriality that would have been noted by any animal behaviorist present. "Rita and Maribeth, this is Lick, LoBall and Franco."

Pretty soon, Cody had his arm around Lilac. Rita and Maribeth were sorted out and spotted between Lick and LoBall, and LoBall and Franco. Another round was ordered as the vociferous vaqueros regaled the maidens with stories of rodeo bravado and derring-do. Cody was sinking into the quicksand of infatuation.

By midnight Lick was drunk, Franco had related his whole

Portuguese lineage, LoBall had eaten eight spearmint Certs and Cody was mired up to his earlobes. We're talkin' cloud nine, straightjacket, last cigarette and blindfold—rapture!

As Cody sat like a space cadet on Pentothol one of the female dancers tumbled into his lap.

"Oh, excuse me!" she said.

Cody helped her lift off.

"Hey, you jerk!"

Cody turned around, still basking in the first plane of anesthesia, just in time to see a right cross four inches from his face!

Friends, forgive the intrusion, but I feel a word is in order here regarding amateur pugilism. Many of us imagine ourselves being forced to fight in defense of a noble cause. We rise to the occasion and vanquish the bully. A small scar, like a saber slash, remains on our cheek as a reminder of that moment of glory.

Or a drunk insults your date. You snort with disdain and walk briskly by, tightening your grip on her elbow. That night you toss and turn reliving what you should have done to defend her honor.

I believe fighting is instinctual. Maybe not as basic an instinct as shopping, but a primitive action just the same. When struck, one strikes back, particularly when the first blow is a surprise.

When you are blindsided at an intersection, you counterpunch.

Cody went backward over his chair and slid like a halibut on a tile floor. He wound up under the next table!

The protagonist, hereinafter known as One-punch Charlie, straightened up. Franco, who was sitting closest to the action, leaped from his chair and jumped on One-punch Charlie's back!

Franco swung both legs around One-punch Charlie's waist and brought his boot heels down on the big man's knees. The men fell forward into the scattering crowd as the band played on—"Hard Hat Days and Honky Tonk Nights." One-punch Charlie might have been a professional football player, because two of his friends fell on Franco like he was a loose ball!

LoBall grabbed one of the big boys by the hair and pulled him off Franco. Atlas turned around and stood up. LoBall let go of his hair. In fact, he couldn't reach the top of his head!

Atlas came up from the basement with an uppercut to the midsection! His fist came knuckle-to-silver with the 1980 Prairie Circuit All Around Champion Trophy buckle that LoBall proudly wore! He broke two bones in his little finger and dislocated the knuckle in his ring finger. The impact carried LoBall two buzzard lengths away!

Lick was on top of the third member of the invading force. Though not as big as One-punch Charlie or Atlas, Billy Goat Gruff surpassed them in ferocious appearance. Billy Goat Gruff was still on top of Franco trying to strangle him! Franco was still on top of One-punch Charlie! They looked like a line of bunny hoppers that had caved in on itself.

Lick had his hands around Billy Goat Gruff's head from behind. He had an index finger up each of Billy Goat's nostrils, pulling them apart like he was setting a gopher trap!

Cody came to with a ringing in his ears. He crawled out from under the table and struggled to his feet. He stumbled and accidentally stepped on Billy Goat's ankle, which was sticking out of the pile like a leg on a soft-shell crab between two pieces of bread.

You could hear the bone snap! Billy Goat Gruff screamed! Atlas spun around and swung on Cody with his broken hand! Cody tripped simultaneously! Atlas connected with Cody's shoulder blade! The long bone in his middle finger cracked at the metaphysis!

Police whistles froze everybody in their tracks! The officers dragged Lick off the pile. Billy Goat Gruff stood up. Tears streamed from his eyes, there was blood on his lip, he couldn't put any weight on his left foot and his nostrils looked like his mother spent the night with a camel!

Franco was flatter'n hammered tinfoil!

One-punch Charlie had two fractured kneecaps and couldn't get up. Cody's eye was swelling and LoBall still couldn't catch his breath. Lick felt suddenly nauseous. He turned to avoid embarrassment and barfed on One-punch Charlie's girlfriend's pantleg, who was kneeling over her wounded gladiator, cooing.

LoBall did the talking.

"No, sir."

"No, sir."

"No, sir."

"Nobody's fault."

"Not much damage, really."

"Yes, sir. Well some."

"We'll pitch in for the chair."

"Yes, sir."

"Tonight? Yes, sir. Out of town. Yes, sir, by dawn."

"Would you mind giving us a few minutes' head start before you release King Kong and Rambo."

"No, sir. Didn't mean to be a smart-aleck. No, sir, I guess they can't travel too good, anyway."

"I just thought—"

"Yes, sir. We're going."

LoBall gathered up Lick and Cody. They balanced Franco between them and split like four caroling winos!

* * *

Ten A.M. Thursday found them all bruised, hung over, on greasy beds in room 306 at the Wanderon Inn, off I-35.

Cody was sitting on the bed in his shorts. More accurately, he was sitting on Franco in his shorts. His mouth tasted like he'd been sucking on a roll of pennies.

"Damn, Lick. Damn, damn, damn! Lick, what do I do? How can I find 'er? All I know is 'Lilac.' 'Course, she probably doesn't want anything to do with me after last night."

Cody was having a sinking spell. His left eye was swollen to a slit and purple. It looked like a canned plum.

"Now wait a minute, Cody," said Lick. "You don't know that. She knows where to find you. Didn't you tell 'er you were up tonight? See, you might be surprised. Besides, it don't matter anyway."

"Lick, she was different! Didn't you see her? She was gorgeous. Delicious, and she liked me!"

"So what? There's millions of gorgeous, delicious women."

"Dammit, Lick, she was different."

Cody felt terrible. He hadn't been that close to something good in so long. His ol' heart was aching.

Longing? Loneliness? Love? Lust? Doesn't really matter which. All require that the object in question be present to be satisfied. And she had disappeared!

July 22
Kansas City, Missouri

That night at the big coliseum, Cody kept studying the crowd. *Hell,* he thought, *there's no way I'd see her, even if she did come.*

During the calf roping Cody was limbering up. They ran the first set of bulls into the chutes and slid the gates closed behind them. Cody's bull was in the next set. He put on his chaps and tied on his spurs. Looping his bull rope on a board behind the chutes, he rosined up his rope and glove.

Concentrate, he thought. *I know the bull. Bucks out straight three or four jumps, then spins to the right. Sit tight and be ready when he starts the spin. Don't be off balance to the left when he makes his move. Have that right spur dug in on the third jump. Good honest bull. He's not a buckle-winnin' draw, but if he's at his best and I am, we could have a chance at the money. Ridable, but don't take him for granted.*

Cody didn't watch the first six bull riders. He concentrated. *Slow, steady breathing. Relax. A vacuum.*

Then suddenly the gates slid back and the last six bulls rumbled in like boxcars! Bull 655, Tonto, was fidgeting in chute number five. Cody sprang to life! Lick was beside him. Cody dropped the loop end of the bull rope over the right side of Tonto, behind the elbow. Lick caught it underneath, through the boards with the hook. Cody ran the tail of the rope through the loop and tightened it up, testing for size.

Just right.

Just then, LoBall McKinney stuck his head over the chute gate. "She's here, Cody," he said, and then was gone.

Cody looked up, looked around, but saw nothing.

She's here, he thought. *She's here! Concentrate. She's here!*

Number 655 stood patiently while Lick tightened the rope. Cody hit a few more licks on the tail with his rosined glove.

"You're next," Lick said quietly.

"Now your attention, please, to chute number five, a Wyoming cowboy, Cody Wing, up on bull number six-five-five, Tonto."

Cody straddled the bull, sitting well back over Tonto's flanks, his boots on the boards. The calm descended over him like it always did at this particular moment. It was timeless and silent. He slid his hand, palm up, into the flat braided loop on the rope. Lick pulled again. Cody nodded. Then he took the tail of the rope across his palm, wrapped it around his hand, put a twist in it and flopped the tail forward of the handhold.

With his right hand he screwed his hat down, and then spit out his chew.

Tonto, you braymer sonuvabitch, I want the best you've got, he telepathed to the back of the bull's head. Then he smiled. *Perfect.*

He slid up on the rope, leaned forward, pointed his toes and furiously nodded his head!

Ol' 655 tensed. The gate swung open. For a split second, Tonto and Cody sat like a statue of Simon Bolívar in a park in Bogotá, Colombia. Then they burst into the arena under the gaze of 9,652 paid spectators! The first jump and deep breath squeezed Cody's left hand like a vise! Cody was settin' pretty. Second jump he spurred! Up on the third jump, spurring! Down, third jump, set right spur, stay to the right. Uptight on the hump. Into the spin, just like the book said. Spur with the left! Tonto tried to stick his head under his tail! Tight spin. Two spins, three, kick, kick high! Cody felt the kick coming, leaned back, ready, no sweat. Spur on the left, tight on right, two more spins! Kick coming, kick coming now! Tonto became completely airborne in a high kicking spin, Cody spurring on both sides, chaps flying, toes out, silver flashing! At the top of the lift-off the whistle blew!

Tonto came down, off balance, spinning to the right with both hind legs off center. Cody released his grip as Tonto hit the ground hard with his left hip! Cody's hand came free and he rolled off to his left. Tonto was on his feet. Cody was on his knees. Less than five feet separated their noses. For two seconds Tonto stared at Cody, shaking! Then the bull snorted and shook his head! *You did it, Tonto. Thanks!* One of the clowns darted between Cody and his eight-second business partner. Tonto ambled off after the clown.

Slowly Cody became aware of his surroundings. The crowd was on its feet, cheering wildly.

"Ladies and gentlemen . . . Ladies and gentlemen . . . A new leader in the bull riding, Cody Wing with an eight-five score!"

The house came down!

Cody took off his hat and bowed to the crowd. He was still smiling.

He watched the last bull rider. A 72 score.

"Drive safely, everyone and God bless. We'll see you back here tomorrow night. Good night."

Cody was taking off his chaps, spurs and glove and gathering up his gear. He was also soaking up the gladhanding and congratulations. He had made one hell of a bull ride! It had to be Tonto's best ever, too. "Best I've ever seen you ride," Lick had said. It was, Cody knew it.

"Cody. Someone to see you," said one of the cowboys.

Lilac stood in the arena, next to the chutes. He walked through the little gate toward her.

He wanted to run to her, slow motion, two lovers in a field of daisies like in the margarine ads, but he walked. A crooked grin on his face and a fading shiner.

She wanted to run toward him, too, like in the margarine ads. Instead she walked up to him, put her arms around him and hugged him. Her eyes were glistening with tears.

"Hey, cowboy, wanna get lucky?"

At her apartment Cody got cleaned up. She set him a glass of wine on the bathroom sink while he was in the shower. He was still on a natural high when he came downstairs and found her in lounging pajamas.

She rubbed his shoulders, held his face, kissed his hands and ran her fingers through his hair.

She was the most beautiful creature Cody had ever seen. She smelled like fresh peaches. She was brown and bathing suit white, smooth as a filly's nose and firm as an orthopedic mattress! When she laughed, it was the sound of wind chimes on a Santa Fe patio.

She made love to him like butterfly wings and new socks, like lime juice and icicles, like a hot tub full of maple syrup.

12

Friday Night, August 6
Great Falls, Montana
The Club Cigar

Three weeks after the Kansas City Summit.

10:15 P.M. Mountain Daylight Time (11:15 P.M. Central Daylight Time):

"Hello. Lilac?"

"Yes?"

"Lilac, this is Cody."

"Cody! Where are you?"

"Great Falls."

"Is that near Kansas City?"

"No, in Montana."

"Oh."

"How you doin'?"

"Fine. I'm doing fine."

"You don't sound too fine."

"I was just a little disappointed. I thought maybe you were back in town."

"That's what I wanted to talk to you about."

"Yes?"

"Lick and me will be comin' back to Burwell and Sidney next weekend, and I'd shore like to see you again."

"Where's Sidney?"

"Iowa. Prob'ly two hours from Kansas City."

"I could drive over and see you."

"That would be great!"

"How long are you staying? I mean, could you come back to Kansas City with me?"

"I haven't got it all figured out yet, but I surely could. We're both up in Abilene on the seventeenth, so I might could stay a couple three days."

"Cody, that would be wonderful! I can't wait!"

"Me, neither!"

"What's that noise?"

"The jukebox. I'm at the Club Cigar. Neat ol' bar here in Great Falls. They claim Charlie Russell used to hang out here. I don't know, everybody in Montana claims to have known him personally."

"What are you doing?"

"Just the usual. Settin' around shootin' the breeze. I just got here."

"Did you ride tonight?"

"Bareback. Might've done okay, too. We'll see after tomorrow night."

"Well, you do good, little buckaroo. Your biggest fan is back here in K.C. rootin' for you!"

"Oh, yeah?"

"You bet!"

"Lilac . . ."

"Yes?"

"Lilac, I really do like you a lot. I've never met anybody like you."

"I think you're pretty special yourself."

"I don't know if I ever thanked you properly for the fantastic time you showed me in K.C."

"Cody, the pleasure was mine."

The operator cut in. "Thirty seconds, please."

"Listen, I'll call you down the road, but save me that weekend?"

"Okay, Cody. I'll be waiting to hear from you."

" 'Bye, darlin'."

" 'Bye."

Click. Buzz.

Cody hung on the phone a few seconds. His heart felt heavy and light at the same time.

"You done?" asked the queued-up cowboy.

"Yeah. Yup, go ahead." He hung up the receiver.

He ambled into the crowded bar. He could picture Lilac. He could almost feel the warmth of lying next to her long browned body. The way she touched him with her long fingernails, tracing patterns on his chest. The way her hair fell around her face, her confident, trusting eyes. Her laugh, really a deep chuckle, that warmed his insides when he heard it. Cody felt a hollow empty longing.

"Hey, you blue-ribbon codpiece! Set yore raggedy ol' butt down here!"

Cody lifted out of his thoughts. "LoBall, what'cha doin'?"

"Set down and have a beer!"

"How you doin', Lo? Haven't seen you since Kansas City."

"Oh, gettin' by. Not winnin' much, though. Don't know how much longer the money will hold out."

"Me, too. Me, too."

LoBall McKinney took a pull on his draw.

Cody contemplated LoBall. He figgered LoBall to be a couple years older than himself, twenty-nine or thirty. Good fellow, honest, easygoing. LoBall was from Oberlin, Kansas, he remembered. Been rodeoing several years.

"Lo, you ever been married?"

"Yup. Twice. One lasted a month. The other a year."

"What happened?"

"Just couldn't quit rodeoin'. They couldn't put up with it."

"Were you in love?"

"You betcher spine-tinglin' cloaca I wuz! The second time, anyways."

"What was it like? I mean, how did you know?"

LoBall put down his glass and stared at Cody. Cody's face was painted a desperate shade of agony.

"You reckon you got bit, ol' pardner?" LoBall asked seriously.

"I don't know. I'm not sure. I don't know what it's supposed to feel like."

"It prob'ly feels different fer everybody. Sometimes it's an atom bomb, sometimes it's a meadowlark's song. Sometimes it sneaks up on you like a sore throat. How do you feel?"

"Well, sort of good and sort of bad. Is it supposed to feel bad?"

LoBall mused a second, wiping the beads of sweat off his glass.

"Yeah, there's a part of bein' in love that's bad. Sad, really. You'd think it would be all happy, but there's a part of it that's sad. Maybe it's suppose to hurt a little. Nothin' comes without a cost. It would be nice if it always felt good, but when you love somebody, when they hurt, you hurt. When they're happy, you're happy. Or you should be anyway. When you get to missin' someone you care about, it's like you peeled the hide off yer heart and all those bad feelin's you never cared about before can slip right in that same hole that love left. It kind of exposes you. You know what I mean? Like before, you were never lonesome or jealous or protective of nothin', so you never had those feelin's, but when you fall in love, you gotta take the bad with the good. Does that make any sense?"

"Sort of."

"Do I know 'er?"

" 'Member Lilac, from Kansas City?"

"Her! Man, do I remember! A died-in-the-wool snowy cottontail!"

"That's her."

"Have you told her?"

"Hell, I've only seen 'er once! Lo, Lick says I'm crazy!"

"Cody. You can't pay no 'tention to Lick. I've known him longer than you, and that pore ol' rat bag is sour on women. He wouldn't know a good one if she danced in his pork and beans!"

"He always has a lot of women. Every town we go to it seems, he has one stashed."

"Yeah, but they don't last long. They figger the pore bugger out purty fast and send him packin'."

"I don't want to end up like that."

"You won't. Somethin' burned him a long time ago. He's runnin' from love and yer runnin' to it!" LoBall thumped his beer down earnestly. "So, how does Lilac feel 'bout you rodeoin'? That's the death of many a cowboy romance."

"I never asked, but you know, I been doin' the circuit hard for nine years and I'm really not gettin' ahead. I been thinkin' 'bout quittin'. Git a job somewheres or go back to the ranch. Maybe goin' to college."

"Yeah, we all think about that some."

LoBall and Cody discussed love on into the night.

* * *

12:45 A.M. Mountain Daylight Time (1:45 A.M. Central Daylight Time):

"Hello, Lilac?"

"Cody?"

"Sorry to wake you."

"Ummmm, that's okay. Something wrong?"

"No. I just wanted to talk to you."

"Okay."

Silence.

"Cody?"

"Yeah?"

"What do you want to talk about?"

"Lilac. I . . . me and LoBall, we talked and had a few beers. I . . . I think I might be a little drunk. But not very drunk! Just a little."

"That's okay."

"Lilac?"

"Yes?"

"How do you feel about things?"

"Things? What things?"

"Important things."

"What do you mean, Cody?"

"Things like . . . uh . . . real feelings?"

"Cody. I think people should always be honest with each other."

"Whattaya mean?"

"They should tell each other the truth."

"I'm really thinkin' about you tonight," he said in a quiet voice.

Silence.

"I'm missin' you somethin' awful," he said in a small quieter voice.

Silence.

"Lilac?"

"Yes, Cody?"

"I think I'm fallin' in love . . ." She could barely hear him. The words faded off through Mountain Bell's spaghetti lines into that black space where true confessions and old memories lie around gathering stardust and wait to be recalled.

"Come see me, cowboy. I'll be here."

" 'Bye, darlin'."

" 'Bye."

Click. Buzz.

Monday
Great Falls, Montana

Monday morning found the boys' pickup headed south out of Great Falls on Highway 89. Destination: an old friend's place in Hardin, Montana, to lay up for a couple of days before making the Rapid City rodeo on Thursday. Hardin sat on the edge of the Crow Indian Reservation, fifteen miles north of where General Custer fired his last shot.

They hit Interstate 90 at two in the afternoon and headed east toward Billings and Hardin. The freeway parallels the Yellowstone River as it courses toward Billings. Beautiful and clear, the river relaxes the traveler and invites a closer look.

Lick and Cody had both placed in the money in Great Falls. They were in good spirits. Lick because he'd bought a new pair of sunglasses that morning, and Cody because he had been bit by the love bug!

Several miles up the road Bill and Doris Peeler had pulled their motor home off the highway into a rest area that was near the mighty Yellowstone. Doris set out a folding chair and poured herself an iced coffee. Bill lifted his spinning rod off its hook over the door, pocketed a jar of Patooshki Fireballs and started upstream.

"Watch out for Melanie," instructed Doris as the mongrel terrior trotted after Bill.

Porcupines lead fairly quiet lives. They nibble, climb trees and rummage around, mostly minding their own business. They do not seek trouble, no more than a tire seeks a nail. But that does not keep trouble from finding them.

The porcupine that now joins our cast happened to be exploring amongst the willers that populated the bank upstream from the rest area. It had a little sip from a stranded pool of cool water and lay down to sun itself. It drifted off to sleep dreaming porcupine dreams. Twitching occasionally, winking off a fly and lazily flopping its tail. Porcupines are never bored. To their everlasting good fortune, they can't tell the difference between boredom and contentment.

"Pull over up here," suggested Cody. Lick turned leisurely into the rest area. He drove several car lengths beyond the parked motor home with Doris sitting nearby.

Our boys got out, stretched their legs and breathed in the cool air. They could hear the river flowing by like a distant locomotive.

Cody started walking toward the motor home. "Where ya goin'?" he asked back over his shoulder to Lick.

"Oh, just down by the river," said Lick. Both of them knew sometimes you just needed a little time alone. Cody watched him go. Lick was relaxed and thoughtful. He'd listened patiently to Cody's analysis of his fledgling relationship with Lilac. Cody needed to talk. Lick had done his part, he listened.

The river had carved out a good-sized gravel bar. No doubt it had been underwater in the spring, but now it allowed easy access to the river's edge. Lick reached the bar and walked slowly upstream, unconsciously soaking up the scenery, consciously clearing his mind.

Bill was casting into the swift current upstream from the gravel bar. He was methodically dragging his baited spinner into likely looking spots.

Melanie stayed near him but explored the brushy bank, sniffing holes and tracks of the residents who populated the neighborhood they'd invaded.

Porcupine lay on his side deep in sleep in the thick willers.

Lick continued his amble up the gravel bar thinking snatches of thoughts that kept him awake at nights, but quickly putting them out of his mind.

Bill moved downstream along the bank. He could not see Lick standing fifty feet away.

Melanie moved downstream through the brush, still circling.

Porcupine entered the flatline plane of slumber. Lick spotted something sparkling in the shallow water. He squatted at the river's edge and realized it was a spinner with two neon-colored salmon eggs lying in a quiet spot. A ten-inch rainbow trout was treading water two feet downstream from the bait, watching it.

Mesmerized, Lick watched the unfolding drama. He became absorbed as the trout beat his wings in the water to maintain his position. Lick momentarily forgot where he was, who he was, or why he existed. He became, for a brief period of time, *one* with the fish. He squatted on the bank of the Yellowstone hypnotized.

Melanie smelled Porcupine. She crept up to the sleeping rodent and sniffed his nose.

Porcupine opened one eye, spied the dog and leaped up! Melanie was so shocked she couldn't bark! Porcupine shot out of the willers onto the gravel bar! With the predator behind him, Porcupine made straight for the only protective cover on the bank! Melanie recovered her voice just as the trout struck the lure and Porcupine dove between Lick's legs!

Bill set the hook and Lick fell back, straddling Porcupine like a Hell's Angel mounting a Harley!

Porcupine squiggled free and shot into the water like a loose ball in the backfield! Melanie stood on the bank and yapped ferociously! Bill was reeling in his catch and Lick sat frozen in place like a butterfly pinned to a cork board!

Melanie's furious barking subsided but not before Cody and Doris came striding toward the ruckus. Bill was just coming out of the willers with the nice rainbow still wiggling on the end of the line. Melanie was sniffing around Lick, who sat bowlegged and leaned back on his elbows. Porcupine had beached himself and disappeared downstream.

"By gosh, nice fish!" observed Cody.

"Oh, yeah," agreed Doris. "Bill almost always catches fish. We're seniors, ya know, so we never worry about a license. I usually cook 'em. We like fresh fish. Sometimes I use cornmeal and fry 'em. Bill's mother used to do 'em that way with catfish, but I like to bake 'em.

A little lemon and butter, some garlic salt. We've got propane, ya know. Nice stove. Maybe you'd like to ..."

By now Cody had realized that Doris was a marathon conversationalist. He looked at Lick who, as yet, hadn't moved.

"You all right, Lick?" asked Cody.

Lick turned his head. Cody saw his face was the color of boiled tongue. Cody put his hands under Lick's armpits and started to lift him up.

"No-o-o-o-o-o-o-o-o!" howled Lick.

Lick's eyes were glistening and saliva dribbled from his mouth. It was then Cody noticed the inside of Lick's legs. From knee to shining knee, up his inseam, and arching across his fly, were uncountable protruding spines!

"Dang! Looks like you sat in a cactus!" said Cody, glancing around for a cactus.

"Porcupine," breathed Lick.

"There must be a hundred stuck in you," said Cody in amazement.

"See if you can pull 'em out," said Lick.

Cody grasped a quill and tugged. Lick groaned. The quill remained firmly embedded.

"Jerk on it," instructed Lick.

Cody did as he was told. The quill came out of the skin but lifted the denim up and stayed fast. When he let go of the quill it repenetrated Lick's leg. He shivered with pain.

"Best get you to a doctor," said Cody.

* ★ *

At 4:45 P.M. Cody was standing at the emergency room admitting desk in Billings Memorial Hospital.

"May I help you?" asked the nurse. She was in her early fifties and cheerful. Cody's mother's age. Her name tag said Betty Jo.

"Well," started Cody, "it's my pardner."

"What's wrong with him?" she asked.

"He had an accident."

"Is he hurt?" The ludicrousness of the question evaded Cody. Besides, it was not his nature to concoct sarcastic replies.

"Yes, ma'am. He was attacked."

"What was the nature of this attack?" she continued, poising her ballpoint above the admittance form.

"It was down by the river," he explained.

"A wild animal? A bear? Mountain lion?"

"No, ma'am," Cody said. "A porcupine."

"Attacked by a porcupine?" She looked up at him above her 1.5x Walgreen half glasses.

"Well, actually he sat on it."

Cody, straight-faced, explained his version of the assault, including Bill's ten-inch rainbow. By the time he'd finished the story, the nurse had dropped her pen, weaved away from the counter and was doubled over in the corner, pounding on the bookshelf breathless with laughter! She scattered paperwork and pencils all over the floor.

"He's out in the truck," said Cody helplessly.

She had another involuntary siege of giggling.

It took a full minute for her to compose herself. As she wrote "Porcupine Attack" under "reason for admittance," tears were streaming down her face.

"We better have a look," she sighed.

Cody led her out to the pickup and opened the back of the camper shell. Lick was bent over the tack box. Cody had arranged a saddle and blanket on the top of it and Lick was laid over it like a roll of carpet on a pack mule.

His legs were spread apart with his buttocks in the air. His hands were braced over the far side.

The nurse peered in and involuntarily said, "Hike!" After a brief moment she recovered and disappeared into the emergency room. She returned with two orderlies and every employee within two miles! As the growing crowd of nurse's aides, residents and ambulatory patients jostled for a better view, the orderlies worked Lick to the back of the truck.

They formed a sling with their arms and carried him like a dead alligator into the large examination room. Unable to lay him on a bed, they set him in the middle of the floor. Lick lay propped up on his knees and elbows as gunshot victims, fracture recipients and alcoholic hallucinators sat up on their gurneys and stared at the human pincushion.

"All right! Break it up!" commanded an authoritative voice. "Nurse, get this rabble out of here! You! Staff, get back to your duties!"

The crowd grudgingly gave way as Dr. Klugman-Smith faced her patient, or more properly, as her patient about-faced her.

"Did he admit himself?" she asked Betty Jo.

Betty Jo had a fleeting picture of Lick coming down the sidewalk, moving crablike through a crowd. She swallowed the bubble rising inside her. "No, Doctor, this gentleman ..." She turned to Cody and broke into uncontrollable snorts. Holding her sides and finally leaning on an unconscious weekend housepainter, she heaved and tried to catch her breath.

"Cactus?" asked Dr. Klugman-Smith.

Cody stared into the intense brown eyes of Dr. Klugman-Smith, twenty-nine years old, hair pulled back in a bun and in her first year of residency.

"Porcupine."

"How ..." she started to ask, but the admitting room nurse burst out with a convulsive peal and plunged blindly through the crowd toward the exit!

Dr. Klugman-Smith walked around to Lick's front end and introduced herself. Lick tried to cock his head but all he could see were her white pants and sensible shoes.

After lengthy discussion and some experimentation they managed to roll up a small mattress for Lick to lie over. They lifted him up on an exam table with him bent over the mattress.

After three futile attempts to pull the quills through his jeans, Dr. Klugman-Smith borrowed a set of side cutters from Hospital Maintenance and began clipping the quills where they protruded through the cloth. Each *click* jiggled the needle-sharp points, causing Lick to emit grunts, then cries and eventually whimpers.

Having completed the pruning, they gently pulled down his pants. They peeled loose like Velcro.

Next came his underwear.

Mercifully, Dr. Klugman-Smith summoned the anesthesiologist on duty and put Lick out of his misery.

Lick was back in high school. The big game for the Vega Longhorns. The crowd watched on in the balmy Texas panhandle Friday night. Lick looked down the line to the left, then to the right, and located the linebacker just over the line. "Hup one, hup two!" He felt the center move. His crotch exploded and Lick flew over the goalpost on his back, large antennae bristling on his body like feelers on a lobster!

"Wake up, Lick," a voice said gently. "You're all right."

Lick opened his eyes and Dr. Klugman-Smith stood beside his bed, clipboard in hand.

"You're all right. We got them all out."

As he stared, she became less fuzzy. He remembered where he was.

"Quills have hundreds of minute barbs. You were under anesthesia for an hour and a half. But we got them all. Eighty-seven, I believe they said. We've given you antibiotics and treated you locally but I'm afraid there's going to be swelling. Especially in your genitals. You took several direct hits in the most sensitive areas."

She went on explaining in gruesome detail the importance of bed rest. Particularly to prevent swelling. Prolonged swelling could result in sterility. Inactivity, keeping cool were the bywords. She added she had prescribed a laxative to reduce straining.

*　*　*

As she left her patient she passed Cody in the waiting room. She tried to speak to him but was seized by what appeared to be a fit, covered her mouth and hurried from the room.

Cody entered and stood by Lick's bed. Lick was on his back with his legs elevated in a sling. He wore a large diaper-looking loincloth.

"Man, who'da thought it," observed Cody. "Well, at least yer not up again till Thursday."

Friends, there are injuries and there are injuries. During my hormone-charged youth, more than once I was able to affect the "Bull Rider's Limp." In my confused mind I envisioned this limp would illicit sympathy and admiration from the opposite sex.

I assume high school and college football players took advantage of sprains, strains, black eyes and casts for the same purpose.

There are all manner of these "glamorous" injuries that add to the projection of the macho image. Even today at poolside, when someone asks about the scar on my shoulder, I modestly say, "Broke my shoulder . . . [pause for effect] riding bulls."

On the other hand, when one of my real cowboy friends accidentally rode his horse up a guywire, resulting in an equine back flip and human broken ankle, he preferred not to discuss it. Of course, his friends made sure everybody in the immediate vicinity knew the gruesome details.

Falling off the cookhouse steps, dropping a rock on your foot or sticking a screwdriver up your nose do not qualify as glamorous injuries. Nor, I might add, does sitting on a porcupine.

Monday Morning, August 9
Kansas City, Missouri

Guess who called this weekend?" Lilac addressed the question to her nine-to-five confidante and fellow secretary, Maribeth.

"Robert?"

"Nope."

"Tim?"

"Nope."

"Who?"

"Cody."

"The cowboy!" said Maribeth knowingly. "Is he coming back to Kansas City?"

"This weekend."

"No kidding! Wait a minute, you ... didn't you have something planned? Tickets to Air Supply?"

"They weren't firm. Tim said he'd call if he could get them. But I guess I'll be busy."

"Serves him right."

"Oh, he's all right. He's a good time."

"Cody," mused Maribeth. "I'll never forget that fight at Jerry's. What a night."

"Maribeth, you should have seen him ride that bull. It was beautiful!"

"Beautiful?"

"It's hard to explain, but that's the only word that comes to mind when I remember it. Guess I've always thought of rodeos as horrid, like bullfights, but I'd probably go to a bullfight now."

"Not me. They kill the poor bull." Maribeth scowled.

"Maybe you're right, but it's the same kind of thrill. The challenge."

"Turns you on, huh?"

"How many people do you know that make a living pitting themselves against something that can kill you? Where your only defense is your own instincts. How many? I can't think of another person I know, personally."

"Oooooh, you got it bad! Did he tell you all that?"

"No. He doesn't talk about it that way. He talked about it, but like he was rebuilding a motor or outlining a sales pitch."

"Like being married to a race car driver or a boxer?"

"Or a matador. But let's not be getting marriage into the conversation," cautioned Lilac.

"Not the marrying kind? Just like every other eligible, conceited chauvinist within ten years of our age!"

"I dunno," answered Lilac, ignoring the diatribe. "He's kind of a drifter. He's had lots of jobs, but only long enough to finance his rodeoing. But, you know, Maribeth, I could almost sense something in him that made me think he's looking for a change."

"What do you mean?"

"The way he talked about his family's ranch back in Wyoming."

"Wouldn't that take the cake? Suave, sophisticated city girl marries Wyoming rancher ... Git along little doggie!" Maribeth laughed.

"There's something about him I really like."

"His cute little buns?"

"No. No, it's like ... well, he's real. Right down to his filthy chewing tobacco and the cow manure on his boots. I never thought about cowboys bein' real. Almost makes you believe there is a Roy Rogers."

Maribeth shook her head and smiled affectionately at her friend. She thought, *I hope this knight in shining armor doesn't have feet of Nike. One of us deserves a break.*

15

I'd rather eat barbed wire than listen to disco." Cody read the bumper sticker on the pickup in front of them. They had picked up Interstate 90 eight miles north of Sturgis, South Dakota.

"Man, what beautiful country!" Cody remarked as the tan hillsides, dotted with clumps of evergreens, surrounded their pickup. Chocolate chips in raw cookie dough.

Lick had good memories of Rapid City. His first big win this year was the Winter Show at the Civic Center, back in February. That thought gave him temporary respite from the current problem gnawing at his nerve ends. One of his special lady friends lived here. Chadron was her name. He saw her two or three times a year and usually stayed with her when he was in Rapid. Last summer she had resigned herself to him and his ways. Part of her feelings for him had died with the realization that her long-term future probably did not include him. But she decided she could handle her own heart and should enjoy as much of him as he let her.

Four days had passed since the porcupine incident. Lick was recovering. He could sit without much pain, though wiggling still hurt. Most of the swelling had gone down, with the particular exception of his dangling participles. They were several shades of bruised blue and yellow. Although they were swollen, he thought it was less than yesterday.

It was also painful, quite so. Movement—walking, for instance—

was awkward. He had been forced to draw out of the bull riding in Rapid City. He remembered Dr. Klugman-Smith's admonition that if he didn't take it very easy, permanent damage could result.

Lick knew Chadron would be disappointed. He'd talked to her last week and they had planned the weekend together. Now he'd have to explain ... *Explain what?* he thought. *That even being near her could render him sterile and forever at half-mast!* "And why?" she would ask, taking it all very personally. Lick could not think the scenario through.

Rapid City sponsors two big rodeos during the year. This summer show was part of the Central States Fair. The boys pulled into the contestant parking off Omaha Street at 6:30 P.M. They gathered their gear. Cody was up tonight.

"Lickity!" Chadron Borglum ran up and gave him a big hug.

"Chadron. How'd you find us so fast?" Lick asked.

"I was watchin' the contestants' entrance and recognized your pickup. How you doin'?" She hugged him and gave him a big kiss. "I've got a great time planned after the rodeo," she said. "Relaxing ... good company."

"Great. I'm ready fer that, Chadron. I need to visit with you about somethin'."

"Fine. We'll have plenty of time. I've got to get back to the booth. I'll catch you after the bulls. Do good, darlin'. Seeya!" She took off.

Following the show Lick found Chadron and they left the rodeo grounds in her car. If she noticed that Lick had drawn out of the bulls, she didn't say anything. That wouldn't have been her style.

"Cody's not coming with us?" Chadron asked. She was a nice-lookin', twenty-nine-year-old brunette who worked for the Rapid City Chamber of Commerce. She'd been ranch raised, a west river girl. She was easygoing and classy.

"No. He's doin' somethin' else."

"Okay." They headed north, out of town. "Let me tell you what's been going on ..." She talked. He remembered one of the many reasons he kept coming back to roost on her bedpost. She relaxed him. Made him feel comfortable. Even their silences were comfortable. She didn't let him get away with half explanations and she encouraged his dreams. She loved him. She had said it. He did not respond in kind. She had only said it once, and not at all in the last several months, but he knew. She let him tell the truth about his feelings, or lack of them, and she never held it against him. He would miss her.

"Now Ron and Rayla are nice folks. You met them last time you were here. He's a rancher and I go out to their place a lot. She's become a pretty good friend, and you'll like them."

They took a right at Piedmont and wound up the road into the hills.

"Tonight," she said, "we're having barbecue and hot tub!"

"Boy, that sounds great!" said Lick. Dr. Klugman-Smith had suggested cool baths. This might be therapeutic if the water wasn't too hot.

"They've got plenty to drink and I brought some scotch . . . You've got a bathing suit?"

"Yup."

Ron Rant and his wife, Rayla, turned out to be all Chadron said they were. A young ranching couple on the family ranch. He was confident, good with cattle and had done some punkin roller rodeoin' when he was younger. He had the makin's of a dignified, successful livestock man.

The hot tub was in the backyard, on a green lawn surrounded by a rail fence. A big Hereford bull stood sleepily watching the party over the top rail. The half-moon silhouetted the hills and trees surrounding the ranch.

Everybody got mellow and Lick almost fell asleep in the temporary arms of Cutty Sark's peace of mind. Ron and Rayla said their friendly good-nights about 12:45 A.M. Chadron snuggled under Lick's arm. They soaked up the hot tub, the crickets, the clean smell and the moonlight for fifteen minutes. Silently.

Chadron started taking off Lick's bathing suit.

"Darlin', I . . . I can't."

She stopped.

"I mean, right now."

She stared at him.

"I'm on medication."

"Are you all right?"

"Yeah, I just have to take this medicine and the doc said no sexual activities for a while."

"What's wrong? Something serious?"

"No. It's just for a few days."

Chadron Borglum had never been married, had an article published in *Scientific American*, or received more than a C in calculus. But she had always done well with deductive reasoning. A selection of possible multiple-choice answers were lining up on the left-hand side of her brain. Some were less than pleasant to consider.

She looked at him sternly, an unfriendly combination of suspicion and injury flickering in her eyes. In spite of knowing better, she hoped the explanation would vindicate him.

"Well?" she prompted.

"Ya see, Chadron, this is gonna sound funny . . ."

Oh, great! she thought. *I share him with who knows how many other women. I get to see him twice a year. I'm ready to pounce on him like a rutting elk and he's gonna tell me a funny story.*

". . . but, last Sunday, after Great Falls, Cody and I were drivin' up I-90 toward Billings. The truck was runnin' good . . ."

Good, you moron, she said to herself. *Great start. Now we're gonna have a travelogue with color commentary by Mr. Goodwrench.*

". . . and we stopped above the Yellowstone—River, that is—and I was walkin' along the riverbank there . . ."

If this has anything to do with laser beams, white buffalo or Jules Verne, it's over, she thought.

". . . so anyway I sorta bent down, squatted actually, and was lookin' at a fish there in the shallow water . . ."

This certainly sounds plausible, she thought. *Although he hasn't said a thing about talking to the fish.*

". . . and the next thing I knew . . . yer not gonna believe this . . ."

Somehow, she said to herself, *I think you're right.*

". . . I sat on a porcupine."

He *was* right.

Lick went on embellishing his explanation, the trip to the doctor, the long ride to Rapid. He offered Cody as a witness and Doris and Bill, though he couldn't remember their last name. The whole story made him sound like a second grader with a huge imagination trying to explain why he had chocolate on his face.

Chadron sat stone-faced.

She slid out from under his arm and looked at him for several seconds. The flames were working across her chest and nibbling at the backs of her ears.

"Sorry," he said lamely.

"Escuse me a minute." She stepped out of the hot tub and walked into the house.

The light clicked off on the back porch. He heard her coming.

"Lick," she said quietly, "close your eyes and slide your head under the water."

He did, without questioning. He could feel the Jacuzzi jets buffeting his wrinkled body. The sound was muffling his thoughts. He stayed under as long as he could hold his breath. He surfaced and opened his eyes. The water looked dark in the moonlight. He heard car tires crunch on the gravel drive. As Chadron backed out, her headlights shined across the hot tub. He raised his hand just as the lights turned and left him in the dark. His hand looked . . . black?

He stood up in the hot tub. Shivering in the chill, he saw a box propped up on the edge. He held it up to the moonlight. RIT Permanent Dye . . . deep purple. He looked at his arms, his feet, his legs, his belly. In the dark he looked black!

He grabbed a towel and rubbed hard on his forearm. No change!

"Damn!" His predicament sharpened his focus. *Let's see . . . I'm ten or fifteen miles from Rapid. I'm freezing and I'm the color of a wino's shirtfront!*

He found his clothes in the garage, dried off and dressed. On the way out of the ranch he checked a pickup for keys and found none. It took him an hour walking bowlegged to get back to I-90. He stopped several times in the moonlight to catch his breath. It was actually funny if you thought about it. At one point, he sat on a rock and laughed. Ridiculous!

Hitching was unsuccessful. People don't pick up hitchhikers at night, no matter what color they are! By daylight he was strolling through the long shadows of the fairgrounds. He couldn't find Cody's pickup, so he slipped into one of the show barns and fell asleep on the straw.

"Mommy! Mommy! Come look at the funny man!"

"Sshh. Don't wake him. Maybe he's sick."

"Mommy, he's purple!"

"What's goin' on here?"

"I don't know. He doesn't look right."

"He's . . . he's purple!"

"He's okay, isn't he? Alive, I mean."

"Yeah. He's breathin'."

"Maybe we'd better get Security."

"Good idea."

"Paging Cody Wing. Will Cody Wing please report to the security building."

"I'm Cody Wing. Somebody paging me?"

"Yessir. Just a moment."

"Cody Wing?" asked the security guard. "We have a man here asking for you."

"Is it Lick?"

"Follow me."

The hallway was crowded. People were taking turns looking through the safety glass on the closed door.

"Excuse me," said the officer as he led Cody through the milling mass into the large office.

Lick sat on the edge of a small steel-and-Naugahyde sofa. He looked like the Minnesota Vikings' dirty laundry!

"Lick?"

"Cody! Boy, I'm glad you showed up. Get me outta here!"

"What happened?"

"I don't want to talk about it!"

"The pickup's outside, c'mon."

The crowd parted in front of the Incredible Hulk! The waves of people gathered in the halls and on the front steps gave way as the convict was hurried to the waiting pickup.

Cody went around. Lick's side was locked. Of course. During the six months it took Cody to slide across and unlock the passenger side, Lick heard the murmurs of the crowd:

"Mommy, he looks like Billy's Popsicle tongue!"

"Shhh, he's probably on drugs!"

"See what happens if you don't eat broccoli!"

"I think it's New Wave, Martha."

"Maybe he's an extraterrestrial?"

Lick slammed the door. "E.T., home."

16

Saturday, August 14
Burwell, Nebraska

By damn, Lick, you oughtta marry *that* ol' girl!" Cody was weak from laughter as Lick recounted the story of Thursday night's adventure. "She's got fire! She'd keep your sorry butt in line!" He continued to laugh and wipe the tears from his eyes. Lick was laughing too, as they drove through the morning sun. Since dawn they had been under the protective gaze of the hundreds of windmills that dot the Sandhills of Nebraska. Now they were driving through miles of cornfield city blocks. They had overnighted at the Remington Arms in Ainsworth, where Lick bought a new razor and shaving kit. His old one had disappeared with Chadron, somewhere in Rapid City. This morning they were ten miles outside Burwell, on Highway 91, when a policeman pulled them over.

"Something wrong, Officer?" asked the Purple Phantom, driving.

The officer looked at Lick's Technicolor face and hands. He leaned over and looked at Cody. "Can you drive this rig?"

"Sure, but what's up?" asked Cody.

"You just follow me into Burwell. You," he said to Lick, "come with me."

"Why?"

"Don't argue, boy. It's nothin' serious. Just for your own protection." He installed Lick in the backseat of the patrol car. Lick asked questions. The officer avoided them. The corn was as high as an elephant's withers along the road.

The Nebraska State Patrol car pulled through the square in Burwell, stopped in front of the Corner Bar and turned off the siren. The contents of the bar poured out into the street.

Lick stared out the back window. Jerry O'Haca opened the door and, with a regal gesture, invited Lick out.

Lick stood on the sidewalk and turned like a heliotrope. "We've been expecting you," said Jerry. He was wearing a purple armband.

Everybody was wearing something purple. They looked like a group of Texas Aggie alumni gone awry on St. Patrick's Day! "I drove all night to set this up, ol' pardner!" said Jerry.

"Thanks!"

"The least we could do! Okay, boys, bring 'em out!" The crowd parted for the coups de grace: personal, passionate, violaceous cheerleaders! Two bouncing, heavy-hipped, Nebraska darlin's marched to the front of the crowd, each carrying a picket sign. One sign said STICK WITH on the front and LICK on the back. The other said LICK on the front and STICK WITH on the back.

They each wore snakeskin boots, mauve leotards, cutoffs and puce knit bikini tops. Silk lilacs were embroidered in their blond manes. Wyla had a small butterfly tattooed high on the right breast, flying into the breach. Twyla had a small snail tattooed high on the left breast, inching into the chasm. Lavender eye shadow and mulberry lipstick completed the ensemble.

"These are your bodyguards!" declared Jerry. To the polychromatic sisters he said, "Girls, never let him outta yer sight!" To the clamoring multitude he said, "Make way for the king!"

Wyla took Lick's left arm and laid her butterfly in the crook. Twyla took his right arm and laid her snail in its crook. The spectators made way.

An old sofa had been placed across two tables in the bar. Lick and the pulchritudinous purple duo were lifted to the throne.

Flam Leetsdale, rodeo photographer, posed him. The rainbow amazons snuggled closer. Everybody bought him a drink.

"A toast!" ordered Jerry. "To the only purple cowboy in the P.R.C.A.!"

Lick's guardians drank demurely as Lick was toasted. Repeatedly. By noon, his five senses were reduced to one and a half.

"How you doin', pardner?" asked Cody.

"Gettin' severely drunk," Lick answered.

"Remember you gotta bull this afternoon."

"Right!" Someone brought him another Velvet ditch.

The lovely maidens kept Lick pressed between them. Each had a hand on his respective thigh. They were wearing identical perfume, Cinnabar, and had begun to perspire.

"Are you really purple all over?" asked Wyla, draping Lick's left arm around her shoulders.

"Yup."

"Even ... down there?" asked Twyla, placing his right arm around her shoulders.

"Yup."

Lick darted his head to the snail and caught a drop of sweat before it cascaded into the gorge. Pictures of a chameleon from an old *National Geographic*, spearing a mayfly, flashed before his eyes.

"Thank you," she said.

Twyla held a fresh draw to his lips and he sipped the brew. She sucked the foam off his mustache and wiped his chin with her knit bikini top.

"Ooooh." She giggled.

"Let me help," said Twyla, maneuvering into position.

(When asked to recall this particular day to his grandchildren, Lick would always smile. Only the warm sensations, devoid of detail, would come back. But that was enough for an old man.)

They made Lick Unofficial Grand Marshal of the parade. His throne was put on the back of a flatbed truck. He and his tinted attendants variously sat, stood and reclined, depending on the wishes of His Highness.

By the time the parade wound through the arena to begin the grand entry, Lick was bareback, blithering and had peed his pants! Fortunately no one could tell, because at least two six-packs had been poured over his head in tribute! He stood, with the aid of his twin entourage, and greeted the crowd, Caesar-like. He raised his glass in recognition of his subjects in the stands. The flatbed lurched! Lick fell backward, his body in rigor, over the back of the sofa, as if someone had toppled a statue of Cortés, sword upraised, coming into Tenochtitlán!

Lick was flying I.F.R. while Cody was pulling his bull rope. "You sure you wanna do this?" Cody wasn't completely sober himself. Matter of fact, it was the drunkest rodeo either of them had seen since the Indian Rodeo in Mescalero, New Mexico.

"Ladies and gentlemen!" Emerald Dune worked his malleable audience. "You are about to see a first. Nebraska's Big Rodeo presents the world's only purple cowboy..." The cheering crowd drowned out Emerald's FM stereo voice. He fine-tuned the volume and went on. "The world's only purple cowboy up on bull ninety-seven D, called Chadron Borglum!"

Lick looked up and caught Emerald's eye.

"Chadron Borglum, in chute number three!"

Lick went back on autopilot. He nodded his head. The spinnin' bull crashed out. Lick stuck to him like road kill skunk on a radial tire! He rode 97D automatically, every nerve and muscle firing! His body a well-oiled machine, oblivious to the emotions of its operator! 97D ducked and spun, dove and stuck! Lick rode him with no mercy! Lick never heard the buzzer. He bailed out to thunderous applause! He lifted his hat, displaying his purple hair. A row of white teeth gleamed under his purple mustache.

He threw his hat in the air! It was his last conscious act.

The night never ended. Lick woke. It was daylight. He didn't know which day. He was in a bed. He didn't know which bed. He lay on his back.

Swatches of vividly colorful memories flipped through his mind like pages in an *Omni* magazine:

> *Lying facedown on the bakery counter.*
> *Standing on top of a human pyramid on somebody's lawn.*
> *Directing traffic in a policeman's hat.*
> *Swimming?*

*Seeing double images and adjusting the knobs for better
reception.*
Roman riding?

His clothes were neatly laid over a nearby chair. His hat gently
placed on a dresser. A purple knit, double-barreled slingshot hung
from each bedpost.

There was a long scratch running diagonally across his belly.
Surely, he thought, chuckling at his early morning wit, *this deserves
a purple heart!*

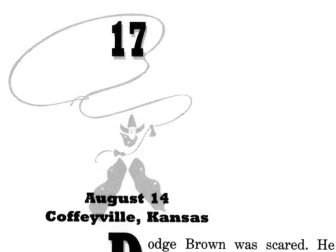

August 14
Coffeyville, Kansas

Dodge Brown was scared. He was teeth rattlin', knee knockin', hair raisin', bed wet-tin' scared! Because he was a local boy, he was allowed to enter the Coffeyville, Kansas, rodeo without being an official card-carrying member of the P.R.C.A. He had been on six bulls in his life. He hadn't decided to rodeo until his nineteenth birthday, last May. He worked for a seed corn company and had just gotten engaged to Dee Dee Stufflebean. This Friday night Dodge Brown was scheduled to buck out on none other than Kamikaze!

Dodge needed no description of Kamikaze's bucking prowess or nasty disposition. Even if he hadn't read the *Sports News,* several cowboys had volunteered their opinion to him this afternoon. It was unanimous; they all suggested he draw out.

Normally, it was unthinkable in the derring-do world of rodeo for cowboys to suggest something as tenderfooted as turn-ing out your stock as a result of fear. Stock was often turned out by cowboys who were scheduled to compete when they got a "bad draw" (a bull or bronc they didn't think would score high enough). They would bypass those rodeos completely. They paid a fine in those cases. But Kamikaze was becoming an ominous phenomenon.

The *Pro Rodeo Sports News* had carried six stories between March 15 and July 28 mentioning the notorious bull. Although the *Sports News* carries pertinent information vital to scheduling for the rodeo cowboy, it contains feature stories as well. When a cowboy is seriously injured it is worthy of mention in the *Sports News*. Kamikaze guaranteed several bull riders press coverage they hadn't sought. But bad news travels fast.

The Nampa Press Tribune, July 14:

Manly Ott, presently ranked fourth in the Pro Rodeo Cowboys Assn. national standings in the bull riding event, was injured last night during the first performance of the Snake River Stampede. He was bucked off before the whistle blew. Officials at Mercy Hospital said he suffered a broken jaw and neck injuries, but is resting comfortably today. The bull that inflicted the damage to Manly Ott is stock contractor Bobby Monday's bull number 1020, called Kamikaze. In the rodeo business, bulls are not usually named and only go by a number, but this bull has gained a reputation and therefore a name. Kamikaze has been on the rodeo circuit for four years and has never been ridden. He has been selected the last three years by the cowboys as a National Finals bull. Kamikaze, according to the cowboys interviewed last night, has a tendency to inflict a heavy toll on those bull riders unlucky enough to draw him. More than five cowboys have been seriously hurt this year attempting to ride him. Snake River Stampede performances continue through Saturday night.

Associated Press Wire, July 20. *Los Angeles Herald Examiner, Omaha World Herald, North Platte Telegraph* and *Kansas City Star:*

In the world of professional rodeo, a certain bull is developing a considerable reputation. Kamikaze, who has been bucking for four years, has thrown off every cowboy who has attempted to ride him. He is dangerous, as demonstrated by the fact that he has injured numerous of those bull riders seriously. The latest is Manly Ott, a bull rider ranked nationally in the standings.

The National Enquirer, July 30:

BULL POSSESSED BY DEVIL!

In rodeo circles, there is a bull called Kamikaze. He strikes fear in every cowboy who attempts to ride this 2,000-pound demon! He has horns over two feet long and an evil eye! He has crippled and maimed many of those cowboys who have been brave (or foolish) enough to climb on his back. He has never been ridden! One cowboy is quoted as saying, "He is the Devil!"

If Dodge Brown read the papers he should have been scared. He did and he was! Dee Dee had tried to talk him out of it.

"Dodge, draw out, honey. You might get hurt and it's not worth the chance."

"But, Dee Dee," protested Dodge, "what if I can ride him? What if? Beginner's luck. I just might be the one who does it. That would be fantastic, with all the gang there watchin'!"

The professional traveling cowboys, who often don't have occasion to discuss much with the local entrants, went out of their way to suggest he draw out. When Dodge told them he figgered on going ahead with it, they just shrugged their shoulders.

Kamikaze wasn't givin' it much thought. He spent the afternoon lazin' around the pens behind the buckin' chutes. He didn't brother-in-law much with the other bulls. He assumed the status of Peckin'-Order Potentate regardless of the company he was in.

If you had a mind to explore the anthropomorphological aspects of Kamikaze, you could compare his thought processes to a piece of heavy construction equipment. A bulldozer, perhaps, or maybe a backhoe with tracks and a three-yard bucket.

Those machines exude power. They have the ability to be surprisingly agile. They are capable of some first-class destruction. This is the basis of their personality.

Just as cables and hydraulics tend to create wear with use, so did memories erode wrinkles in Kamikaze's cerebrum. Each cowboy who mounted him left a unique fingerprint on his brain. Each new trick was printed in his playbook. The counterpunch was programmed.

He didn't know Dodge Brown from Chevy Impala. But unless Dodge tried something no previous rider had done, Kamikaze was prepared.

Kamikaze ambled over to the water trough and took a drink. Several cowboys were leanin' over the fence checkin' out the stock. He studied them for a few seconds. He knew them as interlopers in his territory. He knew them as lightweights who put a rope around his girth. He knew them as frightened rabbits on the arena floor.

But they kept puttin' their hands in the fire.

Like moths, he concluded.

Before the bull riding, rodeo clown and bullfighter Herman Hammer hunted up Dodge for a little chat. "Listen, cowboy, I can't tell you how to ride him 'cause nobody ever has, but when you hit the ground, hit it runnin'! This bull's turned real mean and will try and eat your lunch, so git down and git on the fence! We'll be right there to help you."

Kamikaze was in the second bunch of bulls to be loaded into the chutes. Dodge tried to concentrate. He got some help setting his rope and waited for the announcer to call his name.

"Out of chute number four, a local cowboy from right here in Coffeyville, Dodge Brown, up on three-times National Finals bull, Kamikaze! If this young cowboy rides this bull, he will be the first in the world to do it!"

The crowd let out a cheer and silenced. Dodge nodded his head and the gate swung open.

Kamikaze flew out of the chute, spinnin' like a merry-go-round! Dodge hung on for the first whiplash. The second 180° found him airborne, headed for the fence like a guided missile! He crashed into the gatepost on chute number five, six feet above the ground! Kamikaze wheeled back to his right. He caught Dodge between his horns and threw him ten feet in the air like a rag doll! Dodge, arms flailing, came down over Kamikaze's back! Kamikaze whirled and hooked him as he slid off his rump! Dodge rolled into a ball while Kamikaze continued to gore, pound and drive him into the ground!

The clowns were desperately trying to get the bull off the downed cowboy, but Kamikaze was single-mindedly grinding Dodge into little pieces of arena dirt. Finally Herman Hammer jumped on Kamikaze's back! The bull hooked back toward the new rider! During the momentary distraction, Herman's bullfighting pardner, Smack Knuckles, somehow managed to drag Dodge's inert body out of the eye of the storm. Kamikaze threw Herman off like a slingshot. Herman raced to the arena fence! Kamikaze caught him mid-leap on the inside of his right thigh and lifted him clear over the six-foot steel wire fence! Herman landed in the first row, between two old men from the Elks Club Rehab Center.

$$\star \, {\star} \, ^{\star}$$

At 11:16 P.M. that night, the emergency room doctor came into the waiting room and told Mr. and Mrs. Brown and Dee Dee that Dodge had died during surgery. The boy had a concussion and severe internal injuries. The doctor was sorry.

18

Lyra stood at the edge of the crowd looking at the stage set up in the middle of the street. The band onstage called itself Night-Train Express and they could give a wino a headache! Night-Train Express was building a bluegrass cosmorama: flat pickin' rainbows, fiddle contrails, waves of doghouse bass and a five-string meteor shower! Lyra's eyes wandered casually to the crowd at the base of the stage. She saw the back of a familiar head.

"Lick, you no-good cactus eatin' dog kisser!" she said to herself in surprise.

"What did you say?"

Lyra turned to her left. A dark-haired woman with freckles and blue eyes was staring at her. She held a little girl by the hand.

"Nothing." Lyra laughed. "I just saw somebody I knew."

"Did you say 'Lick'?" asked the mother.

"That's the lowlife's name."

"Is he by any chance a bull rider, this Lick?"

"Yes. Do you know him?"

"Where is he?"

"Over there right under the bandstand. To the right."

The mother looked in that direction. "Yep. That's the Lick I know."

Lick was leaning against the stage looking up at the band. He had a beer in one hand and a blonde in the other.

"My name is Cherry Hills and this is my daughter, Teddy."

"Lyra Block."

"Have you known him long?" asked Cherry.

"Off and on a couple years. He usually calls when he comes through town."

"You live here in Denver?"

"Yes. How 'bout you?" asked Lyra.

"Here, too. I've only known him six or eight months. Seen him three times. I guess he calls me when he doesn't call you."

"Looks like he called somebody else this time." Lyra stared at him again.

Cherry looked over his way. "Lyra. You know what I'm thinking?"

Lyra looked out of the corner of her eye. They both slid into a "why not" sort of grin.

"It would teach the worthless rapscallion a lesson," said Cherry. Then quickly, "You're not serious about him are you?"

"Serious! I see the scoundrel when he comes to town, when *he* wants to! I'd be crazier than he is if I took 'im seriously! How 'bout you?"

"Well, I admit the first couple times I thought he had potential. He's got a little money, or seems to, the way he spends it, and he treats my kiddo like a princess."

"And the princess's mama?"

"Yes. He does have his way."

"I know. I know," said Lyra.

"We always seem to have a good time," said Cherry.

"The loony fool does make you feel like a woman. So many of these men—I should say, boys—don't know the first thing about it. Good ol' Lick."

"Wait a minute, now," said Cherry. "We both have him pegged for what he is, right? The original wild goose. A shirttail in the wind."

"Motion and no emotion. No commitments. Yeah, we both got him pegged."

"So I think we should go over and meet the blonde. What do you say?"

"Right on, sister!"

"Why don't we send Teddy over to see Uncle Lick first? Then we could walk up together!"

Night-Train Express climaxed! "Earl's Breakdown," the last song of the set, broke into a thousand pieces and sizzled into the afternoon sky like a drop of water in a skillet of hot grease!

Cherry, Teddy and Lyra wended through the people seated on the street between them and the bandstand.

"Look at the boobs on her!" exclaimed Cherry.

"No matter. When she's forty, they'll hang like a four-dollar drape!"

"Mama," said Teddy excitedly, "there's Lick!"

"You wanna run up and say hello?"

"Oh yes! Can I?"

"Sure, go ahead."

Teddy ran through the visiting crowd toward him.

"Lick! Lick!"

Lick looked down. "It's me, Teddy!" cried the little girl. He picked her up in one arm.

"Teddy Bear, you little punkin. How you doin'? How nice to see you! This is Wanda. Wanda, this is Teddy."

"Hello, Teddy," said Wanda.

Suddenly, Lick looked around. "Where's your mama, darlin'?"

"Oh, she's comin'. We were wondering when we'd see you again."

"Oh, yeah?" said Lick.

"Oh, yeah?" said Wanda.

"Lick! How nice to see you," said Cherry, blindsiding him. He jerked his head to the left.

"Lick, you ol' coyote! You've been gone so long!" said Lyra, blindsiding him again. He jerked his head back to the right.

"Lyra. Cherry. What a nice surprise!" His face was the color of eight-and-a-half-by-eleven erasable bond.

"Uh, Wanda, this is Lyra and Cherry. Cherry, Wanda and Lyra. Lyra, Cherry and Wanda."

"Hello." Puerta Vallarta sunset.

"Hello." Ski condo fireplace.

"Hello." Ice fishing on Lake Superior.

Now, this might be a good time for the reader to pause and give some thought to a solution to Lick's dilemma. The plausible alternatives are few, the fatal, many.

> *1. He could try to explain: "Wanda, these are two old friends of mine from high school. We were on the track team together. Lyra was a runner, Cherry a sprinter, and I was in the broad jump. Ha, Ha."*
>
> *2. He could faint. Then just lie there till they all drifted away. Difficult to do with a Teddy Bear in your arms.*
>
> *3. He could offer no explanation.*
>
> *He chose number 3. He zip-locked his lips.*

"So ... Wanda, where are you from?" asked Lyra sweetly.

"I live here now, but originally from Louisiana."

"Louisiana. How nice. And you, Cherry?" continued Lyra.

"I live here. Teddy and I." She smiled at Teddy, who was taking a sip of Lick's beer. Cherry bit her tongue and smiled.

"How 'bout y'all, Lyra. Lyra? Is that right?" asked Wanda.

"I'm here in town. How long have you known good ol' Lick?" Lyra spoke as if he were a picture on the wall, a deaf-and-dumb watercolor.

"Probably a year, I guess. August of last year," answered Wanda.

"Oh, really?" said Lyra.

"Oh, really?" said Cherry.

"Have you known him long?" asked Wanda.

"Couple years," answered Cherry.

"We certainly have somethin' in common." Wanda was a good ol' girl, and not stupid, despite the opinion of many less well-endowed snipers. "My feet are killin' me and I've had about all the music I can stand. What say we go sit down and have a beer?"

"Wanda," said Cherry, "I think I like you."

"Lead on, McDuff! Lick, bring Teddy and come along," instructed Lyra.

"Uh, Cherry," mumbled Lick, "how 'bout Teddy and I walk around the booths for a while. We'll find you under those umbrellas?"

"Okay, if it's okay with Teddy."

"Oh yes, Mom! Can I, can I?"

"May I."

"May I, Mom?"

"Yes, you may."

"Wow! Far out! C'mon, Lick. I saw some old shoes to try on!" She led him off by the hand.

"That's unfair, you know," Wanda said to Cherry.

"Well, I admit it, but can I help it if he likes kids?" Cherry smiled.

They ordered a Moosehead, a Heineken, a Michelob Light and sat under the Cinzano umbrella on the bar atrium.

"We set you up, Wanda. Just to harass Lick."

"No sweat. I'd have done the same thing. He is the most unreliable lover I've ever had. Any poor girl who thinks she's gonna get him to stay around the house long enough to sprout roots has lost her mind! Besides, what if you were unlucky enough to catch him! Every time he hit the road, you'd worry about him shackin' up or bringin' home something unmentionable!"

Sometimes conversations like this can be awkward. But these three semiworldly, confident women crowdin' thirty, veterans of the Fern Bar Wars, talked like old roommates.

Two beers later, they were like sisters. Nothing like a common affliction to unite strangers.

"Wanda, why don't you and Lyra come to my place and we'll fix a little dinner. I've got hamburger in the freezer. We can stop and pick up some salad makin's. Wait a minute," hesitated Cherry, "that's not fair. Wanda, you're with Lick. Maybe you have other plans?"

"None that I wouldn't change. This is too good to pass up! A rare opportunity! You know, I admit I'm not too hep on sharing, but since we all obviously know him well, what the hell!"

Teddy came up to the table.

"Hello, kiddo. What'cha got?"

"A balloon, Mom. And Lick bought me these shoes, and this hood ornament. He said it's off a '51 Plymouth. See, it's the *Mayflower*."

"Where's Lick?"

"Oh. He said to give you this." She handed Cherry a note that said "Due to a death in the family, I had to take off right away. Sorry, Lick."

Wanda smiled. "Nothin' to it. Ya know, I make some pretty mean coonass chili, if you still got that hamburger."

"You bet! Let's go."

⋆ ⋆ ⋆

In the fading afternoon shadows a coward slunk off through the parked cars, crawled under a Falcon Futura and pondered all these things in his heart.

19

Saturday, August 28
Payson, Arizona

Welcome, ladies and gentlemen to the third performance of the oldest continuous rodeo in the world! Fast action, great stock, the best rodeo cowboys and cowgirls here in one of the most spectacularly scenic rodeo arenas in our great land!"

The monotonously beautiful high desert mountains and pine trees surrounded the small rodeo arena, and the temperature at one P.M. was standing at a comfortable eighty-three degrees.

Lick was up in the bulls this afternoon and Cody had entered the saddle bronc riding.

Cody had been as successful riding barebacks these last few weeks as Ned had been lucky in love. Neither had scored high enough to buy a bottle of Absorbine Jr.! Cody decided to switch events to the saddle bronc riding to break his slump.

Neatsfoot Hawkins, past world champion bronc rider and presently leading in the P.R.C.A. standings, offered to help Cody.

"Velvet Snide is a good draw, Cody," Neatsfoot was coaching. "He's predictable, but not that easy to ride. He always takes a big jump out of the chute, bucks to the left three or four jumps, then turns back out to the right. Give him plenty of rein or he'll pull you over his head on the first jump."

"How's the turn?"

"Usually smooth, but you gotta watch 'im. I've seen him reverse directions a couple times an' if he does that, you're on your own."

"Good'nuf. I'll be ready."

Cody set his competition association saddle out on the ground. He sat down in it, stretching the stirrup leathers and adjusting to the feel.

Saddle bronc riders enjoy a certain prestige in rodeo circles. Ridin' a saddle bronc is like playing the guitar: it's the easiest thing to do poorly and hardest thing to do well. Neatsfoot was one of the best. He came from Texas, though lots of the good ones grow up in Montana or the Dakotas. . . . He was a personable fellow and had pizzazz. Announcers liked him, rodeo advertisers invested in him, women adored him, men admired him and the crowd loved him! He always put on a show. His personality showed in his work. None of this was supposed to affect the judges' evaluation of his ride, so they said it didn't, but when all was done and said, Neatsfoot was good for rodeo. He stood out like a penguin in a patch of sandhill cranes!

*　*
　*

Velvet Snide was nineteen years old. Born on the Pine Ridge Indian Reservation near Red Shirt, South Dakota, he ran free until he was four years old. They gathered the band that year, branded him and cut him. During the next two years they broke him to ride. But Velvet Snide, whose name at the time was Yellow Star Thistle, had one flaw that predisposed him to verbal abuse by the tribal leaders: the sonuvamare loved to buck! Not maliciously, just gloriously, enthusiastically, with the same joy a peregrine falcon feels when he stalls at fifteen hundred feet, folds his wings and free-falls from the sky!

After two broken arms and futile incantations, it was decided by the tribe that he should be taken to the bucking horse sale in Miles City, Montana.

Yellow Star Thistle distinguished himself and was bought by T. Tommy Calhoot, entrepreneur and stock contractor from South Dakota.

In the last thirteen years, Yellow Star Thistle was selected by the rodeo cowboys to go to the National Finals four times and was Bucking Horse of the Year twice. T. Tommy still owned him. At

Yellow Star Thistle's peak, Tommy changed his name to Velvet (as in Black Velvet) Snide, in response to a little advertising campaign sponsored by a national distiller of white lightnin'.

★ ★ ★

Velvet Snide was in chute number two (there was no number one). Neatsfoot helped Cody get saddled and adjust his hack rein. He threaded a little hank of mane through the braided rein to mark his grip.

T. Tommy rode up to the side of the chute where Cody was waiting his turn. "You got a good one there, son. Watch his first big jump outta the box."

"Yeah, thanks." Cody knew T. Tommy was rooting for the horse. The better ol' Snide bucked, the more the stock contractor's inventory was worth.

"And now in chute number two, Cody Wing, Ten Sleep, Wyoming, on a past Bucking Horse of the Year, Velvet Snide!"

Cody took the rein in his left hand and stuck his toes out over the points of the shoulders. He leaned back and nodded his head. The gate swung open. Velvet Snide rocked back on his hind legs and slammed his butt against the back of the chute! He uncoiled and leaped out! Cody and Snide were airborne!

Lean back an' touch 'im when he hits the ground, Cody thought. Wham!

Pull. Cody brought his spurs from the points of the shoulders plum back to the cantle.

Reach and pull. Three successive jumps and Cody was in perfect rhythm. When Velvet Snide had his tail in the air, his hind feet out behind him and his front feet planted, Cody was ramrod straight, toes out, spurs at the points, and his free arm out behind him held high. When Snide's front feet left the ground for the next ascent, Cody raked his rowels along Velvet's side as far back as he could reach. But something went wrong when Snide made his right turn. Maybe he didn't signal? Maybe T. Tommy had offered Velvet Snide a raise in hay? Who knows? Regardless, Cody was in his backswing when the ol' palomino made a 90° swivel and stuck his nose to the ground. Cody failed to make the swivel and lazy-Susan'd to port side. Velvet Snide took the rein, jerked Cody out over the swells and punched him headfirst into the dirt.

Lick ran over to his crumpled partner. "Jeez, Cody, you all right?" Cody's hat was down over his ears. If his upper plate hadn't stayed in place, he would have bitten off the end of his nose! He stretched his neck and pounded his smashed hat back into a reasonable facsmile of its original shape.

"Yeah. I bit my tongue."

They stepped back over to the fence and watched Neatsfoot make a classic ride complete with flying dismount.

Lick was rosining up his bull rope when LoBall McKinney came up to him. "Howdy, Lick." Lick nodded.

"Listen, Lick. You are really hot this summer. You are flat tearin' 'em up. *Sports News* got you ranked eighteenth now. I ain't doing worth a dang. I wonder if you would watch me ride and see if you could give me a pointer or two? I'm up tomorrow, if yer gonna be around."

"Yeah, I'll be here, LoBall. I don't know what I can tell ya, but I'll watch."

Lick already figured he knew part of LoBall's problem. He just didn't want to win bad enough. He wasn't stayin' with the rough ones when the goin' got tough.

These last few weeks Lick had become possessed. He was quieter, didn't party as hard, and got more nervous before each ride. Cody even told him he was losing his sense of humor! But he was winning, winning consistently.

L92 rumbled into the chutes. Lick's bull. Not a real big bull, kind of a brangus-looking critter, with no horns and a little hump. But he would give a man a good spin.

Lick was concentrating while Cody helped him pull his rope. He still had his mind on it when he and L92 made their grand entry into the arena. Lick rode him automatically. When the whistle blew, he reached down with his right hand to free his grip. L92 kicked and flipped Lick over and off! Lick somersaulted out over the bull's right shoulder, but his left hand didn't come free; he was hung up! L92 continued to buck, jerking Lick around like a tetherball tied to the bumper of a low rider!

The two rodeo clowns were right square in the middle of the dance floor! Bucko Bailey was across the withers from Lick, jerking on the tail of the rope, trying to free Lick's hand!

Wang Snaffle, the other bullfighter, was in front of L92, slapping him on the muzzle to keep him from hooking Raggedy Ann and Raggedy Andy! Bucko gave one mighty yank and they both fell away! L92 wheeled, swinging his head like a scythe, and caught the stumbling duo! Lick took the hardest blow. Wang raced back into the gap and drew L92 off toward the gate. Bucko put his arm around Lick's waist and drug him to the fence.

"Git the doc! Siddown, Lick. Git the doc, he's bleedin'!"

The paramedics slapped Lick on the stretcher and carried him to the ambulance. Cody jumped in the back with them and they sped off.

"What is it, Doc?"

"Might be broken ribs, maybe a punctured lung. See those bubbles of blood in his nose? Punctured lung." The paramedic put his stethoscope to Lick's chest.

"Yeah, could be a punctured lung."

20

**September 5
Hereford, Texas**

Lick got out of the hospital and, for lack of a better place, went home. The doctor in Payson had said he was lucky. *Just what I was thinkin'*, thought Lick.

The punctured lung turned out to be a bloody nose, but his bones didn't fare as well. His take-home pay at the Payson Rodeo had been two broken ribs and two weeks off.

Despite his outward nonchalance, he fretted about missing the five rodeos from which he'd been forced to withdraw. He would have felt that way regardless of his success. But this year, with less than three months to go until the National Finals, he was ranked in the top twenty money winners. To make the finals he had to finish in the top fifteen. Every ride was important.

Home wasn't one of the several places he'd lived in as a boy but where Mom and Dad lived. They had a small but nice house three miles from Hereford, Texas. It had one good outbuilding, eighteen acres of dry-land pasture and a fair set of corrals. They rented.

Lick enjoyed visiting with them both. During the first couple days after Papa had gone to work riding pens in the feedlot, Lick and Mom talked. He looked at photos of his brother's children, old pictures of his parents' youth, of Grandpa Elojio, snapshots of his own youth. His mother had saved Lick's baseball cards. There was a time when he was twelve years old he could name virtually every lineup in the major leagues. Now he couldn't name all the teams. Lick had still never been to a major league game.

"Lloyd's in Amarillo now," his mother informed him.

Lloyd had been his best friend in high school and college. Lloyd had carried their pack of Winstons under the dash of his Ford pickup.

"I thought he was in Chicago."

"Well he's back. He's doing well, I hear. He works in some fancy office building, your papa says. *Pero quien sabe?*" she added, reverting to her father's native tongue. "You should maybe go see him. You can borrow the Galaxy. Your papa saw him go into the office at the feed yard a couple of months ago. So he said hello and Lloyd asked how you were doing. He gave your papa his business card, maybe it has the phone number."

That evening Lick called his old friend and made plans to meet him for lunch the following day.

Lick borrowed the Galaxy and drove to Amarillo. The offices of Hammell, Hammell, Loon and Garvey were on the fifth and top floor of the Luckinbaugh Building downtown. They were commodity brokers.

Lloyd was sincerely delighted to see Lick. To Lick's modest surprise, Lloyd introduced him to everyone in the office and included a flattering discourse of Lick's rodeo career. He was even up-to-date on Lick's present standing and genuinely proud of his friend.

Lloyd had not changed. He had always been a nice person. They went to lunch at a Mexican restaurant. Both ordered a beer; Lloyd loosened his tie.

"Gotta wear the damn thing. Part of the game. Anyway, how are the ribs?"

"Oh, they're healing," said Lick, again surprised that Lloyd knew. "A hazard of the profession."

"You don't know how I envy you," said Lloyd. "Not the ribs, but the rodeo."

Lloyd had been a calf roper. They'd both been on the college rodeo team.

"Whattya mean? Looks to me like you're doin' real well for yourself. Chicago and all. Now you get to come home and have the best of both worlds. How old are your boys now?"

"Six and eight. Both good athletes," Lloyd said proudly.

"Roping already, I bet," said Lick.

"No. T ball and tennis. We bought a house in town. They don't have much interest in horses or rodeo. I wish you were closer. Maybe you could inspire them."

"No more than you, Lloyd."

"Yeah, but I'm so busy. Sometimes I just stare out the window and wonder where you are. Wish I could be with ya goin' down the road."

"It's nice," admitted Lick, "but it's not too lucrative. Takes all your winnin's just to buy the gas."

"I guess. But a new town every night, seein' new country, breathin' real air. Psychin' up to ride. Havin' a beer afterwards. Yup, you sure got it made, my friend. I'm happy for you."

"You ever hear from Alma Lee?" asked Lick.

"Yeah, as a matter of fact I saw her couple weeks ago. She lives here in Amarillo. She said she was workin' in a travel agency."

"You mean she quit teachin' school?"

"Must have. She's married again. Third time, I think."

Alma Lee had been Lick's first love. Their romance spanned his senior year in high school and first year of college.

"So," said Lloyd, "when are ya crackin' back out?"

"I'm gonna try and make Pendleton next week."

They sat silently a minute.

"What are you doin' next week?" Lick asked Lloyd. "Shoot, ya might as well come with me. My pardner's in Iowa right now. I'm gonna meet him in Denver next Monday, then we're headin' west."

Lloyd began to marshal the reasons he couldn't go.

Lick persisted. "You'd like Cody. Good boy from Wyoming. Pretty solid. Kinda like you, I guess. He laughs at my bad jokes and has bailed me out more times than I can count."

"Gosh, Lick, I'd love to, even for a few days, but I can't."

"Aw, that's okay," said Lick. "Just thought it would be fun."

"No, Bea and I have plans. Big shot financial consultant from Wichita is going to be at the office for three days puttin' on a seminar and I'm his host. Oughtta be pretty good for business. Plus the oldest has tennis. Anyway, it would be fun, but I can't."

"No, I guess not," said Lick, feeling a little wistful for his ol' friend and their lost opportunity. "So," he continued, "how do I find Alma Lee?"

Forty-six minutes later Lick walked through the door of Professional Travel. He was in a large open room with three desks, each piloted by a woman talking on the phone. He walked straight to Alma Lee's and sat opposite her in the client chair. She glanced up at him, did a double take, covered the mouthpiece and whispered, "Lick?"

He hadn't seen her for thirteen years. He'd envisioned her as having grown fat or gray or covered with warts. He was wrong! She stood, still shouldering the phone, and stepped to a file cabinet. She looked magnificent! August 12. He remembered her birthday. She'd be thirty-three now.

She sat back down and looked at him as she continued talking on the phone. She had her dark hair pulled back tightly, exposing her large ears. She used to wear her hair in such a way as to hide them. Now they stuck out like wings on a hang glider! She exuded confidence.

She rang off, reached across the desk, grabbed his hand and without a word pulled him into the adjoining storage room. She closed the door, threw her arms around him and kissed him! An onlooker would have thought she was tryin' to lick barbecue sauce off his face! He reciprocated! Within seconds they were rolling on the floor, exploring remembered delights!

They had parted years ago as teenage virgins. Not uncommon then. The world had changed in the intervening decade.

Spent, Lick looked down at her. "Sorry about the button."

Alma Lee was crying but smiling. That's exactly how Lick felt.

They shared an innocence. A secret intimacy with each other that jaded maturity steals from the young. *I can't believe we were so naive* sums up this retrospective wonderment.

"Gosh, Lick, I'm a married woman!" she said, amazed at her own behavior.

"I know."

They stood. He buttoned the front of her blouse. He grasped her skirt belt above her hips and straightened her gig line. She slid her shoes back on and handed him his hat.

"How do I look?" she asked.

Lick thought: *Like a polished masthead on a clipper ship! Like Jayne Mansfield on the hood of a '58 Cadillac! Like Joan of Arc in a bikini! Like a tall iced tea to a thirsty man!*

"Best I ever saw," he said, and he meant it.

They walked through the office to the parking lot. He started the Galaxy. She stood by the driver's side.

"Can I see you again?" he asked, looking up into her eyes.

"Nope," she said, then shook her head, folded her arms across her chest, turned and walked back to her office, never looking back.

He made it to the first stoplight before his eyes began to burn.

Lloyd stood in the kitchen as Bea was chopping lettuce for their dinner salad. The boys were in the den in front of the television. Lloyd was sipping a whiskey and water and telling Bea about Lick's visit.

"He wanted me to come with him for a week. Well, I've got Fred coming for the seminar and Jason's got a tennis match so I told him no. But I thought about it."

Bea kept chopping lettuce. "What a life he must lead. I feel sorry for him."

"Yeah, I guess yer right. Is your Junior League still planning the fund-raiser? Next week, isn't it?"

September 7
On the Plains of Northeastern Colorado

Rock Rypkima, pure Hollywood, walked with Bobby Monday out to the big metal barn behind the rodeo contractor's office. Trailing them were a cameraman and a sound person. The sound person's suitcase bore the stencil PROPERTY OF ROCK TELEVISION PRODUCTIONS.

Rock had to pace himself not to walk ahead of Bobby.

"What we do on 'Those Amazing Animals,'" he was explaining, "is try to entertain the public's curiosity. Kamikaze is certainly famous, but not necessarily a household word." Rock ran his fingers through his silver hair.

Bobby wasn't prone to saying much, so he didn't. Rock felt obligated to fill the silence. "This is certainly a desolate place. Is Brush the nearest town?"

"Yup."

They walked around the barn to a set of corrals. Horses were in several pens. Big heavy horses, unshod, and others, not so big, stood around variously dozing and balancing on three legs. Other pens contained bulls, lying on their briskets or standing. As the crew walked down the alley, the bulls cast them indifferent glances and went back to contemplating the nice day.

"Here he is," said Bobby, stopping.

"Which one?"

"The spotted one."

"Well," said Rock, nervously fingering the gold chain around his neck. "Somehow I'd pictured him bigger." He looked around. "Get your camera set up here, Clint. Maybe get up on this fence behind us so we can get Bobby, here, with Kamikaze in the background."

Rock warmed to the task. He was the producer and though he didn't know anything about rodeo, he knew about filming.

"Bobby, I'll just ask you some questions and we can edit what we don't need."

Kamikaze watched the cameraman move up on the fence hefting the heavy videocamera. A woman scurried behind him. Bobby stood across the fence with another human. The bull knew Bobby. He fed him and made him get in the truck every now and then. Kamikaze recognized his voice. Bobby never got on his back. Kamikaze never associated him with the bull rope or the ride.

Kamikaze kept a suspicious eye on the cameraman. He could sense no fear emanating from the man, but his machine seemed to intrude into Kamikaze's space. It was an uncomfortable feeling. Like someone was sizing him up, but in a different way from the bull riders.

A big glass eye was staring at him. He stared back but the big eye never blinked. It was not intimidated. Kamikaze took a step back. His instinct put him on guard. *Danger,* he thought. *Big eye. Bad intentions.*

"Listen, mister," said Bobby, "I'm havin' second thoughts about doin' this."

"Why?" asked Rock, rapidly calculating the cost of the filming crew's airline tickets from Los Angeles to Denver, the rental car and incidentals.

"This bull is just a poor dumb animal. He happens to be good at what he does. He just doesn't like people. I've seen some of those rags print trash and TV shows like '60 Minutes' crucify innocent people just to get a reaction. Rodeo is my life. It's Kamikaze's life. You might glamorize him or make him look like a monster, neither of which is true."

"No, no, this is a family show," assured Rock. "I think this will make a good segment and show rodeo in a good light. No sensationalism, but some pizzazz."

"Okay," agreed Bobby.

"Beautiful, baby, beautiful!"

One week later. 7:45 P.M. on television sets across the U.S.A.:
Anita, what have you got for us now?"

"Barry, we have a story that is chilling. On the plains of eastern Colorado resides a killer! A killer that is allowed, even encouraged, to maim and cripple humans and never be punished!"

A close-up of Kamikaze's cold eye filled the screen. The camera backed up to reveal the head. The eye was flat black. The camera panned from Kamikaze's horns, over his hump to his rump, then back to present a full body shot.

Anita continued. "Kamikaze is a rodeo bull. What all you urban cowboys will recognize as the model for your disco mechanical bulls. Once every ten days to two weeks, at a rodeo somewhere in the American West, a cowboy bets he can ride this beast. Sometime's he bets his life." She paused dramatically and the camera focused on her serious face. "In August this year, a nineteen-year-old young man named Dodge Brown was killed trying to ride Kamikaze. Kamikaze has never been ridden."

"Bobby Monday is Kamikaze's owner. We asked him how he could, in good conscience, continue to include this dangerous animal in his rodeo performances."

The television screen switched to Bobby leaning against the fence, Kamikaze standing placidly behind him.

"... bull riding can be dangerous ..."

"... certain risks are taken by anyone climbing down on the back of a bull ..."

"I do it for the money ..."

"... sorry for the young man and his family."

"... it's a business ..."

It took a lot of editing to get that thirty seconds, and the cuts between comments were choppy. Bobby, who was never very genial anyway, came across hard.

The film cut to a short interview with the Browns and Dee Dee Stufflebean, who was presently dating a brick salesman in Coffeyville. Next was an action shot of Kamikaze at last year's National

Finals Rodeo, over which a list of Kamikaze's casualties was read.

The report concluded with a repeat of Bobby's last comments. "It's a business . . . do it for the money . . ." The camera stayed on the bull's owner while he spit a brown stream of Red Man at his feet. There was a final close-up of Kamikaze's eye.

"Wow! Anita, that's scary!" said Barry.

"Yes," she said grimly. Then she turned to the audience. "It makes you wonder what they do to him to make him so mean."

"Golly, you're right! Makes you wonder. But stay tuned right after this commercial message to see a dog that actually talks on the telephone! Those amazing animals! What will they do next?"

September 19
On the Road Between Othello and Puyallup, Washington

Cody, I've lost it."

Cody let his runnin' pardner ramble on.

"I had a real shot at the Finals. Now I can't git back on track. I couldn't ride a broken-mouth ewe!"

The headlights sliced a half-moon piece of landscape out of the rainy night like a cookie cutter. The cab defroster warmed Cody's stocking feet, propped up on the dash.

"And today," Lick continued, "I had a money bull and what did I do ... got my two-bit, no-tryin', sorry ash can bucked off!"

"How's the ribs?" asked Cody.

"Feelin' better all the time. They hurt o'course, but a lot better than three weeks ago. No, I can't blame it on the ribs. I've just lost my luck."

"It wuddn't ever luck to begin with."

"Well, whatever it wuz, I ain't got it back."

"Lick, I think you're tryin' too hard."

"Whaddya mean?"

"Ever since late summer, when it began to look like you had a chance, you been real serious. You been a little hard to live with, too. I'm not complainin', I can stand it, but I think now it's interferin' with your ridin'."

"Well, I am serious! I wanna win!"

"I know, but somehow you gotta relax and let the ol' Lick come back."

"The ol' Lick," Lick said sarcastically, "never made the Finals."

"Well, that's just what I think, anyway."

"What do you suggest I do?"

"Number one: ride the best you know how, but when it's over, forget it. You been layin' up in the motel or the back of this pickup, evenin's. Early! You just lay around and think about it till your nerves git shot! I admire you cuttin' back on the booze, but that don't mean you have to give up partyin' with yer friends."

"Jeez, Cody, while I was laid up down at Mother's, I got to figgerin' how much I was drinkin'. I think maybe I got the makins of an alcoholic."

Neither said anything for several minutes.

"Find a spot and let's sleep a little," said Cody.

Lick pulled off Interstate 90 at the next rest stop. The boys parked and laid out their bedrolls in the camper. They cracked the cab window an inch and stretched out.

Cody dug a nearly full fifth of Black Velvet out of his war bag. He took a pull and passed it to Lick, who hesitated, then followed suit.

"Somethin's eatin' you, Lick. Maybe it's the Finals jitters, maybe more, I dunno."

"Cody," Lick said quietly, looking at the camper top, "I'm thirty-two, nearly thirty-three. I've put seven years of my life into bull ridin'. I gave up everything I had to do this. Job, career, family, home. I got nothin' to show fer it except broken bones."

Cody let the echo of the words slip out through the cracks around the camper's open roof vent before he replied. "Remember that time in Jackson when you tackled the bank robber? Jus' clotheslined that big skinny kid? Man, he didn't know what hit him! You settin' there on his chest pointin' his own gun up his nose! He was sure scared! Then the sheriff come runnin' up and arrested *you!*"

"Yeah, the buggers didn't have any sense of humor." Lick smiled.

"How was you to know it was a play for tourists!" chuckled Cody. "An' how 'bout in Phoenix when you took off yer boots and stepped into the lobster aquarium!"

"Yeah, Karen Kay was there that night. Matter of fact, I believe that's when I met her for the first time. Boy, now she was a darlin'! A real keeper. Ya know, Cody, she used to rub my back till I fell asleep. I've reduced everything I know about women to that one single thing!"

"What? Rubbin' yer back?"

"Not just rubbin' yer back, rubbin' it till you fall asleep. When someone makes you feel so comfortable that you forget all the reasons you should be on guard or stayin' awake so you don't miss nothin'! When you feel so relaxed you don't care if you miss it and you know she's kinda watchin' out fer you! You just fade off with her squeezin' the ache and the tired out of you. The perfect woman. You show me a woman that doesn't do that and I'll show you one you got to watch out for!"

"You reckon you'll get married again?" asked Cody.

"I imagine. Hell, I hope so, but now I jus' take it a day at a time. How's Lilac?"

"Good. She's good, Lick."

"She's all right, Cody. I doubt a feller could do any better. You gettin' serious, ain't you, pardner?"

"Could be. It's a little soon to tell."

The conversation ceased. Each mind wandered off into the land of Muzak. God had put them on hold.

" 'Night, Lick."

" 'Night."

"Lick."

"Ummm?"

"You're gonna do all right."

23

September 24
Northern New Mexico

Lick was sober. The first-quarter moon was shinin' its chaste eye down on his stocky frame. They'd made an easy pull down from Washington State. They were both up tomorrow night in Albuquerque. The New Mexico State Fair and Rodeo, a mighty rich one. For a seventy-five-dollar entry fee, the winner might make three to four thousand dollars. At ten o'clock they were about twenty miles south of Farmington, New Mexico, on Highway 44. They were both sleepy, so they pulled over and Cody got in the sack. Lick took a little walk.

Along the vast northern New Mexico roadside he stooped and picked up an old bottle. It was rectangular and flat. He unscrewed the cap and held it to the faint moonlight. Vicks Formula 44. He sat down on a rock and listened to the sounds of the night. Humans had been here for centuries in this high desert land, hundreds of years before Columbus or Alan Alda. Absentmindedly he rubbed the dirt off the encrusted bottle. A whiff of dust puffed out of the top. Mist that smelled vaguely of Vicks VapoRub began gathering from the dust. The mist coalesced into a face. Lick watched, fascinated.

The face was scrinching and grimacing like a baby waking up. It appeared to be floating. The eyes blinked open. It yawned and smacked its lips. Somehow it steadied itself above the bottle. It was the face of a cowboy who'd seen better days. The face spoke to no one in particular. The voice was gruff and had all the enthusiasm of an airport ceiling announcer.

"Rub ol' Pinto, my fine friend,
What's mine is yours, until the end."

The face looked up with tired eyes and studied Lick a few seconds. It glanced around and seemed relieved that Lick was alone. The ragged voice became more pleasant.

"Man, oh man, I'm glad it's you.
I could really use a chew."

Lick handed the gauzy figure his can of Copenhagen. The old-timer rapped a little "shave and a haircut, two bits" on the lid with his knuckles, and put himself a big pinch in his lower lip.

"I smoke clouds to clear my head,
I drink rain before I bed.
Thunder helps me say my vowels,
But Copenhagen moves my bowels."

Without speaking he excused himself. He reappeared momentarily.

"Uh? How are ya this evenin'?" asked Lick. It was all he could think to say.

"Pretty good, I could be worse.
It's hard to talk in rhyming verse."

"You always gotta talk in rhymes?" asked Lick.

"When I don't, my tongue gits tied.
It hurts my throat and pains my side."

"Are you some kinda genie?" asked Lick.

The old figure gave Lick a withering stare with one half-closed eye. His black hat was dusty and sweat stained. There was a ring binder memo pad sticking out of his brush jacket pocket. His face was wrinkled and whiskered. The Copenhagen crumbs clung to his teeth when he stretched his thin lips back. The missing teeth, or rather the few remaining incisors, made him look like a jack-o'-lantern.

"Genie? Genie! Bite yer tongue!
A genie couldn't cork my bung!
Guardin' misfits' what I do!
I'm a hangel, true and blue!"

"What's yer name, brother angel?" Lick was gettin' interested.

"Hoon, brother, it's Calhoon.

Common as a plastic spoon.
'Merican as pecan pie
But Pinto's what I'm goin' by."

"Pinto Calhoon, guardian angel," mused Lick. "Do you do day work by the hour, by the job, 'er what?"

"By the job, but not too long.
I've helped Willie write a song:
'Hangel Flyin' Near the Ground.'
Helped Ali regain his crown,
Helped Knievel cross the Snake,
But everybody makes mistakes."

Lick and Pinto visited awhile in the starlight. It turned out Pinto was born in 1866 in Bonham, Texas. His real name was Barker Francis Calhoon, but not everybody was privy to that information. He had ridden in the Oklahoma land rush of '89, but staked out the site of what was to become Noble, Oklahoma, and ended up with nothin'. He moved around the country a lot, but wound up on a little two-bit ranch north of London, Texas, in 1897. Pinto raised Spanish goats, ran his quail traps and gathered wild cattle.

Somewhere along in the twenties he died of complications resulting from an armadillo bite. Not that anyone ever knew exactly what had killed him, but if they had, they wouldn't have believed it anyway.

Now he was in the "hangel racket," as he called it. He wanted to have "Wings West" printed on his business cards, but Gabriel, the only five-star angel in the regiment, had nixed it, on account of that name being taken by a small commuter airline in California.

The last job he had was for an eight-year-old boy named Jeffrey who had found him in a discarded can of Right Guard (he had been left in a Super Eight Motel by a nervous lover who had gotten his wish with Pinto's help). While under Pinto's watchful eye, Jeffrey came down with tonsillitis and made an F on his spelling report card. However, he did teach his dog how to "siccum" and won $2.35 at recess playin' three-card monte. Pinto was better at some things than others. The tonsillitis was how come he came to wind up in a cough syrup bottle. But he was growing weary of Jeffrey. Hell, he wasn't even old enough to buy beer! Pinto was glad to see Lick.

"I've kinda tol' ya what I do.
Anything I could do fer you?"

Lick pondered a moment. "Well, ya know, Pinto, I'm on a circuit, ridin' bulls. I was doin' good, had a chance to make the Finals. Then I got hurt at Payson. Since then I ain't done good enough to pay my entries. My pardner, Cody, says I'm tryin' too hard. I sure wanted to go to O.K.C., but I gotta git winnin' again."

"Well maybe it ain't meant to be.
At Payson's where you needed me."

"How the hell—'scuze me, how was I supposed to know! Ain't there somethin' you can do now?"

"It just so happens there might be
But what, jus' yet, ain't come to me.
But you could surely help me out
My liver's suffered from a drought.
'Cause milk was all that Jeffrey drank
My belly's gettin' mighty lank.
Let's tend to business, first things first;
A little drink to whet my thirst.
Another thing, if you don't mind,
Accommodations you might find.
Some other place to keep my mug
An' git me out this stinkin' jug!"

Lick opened his Copenhagen can and Pinto Calhoon took up new residence.

"Ride 'em hard an' make 'em buck
Rub ol' Pinto fer good luck!"

Cowboys do believe in luck and superstition. Lick had acquired his good luck charm and he was ready for Albuquerque.

But what about you, steady reader? Do you believe in luck and superstition? Do you always bet your favorite number? Do you knock on wood and throw salt over your shoulder! If so, you are predisposed to believing in the likes of Pinto Calhoon.

Because the real question is, oh, ye trusting, are you willing to follow me further into the depths of this tome knowing that Lick's good luck charm is a . . . what shall we call him . . . a ghost? So

far in this story, I've only asked you to believe that bulls can think. Not a big stretch of the imagination. But now I'm asking you to give legitimacy to a run-down crackpot of an angel. I'm trying to seduce you into believing in his existence like you believe in Moses, Superman or President Buchanan.

When you say your prayers at night do you stop and consider that possibly no one is listening? No! You charge on, blessing this and blessing that, asking forgiveness, seeking comfort so that you may go and sin again.

So following my logic, if you do believe in a higher being, an extended batting slump, hot dice, momentum, Shem, Ham and Jafeth, a kiss for good luck and avoiding black cats, you could give Pinto and me the benefit of the doubt.

It will sure make tellin' this story easier.

Saturday, September 25
Albuquerque, New Mexico

Cody and Lick slipped into the rodeo office at the fairgrounds. "Elveeta, you big dumplin'!" said Lick.

"Lick, honey! Good to see ya! How's the ribs?" Elveeta was rodeo secretary for Bobby Monday's Stock Contracting Company. She was in her late forties and had been Bobby's secretary as long as Lick had been a card-carryin' pro rodeo cowboy.

"Comin' along okay. Still can't raise my arm all the way, but other than that, no complaints. I haven't done much good since Payson, though. That's where I got hurt."

"You've got a chance here," she said. "Do you know what you drew?"

"Nope, never called. We been up to Othello and Puyallup."

"You've got P77!"

"No kiddin'?" said Lick. "Ol' Sunset Strip. All right!"

"You stick a ride on him and you ought to be in the money," she said. "Here's your number." She handed him the nine-by-eleven placard to pin on his back.

"What about me, Elveeta?" asked Cody.

"Let's see here, Williams, Wilson, Wing ... You've got—" A look passed over her face like she had just seen her ex-husband in a crowd.

"You've got ten-twenty."

"Ten-twenty," Cody repeated. Lick looked at his pardner.

"C'mon, Cody," said Lick, leading him to the door.

They glad-handed acquaintances and friends all the way back to the pickup.

"What'ya think?" Lick asked Cody.

"I admit it's a little spooky."

"Yeah. The trash bag's a bad draw." Lick didn't want to encourage Cody one way or the other. Pride is a strange thing. If you're a professional rodeo hand, you live or die on the draw. The chance of Cody ridin' Kamikaze was real slim, and his chance of gettin' hurt was in the definite realm of possibility. Lick didn't want to see Cody get hurt, but he didn't intend on offending him or making his decision for him. If the situation had been reversed, there would have been no question: Lick would try Kamikaze, but he didn't know whether Cody would.

"I reckon I'll try him," decided Cody. Cody and Lick had both tried 1020 before, but not this year. Not since he'd gotten so mean.

They spent the afternoon visiting and waiting for the evening show to begin. Cody got plenty of advice on how to ride Kamikaze. Most of the professional bull riders were careful to circumvent any warnings. Those were unnecessary. They just gave him tips on the bull's bucking pattern and how they'd handle him.

Manly Ott, presently ranked third nationally, in spite of his injury and layoff at the hands of Kamikaze in Nampa in July, went over the bull's bucking technique with Cody.

"He's the wiliest bull I ever saw," said Manly. "He actually thinks. He deliberatedly works you into position, catches you off guard, and dumps you, hooks you or twists you. I've never seen any other bull quite like him. He sideswiped me on the chute in Nampa, not so's the judges could see, but just enough. Got me a skosh off balance, then proceeded to hook me and buck me off. If . . . er, when you make the whistle, get off and run like hell! Fells and Dingo are clownin', so you couldn't ask for none better."

An hour before the rodeo began, Cody was on his way over to the corrals to look at Kamikaze. He spotted Emerald Dune enchanting a group of rodeo queen contestants.

"Cody! How you doin'?" Emerald waved him over. Emerald was dressed in a white satin shirt with kumquats on the yoke. It was unbuttoned to the xiphoid. His designer jeans were tucked inside his python-and-grizzly-bear boots. His Western hat was furry; it looked the way your tongue feels on Sunday morning.

"Girls, this is Cody Wing, bull rider extraordinaire."

The girls giggled appropriately in their color-coordinated boots, Western suits, gloves, makeup and hats. They were sweating more than a bachelor at a wedding.

"Howdy, ladies." Cody doffed his sombrero.

"You up tonight?" asked Emerald.

"Yup."

"Well good! We'll be watchin', won't we, girls?" They smiled and nodded. Cody strolled off when Emerald started into his description of the best banana flambé he ever tasted on Basin Street in New Orleans.

Lick returned to the camper and pulled his can of Copenhagen out of his hip pocket. He rapped the "shave and a haircut, two bits" out on the lid. That was his signal to Pinto Calhoon, G.A., so he didn't have to appear every time Lick helped himself to a chew.

He opened the lid and the dusty mist gathered above it. Pinto appeared in the camper.

"Afternoon, an' howdy do!
Somethin' I kin do fer you?"

"Well, for starters, is there some way you could take a shower? My chew's been tastin' like VapoRub."

"I reckon so. It's been a while.
A little scrub can't hurt my style.
I'll rinse off from front to hind,
But first, let's hear what's on yer mind."

"My pardner, Cody, has drawed a mean mutha. A bad news, triple X, meat eatin', cowboy hatin' spotted braymer! The big-horned head buster killed a kid here a while back and he's hurt plenty others. Cody's gonna ride 'im, but he is sure gonna need some guardin'."

"Guardin' two's against the rules!
It's bad enough just guardin' fools."

"Pinto, he needs it bad. I'm not kiddin' 'bout this bull. Couldn't you jus' help him fer a measly eight seconds? See that he don't git hurt. You know what they say about rules."

"This job don't come without its strings.

Gabriel might clip my wings.
He's mighty strict and has his ways
But he don't work on Saturdays.
What he don't know can't be a crime,
I'll put it down as overtime."

"I'm sure beholden to ya, Pinto. One other thing. I'm up tonight. Got a money bull. If I kin jus' stick it to 'im, I'd be back in the money. I'd appreciate any protection you could give me. By the way, is there anything I could do fer you?"

Pinto closed his eyes in thought. He raised a dirty fingernail and spoke.

"I've helped some folks adjust their fate.
You could bring me up-to-date."

"Fire away," said Lick.

Pinto got out his ring binder memo pad and fished a two-inch pencil out of his jeans. Little scraps of paper fell out of his memo pad like confetti as he thumbed through it. There was a movie ticket stub for the premiere showing of *Rocky III* in Cape Girardeau, Missouri, the address of a Gypsy palm reader in Pittsburgh, and a red business card that said MARIA, LATIN SPECIALITIES, ELKO, NEVADA. His questions concerned people he'd had occasion to offer his services to over the years.

Pinto had gotten mixed up with an ambitious yacht captain from Atlanta during the America's Cup. He had promised the captain he would try to get his face carved on Mount Rushmore. Lick told him that as far as he knew it was the same fearsome foursome etched in the mountain.

"Oh, damnation, sakes alive!
I thought I'd talked 'em into five.
It's my style they try to cramp.
I'll put Ted Turner on a stamp!"

He licked his pencil and made a scratchy, spidery note in his memo pad.

Mario Puzo, author and Hollywood producer, had wanted a leading man for his movie *The Godfather*. He'd asked Pinto to use his influence and obtain Marlon Brando for the leading role. Pinto had gotten confused and brought him Marlin Perkins instead. He had even worked out a side deal with Mutual of Omaha to insure the National Park facilities surrounding Mount Saint Helens. Lick told him Brando had gotten the job, not Perkins.

"Lick, ol' boy, that makes me sad.
Marlin wasn't all that bad.
Could milk a bear, from underneath!
And he'd agreed to fix his teeth.
I trust a man who's good with stock.
He promised me a Piece of Rock!"

Pinto went down the list of those he'd taken under his wing, so to speak, for awhile: Gary Hart, Donald Trump, Anita Bryant, John DeLorean, John Erlichman, Zsa Zsa Gabor's eighth husband, George McGovern, the Seattle Mariners and Kuwait!

Lick answered each question as best he could, and told him what had come to pass. It was a ragged litany and pretty poor references if one was looking to employ a guardian angel. But it didn't faze Lick a bit. He felt fortunate to have Pinto on his team. After all, according to the odds, Pinto was due for a winner.

25

Lick and Cody watched the rodeo from behind the chutes. The other roughstock events at the New Mexico State Fair and Rodeo, bronc and bareback riding, each had two goes. A contestant entered and rode two horses on different days. Due to the large number of entries, the bull riding was a one-header. As the time drew near, the bull riders gathered in the contestants' area behind the chutes. There was a fifth-string banjo tension in the air. Fells Wingtip, rodeo clown and bullfighter, was talkin' to Lick. Others were rosining their gloves and ropes. Cody was doing stretching exercises.

The first load of bulls rumbled into the chutes. The sliding tailgates behind each bull rolled shut with a clunk. The bulls rattled and banged against the boards.

"Seventy-seven's out first, down here in four," Bobby Monday shouted to the scrambling bull riders. He was on horseback in the arena. "Whoever's got 'im, get crackin'!"

Cody's bull wasn't in the first bunch. He knew it wouldn't be. Bobby saved his best for last.

Cody and Manly Ott dropped Lick's bull rope over his bull and looped it. Lick climbed over into the chute and gently placed a boot on the bull's broad back. Then, still supporting himself on the chute, he knelt on 77. Ol' 77 wasn't known as a chute fighter; still, it was good table manners to let him know you were there. Lick adjusted his rope forward until he was satisfied.

Lick was concentrating. He dropped his legs down and scooted up a little.

"Pull! Pull!" he told Cody, who was bent over pulling the tail of his rope. "Good!"

Lick took his wrap and pounded his gloved and rosined fist closed. Sunset Strip was a half Charolais, half Braymer polled bull. He weighed in at 1,840 pounds. That's two hundred and four barn cats, seventeen grass-fat lambs, eleven Saint Bernards, six mule deer, three Berkshire boars, one and a half moose, one Budweiser Clydesdale or half a hippo! The book on the big white bull was that he was a spinner. To the left.

"You ready, Lick, we haven't got all night," chided Bobby Monday from the arena side of the chute. Lick ignored him. *Remember*, he thought, *whose side Bobby is on*. He slid up on the rope. Ol' 77 had his nose to the ground.

Lick took his right hand off the chute and rubbed the Copenhagen can in his shirt pocket. *Ride 'em hard and make 'em buck. Rub ol' Pinto fer good luck.*

He put his free hand back on the railboard, his only escape route.

"Git his head up," said Lick.

Cody slapped the back of the bull's head three times. He raised his head. Lick dropped into the vacuum of concentration. He spit out his chew.

"Cowboy up," said Manly into the whirlpool surrounding Lick's senses.

"Do it, Lick," encouraged Cody.

Lick nodded his head.

The chute boss, afoot in the arena, who had been watching Lick intently, slipped the latch and pulled the gate wide open instantly. Bull 77 roared into the arena! He took two short jumps and flung himself into a whirling dervish! He spun back to the left. Lick sat tight. *Squeeze*, he thought. He squeezed his legs. *Lift*; he lifted up on the rope. The split second before the huge body jerked him into another 180° whiplash, the massive head feinted in the direction of the intended orbit. Lick kept his eyes glued to the back of the bull's head. Reaction time was measured in nanoseconds. The hulking ropes of muscle beneath the rolling skin flexed and stretched beneath Lick's seat. He bit in with his left spur at the precise moment and spurred with his right. His right chap leg flapped furiously! Watching the great white head for that same moment to reappear, he bit in and spurred again!

Everything became slow motion. He was on a gently turning merry-go-round. He became aware that it was taking longer and longer between his opportunity to spur. He waited patiently. The bull was rocking gently. At one moment, he was high in the sky, climbing, climbing, then the gentle roller coaster ride back to Earth. Time to spur again. The great muscles bunched and released in waves beneath him. Lick felt a tremendous sense of satisfaction course through his body. *Hey! This is what I do*, he thought. *This is what I'm here for. Nobody can take this away. I am there.*

The buzzer rudely interrupted his magic moment! He descended into reality. Ol' 77 was jerking and pounding him! He was still spinning hard to the left. Lick needed to go off into his hand, to the left, to prevent hanging up. The eye of the hurricane, however, was also on his left, so he reached down with his right hand and loosed the wrap. He opened his palm and bailed off the right side.

Fells and Dingo were right there to take 77 off the rider. Nonetheless, Lick hit the ground running and sprinted to the fence. It wasn't until he was safe that he realized the crowd was on its feet, cheering. The cowboys, his peers, on the fence, were all grinning ear to ear like a photographer had ordered them all to say "Wheeze!"

His mind began to pick up Emerald's creamy smooth, spreadable voice: "... *like it!* That's rodeo at its finest! Let's see what the judges say."

Each of the two judges were allowed to give a maximum of 25 points to the bull and 25 points to the rider, for a total of 100 points. They told the runner their scores, he tallied them up on a small blackboard and held it up for Emerald to see.

"Ladies and gentlemen, your new leader in the bull riding here at the New Mexico State Fair and Rodeo, an eighty ... three!"

The crowd's hoopin' and hollerin' refilled Lick's confidence tank. It went from two quarts low to overfull! Just that quick he was back on the trail to the National Finals and Pinto was goin' with him!

Cody was behind the chutes, stretching. He was definitely scared. His movements were mechanical, his skin was blanched. Lick put a hand on Cody's shoulder, stopping his leaden exercise. He spoke quietly into Cody's ashen face.

"Cody, I know this is gonna sound like I been smokin' pigweed, but I want you to do somethin' fer me."

"What?" Cody was rigid as a bathroom tile.

"I got a good luck charm."

"What?" His eyes were all pupil.

"I'll tellya 'bout it later. His name is Pinto. He's in my Copenhagen can."

"What?" Cody was still unable to blink.

"Just rub ol' Pinto fer good luck." Lick proffered the can. "Jus' do it."

Cody rubbed.

Lick slapped Cody gently on the cheek. "C'mon, pardner. You kin ride this bag o'bones. He's jus' like any other bull. You've rode a million of 'em. You're jus' the cowboy who can ride him. Now git yer rope, here he comes."

Cody's spring was one turn too tight. *Just relax,* he told himself. *Sure,* he answered. He had drawn ol' 1020 two years ago but he honestly could not remember the ride. He'd gotten bucked off, of course.

Cody watched Kamikaze come into the chute. The big spotted braymer fought it all the way. He banged his horns on the planks and the iron pipe. He kicked the tailgate repeatedly.

If yer tryin' to make me nervous it won't work, Cody telepathed to the back of Kamikaze's head.

Loud teeth, noted the bull.

Matter of fact, continued Cody's brain waves, *this may be our big night, Hog Belly. I am so psyched I b'lieve I could ride a beach ball in a hurricane. I'm stuck to you like glue. When I'm done they'll retire you to a dairy! Little kids will ride around on your back for a nickel apiece! You'll be known as Bozo the Stumbler!*

They'll put mascara on your face and paint your hooves red. Dress you in frilly stuff and puff up your tail with hair spray.

You'll remember tonight, Burger Brain. Yer all downhill from here!

Lick interrupted. "Okay, pardner, it's time."

Cody eased over into the chute. As soon as he touched the bull's back, Kamikaze started throwing his head. Cody dropped down on his back.

"Pull! Again!" he instructed Lick. "Again, okay."

Cody's hand was set. He slid up on the bull rope. Kamikaze smashed Cody's leg against the gate. Cody nodded his head. The gate slammed open.

Kamikaze didn't move a muscle! The crowd was silent, anticipating.

Hog Belly? came the low-frequency waves from the bull.

They rolled into Cody's autonomic receptors and printed out, *Watch this . . .*

Suddenly Kamikaze bellowed! A fearsome, bone-chilling, neck-tingling, malevolent warning! The long inhuman wail echoed eerily through the lighted arena!

Kamikaze dropped to his knees! The ground man started to close the gate. With less than three feet left to secure the latch, Kamikaze rose like a missile fired from a nuclear sub and crashed out of the chute, knocking the gate man on his back! He bucked two spectacularly high jumps and stopped stock-still!

Bozo, hey? Kamikaze thought. He was stopped no more than half a second, but it was enough. He knew what he was going to do next. The hapless Cody didn't have the slightest idea. Kamikaze reared up like Trigger. *Bulls don't do this,* thought Cody as he slid perceptibly back off the rope.

Syonara, hawk bait! A quick gyration to the right and Cody hit the ground with both hands! He was up and on the fence before Kamikaze completed his circle.

Cody clung to the highest rail panting like a hot dog. He watched over his shoulder as the massive bucking machine trotted toward him. The muscles rolled and bunched beneath the skin. The almost Appaloosa spots that covered his hide would have made him appear clownish except that your stare was drawn to his face.

The spots had arranged themselves into dark furrowed brow lines like a blindfold over both eyes. His muzzle was black. He looked like a gargoyle wearing a Lone Ranger mask.

He stopped and looked up at Cody. Cody was quivering slightly. Their eyes met, Cody's fearful, Kamikaze's deep and inscrutable. *Burger Brain? Humph.*

The big bull swung his heavy head toward the out gate and trotted off. Cody sagged.

* * *

Lick patted his pocket and let out his breath. "Thanks, Pinto." There was a faint effluvium of VapoRub in the air.

September 26
Albuquerque, New Mexico

The bull riding championship of the New Mexico State Fair and Rodeo paid $4,503. The win put Lick in eighteenth place in the world standings. It brought his total to $24,376. The men in nineteenth and twentieth place had $23,455 and $21,512, respectively. The man leading the bull riding had collected $73,295 to date. But the key number was fifteenth place. To compete in the National Finals Rodeo, held December 4 through 13, you had to be one of the top fifteen money winners in your event. There are approximately 8,500 card-carrying members of the Professional Rodeo Cowboys Association. Three to four hundred of these men and women made enough money to rodeo full-time.

The man standing in fifteenth place had earned $27,225.

At the conclusion of the Grand National Rodeo held in San Francisco's Cow Palace October 29 through November 7, the annual professional rodeo season ended. Competitors' earnings would be tallied and the top fifteen would be invited to the Finals.

Lick and Cody regularly studied the *Rodeo Sports News* to plan their itinerary. Each rodeo had a deadline to enter. On average the rodeo secretary required ten days' notice. The major rodeos needed to be entered thirty days in advance. The P.R.C.A. had a computerized system in Colorado Springs that helped these traveling athletes keep up and get entered. It required only a telephone call.

While Lick was laid up in Hereford with his cracked ribs, he had planned his schedule up through the Cow Palace in San Francisco.

He drew a big calendar that covered the last six weeks of the season, from September 26 through November 7. He wrote down every rodeo scheduled on each day that had a winning payoff of a thousand dollars or more.

He planned to go to Memphis, Pine Bluff, Oklahoma City, Omaha, Bonafay, Waco, Texarkana, Little Rock, Minot, Portland, Dallas, Billings, Bismarck and San Francisco. He and Cody hashed it over and figured which ones Cody could enter and still be able to drive to the events Lick would be flying to.

He calculated the required entry fees: twelve to fourteen hundred dollars, and commercial flight expenses another fourteen hundred. Plus his share of the gas and incidental costs. He'd have to win along the way. He had less than two thousand dollars in the bank.

Some cowboys earned over fifty thousand a year competing at a hundred rodeos. Many rode in a lot more and didn't make that much. Lick usually averaged a hundred and ten. If he was going to make the Finals, he was really going to have to press in October. The other bull riders ranked fifteen through twenty knew the same thing. It was going to be tight.

Cody drove Lick to the airport in Albuquerque this fine Sunday morning. Lick climbed aboard the big silver bird to Memphis, the start of a meandering odyssey that would cover thirteen hundred miles, give or take flat tires and lost luggage, in less than six weeks.

Friday, October 1
On the road from Oklahoma City to Omaha

What's botherin' you, Cody?" asked Lick. "You ain't said five words all mornin'."

"I feel kinda rotten 'bout last night," he answered.

"What! I wish you'da said somethin'! I'da gladly swapped you. That dolly I's with couldn'a been over twenty-one. Like talkin' to a recorded message!"

"I didn't mean Harvetta. She was real nice. Matter of fact, I didn't even sleep with her!"

"Well, no wonder you feel dumpy."

"No, I woulda, but she didn't want to. But I would have. All the time I was talkin' and huggin' her, I kept thinkin' 'bout Lilac."

"You jus' didn't git drunk enough. That's simple," said Lick.

"No, dammit! That's not it. It's not that simple. I've got the lonelies all the time. I keep wishin' I was with her, or she was with me." Cody sighed. "Lick, what would you think if I was to git married?"

Lick looked over to the passenger side. Cody was sitting up on the edge of the seat, hands clasped and looking like Father O'Flanigan at a paternity suit.

"Married?" asked Lick.

"Yeah, married."

"Hummm, I don't know. I guess it has to happen to everybody at least once."

"I'm thinkin' 'bout askin' her."

"When?"

"I'll see her Sunday night, spend two or three days at her place before I meet you in Texarkana."

"No, I mean when would you git married?"

Cody loosened up a little and smiled. "I thought maybe during the Finals. Have a big blast. The folks could come down."

"You gonna quit the circuit?" Lick asked, keeping his eyes straight ahead.

"Yep. If I get everything set. Maybe I'll go back to the ranch. Dad's gonna be fifty-eight next month. He could use the help. Long as we had a place to live, I'd be okay."

"You reckon Lilac could handle livin' out like that?"

"Yup, but I never asked her yet. Both her folks are dead. She's got a brother in Saint Louis and an ex-husband in Omaha. There's nothin' keepin' her in Kansas City."

"In that case, I say ask 'er! We'll have a celebration like you never saw. We'll party till our knees are sore!"

"You really think I should?" Cody asked, brightening.

"Ya damn right! If that's what you want, go after it!"

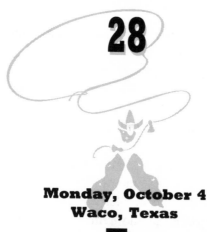

28

Lick had flown into Waco from Bonafay, Florida, and was watching the last of the bull riding. He felt a hand on his shoulder. He turned his head. Cody was standing there. His clothes were rumpled, his eyes bleary and bloodshot.

"What the hell!" said Lick. "I wuddn't supposed to see you till tomorra!"

"She turned me down, Lick. I ast 'er and she turned me down."

"Cody, I'm sorry!"

"I ast 'er Sunday mornin'. Saturday night had been so wonderful. We talked and everythin', so the next mornin' I ast 'er. She said no. I drove straight through."

"Let's git a room somewhere," said Lick. "You look like you been drug through a knothole. Get some rest. It'll look better in the mornin'."

Lick grabbed his gear and they took the pickup to town. They found Franco and Pork Chop at one of the overcrowded motels and moved in. Cody went right to sleep.

Lick took Franco and Pork Chop to Acosta's BBQ and Cantina. They sat around licking their fingers and discussing Cody's plight.

"I was there when he met her that night in Kansas City. Had the big fight with the football team," remembered Franco. "A girl that good-looking is sure to have all kinds of men chasing after her. Maybe she doesn't think he's good enough for her?"

"That's crazy!" said Lick. "Cody's one of the best men ever strapped on a pair of spurs! You guys know that!"

"That's fer sure," said Pork Chop. "He'd give you the shirt off his back. He never gets mad."

"Boys, I know him better than anybody," said Lick. "He is a genuine, silver-plated, good ol' boy. Good hand with stock. Got good folks. He's talented and he loves her!"

"Maybe something is the matter with her," volunteered Franco.

"Dang sure must be!" said Lick indignantly. "If she can't see he's a good man, she needs her head examined! If he was like me, or even you, Franco, I could see her passin' 'im by, but not Cody! I know fer a fact he'd be true to her and treat 'er right!"

This tawdry triumvirate sat and extolled Cody's virtues and questioned Lilac's wisdom until 11:30 P.M.

"We oughtta call her," suggested Pork Chop.

"Better yet," said Lick, "we oughtta go see her, and there's no time like the present! Any y'all feel like goin' fer a drive?"

Pork Chop agreed to stay with Cody until they got back. Franco and Lick had both drawn bucking stock for the following night in Waco. They took Cody's pickup and started north on I-35 at 12:01 A.M. digital time.

It was 110 miles to the Dallas–Fort Worth airport. They pulled into American Airlines's unloading zone at 2:35 A.M. The earliest flight was number 298, departing at 7:00 A.M. Lick bought two tickets at $124 each. They buzzed and jangled their way back and forth through the hijacker's keyhole until they were depleted of any pig iron, hubcaps, Copenhagen lids, belt buckles or live ammunition. They lay down in the waiting area. It was furnished in neon gloomy.

"Lick, how do we know how to find her?"

Lick slid his hat back off his eyes and looked at Franco, "What?"

"How do we find her?"

"I guess I don't know. I never thought of that." He looked puzzled.

"Maybe Cody's left her address in his truck," suggested Franco.

"We better take a look!"

In the jockey box was a map of Kansas City. It was fresh. Up at the top was written "L.H. 1918 N. 76th Dr. Apt. 26."

"L.H. That's probably her," said Franco. "Did you find any-thing else?"

Lick was scouring the jockey box for scraps of paper in the dim interior light. He crawled over into the camper and searched, to no avail.

"Well," Lick said, "if that's all we got, then it's enough."

Tuesday, October 5
Kansas City

"Wait here," they said to the cabdriver.

Lick and Franco tromped up the stairs to Apartment 26. It was 9:36 A.M. Nobody was home. A neighbor walked down the stairs. She knew where Lilac worked. God often takes care of the innocent well-intentioned. Lick had her explain it to the cabbie. The meter already read $22.50.

Lilac and Maribeth looked up in surprise as the two disheveled figures pushed open the glass door into their office. The invaders were dressed like cowboys; both needed a shave. They looked like they'd wadded their shirts up and carried them in their pockets for a week! They were vaguely familiar to Lilac. They stomped over to her desk.

"Lilac?" asked Lick.

"Yes?"

"We need to talk to you."

"What? Why?"

"It's about Cody."

"Oooh, now I remember. You're Lick and I know you too."

"Franco, ma'am. I met you during the Shriners' Rodeo," said Franco. She looked back at Lick. "What about Cody?"

"He's plum lost his mind over you."

"We talked. I hope he didn't do anything foolish."

"Foolish! He fell in love. That night at the bar he fell in love! From the very first. I thought he was loony, no offense, like some-body spiked his punch!"

"Did he ... did he tell you what he did?" she asked.

"Yup. Said you turned him down."

"I told him I just didn't think our life-styles were compatible. I knew it would hurt him, but it's the truth."

"Lilac," said Lick, "I don't know what I can do to make you change your mind, but I'm here to tell ya, if you let him git away, you'll be kissin' off just about the most decent, honest, sincere, hardworkin'—"

"Brave, kind, considerate ..." interjected Franco.

"... Lovin', true-blue, intelligent, talented ..." continued Lick.

"... Bronc stompin', bull ridin' ..." added Franco.

"... good-hearted man I have ever known!" said Lick. "And I've known a few!"

"Is he outside?" asked Lilac.

"He's asleep in Waco, Texas."

"How'd you get here?"

"That's not important. What's important is that his ol' heart is achin'. He thought you felt the same way about him."

"I really care about him. He's everything you said. He makes me happy. I love his singing, and he is so considerate."

"He's willin' to quit rodeoin' for you! He's ready to carry you back to Wyoming to his ranch. He'd do it, too!"

"I know. He told me."

"And you still turned him down!"

"I've only seen him four times! I'm not sure how I feel. What if I don't like Wyoming? It would be worse to go and then be unhappy."

"Who says?" asked Lick. "Go. If it don't work out, it don't work out. You can always leave."

"That would hurt Cody."

"Worse than he feels now?" asked Lick.

"Yes. And what if he's not ready to settle down? What if he stays on the ranch for six months and get restless and wants to rodeo again?"

"So what. Go with him."

"I can't live like that."

"Like what?"

"On the road. No security. I want a man who's home with me. A home, a family. Besides, I like to work."

"You can work."

"I can get a job in Ten Sleep, Wyoming?"

"I said you can work!" said Lick. "Lilac, I wanna tell you from the heart, there's not many men I'd be standin' here for. Matter of fact, I can't think of a single other one! No offense, Franco. I'm not real gung-ho on anybody gettin' married. Most fellers that get turned down, I figger it's just their good luck, only they don't know it. But some men are the marryin' kind. What I'd call good family men. They're true to their wives, they like workin' in one place. They're good with kids, they belong to the volunteer fire department, the Kiwanis Club and the church. They're dependable husbands and pillars of the community. Everything I'm not. But I can recognize one when I see him. I've lived with Cody for nearly two years and he's real. You couldn't go wrong."

"That's very touching, Lick," Lilac said. "It's also quite a tribute that you would come up here from Waco to speak for him. You must think very highly of him."

"We're friends. You can't be more than friends."

"I told him I enjoyed seeing him, but I honestly didn't think there was much future in our relationship."

"Well, Lilac, if you can't see a future in that kind of man, maybe you don't deserve one that good!" Lick turned to go, then looked back at her. They held each other's eye for several seconds. She didn't blink.

"C'mon, Franco. We're wastin' Cody's time." They walked out.

29

Tuesday, October 5

Franco and Lick took Delta and Henry Ford from Kansas City to Waco. They were back at the motel by 6:00 P.M. Pork Chop came out to the pickup.

"He's been in there all day. Won't eat nothin'. I had some good tequila, 'bout half a fifth. He drank it all," Pork Chop reported.

Lick went into the room.

"Cody, how ya feelin'?" he asked.

Silence.

Cody didn't say a word. He wouldn't even look at Lick. Lick came back outside.

"He won't talk to me," he said.

"He hasn't said a word all day," said Pork Chop.

"Keep an eye on him, will ya, fellers? I gotta think a minute," said Lick. He climbed into the camper.

"Shave and a haircut, two bits," he telegraphed on his Copenhagen can. Pinto formed into his seedy image. Lick wrinkled his nose.

"Jeez, Pinto! Why don't you take that bath like I asked you? You smell like a three-day-old Absorbine bandage!"

"You woke me to tell me that!

Kiss my foot, you little gnat.

I'll git by, I don't need you.

I've got better things to do!"

"Aw, hell," said Lick. "Cool down. I'm just edgy. I got another problem."

"Might've guessed, you worthless whelp.

You only knock when you need help."
"It's Cody again."
"Your ears bad? I've told you, son,
My license's only good for one."
"I know, I know! But hear me out! Maybe you can give me some advice." Lick told Pinto of Cody's love affair, his expectations, his tragedy and his present condition.

"You got any suggestions?" he concluded.
"Seems to me, if I hear right,
Cody needs a bride tonight.
From my view, it matters not
Who it is or even what."
Pinto drifted back into his can.

"What?" Lick sat and absorbed the wisdom of the spirit who had advised the designer of the sleeveless parka. After due consideration, he came into the room and presented his plan to Franco and Pork Chop.

"Cody's getting married tonight," he announced.

They produced a bottle of distillate from the mescal plant (a variety of the maguey) on the way out to the rodeo grounds. Each took turns nursing the morose Cody Wing while the others competed. Word spread among the cowboys.

At the conclusion of the rodeo the stands emptied and fifty or so cowboys and cowgirls gathered at Cody's pickup.

Lick stood in the back of an adjoining pickup bed and explained Cody's turn for the worse.

"We need a bride and a preacher," he said.

The crowd raised their beer cans in agreement.

"Part of y'all scatter and find a suitable bride for this, the finest of our lot. Emerald," he said, and pointed to Emerald Dune, rodeo's answer to Jimmy Swaggert (radio evangelist and cousin to Jerry Lee Lewis and Mickey Gilley), "have you ever performed a wedding ceremony?"

"Nope, but I'd sure be willin' to try," declared the announcer.

"Good. I'll be best man. Gather up some bridesmaids and a bouquet of flowers. Turn on the lights in the arena and we'll make a wedding chapel in front of the chutes."

Half an hour later the wedding committee was interviewing prospective brides. Chaco Tortuga had offered his roping horse, Branch. A dogging steer had been considered. Wyoming Montana escorted a fourteen-inch Brazos River carp to the reviewing panel. Someone brought in a possum that had laid in the fast lane for three days. Twenty-three-year-old Nostra Fillip had offered her forty-five-year-old body as Cody's Cleopatra. She was placed on the list between the carp and the possum.

Good ol' LoBall had finally returned from his citywide search with what all agreed to be the best selection. He had found her at Piggly Wiggly, looking back at him in the fresh meat department. Her skin was smooth to the touch. She had a long tapering neck and shapely legs. And her breast: pulchritudinous and white as porcelain!

"What's her name, LoBall?"

"Butterball!"

Since Cody could not stand of his own accord, a rope was looped under his arms and draped over the chute braces under the announcer's stand. Butterball was similarly strung by the tail, eye level to the oblivious groom.

A small bouquet of shin oak twigs were placed in her enlarged giblet holder like roses in a vase.

Butterball rotated gently on her supporting string. One of Cody's toes reached the ground and he hung and swung slowly, inscribing a meandering infinity sign in the arena dirt.

Lick and LoBall stood solemnly next to the swiveling Cody, occasionally pressing the fifth of Cuervo Especial to his slack lips.

Nostra Fillip, Branch the roping horse, and a hog-tied Spanish goat were the bridesmaids. They stood at Butterball's side.

Flujencienta Rojas was recording the wedding ceremony for Polaroid posterity.

Emerald took his place in front of the bride and groom.

"Ladies and gentlemen," he began, casting a puzzled glance at the bridesmaids, "we are gathered here, an' it ain't often that so fine a group is ever gathered as this. . . . Gimme a little swig, there, Lick. Thanks. It ain't often that we poor peripatetic souls, who make our meager livin' gettin' pounded and pummeled by all manner of mean, ugly and often stupid brutes, are given the opportunity to pay tribute, and I do mean tribute! It is an honor that we are here to witness, to attend the uniting of our friend, one of us, the nearly great Cody Wing, and his darlin' bride, née Miss Butterball.

"Usually when one of our kind gets hitched, he slinks off like a hip-shot coyote and winds up in an ol' bore hole plowin' ground or settin' posts. Neither of which—I say, neither of which—is a suitable or worthy end for the great American cowboy!

"Do I hear an amen!"

"Amen!"

"Gimme another shot of Crow. Thanks.

"Now we are here to join this man"—Emerald was looking at the back of Cody's head at the moment—"and this turkey in the time-honored, civilized institution of marriage.

"Who offers this bride to be wed?"

"I do," said a thick voice near Lick. Lick smelled VapoRub in the air.

"Before I unite this beautiful couple, is there anyone among you who has any objection?"

"I think it is preposterously silly."

All eyes turned to the rotten apple. It was Ned! Big Handy Loon was standing behind Ned. Big Handy placed a bear claw on each side of Ned's hat brim. He pulled it down with so much force, the brim tore off Ned's hat and encircled his neck like a wreath! The crown completely covered his eyes and bent his ears out like a rabbit standing on his head.

"Any other objections?" asked Emerald.

"None," said Ned.

"Do you, Butterball Histomoniasis, take Cody as your lawfully wedded spice?"

"She does," said Nostra Fillip, always the bridesmaid.

"Do you, Cody Wing ... turn him around this way, Lick ... do you, Cody Wing, take Butterball as your lawfully wedded turkey?"

A thin glimmer of light shown in Cody's eyes, like a night flight over Yaak, Montana, at 35,000 feet. His lips began moving. The sound was out of sync with the picture. "Lilac? Is it you-o-o-o?"

"The ring please." Lick peeled Cody's Timex off his limp wrist.

"You may place the ring on her, her ... uh ... ?"

Lick helped Cody manipulate the expandable watchband over Butterball's upraised thigh.

"I now pronounce you man and turkey. You may kiss the bride."

Lick turned Cody toward Butterball. He pressed Cody's head to Butterball's cool, inviting skin. Cody licked her.

Nostra began to cry.

They carried Cody and his bride to the camper, placed them side by side on a pillow and left them to consummate their union in privacy.

The reception continued until dawn, when Lick climbed into the pickup and pointed it toward Texarkana.

30

October 6–23
On the Road

Cody did a lot of hurting the next three weeks. Lick pushed him hard and kept his mind occupied. They made the Texarkana rodeo October 6, then Little Rock, Minot, Portland, Dallas, Billings, and rode October 22 in Bismarck, North Dakota. Cody missed Minot and Portland. Lick had flown to them.

Lick regained his confidence and was back on track. Cody drank more than usual for him, philosophized and carried his heart around gently. He wrote twelve songs in the two and a half weeks! Songs with titles like: "You've Put My Heart on Hold," "You Kissed My Lips Then Kissed Me Off" and "Another's Feeling You and That's Why I'm So Blue."

Lick even got into the songwriting mood. All he could create was the first line and Cody thought he had heard it somewhere before. It went: "I'm so miserable without you, it's like you never left."

The two friends spent many hours and miles discussing Cody's love life. Lick didn't hesitate to give advice. Fortunately, Cody knew when to listen to him and when not to.

31

Sunday Afternoon, October 24
Kansas City, Kansas

Lilac's dog barked like a seat belt buzzer in a '73 Lincoln. She slid off the couch, turned down the game and answered the door.

"Cody!"

"Hi, Lilac." He stood in the doorway, hat in hand.

"I . . . I wasn't expecting you."

"I wanted to talk to you."

"Of course. Come in!"

The lazy afternoon sun made her front room warm.

"Something to drink, or eat, maybe?" she offered.

"No thanks. I don't plan to stay long, but I . . ." He'd practiced all the way from Bismarck how he was going to address her. "I think I might have been too soon, uh, too hasty, in asking you to consider marrying me." He blushed. "It's just that I never felt like this about anybody. I figgered you had felt the same way, but I had no right to assume that . . ." He hesitated. She looked at him, bright-eyed, not speaking. He hurried on. "And I wondered if maybe we could forget I asked and we could see each other again?"

Lilac smiled sadly. "Cody, I like you very much. You are a special man. But we don't know each other very well. I don't think I'm prepared to move to Wyoming and live on a ranch . . . with your parents. I'm not sure I would ever be prepared to do it. It's not fair to you to lead you to believe otherwise.

"I'm satisfied with my life, at least right now. Ten years from

155

now I might regret not going with you. But in those same ten years I might regret living in Wyoming. I have to be honest with you. I'm a city girl. You're a country boy."

"Okay, okay," he said. "Could we forget that I asked and just let me see you again, every now and then?"

"One day at a time?"

"Yup. One day at a time."

"No promises? No expectations?"

"This agreement can be canceled on five minutes' notice by either party," said Cody.

"I'd like to think about it," Lilac said.

"Certainly." Cody stood up and turned toward the door, hiding a little tear of disappointment.

"Cody," she said to his back.

"Yes?"

"I've thought about it."

"Yes?"

"Gimme a hug, cowboy!"

Excuse me, friends, but I should like to point out that we are in a critical stage of this relationship.

In the Guidebook of Love: Step one is discovery and declaration.

Step two is relax and let it happen. Lilac is having trouble with step two. She is guarding her heart with the regulations set forth in the Presidium of the Practical. These regulations are filed in the brain between "Heartache Memories" and "Status Quo."

They are meant to protect. Lilac knows she should not be tempted by some elusive fairy-tale hints of love ever after. She knows it . . . but she hesitates. She steps back and takes a deep breath.

Cody, on the other hand, never saw the sign that read CAUTION: LOVE AHEAD, USE LOWER GEAR. His emotions boiled out of his heart and rolled like magma over every warning thrown in their path. His love was uncontrollable until she simply held up her hand and stopped his landslide halfway down the slope. Cody's chest is fluttering, his mind is teetering, he is balancing on the edge of his heart. He gains control of himself, steps back and breathes deeply.

Love is so fragile at this moment that the weight of an old boy-

friend's finger on a touch-tone phone can make it dissipate like morning fog.

Even a single reference to a future filled with new adventure can drive the timid heart to retreat to the comfort of familiar pillows.

At this moment the door to love is ajar.

They both sighed. Cody touched Lilac's long fingers. They stepped through the door together.

Monday Morning, October 25
Kansas City, Missouri

"Cody came by yesterday," said Lilac.

"Oh, really?" said Maribeth.

"Yes. We've agreed to see each other, without any strings attached."

"Do you think you can do that?"

"I think so. He seems willing. I told him I just wasn't ready for a deep relationship."

"Is he?"

"Yes, very much so."

"He's about the only man I know who is!"

"He invited me to come to Wyoming with him for Thanksgiving."

"You're not going, of course! You told me how you'd probably hate Wyoming."

"Well, I ..."

"If I were you, I'd sure avoid the temptation," said Maribeth with a sly smile. "It would be terrible if you liked it."

Lilac looked at her and grinned.

32

Saturday, November 6
Grand National Rodeo at the Cow Palace
San Francisco, California

It all came down to the last bull ride. Shang Lutz, according to Lick's calculations, was three or four hundred dollars ahead of him in the national standings. Shang was in fifteenth place, Lick in sixteenth. The bull riders in seventeenth, eighteenth, nineteenth and twentieth had been eliminated during the first two goes at the Cow Palace. Both Shang and Lick had been sent preliminary invitations to the Finals in OKC. The man who finished sixteenth would be notified after this rodeo that his only official capacity at the Finals would be hawking Snow-Kones in the cheap seats!

* * *

He and Shang would find out which bull they had drawn tomorrow morning. Tonight Lick had no intention of doing anything that would violate his training rules.

At the end of the rodeo tomorrow night Lick would slide from the statistics or be standing where he'd never stood before.

His good intentions included a glass of warm milk and a good night's sleep.

He had good intentions but weak resolve. He rose from his insomniac's bed at 1:30 A.M. and prowled the hotel hallway until he found a party in progress.

$\star \; \star^{\star}$

6:36 A.M. Sunrise slid in around the corners of the hotel curtain and woke him. Cody was snoring in the other bed. Lick lay under his covers, shifting uncomfortably, unable to go back to sleep. At 8:30 he got up, fuzzy-mouthed, eyes burning. He rattled around the room like a man in a motorized wheelchair.

After several busy signals, he reached the rodeo office to ask about his draw for that evening rodeo: 007LB10, not good news. He was a mediocre bull. If Shang drew a better bull in the short go, Lick's chances of going to the National Finals would be about as good as being appointed ambassador to Great Britain. Lick left the room without waking Cody. He went out to the sidewalk and wandered up the street.

"Shave and a haircut, two bits." He put in a call to his guardian angel.

"Ah, my friend. Bee-yoo-tee-full day!
Looks like it's all goin' our way!"

"Pinto," asked Lick, "what's that smell?"

"Polo, son, Polo cologne.
Only the best fer yer chaperone."

"Shore is potent stuff. Guess it's better than VapoRub, though."

"A pleasant change, to say the least.
Polo tames the savage beast.
Prickly pear and cactus claw
Tell me, son, who'd you draw?"

"007LB10," said Lick glumly. Pinto whipped out his ring binder memo pad and flicked through the lined pages. A yellowed black-and-white photograph of the Birdman of Alcatraz fluttered to the sidewalk.

"Oh, Oh, Seven, L, B, Ten.
Not too good my bumbling friend."

"I know," Lick sighed. "This is it. Tonight. For all the marbles. I have to finish higher than Shang Lutz in the short go and the average. Otherwise, we don't go to OKC."

"What do you intend to do?
You drew the bull, it's up to you."

"Ride him, I guess."

"You're dang right! You ride 'im hard!
Ride that bull an' I'll stand guard.
Spur 'im like a hurricane
Was in your shorts and in yer brain!
Lock up tight! Make 'im buck!
Only you can change yer luck!"

"What if Shang draws a better bull?"

"You bet yer wad he's tryin' to!
Just do the best that you kin do!"

"Right. Yer right, Pinto, ol' man. I'm the only chance I got." Lick smiled a little.

"By the way, I like yer new perfume. Even if it smells like a debutante's laundry."

"You measly, weasly parasite . . ."

Lick just snapped the lid on tight.

★

The Cow Palace crowd was big and rowdy at the Sunday night performance. This was a big money show and important to plenty of cowboys who knew it was their last chance to make the Finals.

Lick had spent the afternoon in his room sleeping and forcing himself to rest. He hadn't eaten all day. Now he stood in relative calm behind the bucking chutes waiting for the bulls. His was in the first load. Shang had drawn W6, ShugaVelvet, an eliminator, hard to ride. If Shang could ride him, he'd probably beat out Lick. Lick's bull did not have a reputation for winning rodeos, but he should be easier to ride. Lick was talking to Shang while each buckled on his chaps and readied his gear.

"I'd almost trade you, Lick," said Shang.

"I was thinkin' the same thing," Lick replied. "I been on W6 twice. Bucked off both times. He fights the chute."

"Yeah, I know. It's not my first time on him. I had him in Fort Worth."

"You ever been on LB10?" asked Lick.

"Rode him once. Drew him again, but turned him out. Best I

recall, I marked a fifty-eight. Couldn't get him to do much. It would help if the clowns turned him back, otherwise he'll go straight."

The first load of bulls rumbled into the chutes.

"Guess I better get to work," said Lick.

"Lick . . ." started Shang. Lick looked at him. They held each other's gaze. The space between them was filled with mutual respect.

"Yes?" asked Lick. Shang stuck out his hand and Lick shook it.

"Ride 'im, cowboy."

"Thanks."

33

Lick and Shang each did the best they could. They played out their small drama at the far side of the bigger stage. They had record crowds at the Cow Palace. A seventeen-year-old girl on a big rangy horse won first in the barrel racing. A spectator was mugged in the parking lot. Manly Ott, bull rider, continued his slump.

Lick rode his bull. He scored an anticlimatic 63 points. He and Cody stood on the deck behind the bucking chutes and watched Shang Lutz ride. ShugaVelvet lived up to his reputation. He bucked hard, spun crooked and tried to kill Shang after he bucked him off. But buck him off he did, four seconds into the eight-second ride.

Cody was ecstatic! He was so happy for his friend he could barely contain himself! He pounded and hugged Lick, stepping on his toe and mashing his hat! Lick just stood there with a supercilious look on his face, a little embarrassed.

Lick's qualified ride placed him in the average, which upped his total winnings for the year to $33,763. That was $632 ahead of Shang, who fell to sixteenth place overall.

They saw Shang Lutz a few minutes later behind the chutes.

"Good ride, Lick," said Shang. "Congratulations!" His goodwill was genuine. Shang was twenty-three years old and destined to attend several National Finals in years to come.

"Thanks, Shang. You almost rode 'im, didn't ya?"

"Yeah, almost. Next time. Tear 'em a new one in Okie City. You deserve it." Shang shook hands and headed off.

"Let's git on with the party! We're gonna celebrate tonight!" said Cody.

"You go ahead. I'll be there in just a minute."

"Okay, pard."

Lick walked into the arena. It was over. Cowboys, spectators and maintenance people were moving in all directions, like they had someplace to go. He felt small in the big coliseum.

Lick spoke to himself in a small, quiet voice. "You made it. You may not have deserved the good luck, but you made it.

"Lord, I owe ya. You've always been there. I know I'm not always there for you. But every time I need to talk to you, you listen. Sometimes I know you're tryin' to call me and the line is busy. My life's good. I'm a simple man on a lucky roll. I know I'll have to pay you back sometime. Maybe I'll be ready when the time comes. Anyway, for now, I thank ya for standin' by me. Amen."

Lick stood there another minute or two until the nagging emptiness sent him trotting after Cody and the security of friends. Victory and achievement were meaningless when you couldn't share them.

Lick climbed into the pickup with Cody.

"Pardner, I wanna be the first to toast ya!" Cody uncapped a fifth of Jim Beam and made it bubble. "I'm so proud of ya, I could bust!"

"Thanks, Cody." Lick took a swig. "Where to?"

"The party, where else!"

34

November 18
Houston, Texas

Into each life some rain must fall.

Sympathetic reader, have you ever been the helpless victim of some grand design? Does the term "eminent domain" make you shudder? Did the new truck bypass leave your little Main Street business high and dry? Did they find an endangered species in your pasture and condemn your farm? Did they raise your taxes? Close your bank? Cancel your favorite TV show?

And who did these deeds that so affected you personally? The answer is, dear friends, the infamous "THEY." They who are the wheelers and dealers, the seedy and greedy, the lickers and stickers, the kissers and pissers!

The honor bending, condescending, all important, influential, anonymous They. When They, these influential people, do something, they usually make waves. Innocent bystanders get washed away with the tide. That is not to say that influential people are mean-spirited or uncaring. They are simply unconscious of the far-reaching consequences of their little amusements.

In Houston, on this November night, a thunderhead was building that would nearly drown our bull ridin' hero.

Read on. . . .

Clive McDill was a good man, with eight grandchildren, 136 oil wells on three ranches and a standing order for two new Cadillacs every October.

He loved his grandchildren, his oil wells and his Cadillacs. He was a charter member of the Texas Cattle and Oil Club. This year he had assumed the chairmanship after fellow member Billy Ray File had been appointed ambassador to Lagos.

The Texas C & O, as it was called, was as exclusive as the Association of Left-handed Astronauts Who Have Walked on the Moon.

Clive brought the meeting of the Texas C & O to order. Twelve men sat around the conference table on the thirty-fifth floor atop the Texas Red Petroleum Building. The reflection of Houston's night lights sparkled on the large window at the end of the room. An elegant stained-glass light fixture hung over the shiny oak table, giving the impression that one was in a pool hall and not a corporate boardroom.

Bourbon and scotch were in crystal decanters on the side table. Cigar smoke made its presence known in spite of the humming air-quality filters.

"Boys," said Clive, "y'all know how much fun we have bettin' the ponies at Ruidoso, an' how we been lookin' fer another little event we could calcutta."

The members nodded noncommittally. Each year before the quarter horse futurity at Ruidoso Downs race track in New Mexico, they held their own private betting pool. The starting horses in the race were auctioned off to the highest bidder. The members would begin with the favorite horse and bid amongst themselves, continuing until all of the entries were bought. Then all the money would be pooled. After the race, those who had bid the highest for the horses that won, placed and showed would divide the pool. These were rich men and the pool was deep.

Clive continued. "The committee, Bosco, Jim Bob Tom Ed and me have come up with a possibility that might be right down our alley. Jim Bob Tom Ed, would you kindly explain our proposal to the boys."

Jim Bob Tom Ed Luckett, cattle rancher from Crane, Texas, rose. Jim Bob Tom Ed ran twenty-eight-and-a-half cows per oil well on his place south of Midland and made a pretty good living. "Thankya, Clive," he drawled. "We figgered we could pick an event at the National Finals Rodeo next month, say the bull ridin', and calcutta the fifteen finalists. Each one of us could buy a finalist, maybe two, and the winner would be determined by the amount of money won by the rider during the ten days at the National Finals. Each rider starts out even. Pay three places in the calcutta: win, place and show."

"What they've won to date, the rest of the year, don't have any bearing on the calcutta?" asked Dicky Lee Limenuts, president of Dicky Lee's National Gas and Brangus.

"Nope. 'Course, the bull rider with the best record goin' into the Finals might bring a little more in the auction," answered Jim Bob Tom Ed. The good ol' boys around the table chuckled.

Smiley Horrocks pushed his 6'4" lanky frame back from the table. "The cowboys don't know nuthin' 'bout this and we don't tell 'em, right!"

"Right. Anybody caught tryin' to interfere will forfeit his membership in the Texas Cattle and Oil Club.

"Everybody understand the rules? Good."

Ah, sure . . . we all understand, don't we, fellow readers? We understand the good ol' boys are just havin' a little fun. How could it possibly affect the little people? Wait and see.

Clive handed each of the members a list of the top fifteen bull riders showing their standings going into the National Finals and the amount of money won by them to date. He let everybody study the list for a few minutes.

Halfway down the table Hoss Bendigo sat beside his cousin, Jaybo Marfa. Hoss was trying to explain the proceedings to him. Abandoning the details, he concentrated on coercing his not-too-bright cousin to buy the second bull rider to be auctioned off. Hoss, himself, planned on being the highest bidder for the number-one-ranked bull rider.

A flicker of understanding crossed Jaybo's eyes and he took the bait. Jim Bob Tom Ed stood up and terminated the table talk.

"You ready, Sam?" asked Jim Bob Tom Ed.

"Yup, if y'all are." Sam Houston Pinzgauer, auctioneer, Longhorn raiser and offshore drilling magnate, stood up.

"Okay, boys. We're gonna go down the list, one through fifteen. All bids are final and we'll need a check by December first. Clive is keepin' the books."

"First up for bids is Smokey Brothers. Won eighty-one thousand, two hundred and thirty-nine dollars this year. What am I bid? Will you bid twenty-five thousand? Twenty-five, bid twenty-five, twenty-five. Thank ya, Hoss, now fifty ..."

Smokey Brothers brought $210,000.

One hour and fifty minutes later, Clive handed a typed copy of the calcutta results to each member. The bids ran from $210,000 for Smokey all the way down to $18,000 for Lick in the fifteenth place.

The total pot, which would be split 50-30-20, was $1,859,000.

On the way to their car following adjournment of the Texas C & O, Hoss was givin' Jaybo the "Good Dog" treatment. "Ya done jus' right, cuz, we got the number-one and number-two cowboys in the pot. One of us is bound to be in the money. Ma's sure gonna be tickled!

" 'Course, if it gits right down to it we might have to hedge our bets a little. A little burr under the blanket, so to speak." Hoss chuckled.

"Ya really think Ma will be tickled?" asked Jaybo, who always worried what Ma would think.

"You betch'er hat!" answered Hoss.

"That'll be great, if Ma's tickled," concluded Jaybo, smiling. "Jus' great."

Wednesday, November 24
Worland, Wyoming

The boys had ridden in three more rodeos before the Thanksgiving lull: Brawley, California; Sioux Falls, South Dakota; and the American Royal in Kansas City. Then Lick took off to spend the holiday with a belly dancer in Hailey, Idaho.

Cody stood in the small airport waiting room in Worland, Wyoming. It was 11:15 A.M. The airplane was half an hour late.

"Frontier flight 915 from Denver now arriving."

The reliable Convair 580 touched down. Smoke puffed off the tires on impact. It taxied up and shut down the props. Lilac was third and last to debark.

Cody saw her and his heart skipped a beat. Her long brown hair was pulled back behind her ears and blowing in the wind. She was a tall woman, but she walked erect, shoulders back, with long strides. She had on a long coat and dark pants. She was wearing fashionable Western boots.

"Hi, Cody." She smiled.

"Hello, darlin'." He gave her a hug.

He shuffled a minute. "You got bags?"

"Two. I didn't know what to bring, so I brought more than I'll need, I'm sure."

"That's okay. We've got plenty of room."

He tossed her bags in the back of his blue pickup and they drove east toward the Bighorn Mountains.

"I'm a little nervous, Cody."
"I know, but it'll be all right."

Meeting potential in-laws. What could be worse? Possibly taking the final exam in bio-chemistry? Contracting malaria? Stacking twenty tons of moldy hay? Scheduling a hemorrhoidectomy? Spending the winter in a sheep camp? Given a choice, most normal people would rather be stabbed to death with a table fork than meet potential in-laws!

It is no wonder Lilac has butterflies. In her worst nightmares she envisions them living in a cave cooking big hunks of antelope liver over a cow chip fire. The father-in-law belching and grunting, the mother-in-law shuffling around shooing bats off the skewer while the children skitter and screech like Rhesus monkeys!

She realizes that the mother-in-law will only be pleased if the new daughter-in-law is like her. The father-in-law may have a different opinion depending on his relationship with the mother-in-law. Assorted aunts, uncles and grandmas can all sway the evaluation. Younger siblings can bolster or erode a family's approval. Did she pick up the baby? Did she help with the dishes? Did she listen to Uncle Albert's jokes? Did she like sister's corn bread?

Potential wives are usually evaluated as potential mothers. First impressions aren't formed on the fact that the candidate may have a Ph.D. in nuclear physics or own her own shoe store. No. First impressions hinge on the initial response to questions that often begin:

"My son tells me that you are a supreme court justice, the first person to cross the Pacific in a hang glider and have been nominated for the Nobel Prize in literature. That's nice . . ." says the mother-in-law, who hesitates, then, ready to resign herself to disappointment, reluctantly continues, "But can you chew buffalo hides and make your own jerky?"

Lilac knew all these things and pondered them in her heart.

"Cody, we're still on one day at a time, right?"
"Yes, ma'am. I'm not tryin' to put any pressure on you. I hope

you have a good time. I've told the folks that you're just a friend, so they shouldn't harass you too much.

"Knowin' them," he continued, "they'll just fit you right in and you'll feel comfortable."

"Good." She reached over and kissed his cheek. "It's nice to see you, cowboy. Where will we be sleeping? What arrangements, I mean."

"You might be in Kaycee's room, my little sis. I'll be on the couch. Sorry."

"That's okay. I understand." She slid over and sat next to him.

The weather was clear and fifty-two degrees. They turned off onto the ranch road. Cody took them up another side road up a draw. He stopped at the base of a little meadow. The sun was shining through the windshield. He took out a mattress from the camper and covered it with his bedroll. He laid them out in the meadow. He and Lilac lay on their backs, side by side, looking up at the sky.

The sky was blue. Migrant clouds stood at parade rest, like cottonwood silk on a municipal swimming pool at dawn; no ripples.

"Lilac, this is what I love. This is where I belong. My roots are in these mountains and hard ground. I've banged around the country these last few years and seen all of it I care to see. I'm tired of it. I'm tired of the long nights, the bad whiskey and the endless road. My body hurts, neon gives me a headache.

"If I'd been one of the best, maybe it would be different. But my bones ache, I live from one rodeo to the next, always bettin' this one will make me enough to enter one more.

"I'm ready to come home. I'm ready to try and amount to somethin'.

"Lilac, I love you. I love you more than anything I've ever seen, known, tasted or rode. Since I met you, I know what it means to love.

"I wanna marry you. I want to have kids. I want to teach 'em to ride colts, track lion, punch cows, rope steers, play guitar and love this wild Wyoming country. I wanna sleep with their mama every night.

"I know we've got a deal. I'm not gonna back out on it. I promise not to talk about it again, but I want you to know how I feel. You are the best thing that's ever happened in my life."

Cody's open-faced honesty and quiet confession pierced Lilac's self-defense. He touched her heart. She squeezed his hand and lay there in the feather bed of his love.

He rolled onto his side and unbuttoned her coat. "We're not in a hurry," he said.

* * *

"Mama, this is Lilac ..."

"Come in, sugar, outta the chill. Call me Chick. Roscoe and the boys are up on Willer Crick. They'll be in by supper.

"Have you kids eaten yet? Probably not, huh? Cody would never think of stoppin' off for a bite. Worse than his dad! Can go for three days without thinkin' of eatin'.

"You've been comin' this way a long time, haven't you, darlin'? You know that though, of course.

"Sit down, honey, I'll heat up some Hamburger Helper and stringbeans. You like peach cobbler? Cody's favorite. I always make up two or three when he comes home.

"Cody, put her suitcase in Therm's room. You two boys can sleep on the sofa.

"Now, Lilac, tell me about yerself. You sure are a pretty thing."

Lilac spent five days bein' tossed and tumbled amidst the busy, happy Wings. They assimilated her like a snowflake on Powder River Pass! She was asked to help. She made the turkey dressing and pumpkin pie. She learned to play dominoes and rode to the head of Cedar Creek. She saw her first elk, mule deer, antelope, porcupine, jackrabbit, eagle, buzzard and pheasant. She ate her first venison and Rocky Mountain oyster. She talked for hours with Cody's little sister, Kaycee, who was hungry for sophisticated conversation.

Lilac was taken to a real country dance, met someone who had never heard of Neil Diamond and did something on horseback she didn't know you could do!

36

Friday Night, December 10
Oklahoma City, Oklahoma

Lick had a room reserved at the Sheraton during the Finals. Cody was staying with him. Cody saw to it that Lick was sober, rested, and celibate. Pinto saw to it that he was safe. They kept his socializing to a minimum and his partying proper. Lick could have applied for membership in the Campfire Girls!

Friday night they were all back in the room by 10:30 P.M. watching a "M*A*S*H*" rerun. Lick had ridden his bull earlier that night and won second in the go round. It paid $2,439.

Lick was sore. He had climbed on seven bulls in seven days. Not just your everyday run-of-the-mill eighteen-hundred-pound thrashing braymer, but each one of the top hundred bucking bulls in the rodeo game. They had been selected to represent the best stock the rodeo contractors had to offer. After all, it was their showcase, too!

Every person competing, be he roper, rider, dogger or roughstock rider, was wound up and ticking like a two-dollar watch! A high sense of drama hung over every conversation, keeping the cowboys on the edge of hysteria. Friends, supporters, fans and family suffered the tension vicariously.

The physical pain and nervous exhaustion was cumulative. It was the true test of Ban and Certs! Each competitor had to bring himself to a mental and physical peak nine days in a row. Hallways and rooms began to smell of liniment and DMSO. Rolaid wrappers piled up in the butt cans.

At the coliseum a training room had been designated. In the hour or two before the rodeo it filled with contestants. Roughstock riders, mostly. There was so much black and blue, bandages and tape, and creaks and groans a visitor would think he was in a battle zone!

Allow me, friends, if you will, to expand on pain, on playing hurt. Rodeo is not a team sport. If the quarterback injures his elbow and is on the bench for three weeks, the game still goes on, the team still takes the field and the quarterback still gets paid.

If the bareback rider injures his elbow no team physician writes him an excuse. His game is canceled. His horse is turned out and his money goes back in the pot.

National Finals: ten performances, nine days in a row, ten chances to win. Chances to win, did I say? Fifteen first-class cowboys ride. Each performance pays only the top four places. Even if you rode your bull every performance, you could still score out of the money.

And even if you don't score you still get beat up. Playing with pain? You have no choice. The coach can't pull you out; you're the coach!

I could turn around and tell you that they don't do it for the money. You'd laugh, unless you'd climbed mountains, danced in a chorus line or circumnavigated the Earth in a one-man sailboat.

Grit, drive, desire and determination fuel the fire that burns inside the gladiator until it is so intense that pain is overcome. Each night, for each performance, he must stoke that mental fire.

High risk? Mental fire? Playin' hurt? Low pay? What kind of game is that!

It's rodeo. The cowboy's answer to organized sports.

Lick had drawn seven bulls up through this Friday night. He'd made the whistle on six head. Three other bull riders had ridden six bulls: the first- and second-place bull riders in the world standings coming into the National Finals, Smokey Brothers and Lennox Wildebang, and the fifth-place finisher, Wyoming Montana.

Although all four men had ridden six bulls so far, Smokey was ahead in the average for the National Finals Championship. Their scores for each ride were totaled to determine their standings in the average.

At the conclusion of each performance, the cowboys drew for tomorrow's bull. Officially forty-five rides remained, forty-five bulls to be drawn for, including the Bucking Bull of the Year, number 1020, Kamikaze. Some poor, unlucky, hind-tit sucker was going to draw that cowboy killer and put his body on the line! It gave each potential victim a queasy feeling. But this queasiness didn't last long among these brave vaqueros. The odds against drawing Kami-kaze were fifteen to one.

CL75, Bugger Velvet, had bucked off Lick in the third round and reinjured his ribs. He'd been wrapping them faithfully before each ride, but each successive night the pain grew worse. Cody had been taking care of Lick like he was an only child.

Cody put down the telephone. He'd turned down a party invitation for him and Lick.

"A little drink would relax ya, pard," Cody said, pouring Lick a shot of Johnny Walker Red over ice.

"Thanks." Lick grunted.

"Still hurtin', huh? Does it hurt to breathe?"

"Yup, but I'm all right."

"Ya damn shore are! You're doin' fastastic!" Neither alluded to Lick's present status in the top four: bad luck.

"Any suggestions 'bout tonight?" asked Lick.

"Hell, you're ridin' better than you ever have! Those ribs must be forcing you to stay over yer rope!"

"When's Lilac comin'?" asked Lick.

"I'll pick 'er up tomorrow at noon."

"You gotta place to stay? You can stay here, ya know, if Lilac can handle it."

"We'll see. Nothin' fer you to worry about." Cody paused. "I never did thank you for goin' up to Kansas City after I'd ... I'd made a fool of myself."

"No sweat. Didn't do much good anyways."

"Maybe it did. She's comin' here and she went to Wyoming with me for Thanksgiving."

"How was that?"

"Thanksgiving? Good, I guess. She got the full dose. She knows what it would be like if she ever decided to marry me."

"You still tryin' to talk 'er into it?"

"No. We don't discuss it. I promised her I'd not mention it unless she wants to talk about it."

"You've been pretty straight-arrow. Maybe it's to help me, but if you wanna snort in some ol' dolly's flanks, don't let me stop ya!"

"No! You're not stopping me. I just don't feel the urge. Actually, it's helpin' take my mind off it, stayin' here and keepin' you outta trouble."

"You reckon she's bein' as true and pure as you?" asked Lick.

The question hit Cody like a fist in the chest! He hid it well. "I don't know. She's made it clear we've got no hold on each other."

Lick laughed. "Well, you're a better man than me! Matter of fact, I could use a little lovin' right now! This place is crawlin' with sumptuous darlin's, one of 'em with my name tattooed on the inside of her upper lip! I've been here a week and been brushed up like an ol' bull in the willers!"

"You're winnin', pardner! Maybe what yer doin' is the right thing."

"I don't know, dammit. I ain't been drunk once, loved at all and I've slept more than a man in a coma! I'm supposed to be enjoyin' this! This is my last fling!"

"Last fling?" asked Cody. "You gonna quit after this?"

"I been thinkin' on it," Lick admitted, mad at himself for the slip of the tongue. "I'm gettin' too old to keep hurtin' this bad. But I don't know what I'd do. Bull ridin's the only thing I'm half good at. I figger I'm good for another year or two, unless I get hurt again."

He sighed. "What about you? You still goin' back and run the ranch?"

Cody shook his head slowly and said, "It all depends on Lilac."

37

Saturday Morning Early, December 11
Oklahoma City, Oklahoma

Hoss Bendigo pulled into a handicapped parking space and turned off his lights. The Eldorado glowed silver under the vapor lamps in the parking lot. No one else was visiting the Cowboy Hall of Fame in Oklahoma City at 4:30 in the morning.

"Are you sure these guys are reliable, Hoss?"

"Shootfahr, cuz, 'course I am! The lawyer gimme Slyzack's name and he personally picked 'em fer us."

"But Slyzack's locked up in La Tuna!"

"These peckerwoods are from Dallas, the Big D! They're hand-picked! And only a thou a day. Not much to protect our investment."

"I wished Ma wuz rightcheer. She'd know if we wuz messing up."

"Shootfahr, trust me, Jaybo," encouraged Hoss.

Hoss and his cousin, Jaybo Marfa, had inherited their oil ranch in Wharton, Texas. Hoss was smart, but shady; Jaybo had trouble keeping score in the game of life.

Jaybo's real name was Jim Bowie Marfa. His mother, now deceased, had been president of the Daughters of Texas in 1951 and a shrewd businesswoman. In addition to her son, whom she called JayBoy, she had raised her nephew, Hoss, as her own, after his mother ran off to Shreveport with a wildcatter. A group of lawyers, friends of Jaybo's mom, now ran the company.

"So what's these two Dallas woodpeckers gonna do?" asked Jaybo.

"Git out yer list, Cuz. I'll 'splain it to ya. I bought Smokey in the calcutta. You bought Lennox. Number one and two. We paid over two hundred thousand apiece, right?"

"Now ... try to understand this, Jaybo ... each bull rider's been on seven bulls. They've got three to go. Our boys have ridden six bulls each. There's only two other riders who've ridden six bulls each. Follow so far? So, just to help *our* boys out, we set a few traps along the way for them other two cowboys. Nuthin' serious, just kinda a wrench here an' there to make sure they don't ride as many bulls. See?"

Jaybo thought it over. "I'm not sure I understand, Hoss."

Hoss sighed. "These boys from Dallas toss a few tacks in the road. Apply a little gentle pressure, you know. Then we win. You wanna win, don'cha?"

" 'Course I do, Hoss. You know that."

"Well, then, trust me. Have a cheroot."

As Jaybo lit up, the plan disappeared into his cranial vault like a firefly into a black hole.

★

"That must be the cats there," observed Hoi Solomon Rosofsky.

He sat at the wheel of a rented four-door AMC Concord. The heater wasn't working and Hoi Sol was cold. He steered toward the parked car. "Man, look at that Cadillac! Nice set of wheels. Might git one like that myself someday, but in panther black."

Hoi Sol was not talking to himself. His traveling companion, Thorhild by name, sat hunched in the passenger seat. Thorhild bent his head slightly to keep from touching the headliner and his knees pressed against the dash. He had thick, very light blond hair, ice-blue eyes, a cross tattooed on his thumb and a nose like a gravy boat.

"Nice of Slyzack to throw a little work our way," continued Hoi Sol. "I'll tell ya, bro, it's been thin. Things are changin'. I mean, when was the last time we rousted some liddle mom-and-pop business. Hell, everybody's carryin' firearms! The corner drugstore now belongs to an international conglomeration that doesn't give a flyin' filch whether they get held up or not!

"And when was the last time you broke somebody's arm? Every-body's got a lawyer! I don't know what it's all comin' to, ya know? We're losin' our traditional values. Extortion, a little payola, some strongarm. Now they steal more with computers than you can make hijackin' an armored car!" He sighed sadly.

"Maybe it's drugs or TV preachers. Somethin' has taken folks' minds off unscrupulous behavior or petty revenge." He glanced at Thorhild, who was staring straight ahead. "I mean, nobody robs a church anymore."

Hoi Sol pulled in perpendicular to Hoss's Eldorado. He could see two heads illumined in the front seat. The Cadillac's doors opened. Hoss walked around to Hoi Sol's window.

"Y'all Slyzack's boys?" he asked.

"That's us, brother."

Hoss climbed in the backseat. Jaybo came in after him.

"I'm Hoss and this is Jaybo ... uh, Jim."

Hoi Sol adjusted the rearview mirror to better see the gents in the backseat. Hoi Sol immediately noticed the Texans' attire. It was Hoi Solomon Rosofsky's curse. He was preoccupied with clothing. He came by this preoccupation naturally. He was descended from a long line of tailors. His grandfather was a Russian Jew who had immigrated to Houston. Hoi Sol's father had learned the trade, moved in the fifties to San Francisco, where he worked for a large dry goods store. His father had made a buying trip to Hong Kong, where he met and married the working daughter of a Chinese haberdasher. They returned to California and soon moved to Los Angeles, where they started their own business making fine men's clothing. Hoi Sol was born thirty-nine years ago in L.A. and grew up on East Eighth Street in the middle of the garment district. As a baby Hoi Sol slept on the cutting table while his mother and father were cutting fine suits. His diapers were tailored from scraps of white silk left over from shirts his mother made.

For the meeting tonight, Hoi Sol had chosen one of his seventeen hand-tailored suits made by Rosofsky's Fine Clothing for Men, Los Angeles. It was midnight blue with subtle metallic green highlights. To compliment the ecru hand-made silk shirt—with stays, of course—he wore an Italian silk tie just a shade lighter than midnight blue with echoes of metallic green. Unseen were the coordinated silk socks and silk boxer shorts, a luxury he'd acquired the taste for while in diapers. A dark homburg and sleek Italian shoes with only four shoestring eyelits rounded out his top and bottom.

He had inherited his mother's dark slanted eyes and his father's thin face. Though he kept trying, he had a horrible time growing a mustache. His chin was slightly recessed and his neck was scrawny. Tonight he wore a long silk-lined cashmere scarf, exactly matching the midnight blue, which he wrapped once around his neck. He had fancied himself a little like Al Pacino in *The Godfather* when he'd checked himself in the dressing mirror earlier.

In fact, he looked more like a weasel in a peacoat sleeve.

Hoi Sol stared at the reflection of the two Texans. Ever since coming to Dallas from Los Angeles via Las Vegas seven years ago, he'd tried to understand the Texans' mode of dress. He'd given up. Hoss was wearing a bolo tie with a turquoise stone the size of a largemouth bass. Hoi Sol was sorely tempted to turn around, reach over the seat and jerk Hoss up by the mink lapels of his hair-side-out Hereford-skin vest and offer some much needed sartorial guidance: "Can't you see that you look like sticky Christmas bows on a naked fat boy? Your hatband weighs more than a carpenter's belt! That elk horn sterling silver belt buckle in the shape of Lake Texoma belongs on a trout line in the Bay of Fundy! Have ye not heard of good taste, understated ostentation, scrofulous affectation! . . . 'Seek elegance rather than luxury, and refinement rather than fashion; to be worthy, not respectable, and wealthy, not rich' . . . In the words of the immortal William H. Channing, '*That* should be your symphony!' "

Hoi Sol considered it, but instead he said, "I'm Hoi Sol and the little guy here is Thorhild."

"Please to meetcha," said Hoss.

"So, what's the job?" asked Hoi Sol, acting brains of this dynamic duo.

Hoss leaned forward. "My cousin and I have a wager with some other gentlemen and we'd like to hedge our bet. There's two cowboys entered in the bull ridin' here at the National Finals that we don't want to win any more money. They've got three more bulls to ride and I'd just as soon they didn't ride 'em. Get the picture?"

"I think so," said Hoi Sol. "You want 'em iced? That'll take more than a grand."

"No, no!" Hoss said quickly. "Just don't let 'em score."

"How do we find 'em?"

"They've got three rides left," explained Hoss. "Two today, Saturday, at one-thirty and eight P.M. Then the last one Sunday afternoon at one-thirty. You boys find 'em this morning and do whatever you have to do. If you keep these two bull riders from their appointed rounds there will be a ten-thousand-dollar bonus. You savvy?" He paused to let it sink it.

"This is real important to me and Jaybo here." He handed an envelope over the seat. "Here's twenny-five hunnert in advance."

"Who are these cowboys?" asked Hoi Sol.

"Give 'em your list, Jaybo. They're number five and number fifteen."

Hoi Sol switched on the dome light.

"Wyoming Montana and Lick . . . ?" he read. "I can't read this. Looks like you spilled something on it!" He looked back at Jim Bowie Marfa.

"That's, uh, barbecue sauce, I think," said Jaybo.

38

Saturday Noon, December 11
Oklahoma City, Oklahoma

Cody had just left for the airport to pick up Lilac. Lick lay back on the hotel bed. He planned on walking over to the coliseum about one-thirty.

The door knocked. He answered.

"Room Service," said the lady.

"I didn't order anythin', ma'am."

"Is this twelve-twenty-five?"

"Yup!" Lick looked her over. She didn't look like a waitress. She didn't look like a maid. She certainly didn't look like a Hutterite missionary!

Lick's visitor smiled. "I was told to come up here and entertain you," she said. Now he knew what she looked like! "Compliments of Cody," she added.

"Well, bless his randy ol' heart! Come on in!"

Willa Dean slid into the room like magma down a slope. She was 5'5" wearin' high heels. But she was a big girl! She shook her long wavy blond mane, then looked at him steadily.

Her fur coat slipped off like a shedding snake's skin.

She was wearing a sleeveless, strapless blouse of some kind. From shoulder to shoulder, acres of porcelain skin filled the landscape and Lick's approving eye eventually disappeared into the décolletage. The silky blouse did little to hide the articulated infrastructure that reached up in support like two catcher's mitts awaiting a pop foul.

A wide elastic belt separated this magnificant top from the equally spectacular bottom. It—the bottom, that is—appeared broad and smoothly encased in a short dark form-fitting skirt that ended just above the knees. This entire display of colossal comeliness balanced on shapely legs as stout as marble columns.

When she walked away it was the driver's-eye view of a wheel-horse pullin' against the tugs.

I know, y'all are trying to envision from my description just how big Willa really was. Surely you appreciate that I would never be so indiscreet as to tell you what she weighed. I have mentioned she was big. Was she fat? Well, I would never describe Willa that way, because I want you to picture her as truly beautiful. Big, and truly beautiful.

If Funk and Wagnall's needed an illustration to accompany the term "seething pulchritude," she would be it.

Lick was impressed.

"Wow," he said appreciatively. "You are amazing."

"Thanks, cowboy. You have somethin' to drink in here?"

"A little scotch do ya?"

"You're talkin' my language.... Join me?"

"Oh, I don't know. I gotta ride this afternoon and tonight. I better not," he explained.

"Honey, yer wound up tight as a hippo's girdle. You need to relax. That's what Cody had in mind. A little drink, a hot bath, a little harmless recreation."

"Well ... yeah, sure. Yer right. Might be just the ticket."

He poured the drinks in the hotel glasses and gave her one. "Sorry, no ice," he apologized. They sipped.

"Let me help you get comfortable," Willa offered. She pulled his shirt off over his head. He put his arms around her waist and squeezed. "Careful," she said. "I'm precious."

A few steamy moments later Lick was in the bathtub. He was breathing heavily and felt light as a bag of jellyfish bones.

"Let me go get our drinks," Willa said.

He lay back in the tub and watched her magnificence depart.

She returned with their glasses. "Drink this and let me give you a scrub."

He downed the scotch in two gulps. Willa picked up his leg and started by soaping his foot, a toe at a time. Then she continued up the leg.

By the time she finished his second leg, he was in never-never land. The particulate count in his hemoatmosphere was registering "Don't go out today!" He was babbling incoherently and smiling when the phenobarbital she had stirred into his drink overloaded his circuits and blew the fuse in his brain! He remained at half-mast.

She put on her blouse and jacket. Then she dialed a hotel number. It was answered on the first ring.

"Hoi Sol? . . . Yeah . . . he's ready . . . Right . . . Bring the money," said Willa.

Cody kept scanning the contestants' area for Lick. The Saturday afternoon performance was already into the saddle bronc riding.

"Dang, Lilac. Where's he at! Maybe I should check the room again."

"You've already called three times," said Lilac. "Maybe he's visiting with someone. He doesn't have to ride for another hour, you said."

"Yeah, but it's not like him. I'm goin' down and look again."

"Whatever you think, Cody. I'll wait here."

Cody made his way down behind the bucking chutes. Manly Ott had reinjured his neck and been forced to turn his last four bulls out.

Manly was standing with the clowns, rigid in his neck brace. Cody approached.

"Manly."

"Hi, Cody."

"Have any of you seen Lick?"

"Since when? I saw 'im ride last night."

"I mean this afternoon. The last hour or two."

"Nope. Sure haven't."

"No?"

"Nope."

Cody walked all the way back to the hotel room. Lick's gear bag and bull rope were on the floor where he'd put them last night. His hat lay on the television.

His hat? thought Cody. *He must be in the hotel somewhere. Maybe shacked up, the crazy cockeyed lunatic! This is no time to be ruttin' and rubbin' his horns on the tree!*

He had the hotel operator page the restaurant, bar and lobby. No luck, no Lick. By the time he returned to the coliseum, the bull riding had begun. He sat down beside Lilac, agitated.

"Somethin's wrong. I know it. He'd never miss this. Not for all the tequila in Guadalajara!"

Smokey Brothers came out on a big Santa Gertrudis spinning bull. He made a beautiful ride and marked an 83, which would eventually split first in the eighth go-round.

Lennox Wildebang bucked off, and during Wyoming Montana's ride a strange thing happened: his bull rope broke! Just as the gate pulled open, the rope came loose in his hand! The bull threw him into the gatepost and knocked him unconscious. The ambulance had to cart him off.

Bull ropes don't break! Closer inspection by the judges revealed Montana's rope had been cut nearly in two where it was knotted to adjust for length. It was not cut enough to break when it was pulled up to seat the rider, but when the bull took a breath and flexed, it popped like a piece of cotton thread! The judges conferred and decided to say nothing about the insidious tampering unless an official protest was registered.

39

4:00 P.M., December 11
Oklahoma City, Oklahoma

By four o'clock Cody and Lilac were up in room 1225.

"We've got to do something!" Cody was furiously pacing.

"Sit down, Cody," said Lilac. "Let's figure this out." Cody sat on the bed. "All right," she continued, "now it has to be some emergency. How about a death in the family? Maybe he got suddenly ill or an accident?"

Cody jumped back up. "Right. He might have fallen and got amnesia. Or food poisoning. If it was his folks, he'd have left a note. Call the hospitals, see if they know anything. Call the police. He might'uv got in trouble. I'm goin' downstairs and see if the hotel help has seen 'im. I'll be back in an hour."

* * *

Lick opened his eyes. All he could see was white. There was a cloth over his face. He felt a pain in his shoulders. Trying to move his hands to pull the cloth off his face, he realized his arms were secured behind his back at the wrists and elbows. His ankles were also taped. When he moved, the bed he lay on moved!

Clearing his mind, he tried to recall: *Where am I? Oklahoma City. Daylight? Cody left to pick up Lilac at the airport. Room Service. Room Service! Willa Dean! Gorgeous. We made . . . no . . .*

185

we . . . I . . . took a bath. I musta dozed off. Willa Dean! He smiled. *She must be afraid I'm gonna try to escape!*

"Willa Dean," he called. "Come here, you Greek goddess!"

He heard footsteps. Footsteps on a rug? Someone placed a hand on his blanketed butt and pushed. His bed swayed back and forth! He was in a hammock!

"She couldn't make it," a thick male voice said beneath him.

Lick got goose bumps. The hair stood up on his neck.

"Who is it?" asked Lick, trying to hide his rising panic. *Probably just the boys makin' a joke,* he thought, embarrassed.

"Cody, are you there?" he asked seriously.

"Nobody here but us chickens," said the voice.

"Where am I?"

"With friends."

"Who are you?"

"Friends."

"Well, boys, you pulled a good one on me, but I've got a bull to ride about one-thirty." Lick laughed nervously.

"It's a quarter to five, little buckaroo. I think you missed your appointment."

"What!" Lick tried to sit up and the hammock moved jerkily beneath him.

"I'd be careful if I were you. You're six feet off the ground."

"What the hell are you doin'?"

"We're going to stay with you until tomorrow afternoon."

"But I'll miss my bulls."

"That's the idea, cowpoke."

"But why me?"

"Orders."

"Orders?"

"You need anything, you just call," the voice said pleasantly.

"I have a splittin' headache," Lick heard himself say.

"Good. It'll keep your mind busy." The footsteps left. Lick lay still, thinking. *Me? Why me? Why anybody? What for? Who?* His head was pounding. He quit thinking.

✶
✶
✶

Cody rejoined Lilac in the hotel room. She recounted her fruitless telephone search.

"Nobody downstairs knows anything," he said.

"Let's add up what we know again," she suggested.

"Okay. He was here in bed at eleven this morning when I left to get you. He left his hat. Very unusual. That might mean he's still in the hotel if he left of his own free will. He took his boots, pants ..." Cody looked around the room. Lick's pocketknife, change, wallet and Copenhagen can lay on the dresser. "He'd never leave without his Copenhagen! Much less his hat!"

"He might have forgotten them," Lilac offered.

"No way! He was carryin' his guardian angel around in his Copenhagen can! That was his good luck charm!"

"What do you mean?"

Cody tried to explain Pinto Calhoon, G.A., to Lilac.

"What! You don't believe that stuff, too?"

"I don't guess so. I've never seen him, but Lick believed. Enough so's I know he wouldn't go without his guardian angel!"

"I knew you said he was coyote, but I didn't know he was crazy!"

"He didn't leave of his own free will," Cody said, finally facing the truth.

"You mean somebody kidnapped him?" asked Lilac incredulously. "Why would anybody kidnap him? Does he have money?"

"Some, but not enough to hold for a ransom. Maybe it was one of the women."

"What women?" asked Lilac.

"He has had lots of lady friends and they don't always part on the best of terms."

"They'd kidnap him? Personally, I can't see that. Is there somebody else that would want to keep him from riding today? Even as a joke?"

"Keep him from riding today ..." Cody repeated. Thinking out loud, he said, "If they were gonna keep him from riding today, they'd have to keep him from riding the rest of the Finals tonight and tomorrow, too."

"Why would anyone do that?"

"He's done real well in the Finals so far. He's won a first, a second, and a fourth in the go-rounds and is standing third in the money won. But more important, he's ridden six out of seven, now eight, bulls. Only three other bull riders have a good shot at the top money. The man that rides the most bulls and scores decent usually wins close to ten thousand dollars. Smokey rode today, so he's ridden seven out of eight, Lennox bucked off, so he's still six, and Wyoming Montana, the cowboy whose rope broke and was taken to the hospital, had ridden six." Cody began to pace up and down the room.

"Theoretically, somebody who'd ridden five bulls so far could ride his last three and finish with eight, but the odds are against it. These are tough bulls and the boys are gettin' worn down, beat up and tired." He paused a moment.

"Wonder why Wyoming's rope broke?" he said slowly. "I've never seen that before. He was in the runnin' for the average like Lick. He was behind the other three in total points, but he still had a good shot at it."

Lilac stared at him. "Cody ... maybe somebody didn't want Wyoming to win. The same somebody who doesn't want Lick to win. Who'd benefit if they dropped out?"

"Smokey, Lennox and anybody else who had a shot at the average. But no cowboy would do that. They just wouldn't." Cody started pacing again. "Smokey's new, but he already has the overall buckle won and Lennox is straight as a Texas ranger. No, I can't believe any of the finalists would resort to ... to foul play."

"Maybe Wyoming's rope was tampered with," said Lilac. "Both he and Lick were eliminated in what you might call unusual ways. Sounds like more than coincidence to me."

Cody just looked at her without speaking.

★ ★ ★

Cody and Lilac attended the Saturday night rodeo. They left a message on the desk that they were expecting an important call. Cody was tense and his concern infected Lilac.

Lick never showed. They watched the bull riding in pain. Wyoming was still in the hospital. Smokey and Lennox both bucked off.

⋆

10:30 P.M. Saturday night. The phone rang in the small motel room. Hoi Sol answered.

"Yes?

"Thanks.

"He's in the next room. He'd come to the phone, but he's, you might say . . . tied up!" Hoi Sol allowed himself to chuckle.

"Right, I'm going by during visiting hours tomorrow to make sure he's still out of the picture.

"Sure. We'll come see ya tomorrow night, midnight. Same place.

"You bet. All part of the service.

" 'Bye."

Thorhild lifted Lick out of the hammock and hopped him to the john for a whiz. They left him taped up and blindfolded. Lick was cramped, but his circulation was still good. They put him back in the hammock and tucked him in. He didn't sleep well.

⋆

Cody and Lilac went back to the hotel room.

"Cody, there's nothing we can do."

"He might call," Cody said hopefully.

She put a hand on his shoulder. He slumped.

"Go to sleep, cowboy. You need some rest. We'll start early and find him tomorrow."

"He's like a brother to me. I don't know what I'd do if something happened to him. He's always been there to help me. Now he needs me, I just know it, and I can't do a damn thing!" Cody felt as useless as a painting in a blind man's house.

"Close your eyes." Lilac turned him over and rubbed his neck until he finally relaxed and slept.

40

**1:15 P.M., December 12
Oklahoma City, Oklahoma**

Four ... three ... two ... one ... cameras rolling!" The man with the earphones pointed at Will Yunk. Will had been World Champion Bull Rider and All Around Cowboy in his day. He used to wear Levis that buttoned up the fly. Later he wore Wranglers that faded after two washings. Now he wore name-brand designer jeans, his own name! He had an entire line of clothing with his name on it: boots, hats, vests, leather coats, fancy shirts and even Yunk Junk. Yunk Junk was costume jewelry for hats. It had become very popular with the straw hat/leisure suit group as well as Oklahoma truck drivers. Their hats jingled and shook like a Moroccan bride with a limp!

It was amazing to most of Yunk's friends that his clothing line showed artistic refinement. They had known him when he wore the same gaudy shirt ten days in a row and never wore socks. Putting an expensive, tasteful, well-fitted Western shirt on Will was equivalent to sprinkling croutons on a cow pie! But Mrs. Yunk, Will's wife, had a good eye for style. She dressed him and ran the business.

Will spoke into the microphone and addressed his taped television audience. "Welcome back to Rodeo TV Network," he drawled. Will turned to his co-anchor, Thermal Bind. "Thermal, the big story here at the Finals is shaping up in the bull riding. Going into this tenth and final go-round, Smokey Brothers has ridden seven of his nine bulls and has the highest dollars. Lennox Wildebang, having ridden six bulls, is second in total dollars, followed by two other cowboys who still have a chance."

"That's right, Yunk," said Thermal, taking the electronic baton. "But neither of them has ridden in the eighth or ninth go. If either of them or Lennox have a chance to win top money, they must ride their bull today and Smokey has to buck off. As you know, Wyoming was injured yesterday in a freak accident and is still in the hospital with a concussion. That leaves only Lennox and Lick with the possibility of catching Smokey. Lennox has drawn a good bull, but, according to our day sheet, Lick has made the worst possible draw of the finals. He's up on Bobby Monday's bull of the year, number ten-twenty, Kamikaze! The reason I say this is the worst draw is that this bull has never been ridden! I wonder if Lick even knows that he drew Kamikaze?

"But Yunk, all Smokey has to do is ride his bull today and he will likely take home the top money," wrapped up Thermal. "We wish all the bull riders the best. And now ... we'll be right back with the calf roping after this word from Hesston...."

41

*I*n the annals of sports history the losers disappear from memory as fast as lightning leaves the sky. Who lost the War of 1812? Who did Jesse Owens outrun in the 1936 Olympics? Quick, friends, name one Superbowl opponent of the '75, '76, '79 or '81 Pittsburgh Steelers. Matter of fact, who lost last year's Superbowl?

There are exceptions to the forgotten-loser rule, mainly those who are notable because their losing was so unexpected: the 1967 Baltimore Colts, Sonny Liston, and Tornado.

They are remembered in part because they were the dragons slain by Joe Namath, Cassius Clay and Freckles Brown.

Tornado was a bull that had bucked out over two hundred times and had never been ridden. Let me allow that to sink in. It would be the equivalent of a pitcher facing two hundred of the best hitters in the league, one after the other, and striking them out . . . every one.

Or the equivalent of Martina Navratilova winning two hundred games in a row. Not two hundred sets in a row, not two hundred matches in a row, two hundred games in a row.

I can't even spell my name right two hundred times in a row!

When Freckles Brown rode Tornado at the National Finals Rodeo in Oklahoma City in 1967, it was Charles Lindbergh, Admiral Perry and Saint George all rolled into one! It was the indelible rodeo moment.

Kamikaze is a figment of my imagination. Tornado is real. So if fiction imitates life we can imagine that if some lucky bull rider were to make a qualified ride on ol' 1020, that cowboy would have a place in fictional history. But Kamikaze would be remembered as well.

None of this was going through his bovine brain as Kamikaze stood in one of the stock pens that were a part of the OKC coliseum. Mount Everest doesn't leaf back through its scrapbook and reminisce about Sir Edmund and the Sherpas. Plymouth Rock doesn't dwell on its place in the brief human history of Massachusetts. It will be there long after the Kennedys have become Republicans.

Kamikaze, however, had a sense that this rodeo was different. It was his third trip to the National Finals here in Oklahoma City. He was familiar with the pens, the chutes, the arena, the crowd and the smell of the dirt.

During an unprecedented ceremonial exhibition he had been run into the darkened arena and spotlighted in front of the crowd. He was not pleased and stomped around swinging his head, holding it high, ears alert to stimuli. He could not understand the dramatic poem dedicated to him and his worthy adversaries. It was meaningless droning. This prerodeo entertainment was the idea of Wooley Boogin, known as the P. T. Barnum of rodeo producers. It was dramatic and pleased the crowd enormously.

To Kamikaze, all this hoopla was an irritation.

On this Sunday afternoon he was aware that he had not done anything yet. Other bulls came and went. He waited patiently. He would be ready if they called on him. No onerous premonitions disturbed him. He had become comfortable in his pen these last few days. He was not nervous.

He could see cowboy after cowboy walk or ride by, sometimes stopping and staring or pointing him out to others. They'd sit on the fence and watch him.

Like birds, he thought. *BOO! They'd flutter away.*

42

Sunday Morning, December 12
Oklahoma City, Oklahoma

Cody had been awake since 5:30 A.M., looking at the ceiling. He and Lilac ordered Room Service breakfast at 8:30. They ate in bed. They went over and over the possible reasons for Lick's disappearance. Exhausted, Lilac asked Cody about Pinto Calhoon. Cody explained again.

"You mean Lick thinks he lives in his Copenhagen can?" asked Lilac.

"Yup."

Lilac slid off the bed, her long nightgown flowing, and picked up the can. She opened it, sniffed the contents and made a face.

"He always taps the top before he opens it," said Cody.

"What do you mean?"

He took the can and did "shave and a haircut, two bits" on the lid. He opened it.

The strong wave of men's cologne hit her delicate nasal passages. "Polo!" she exclaimed.

"What?" said Cody.

"Polo's correct! How nice to be whiffed at!
Her olfactory sense is not to be sniffed at!"

Pinto's head and shoulders floated together like a jigsaw puzzle in a smoky room. They formed into his image and rippled.

"Pinto?" asked Cody.

"Pinto Calhoon, please hold the applause.
Guardian angel, but not without flaws."

"Why aren't you guardin' Lick? He's disappeared!" said Cody, obviously disturbed.

"Disappeared? Wiped out in his prime?
How did it happen? I've lost track of time."

"Yesterday morning. He's missed two go-rounds. He's got one bull left and a chance at the money this afternoon!" explained Cody. "I can't find him anywhere!"

"Spare me the anguish, the sentiment, too.
First things first, who the devil are you?"

"Cody. An' this here's Lilac."

Pinto raised a gnarled claw and tipped his hat.

"You're pretty as an Easter ham.
I'm surely pleased to meet'cha, ma'am!"

"Thank you," she whispered, staring.

"Pinto," implored Cody, "do you have any idea how we could find Lick? Any place for us to start? You were in the room, in yer can, when he left. He left his hat, his Copenhagen, his money, even you! We think maybe somebody kidnapped him to keep him from ridin' his last three bulls."

"Other angels, not unlike me,
Are guarding humans constantly.
Perchance another might recall,
So I'll put in a conference call."

Pinto whirlpooled clockwise back into the Copenhagen can like dirty bathwater down a drain. His voice came up from the well:

"If I'm expected to help him, kid,
Gimme a break and close the lid!"

Cody did.

"Conference call? Other guardian angels? I must be dreaming!" said Lilac.

"Do you believe in gravity?" asked Cody. "Evolution? Life on other planets, God, Santa Claus, electricity, ESP? That momentum equals mass times velocity?"

"What?"

"If you do, then it's not hard to believe in guardian angels."

Fifteen minutes ticked by. Cody tapped out Pinto's code. He reappeared, brushing Copenhagen crumbs off his shoulder.

"Did you find anything out?" asked Cody anxiously.

"A Russian ballerina great
Assigned to guard a Viking's fate
Said she might have seen ol' Lick
An' he's taped up and feelin' sick.
He's hangin' in a swingin' bed
With pillowcases on his head."

"Pinto! Did she say where Lick was?" cried Lilac.

"He's with the Viking, she knew that.
But not just sure where they are at.
Some motel that's not too neat.
McDonald's is across the street."

"Anything else?" asked Cody. Pinto shook his head. Cody capped the can and stuck it in his pocket.

"Git crackin', darlin'. We're gonna find our pard if we have to go to every McDonald's in town."

"How do we know he's even in Oklahoma City?" asked Lilac, pulling on her jeans.

"We don't. Grab the phone book."

★ ★ ★

There were twenty-eight McDonald's in Oklahoma City.

They drove to the first five. Each was teeming with teenagers like an adolescent anthill. None had "not too neat" motels across from them. It was 1:15.

"Cody, this is not gonna work," said Lilac. "Let's get a cab. The driver should know the town better."

They found a cab downtown. They explained what they were looking for. The cabbie knew of two places that fit the description. Off they went!

The first McDonald's was across the street from a used-car lot. The second one the cabbie took them to was off Fifty-fifth Street, a few blocks north of the zoo.

"That's gotta be it," said Lilac excitedly.

The sign said CHARLIE & DI'S MOTOR COURT. It was 1940s vintage white stucco with scrubby landscaping and a red dirt lawn. There were eight motel room doors numbered 5 through 26. Cody asked the cabdriver to wait and gave him a twenty-dollar bill. Rooms 7 and 18 had the curtains closed. Lilac explained her plan to Cody. He held her purse and coat.

She walked up to room 7 and knocked. An elderly woman answered.

"Towels?" asked Lilac.

"Powells?" said the woman, cupping her ears.

"Towels," Lilac enunciated.

"No Powells around here. They moved."

"No, towels!"

"Bowels?"

"Not bowels, towels!"

"Bowels moved, too. Friday afternoon. Wait a minute." The old lady turned and spoke to someone in the room behind her. "Elsie, there's a traveling laxative salesman here. You need anything?" She turned back to Lilac. "Guess not, honey, thanks anyway." She closed the door on Lilac.

Lilac walked down the row to number 18 and knocked. The veneer was peeling off the wooden door front. It opened and was filled top to bottom, side to side, with Viking!

He was a head taller than Lilac, which made him close to 6'8". As his mama would have said, "A big-boned boy." He was neither musclebound nor sloppy fat. He was clean-shaven with light blond hair that reached to his shoulders. His brow beetled over his light blue eyes. His nose cast its own shadow. He neither leaned nor bent in the doorway. He balanced on the doorjamb, a good portion of his size fourteen triple-E Redwing lace-up boots hanging outside. He wore generic blue jeans and a nondescript flannel shirt the size of a hay tarp. He was tieless.

Thorhild's forehead furrowed as he looked at Lilac.

"Towels?" Her voice sounded like Minnie Mouse.

His head rolled from side to side, like a half-ton wrecking ball.

"Thanks," she squeaked, and walked back toward the office. The door closed behind her.

She ran to the cab! "Cody! He's big as a house!"

"Who?"

"This giant man. He could be the Viking Pinto was talkin' about. What am I saying?" she asked herself in surprise.

"Viking? It's the right place, then! Pinto, you scarpacious ol' side-winder, you were right!"

They went around behind the long building and peered in the back room window. They could see the hammock and the wrapped carcass through a part in the curtain.

"It's him!" said Cody.

"Is he dead?" asked Lilac anxiously.

"No," said Cody, squinting at the mummy.

"What are we going to do? Call the police?"

"I don't know. Probably should."

They walked around the end of the building. The Viking was walking across the red dirt toward the McDonald's on the other side of the street. A four-door AMC Concord was now parked in front of room 18.

"Come on," whispered Cody.

They ran to the room. The door was ajar. Cody pushed it back quietly and stepped in. He heard that universal sound that supports the flawed concept of biological male superiority. That audible splashing that demonstrates why the human male can remain vigilant even during peaceful moments. That ultimate display of evolutionary distinction between the *Homo sapiens* male protector and his female counterpart: the standing pee.

Cody opened the sharp blade of his Old Timer pocketknife and handed it to Lilac. He pointed to the bedroom and then his wrists. As Niagara Falls continued to resound in the background, Cody pointed to himself and toward his crotch. Lilac nodded to indicate she understood his hand gestures. Of course, had he done the same thing in a crowded restaurant she might have never spoken to him again.

Cody stealthily walked over to the bathroom door. Hoi Sol was unself-consciously tinkling his heart out. A cardigan sweater was draped neatly over the back of a tattered sofa.

That explains the AMC Concord, which wasn't parked there when we arrived, deduced Cody.

Before going into the bathroom, Hoi Sol had changed from the sweater into a forest green silk smoking jacket with maroon lapels and sash. It had been in the latest package from his mother. Knowing he might spend the day lounging about the motel room, he had dressed with the beautiful smoking jacket in mind. An ivory white silk shirt, gray wool slacks and silk tie in the same forest green with a maroon paisley pattern. He accessorized with matching Armani belt and slip-on loafers in cordovan.

Cody studied this well-dressed free-lance felon. He could see Hoi Sol's reflection in the mirror. Hoi Sol had his eyes closed and seemed to be meditating.

Cody put one foot into the bathroom, raised his arm and tapped Hoi Sol on the left shoulder. Hoi Sol turned his head sharply to the left. Cody reached over Hoi Sol's right shoulder and grabbed him by the designer tie! In one swift motion he jerked on the tie and stepped back out the door, pulling the hapless Hoi Sol in his direction.

With his left hand, Cody closed the bathroom door, slamming it on the tie! Cody hung on to the tail of the tie like a kite flyer in a high wind. He jerked and felt Hoi Sol's head smash into the door. The tie prevented the door from latching, which allowed Cody to repeat the gesture three times before his opponent had the chance to fight back.

"The tie! The tie!" came Hoi Sol's strangulated screams. "You schmuck! You'll fray the silk!"

Whack!

Cody had one hand on the door handle, a foot against the doorjamb and a fist full of tie. "Cut him loose!" he shouted to Lilac, who had disappeared into the bedroom.

She found Lick swinging in the hammock.

"What's that racket?" he asked, frightened. "Who's there?"

Lilac steadied the hammock.

"Lilac . . . and Cody," she whispered.

He swung his legs over carefully, expecting a long drop. He was only two feet off the floor. A cheap trick.

Lilac unwrapped his blanket. All he was wearing was a pillowcase and a pair of the Viking's Fruit of the Looms. She cut the nylon-reinforced wrapping tape between his legs, his elbows and his arms. He tried to pull the pillowcase off.

"Wait," said Lilac, "they've got it taped around your neck. I'll cut it if you sit still. I don't want to hurt you!"

Hoi Sol was swearing. "You backstabbin'..." Cody pulled: *Whap!* "Kicker...!" *Whap!* "... of crippled dogs! You made me ruin my good pants! Careful with the tie! Umph! You're a dead man when I git my hands on you!"

The bathroom captive was pulling hard to open the door. Cody suddenly released the handle. The door flew open twelve inches. Cody jerked back hard on the tie. The door's edge hit Hoi Sol on the right eyebrow with a crunching thud! "Yeow! You putz! Blood?" Hoi Sol's angry voice turned panic-stricken. "Blood? Oh, no! My new smoking jacket! Where's a towel?"

"Let's go, quick!" Cody shouted to Lilac.

Lick took the knife from Lilac, held the pillowcase up and cut the top off it like he was castrating a bull calf. The rest of the pillowcase dropped down around his neck.

She grabbed his arm and raced for the door.

"Co-de-e-e!" she screamed.

Cody slammed the door on Hoi Sol's tie and followed them out the door.

Thorhild was returning from McDonald's with an industrial-strength order of Big Macs and fries. He saw Lick and Lilac running toward the cab, though Lick was mincing in zigzag fashion on his bare feet. Lilac was urging him on. "The rodeo has already started but we still might get you back in time to ride your bull. Come on, Lick, hurry!"

The cabdriver spotted Lilac accompanied by a barebacked, bare-legged, barefooted spook in his underwear. They were headed his way. He had second thoughts about waiting. Suddenly his left-side rearview mirror was filled with the figure of a large person hurtling! On his mirror was printed the warning OBJECTS MAY APPEAR LARGER THAN LIFE. Not today, Charlie!

"Time to go," concluded the cabbie, shifting to D and stomping on the gas. Dirt and gravel kicked up behind, hitting Lilac.

Both she and Lick caught sight of Thorhild bearing down on them. "This way," she said. "Run!"

Cody ran out the door. He saw Lick and Lilac swerve away from the departing taxi and start up the side of the road. What he assumed to be "the large Viking" was in hot pursuit.

Cody heard the bathroom door open behind him and footsteps pounding across the linoleum. Cody accelerated, falling in behind Thorhild in the chase.

Hoi Sol paused in the doorway holding a towel against his right eye and under his neck in the vain attempt to protect his clothes. "Get the bull rider!" he shouted at Thorhild. "Forget the other two."

Hoi Sol reached back to close the motel door as he started for the AMC Concord. His sash caught in the doorjamb and when he stepped off the concrete step in front of the door he spun sideways. He hit the gravel on his back and rolled, scuffing his loafers, abrading his smoking jacket and ruining his day.

He climbed into the car and started it, still holding the towel to his face. He checked himself in the rearview and realized he'd forgotten his hat! He gently ran his unoccupied hand through his hair, palpating the bald spot. It was like Achilles feeling his heel. Hoi Sol's confidence ebbed slightly. He pulled out on the road.

The motel parking lot abutted an undeveloped area of thick woods. Cedar, oak brush, hickory and maple trees extended to the north along the highway. No sidewalk bordered the road but a wide gravel path meandered along between the curb and the edge of the woods.

It was along this leaf-strewn path that Lilac and Lick were kickin' up cinders as fast as they could! They were a hundred yards ahead of Thorhild.

Lilac was taller than Lick, with longer legs, but he was keeping up despite his handicap. He was barefooted and one hand clutched the elastic on the Viking's borrowed shorts.

Cody was ten yards behind Thorhild and gaining! Hoi Sol was pacing the whole bunch from the road. He was leaning out the window holding the white motel towel under his chin, shouting encouragement to his partner. "Run, Thor, get the one in your underwear! I'm gonna kill the one behind ya!"

Thorhild threw the McDonald's bag over his shoulder. Cody caught it on the fly!

He fished out a Big Mac and bounced it off the Viking's bare head! Special sauce and a dill pickle clung to his hair. Cody went over left tackle and drilled a strawberry shake just above the numbers! The Pepto-Bismol-pink sludge ran down the back of Thorhild's neck, but he remained oblivious to his assailant.

Cody darted in and out, rocketing the contents of the paper sack at the hurtling hulk like a sparrow harassing a hawk in flight!

Up ahead, Lilac and Lick had taken a fork in the path that veered down an embankment and into the woods.

Thorhild slid down the embankment. Cody reached the top just as Thorhild hit the bottom. Cody never slowed. He leaped toward the lumbering Viking, who tripped at precisely the wrong moment. Cody sailed over Thorhild's fallen body and skidded on the leaf-covered ground like a hockey puck!

Thorhild scrambled to his feet and accidently stepped on Cody's ankle as he rejoined the chase. "Sorry," he said. Cody grunted and scrambled after him.

A car door slammed out of sight, behind them! "Get the bull rider, Thor! I'm right behind ya!"

Not far up the path they could both see Lick and Lilac dropping over the other side of an eight-foot cyclone fence. Thorhild was four feet up the fence when Cody made another flying leap and got his arms around the Viking's neck. The giant never slowed his ascent.

"Look out, Cody!" shouted Lick, watching from the other side.

"Git goin'," Cody hollered. "It's you they're after!"

At the top, Thorhild hooked an arm over the wire, got a little leverage and elbowed Cody in the ribs.

Cody grunted and crashed to the ground on the top of Hoi Sol, who had just arrived and stood below trying to unfold his knife.

Hoi Sol howled. "You clumsy flatheaded bumbling clutz! Now you made me stab myself!"

Cody rolled off him and looked at the switchblade stuck in the meaty part of Hoi Sol's thigh. Blood was soaking into the Edinburgh fog-gray wool pantsleg his mother had hand-sewn just for him. Hoi Sol paused a moment, looking at the slacks. "They were wet anyway," he sighed.

"Yep. Sure were," agreed Cody.

Cody leaped up and scaled the fence! He dropped over and spotted the others running through the trees! He pursued! Hoi Sol pursued more slowly.

The KEEP OUT! NO TRESPASSING! sign went unseen and unheeded. That was unfortunate for the Oklahoma City Zoo.

Sunday Afternoon, December 12
Oklahoma City, Oklahoma

It was forty-eight degrees and sunny this fine Oklahoma Sunday afternoon. Strollers walked the wide concrete path in fall coats enjoying the zoo's ambience. It was a peaceful scene.

Imagine, if you will, a couple sitting on a bench soaking up the sun. Their two children are across the walkway feeding peanuts to their ancestors, the howlers. Pigeons coo nearby.

Suddenly there is a disturbance in the aviary! Bounding from the raptor section comes a Halloween hundred-yard dash! As the couple gape, five almost human figures fly by them!

Lilac was in the lead. With her long hair flowing and her graceful stride she looked sleek as a hood ornament. Lick was less than ten feet behind her, pounding the sidewalk with his bare feet! His punctured pillowcase was still taped around his neck and flutterin' in the slipstream. He held a handful of bunched-up elastic at his waist, which kept Thorhild's underwear modestly in place.

Lilac slowed enough for Lick to catch up. She spoke between breaths. "I don't know ... uh, hu ... where I'm ... uh, hu ... going ... uh, hu ... find a ... uh, hu ..." "No cop," puffed Lick, imagining the skeptical response their explanation would elicit.

"Ya see, Officer. I'm competing in the National Finals Rodeo. I'm one of the top fifteen professional bull riders in the country and I was kidnapped by these two gentlemen following me. Well, come to think of it, I think it's them. I've never actually seen their

faces. Anyway, the final rodeo performance is this afternoon and my friends here, Cody and Lilac, rescued me and we're on our way back to the rodeo grounds, if we can find it, that is. . . . Maybe you could help us catch a cab, 'cause I'm seriously running outta time, what time is it? . . . I'm late, I'm late . . . for a very important date. . . . See, I still have a chance to win the average, or I did before I was kidnapped, and I'd really like to ride my last bull, so that's what I'm doing here. . . .

"No . . . 'course not! I've never used drugs. I don't have time to take the test! Well, I don't know, a pillowcase, I guess. I don't know where the underwear came from . . . a sumo wrestler, perhaps. . . . Look, Officer . . .

"We've . . . uh, hu . . . got to . . . uh, hu . . . find a way . . . uh, hu . . . outta here . . ." continued Lilac. "You still . . . uh, hu . . . have a chance . . . uh, hu . . . to win it all!"

Lick looked over at Lilac as they ran side by side. The realization of what she said sunk in. His eyebrows shot up questioningly.

"That's right . . . uh, hu . . ." she said. "That's why . . . uh, hu . . . we've got . . . uh, hu . . . to hurry!"

The couple on the bench watched Lilac and Lick race down the broad sidewalk and disappear around the bend. They heard big slapping footsteps, jerked their heads back to the left, and watched Thorhild thunder by!

Cody followed, arms pumping furiously, knowing he must prevent this persistent Viking from knocking Lick out of the game. His friend Lick, who really had a chance to do what neither of them ever allowed themselves to think about: make history . . . get in the record books . . . a little bit of the "Big Time." Cody got a warm, fuzzy feeling and picked up speed. *Lick will make it,* he thought, *or I'll die trying!*

As the couple watched Cody tear off after the others, Hoi Sol limped by as if an afterthought. He presented an odd eyeful in his forest green smoking jacket, tattered bloodstained pants and thinning flyaway hair. Hoi Sol paused, cupped his hand and shouted down the empty sidewalk, "Git the bull rider!" He glanced over at the couple, who sat dumbfounded. Hoi Sol growled at them and took off in a sort of skipping gait.

The man on the bench turned to his wife. "Probably another celebrity ten-K. I heard about it on TV, I think." The wife nodded dutifully, knowing her husband was full of night soil.

Elsewhere, two security guards were communicating on their walkie-talkies. "I don't know, Harry. They were headed toward the ungulates!"

Lick had increased his lead on the Viking. He veered off the walkway and down a slope into a brush thicket. He crossed a trickling stream in high gear and climbed up the opposite slope. Another eight-foot cyclone fence blocked his path. He scaled it and started running across a big open pen of assorted lame and convalescing llama, roe buck, dik-dik, mule deer, eland, impala, bighorn and one blue gnu with a snotty nose!

I'll be durned, thought Lick. *I'm in the hospital pen!*

He looked back over his shoulder to see the Viking doubled over the top of the fence, his fingers locked in the wire. Cody and Lilac each had one of his legs and were pulling against the tide!

At the far side of the enclosure was an institutional-looking frame structure. Lick, panting heavily, entered through a loading door in the back. Several cloven-hoofed critters were in individual pens enduring various stages of illness or recovery. The building turned out to be the vet shack.

Lick was in the treatment room. Along the far wall ran a counter with bottles of medicine, boxes of pills and record sheets. Several 60-cc disposable syringes lay soaking in a blue solution. On a plywood wall behind him hung all manner of medieval treatment and restraining devices: sheep hooks, hog snares, coils of cotton rope, halters, twitches, lip chains and two nylon lariats.

Lick peeked back through the door. Somehow Thorhild and Hoi Sol had taken the lead and were running side by side across the enclosure headed for the vet shack. Lick thought he could see Cody still on top of the fence and Lilac below him.

Lick reached above his head and pulled down one of the lariats. It had farmer knots in it, but he managed to get the rope shook out and built a loop. On the far side of the wide entranceway was a fifty-five-gallon drum of propylene glycol. He threw his loop over the barrel. On the near side of the entrance was a six-inch steel post about four feet tall. It was sunk in the concrete floor. Lick flipped the standing part of the rope over the post. He let the rope slack to the ground across the entrance. Holding on to the tail of the rope, he stepped back about three body lengths from the trap. He was the bait.

Hoi Sol and Thorhild came sprinting through the door side by side. They saw Lick and never broke stride. As soon as the hunters appeared in the doorway, Lick squeezed the tail of the rope with both hands and jerked! His borrowed underwear dropped to his knees! The rope pulled taut at knee level. Hoi Sol and Thorhild hit the trip together and catapulted forward, arms outstretched, sliding into home plate! The force on the rope pulled over the fifty-five-gallon drum. It fell on the back of Hoi Sol's leg with a crunch! The plastic pump and spout broke off and the slippery, sticky contents gurgled out on Hoi Sol's pants.

"Great balls of flaming, sulfurous bat guano!" screamed Hoi Sol, resigned to buying new threads.

The Viking was single-mindedly clawing and crawling toward Lick's feet! Lick popped him on the head with the tail of the rope! Special sauce splattered! Lick pulled up his shorts and grabbed a halter off the wall!

The Viking looked up with determination in his eyes! He lunged for Lick's ankle! Just as he did, Cody broad jumped into the middle of Thorhild's back!

Hoi Sol looked up from his crocodilian position. He started to shout at his villainous cohort. "Get—" Before he could finish, Lilac cleared the barrel like an Olympic ice skater and mashed his face into a fresh pile of water buffalo droppings!

"Go! Go!" shouted Cody.

Lick went out through a door at the side of the animal hospital! He found himself in the surgery room. A door to his right opened onto a loading dock, a door to his left led down a small alley with individual animal pens bordering it. He went to his left. He passed two wildebeest and a whitetail doe with fawn. He read the treatment chart in its aluminum folder on the last pen:

NAME: Mohammed

SPECIES: Bactrian camel

COMPLAINT: Haematoma of the tail

RATION: Normal feed and water

Mohammed lay on his brisket, placidly chewing his cud. Lick opened the gate, eased up to the camel's head and buckled on the nylon halter. He took the tail of the lead rope and tied it back to the halter, making a rein. Pulling up his undies, he crawled on between the two humps.

"Giddyup, Mohammed!" Lick spurred the animal's flanks with his bare feet! Mohammed craned his neck around, belched and tried to bite Lick's knee!

"Cody!" Lick yelled. Cody appeared in the doorway. "Hold the door!" At that moment the Viking ran through it!

The sight of the furious warrior rushing down the alley finally inspired Mohammed to rock to his feet! Lick pounded on Mohammed's ribs! They trotted out the gate and sideswiped Thorhild, who lunged desperately and grabbed Mohammed's tail. Mohammed's tail had just been operated on yesterday morning. It was swollen and painful. Mohammed brayed and cow-kicked Thorhild in his progeny bank! The Viking paled and released the tail.

Lick astride Mohammed coursed through the door into the surgery room. Lilac was on the other side of the room holding the other outside door open.

Like the Ghost of Train Wrecks Past Hoi Sol staggered into the middle of the surgery room! He bolted around the table and threw himself in front of Mohammed, blocking his way. Mohammed stopped. Hoi Sol reached out his hand.

"Nice camel. . . . Good boy . . . ," whined Hoi Sol ingratiatingly. Mohammed spit a fetid lunger at Hoi Sol's pleading countenance! Then he gave forth a salivaceous razzberry, soaking Hoi Sol's wrinkled tie and shirtfront. Mohammed clamped his ruminant jaws down on Hoi Sol's outstretched fingers and shook vigorously. When the camel unceremoniously released his grip, Hoi Sol fell over backwards!

"Hang on!" yelled Cody! He touched Mohammed's rump with an electric stock prod! Camel and rider shot out the door, leaped off the loading dock and loped up the driveway!

"Harry, do you read me? One to two . . . Harry?"

"Go ahead, Joe."

"Some naked maniac is headed toward the front gate! He's on a camel!"

"I'll cut him off! Over."

Mohammed was running like Whirlaway when he reached the main entrance of the Oklahoma City Zoo!

"Stop! You can't leave here with that camel!" shouted the security guard as he watched Lawrence of Roswell, pillowcase flowing, loincloth billowing, clear the turnstile and a honeymoon couple from Tecumseh. Man and beast disappeared across the parking lot!

Lick took a left on Eastern Avenue. Mohammed had an easy rocking gait. They rode down the middle of the street in the fast lane. Mohammed had no fear of cars and ran every red light. At the intersection of Thirty-sixth and Eastern he took to the air like a steeplechaser and cleared a black 240Z. Lick and his steed made a wide turn and galloped two miles up Twenty-third Street, collecting a growing entourage along the way. When they swung into Broadway, against the traffic, the Channel 5 news team was set up and filming!

It was a mile and a half from Twenty-third Street to the Myriad Convention Center and the National Finals! The bank time & temperature sign said 3:21 P.M. It was 3:31 when they rode through the contestants' entrance and 3:40 when they pounded up the corridor that led to the arena.

Lick pulled back on the rein, to no avail! Mohammed took his head and picked up speed! Looking down to the end of the tunnel, Lick could see the arena and hear the crowd. The arena gate was closed.

"He-e-e-E-E-L-P!"

Lick could see two white eyes peering between the gate boards. The gate swung open with seconds to spare. He galloped into the arena!

A clown was doing his act in the arena with a dog and a monkey. The monkey was riding the dog around the coliseum floor. The announcer was narrating the act:

". . . And what's this?" the announcer fumbled when he saw the newcomers. He glanced at his script; no help. "A monkey on a camel?"

The camel and the dog loped side by side and both came to a halt in front of the clown. Snap Wilson, rodeo clown, looked up at the strange figure astride the camel. "Is that you, Lick?" he asked with wonder in his eyes!

"Yup."

"Where you been?"

"It's a long story. Am I too late?"

"No. No! The bull riding's next." The clown turned to the announcer and shouted, "Emerald ... it's Lick!"

A cheer went up from the chute area. One of the pickup men rode out and Lick climbed up behind him in the saddle, simultaneously mooning sections F through M.

44

As Lick thundered down the tunnel on Mohammed, he passed his date. Kamikaze looked up, startled. Streaking from his right to his left came an odd sort of horse carrying a nearly naked white boy!

Kamikaze snorted in surprise and backed up a couple steps as the apparition raced on by.

What was that? he thought, aware that his pulse was pounding from the fright.

For a few fleeting seconds the big bull reflected on what he'd just seen. He was slightly offended that a horse had caught him off guard. In the swirling world of Kamikaze's prejudices, horses ranked beneath sheep. His logic was bovine clear: a horse's subjugation to a species as physically inept as humans only confirmed its stupidity. Plus the way horses constantly complained about everything from inadequate working conditions to poor circulation made them tiresome company.

Not to mention how dorky they looked! Goofy little single-toed hooves, big floppy lips and a head like a hornless rhino! And the specter that had just raced by him seconds ago was the dumbest-lookin' horse he had ever seen! He had ears like a pig, lips that could eat peanuts through a picket fence and he smelled like a burnt carpet!

But there was something familiar about the bare-skinned bucka-roo in the big white wild rag. His scent was as unique as his mama's moo. A few of the cowboy's odiferous molecules lingered in the air. They were gathered up by inhalation and sent to the olfactory decoding section of Kamikaze's brain.

The red light of positive ID began to blink. Lick registered on the screen as: BULL RIDER ... BUCKED OFF ... TWICE ... ESCAPED.

* * *

Just then Kamikaze heard the gates rattle and the next thing he knew he was being taken along with his pen mates to the arena. Standing single file with the other bulls in the narrow alley with six-foot sides, Kamikaze couldn't see much. He was aware of the scaffolding and lights on the roof of the coliseum. He could hear the big noise of the crowd. He could sense the tension. One by one the bulls worked their way into the chutes. Kamikaze stopped at chute number five.

As soon as the gate clanged behind him he smelled the bull rider that had given him the momentary distress back in the pen. Kamikaze had recovered from the embarrassment and had begun to resent the attack on his macho. The smell of that bull rider hit him like a gust off an estrus heifer!

He reacted instinctively, swinging his massive horns at the rider trying to loop the rope around his girth, banging back and forth in the tight box and bellowing!

Suddenly Kamikaze realized that he was losing his self-control. He stopped the chute fighting and stood still. He felt the bull rider lean over and feed the tail of his bull rope through the loop. Mixed with the molecules that identified him, Kamikaze smelled something else on the man ... fear.

That's right, cowboy, telepathed Kamikaze, cool as a cucumber. *Yer dead meat.*

45

Afternoon, December 12
Oklahoma City, Oklahoma

Cody and Lilac paid the cab at the gate and hurried up one of the spectator tunnels. They stood in the portal entrance looking down at the arena floor. The bull riding had started.

"Oh, Cody, I hope he made it," said Lilac.

"Me, too, darlin'," said Cody. "If he didn't, it's too late now."

They watched Lennox Wildebang buck off one of T. Tommy Calhoot's best bulls, Velvet Whacker.

"There's Lick!" said Lilac. "By chute number five!"

Four more bull riders rode and then the announcer introduced Smokey. "And now from LeBec, California, presently leading in the World Standing and leading here at the National Finals, Smokey Brothers! He's drawn a Maid Brothers bull called Pecan Punch! Ladies and gentlemen, this ride may be for all the money!"

Lilac gripped Cody's hand. Smokey rode the full eight seconds.

"That's it," Lilac said dejectedly.

"I don't know," said Cody. "Looked like he slapped him to me!"

"A tough break," intoned the announcer. "The judges say he touched the bull with his free hand . . . an automatic disqualification. No score for Smokey Brothers." The crowd groaned.

"Our last bull rider has a chance to take the lead but he's got his work cut out for him. He has drawn a bull that has never been ridden! Number ten-twenty of Bobby Monday's string . . . a bull called Kamikaze!"

The whole coliseum grew silent as Emerald announced Lick in chute number five.

Will Yunk and Thermal Bind spoke in hushed tones in front of the Rodeo TV Network cameras.

"Ladies and gentlemen," said Thermal. "You could hear a pin drop in this huge auditorium. For some as yet unexplained reason Lick turned his last two bulls out. He arrived at the arena minutes ago on a . . . a *camel!*"

"A two-humped, double-toed, split-lipped, nonfiltered camel!" added Yunk in amazement!

"Both Lennox and Smokey failed to score today," continued Thermal, "leaving Lick the last chance at top money. He needs to ride this bull and score well. According to our statisticians, if he marks a seventy-nine or better he'll win the average. If not, he'll place third overall. . . ."

"Bare butt, stark nekkid, flag wavin', flyin' in on a fork-ed footed camel! Folks, you never seen nothin' like it!" crayoned Will Yunk, color commentator!

"However," Thermal broke in, glaring at his partner, "Lick is facing formidable odds. The bull he has drawn is the Buckin' Bull of the Year, unridden in four seasons, the one and only . . . Kamikaze!"

"Ride the sumbitch, Lick!" blurted Yunk, misplacing his professional objectivity. "Ride him till he'll pull a plow!"

Four rows up in a reserved box, two beefy characters puffed their cigars.

"Shootfahr, Jaybo. If he rides this bull it'll cost us a cool million!"

"How'd he git here anyways, Hoss?"

"On a camel, you moron!"

"Yeah, but . . ."

"Shootfahr! Wait'll I ketchup with Slyzack . . ."

Five miles away, two low-rent hoods were standing beside their rented AMC Concord. Hoi Sol threw a rock at the No Trespassing sign posted by the Oklahoma City Zoo. He was scraping at some nameless muck on his forest green silk smoking jacket with a flat stick.

"Peed on, hit by a door, stabbed with my own knife, run over by a barrel, stepped on, wallowed in wild animal droppings, bit and spit on by a camel . . . What a terrible day." Hoi Sol turned to the Viking. "You've got a pickle in your hair."

"Don't feel bad," offered Thorhild. "Could happen to anyone."

"Thanks, Thorhild. By the way, where are you from anyway?"

"Minneapolis."

"What's Thorhild mean?"

" 'Works construction.' "

* ⋆ ⋆

Lick stood over Kamikaze in borrowed socks, borrowed boots, borrowed spurs, borrowed shirt, pants, chaps, glove and a borrowed hat. He burned borrowed rosin on the borrowed bull rope.

Kamikaze stood quietly. He felt the rope tighten around his girth and heard the cowbell jangle between his front legs. A light spot of weight settled on his back. He allowed it. More tightening and pulling of the rope followed. The loose strap around his flanks was adjusted. He switched his tail.

Lick slid up on his left hand. Kamikaze snorted. Lick dropped his legs down over each side. Kamikaze tensed.

Up in the stands, Cody fingered Lick's Copenhagen can. "Rub ol' Pinto for good luck," he said as he did it.

Lick cleared his head. The last twenty-four hours vanished. *Concentrate!* He looked at the back of Kamikaze's head. *The only way to ride you, pardner, is to be there when you make your move.*

Concentrate . . . the spiritual peace settled over the moment. Lick was ready. He nodded his head. The gate opened and the crowd roared!

Kamikaze propelled himself out of the chute . . . airborne! Before his front legs hit the ground, he whipped his tail end high in the air and landed with a thud, facing the chutes! Lick sunk his spurs into the bull's ribs! 1.000 seconds had elapsed.

Bull number 1020, king of the hill, top of the heap, tucked his head and whirled to the left, spinning so fast he looked like a roulette wheel! Lick's left spur was locked hard behind Kamikaze's elbow. Kamikaze set his hocks and skidded like a three-year-old colt at the Cutting Horse Classic! The Bucking Bull of the Year felt the cowboy's left heel slacken pressure. 3.090 seconds.

Kamikaze snapped his hindquarters straight out! His spinal column popped! It sounded like a switch engine taking slack out of a train of coal cars! He felt no pressure on either side from Lick's spurs. Kamikaze hopped forward like a deer and pulled Lick off his hand that was locked in a death grip to the bull rope. He kicked high with his hind legs! He felt the unwanted rider lift clear off his back! 4.900 seconds.

The instant the bull's feet hit the ground he felt the cowboy's seat hit his back and slide up under his hand. Two glinting steel rowels gouged at the thick skin on either side of his chest! Kamikaze bellowed in rage! 5.560 seconds.

The crowd surged to its feet hysterically cheering.

"We are witnessing a spectacular ride!" shouted Thermal Bind. The goose bumps came up from the back of Yunk's ankles and rolled in waves to the top of his scalp. "Stick it to 'im, Lick!"

The spectators watched the battle, captive to the adrenaline rush. That vicarious high physically lifted them out of their seats. A whirling, thrashing, bucking inferno churning up the arena dirt! The sight of such raw ability and naked will reduced each onlooker to his own primitive instincts. It was like watching an electrical motor operation out of control: sparks flying, the armature smelling like hot copper! Blue light! Shrill wailing! The crowd watched from the stands, secure in the fact that the action would never leave the arena floor.

Kamikaze hooked back with his two-foot horn and missed Lick's chin by an inch! Lick raked the bull again! Kamikaze spun tight to the right, pumping up and down! Lick was pounding his left heel into Kamikaze's side! Through gritted teeth Lick spat out, "Make yer move!" 6.250 seconds.

Kamikaze bucked out straight. Lick reared clear back and felt the small of his back come in contact with the broad smooth muscles of Kamikaze the cowboy killer! With silver flashing, chaps flying and knees pumping, Lick spurred the bull like a crazed bareback bronc rider!

Kamikaze ran headfirst into the arena gate beside the chutes! The crash could be heard in the cheapest seats in General Admission! Lumber and steel tore away with a sickening groan! Splinter and pieces of horn filled the air! The Bull of the Year spun back into the arena like a man-eating shark gliding into the shallow end! 7.150 seconds. Kamikaze was about to lose his cool!

46

December 12
Oklahoma City, Oklahoma

Kamikaze put every ounce of energy he had left into a last high wheeling buck. He sunfished and showed his cetacean underbelly to the announcer's stand. Lick stuck to the bull's back, his left arm supporting his whole weight! Bull and rider were parallel to the ground! The buzzer resounded in the arena: 8.000 seconds!

Lick bailed out in midair! Man and bull hit the ground simultaneously! Kamikaze was looking for Lick. Lick was looking for the exit. He raced for the chutes.

The big spotted bull charged after Lick, ignoring the bullfighting clowns bent on distracting him. Lick leaped for the top rail! Kamikaze caught him between his horns just as Lick made his jump! The force of the impact propelled Lick into one of the chute's vertical iron pipes, ten feet above the arena floor. Lick was madly scrambling over the chute gate! Kamikaze was trying to climb the gate after him! A gang of cowboys were pulling Lick over the back of the chute. He fell over the back boards headfirst.

Pandemonium reigned! The roaring and stomping crowd, including Emerald Dune, Will Yunk, Smokey Brothers and Bobby Monday, was making so much noise they woke up people in Tulsa! Once Kamikaze was safely out of the arena, the cowboys pushed Lick back out. He walked front and center and slowly took off his hat and tipped it.

All eyes were on the Winston Scoreboard. The numbers flashed. Lick had marked a ninety-seven!

Well, friends. He did it. Our hero did it. He moved the unmovable mountain. Wrote the unwritable song. Rode the unridable bull. A common man like the common man in all of us did the impossible. Do you think the crowd that watched those indescribable eight seconds didn't tear the roof off the stadium! I mean they shook the rafters and rattled the bedrock! They poured beer on each other and kissed their ex-husbands. Women fainted and cowboys cried. It was a moment in time frozen for posterity. They will tell the story of that eight-second ride the rest of their natural lives because they were there. "Yup," they'll say with a wistful smile and a far-away look, "you should'a been there."

Lick stood in the spotlight. He made no effort to collect his thoughts or memorize what was happening to him. He was capable only of absorbing the adulation of the crowd. He opened every sensate door in his body. The rapture of the crowd, their open admiration, their respect and affection rolled into his hungry soul in waves. It seeped into his marrow. It penetrated the recesses of his rusty feelings so long unused. It tore out brittle walls built over years of bitter heartache and slogging ambition. He filled to overflowing.

The clamor began to fade. Lick remained standing center stage long past his cue to depart. The crowd became quiet. Cody vaulted into the arena from the grandstand seats. He walked up to Lick, hand out, like he was approaching a spooky colt.

"You all right, Lick?"

Lick was staring at the far end of the big coliseum with unfocused eyes. Tears ran down his cheeks. Cody shivered. He put his arm around Lick. "C'mon, pardner." They walked side by side out of the arena.

Kamikaze stood in the pen with several other bulls. A big beefy brindle Braymer sidled by and cracked horns with him. Kamikaze backed up a step. They knew. Something had changed. He sensed there would be new nominations for the peckin' order soon.

He saw two cowboys stop and look through the boards at him.

One of them registered immediately! *Bull rider ... bucked off ... twice ... rode ... once ... escaped ... two out of three.*

Kamikaze gave a quick glance at the brindle bull, pawed the ground twice and charged the fence! Cody and Lick fell back as dirt pelted them! Kamikaze stood staring unblinkingly at Lick. He could smell that the fear was still there.

Big shot! He bored his brain waves into Lick. *With fences and ropes and clowns and spurs and horses. But you and I know you won't set foot in here. Brave rabbit. Go back to your hole and tell your stories. Maybe you will look strong in the company of cottontails.*

He swung back from the fence and walked toward the feed bunk. The brindle bull stepped back. Not far enough. Kamikaze swung a horn into his shoulder. Brindle backed clear to the corner of the pen!

Kamikaze looked over his shoulder toward Lick, who stayed back a safe distance from the fence. The other bulls stood watching quietly.

He swung his massive head around, awaiting any challenge. Seeing none, Kamikaze walked to the hayrack.

★ ★ ★

Lick's victory was not without cost. He had separated his collarbone from his shoulder when Kamikaze slam-dunked him into the pipes above the bucking chute. The ambulance delivered him to the hospital.

Lick returned to the party in progress, arm in a sling, with the stern admonition from the doctor not to eat or drink anything after 6:00 P.M. His surgery was scheduled the following morning at 8:00 A.M. Lick got knee walkin', blood pukin', commode huggin' drunk!

He spent the night with a woman who wanted to show him her tattoo. He passed out before he got it uncovered!

Cody and Lilac partied until midnight and retired to room 1225. They crawled under the covers, sharing each other's warmth.

"Do you think Lick will ever change?" she asked Cody.

"Whattya mean?"

"Get married and settle down?"

"Stranger things have happened."

"Gosh, that was disgusting the way he drank tequila out of that girl's shoe." She laughed.

"Yeah, disgusting!" Cody agreed. He started laughing, too.

"I can't imagine any woman putting up with him for long. I'm glad you're not like that!"

" 'Settle down' is the key phrase here. He's not ready. Till a person's ready to settle down, they'd make a sorry mate. But Lilac, don't ever worry 'bout ol' Lickity. Worryin' about him is like worryin' about the weather.

"He may never amount to much by some folks' standards, but he's the kind of man who'll be there for ya when the chips are down. Wherever the ragged ol' coyote winds up, he'll always have me to help him, if I can."

"You love him, don't you?" she asked.

"Lilac, there's only one person outside my family that I love more than him. That's you."

Silence slid between them, separating their thoughts. Finally Lilac spoke.

"Cody, would you propose to me again?"

Cody sat up. "What! When?"

"Now."

"Lilac, would you marry me?"

"Cowboy ... this is your lucky day!"

47

So there you have it. A simple story of two cowboys chasin' a dream. I added a little violence in the form of action, a little intrigue in the form of plot and a little sex in the form of love. That's all part of writin' a book.

But it should be easy to tell that I am a real rodeo fan. As a past participant and as an appreciative spectator. But mostly I enjoy rodeo and the real-life cowboy life-style that it imitates because of the people and the animals who live in it.

When it's all said and done this book is about two of those people and how they take care of each other.

Friend is a word . . .

> that I don't throw around
> Though it's used and abused, I still like the sound.
> I save it for people who've done right by me
> And I know I can count on if ever need be.
>
> Some of my friends drive big limousines
> Own ranches and banks and visit with queens.
> And some of my friends are up to their neck
> In overdue notes and can't write a check.

HEY, COWBOY, WANNA GET LUCKY?

They're singers or ropers or writers of prose
And others, God bless 'em, can't blow their own nose!
I guess bein' friends don't have nothin' to do
With talent or money or knowin' who's who.

It's a comf'terbul feelin' when you don't have to care
'Bout choosin' your words or bein' quite fair
'Cause friends'll just listen and let go on by
Those words you don't mean and not bat an eye.

It makes a friend happy to see your success.
They're proud of yer good side and forgive all the rest
And that ain't so easy, all of the time
Sometimes I get crazy and seem to go blind!

Yer friends just might have to take you on home
Or remind you sometime that you're not alone.
Or ever so gently pull you back to the ground
When you think you can fly with no one around.

A hug or a shake, whichever seems right
Is the high point of givin', I'll tell ya tonight,
All worldly riches and tributes of men
Can't hold a candle to the worth of a friend.

ABOUT THE AUTHOR

As America's best-selling cowboy poet, Baxter Black has taken the art of rhyme one step further, using his lunatic wit and animated delivery to create a whole new field of entertainment. Black has published eleven poetry books, is a regular commentator on National Public Radio, and appears regularly on national television shows.

Raised near Las Cruces, New Mexico, Black grew up in and around the livestock business. He became a veterinarian, dispensing his medicine and practicing his humorous songs and poems on countless cowboys who worked with him on ranches and feedlots around the mountain West. Before long, Black was spending as much time entertaining as he was doctoring livestock. Choosing the cleaner of the two options, Black hung up his plastic sleeve and jumped head-first into show business. He hasn't treated a case of foot rot since. *Hey, Cowboy, Wanna Get Lucky?* is his first novel.

JUNIOR

Now, Junior is tough and can't git enough
   of lively confrontations
And bein' his friend, I'm asked to defend
   his slight miscalculations.

Among his mistakes, too often he makes
   none of his business ... his.
So I counsel restraint 'cause sometimes he ain't
   as tough as he thinks he is!

Like the time he cut loose in a bar called the Moose
   in Dillon on rodeo night.
I stayed on his tail in hopes to prevail
   and maybe prevent us a fight

But Junior's headstrong and it didn't take long
   'til he got in a debate
Involving a chair and big hunks of hair
   and startin' to obligate

His friends, I could see, which only was me!
   A fact I couldn't ignore,
So takin' his arm to lead him from harm
   I drug my pal to the door.

No one disagreed and I thought that we'd
   made our escape free and clear
But he turned to the crowd and said good and loud,
   "Who is the toughest guy here!"

Not the smartest remark in a place this dark,
  ol' Junior had gone too far!
No one said a word but I knew they heard
  'cause all heads turned to the bar

And there in the hole like a power pole
  stood the pressure for all his peers.
"Ugly for Hire" and he wore a truck tire
  that came down over his ears!

He had on some chaps with big rubber straps
  but over his arms instead!
And sported a pattern like the planet Saturn
  his eyebrows went clear round his head!

His good eye glared while his nostrils flared
  like a winded Lippizan
Which lent him the air of a wounded bear
  whose pointer'd been stepped upon!

A Crescent wrench swung from where it hung
  on a log chain wrapped round his neck,
Along with a claw, a circular saw
  and parts from a Harley wreck!

With his Sumo girt he needed no shirt.
  Hell, he had no place to tuck it!
And wonders don't cease, he wore a codpiece
  made from a backhoe bucket!

He was Fantasyland, the Marlboro Man
  and heartburn all rolled into one!
From where I was lookin' our goose was cookin',
  our cowboys days were done!

Then he spoke from the hole like a thunder roll
  that came from under the sea,
He swallered his snuff . . . said, "If yer huntin' tough,
  I reckon that'ud be me."

I heard a pin drop. The clock even stopped!
  Silence . . . 'cept for me heavin'.
But Junior, instead, just pointed and said,
  "You! Take over, we're leavin'!"

STELLA CAMERON

CHARMED

AVON BOOKS NEW YORK

AVON BOOKS
A division of
The Hearst Corporation
1350 Avenue of the Americas
New York, New York 10019

Copyright © 1995 by Stella Cameron
Published by arrangement with the author
Library of Congress Catalog Card Number: 94-96359
ISBN: 0-380-77075-X

First Avon Books Printing: April 1995

AVON TRADEMARK REG. U.S. PAT. OFF. AND IN OTHER COUNTRIES, MARCA REGISTRADA, HECHO EN U.S.A.

Printed in the U.S.A.

RA   10   9   8   7   6   5   4   3   2   1

CHARMED

His lips were at first delicately teasing, then firmer, more insistent. Pippa stopped breathing. She slipped her hands up his arms and around his neck, wishing this could go on and on.

A thundering crash shocked Pippa rigid.

"In God's name! If this don't beat all!" the Duke of Franchot roared. "Ravishin' me betrothed in me own conservatory! Last night you were saved, you cur. Now I shall have what I intended then. I demand satisfaction!"

"And you'll have it." Mr. Calum Innes gently disengaged himself from Pippa and faced the duke. "I believe dawn is the preferred hour. Tomorrow. And since the choice is mine, we shall use pistols."

Praise for Stella Cameron's
BREATHLESS

"BREATHLESS sizzles"
Romantic Times

"This sexy romantic suspense
will keep you on the edge of your seat."
Rendezvous

For Suzanne Simmons Guntrum
and the "twin" we share

We are all in the gutter, but some of us
are looking at the stars.

—Oscar Wilde

❧ Prologue

Cornwall, 1789

"*They will* kill you for this," Guido told her. Doubled over, he gasped with every running step he took. "Kill *us*!"

Rachel didn't laugh. She usually laughed when he tried to guide her. "They'd likely kill us if they caught us," she agreed, darting behind a thick hedge brilliant with summer leaves even in the mist of a damp Cornish evening. Holding the bundle she carried to her chest, she said, "But we'll not be caught. Why did you come to look for me? I did not ask you to follow me this night."

"I saw that you were gone and I was worried." He knew she did not want his concern, yet he could not help but tell her. "Miranda saw you. She saw you meet someone. And afterward you came this way with . . . with something in your arms."

"Miranda sees too much that does not concern her. And she says too much. So does Milo. They should keep their eyes and their minds on their spells. I have already told you I agreed to do what I was asked to do. Now it is done. Enough of this talk."

Guido shook his head. If only she would let him care for her.

In the cover of the hedge, they crouched, side by side, and

1

looked up at the fantastic, soaring pattern of white stone towers and turrets that was Franchot Castle.

"I cannot believe you found a way inside that fearsome place and that you did not get lost," Guido said, thinking of the hundreds of rooms and passageways and staircases and halls that made up the great building on its hill above the sea. "It is a miracle you were not noticed. Why would this friend of yours ask you to do such a thing?"

A whimper came from the bundle and Rachel raised the child to her shoulder. "I said nothing about a friend," she told him. "I said I knew her and that she wanted me to perform a service for her. She has already paid me well for this. I have more gold than we could gather in a year of passing our cup at the fairs."

"The fairs are good to us," he grumbled.

"We travel from town to town. We have no home and we are scorned by all who look upon us."

"People are glad when we come." This argument was not new. "Each year they await us. We make them happy and we are happy enough ourselves."

She gave a short, harsh laugh. "*You* are happy. *You* are not the one around whose body the snakes curl. *You* are not stared at by men who do not come to see the snakes."

He felt peevish. "I am the snake man. You are my assistant. When you came to me, you were glad enough for a place where you could be safe from that creature who used you."

"I am not safe," she muttered. "I will never be safe."

He wished he could calm her, please her, but there was no pleasing Rachel, and she wanted nothing from him but the meager security he could offer. She did not want what he so desperately longed to give her—his love.

"Come," he said, his throat tight from breathing too hard and his heart still pounding from terror. "Soon the child will be missed and all at the castle will be alerted. They will come for us, and the first place they will look is the camp. What shall we do? I should have stopped you."

"You could not have stopped me, because you did not know what I intended to do—and they will not come. They will never know what I have done, I tell you."

Turning their backs on the castle, they continued on, stooping low. The baby cried now, softly but steadily, and Rachel made clucking sounds.

"I ask you again," Guido said. "*Why* did the woman ask you to do this?"

"I told you, as a service and she paid me."

"You anger me with your deliberate foolishness, Rachel. The woman wanted the child taken from its mother. For what reason?"

"The child's mother is dead now," she reminded him. "And I cannot answer your question, because I do not know. Anyway, it is of no interest to me. We should go by separate ways now. It will be best for me to enter the camp alone and from a different direction than expected."

He coughed. The moist air of Cornwall always tightened his lungs. "You will not be able to hide the child from the others."

"I know." She looked anxiously about. "Please leave me."

"What will you say? What if they guess who he is?"

"He is *nobody* now," she hissed. "He is nothing, just like us."

"He is a—"

"Hold your tongue! And leave everything to me. We will have money to buy a better horse now—and perhaps new shoes for ourselves."

"The child will need—"

"The child will need nothing." Her voice had lost its life.

He grasped her arm and pulled her close. "Babies grow. Soon he must be clothed, and he will also eat. The more he grows, the more he will eat."

"He will not," she declared, her black eyes burning into his.

A coldness curled inside the man's belly. "Boys have large appetites."

"Yes, but we shall not be concerned with such matters. I was paid well, my friend. *Very* well."

A small flare of hope warmed him. "I suppose that is why the parcel the woman gave you was large—because it contained so much gold. It must have been heavy. Quickly, take me to the place where you hid the gold. We must get away from here."

"The parcel did not contain gold. It held a child. An infant boy."

He rubbed a hand over his eyes and made himself concentrate. "You took the child into the castle? Then you brought him out again?"

Hunched over, Rachel began to walk once more. "I took *a* child in. I brought a child out."

The meaning of her words became clear, and his heart turned in his breast. "You are mad, truly mad, if you think they will not notice the difference."

"They will not." She laughed shortly. "They are people who pay strangers to care for their babies. Those strangers—if they should notice something amiss—will never admit that they allowed their charge to be stolen and replaced with another infant."

Guido took a shallow, difficult breath and said, "And now you are to pass this child along to someone else? Someone else who will worry about food for a growing boy? You were paid a great deal for a task soon to be over."

"No. And yes. The task will soon be over. I was paid a great deal because I am to ensure that the child disappears." She splayed the long fingers of one hand over the writhing baby. "The woman said to be certain the body is never found."

🌳 One

London, 1823

"*His Grace* the Duke of Franchot," the footman announced nasally from the entrance to the packed music room.

"He is here," Calum Innes said, so softly that only the man to whom he spoke could hear him. His next breath seemed the most difficult he'd ever taken. "His Grace the Duke. The man who is living my life."

"Ah," Struan, Viscount Hunsingore, murmured thoughtfully. He draped a heavy arm around Calum's shoulders and said, very low, "Shall you want that life back, d'you suppose?"

Calum regarded the strapping blond man who strode through the parting crowd in the blue-velvet-and-gilt room at Chandos House. "That remains to be seen," he said, although until this instant he had been almost certain his only interest was in observing in the flesh—just once—the man who had taken his place when they were both infants. "He is a prancing ass," he added, none too softly.

Struan chuckled. He flipped the backs of his fingers across Calum's chest as if brushing some minuscule annoyance from the perfectly fitted black evening coat. "Have a care," he said for Calum's ear only. "The man is known to be dangerous,

5

and you cannot be certain you are right about this so-called discovery of yours."

"I *am* certain."

"You have no proof."

Calum raised his chin. "I shall get it. Look at him. He goes directly to the prince, as if his arrival must be the only one awaited."

"Esterhazy seems not to mind," Struan commented, studying the jewel-bedecked Austrian ambassador. "I'd say this isn't their first meeting. No doubt they've a deal in common—great men together, hmm?"

"I fail to see any humor here," Calum said, stiffening his back. "The man's a strutting cockerel and I hate him."

"You *want* to hate him," Struan amended. "But I doubt you want to hate the lovely Lady Philipa. Such abundance, hmm? Abundant hair, abundant eyes, abundant lips. Abundant white flesh. Ah, yes, such flesh. Breasts such as those might be more than most men could . . . handle?"

"For an ex-priest, you are remarkably free with your assessments of the female form."

"*Ex*-priest. Yes, indeed, *ex*. Let us not forget that I was a priest for a short time and that I ceased to be a priest some time ago." Struan's dark eyes glittered with laughter. "*I* acknowledged my fleshly weaknesses. When will you confront yours, my friend?"

Calum deliberately looked away from the viscount's clever, handsome face and concentrated instead upon the man known as the Duke of Franchot—and the voluptuous blond woman who clung to his arm. "Popinjay," he said of the duke.

"Come, now," Struan said. "Do not evade what may be the more important question here. What think you of his fair fiancée?"

"Garish," Calum remarked shortly. "Too free with the paint pots." But he continued to study the woman. He'd like to say she was nothing to him. That would be a lie.

"That may well be," Struan agreed. "Yet a man's bed would be the warmer for her presence there. And if her thighs are as white and round as her breasts, well, one can imagine the delights a man's ship might find in such a harbor."

"I liked you better as a priest," Calum said curtly, but he

felt the quickening between his own legs nonetheless.

Franchot spoke with Prince Esterhazy as the equal he clearly considered himself to be. Whilst he spoke, he looked around, inclining his head at men whose eyes he caught, and assessing women with insolent openness.

The orchestra burst forth afresh and dancers surged to the floor, their shimmering finery vying for supremacy. Plumes swayed and jewel-studded turbans winked. Silks and satins and sumptuous brocades swirled together. For each splendidly adorned female, a richly dressed gentleman, frequently noble, directed the progress.

"Now you have seen him," Struan said, staring straight ahead, "no doubt we may leave?"

"Not quite," Calum said, still studying the object of his interest. "She clearly adores him. But he is not attentive to her."

"He behaves like a man who has tasted the fruit and knows he may continue to sample at will."

Calum frowned.

"Ah, yes," Struan said. "That troubles you, doesn't it? You are thinking that the man has taken something else that should have been yours."

Calum could not bring himself to answer.

"Odd," Struan said. "I'd have expected a man like Franchot to choose a more elegant female as his duchess. One with a more subtle grace."

"She has no grace at all," Calum replied darkly. "And he did not choose her."

"No, no, of course not. What am I thinking of? The betrothal took place at the time of Lady Philipa's birth. And she comes with a huge dowry, I'm told."

"Absolutely huge, my dear fellow," said a man who stood nearby. A mincing creature corseted into a ridiculous pigeon-breasted silhouette, he turned his powdered and rouged face upon Struan. "Have we met? I am Wokingham. I'm sure I remember you from somewhere or other."

"Hunsingore," Struan said, unsmiling. "I doubt if we've met. Kirkcaldy is our seat."

"Scotland!" the man said, pursing red lips. "You must be Stonehaven's boy."

"Stonehaven's brother. My brother, Arran, succeeded. Our father died some years ago."

"Ah, forgive me. Time rushes away from us. You were interested in Lady Philipa Chauncey?"

Struan cast Calum a brief, warning stare. "I was merely curious. After all, it is supposedly to be the event of the year—this marriage between two such old families."

"More of an event for Franchot than for the girl, I fancy," Wokingham said. "The world knows old Chauncey's Cornish lands march with the Franchots'."

"And that is of significance?" Calum asked, smelling a man who liked to show himself an authority on the prevailing *on-dit*.

"Significance!" Wokingham thrust forward a hip and guffawed. "I thought *everyone* knew."

Calum restrained himself from saying that he was no one and said instead, "Refresh my memory."

"Franchot needs the port to get all that lovely tin of his out of Cornwall in a timely fashion, don't y'know." Wokingham feigned boredom at this point, but his little eyes glittered. "It's on Chauncey's land. All well and good when the Franchots were in the business of protectin' the Chauncey estate from invaders. The Franchots got free passage overland and the freedom to come and go from the ChChaunceys' port as they pleased. Not much call for protection from invaders anymore. That could change the nature of things, don't y'know. But the present duke's father had the wit to suspect he'd best make sure his path to an easy port didn't pass into greedy hands—greedy hands that owed him nothing."

Calum waited for Wokingham to continue and, when he didn't, said, "You mean Lady Philipa's father made all of his lands her dowry?"

Wokingham staggered under a fresh gale of mirth. "Strike me, no, m'boy! Chauncey's not about to let go of his Yorkshire holdings. But the Cornish parcel goes with the girl, and that means it goes to Franchot on the day he marries her. He'd probably find a way out of the match—agreement or no agreement—if his future didn't depend on that port."

"The terms of the arrangement would not seem entirely

onerous from his point of view," Struan remarked. "She is
certainly a memorable creature."

Wokingham raised a brow. "You think so?"

"I do indeed." Struan nodded toward Franchot and his
companion. "There seems almost more of her than should be
remembered by only one man, wouldn't you say?"

Wokingham followed Struan's gaze and smiled hugely.
"You think that . . . Oh, no, m'boy, not at all. *That* isn't the
fiancée. She's Lady Hoarville, don't y'know. Old Hoarville's
widow. Should be a lesson to older gents who still like to
poke a lush young piece. Did for him in short order, I can tell
you."

A flunky removed the potpourri warmer from the fire and
held it aloft as he progressed through the guests. Musky san-
dalwood and the scent of roses wafted heavily on already too-
pungent air. Calum began to feel too warm. The crush swayed
together and voices soared in a shrill babel over the music.

Calum said, as much to himself as to Wokingham, "You'll
have us believe the . . . the duke attends a ball in the company
of a woman to whom he is not engaged?"

"It's the truth, m'boy. If you knew Franchot, you'd not be
a whit surprised. His father had his wild moments, but there
was never a doubt he was a gentleman with a scholar's soul.
This son is a rakehell to the bone. The Chauncey gel's over
there."

Calum felt a coldness between his shoulder blades. He
turned to survey the crowd behind him. "You mean," he said
slowly, "that Franchot's fiancée is already here and he's arrived with another woman?"

"I'd lay odds that those two are fresh out of her bed. Makes
sense he'd feel obliged to bring her."

Calum ignored that and asked, "Which is Lady Philipa?"

"Hmm." Wokingham tapped a beringed finger against his
slack lower lip. "Ah, yes, there she is, pretendin' to be part
of the statuary in that window alcove. Evidently Franchot's
grandmother—the dowager—is bringin' the gel along. I see
Her Grace sittin' with Countess Ballard. Just to the right of
the window. Lord Chauncey's an explorer, when he's not per-
formin' some sort of service for our Fat Friend's lot. Widower.
Love of his life—the wife—so the story goes. Wouldn't think

of marryin' again. Just the one offspring. Another man would consider it his duty to produce a male heir, but not Chauncey. Happy enough to leave it all to the one female and Franchot.''

Calum was too engaged in searching for a lady trying to impersonate a statue to listen particularly closely to Wokingham's diatribe. "Which particular window alcove?" he asked.

"Over there," Wokingham said, pointing rudely. "Beige gown. Black hair. Absolutely forgettable—except for the diamonds. Chauncey supposedly gave the gel the family diamonds and told her to get some wear out of 'em. Dashed strange fellow, Chauncey.

"Word has it the daughter's been allowed to just about bring herself up. Now Chauncey's not even in the country. Supposed to get back in time for the nuptials—not that I'd place any money on that.''

"We really ought to be getting along," Struan put in.

The edginess in his friend's voice was impossible to miss, but Calum ignored it anyway. "Beige dress," he said, scrutinizing one female after another. "Black hair. Diamonds . . . Oh, my word, *diamonds.*''

"Wouldn't miss those in a crowd, would you?" Wokingham remarked, looking down his immensely long nose. "No man would pass up a chance to put those pretty baubles into the family coffers. 'Course, everyone knows Franchot's coffers are already deep enough to drown in. But he needs Lady Philipa's port. Not that there's any danger of Franchot not getting the gel *and* the diamonds, I suppose. Disaster for him if there was.''

Calum heard what Wokingham said but found he'd lost interest in a flow of information that should concern him above anything else in life.

Lady Philipa Chauncey was tall and slim, possibly overslim. Her hair was, as Wokingham had said, black. Black and shining and drawn smoothly away from a sharply boned face that appeared entirely devoid of paint.

The diamonds in question formed an astonishing webbed collar with multiple points all but touching the modest neckline of the lady's simply cut satin gown.

"Bit of a toadeater, what?" Wokingham said on a sigh. "Can hardly blame a fellow like Franchot for preferring La

Hoarville, but dash it all—not quite the thing to flaunt it in front of the gel, eh?''

Calum set his teeth together and observed Lady Philipa narrowly.

Lady Philipa observed her fiancé and his companion.

"Looks dashed upset, if you ask me," Wokingham said. "They say she's a quiet little thing. Bookish, or some such nonsense. Keeps to herself. But you can tell she's got eyes for the duke. Oh, yes, she's all aflutter over him."

"I wouldn't have said so," Struan commented from behind Calum. "I'd have said she was . . . well, what would *you* say Lady Philipa was, Calum?"

"Animated," Calum responded, surprising himself. "I'm damned. She looks animated. And *impatient.*"

"My thoughts exactly," Struan said. "And now we should leave."

Calum turned so that Wokingham could neither see his face nor hear what he said. "Have patience, Struan. We are barely arrived. Surely it wouldn't be polite to leave so soon."

Struan's chest expanded with his next breath. "I don't think I like the look in your eye. You promised me that if I could arrange for you to see him—just *see* him—you'd be satisfied. You said your quest would be done with."

"Thank you for securing our invitation," Calum said, smiling benignly. "But I find I must have lied to you."

"I *knew* it," Struan said. "I should never have had any part in this."

"I didn't ask for your help," Calum reminded him. "I had, on previous occasions, managed entrance to London's soirees quite nicely. I am not entirely without contacts other than you, m'lord."

Struan gave a disparaging snort. " 'A damnably dangerous rogue' seems to be the reputation I heard applied to you, my friend. And by more than one sharp-eyed papa, if I'm not mistaken."

"I was not referring to the rakehell days of my youth," Calum said, feeling peeved. "I had in mind my bride-gathering adventures on Arran's behalf. But no matter. Why not go back to Hanover Square and await me there? I promise I'll get into no mischief in your absence."

"You are by no means far enough into your dotage for me to trust you in this company. Come with me—*now*."

"I cannot."

"Why?"

Calum crossed his arms and rested his chin on a fist. "I cannot come with you because I was probably mistaken. This may well be only the beginning of what I must do."

Struan groaned. "Franchot is a villain. He is debauched and depraved. Dueling is but one of his illicit pastimes. I beg of you, do not do anything to capture his attention. Not until or unless we are fully prepared to deal with him."

"I shall bear your warnings in mind."

"What am I saying?" Struan moaned. "*We* shall never deal or do anything else with him. You gave me your word that a look at the fellow was all you required. Then, you said, we should leave instantly."

"I have always had a way with fairy tales," Calum said, once more looking at Lady Philipa Chauncey.

"You do not and never have had a way with fairy tales." Struan was clearly incensed. "You are—or have become— the most thoughtful and even of men. You, and only you, kept my brother from allowing his inheritance to pass into our loathsome cousin's control. You have been our guiding influence since Father died and—"

"And I am only a man, not a saint." *Animated.* And incredibly impatient. That was exactly how he would sum up Lady Philipa Chauncey's present mood. "Excuse us, would you, my lord," Calum said to Wokingham. He held Struan's upper arm firmly and led him to a place where they stood directly between Lady Philipa and her fiancé.

"Good God!" Struan immediately turned his back on the girl. "Think, man. If you've anything to think with, that is. She will see you staring at her."

"She is preoccupied," Calum said, and his eyes went to a rapidly tapping satin slipper.

"Probably horribly embarrassed," Struan said. "Mortified, no doubt. Made a display of in front of half London."

"It is not she who is a disgraceful display. And she knows it. The lady is, unless I am much mistaken, bored by the proceedings and anxious to attend to matters she considers more important."

Struan poked a hard forefinger into Calum's shoulder. "You, sir, have developed an amazing imagination. You know nothing about any of these people and what they may or may not think or want."

"She spends time in the fresh air," Calum said. "Her skin is that light skin of the very dark-haired, but it is healthfully clear. Her eyebrows are black wings—very delicate."

"Oh, *my* God!"

"Her nose is rather sharp, but not at all displeasing. Her chin also. Overall, her face is oval with the type of hairline that arches from a central point. Really quite engaging."

"You have never . . . At least, you have almost never shown any interest in a particular female. Not since Alice—"

"Kindly do not mention that episode. Lady Philipa's cheekbones are rounded. I like that. Her mouth is fuller than is fashionable. I like that, too. And deep blue eyes with such dark hair have always intrigued me."

"Wokingham said she was forgettable."

Calum breathed in slowly through his nose. "He was wrong. She is understated. A little fragile of build, perhaps, but pleasing. I fancy she would be soft. Rather like a supple, blue-eyed black cat. Mmm. And she clearly has spirit. I like that, too."

Struan's finger jabbed Calum again—like an iron spike. "Where are you coming by these remarks? I have never heard you speak so before."

"I have never before looked upon a woman who was betrothed to me on the day of her birth."

"Oh, *my God*!"

"Do stop saying that."

"You have fabricated an existence for yourself out of God—out of who knows what gossip and rumors. There is no proof that you are anyone other than Calum Innes."

The familiar turning started in his belly. "Calum Innes, man without a past."

"Your past is with *us*. With the Stonehavens. You became one of us when you were but a small boy."

"You have been good to me," Calum allowed, and meant

every word. "But I am not one of you. I am a man who was left, a child sick unto death, upon frozen ground in Castle Kirkcaldy's stable yard. Left dressed in rags and with only a worn scapular to guard my body and soul. And the name I have been known by is a lie. A note in a poor hand thrust inside my clothing. Calum Innes. *Not* my name, I tell you."

"Calum—"

"She has remarkable eyes."

"She will *see* you looking at her."

"She already has," he said, and felt a stillness form around him.

"Good *God*," Struan hissed. "Please come away. *Now*."

"And allow her to be twice spurned in one night? I think not."

Her foot had ceased its rhythmic tapping. She did not blush, or lower her face, or flutter her thick black lashes. She did not finger the fabulous diamond collar or flip open her beige lace fan.

Her lips did part a fraction, show small white teeth—just a fraction. Her eyes rested squarely, curiously, on his, and Calum's right hand went to the part of his stomach covered by his white waistcoat.

"Calum?"

He ignored Struan and walked with determined step to stand a short distance in front of Lady Philipa Chauncey.

The top of her smooth black hair would reach his chin. From his new, closer vantage point, he saw blue lights in that hair and noted the absence of fussiness. Coiled at her crown and secured with a simple, if diamond-studded, comb, gleaming curls fell loosely to her shoulders.

Without intending to, he approached and offered her his hand.

She took it and allowed him to draw her close enough to force her to raise her face to look at him.

Her black lashes cast a smoky veil across the dark blue of her eyes. Some might find her unremarkable; Calum was not one of their number.

"Where did we meet, sir?"

For several moments it was as if he'd heard her light, clear voice in some other place—at some other time. Then he remembered to smile. "I was going to ask the same of you, Lady Philipa."

She had begun to smile, but her expression became serious again. "I was right, then. We have met. But you have the advantage of me, sir, for I do not recall your name."

"I am Calum Innes." He bowed. "May I have the honor of this dance?"

Without the expected glance in her chaperon's direction, she folded her hand entirely into his and walked with him to take a place among the couples who were beginning the whirling steps of a daring waltz.

Calum hesitated only a moment before placing a hand at his partner's waist.

Her eyes widened and he saw her draw a short, sharp breath. But when he smiled, she smiled back and then concentrated so hard on the steps that her brow furrowed and she held her bottom lip in her teeth.

"You weigh nothing, Lady Philipa," he remarked as he swung her around. "And you are clearly very practiced in the waltz."

Her face came up. "It is unkind to make fun of a clumsy bumbler, Calum Innes," she said, and laughed.

Calum forgot to move.

When she laughed, her eyes closed and her nose wrinkled. Pure delight washed any hint of sharpness from her features. And the sound was as abandoned and full as the laughter he had heard among sweet-voiced village girls at Kirkcaldy.

He tightened his grip upon her and turned her effortlessly, glided with her across the floor with more grace and command than he'd known he possessed.

"There, you see," he said, laughing himself now, "you are a nymph of the dance. You fly as an imp of music through the night."

"And you lie, sir," she said, then bowed her head as a blush rushed over her cheeks. "Forgive me."

"I will not," he informed her. "Not until you apologize appropriately."

"And how shall I do that?"

His throat grew dry. "By agreeing to see me again. By allowing me to call upon you."

Her lips remained parted and he could almost hear her tumbling thoughts. She did not know how to answer. That, at least, was a boon.

"Where did we meet?" she asked at last. "*Did* we meet?"

"I don't know," he lied. "Did we? Or is it just that we ought to have met, because we are clearly so perfectly suited to each other?"

"That is an inappropriate comment, sir."

He felt rash. "Pretend it is not inappropriate. I should like to know a great deal about you, Lady Philipa."

She had grown pale. "Please tell me where we met. We haven't, have we?"

"No," he told her seriously. "But I felt as if we had, didn't you?"

"Yes."

"And I wished we had. I still do. I'm glad we have." Banter with females was not a skill he'd had any opportunity to perfect of late, yet talking to this girl was remarkably effortless.

"I am engaged to be married," she said, looking entirely unhappy now.

"Ah." Calum kept a smile in place and whirled her around and around. "Then I am desolate. Point the lucky man out to me. I shall congratulate him, then demand that he give you up."

Anxiety and humor flitted by turn across her face. Her fingers curled on his arm. "You are a flattering scoundrel, sir. But . . ." She hesitated, then shook her head. "I am also glad we met, even if only for a dance. I should have hated to look back on my life and remember not a single dance purely for pleasure and with a man who wanted nothing from me." Her lips snapped together and something close to horror made her eyes bright.

In that moment Calum was aware of the crush of dancers only as a distant, undulating pattern of colors. The music faded to the outside of the small space he shared with Lady Philipa and with her alone. She wasn't happy. She felt no power to change her future. And the man who was to take her bright spirit, to trap and to tame it, had no right to claim her.

Calum didn't know exactly when, but the music had stopped.

The dancers had drawn a little distance apart from him and Lady Philipa. The rustle of rich fabrics came in sibilant waves upon the rise and fall of whispers.

"You there, sir," an autocratic voice demanded. "I'll thank you to release my fiancée."

Even as Calum's heart pounded, a part of him reveled in the opportunity that was upon him. Keeping a hand at Lady Philipa's waist, he turned, knowing the man he was about to face.

His Grace the Duke of Franchot gave his "fiancée" the briefest of nods and a stare that promised unpleasant things to come. "What can you be thinking of, my dear?" he said, and to Calum, "You, sir, are a knave. Do you pretend not to know that an engaged female's attentions belong to her betrothed?"

Calum looked into cool, pale blue eyes and knew absolute loathing. "The fault—if there is any fault—is entirely mine," he said. "Please do not upbraid Lady Philipa for an innocent—"

"Silence!" the man roared. His height and breadth were considerable, but there was a softening about the handsome lines of him that suggested too great an appetite for rich food and drink. "When you address me, it will be as Your Grace. Not that you will have a great deal of cause to address me. I asked you a question about your understanding of betrothal."

Calum took his hand from Lady Philipa's too-warm body and executed a careless, abbreviated bow. "You said that an engaged female's attention belongs to her betrothed." He turned a deliberate eye to Lady Hoarville, who stood a few feet from the duke, her coarsely beautiful face folded into puckers of discontent. "As I was saying"—Calum inclined his head to her but spoke to the duke—"the engaged female's attention belongs to her betrothed."

"It is fortunate you have such a clear memory." Franchot held a fine white doeskin glove in one fist.

"Indeed," Calum agreed. "I would add that, as I understand the subject, harmony between the sexes is most likely to be achieved when there is *mutual* attention. Given that, I assume the harmony between you and Lady Philipa must be enviable.''

Utter silence fell.

Calum saw the duke's hand, holding the white glove, rise. The man's pale eyes riveted the object of his current loathing.

Franchot was going to call him out.

The hand began its deliberate descent.

"Oh, good grief!" a male voice said loudly. A blur of black and white stumbled between Calum and Franchot. "Hell and damnation," the man exclaimed, his arms flailing. A veritable fountain of champagne shot from an overlarge glass to douse the duke's perfectly arranged blond tresses and drip down his shocked face onto his formerly immaculate, ruby-studded stock, his midnight-blue coat and his gold-embroidered waistcoat. The red-and-gold silk sash, emblazoned with the jeweled emblems of his rank, might never recover its original splendor.

"Good *God*!" the duke sputtered, striking at his assailant. "Bloody clumsy oaf. Get your hands off me!"

"Forgive me." Much flapping of a pristine kerchief followed. "Do let me blot your rubies."

Muscles in Calum's cheeks twitched. A giggle from his side made him glance at Lady Philipa.

"*Off*," the duke roared. "*Off*, I tell you . . . you . . ."

"Hunsingore, Your Grace. Viscount Hunsingore."

Struan aimed a malevolent glare at Calum, who obligingly turned away . . . and walked into the arms of smiling Anabel, Lady Hoarville.

❧ Two

"*I'd be* delighted to accompany you to the supper room," Lady Hoarville said, resting her hands on Calum's arm and looking up at him through blackened lashes. "I do believe I'm really quite hungry."

Calum thought to look over his shoulder, then changed his mind and returned the lady's flashing smile. Under his breath, he said, "How kind of you to join in my rescue."

Lady Hoarville placed one white-gloved hand on Calum's arm and pointed them away from the continuing scuffle between Struan and Franchot. "He would have called you out, you know," she said very softly. "Etienne is exceedingly headstrong and passionate. Passionate in *everything* he does." She peeked at Calum.

"No doubt." Even had he wanted to, and he didn't, Calum could not have failed to see the truly extraordinary proportions of the lady's mostly revealed breasts. Sprigs of green satin leaves ornamented her lilac lace gown, the bodice of which was exceedingly tight. The resulting effect was rather that of too much pale blancmange resting precariously in a too-small dish.

After what seemed a lengthy time, they passed from the music room to the supper room, where several long tables bore lavish displays of extravagant edible delights.

Calum halted. "I really do appreciate your kindness, madam, but I cannot take you away from your companions." He did not add that he was not a man who walked away from conflict, and had Struan not appeared to be on the verge of apoplexy, he, Calum, would be asking his friend to act as his second.

"Fie." The moue was accompanied by a small dip of her knees and a smart rap of her fan on Calum's chest. "You would use me and desert me, sir? I am wounded."

"I believe the time has come for me to leave."

"No! No, I forbid it. Not until I have found out absolutely everything about you."

Not for the first time that evening, Calum felt a prickling climb his spine. "I am a dull fellow, I assure you," he told her.

She wandered to the closest table and selected a small cake coated with pink sugar. "You are not dull to me," she said, and applied the tip of her pointed tongue to the sugar. Slowly, she licked a circle around the glacé cherry at the cake's center. "Perhaps *I* am dull to you? Oh, dear, yes. That must be it. You are bored by my company."

"Not at all." Franchot and Lady Philipa totally absorbed him; otherwise he was bored with the entire proceeding. He was also aware that, for some obscure reason, this woman wanted something from him. "Shall I return you to the ball?"

"What is your name?"

There was danger here—he could feel it. "Calum Innes," he told her. Perhaps the danger he felt arose only from knowing that this woman was a very "close" acquaintance of the man who, only minutes earlier, had been on the verge of challenging him to a duel.

"You know Lady Philipa, don't you?" Lady Hoarville asked.

The reason for her interest in him began to take shape. "Surely you intend to honor me with your name, madam?"

The whole of the little cake disappeared into her mouth and she chewed. Beckoning, she drew a footman nearer and took a glass of champagne from the silver tray he held. This she gave to Calum before taking a second glass for herself.

Without speaking, she proceeded to a doorway near the towering white marble fireplace and indicated for Calum to

follow. Reluctantly he did so and found himself in a sumptuous green brocade sitting room.

"I am Lady Hoarville." The door was closed behind him
with a firm thud. "Anabel. You may call me Anabel."

"Why?"

She moved to the center of the room and faced him.
"Because I like you, of course." Her bright blue eyes became
innocently round. "And I think you are coming to like me,
too. Just a teensy bit?"

Calum was overwhelmed by a feeling that he had wandered
into an elaborate theatrical production—a farce—and that he
was being manipulated to play a part of the lady's choosing.

"Is it simply *Mr*. Calum Innes?"

"Yes," he said without hesitation.

"How fascinating."

"That I am simply *Mr*. Calum Innes? Or that I am here at
all?"

"That clearly you are intimately known by Lady Philipa,
while I do not know you at all." She sipped champagne and
looked at him through popping bubbles. "*I* know *everybody*
who is *anybody*. Yet I do not know you."

How very important it was for people such as Wokingham
and this woman to count themselves among their select "anybody" circle. "Perhaps, my lady, I am not anybody," he suggested, not without enjoyment. "Wouldn't that account for the
situation?"

She laughed, and Calum immediately remembered how
Lady Philipa's laugh had sounded. The comparison was as if
between a penny whistle and a flute.

"Oh, Mr. Innes," Lady Hoarville said, inclining her head
to let her mass of blond ringlets trail over a round, white shoulder. "You tease me. When did you first meet Lady Philipa?"

"Tonight," he said promptly.

"Come, come, now." She sauntered about the room, watching him all the while, and finally posed beside a tufted chaise.
"Did she pay you to dance with her?"

He was too shocked to respond. Slowly, he put his glass on
a mahogany teapoy.

"Aha! I see I finally have your attention. It won't work,
you know. Not without a great deal of insight into the man,

and you may be assured that Etienne doesn't give a fig for his silly little intended, one way or the other.''

Calum opened his mouth and shook his head.

"She may think she's won some sort of victory by gaining his attention, but she cannot steal his affections from me. Etienne and I have known each other for a very long time. This annoying betrothal was not of his making, and Lady Philipa would do well not to practice calling herself Duchess yet. Etienne and I, we are . . . we are like a fine musician and a perfectly tuned instrument. We belong together."

"I see," Calum said, sensing that the woman's jealousy could become a useful weapon against Franchot—should a weapon ever be needed. "Might I know which of you is the, er, fine musician and which the perfectly tuned instrument?"

She tossed her head and three long green ostrich feathers floated around her hair. "How much did she pay you?"

Poor Lady Philipa. What very unpleasant people she counted among her acquaintances.

"How much?" Lady Hoarville pressed.

"Nothing."

"Chivalry from a paid courtier?" She snorted. "How admirable. By now he will have sent her packing back to Pall Mall with the horrid old dowager. So the little charade you arranged will not have accomplished a thing, you see."

Calum's jaw ached from clenching his teeth. "Tell me, Lady Hoarville," he said, "why exactly do you think Lady Philipa Chauncey would pay me to dance with her?"

"I told you. In order to try to steal the duke's attention from me. She is jealous."

"Why should she be jealous? Regardless of your wishes to the contrary, she is his fiancée, I believe. She is to marry him at the end of the summer, isn't she? Surely you don't think you can do anything to change that."

"I think Lady Philipa fears she may lose what she has always expected to gain from poor Etienne." Cunning entered those guileless blue eyes. "You know all this. And you arranged what happened out there."

"You are wrong," he assured her. "I do not know all this. And I arranged nothing. The clumsy gentleman who spilled champagne on your passionate friend has been my companion since we were children. He is Struan, Viscount Hunsingore, and he invited me to accompany him this evening. I had never seen Lady Philipa before tonight."

"Hunsingore," Lady Hoarville repeated. "How do I know that name?"

"You heard him announce it."

"No, no." She flipped her fan impatiently. "What made you decide to ask Lady Philipa to dance?"

He felt protective of Lady Philipa and immediately knew the insanity of any such feeling where she was concerned. "I asked her to dance because I found her appearance pleasing and because she was not already dancing."

"You are not English," she said suddenly.

Calum raised his brows. He could not say that despite his subtle Scottish brogue, he was most definitely English, that he had been born in Cornwall and that the man whose identity and origins were truly a mystery was, even now, posturing in Prince Esterhazy's music room.

"Are you a Scot?"

He nodded. "I have lived most of my life at Castle Kirkcaldy." The truth always simplified matters. "The late Marquess of Stonehaven was my guardian."

"Hunsingore," she exclaimed. "Of course! He is the younger brother of the present marquess. How are you related to them?"

So many questions. "I told you. I was the late marquess's ward. Later I became his son's ... advisor." It was close enough.

"But surely there is some blood tie? Through your mother, perhaps?"

"None at all. I was a foundling." As he said it, he faced her squarely and planted his feet. "I am, my lady, nobody. Nobody at all. Now, if you will excuse me?"

"Yet you have the bearing and presence of a man very much certain of himself. And you presumed to ask a noble lady to dance?" She clucked, then perched on the edge of the chaise. "I do not think I believe you, Mr. Innes. There is much more here than you are prepared to divulge. Would it make you more talkative if I told you that I will not repeat anything you tell me to the duke?"

"I doubt it."

"Humor me, Mr. Innes." She paused with her lips parted. A crease formed between her arched brows. "Innes? I'm almost certain I have known an Innes."

"It's a common enough Scottish name."

The closed fan was leveled at him. "We have met before."

"It seems," Calum said with a sigh, "that I am either most memorable or exceedingly forgettable. We have not met before."

"And you stand by your word that Lady Philipa did not hire your services to incite the duke's jealousy?"

"I do indeed."

"You certainly did make him angry, didn't you?" A dimple appeared in her left cheek. "He does so despise anyone who crosses him."

Calum almost felt sorry for Franchot. He was dallying in malicious and greedy arms. "No man likes to feel the fool."

"Are you wealthy, Mr. Innes?"

"I . . ." He had the adequate bequest left to him by the late Marquess of Stonehaven, but that was not this woman's affair. "I am an independent man."

"An independent *poor* man? Or an independent *rich* man? The latter is so much more appealing, wouldn't you say?"

"Undoubtedly."

"But you are not of the latter variety?"

"I'll take my leave of you."

"Not unless you want me to tear my dress and scream."

Calum stood quite still. As he watched her, Lady Hoarville pulled the bodice of her gown down, baring her breasts.

"*Madam!*" He stepped backward, jamming his heel against the door to ensure it remained closed.

"I see I have overwhelmed you. It is invariably the case." She reached up to jerk several curls loose and let them fall over the swell of one breast. Her large pink nipple thrust between shiny strands. Lady Hoarville took the tensed flesh idly between a finger and thumb, then rested her head against the chaise. "Why don't you join me, Mr. Innes? I know you would enjoy this even more than I."

He could walk out on her and risk the outcome.

"Oh, I've embarrassed you," she said, her voice husky.

"All I intended was to make certain I had your full attention."

"You do," he said shortly.

"Good. Then I think we should talk a little business."

"There is no business that we could possibly have in common."

"Oh, but there is." Somewhat laboriously, she got to her feet and approached Calum. "You have presented me with an absolutely marvelous solution to the biggest dilemma of my life."

"I suggest you attend to your gown, Lady Hoarville."

"*You* attend to it," she said, coming to stand toe-to-toe with Calum, her body layered intimately against his. "You are a very handsome man, Mr. Innes."

He stared down into her face, and lower.

"Yes," she whispered. "You see something you want, don't you? And you shall have it, dear man. All of it. In time." Her fingers trailed up his thigh until she could explore the solid contours of his manhood.

Calum grunted and reached for her hand.

She squealed and rocked against him, parting her thighs to straddle one of his. "We must be quiet," she said, giggling. "Or they will come and find us. What will you say if they do?"

He abandoned her darting hand in favor of dealing with the bodice of her gown. When his fingers passed over a crested nipple, she gave a little shriek. He pressed his lips together and dipped to grasp the neck of the dress.

"We are going to be well suited." She sighed. "Oh, yes. But first you must do what I tell you to."

As he hauled the lace back into place, she trapped his hand inside, molded it to her flesh and began to pant.

Several more minutes of erotic struggling elapsed before the "lady" was more or less clothed again.

"So," she said, smiling while she made an effort to restore her hair. "Now you know how quickly and easily I can ensure your cooperation."

He couldn't help asking, "What exactly is it that requires my cooperation?"

"Surely you've guessed. You've given me a marvelous idea." She slipped a hand between his legs and squeezed.

Calum's flesh sprang harder than ever, but he regarded her unflinchingly. "No doubt you're about to enlighten me about this idea," he said.

"Don't you know already?" She spun away and clapped her hands. "I want you to do what I thought you were doing. I want you to pretend to woo Lady Philipa Chauncey—*Pippa*, as she so strangely prefers to be called."

The town coach rumbled over London's cobbled streets, sending its occupants swaying against luxurious, deep red leather squabs. A white moon silvered the facades of the shops and gentlemen's clubs on St. James's Street. Despite the tension that turned her stomach, Pippa took note once more of the famous bow window at White's but could not see if anyone was seated there.

"Justine should have come tonight," she said impulsively. The Dowager Duchess of Franchot's silence had swelled to fill the coach, and Pippa could hardly bear it. "She doesn't go about at all." She spoke of Lady Justine Girvin, the duke's sister, a shy but charming woman who seemed completely terrified by London.

Pippa tried again. "I think Justine is lovely. I'm certain she would enjoy dressing for a ball. She'd be bound to draw the attention of some very suitable gentlemen."

"Justine is four and thirty," the dowager said in her brittle voice. "Little short of five and thirty. Hardly marriageable material. She hated balls when she came out, and to as much as consider her attending a ball now is ludicrous."

Pippa took a breath that burned her tight throat. "I'm very grateful to her for coming to London to greet me. I can tell it's difficult for her to be here."

"We all must do things that are difficult when duty demands them," the dowager said.

Like marrying a man you don't know, but whom you are positive you will detest when you do know him, Pippa thought. She wound and unwound the tiny lace handkerchief she'd pulled from her reticule.

Who was Calum Innes?

She pressed a fist into her middle and realized with amazement that tears prickled in her eyes.

Why would wondering about a stranger make her want to cry?

She never cried.

Why had he chosen to dance with her when he could have asked someone beautiful?

The coach made the turn onto fashionable Pall Mall, and here the moon cast the white buildings in icy splendor.

"I cannot imagine what Etienne was thinking tonight, Philipa," the dowager said. Rigidly upright, her small form was turned away from Pippa, so that her stern profile stood sharp against the moonlight. From the moment when she'd brushed the duke aside and hurried Pippa from Chandos House, she hadn't initiated conversation—until now.

"Posturing," she said in a thin voice. "Ordering. *Demanding*. All but calling a man out! My grandson and I are going to have a long discussion when he arrives home—whenever that may be."

It could not possibly be late enough for her liking, Pippa thought unhappily.

"That young man," the dowager said. "The one you danced with. Where have I seen him?"

"Nowhere," Pippa said in a small voice, thoroughly miserable now. As soon as she'd first looked at Calum Innes, she'd found it impossible to think exclusively of anything or anyone else. "He simply asked me to dance and I agreed."

"Hmph. I can't imagine *what* you were thinking of, I must say."

"Not wise, I know, but I just didn't think. And it was a perfectly decorous dance, after . . ." Her voice trailed off. The waltz had definitely *not* been particularly decorous. *Thank goodness!* she wanted to shout. Thank goodness for a man so confident that he made her feel confident. Thank goodness for a man who'd made her forget she was clumsy. Thank goodness for a man who *looked* strong and *felt* strong and who had about him an air of purpose that had nothing to do with self-importance.

"Etienne must be made accountable for his behavior," the dowager remarked. "For all our sakes, he simply *must* stop keeping company with that—" She stopped abruptly.

Pippa didn't dare say what she thought, which was that the

Duke of Franchot and Lady Hoarville seemed well matched
and that she'd be happy to give them her blessing. Oh, if only
Papa would simply *give* the wretched Franchots a path across
Chauncey land to the port, and a right to use it *without* making
marriage to Pippa the asking price, for goodness' sake. She
worried the strings of her reticule. She had never seen the
dowager duchess so upset. Why, in the four weeks since Papa
had deposited Pippa at the Franchots' Town home, the dowager duchess had never spoken a harsh word about her grandson—until tonight.

"Such a bother," Pippa muttered, and was grateful when
the old lady showed no sign of having heard.

The coach ground to a halt before Franchot House, and the
footmen leaped nimbly from their posts to place the steps,
open the door and hand down the dowager and Pippa.

The butler admitted them to the building, saying in hushed
tones, "Good evening, Your Grace. My lady. So early? I trust
there has been no difficulty?"

"No difficulty at all," the dowager declared.

Their evening slippers rustled on black-and-white tiles in a
marble vestibule lined with Franchot family busts, each one
ensconced in a blue-enameled alcove.

"Very well, then," the dowager said, snapping the fingers
of her gloves free, one by one. "It is a lady's place to make
the best of it, don't y'know."

"Yes," Pippa agreed softly, knowing without being told
that the second "it" referred to her future husband. "Papa
alluded to that being the case. Such a bother."

The dowager duchess gave Pippa one of her bemused stares
before saying, "Yes. Well, then, you'd best go to your bed.
One hopes that impossible maid your father supplied will have
had the sense to await you."

"Nelly is very satisfactory," Pippa said, not caring that she
sounded as defensive as she felt. "Papa always gives deep
thought to matters involving my welfare."

"As you say. I shall appeal to Etienne's finer nature. Things
will progress tolerably well then, I'm sure."

Pippa was not sure. Pippa was suddenly deeply anxious.
"Does this mean the wedding may occur sooner than expected?" She held her breath.

"Not a bit of it!" The woman's exasperated breath sounded explosive in the quiet house. "That would be the end. All the tongues in London would wag."

"They would?"

"They would think you—" The dowager cleared her throat. "There are still many matters upon which I must instruct you. Yes, well, then . . . Yes, many things. It is unfortunate that you grew up without close female relations, but I shall not shirk the unpleasant duties that befall me. I shall certainly not shirk them, since the future of the Franchots is at stake."

Before Pippa could ask if so ominous a statement referred to anything other than the importance of her dowry, the dowager touched her cheek lightly and turned to climb the stairs. Pippa waited a discreet time to allow her future in-law to ascend to her apartments—on the floor above Pippa's—then ran lightly upstairs and along the corridor to the bedroom that was too cold and too elegant for her taste.

Nelly Bumstead all but capered in her excitement at Pippa's return. Smaller than her mistress and fair, with brilliant gray eyes, she shot up from a window vantage point of the street and plucked Pippa's satin reticule from her wrist.

"You need not have waited up for me, Nelly," Pippa said.

"Oh, go on with you, my lady." Nelly's broad, North Country vowels were warm and comfortably familiar to Pippa's ear. "I'd as soon cut off me own head as not be waitin' when you got back from that ball. Exciting, was it?"

Pippa sighed and allowed herself to be divested of her velvet cape. "All a lot of bother," she said.

"Oh, go on with you, my lady. Surely there was a crush of the quality." Nelly bobbed in front of Pippa to look directly into her face. "And lots of lovely gentlemen? Were there lovely red uniforms and gold braid and such? I thought when I came to you as there'd be all sorts of fancy affairs t'see, but—"

"My father has always been quiet," Pippa said, and thought "preoccupied" would be more factual. "Since my mother died, that is. When she was alive, Dowanhill was filled with laughter much of the time. Papa has told me so."

"Aye, I know," Nelly said, sounding anything but mollified. "Me own mam told how Dowanhill used to be the live-liest estate in all Yorkshire. D'you suppose there'll be more goin' on at that high-and-mighty''— Nelly covered her mouth and ducked her head—"I mean, at the duke's castle? I only wondered because he's hardly at home here in London."

"I have no idea what the duke's habits are at Franchot Castle," Pippa said. She did know that she wished she never had to find out. "His lands are beautiful—as beautiful as our Cornish property, and much larger, of course. We are neigh-bors there, I suppose. When Mama was alive we went to Cloudsmoor every summer. After . . . Well, since then, we've rarely visited Cornwall and we have never kept social com-pany with the Franchots." How odd that statement sounded, when the two families had connections reaching back for cen-turies.

"So you do know the countryside there, my lady," Nelly said.

"Quite well," Pippa agreed. "I always enjoyed exploring the wild hills around Cloudsmoor. But I do wish we could return to Dowanhill," she added, without having intended to say such a thing.

"Oh, my lady," Nelly said, and her eyes clouded with worry. "Come and sit by the fire. I'll take off those slippers and rub your feet. You always like that."

The room was done in rose tones, which Pippa liked well enough. She did not like the soaring crown canopy on the bed that made her feel as if she were lying at the bottom of a tower, or the stiffly upholstered chairs and gilt tables that did not encourage one to relax at all. Nevertheless, she did as Nelly suggested and sat in a wing chair near the fire.

"Lady Justine brought you a present," Nelly said. She nod-ded at a table to one side of the chair. "Said to tell you she hopes you won't think her forward in giving you something she made herself."

"Oh." Pippa picked up a miniature fashion doll with a rosy china face and black hair gathered into ringlets above each ear.

"Not the doll, of course," Nelly said. "She didn't make that, but she dressed it for you. Lady Justine said to explain as she saw the gown in Ackermann's Repository and she thinks you'd look lovely in one just like it.''

Nelly paused for breath, and Pippa exclaimed over the wonderful detail of the perfectly fashioned clothing. ''This is the new poppy color,'' she said of the India muslin gown. ''The gold lace trim is exquisite. I should *love* such a gown.'' And the dowager duchess would go into the vapors at the idea of Pippa's wearing anything so daringly modish.

''You'd look a treat in it, too,'' Nelly said with the rush of loyalty Pippa had already come to love. ''With your black hair and white skin, you'd be as pretty as a picture.''

Pippa smiled shyly and touched the doll's gold-and-poppy-colored crepe turban and examined the tiny pearls Justine's nimble fingers had placed as earrings. ''Lady Justine is clever,'' she said and sighed. ''And kind. I hope I can be a friend to her.''

''You've a heart of gold, my lady,'' Nelly said. ''There's not a body alive as wouldn't be proud to have you as a friend.''

Would Calum Innes be proud to have her as a friend? Pippa shook her head and cradled the doll in the crook of her arm.

Nelly lifted her mistress's feet and set them on a small stool. ''I expect you've fair danced your feet off at that ball,'' she said, removing the beige satin slippers the dowager had chosen to match the gown Pippa so disliked. ''You'll have been glad Her Grace arranged for that barley-brain of a dancing instructor to come and teach you the steps and such.''

''Yes,'' Pippa said distractedly. ''Not that he's made me less clumsy.''

''Go on with you, my lady,'' Nelly said. ''If you occasionally knock a thing or two over, it's because you're nervous, naught else. I just know you enjoyed the ball.''

Pippa could not begin to explain to practical, if romantic, Nelly that she was lonely and homesick and that her heart ached, not for London balls, but for the gardens of Dowanhill, where she'd learned to fill the solitary years of her young life and where she had created her own world.

''Were the dresses ever so lovely, my lady?''

''Ever so,'' Pippa said.

Nelly sighed hugely and ran a hand over thick blond hair

that never seemed to want to remain where it was pinned. "And the gentlemen were lovely, too?"

"You are altogether too concerned with gentlemen," Pippa observed, but kindly.

"I know." Nelly smiled and her pretty face glowed. "I'm glad I've my dreams for company. As long as you've your dreams, you're never lonely or disappointed, I always say. Of course, you don't need dreams, because your life's going to be a fairy tale, my lady."

How could a large, angry-looking man who clearly preferred the company of another female provide Pippa with a fairy-tale life, or even with a moderately pleasant one? "I think dreams are the best," she said. "Dreams are your own, and if you dream when you're awake, you've got some control over them."

Nelly, kneeling before Pippa, paused in her firm massage of her mistress's feet. "D'you dream, too, then? You sound for all the world like you know how."

"I dream," Pippa agreed, and remembered how Calum Innes's big, firm hand had felt at her waist.

"Did you dance every dance, then? Of course you did."

"I danced once," Pippa replied before she could stop herself.

"*Only once*?" Nelly dropped Pippa's foot unceremoniously onto the stool. "*Once*? Whatever did you do the rest of the time? I'd have thought the duke would keep you floating around the floor all night, just so he could show you off."

Pippa smiled and impulsively leaned over to kiss Nelly's cheek. The maid looked so taken aback, Pippa was embarrassed.

"Perhaps the duke wasn't feeling himself," Nelly suggested, resuming her massage of Pippa's feet. "Is he lovely to dance with?"

"I don't know."

Again Pippa's foot was dropped. "Y'don't know?"

"I've never danced with him."

"But you said you danced with him *once*."

Heat began building in Pippa's cheeks. "I said I danced once. I didn't say it was with the duke."

Nelly sat back on her heels and regarded Pippa with open

fascination. "You danced with someone else?" she whispered. "Another *man*?"

Pippa flipped a hand. "It was nothing."

"Did you know him before?"

"No."

"*No*? You danced with a man you didn't know? Who was he?"

The warmth in Pippa's face spread steadily over her entire body. "I told you, I don't know. And it isn't important. We won't meet again." She felt a slow, cheerless turning about her heart.

"You must have found out his name." Nelly drew up her shoulders. "Not that it's any of my business. Not that I ought to ask at all, even."

"Calum Innes." Pippa stared into the fire. "Of Scotland, I think."

"Of Scotland? Scottish gentlemen have such lovely voices, don't they?"

"Lovely," Pippa agreed. "It suits him. It's warm and low and serious. But he laughs so beautifully." Her father had been the only man in her life, and he'd never been given to laughter.

"What kind of dance did you dance?"

"A waltz."

Nelly gasped and her hands flew to her cheeks. "Go on with you. You danced a *waltz* with a man you don't know? *My lady*!"

Pippa frowned. Was that so very shocking? "Yes," she said. "He is a gentleman and the dance was delightful." That explained *that*.

"And you'd do it again," Nelly said with awe. "I can see it in your eyes. Is it as fast and free as they say—the waltz?"

"Very fast and completely free."

"But you'll not be seeing the gentleman again."

"Never."

"How can you be sure?"

"I'm sure," Pippa said, remembering the thunderous expression on the Duke of Franchot's face. "Quite sure."

"Calum's a lovely name."

"Lovely."

"I expect he was tall, my lady."

"Very tall."

"And dark?"

"His hair is dark red. Or perhaps exceedingly dark brown, but a little red when the light touches it."

Nelly sighed. "You're going to dream about him."

"Yes . . . *No*. Absolutely not!"

"Of course not," Nelly agreed quickly. "Why would you dream of a strange Scotsman when you've a dashing English duke about to make you his duchess?"

Why indeed?

"I fancy gentlemen with shoulders that don't need any padding myself," Nelly announced.

Calum's shoulders were broad and muscular. "Mmm. He wore a black evening coat. Very plain, but of perfect cut and fit. His shoulders are so . . ." She drifted for an instant. "Yes, his chest is also very nice."

"Lovely," Nelly said. "I can almost see him. Does his hair curl?"

"A little. Just enough. When he laughs, dimples show beneath his cheekbones. His face is lean and full of wit."

"Lovely," Nelly sighed. "Did you happen to notice his mouth?"

"Oh, yes. Wide. And very firm. The lower lip is fuller than the upper lip, and the very corners tip up the tiniest bit, as if he were in danger of smiling—even when he is so serious." Pippa's heart drummed; she heard the rhythm in her ears and felt it beneath her skin.

Nelly rubbed the toes of Pippa's left foot with steady concentration. "I don't suppose there was an opportunity to look at Calum Innes's legs."

"Oh, yes. Solid. I can imagine him on horseback. I'm sure he is an accomplished rider. His hair would be tossed and he'd laugh at the wind." She caught her breath and let her eyes close. "I should like to ride beside him and watch him laugh at the wind."

"But you won't see him again."

"Absolutely not. Never. I cannot, because I am to marry the duke. I am a very lucky girl."

"Very lucky. Did he say—Calum Innes, that is—did he say anything *lovely*?"

Pippa breathed in deeply. "Only that I danced like a nymph and that I flew like an imp of music through the night."

"Oh, *my lady*." Nelly sighed.

"At least he said something like that."

"Lovely." There was reverence in Nelly's voice. "But you won't ever see him again."

"Oh, no." How could it be that for a few minutes one could be so perfectly happy, then know that such minutes would never be repeated? "He wanted me to make him a promise."

"What kind of promise?"

"It was because I accused him of telling a lie—and for calling him a scoundrel." She smiled. "For flattering me. Then I apologized, but he said my apology wasn't enough."

"He wanted something more?"

Pippa worried her bottom lip. "He wanted me to say I would see him again."

Nelly stopped rubbing entirely. "And did you?"

"No. Absolutely not." She hadn't, had she? "At least I didn't really. No . . . no, not exactly."

❧ Three

𝒫ippa stood on her toes and jiggled. The morning sun teased the bobbing heads of daffodils that marched with annoying precision along the tidy pathways in the gardens behind Franchot House.

"*Bother*," Pippa said.

Nelly was instantly at her side. "Come again, my lady?" She was all smiles and rosy-cheeked good humor.

"I said, *bother*," Pippa informed the girl. "It is all such a bother. London and ugly dresses and doing what's *done* and saying what's *said* and not appearing too intelligent and—and—and these dreadful gardens!"

Nelly's smooth brow ruckled. "Dreadful? Why, they're as neat as a pin, they are. See how tidy they've planted the flowers. And how the trees match."

"Yes," Pippa agreed, scowling. "They do *match*, don't they? What, I wonder, would Mr. Capability Brown say about the way this garden *matches*? An elm to the right and an elm to the left. Not an inch more to the right than to the left. A lilac bush on that side of the path and a lilac bush on the opposite side of the path. Oh, how I miss my marvelous Downhill!"

"Because it's all so wild, you mean?" Nelly asked dubiously.

"Because it is exactly as it should be. Land made as beautiful as it can be by working with nature. All that is required

36

for the complete pleasure of the eye is the emulation of nature, Nelly. In nature, the flowers are not planted in silly rows like silly soldiers. They grow in free fields here and there and they mix, one with another. The land rises and falls—woods in one direction, open fields with grazing sheep in another, a lake in another. And always the trees . . ."

Ignoring the fine India muslin of her boring pale pink dress, she dropped to her knees and pushed her fingers into the soil. "There is nowhere to *be* here. No one who *needs* me."

"Ah," Nelly said sagely. "Now I understand, my lady. You're missing your woods. That's it, isn't it? You want a place where no one can find you, like you had at Dowanhill.

"And you did so love helping the little ones in the village. I don't suppose a duchess would be likely to spend her time giving lessons to village children."

Pippa closed her mouth tightly. She would not speak of what she had been forced to leave behind, but she would think of it nevertheless. And she would pray every night that at Franchot Castle she might manage to escape into the woods and find again some of the places she'd relished in childhood visits to Cloudsmoor.

But even if she could wander free in Cornwall and claim a special place for herself, how could she find a way to fill the empty places in her heart that had belonged to the children of Dowanhill?

Grateful for the shielding brim of her chip bonnet, Pippa closed her eyes and willed away the sadness. She was to be Her Grace the Duchess of Franchot. That would become her life's work . . . whatever that meant. It would certainly *not* mean dreaming about a man with intense dark eyes who seemed to have charmed his way into her undisciplined favor.

After a long silence, Nelly said, "I do hate to see you so unhappy. You've not been yourself since last evening. I expect you're unsettled by thinking about that fine Mr. Calum Innes."

"No such thing!" Pippa filled a fist with earth and squeezed. "I have more important matters to consider than a casual encounter with a man whose acquaintance I'm never likely to make again." She should never have mentioned him.

"Aye," Nelly said faintly. "I only thought—"

"Perhaps you should think less. Thinking in females is *not* considered particularly admirable. You'd do well to remember that. Why——" Pippa stopped and bowed her head. "Forgive my snappishness, Nelly. I'm not quite the thing today, I'm afraid."

"You've too much to deal with," Nelly said. "A body needs people of her own around her when she's t'be married. You've naught but strangers. The dowager's——well, I've no doubt she's a good heart, but it's not the same as havin' a mam of your own to tell you the way of things."

All true, but Pippa dared not allow any self-pity. If she once gave in to the panic she felt hovering just outside her composure, she would be lost.

"That dress will be ruined, my lady." The happiness had left Nelly's voice, and Pippa regretted that.

"You're right," she said brightly, springing to her feet. "Thank you for making me feel better. I'd best wash my hands and see if I can hide any damage to the dress. Come along, Nelly. I don't suppose you've seen an apron anywhere in this bothersome house?"

"Aprons aplenty," Nelly responded. "But they all belong to maids."

Pippa looked toward the house and wrinkled her nose. "Here comes Finch." She glanced from the approaching butler to her skirts and noted, with dismay, that muddy spots marked the place where she'd knelt. "Oh, this is all *such* a bother," she mumbled.

Finch arrived at a stately pace and bowed as he offered her a single card upon a silver tray.

"Thank you, Finch," Pippa said, and winced as dirt from her fingers smeared the card and dusted the shimmering tray.

The corner of the card was turned down.

Lord-a-mercy! At this moment, while Pippa stood in the gardens of Franchot House, her hands and dress filthy, Mr. Calum Innes, of Hanover Square, stood inside that house awaiting Pippa's response.

"My lady?" Finch inquired in his reverberating baritone. *Here*.

Was the duke at home? She didn't know. She knew almost nothing at all about him. Only yesterday——at precisely noon——she had encountered him on the stairway as he returned from a night's revelry. He hadn't as much as wished her a good day.

"My lady?" Finch repeated.

What if the duke were at home and he chanced to appear in the hallway and see Mr. Innes?

What if the duke returned while Mr. Innes stood in the hallway?

"Oh, bother," Pippa said.

"My lady?" Finch inquired.

"Yes," she said, completely befuddled. The duke had been so angry with Mr. Innes for dancing with her that he'd been about to call him out!

Finch had already turned away and begun to retrace his steps to the house.

"This is desperate," Pippa said, looking wildly around. "Disastrous. Devastating. Calamitous. Catastrophic. *Finch*!"

Finch, well on his way back to the house, didn't even check his stride.

"Oh, bother, bother, *bother*." Pippa whirled about, and whirled again. She stood, her fingers twined tightly together, staring toward the terrace.

"What is it?" Nelly asked. "What's disastrous . . . and all those other horrible things?"

"It's—" No, she must be calm. A clear head had always been her most valued asset. God knew she had none of the other attributes a young lady needed to be a success—except the silly dowry that had brought her to this frightful fix. "I must return to the house at once. Come with me, Nelly. Whatever you do, remain calm."

"Yes—"

"Show no sign of agitation." Pippa's feet flew along the pathway. "It would be best to appear slightly bored, as if whatever is happening—*if* anything happens—as if this were the type of thing that occurs every day. Do you understand?"

"No."

They'd reached the steps leading to the terrace and Pippa glanced anxiously at Nelly before racing up, crossing the terrace and entering the lush conservatory that was her favorite spot in the house. "I shall simply have to tell Finch to send him away," she said. "At once. Before the unspeakable can occur."

Pippa had walked almost the length of a palm-lined aisle when a deep masculine voice said, "No need at all to announce me. I'll find my own way from here."

She stopped, looking for an escape, and Nelly ran into her heels.

He appeared in the doorway, took the two stairs down into the conservatory in a single stride and saw Pippa.

In daylight, with plant shadows playing over his features, he was even more compelling than she recalled.

The absolutely best thing for this hazardous moment would be to pretend she did not even remember him.

"Good morning, Lady Philipa," he said.

Her heart had surely stopped.

"I do hope I'm not calling too early."

Her heart had definitely stopped. His cheekbones slanted. She hadn't noted that, or if she had, there had been so many other things to contemplate that she'd forgotten. Yes, he did have the most marvelous cheekbones. And she hadn't made as perfect a memory picture of his mouth as it deserved. If a man's mouth could be said to be beautiful, then she would most certainly say it of Calum Innes's mouth. Sharply defined along its edges, the lips curved most . . . most . . . they *curved*.

And his eyes were almost black, with curling lashes . . . Black and penetrating and . . . questioning?

Pippa remembered her plan and half-turned away. "This is the way to the gardens, sir. Possibly you intended to go the other way? Or perhaps you are in entirely the wrong house?" Ooh, how foolish that sounded.

Mr. Innes inclined his head. "I think not."

"I *know* not," Nelly announced suddenly. "You're not seeing plain, my lady. I told you not to stand out there staring into the sun. It's affected your sight. It's Mr. Calum Innes. I'd know him anywhere."

Pippa folded her arms around her middle and tried not to cringe.

"Look at him," Nelly instructed. "Very tall with very broad shoulders. No need for padding, my lady. Just like we talked about."

"Nelly, I don't think—"

"I know, my lady. And I'm trying hard to do as you told me and stop thinking, too. But it's hard. There is red in his hair. And his legs—"

"*Nelly*!"

The maid dropped a hasty curtsy and said, "Yes, my lady," before withdrawing a few yards.

Pippa turned back to Mr. Innes. "Forgive me," she said. "As Nelly said, the sun . . . Oh, what complete twaddle! Of course I know who you are. I knew who you were the moment you appeared . . . before you appeared. Finch brought your card, so naturally I knew."

"Please," he said, so very gently. "Don't overset yourself. I have surprised you."

"That is no excuse for playacting and falsehood," she told him. "My father always insists upon honesty, and I've liked him for it. Honesty sets out the proper way of things. Honesty makes living inside oneself more comfortable."

"No doubt," Mr. Innes agreed.

"I was flummoxed because the duke was angry with you last night—with *us*. When Finch brought your card, I was immediately concerned that His Grace might see you and renew his attempts to duel with you." There, she had been truthful, and . . . and it did not make her feel one whit less afraid.

Mr. Innes's expression had set into deeply serious lines. Pippa decided she liked his face as much when he was serious as when he laughed.

He came close and rested a booted foot atop the low wall that contained planting beds. Leaning forward—very close to Pippa—he propped a forearm upon his thigh.

Mr. Innes had strong-looking thighs, with long, hard muscles that flexed along the top . . . and beneath. His bespoke top boots fitted snug to equally strong-looking calves.

Pippa shifted her eyes from Mr. Innes's braced leg to the ground.

"Lady Philipa," he said, "what did the Duke of Franchot say to you last night?"

"Nothing."

"*I* am not an angry man, my lady. And, like you, I prefer

honesty whenever there is a choice. Tell me how the duke showed you his anger.''

She did not know how to answer him.

His touch, light on her cheek—fingertips brushing to her jaw and on to the point of her chin—made Pippa draw a quick breath. Still she could not look at him.

''I want to know if you are being treated unkindly,'' he said.

She shook her head. ''No. No, I am not being treated at all.'' Fie, why did she find herself telling this man whatever came into her head?

A purposeful tug on her bonnet ribbons startled her and she did glance up. ''Mr. Innes?''

''Lady Philipa?'' The ribbons were loosed and he swept the bonnet off. ''There is little sun in here. And you have the loveliest hair. It is too bad to cover it.''

Pippa blushed and looked around for Nelly—just in time to see the girl slip from the conservatory and onto the terrace.

''So you described me to your maid.''

The blush throbbed. ''Yes, I did. I told her we danced a waltz, too.''

''I'm flattered. With all the men you must have danced with, it cannot be easy to remember every one.''

''I danced only with you and you know it. Now you are being dishonest.''

''Perhaps. Nevertheless, I am flattered. I came to satisfy myself that you were safe.''

Pippa frowned at him. ''Why would I not be safe?''

''You said yourself that the duke was angry. I feared he might speak harshly to you.''

''He never speaks to me at all,'' Pippa responded promptly. ''I mean . . . To be truthful, Mr. Innes, the duke and I are barely acquainted. Actually, we are not acquainted at all. We were betrothed at the time of my birth. Apart from our both being present at several gatherings when I was a small child, we had not met until four weeks ago.''

He still stood exceedingly close. His eyes changed with the light; sometimes they were black, but sometimes they glinted almost dark green. ''The duke is very fortunate,'' he finally said. "When he saw you four weeks ago, he must have marveled at his luck."

"You are a shameless flatterer," Pippa said, but she smiled—just a little.

"I tell the truth." His gaze shifted to her mouth. "There is a sweetness in you. I think that sweetness, once tasted, would bind a man to you in his need to taste again and again."

Pippa was unschooled in the art of coquetry. She knew nothing of the light, feminine chatter she'd been told was expected at moments when men spoke pretty words they could not possibly mean. She did know that this was a moment that should not be happening.

"I would like to be your friend, my lady," he said, his voice vibrantly, softly, deep. "Do not fear me. I will never hurt you."

"No." The headiness she felt must come from the moist air in the conservatory. "I know you would not hurt me. But it would be best if you did not say these things."

"You tell me the duke does not speak to you. Why is that?"

Pippa fought for breath. "I don't know."

"He has not told you how beautiful you are?"

"No. But I am not beautiful. Pleasant to look at, I believe, but nothing more."

"You are beautiful." He leaned a little closer. "There is no artifice in you. No guile. Can you imagine how intoxicating a man might find a woman such as you?"

"I . . . No." She should move away.

"The duke doesn't even say pretty things to you when he kisses you?"

Pippa wrinkled her nose. "He has *not* kissed me, sir."

Closer. His beautiful mouth came closer, and his eyes were like night on deep water. "He has not even tried?"

She didn't wish to think of that. "No. Yes, but . . . He did not exactly . . . *kiss* me."

"You didn't want him to kiss you?"

"No." Ooh, the trembling in her stomach was very queer, and in her legs, too.

Mr. Calum Innes's mouth touched Pippa's so lightly that when her eyes drifted shut, she was not certain there had been a touch at all.

"Mr.—"

"Calum," he said against her lips, stopping whatever else she might have said. "I should very much like to kiss you, my lady. If I may?"

Pippa shut her eyes tightly and tipped her face up to his.

He'd spoken of sweetness. Did he know how sweet his own mouth tasted? Did he know that as his lips moved carefully on hers, Pippa's skin tingled? The very tip of his tongue passed along the soft, exquisitely tender place where her lips were slightly parted.

How sweet. How gentle. How she must stay here, like this, with his mouth on hers—*forever*.

Their breath joined.

Pippa breathed him in, and felt him take back air that had been hers.

His hand settled at her waist, slid around, eased her against him until her hips met the place where his hard thighs joined. There were shapes and textures to him that were different. Pippa had never been held close by a man, had certainly *never* seen a man unclothed, but from the feel of Calum Innes, that might be quite . . . stimulating?

"Lovely," he said against the corner of her mouth. "So lovely. I should like to hold you—really hold you."

"You *are* holding me." Pippa looked into his eyes and saw pure black now. Her heart flipped over, and her stomach. The strangest sensations were deep inside her, and she knew that only Calum Innes could be and do whatever those sensations demanded. Seeking, she followed his face with her own until she could place her mouth beneath his once more. "Please kiss me again," she whispered.

"Gladly." This time the quality of the kiss changed. His lips were at first delicately teasing, then firmer, more insistent.

He rubbed her back, lifted her hair to stroke her neck and brought his hands to rest beneath her arms.

Pippa stopped breathing. His thumbs had settled on the sides of her breasts. Slowly, he rubbed the soft flesh that no man had ever touched in such a way. She slipped her hands up his arms and around his neck, and wished this could go on and on.

A thunderous crash shocked Pippa rigid.

In a voice that jarred her spine, the Duke of Franchot roared, "In God's name! If this don't beat all! In me own house! Unhand her, you cad, and face me."

Instantly Calum Innes made to set her from him.

Pippa clung. She clung to his neck, dropped her head back, rolled up her eyes and plummeted toward the ground with the full force of her insubstantial weight. The result was exactly as planned. Mr. Innes swept her up into his arms.

"Hell and damnation," the duke sputtered. "Ravishin' me betrothed in me own conservatory. Last night you were saved, you cur. Now I shall have what I intended then. But not until you tell me what you hope to gain by pursuin' my intended."

Pippa began to pant and sigh. She brought her eyes into focus on Calum's face and sighed. "Oh, thank you, sir. I cannot think what came over me. I do not normally swoon, I assure you."

"Swoon?" the duke snapped. "No doubt this blackguard frightened you into a swoon. Creep up on you, did he? How did he get into this house, that's what I'd like to know? And where's Grandmama? And that fool of a maid of yours?"

"I'm here, Your Grace," Nelly said from somewhere behind Pippa. "My lady fainted dead away. We were coming in on account of her feeling the sun, and she swooned. This gentleman was just catching her. Wasn't it lucky how he was here when—"

"Enough of this foolishness," the duke broke in. Still dressed in the clothes he'd worn to the ball at Chandos House the previous night, he hauled Pippa unceremoniously from Mr. Innes's arms and stalked into the sitting room behind the conservatory. "I'll thank you to say nothing more, my lady," he announced, setting her down with a thud on a rose-colored chaise.

"I don't advise you to hurt her, Franchot."

Mr. Innes's words rang in the high-ceilinged room. Terrible words that spelled awful consequences. Pippa watched the duke's face as he slowly straightened. His blue eyes met hers and she saw the man's deep coldness. And she saw that although he looked at her, he did not see her.

"I beg your pardon?" he said, facing Mr. Innes. "Surely I

have misheard you. You could not possibly have told me how to deal with my fiancée.''

"If warning you to be gentle with her falls into the category of telling you how to behave, then yes, *Your Grace*. Yes, I told you how to deal with a gentle lady."

"Insolent swine," the duke said. "Name your seconds—"

"Etienne!" Lady Justine hurried into the room, her limp more pronounced than usual. "Etienne, there you are. I have been awaiting you all morning."

Pippa stared at her future sister-in-law in amazement. Never, in the four weeks since they'd met, had that lady shown the slightest animation or disquiet over anything. Justine was, Pippa had decided almost upon their first meeting, the most painfully withdrawn and possibly the most unhappy woman she had ever met.

The duke's perplexed expression suggested he was as surprised as Pippa by his sister's agitated appearance. "Are you ill?" he said, and sounded as if he might actually be concerned.

"I . . . no."

"You are quite winded, Justine." The duke, his grand evening garb showing signs of the many hours that had passed since he had donned it, cast a glare at Mr. Innes before approaching his sister and eyeing her closely. "You do not look yourself. Your face is flushed. Are you feverish?"

Justine pressed her thin hands to her cheeks. "I am well, thank you," she said, and this time her voice shook a little. "It's just that I have grown unsettled waiting for your return. There are some important things that I think we should talk about."

"*Now*?" Disbelief coated the duke's voice. "Can't you see there is a matter of consequence occurring here?"

"There most certainly is," Justine agreed. The limp did not detract from her dignity as she went to seat herself at the foot of Pippa's chaise. "Introduce our guest, please."

Silence followed the request.

Justine's dark hair was thick, and despite all efforts to restrain it, curls always sprang free around her face. It was assumed that, at thirty-four, she was doomed to spinsterhood, yet Pippa never looked at Justine's striking face and tall, slender form without thinking that there must be many a man who would be proud to have her at his side.

At this moment, Lady Justine Girvin looked positively blooming and . . . Pippa was suddenly certain that this even-tempered, perpetually serene and mannered lady was *furious*.

"*Introduce* him?" The duke looked around as if for an explanation of his sister's insane behavior.

"I believe it is usual to introduce visitors, Etienne."

Justine drew herself up very straight, and Pippa's eyes were drawn to the remarkable spectacle of several leaves caught in the back of the other woman's hair. Pippa glanced at Justine's feet and saw what she expected to see—damp slippers.

The pieces fell together. Justine must have been in the con-servatory when . . . Pippa felt herself blush. Justine had very probably hidden among the plants and seen Mr. Innes kissing Pippa. Afterward, when the duke had stormed in, his sister must have raced outside and across the still-damp grass to the door that would allow her the speediest access to the house.

So that she could arrive in time to interrupt the duke's in-evitable angry tirade? How extraordinary.

"This is Mr. Calum Innes," Pippa heard herself say. "Mr. Innes, this is my future sister-in-law, Lady Justine Girvin."

"It's a great pleasure to meet you, Mr. Innes," Lady Justine said in a strong voice quite unlike her own. "Should you care for some refreshment?"

The duke made a sputtering sound.

Mr. Innes, who until the arrival of Lady Justine had ap-peared for all the world to be as calm as if he were seated at the breakfast table reading his morning paper and about to enjoy a plate of buttered eggs, simply watched Lady Justine and said absolutely nothing.

"Where do you make your home, Mr. Innes?" Justine asked.

Pippa stared at her.

The duke gaped.

From a corner came a snuffle that reminded Pippa of Nel-ly's presence.

"My home . . ." Mr. Innes took a step toward Justine and reached for her hand. When she gave it to him without hesi-tation, he held it and looked into her face intently. "Recently

I have been living in Hanover Square, my lady. I grew up at Castle Kirkcaldy in Scotland. Lord Stonehaven—the father of the present marquess—accepted me into his household when I was a small boy and became my guardian. I was a foundling, ma'am.''

Justine smiled, an event so remarkable that Pippa's hand went to her throat. When Justine smiled, her dark eyes shone and dimples appeared in her cheeks.

"From the way you speak of him, I would say you greatly admired your guardian, Mr. Innes," she said. "I appreciate your openness about your beginnings. Many men would not be so forthcoming."

Justine liked Calum Innes.

Pippa swallowed and tried to order her thoughts. Justine liked him for the man she had instinctively perceived him to be, not in the romantic manner that had drawn Pippa . . . She caught the tip of her tongue between her teeth. There could be no excuse for allowing such thoughts.

"You have hurt your leg, my lady," Mr. Innes said. He still held Justine's hand—in both of his now. "Were you injured recently or very long ago?"

Nobody mentioned Lady Justine's limp.

"Look here," the duke sputtered. "Kindly remove yourself from my sister's presence. At once. Dashed impertinence, asking personal questions of a lady. Embarrassin' questions, too. Come with me and we'll finish arrangin' our business."

"It happened at Franchot," Lady Justine said, as if her brother hadn't spoken. "Franchot Castle. It's in Cornwall. On the coast. We used to go with our nurse to the beach."

"No need to drag all that up now," the duke said loudly.

Pippa studied him and felt sick. His face was red, his eyes puffy. She had seen gentlemen of her father's acquaintance appear thus. Papa had always been most disparaging after their departure, speaking about the evils of strong drink and what he termed "careless living." Pippa wasn't sure what "careless living" was, but she suspected the Duke of Franchot indulged in it to a considerable degree.

Using Mr. Innes's hands to steady her, Lady Justine got to her feet. "My leg became trapped between rocks. The tide was coming in. The more I struggled, the more trapped I became."

"All over with now," the duke said.

"Yes," Lady Justine agreed. "All over with now. My leg was broken in that complicated way young children's limbs break, and it did not heal well." She gave Mr. Innes's hands a firm shake and removed her own. "But I did not drown, so all is well, you see."

Mr. Innes was very quiet. He continued to study Lady Justine intently, and Pippa had the strangest feeling that he liked her, too.

"Very well," the duke said. "Since you ladies seem determined to turn a serious event into some sort of polite circus, I shall simply have to finish business here. Name your seconds, sir."

"I believe I feel much better," Pippa said. Rapidly and not particularly gracefully, she scrambled to her feet and addressed the duke. "Your Grace, there has been a misunderstanding. Mr. Innes came here because he was concerned about the events of last evening. Isn't that so, Mr. Innes?"

Calum's gaze shifted to her. "That's so."

Pippa stood beside him and rested a hand on his arm. She knew her mistake when the mere warmth of him made her feel a little numb all over. "Um, Mr. Innes is a most reasonable man." Her eyes met his and she swayed toward him a little. He covered her hand on his arm.

"Look here!" the duke said. "I don't know what kind of man you think you're dealing with, but I'll have no more of it. You are trifling with the affections of the woman who is to become my duchess, and I demand satisfaction."

"And you'll have it," Pippa said, silently beseeching Mr. Innes to cooperate. "Won't he, Mr. Innes? You'll explain how you came to—"

"To apologize," Lady Justine announced, also on her feet. "Mr. Innes came to apologize for any offense he may unwittingly have committed, Etienne. Isn't that a sensible gesture?"

"Very sensible," Pippa agreed. She could not help staring at Mr. Innes's mouth—and remembering how it had felt and tasted upon hers. "Lady Justine has the entire episode exactly right. Mr. Innes came to ask you to forgive and forget, Your Grace.''

"Above his station," the duke muttered. "But under the circumstances, I can be a generous man. Just be certain I never set eyes upon you again, Innes.''

Mr. Calum Innes gently disengaged himself from Pippa and moved across soft, rosy silk carpet to stand before the duke. "I intend," he said, "to be certain that you lay nothing *but* your eyes upon me, sir. *Ever*. I believe dawn is the preferred hour. Tomorrow. In the absence of another, Viscount Hunsingore will stand as my only friend. Since the choice is mine, we shall use pistols.''

❧ *Four*

"*I knew* I should never have agreed," Struan said morosely. He sat huddled in a corner of the shabby hackney carriage Calum had secured to drive them in anonymity to Whitechapel.

Preoccupied with the events that lay ahead this night and at dawn, Calum barely heard Struan's lament—one of a stream of laments kept up since Calum's return from Pall Mall in the early afternoon.

They were on their way to see a brother and sister he had tracked during his search for his true identity. These two followed the fair circuit around the country, selling preparations "guaranteed" to accomplish all sorts of marvelous results, from curing the ague to rendering an ugly nose a thing of beauty. Milo and Miranda—they denied any other names—could very well hold the key to what Calum sought. That they would readily give him that key was gravely in doubt.

"When will I learn to follow my own very good judgment?" Struan persisted. "After all, I'm a man to whom others have been known to turn for advice. And I've given it and been congratulated for my level head. A reasonable man. A reliable man. A—"

"A man who is about to be throttled if he doesn't keep his sermons to himself," Calum interrupted. "A man who seems to have forgotten that only last year he returned to Castle Kirkcaldy pretending he was still a priest."

"But that was—"

"That was what many would have called sacrilege. You came home and allowed Arran to believe the entire responsibility for producing an heir and maintaining the estates in the family continued to rest upon his shoulders. You *tricked* him into marriage."

"*I?*" All trace of apathy left Struan and he pushed forward to sit on the edge of the seat. "*I* tricked him? By God, that's rum. *You* came to London and *secured* a bride for Arran. *You* tricked him into believing she fully understood what an impossible recluse he is. And you'd already tricked *her* into believing she was marrying an old man who would want nothing from her other than a cool hand on his brow and a few soothing words to ease him through the remaining days of his life." Struan paused for breath before continuing. "And you told poor Grace that Arran's remaining days would be short."

"Finished?" Calum asked pleasantly.

"Yes."

"I tricked no one," Calum said. "I merely worked a little magic—more by what I didn't say than by what I did say—and I brought two wonderful people together. Do you deny that Grace Wren was the perfect choice as Arran's wife?"

Struan mumbled something, then said, "No, I don't."

"Do you deny that Arran and only Arran could have made the perfect husband for Grace?"

"Enough of this," Struan snapped. "Let's get back to the business at hand."

"*Is* Arran a good husband to Grace and an admirable father to their daughter?"

"He's been a father only for a few weeks. But yes. Yes, Arran and Grace bring me as much pleasure as they bring you. Not that I see what this has to do with the fiasco you have brought upon us. A *duel*, in God's name. *A duel*!"

Calum grimly resolved to avoid that topic at present and said, "You made an accusation."

"*I?* It was you who called my behavior sacrilegious."

"And so it was, but enough of that." Calum peered through soot-coated windows at the jumble of mean buildings they passed. The night streets were as busy here in the city's East End as they'd been up west, but there was little similarity

between the nobs coming and going around Hanover Square
and the present ragtag company.

"I do not regret visiting Pall Mall this morning," Calum
said, thinking aloud. "I would do it again."

"If only you'd said something. *I* would have found a way
to stop you."

Calum did not bother to argue that no one could have
stopped him. "Lady Philipa is beautiful."

Struan beat a tattoo on his thigh with his fingers. "I think
there is some wisdom that suggests that beauty is a subjective
issue. You should never have gone there."

Duel aside, his encounter of the morning had left Calum
more shaken than he could have imagined possible. "She
cares nothing for that man," he remarked.

A disgusted grunt was Struan's only response.

"I believe she hates him."

Another grunt.

"He needs her. Without the security her dowry brings to
his affairs, his fortune would eventually begin to dwindle."

"This is nothing to me *or* to you."

"It may become a great deal to me," Calum said curtly.
"Clearly the lady does not hate *me*."

Struan's face came up. "What are you implying?"

What was he implying? That he could and would take Franchot's place with Lady Philipa? "I was merely voicing my
thoughts," he said finally. Franchot needed Lady Philipa; he
did not *want* her, of that Calum was certain. The possibility
of taking what the man needed held great appeal.

"I must find a way to turn you from this folly," Struan
said.

Calum barely heard his friend's words. Could he bring himself to use Lady Philipa Chauncey? For the pleasure of having
an advantage over Franchot? A huge advantage?

"With your death arranged for the dawn, we now go in
search of your so-called witnesses," Struan said. "I cannot
believe I allowed you to trick me into this little escapade."

"I did not trick you. I told you I was leaving. You did not
want me to go alone. I said you might come also, and here
you are—to my discomfort."

Struan scowled. "How much farther do we have to go?"

"We'll be there soon enough. I hope I've calculated the dates correctly."

"I hope you haven't," Struan muttered. "It isn't too late to turn back."

Calum thought for a while, then said, "It was too late when it first began. And that was before you were even born."

"If only you would abandon all this, Calum. The pieces seem to fit, but you cannot be sure of these stories you have been told."

"So you say," Calum replied. "Yet I *am* sure. And after you hear them for yourself, you will not be so quick to put them aside."

"We shall see," Struan said. "Are you finally prepared to tell me what passed between you and the Hoarville woman last night?"

"Whitechapel High Street lies ahead." Calum didn't want to think about the proposition Lady Hoarville had made.

"Dash it, Calum, you are a sly dog. First you spend years secretly gathering all this information on your so-called beginnings—"

"They *were* my beginnings."

"Perhaps. Then you run off to God knows where, following fairs and traveling players. Hell and damnation, man, how can you expect us to take the word of some witch-doctoring pair seriously?"

"They aren't witch doctors. They make charms and . . . and spells," he finished under his breath.

"Exactly. Witch doctors. Look here, old chap, you're obviously very keen for any story you can believe. These mountebanks ply their trade by feeding the desperate needs of others."

Making fists on his thighs, Calum turned his attention entirely upon Struan. "Damn you," he said furiously. "I owe my life to the Stonehavens, but I don't owe *you* the right to call me a fool."

"I didn't call—"

"That is exactly what you have called me."

Struan bridled. "You are entirely too defensive. And it is that defensiveness which convinces me I am right. You have been duped by these charlatans, and unless someone intercedes, the road you are choosing to follow will lead to dire consequences.'' He took off his hat and tossed it down beside him. "*Deadly* consequences, even. If you insist upon going through with this dueling madness in the morning, you may be fortunate enough to escape with nothing more than a wound. But if you then insist upon confronting Franchot with some outrageous announcement about the circumstances of his birth, the man *will call you out again.*''

"Let him.''

"In God's name! Think, man. Franchot's reputation is legendary. He's said to have killed three men and wounded too many others to count. If you force his hand a second time, you may depend he'll add you to his list of deceased enemies. And this supposes you would not merely be gathered up— wound and all—and tossed into a madhouse with nothing but screeching lunatics as companions.''

Calum swallowed with difficulty. "I am perfectly sane.''

"You know you are. *I* know you are. But a man who has lived his life as a duke, accepted by all as a duke, would doubtless get an audience for his view that you were not in possession of your senses if you demanded to take his place.

"These people we supposedly go to see, how much did you pay them for their little story?''

"I . . .'' Damn Struan. He had the ability to make even Calum doubt what he knew to be true. "I gave them a small token of my thanks for their help. Nothing more.''

"I knew it,'' Struan exclaimed. "And I'll wager they are rubbing their hands this night while they wait for the next installment from their latest fat pigeon.''

"They do not know I'm coming,'' Calum blurted out.

The carriage wheels bounced into a deep rut, throwing Struan forward. Calum caught his arm and shoved him upright.

"You told me,'' Struan said, altogether too calmly, "that this Milo and Miranda had rooms on the Whitechapel High Street and that they would be there this evening.''

"Yes. I didn't say they knew I was coming to see them.''

"How do you know they will be there at all?''

Calum filled his lungs while he thought about his next announcement. "They live in a certain lady's house. I visited there several days ago and ascertained that she expected them to return today. Evidently they use their London rooms to prepare the—er—preparations they sell at fairs and markets.''

''You do not think it might have been more appropriate to send word and arrange a meeting?''

''No.''

''So adamant?''

''They might not have agreed to see me.''

Struan made an exasperated noise. ''You speak in riddles. First I understood that you were all but expected, then that you were simply playing a game of chance as to whether these creatures will be available. Now you lead me to believe that they may have some reason to refuse to see you at all.''

''You did not have to come with me,'' Calum said, feeling truculent.

''I most certainly did. Someone must attempt to save you from your own folly, and in consideration of that noble aim, I propose we have the driver turn about and return us to Hanover Square. And then we will arrange to leave London before morning.''

As Struan finished speaking, the hackney rumbled to a swaying stop and the driver yelled, '' 'Ere you are, guvs.''

Before Struan could argue further, Calum jumped down from the carriage and paid the fare. ''Await our return,'' he told the coachman. ''You'll be well compensated for your trouble.''

''Damn foolishness,'' Struan said, joining Calum in the rubbish-strewn gutter. ''What the hell is this place?''

The place was a narrow, five-story building squished between similar neighbors. Similar in size and proportion, but in no other manner.

The ground floor of Mrs. Lushbottam's establishment sported two lighted bay windows separated by a gilded front door at which twin bronzed cats stood sentry duty. A sign prominently displayed in one window promised: THE PERFECT SIZE AND SHAPE FOR EVERY GENTLEMAN. OUR LADY TAILORS FIT TO YOUR DEMANDS. WE WELCOME THE MOST SINGULAR DESIGNS. NO REQUEST DENIED.

''Good Lord,'' Struan murmured. ''A brothel.''

In each of the rosily illuminated windows sat two women, apparently talking over their sewing.

"Innovative, wouldn't you say?" Calum said, deliberately offhand. "And quite *the* establishment among a certain set— has been for many years, so I'm told. I understand the resident ladies enjoy challenge. Apparently they cater particularly effectively to the exceptionally large gentleman. So Mrs. Lushbottam told me, anyway."

Struan twirled his hat on his cane and cocked an eyebrow. "In that case, it's doubtful we'll encounter great competition to ascertain our measurements."

Calum grinned and tipped the brim of his own hat lower over his eyes. "No competition at all, old friend. Some things are obvious. But I shall as ever be humble when I place myself in the hands of the grateful winner."

He ducked beneath Struan's playful swing and dashed to rap at the gilded door. "Observe," he said. "Even now they clamor about who will best accommodate the astonishing demands my proportions present, to say nothing of the quality of the material a Corinthian like me commands."

"We shall continue this . . ." His lips still parted, Struan paused to stare directly into the great brown eyes of an olive-skinned beauty who had risen from her chair to stand next to the window. "Good God," he murmured. "What an exotic creature."

Calum rapped again.

"Look at her, Calum."

He did look, just as the dark-haired female spread a slender, long-fingered hand on the glass. With her other hand she gathered a black velvet cloak tightly together at her neck, all the while staring intently at Struan. Calum swallowed and said, "We are here to attend to business."

"Indeed," Struan said, sounding breathless. "How fortunate that part of that business is to enjoy the simple pleasure of looking at scenes along the way."

"*Look*," Calum said, doing so himself. "But do not think of doing anything more. This is no place to tarry for reasons other than that which brought us here."

Struan wasn't listening. "Calum, I want to meet her."

"*Meet* her?" Calum said, disbelieving. "A man doesn't *meet* women like her. She's a—"

"*Don't* say it. Her face is like none I have ever seen. She is a work of art."

At last the door opened, and Calum all but prayed his thanks aloud. Hooking his arm unceremoniously through Struan's, he hauled him to confront the overwhelming Mrs. Lushbottam.

"Good evening, madam," Calum said, bowing and exerting pressure on Struan's arm to ensure he did likewise. "You will perhaps remember that I called two weeks ago?"

When the woman didn't answer, he slowly looked up, all the way up to her thin, darkly roughed cheeks, heavily painted brows and mottled nose, a nose that cleared the top of his own head by an inch or more. Mrs. Lushbottam was at least six and a half feet tall. Her shoulders were narrow, her chest concave and her hips nonexistent. She wore a severely cut black silk gown inlaid with gussets of heavy lace. The same lace was employed as a mantilla attached to the black bone comb skewered into dull black hair atop her head.

Finally she sonorously inquired, "You came for a fitting?"

Calum turned a laugh into a cough.

"Yes," Struan said quickly. "A fitting."

"*No*," Calum said, equally quickly, glowering at his companion. "No, thank you, Mrs. Lushbottam. Unfortunately, we don't have time to avail ourselves of the, er, your talented staff tonight. Don't you remember me? I was here in January and again two weeks ago. On that latter occasion you informed me that your lodgers were due to return about now. Did they? Return?"

"Possibly." Her voice had the quality of a low-pitched wind gusting in a stovepipe.

"What is her name?" Struan asked suddenly, stepping into the house and drawing Calum with him.

"I told you," Calum said, becoming infuriated. "Mrs. *Lushbottam.*" That lady had moved aside and folded her arms.

"No," Struan responded, and Calum discovered it was not at Mrs. Lushbottam that his friend looked. "*Her* name? Mrs. Lushbottam, may I please meet that girl?"

The girl Struan spoke of had stepped through a door that closed the bay window off from the square vestibule into which the front door opened. She trailed fluidly across a thick carpet patterned with huge pink roses and lattices of green leaves.

"Milo and Miranda," Calum said, growing truly disturbed by the intensity in Struan's dark eyes, in the lean lines of his face. "Mrs. Lushbottam, may I take it that they are at home?"

"Why not go up and see?" she told him. "Top floor. I'm sure you remember the way."

"Yes, yes. Thank you. Come, Struan. It's growing very late."

He started up the stairs, but realized Struan wasn't with him. "Come on, man," he said impatiently. "We have things to accomplish this night."

"Mmm."

"Things to accomplish," Calum repeated loudly.

"You like what you see," Mrs. Lushbottam said to Struan. Satisfaction coated her words. "Ella is not one of my regular craftswomen."

"No," Struan said indistinctly. He walked toward the girl as if she were a fisherman drawing in a line and he the fish she had caught. "Ella? A graceful name. It suits you."

"As I said," Mrs. Lushbottam continued, "Ella is a most unusual treasure who has been entrusted to me."

Calum shook his head in frustration. Struan had always been the idealist. It had been that idealism that had won him, if only for a short time, for the Church.

"May I . . ." Struan did not take his gaze from the young woman. "Could I talk to you?"

"She talks to no one," Mrs. Lushbottam announced. "She owes her safety—her very life—to me. That is my affair alone. But she talks to no one."

Calum's interest was aroused. "Come now, madam. Mystery is all very well, but surely we are not dealing with anything more unusual than a"—he glanced at Struan—"a lovely creature who is one of your better sources of income?"

"No!"

Mrs. Lushbottam's pronouncement stilled Struan, who had taken an aggressive step toward Calum.

"Ella is an innocent," Mrs. Lushbottam said. "She will

remain an innocent until . . . until *I* receive the right offer for her. Until then, she is under my protection.''

Calum tasted the acid of disgust. The old crone had acquired a prize and she intended to sell that prize to the highest bidder. ''Struan,'' he said warningly, reading his friend's mind, ''this is a night filled with odd adventures. Let us take the time we need to consider what they all mean. *Later*. For now, come with me.''

Mrs. Lushbottam clicked her fingers at Ella, and the girl glided away through double doors into a room from which came female laughter and the rumble of male voices.

''I will join you later,'' Struan said.

''An excellent idea,'' Mrs. Lushbottam said. ''You go on up, Mr. Innes. Your friend will be in good hands—down here.''

''*Struan*,'' Calum said, noting that the proprietress had remembered him well enough from his last visit to recall his name. ''I need you with me for this—*discussion*.''

''They aren't back yet,'' Mrs. Lushbottam said, her thin chest rising on a sigh. ''You can always wait with your friend here.''

Infuriated, Calum went to Struan's side. ''You told me they were in their rooms, madam.''

''I told you to see if they were.''

''But you know they are not.''

She scowled, drawing her heavy brows together over very pale, deep-set eyes. ''The affairs of those two are not *my* affairs. They pay their rent and don't give me any trouble. That's all I've got to say on the matter.'' She seemed to consider before adding, ''Stay or go. It makes no matter to me. But I will tell you that they'll return within the hour. Come back then, if you like.''

Struan continued to stare at the door through which Ella had disappeared. ''We will wait, thank you,'' he said with a short, hard look at Calum. ''Come. What can it hurt to spend an hour in the pleasant company of Mrs. Lushbottam's lady tailors? I find I have been too long removed from a little stimulation.''

''Well,'' Mrs. Lushbottam said in a confidential tone, ''if it's stimulation you want, sirs, then by all means, do become my guests. I think you will find the quality of what we offer unusually fine." She concentrated on Struan. "And for you, there may be a most intriguing opportunity."

Calum considered arguing further, but discovered he was more than vaguely curious about what lay on the other side of the double doors. "You will inform us when Milo and Miranda return?" he asked.

Mrs. Lushbottam waved them regally before her. "I'll let you know, sirs."

Five

The room beyond the doors was surprisingly large and appeared to occupy most of the ground floor of the house. Calum had seen his share of pleasure houses and, despite the rumors he'd heard to the contrary, had expected nothing more than a display of faded prostitutes disporting themselves with men unable to afford a higher-class establishment.

But this was no collection of either overused doxies or men with shallow pockets.

"Gad," Struan muttered, inclining his head toward a company of brilliantly dressed men and women—some of whom Calum recalled seeing at Chandos House the previous evening—who lounged drunkenly on divans arranged in a circle. "Isn't that . . . ? Bloody hell, it *is*. Our princely host himself."

"I had no idea," Calum said as several of the company noticed his arrival with Struan and offered knowing nods of greeting. "Damn, but this is irony. I'll lay odds Franchot wouldn't be a stranger here. And I'll lay equal odds he'd expire if he knew what is known by the people we came to see in this very house."

"Make yourselves comfortable, sirs," Mrs. Lushbottam whispered hoarsely. "Our next offering is about to be displayed."

Struan led the way to an empty divan within easy reach of the doors. No sooner were they seated than two blond beauties materialized from a curtain-draped corner to join the newcomers.

From behind, Mrs. Lushbottam said, "Camille and Daphne will see you get anything you require. Enjoy yourselves."

Before Calum could react to the ministrations of Camille or Daphne—the ripe-bodied creature who set to work loosening his cravat and waistcoat made no introductions—a musician entered to sit, cross-legged, on the floor. Dressed in cloth of gold with a matching turban, the swarthy-skinned man played haunting scales on a wooden pipe of a variety Calum had never seen before.

"Thank you, no," he told his companion as she attempted to unfasten his trousers. She stopped instantly and knelt beside him on the divan, smiling as if she had never seen a more desirable sight than Calum Innes.

He tried to ignore her. Within moments, the task became simple.

From the curtained corner emerged two females, dressed in identical white robes. Their black hair was demurely braided into coronets atop their heads. Hand in hand, they progressed to the very center of the circle and stood there, silently surveying the audience, an audience grown expectantly intent.

Calum looked at Struan, who raised his eyebrows while trapping the wrists of his assigned attendant in one large hand. Calum noted that his friend's neckcloth and shirt hung loose.

An eager gentleman's cry of "Let's see what you've got, then" was shushed by others present.

The black-haired girls faced each other, apparently passive, before one grasped the neck of the other's robe and began to tear. In an instant, the calm of the moment disintegrated. Urged on by shouts of encouragement from both the men and the women in the audience, the performers grappled with each other's clothing, gradually stripping it away. Braids loosened and fell in slithering waves over bared shoulders. With a great ripping tug, one girl's high, pointed breasts were completely revealed.

A raucous roar arose, and a lady who had arrived as a guest was similarly divested of her bodice by the men who sat at her sides. Giggling, she writhed in obvious pleasure, with the result that her two companions announced their decision to "share the bounty," and fell to suckling a breast apiece that was indeed bounteous. The lady cradled the heads of her lovers and gave up ecstatic cries.

Even as Calum felt his own sex leap, he checked over his shoulder. Mrs. Lushbottam continued to stand guard at the doors. To Struan he said, "This is monstrous. Excessive. They have all come for this display."

"As you say," Struan agreed. "The women appear as enthralled as the men."

The grappling females in the center had fallen to the floor and were soon completely naked. Their bodies had been oiled to white slickness, their nipples rouged deep red.

A mystical Eastern quality entered the piper's music. With the rising and falling of the notes, the fighters contorted, spreading their legs to display their most secret places and calling to the onlookers to join them. Soon one young buck rose to the occasion and entered the fray with his breeches already around his knees and his sex jutting.

As if by a prearranged signal, one of the girls pretended to hold the other down while the eager fellow drove home his manhood, yelling like a man running another through in the heat of battle.

The woman at Calum's side made a grab for his penis and he came close to losing control. He pushed her, harder than he had intended, but the violence only seemed to incite her afresh. His vision of the copulation on the floor was obscured by the breasts thrust into his face, and as he reached to push them away, the girl took her advantage and snaked a hand inside his breeches.

His next push sent her sprawling from the divan, but rather than anger, she showed only mounting sexual frenzy. Turning away from him, she moved to a flanking divan on which a man who had been at the Esterhazy ball sat with a lavishly dressed creature who fingered his crotch while she avidly watched the display on the floor. The woman who had left Calum pushed up the aroused female's brocade skirts to reveal plump thighs above lace stockings. When that lady pretended an attempt to cover herself, the prostitute tugged down the jewel-encrusted bodice of the other's gown.

Instead of protesting, the lady swayed forward, squealing

loudly while she fumbled with the blond creature's clothing.

"My God, Struan," Calum managed to gasp, "I've never seen anything like this."

"That beautiful girl is here somewhere," Struan responded. "I want to take her away with us."

"Don't be a damned fool."

Fresh shrieks of excitement arose as a splendid young man, little more than an adolescent, was produced. The females who had started the "offering" rapidly readied the boy, stripping and stroking him until he thrashed and grabbed for them in turn. Always they evaded. Then, without warning, a disheveled onlooker—clearly long past caution—spread herself upon the carpet and held up imploring arms until the boy entered her.

The insane roars of pleasure penetrated Calum's nerves and he stood. "This is more ugliness than even I can stomach," he told Struan, who was just as quickly on his feet. "I'd as soon wait for my *witch* doctors in the street."

Struan nodded, but kept watch on the room.

"Forget her," Calum insisted. "It is all an act, don't you see? She is one of them. One of *this*. A fake virgin paraded forward for some sort of depraved ritual. These people are all of a kind. Unless I am much mistaken, they come for these orgies regularly. Nothing here was unplanned. They all expected to participate."

Calum turned away, but Struan caught his arm. "No," he murmured. "No, she should not be here."

Calum followed the direction of Struan's anguished stare. Led by Mrs. Lushbottam, Ella, blindfolded and still dressed in the black velvet cloak, haltingly entered the room. As if a cold wind had passed over the scene, the writhing gradually subsided. Participants in the debauchery slowly eased away from one another and, fastening what clothes they could reach, made a space among them.

"We trust you have enjoyed our little entertainment," Mrs. Lushbottam said, her lipless mouth parting in what might have been a smile. "Now for a very special treat before I send you home to your beds. Some of you have been awaiting this moment. I had not intended it to come tonight, but"—she looked directly at Struan—"I do believe it is time to begin the bidding."

"*Bidding*?" Struan said under his breath. "By God, she intends to auction the girl off."

"You might as well understand that I am by no means ready to accept offers for my greatest treasure. However, times are difficult and I must be sensible. Please, those interested should write the nature of that interest—in detail—on their cards and leave them in the crystal dish that has been placed by the front door."

Utter stillness had fallen again.

"Ella," Mrs. Lushbottam said, removing the girl's blindfold, "it is time to take off your cloak."

The girl's golden face with its great, dark, almond-shaped eyes turned a paler shade. She clutched the neck of the robe even tighter.

"Ella is an innocent," Mrs. Lushbottam announced with audible relish. "Such a prize. Take off the cloak, child."

For another instant the girl hesitated; then she parted the velvet garment, pushed it back from her shoulders and let it fall.

A collective sigh rippled around the room, punctuated with exclamations of awe from women as well as men.

Beneath the robe, a modestly cut gown gained the effect for which it had been designed. Of cobweb-transparent red muslin, rather than cover the astonishing body beneath, the filmy gown cast a rose-tinted glow over golden skin. Dampened, the fabric clung to uptilted nipples that had hardened under the crowd's scrutiny. The girl's breasts were perfectly round and provocatively pointed at the tips in a way that sent the tongues of many men present in hungry circles around their lips.

A triangle of black hair showed clearly at the juncture of slender thighs.

When Ella made futile attempts to cover herself, Mrs. Lushbottam turned her around to display her rounded bottom, and Struan took a violent step forward. Calum restrained him. He put his mouth close to the other man's. "You cannot make a move here. Take my word. Nothing is going to happen. That crone is accomplished with her tricks. She intends to do exactly as she has promised. The stakes will dizzy many heads before she sells this Ella's so-called untouched charms.''

"I'm going to pay whatever the woman asks.''

Calum groaned. "And you will be paying what has doubtless been paid many times before. Heed me, *please*. I have seen more of this world than you.''

"You do not know how much of this world I have seen," Struan retorted, and not for the first time, Calum was puzzled by an unaccustomed distance he felt between himself and his boyhood companion.

"Perhaps," Calum said finally. "That is obviously of no account now. She is leaving. It is my guess that this show takes place from time to time and that it always nets the woman a treasure in attempted bribes. Forget the girl. She could leave if she wanted to. Remember that.''

"It is you who are naive," Struan said. "There are things in this world about which you know nothing.''

Calum didn't argue that his eyes were as old as those of any man who had been about in their particular world for four and thirty years.

With the departure of Ella, revelry broke out once more, and Calum, with Struan at his elbow, escaped gladly into the foyer.

Entering from a door behind the staircase, Mrs. Lushbottam joined them. To Struan she said, "No doubt you will be leaving your card, sir. It'll take a generous man to win my Ella. Remember that and plan accordingly. Your parties have returned, Mr. Innes.''

Calum frowned, then registered what she'd said. "Very well. Come, Struan, it's time." It had been more than an hour already. One look at his companion's face promised more trouble to come unless he could be persuaded to forget Mrs. Lushbottam's succulent "offering.''

Struan climbed the ten flights of stairs to the top story quietly enough. Perhaps he would regain his senses more rapidly than Calum feared he would.

The door Calum sought was at the end of the narrow hallway where the ceiling beneath the attic sloped down far enough to make it necessary for him and Struan to bow their heads.

Calum knocked, and jumped when the door flew open and

he was faced with the stooped, white-haired form of Milo, the Mystical Healer, Detector of Ills, Bearer of Forgotten Powers. Calum knew this title from the painted boards he'd seen displayed on the sides of the cart Milo and his sister, Miranda, used for their unending round of the fairs of England, Scotland and Wales.

Milo peered up at Calum from beneath jutting, shaggy brows as white as his hair. "You," he said, his mouth turning down. He attempted to slam the door shut, but Calum's booted foot happened to be in the way. "We told you not to come back," Milo said. "You can do us great harm and we cannot help you further."

"Is it him, Milo?" a querulous voice asked from the dim recesses of the room beyond. "Is it the child?"

"Sleep," Milo ordered, frowning ferociously at his visitors. "Go. Now. My sister is exhausted. Our life isn't easy. We don't need your meddling to make it worse."

"Miranda is ill?" Calum asked, feeling some guilt at knowing that his primary concern was the possibility of losing his one definite source of information.

"She's tired, is all," the man said. "Go away."

"Red-haired one?" the woman called. "Is that you?"

"Yes," Calum said, forcing his way past Milo. "Come, Struan, and meet my friends Milo and Miranda. They travel around the country with fairs and sometimes with troupes of traveling players. They make marvelous potions that help all manner of ailments, and wherever they go, people await their coming with great hope." He noted a softening in Milo's stance and approached a narrow bed on the far side of the small room.

"It is you," the woman in the bed said. Unlike her brother, her sand-colored hair had not begun to turn gray. She appeared still young, although closer inspection revealed a network of fine lines on her handsome face. "Who is with you?"

"This is . . ." Calum hesitated, looking at Struan.

"I am Struan, Viscount Hunsingore," Struan said without hesitation and offered the woman a polite bow. "Calum has told me about you. I wanted to come with him. He tells me you know about the place and circumstances of his birth."

"Say nothing more." Milo spoke loudly and shuffled to the

side of the bed. "I told you, Miranda. Say nothing more, or we shall be punished. *She* will punish us."

"It is so long ago now," Miranda said, making an effort to sit up. "The time has come for justice to be done, just as I always knew it would."

"She warned you to say nothing," Milo insisted, wringing his bony hands.

"Hush," Miranda said, but she smiled gently. "No one has seen her since . . . Not since she left."

"They've seen Guido and he insists she lives still, and that she wishes only to forget."

"Then she should have considered her actions before she committed such a crime," Miranda said. "There are evil things I am powerless to change. But it is time to right this wrong. I feel it. I have felt it ever since the child found us."

"Child?" Struan said, clearly puzzled.

"The child who was brought to the camp beneath the hill where Franchot Castle stands," Miranda said.

Struan frowned deeply and met Calum's eyes.

"Sores," Milo said, his voice rising to a wail. "Wounds and festering. Bones that break at a touch. Fingernails and toenails that fall out in the breeze. Eyes that will no longer see. All these were promised to us if the silence were ever to be broken."

"Rachel is no more!" Miranda said sharply. "She has not been seen in many years, not since the boy was sick and she took him to find help."

Rachel. Calum heard the name and took it to his heart.

"I tell you she is not dead," Milo declared with desperation. "I tell you that if you break the silence, she will find us and torture us. And there are others to whom even Rachel answers who will finish what she starts."

"Guido told this?" Miranda asked.

"Yes," Milo said with finality. "It is already rumored among the players that the boy who was left in Scotland did not die and—" He clapped a hand over his mouth, and veins stood out in the papery skin at his temples.

"The boy who was left in Scotland," Calum said, dragging air into his aching lungs. "What boy who was left? Miranda told me of a baby who was brought to your camp near Franchot Castle in Cornwall. She said the baby came after the Duchess of Franchot had given birth and then died within days of that birth. Then Miranda would say no more. I implore you. Tell me all you know. I shall have no peace until I can understand everything."

"We cannot help you," Milo said. "Go away and leave us alone."

"You think I was that baby, don't you?" Some of this had been all but admitted. Now Calum wanted absolute confirmation. "Was I brought to the camp by the woman Rachel?"

"Do not say another word," Milo implored his sister. "What is finished is finished."

"I shall have to think," Miranda said, and she fell back onto her pillows. "I have been ill with a fever. Now I must gain my strength again."

"Tell me if this Rachel brought a baby to your camp in Cornwall thirty-five years ago."

Miranda closed her eyes and said weakly, "Yes. Now leave me."

"Go," Milo insisted.

"Why did you think I was the Duke of Franchot?"

"For several years the child grew among the players and the performers," Miranda said. "He grew strong and happy. We all cared for him. He carried the pan among the audience and they gave generously because he made them smile."

Calum turned aside. *Colored cloth. Stars in dark skies. Fires. The scent of smoke and the crackle of sparks. Costumes that swirled, red and yellow and gold. Coins on headdresses. And coins that clinked against metal in the pan he held. Laughter. "You are young to be so sure of yourself, my boy." "See how he holds himself? Like a prince strutting among his subjects rather than a beggar-boy among his betters."*

The pictures and the voices did not come often to his mind, and never had they been as vivid as in the moment just past. "You traveled to Scotland, didn't you, Miranda? The boy traveled with you."

She tossed restlessly.

"Can't you see she is exhausted?" Milo said, and Calum heard genuine concern in the old man's voice. "Leave us, I beg you, so that I may tend her."

"Let me help," Calum offered. "Let me arrange a more comfortable place for you. And good food and warmth."

"We are warm here," Milo replied. "I thank you. But I am well equipped to tend my sister's sickness."

Calum looked dubiously into Milo's bright blue eyes. "Answer me one question, and then I will go. For now. I was told by certain people in Scotland that a boy was seen with a traveling troupe near the village of Kirkcaldy. They were not expected there, but had chosen to stop because one of their number was exceedingly sick."

"I cannot speak of this."

"The sick one was the boy," Calum persisted. "And he was taken to Castle Kirkcaldy and left in the stable yard because it was feared that he was dying. Someone cared enough about him to hope that the people at the castle would take him in and somehow save him."

"No."

"That child had come into the camp near Franchot Castle five years before, and Miranda has reason to believe he was heir to the then Duke of Franchot, but that he was stolen from his cradle."

"*No*, I tell you."

"Yes." The voice, Miranda's faint voice, came from behind Milo, and they all turned to look at her.

"Tell me," Calum begged.

"The baby may have been a noble baby," Miranda said. "And that baby became the boy who was left at Castle Kirkcaldy."

"And *I* was that boy," Calum said, making fists at his sides. "I ask only for a chance to know for sure who I am. Perhaps then I can find peace."

"Or the beginning of a quest that may cost you your life— if you don't lose it tomorrow morning," Struan said, ramming his fingers through his hair. "I beg you to come with me, Calum. This night is going to cost us both dearly."

Calum knew his friend was seeing a silent, dark-haired beauty, yet he could think clearly of nothing but the closeness of the truth about his identity.

"You must go now," Miranda said, her voice stronger. "I have told you I will consider all these things, and I will. If I decide it is wise—and safe—I will help you."

"When?" Calum asked in desperation.

"That will depend upon a great many things. We must discover for sure whether our lives will be in danger if we tell you more."

"Where is this Rachel?"

"Ah," Miranda said, smiling a little. "You have realized that she is the answer. But I cannot tell you where she is, or if she is anywhere at all. For the first, if she still lives, we may never come to you. If she does not still live, our coming to you may be fruitless in your cause. In the end, only Rachel can prove if you are who you think you may be."

"But is there nothing you can do to help me without her?"

"There was something, something Rachel would not have dared to destroy. Perhaps we can discover where it is. It might be proof enough, or it might not. But do not press me further now."

Calum looked at the stained ceiling. "What is this something?"

"I cannot tell you."

"Very well." He could not continue to fight, not tonight. "Tell me one thing and one thing only, and we will leave."

"No," Milo shouted. "Get out."

"One thing," Miranda agreed.

Calum stared hard into her clear eyes. "Do you believe I am the rightful Duke of Franchot?"

Her lips parted, and for an instant he thought she wouldn't respond. Then she said, "Yes."

❧ Six

"*Pippa!*" *Lady* Justine entered Pippa's chamber without knocking, closed the door and leaned upon it. "Something very dangerous is occurring."

"What is it?" Pippa asked, going to Justine and tentatively touching her hands. "Has something gone wrong with our plan?"

"Not yet," Justine said. Her face showed signs of desperate strain. "Nelly is standing guard."

"But it is not time for us to start dealing with—"

"Do not speak aloud of that," Justine implored. "Not when so much depends upon the outcome. Not when we shall, very likely, find ourselves banished to the dungeons beneath Franchot Castle if we are discovered."

"Ooh, bother!" Pippa bounced in her agitation. "I shall not allow any such thing to happen to us. And I cannot bear to wait another moment."

Justine held up an imperious finger. "We will commence soon enough." The words were reasonable. Her voice held barely restrained panic. "It is not time, but there is someone below—in the gardens—who must be persuaded to leave forthwith."

Pippa grew quite still. "In the gardens?" she squeaked. "At past midnight? How do you know there is someone in the gardens who must be persuaded to leave?"

"Because he had his servant come to the kitchens and ask

for Nelly. The man asked for Lady Philipa's maid, mind you, as plain as that!''

"Oh, *my*." Pippa's hand went to her throat. "It's him, isn't it? Calum?''

"Calum, indeed," Justine agreed. She looked away. "He pleases you a great deal, doesn't he?''

Pippa felt herself redden. "He is gentle and kind . . . and manly," she finished quickly, casting aside caution.

"Yes, I see that you do indeed *like* Calum Innes. The man is charming and I liked him on sight myself, but he shows very poor judgment in coming here so late at night—particularly on *this* night."

"I have put you in a most difficult position," Pippa said unhappily. "Only bear with me tonight and I shall not press you into further intolerable service on my behalf."

Justine smiled and her dark eyes glistened. "I do not find service on your behalf intolerable. I am happy to help you. You are the brightest creature who has ever entered my life and I want the best for you. I only wish—" She broke off and looked away.

"You wish?" Pippa pressed.

"I . . . I only wish I were more brave," Justine said, sounding remarkably brave already. "But we really must persuade Calum Innes to leave our gardens. Tonight, of all nights, it would be catastrophic if he were as much as glimpsed in the vicinity of this house by someone who then told Etienne."

"Oh, *my*." Pippa whispered. "This calls for extraordinary measures. I must persuade him to leave without delay."

"I agree," Justine said. "Put on a cloak over your gown and run down the back stairs. I will watch in case someone comes looking for you. There is a little door at the bottom of the stairs that leads into the potting shed. Only I seem to remember it is there."

"Is that the door you—" Pippa changed her mind about asking that question.

"It's the door I used to enter the house after Etienne's return this morning," Justine said matter-of-factly. "Let us not dally with further discussion. The potting shed is hidden from the rest of the gardens by a hedge. Calum Innes is waiting for you there. If he goes nowhere else, he will not be seen."

"I will make him leave at once."

"He should use the door by which he entered from the alley. The one in the side wall near the shed."

"He will. I'll insist."

Donning a gray wool cloak, Pippa swirled out of the chamber and slipped along the corridor. From lower regions of the house came the raucous bellows of the Duke of Franchot and his friends, who had been gambling and drinking for many hours.

Justine followed Pippa as fast as her lame leg would allow and showed her the way to the back stairs. Very soon Pippa pushed through a stiff door into a dusty shed where the air was thick with the smells of earth. Old, dry earth. Evidently the shed was not used much anymore. As Pippa went toward grimy windows that shone dully in the moon's light, thick swags of cobwebs caught at her hair and brushed her face.

The door to the garden had a window. Through it Pippa saw the dark shape of a tall man. While she stared, he turned and his profile was sharply etched by moonlight.

How could two men be more different than Calum Innes and the Duke of Franchot?

How could it be that one—unwittingly, it was true—held her heart in his very hands, while the other was about to own every part of her *but* her heart?

How could she send away the man she . . . the man she could probably love?

Pippa approached the door, turned the handle and pulled it open. Cool, clean air bathed her.

Calum was already striding to meet Pippa. Before she could take another step, he arrived before her and pushed back her hood. "I had to see you," he said, his voice deep with some emotion. "Thank you for coming to me."

She must not admit that she wished she need never leave him again.

Gently, so gently, Calum touched her hair. "You cannot know how this moment feels," he murmured, his gaze settling on her mouth.

"I—"

Whatever she might have said was obliterated by the sealing of her lips by Calum's. His enfolding arms held her in a crushing embrace, but she discovered she enjoyed being crushed by him.

He kissed her long and deep. Every slanting stroke of his mouth upon hers searched for her response, and as best she could, she gave him what he searched for.

Pippa rose to her toes and twined her arms about his strong neck. Calum's chest was a warm, solid, unyielding wall that absorbed the pressure of her soft, slight form and made her feel as she had never felt before. His big, hard body made Pippa feel very feminine and very protected—and she found she liked those feelings a great deal.

"Did I bring you from your bed?" he asked gruffly when he finally lifted his face a scant inch or so from hers. "I told your maid she must bring you at any cost. She is a clever girl. She understood my urgency without a lot of questions."

"Nelly is clever," Pippa agreed breathlessly. She touched his lips with shaky fingers and he kissed their sensitive tips. "Oh," she murmured, and her eyes drifted shut.

The next kisses she felt were on her closed eyelids. "I wasn't in bed," she told him. "I have been too worried about tomorrow to sleep."

"I—want—you," he said against her cheek. He slid his arms beneath the cloak and pressed her against him. "I tried to stay away, but I had to come because I cannot bear to think of you here. Here, with *him*."

And she could not bear that either, but what choice did she have? Pippa nuzzled her face beneath his jaw and tasted salt on his skin. She loved the feel of him, the smell of him. He was big and hard and warm, and his scent was of leather and clean linen and something undefinable that was unique to Calum Innes, something totally male and totally intoxicating to Pippa.

She parted her lips to touch her tongue to the strong pulse in his neck and he groaned.

That groan excited Pippa. Heat began to gather low in her body. A most surprising sensation. "Calum," she said, holding his shoulders. She tested the contours of his neck with the very tip of her tongue—all the way to the cleft in his chin.

Calum groaned again. There was satisfaction in that groan, and something more—or something that asked for more.

Pippa felt suddenly bold. Leaning away for a moment, she looked at his face. His eyes were closed. Making the best of her advantage, she bobbed up to her tiptoes, urged his face down and kissed him full on the mouth.

Instantly his lips parted and with yet another groan, he slipped his tongue deep into her mouth and rocked her face with the force of his ardor.

And he did something else, something most extraordinary. Calum's hands went to Pippa's bottom. They went there and held her in a shockingly intimate manner. And while his hands spread, the fingers surrounding and pressing and molding her, he brought "That" part of him against her belly.

He was very large and very hard—and very hot. And Pippa was mad with the desire to know a great deal more about That.

"Come with me," he said, and drew her lower lip between his teeth. Gently, he nipped and slowly released her tender flesh. "Come away with me now. I came here direct from Hanover Square. I left my friend Viscount Hunsingore there and had the cab bring me on. We should return to set Struan's mind at ease, then make our escape."

Pippa could not get any air into her lungs. His fingers were steely, but she craved that steel. And she craved it probing her.

"The hackney is in the mews. We can be away before anyone misses you."

Pippa had never drunk intoxicating liquor. If she ever did, she was certain it would make her feel like this. "Kiss me again, Calum."

"It grows very late, dear one. Someone is bound to notice your absence and raise the alarm soon. Let it be an alarm that should be raised. Let it be because you have left and they cannot find you."

A still place formed in the center of all her hot, whirling wanting. "Left?" Surely he was funning her. "Me? I cannot leave."

His grip on her bottom slackened. "This is not a good place for you. The man you are engaged to marry is not a good man."

"No . . ." What was she saying? "The duke is my fiancé."

"Yes. And I'm asking you to leave him and come to me."

Cold reason doused every vestige of warmth within Pippa. "I'm sorry," she said, pushing very firmly on his chest. "What can have happened to me? What can I be thinking? Please, I beg you, step away from me."

Moonlight showed her the play of emotions on his handsome face. "You were thinking that you feel something for me, Pippa. That is what you like to be called by your friends, isn't it? Pippa?"

"Yes," she murmured, beginning to shiver. "Please. Leave at once by the side gate and do not make any sound. The duke must not know you have been here."

"Why?" He laughed aloud as if to thwart her warning. "Because he may *hurt* me? I am not afraid of your dashing duke."

"He is not dashing," Pippa said in a small voice. "He is not nice at all. But he is the man my father has told me to marry. The choice is not mine. We both know as much. What I have done here tonight, with you, has been wrong. The fault is mine and I beg your forgiveness."

"My forgiveness?" he snorted. "That's rich. You are an innocent. You know nothing but the natural yearnings of your own passionate body and soul. There is no *fault*. If there were, it would be mine. Leave him."

"He would hunt you down and kill you."

"I want you to be my wife."

She gasped, and the beating of her heart was so furious she was certain he must hear it. "You are rash, Calum. And you are a danger to yourself, which is all that truly concerns me. Leave me, I beg of you. And never try to see me again. Leave London this very hour and return to Scotland."

He grew quite still. "Return to Scotland? You mean, turn and run from your proud betrothed because I should fear him?"

"I mean," she said, each breath searing her throat, "that I cannot have what I want, but I can implore you to make sure the duel does not take place in the morning."

"You deny my proposal?"

"I am already promised to another." Her speeding heart would surely break.

"You will not reconsider and come with me?"

Never could she have imagined a man such as this caring for her, caring for her so much. "I will not consider coming with you," she told him. She would not consider placing him in the mortal danger such folly would surely draw in its wake.

"I see," he said quietly. "Will you tell me one thing? In complete honesty."

Pippa nodded.

"Have my attentions caused you pain?"

She bowed her head. They had caused her joy that was agony—and pain that was an unbearable pleasure. "No," she told him. "No pain."

"And you will not regret sending me away without you?"

"I—" She must say what was necessary, then deal with what must be done once she had dispatched him. "I am much enamored of you, Calum, but I am a sensible female. I shall not dwell on what might have been."

"I see."

She knew he did not see at all. "Will you do as I ask and leave England?" she asked.

"No."

Her fists clenched against her middle. "*Please.*"

"Never. My honor is greater than that man's. I shall never run from him unless it is with you at my side."

And if she were at his side, the duke would surely track them until he could destroy Calum and "forgive" Pippa, who would have been "lured away against her wishes." The words might be different, but she knew that whatever words he used, the duke would find a way to keep what he considered his. After that and with Calum dead, Franchot would magnanimously marry her, and her life would be every bit as empty as it would be in a few moments when Calum walked away from her.

"Pippa?" he said.

She pulled the hood over her hair once more and wrapped the cloak tightly. "Go," she told him, shaking with the effort of holding back tears. "My destiny was made before my birth. Obedience to my father demands that I fulfill that destiny."

"Is that your final word?"

Pippa raised her chin. "It is."

"As you will, then," Calum said. "I'll take my leave of

you, my lady. And I'll look forward to meeting your future husband with the dawn.''

Through a film of tears she watched him leave. At the sound of the door to the alley closing, she started after him. ''Calum,'' she whispered urgently.

The voice that answered her came not from the alley but from the potting shed. ''Pippa, Pippa, come quickly.'' Looking around, Justine hurried toward her. ''He's gone?''

''Yes.''

''Praise be. We must hurry.''

Pippa took the hand Justine offered and allowed herself to be led back inside. ''Has something happened?''

''I think it's about to. Nelly said she heard Etienne calling for you. She said he sounds . . . Oh, Pippa, he announced that he was going to *visit* his *bride*.''

Pippa smiled in the gloom. She had never considered herself particularly brave before, but tonight she had courage to rival a lion's. If the duke tangled with her tonight, he would regret his actions.

In fact, whether or not he tangled with her was of no moment at all. By the time she finished with the Duke of Franchot, he would regret not only his actions, he would regret the moment his future had been linked with hers and every subsequent act of his that had caused her to hate him!

❧ Seven

"*Seconds?*" *Arran* Rossmara, Marquess of Stonehaven, thudded back and forth across the study in his Hanover Square house. "Bloody hell! I *knew* something was wrong. I *knew* the two of you couldn't be trusted not to do something bloody crackbrained without my guidance."

Still reeling from the shock of arriving back from Pall Mall to be confronted by Arran, Calum bristled at his old friend's tone. "Some things are beyond your control," he retorted. "Evidently Struan has mistakenly told you too much about my affairs here."

Arran's mouth became white-rimmed with rage. "Wrong-headed *buffoons*," he growled. "Where were you when I arrived? Answer me that. What fool's errand are you returned from now?"

"That is my business," Calum said, shooting Struan a stare that warned him to say nothing about the "rash" visit to Franchot House.

"I *demand* a full explanation," Arran said, his nostrils flaring.

"Steady on, old chap," Struan said mildly enough, although his lips were thinned against his teeth. "We aren't children and you aren't our parent."

"And this is no affair of yours, Arran," Calum put in, feeling anything but mild. "I asked Struan to act as my second tomorrow, not you. I had no idea you intended to descend upon London in the middle of the night. You are not supposed—''

"*Don't* presume to tell me what I'm supposed to do," Arran bellowed. His dark hair, as ever constrained in the unfashionable but roguishly dashing tail at his nape, had a wild, windswept appearance. "If you'd told me the truth of what you were about, I'd have stopped you from leaving Kirkcaldy."

"You could not have stopped me," Calum said.

Arran breathed loudly. "And you, Struan. *You* should have informed me directly you knew what was afoot here. Of course, I blame myself. Grace was right. I should have listened to her earlier."

Calum raised his brows at Struan and said to Arran, "And what did our fair little Grace say that was right in this instance?"

"She said that only something dire would keep the two of you from being present to dote upon your new niece. And she said her otherworldly instincts told her there were influences at work that could do you harm. She spoke of you in that regard, Calum."

"Oho," he said, walking to the desk with exaggerated steps. "Grace's otherworldly powers are now the approved wisdom at Kirkcaldy? That blond elf of yours has you wound around her pretty fingers, Arran. Your love for her has poached your brain. Not that I don't think a brain thus poached might not feel exceedingly well treated, but the condition could interfere with logic."

"Have you finished?" Arran asked, advancing. "*Poppycock.* In case you didn't hear that, I'll repeat: *poppycock.* You know as well as I do that Grace has a gift for sensing things that most others do not sense. And you know that when she says there is something afoot, she is almost invariably right. And she was right this time. Thank God I listened to her at last. And thank *God* I chose to finish my journey here tonight rather than bedding down at an inn until morning."

Struan turned away and waggled his head. It took little imagination for Calum to visualize him soundlessly parroting Arran's words.

"I think you are annoyed with us for being absent during

little Elizabeth's first weeks of life and that you are come to demand that we leap to heel and return to Scotland at once," Calum suggested. "What else would induce you to leave your adored wife and baby—*and* your music?" Arran's brilliant secret life as a musical composer had been his driving passion—until the intrusion of Grace Wren into his strange, and insular, nocturnal existence.

Arran scowled. "Do not change the subject. You've got yourself into a pretty pickle and it's just not on. Do you understand me?"

Calum had to smile at this man who, even more than Struan, had always been of greater importance to him than his own life. "Still looking after me," he said. "I'm touched."

"You are a bufflehead," Arran said. "There is to be no duel, and that is all that will be said on the subject. Pack whatever you must take. We leave at once. We can be out of London within the hour."

"No."

"You, too, Struan. You should not have aided Calum in this foolishness."

"No," Calum repeated. "I am not leaving. And I will be in Hyde Park at dawn. I hope Struan will be with me, and it would please me greatly if you would come also, Arran."

"We can't let you do it," Struan said, turning to face Calum. "I don't like to refuse you anything, but I'm with Arran in this. He's right. You must leave at once."

Calum opened his mouth, but couldn't decide what to say.

"It isn't only Franchot," Struan said to Arran. "It's the man's fiancée, Lady Philipa Chauncey. Lord Chauncey, the explorer, is her father."

"Yes." Arran frowned. "What has she to do with Calum?"

"He met her last night at Esterhazy's. That's what this duel nonsense is about. He danced with her. Franchot saw and objected and tried to call Calum out. I managed to stop him."

"But—" Arran raised one of his long, strong musician's fingers and jabbed it in Calum's direction. "Why did you just burst in here babbling about a duel if the whole thing was called off last night?"

"He went to Franchot's house this morning," Struan said. "Why?"

"To see the girl."

Calum said, "Shut *up*, Struan. I can answer any questions Arran has for myself." Another moment and Struan would be babbling about Calum's latest visit to Pippa. He could scarcely bear to think of it himself. Part of him mourned her denial of him. Another, very strong and quite foreign part of him was beginning to resolve on the side of using Pippa's obvious attraction to him for his own ends.

"He hasn't stopped thinking about her since last night," Struan said, undaunted by the hard stare Calum gave him. "Have you?"

"I . . . no, dammit. Not that it's any of your business."

"You promised me that once you'd had a look at Franchot, you would be satisfied." Struan was deadly serious now. "You've changed your mind, haven't you?"

Calum remembered Miranda's parting words. "Yes, I've changed my mind."

"Struan has been talking to me about this madness you've involved yourself in," Arran said. "Even if there's a shred of truth in what you've decided to believe, there is no way to prove it. Set it aside, Calum. Come back to the good life you have and forget all this."

Calum let his head fall back and sighed aloud. "I cannot."

"It's the girl, isn't it?" Struan asked.

He hardly knew what he thought anymore, except that he couldn't walk away from the life that was truly his. And he knew he was truly the Duke of Franchot.

In a familiar gesture, Arran tugged loose his neckcloth. He shrugged his austerely cut green jacket from immensely broad shoulders and tossed it onto a chair. "We have time," he said, dropping into an upholstered gilt chair that seemed too small for him. "Whatever help you need sorting this out, you shall have, Calum. I was wrong to try to hurry you through it."

"Thank you." Calum didn't feel grateful. He felt a need to sleep before the trials of dawn, and he felt anxious. More than anything else, he wanted to remove Lady Philipa—and Lady Justine—from Franchot's clutches.

"I have a sister," he said simply. "Can you imagine how odd it feels to be confronted with a woman who is your sister when you have lived as a man without a history, let alone a sister? Her name is Justine. She is slender, with a clever face. She limps because of some childhood injury. Wait till you see her. You will know her at once. I expected one of those people to exclaim at the likeness between us. I know she felt some affinity for me.''

Arran pushed himself to his feet. ''This is worse than I thought. You are deluded.'' Shaking his handsome head, he went to pour cognac into three glittering crystal glasses. ''What possible grounds can you have for assuming this woman is your relation?''

''The only grounds I need,'' Calum said. ''She is there in Franchot House and she was introduced to me as the Duke of Franchot's sister. *I* am the Duke of Franchot.''

''You *think* you are,'' Struan said.

''I know I am. You heard what those people said last night. What Miranda said. Did you tell Arran?''

''Yes. He isn't any more convinced than I am.''

''You will both be convinced when she brings me some proof.''

Arran pushed a glass of brandy into Calum's hands. ''What do you think you will gain by dueling with Franchot?''

''I will kill him. That will end a great problem.''

''Good God!'' Arran drank deeply of his own cognac. ''You are not yourself. Kill him? You are a gentle man who abhors violence.''

''It was not I who called him out . . . not at first. I simply accepted.''

''And you think that by removing the man, you can make your claims more readily believed?''

Calum laughed harshly. ''Unfortunately, no. If I kill him, I'll likely be accused of doing so to make certain he cannot defend his right to the title.''

''Franchot has killed three men in duels,'' Struan observed. ''Please, Calum, go with Arran to Kirkcaldy. *Now*. Forget all this. And *think*, man. What could that witch woman possibly produce that would prove your right to the Franchot title and all that goes with it? Infant toenails, perhaps? A lock or two of infant hair?''

Calum set his jaw stubbornly. ''I know she has proof of my

identity. And I feel in my heart that she will decide to find it for me.''

''Reason with him,'' Struan urged Arran. ''Make him go with you.''

''We will all go,'' Arran said.

Struan regarded the cognac in his glass. ''I cannot. Not immediately. I will follow as soon as I can.''

Calum strolled to stand between Arran and his brother and looked directly into Struan's face. ''Did you place a card on the lady tailor's crystal tray?''

A faint swath of color appeared on each of Struan's cheeks. ''This is neither the time nor the place to speak of that.''

''What lady tailor?'' Arran asked. ''What tray? What is all this?''

''It is a joke,'' Struan said rapidly. ''Calum refers to a certain game of chance at an establishment we visited. It is of no importance.''

Calum saw his opportunity and pressed it to the hilt. ''We'll set that aside for a moment. Think again, Struan. Do you not believe, at least a little, that I am the Duke of Franchot?''

''I—'' Struan glared. He rested an elbow on the fireplace mantel and let his glass dangle. ''Well, I suppose there is some possibility . . .'' He allowed the sentence to trail off.

''Did you tell Arran about my travels? How I learned that the people who were presumed to have left me at Kirkcaldy were not, as we once thought, tinkers? Did you explain that Grace's maid told me how her father had spoken of talk in the village, about a group of performers in the area who had been seen earlier in the market at Edinburgh?''

Taking his time, Arran refilled his glass and strolled to sit behind the desk. He pulled a sheet of paper toward him and checked the standish for ink.

Calum's temper rose. ''These performers followed the fairs and were on their way north when, for no reason any of the Kirkcaldy people knew at the time, they broke away from the others and set up a small camp near the village.''

''Grace's maid told you all this?'' Arran began to write.

''She did. And Robert Mercer—one of your tenants—told me that his father had spoken to him of the event. The players performed. A snake act. A dancing bear. A brother and sister who dealt in remedies, and a group of acrobats." When Arran didn't respond, Calum pounded his fist on the desk. "There was a small boy with them who was kept near the fire. He appeared to be ailing. Robert Mercer's father said the boy was with the snake man's assistant."

"Interesting," Arran said. He had stopped writing.

"Mrs. Moggach—our esteemed Kirkcaldy housekeeper who has never regarded me as other than an *'upstarty laddie'*—took pleasure in confirming that *everyone* knew I was a snake man's brat."

Arran fiddled with the pen and soon a string of notes flew across the page where, moments before, he'd commenced to write what appeared to be a letter.

"Damn you, Arran!" This had always been the way. When confronted with the world, Arran retreated into music. "I have traced those people back through thirty-five years to find myself. Now that I have done so, I shall *never* rest until I prove it to the world."

"You said all you wanted was to see Franchot," Struan said explosively. "You *promised* me you had no interest in changing places with him."

Arran tossed down the pen and leaned back in his chair. "You are Calum Innes. You are our brother in every way except in name. My father made provision for you, and *I* need you. I put it to you that you *are* or were the son of a snake man, or whatever, but that you have become determined to prove otherwise. There is no shame in your birth, my friend. We will never discuss the matter again after today."

Black rage overwhelmed Calum. He snatched up the paper from the desk and saw that Arran had started a note to Franchot. " 'Please be advised,' " he read aloud. Arran had written nothing more except notes of music. "Please be advised of what? That the mind of Mr. Calum Innes is unbalanced and his actions should be dismissed?

"Listen well, Arran. And Struan knows this as surely as I do. I found Milo and Miranda, the brother and sister who sold remedies, the pair who were remembered by Robert Mercer's father—and by the father of Grace's maid. And Miranda spoke of an infant brought to camp at a fair held near Franchot Castle thirty-five years ago. Brought by the snake man's assistant—

who had not been increasing. This occurred a matter of days after a son was born to the Duchess of Franchot. Miranda said the mysterious infant was noble.''

''Noble?'' Arran swept wide an arm. ''And how would one know a noble infant from any other?''

''Do not scoff.'' Very deliberately, Calum tore the paper in half and let the pieces drift to the carpet. ''I am not the snake man's child. I am the Duke of Franchot. If I had ever doubted it, the sight of my sister's face has quelled such a doubt.''

Arran jerked forward suddenly and planted his forearms on the desk. ''If I were to consider that you are who you think you are—*if*, mind you—then who in God's name is the man who took your place?''

''When we know that, we shall know everything,'' Calum said. ''We must pray that these traveling players do not alert whoever committed the crime against me.''

Struan had been silent for a long time. He muttered an oath and strode to stand beside his brother. ''What have I been thinking of? Whoever did this must never know of your suspicions, Calum. They obviously have everything to lose if they are unmasked.''

The satisfaction Calum felt at this change of tune was poor comfort, but it was something. ''Agreed,'' he said. ''This false Duke of Franchot did not begin the travesty. Someone else placed him in my stead, and that person stood to gain greatly by having me removed. If whoever the villain is finds out about me too soon, my life will be in grave danger. I shall not reveal myself until I have absolute proof of my identity and can announce it to the world.''

''Very wise,'' Arran said. ''And you will be certain to make every effort to look after the health of the current holder of the Franchot title? You understand that there are—if you are correct—many elements about which you know nothing. But you do know that his death would doubtless force a desperate hand.''

Calum understood very well. ''I will meet the man tomorrow,'' he said. ''And somehow I will satisfy my honor *and* spare his life.''

''And our task,'' Struan remarked, ''is to keep watch for

the man behind the duke. There *is* someone who will become
an obvious culprit if we observe carefully.''

"How right you are," Calum observed.

"And finally you realize that, regardless of your identity, I
am afraid for your safety." Arran smiled grimly. "We will
manage the business of the duel. Then you will tread very
carefully, my friend—and we will all watch your back."

At dawn, they were a company of three.

Calum rode, flanked on his right by Arran and on his left
by Struan. Their horses' hoofs rang dull on streets where only
those about the business of their betters ventured forth at so
unkind an hour.

There had been no conversation since Arran, with Struan
his echo, had made a final plea for Calum to change his mind
and avoid this duel. Then they had left Hanover Square, riding
out beneath a pall of smoky, mauve-tinged fog.

They approached the Park by the way that led past Glouces-
ter House, and Calum noted its bulk only as a great, pale
marker that stared over what might become the last landscape
his eyes ever gazed upon.

Arran took the lead now, for all the world as if he were in
a hurry to be done with the business at hand—regardless of
the outcome.

Wordlessly, Struan and Calum fell in behind. The houses
of Mayfair were swallowed by the livid fog, and the trio
moved onto earth packed hard by the prancing mounts of the
privileged. A dozen hours would pass before the next daily
parade of impeccably garbed riders.

By then, Calum thought, he might be in his last, long, cold
sleep.

"For God's sake!" Arran wheeled around and cantered
back to head them off. "Once more I beg of you, Calum, give
up this foolishness."

Struan caught at the bridle of Calum's horse. "Listen to
him," he implored. "There is no shame in refusing to satisfy
an idle fool with a murderer's cowardly heart."

"And why pistols?" Arran asked.

"It would appear that even I know more of the times than
either of you." Calum laughed without mirth. "Franchot is

rumored to be the only man alive who still chooses the sword. That, and the fact that he has made each of his kills with the sword, may have swayed me toward pistols.''

''You never even cared for the shoot,'' Struan argued. ''I cannot remember you ever with a weapon in your hands.''

''It's true I have no stomach for blood sports,'' Calum admitted. ''But you insist I am a Rossmara in all but name, so is it any wonder I prefer to bow a fiddle than shoot an arrow— or a musket? You are both men of music and peace, and so have all your family been. Come. Dawn is upon us.''

He urged his mount around Arran's and set off. The sounds of hoofbeats were muffled on the damp air and he blinked against moisture that wet his face.

Arran was the first to catch up. ''No lord of Stonehaven has ever failed to bear arms when needed,'' he said, more forcefully than should have been necessary. ''There has never been a suggestion that we are cowards.''

''I rest my case,'' Calum declared, lengthening his horse's stride. ''No member of the family—or in my case, no man under the close protection of the family—has failed to bear arms when needed. *I* am not a coward, and therefore, this morning I must bear arms. Fear not; I have held a pistol more than once and I am a fair shot.''

''When—''

''The subject is closed,'' Calum said, cutting Struan off. ''And the appointed place lies not far ahead. Beyond the beeches.''

''Gad,'' Arran muttered. ''I don't like this. Give me a Scottish hillside, the heather and the broad sky any day over this crowded little land inside its cloudy bowl.''

''I'm about to fight for the sport of sparing a man's life and *he* waxes poetical,'' Calum said of Arran, sighing loudly. ''One would think my hide was of less interest than *his* comfort.''

''You'll spare him if he doesn't *kill* you,'' Arran snapped. The heavy stand of trees gave way to a grassy clearing. Calum dismounted, tethered his horse and started steadfastly toward open ground. The fog completely cut off the sky, trapping the fuzzy scene beneath a sulfuric mantle.

His friends joined him, clapping together their gloved hands and turning to search for signs of Calum's opponent.

Minutes passed.

The slightest of breezes tore strips from the fog and threaded them through the trees.

"What hour is it?" Calum asked.

Struan searched beneath his cloak and produced a watch. "It is time," he said grimly, scanning the circle of trees.

Arran set down a lumpy bag made of rough black fabric.

"What's that?" Calum indicated the bag.

"Nothing," Arran and Struan said in unison.

Calum walked a slow circle around "nothing." "Franchot's seconds are to bring the pistols?"

"Correct."

"And I shall be the first to choose?"

"Correct," Struan said.

"So the bag does not contain pistols?"

Arran shook his head. "No."

"Perhaps you thought to have a feast prepared," Calum suggested. "No doubt there is a blanket somewhere about you that we shall use to sit upon when we eat our picnic."

Struan frowned fiercely at nothing in particular.

"It's just a precaution," Arran said. "Just in case."

Calum was almost certain he heard rustling coming from the bag. "There's something alive in there!"

"Of course there isn't," Arran said, laughing. "He's lost his mind, brother. Completely. Living things in bags. Hah! Insane."

Struan was quick to agree. "Quite. We should probably subdue him and carry him back to Hanover Square." He looked at the watch again. "The hour for the meeting has come and gone."

"Indeed," Arran agreed. "Definitely come and gone."

Disquiet climbed icy steps up Calum's spine. "Franchot's honor is everything to him. Were it otherwise, we should not be here. He would never risk his reputation by not coming."

"I suppose not." Struan didn't sound a happy man. "But the fact remains that he is not—"

"Someone's coming," Calum said, hearing his voice as if it belonged to another.

Arran and Struan swung around in opposite directions.

"Where?" Arran asked.

Calum indicated the trees to his right. "Moving over there. See? Going from trunk to trunk. Watching us."

Struan swept off his hat and wiped the back of a sleeve over his face. "Probably a damnable footpad. Looking for some fool who can be easily parted from his goods."

"I see him, too," Arran said, narrowing his green eyes. "If he's a footpad, then I'm an Englishman."

Calum almost smiled. "In that case, we are not looking at a thief, my lords."

As he spoke, the figure separated from the trees and sidled, head lowered, steps hesitant, toward them.

"What in God's name is this?" Arran said. "A beggar?"

"His clothing is plain, but I'd not take him for a beggar," Struan said. "The creature is a boy, not a man."

"The creature is ignorant or a fool to be here, alone, and approaching three strangers." Calum walked to greet the newcomer. "You. State your business."

A hoarse, cracking voice announced, "A message from my master, sir."

"And your master's name?" Calum asked.

"The Duke of Franchot."

Calum heard Arran's soft oath.

"Give it to me." Calum held out his hand. The boy had stopped some yards away. "Come along. You've no need to be afraid of any here."

"I'm to tell it to you, sir," the crackly voice said. "His Grace wishes you to know he's thought better of this morning's affair. It should best be forgotten."

"Damn me," Struan said.

"Bloody coward," Arran remarked, as if disappointed.

Calum advanced slowly upon the boy. "Did your master explain this—*change of heart*?"

"It was probably because he wasn't . . . No, sir. He didn't explain."

"I see." Several more steps took Calum close enough to see a thin neck above a green woolen stock. The youth's top hat was of best-quality beaver and his jacket was of fine, dark green wool. For one so small, the white doeskin breeches fit extremely snug.

"I'll be off now, then," the boy said.

Before Calum could respond, thunderous hoofbeats sounded and a tall man astride a dappled gray broke into the clearing.

"They're coming after all," Arran said sharply, and swept up his black bag. "The boy was a deliberate diversion. The bloody blackguard sought to throw us off guard."

"Indeed," Struan agreed.

Arran yanked open the bag and shook it. "We'll show him diversions!" he shouted triumphantly.

Calum fell back before a cloud of flying black creatures that flapped their webbed wings and swarmed skyward in a clotted cloud.

"What in God's name?" He threw his hands over his head. "*I* am insane? *Bats?*"

"Too soon," Struan moaned to Arran. "*Not* until they face off. We agreed not to release them until then. Now the effort is wasted."

"Oh, good Lord," Calum said, although no one appeared to hear him. "Diversion upon diversion. All the world is filled with fools—except for me."

Apart from checking his horse's stride for an instant, the approaching rider hardly seemed to note the ascending host of winged rodents. When he drew close, he called, "Innes?" and pulled up in front of Arran. "Are you Innes, man?"

"I'm Innes," Calum stated, noting that the boy seemed rooted in place. "Calum Innes."

"Lord Avenall," the man said, dismounting. Clearly out of breath and, if Calum wasn't mistaken, ill, he clung to his mount's reins as if he'd fall without them. Finally he managed to gasp out, "Thank God I'm not too late."

"Who are you, sir?" Arran asked. "What is your business here?"

"I am Saber, Lord Avenall. Etienne . . . the Duke of Franchot, is my cousin and guardian. No matter about that. He . . .." The young man tried and failed to straighten his leanly built body. With one hand he pushed tangled black hair away from his eyes. "He cannot come. I beg you, sir, do not speak of this until His Grace is able to make his own explanations."

"*Able?*" Calum felt the boy shift, but had eyes only for this Lord Avenall. "What do you mean, *able?*"

With difficulty, Avenall hauled himself back into the saddle. "I must leave," he said, leaning over his horse's neck. "Only do as I've asked, I beg you. Before the day is out, you will hear more, I promise you."

"He's begged off." Arran's tone held pure disbelief. "Damn it all, the bloody coward's begged off."

"No!" Avenall declared, his handsome face twisted with obvious pain. "No, I tell you. That is not the way of it."

"Here." The boy's sudden, squeaky utterance and his twisted lope toward the horseman surprised Calum into silence. A thin hand shot out to thrust an envelope at Avenall. "Take this to His Grace. I was on my way to do it myself."

Rid of his missive, the boy thwacked the flank of Avenall's horse. The beast wheeled away and started into a gallop, its rider clinging to the mane as if foxed. Calum stared after him and thought of the potentially increasing circle of his family by birth.

"I'll be," Struan murmured. "Saved by—"

"Not by *bats*, in God's name," Calum said.

Arran appeared aggrieved. "We were at pains to gather them from a nearby church tower. They'd have disrupted any duel—"

"If you hadn't loosed them too soon," Struan cut in. "No matter. Franchot begged off and all is well."

"We shall see," Calum said, pointedly indicating the "messenger," who was, even as they spoke, hurrying away. "Time to return to Hanover Square, gentlemen. It appears this morning's work is done here." In a low voice he added, "I think I should ensure our young messenger's safe return home, don't you?"

Arran looked blank.

"Good Lord," Struan said slowly. "Of course. I see it now. I think you should thank God for your good fortune, Calum. Make sure she . . . Watch her from a distance. Don't meddle further."

"Her?" Arran peered at the retreating figure. "*Her*?"

"Yes, Arran," Struan said. "That is a woman. Come

away. We'll await you, Calum. Do nothing foolish.''

"Trust me," Calum told him. "And later we shall discuss bats in bags and other uninvited diversionary tactics." With that, he set off after Lady Philipa Chauncey.

Eight

Men were such arrogant fools.

Pippa reached the trees and began threading her way among them.

Men were nothing more than overly large boys. Boys did nothing but think up nasty games from morning till night, and the fact that they grew large enough to be called men did not stop them from thinking up nasty games. Only when they were men, their games could become deadly.

"Hold up, there!"

Pippa heard Calum's voice and, at the same instant, the sound of his boots on wet ground.

Despite the fog, young daylight seeped down in shafts. If he got too close, he would know her for sure.

She began to run.

"Hold!" Calum shouted. "Please. You know you have nothing to fear from me."

Pippa had *everything* to fear from him—and from herself when she was near him. "I've got to get home, sir," she managed to croak. "Please don't detain me. I'll lose my place if I'm late."

"I think we've played this game long enough"—his hand descended upon her shoulder—"don't you, my lady?"

"Yes." She stood still. "I probably didn't even need to come. I wanted to be certain there'd be no repeat of this morning's foolishness, that's all."

96

"I had not expected to see you again so soon . . . Pippa."

Heat built in her face and she remained with her back to him.

"Very well," he said, slowly turning her to face him. "We will not speak of our last meeting—yet. What on earth would cause the duke to risk his precious honor by failing to meet me as arranged?"

She didn't know how to answer—not honestly.

"I don't trust him, y'know," Calum said. "Pardon my referring to your fiancé in such terms, but I don't. This is all to gain him some advantage he didn't think he had today."

"No, it isn't," she told him flatly.

"He'll demand satisfaction at a later time. That is the only likely outcome. He has deliberately sought to try my nerve. And he has lost. You may tell him that."

"He did not send me," she said in a small voice. "He has dishonored himself. The upper hand is now yours, Calum. Should the duke seek to prove otherwise, you have only to call upon your friends, who can prove—together with Saber Avenall—that you were here and the duke was not."

"You seem certain of all this." He stood very close to her. "What of the letter you gave to Avenall?"

Pippa stared directly at his white shirtfront and austerely simple cravat. "I am certain." Of the letter she said nothing.

"You discussed this with him."

"In a manner of speaking."

With a gloved forefinger, he gently raised her chin. "Will you please confide in me? I am not your enemy, Pippa. I think we are both very well aware of that. Explain what has happened here."

His voice, so deep yet so soft, curled warm and tingling into her stomach.

"Pippa?"

She would not look up at him. "This is such a bother. Such foolishness. *I* feel so foolish."

"Don't."

"How can I do otherwise? Running about dressed as a boy, like some character in a bad romantical novel. I wouldn't have considered such silliness, but I didn't know what else to do. For a moment when you were with me last night, I hoped you would agree to . . . Yes. Well. I did think I had a chance of getting away with it if I spoke quickly and left quickly.''

''But Avenall spoiled your theatrics, is that what you mean? You are fortunate. Had he not been so obviously physically distressed, he'd doubtless have recognized you—as I did.''

This time she did look up into his black eyes. ''I am not fond of being treated like an annoying child, Calum. Kindly adjust your tone and your choice of words when you speak to me. *If* you ever have cause to speak to me again.''

There, she had told him and she sounded most collected.

His hand, tightening on her shoulder, ensured that she could not march away as she'd intended.

''Good day to you, sir.''

She looked at his firm mouth with its ever-so-slightly up-tilted corners and did not feel at all collected.

''It is not a good day,'' Calum said. ''It is, and has been, one of the worst days of my life. Although it does begin to show a little promise again now. Could you perhaps remember to call me Calum rather than 'sir'? At least when we're not in the company of others?''

She felt him, his strength and the powerful life within him. He made her want to *touch* him! Pippa held herself rigidly straight and replied, ''I'm very glad you are of an optimistic turn of mind.'' She ignored his request for her to use nothing other than his given name.

''It is you who make the day brighter, dear one,'' he said clearly. ''I find that when I look at you, there is this certainty that no obstacle would be too large for me to overcome. I do believe I could fight several duels in a morning for you.''

Her heart turned completely over and stopped. Yes, she was certain—her heart had stopped.

''This is most odd,'' he continued conversationally. ''I don't recall ever feeling quite like this before. What do you suppose it means?''

She swallowed, shivered, shifted from foot to foot in the boots that had evidently belonged to Saber Avenall when he'd been a boy and which were too big for Pippa. At least Saber hadn't shown signs of recognizing his cast-off clothes.

''What, I ask you?'' Calum pressed. ''I'm asking for your help in diagnosing this condition.''

"Arising too early," she suggested. "Or possibly not going to your bed at all. And you may be hungry. Did you have breakfast?"

He didn't respond to her suggestions, but merely swept off her hat and regarded her with his head tilted to one side. "Duels would be nothing," he declared. "Wrestling with lions might be more of a challenge."

He did not sound at all like himself. "The duke was wrong to bring about a duel," she said. "And when he did so, he produced a desperate situation. A shocking *bother*. All I did was deal with that situation. It's my way, d'you see—dealing with bother in a sensible manner."

"Is it?"

"Oh, yes. I've had to learn to do that. My father has always been a busy man. I like him for that, of course, but there was never any time for him to deal with foolish female nonsense, so I simply had to learn not to allow it. I do not tolerate female foolishness, or any foolishness at all—in myself or in any other."

"I'm impressed."

"People are."

"You're so humble."

She nodded. "My father has always believed in humility. I like him for that."

"Arran would approve of your coiffure," he told her.

"That large man?" She touched her severely drawn-back hair and checked the ribbon that restrained it at her nape. "Who is he?"

"The Marquess of Stonehaven."

"Ah." She recalled some mention of him at the Esterhazy ball. "The Scot?"

"The same. Could you, do you suppose?"

She missed his meaning. "Could I what, sir?"

"Always call me Calum when we are alone? Until you are comfortable using my name in front of others, too."

"We should not be alone again," she told him testily. "But . . . Calum, I should return to Pall Mall."

"Do you want to?"

"I want—" Her eyes felt alarmingly as if they were filling

with burning tears. How could that be? "I am glad—no—
grateful that there was no duel."

One of his hands closed over hers where she'd pressed it
against her stomach. "I cannot forget our kisses, my dearest
Pippa. Yesterday morning, or last night. You are so warm
where I've touched you—and so *hot*, I think, where I have
not touched you. As yet."

Pippa breathed in sharply. Some of what he said was plain;
much was a confusing riddle.

His thumb stroked the back of her hand, traced the rise and
fall of each knuckle. "Are you at all happy?" he asked so
softly that she leaned a little closer. "I know you do not admire your fiancé. But is he—is Franchot kind to you?"

A lump swelled in her throat until she felt she might never
swallow again. She coughed and averted her face.

"Is he? My dearest—"

"If we were ever to be alone," she said rapidly, "as we
were last night and are now, but probably never shall be again,
then I should always enjoy hearing you say my silly little
name. Pippa. Very silly, but the name my friends like."

"I like it, too. There is nothing about you that I do not
like."

She glanced quickly up at him. His lips remained parted to
show the edges of square teeth. Where his mouth tilted at the
corners, curved lines formed. Had he smiled a great deal in
his life? She liked to think that he had.

"Does that cause you any happiness?" His breath raised
his broad chest inside the simple but perfectly cut black coat
he wore beneath a many-caped cloak. "That to me you are
perfect?"

"I like the way your voice sounds when you tell it. And I
like the way your eyes grow even darker."

The lines beside his mouth deepened, but his smile didn't
narrow his eyes. Moistness in the air glistened in his curly hair
and on his eyelashes. The same moisture wet his skin.

"There is something . . ." What did she mean to say? That
there was something mystical in this moment? "I am a very
sensible female," she said instead.

"I'm certain you are, Pippa." His smile widened even
more, and with the backs of his fingers he stroked her cheek,

stroked away escaped strands of her damp hair. "Oh, yes, I'm sure you are most sensible. If being *sensible* can make a woman the most desirable creature in the world to a man—to this man—to me."

"This should not be happening again," she told him, but when he spread his hand over the side of her head and bent to press his lips to her brow, her eyes closed. "I was most determined that there would never again be such an unseemly closeness between us. And I have gone to so much trouble to ensure Franchot cannot hurt you." And she leaned closer.

"Tell me about your trouble."

Reason struggled to stay alive. "I cannot."

"You can."

"I must never speak of this again. And I must go back."

His lips moved to her temple, to the hollow in her cheek, to her jaw. "Could it be that you came this morning merely to fulfill an obligation?"

"Obligation?" She felt . . . *drugged.*

"To see me again. We agreed you owed me another time with you to erase your insult to my honesty at the ball."

He was attempting to trick her in some manner. "I have already seen you again—at Pall Mall. *Twice.*" To be tricked by Calum Innes was to be in heaven. "The first meeting was dangerous and caused a great deal of bother. The second meeting was simply . . . *dangerous.*"

"No, no," he whispered against her ear. "That will not do at all. Our last meeting was far more than simply dangerous. It was ecstasy. You sent me away, but I do not think I am ready to give up on you quite yet, my Pippa. But as to the other, I'm certain your admirable father would expect nothing less of you than that you accept responsibility for the discharge of your own obligations."

"To see you again?" Pippa inclined her head, the better to feel his mouth upon her ear. "I did see you. You know I did."

"*I* saw you," he told her, and there was laughter in his voice. "*I* came to you. *Twice.* That is not at all the same thing. *You* were to see me, don't you know?"

"Words, Calum Innes. Only words. I do not muddle easily."

"I cannot forget the feel of your lips on mine. Or their taste."

This was so reckless, but she could not make herself care. "I cannot forget, either." Pippa opened her eyes and looked at him direct. "I have been receiving instruction on the ways of the world, Calum. It is entirely wrong for me to say so, but I would like, just once more, to feel . . . I should like to do it again, please."

Shades of darkness shifted within those black eyes, and mist-slicked lashes flickered, a little. Without a word, Calum Innes's eyes closed and a singular expression passed over his features. Sweet, intense ecstasy? Pippa wondered if she knew what sweet ecstasy was. Her heart speeded. Sweet ecstasy that became sadness—or aching need? And then his mouth pressed hers and she saw nothing more, only felt, only felt the supple shifting of his lips against hers, only tasted the sweet, mist-dampened taste of his lips on hers.

Pippa tried to sigh, but could not find new air. Heated, flushing, she started when Calum threaded his fingers between hers and held her hands tight against her thighs. His face moved hers, raised hers, brushed hers with skin so subtly different from hers. Male skin, a little rough where his jaw grazed her tender skin.

His lips parted—slightly—parted, so that the edges of his teeth touched the sensitive inside of her lower lip. And then his tongue sought the same spot—so very carefully, so lightly.

There was more.

Just beyond her reach. Just outside what he knew she wanted, there was more. Why didn't he know what she wanted? Why couldn't she tell him?

"I . . ." she murmured.

"Mmm?" He breathed softly, dipped to place a dozen tiny kisses along her pulsing throat. "What is it, Pippa?"

She could not tell him what she wanted, because she did not know.

He released her hands and held her waist. "That man is a fool," he said.

She did not understand.

Calum shook his head and brought her fingers to his lips,

then kissed—with great concentration—each one. "This will not be enough, you know."

Pippa looked up at the treetops. The fog had almost dissipated. Patches of sky showed. "It's all going away," she said. "But it has to, doesn't it?"

"No," he said, as if he understood her perfectly. "No, it doesn't have to go away. Not yet and not forever."

"We will not meet again after today."

"Oh, but we will, my dear lady."

"I am to be married."

He fingered her throat and brought his thumbs to rest beneath the point of her chin. "You are indeed."

"So you do understand that this is wrong? The blame is mine." And she must turn from him, run from him. *Now*.

"We will speak more of this soon." The light that seemed to see only her did not leave his gaze. "Why did Franchot not come this morning?"

"Oh, that." She could not concentrate.

"Yes, that. What manner of coward hides behind a woman's skirts?" He grinned and glanced down. "Or breeches?"

Pippa straightened her shoulders. "Would you have me believe you consider a woman less your equal than a man?"

For a moment he appeared nonplussed. His hands fell to rest on her shoulders. "I merely mean that no man should hide behind a woman. There is no doubt as to the weaker of the sexes, is there, Pippa?"

The dreaminess lifted, and the spell. "There is no doubt that women are physically less strong than men, Calum. But that, I *know*, is where the disparity ends."

He made a short bow. "I respect your right to your own opinions. In fact, I find your sprightly manner enchanting."

Enchanting? Really, even when one felt totally at one with a man for the very first time, he had to ruin the moment by exhibiting his ridiculous belief in wretched male supremacy.

He shook her lightly. "Come, do not be angry with me."

"I am *not* angry. *You* are misguided, but we will not discuss this further. I know it is no use to try to persuade you of the obvious. My father always warned me that my life would be easier if I didn't insist upon declaring my . . . Anyway, I have always liked my father for being so direct."

"A wise man," Calum remarked. "It grows light, Pippa. I want to ensure you arrive home safely. But first, *please* tell me where Franchot is."

She marshaled her most serene countenance. "Certainly. He is in his bed . . . when he is not out of his bed." She shrugged. "But then he is back in his bed. Or so I believe, for, of course, I have not seen him there."

"Of course," Calum said, and his deep frown assured her that he was no wiser than before she'd begun her explanation. "You intrigue me, Pippa. Sincerely, I wish to know where my opponent is. And his other second."

"I have told you where he is. By now poor Saber will have returned to the same place. And Henri St. Luc—His Grace's other second—is also there."

"And where—"

"Good day, Calum. I have enjoyed knowing you for a little while." She turned from him and began walking away.

Calum caught up and fell in beside her. "You will not be able to forget our kisses, y'know. Neither will I."

"We must. I am—that is, I have not been myself. It was the strain of this morning's events—and those that took place in the gardens last night."

"If you were not yourself, I intend to help you not to be yourself very frequently."

Fear began its cold journey through her veins. "Please leave me now, Calum."

"Alone? In Hyde Park, while the night's villains are still abroad? *Never*." He took her elbow.

"Forget what has happened, I tell you. I have not been myself."

"Ah," he said, chuckling. "But I have been very much myself. And I should like to kiss you again and again."

How could she have forgotten herself so outrageously? "Give me your word you will stay away from me." She began to run.

Calum kept up by lengthening his stride. "Why would you ask such a thing?"

"Because I care about you," she said before she could stop herself. "I mean, because I don't want anything to happen to you."

"Thank you, sweet one." He pulled her to a stop and swung her to face him. "Do you want to marry this man?"

She could hardly breathe at all. "I was betrothed to him at the time of my birth."

"So you have already told me. *Do* you want to marry him?"

"It is expected of me." Her heart hurt.

"Pippa, do you *want* to marry Franchot?"

He must stop. She covered her face. "My father always—"

"Yes," he cut her off. "Yes, you like your father for always deciding what is best for you, and that is exactly as it should be. But, and I beg you for your honesty, *do you want this marriage*?"

"No!" She fell back a step. "No, no, *no*."

He pulled her against him so fiercely she tripped. He caught her and wrapped her in his arms. "Sweet one. What a miracle you are. If only I could tell you—" He buried his face in her hair.

"Tell me what?" Pippa managed to gasp.

"You *will* see me again," Calum said. "Again and again. You and I are sealed together, do you understand?"

"No . . . yes, perhaps."

"Oh, yes. You and I are sealed by fate to walk together through life. And I will make your life very good, sweet one. Just as you will make my life all that it can be."

She did not understand. "I will do what I must do, Calum."

"Yes." But he looked *happy*. "You will do what you must do. What you were always intended to do."

"I will never disappoint my father."

"How could you disappoint anyone?" Catching her hand, he led her quickly through the trees to a horse that quietly cropped the shaggy grass. "I'll get you back," he said, lifting her to the horse's back and leaping up behind her.

"We can't go like this," she protested. "We might be seen."

"Ah, yes." At that he rode a distance and dismounted to retrieve her top hat. Seated behind her once more, he plopped it on her head, arranged her in the most intimate manner between his thighs and set off. "I am a man no one knows, riding with a boy no one knows. Possibly a man with his son? Fear not. I shall release you a distance from Franchot House.''

Pippa's doeskin breeches stretched much too tightly over her bottom. And her bottom fitted much too neatly against That part of Calum Innes that had so fascinated her from their first touch.

"You will send for me if you need me?" Calum asked, bending his head beside hers. "Do not doubt that I will come to you at once."

"I will not need you."

"Then I will come as soon as I've done what must be done."

He was such a puzzle. "You will never be able to come for me. This must be enough. This must be all."

She felt him laugh. They had reached a corner that was perilously close to her destination.

"I will set you down here," he told her, drawing his great horse to a halt. "But I will watch until you are safely inside the house."

"I must enter from the gardens," she said.

"Just so."

His arm tightened around her and he shifted to dismount.

Without meaning to, Pippa gripped the horse's mane in one hand and Calum's sleeve with the other.

"What is it?" he asked, concern heavy in his deep voice. "Are you afraid? Only say so, and I will take you with me now."

He was headstrong. She must be wise for both of them. "I am not afraid."

"There is something you want, then? Tell me."

"I want to . . ." Oh, she could *not* believe herself. "I want to thank you for your kindness," she said quickly and slackened her grip.

He dismounted and lifted her to stand before him. "You're certain that's all you want to say to me now?"

"Yes." But what she wanted to do was run her hands over him. All of him. A heaviness pressed downward inside her lowest places. Goodness, what could it be that made all this happen? She wanted to run her hands—and her lips—*all* over him, and she wanted to do so when he wore no clothes. Not a single item. Not a *stitch.*

"Good-bye, then, Pippa. For now."

"Yes. Good-bye." She began to run. "Good-bye!"

She was completely mad. Only a mad female would have such evil thoughts, and she knew they were evil even from the rather peculiar teachings the dowager had given her on the subject of intimate behavior between husbands and wives.

At the entrance to a passageway leading to the rear of Franchot House, she paused and glanced back. Calum stood there, bareheaded, his hand raised in a wave.

Pippa gave the most insignificant of waves in return, ducked her head and sped to the little gate in the high wall around the gardens.

Mad, mad, *mad*!

An evil, carnal spirit. Why, the dowager had informed her that all men were evil, carnal spirits who required the sacrifice of a woman's body to satisfy the appetites of those spirits. The dowager had said, in a voice one might use to discuss a nuncheon menu, that it was a woman's duty to lie supine, retaining only those garments her husband permitted her to retain, whilst he "did with her what he would." The inference—or so it had seemed to Pippa—was that "what he would" might entail a considerable amount of touching one—with various parts of himself. She visualized Franchot's moist lips and equally moist palms, and shuddered.

Shunning the unpleasant thought of going into the house by the nasty potting shed again, she had decided to trust the activity she knew prevailed inside Franchot House as an adequate diversion and use the conservatory for her departure and return.

She crept along in the shadow of a tall hedge. Then came the part that was most critical. This was where she had to leave the cover of the topiary gardens and dash across open lawns to the terrace and the conservatory.

Pippa began to run.

On the one occasion when Franchot had attempted to kiss her, she had turned her face away and his wet mouth had slithered across her cheek to her ear—which he proceeded to bite rather painfully. And whilst he did all this, he contrived to clutch—equally painfully—at one of her breasts. Pippa wrinkled her nose and felt quite sick at the memory.

She gained the terrace, and then the conservatory door.

Then she was inside with the door closed behind her.

Blessedly, there was no one in sight.

As a wife, she was supposed to submit to beastly pawing from her husband, and she did not like the thought of that one bit.

With such haste that she began to pop buttons, Pippa ripped off Saber's green coat and divested herself of the woolen cravat.

Really, she was *so* puzzled by herself. She considered the idea of her husband touching her bare skin abominable, yet . . . Oh, dear, what a bother all this was. *She wanted to run her hands all over Calum Innes's bare body. She wanted to "do with him what she would."* Whatever that might be.

Lady Philipa Chauncey was an evil, carnal spirit.

Really! Who would have thought it?

She retrieved the apricot velvet mantle she'd hidden in a cupboard where the gardeners kept supplies and slung it around her shoulders. Sitting on the edge of the nearest planting bed, she hauled off the boots.

Before she could pull on her slippers, the door into the conservatory from the little salon opened. Shaking in her agitation, she finished putting on her shoes and turned to stuff Saber's coat and boots into the cupboard.

"Pippa!" Justine whispered hoarsely. "Thank goodness. I was so afraid you wouldn't get back before someone came looking for you. I've had to put that poor little maid of yours to bed and have the housekeeper told she's ill."

"Why?" Pippa asked, alarmed.

"Because she's frantic with worry about you, of course. As am I. What exactly did you do to them?"

Pippa shut the door on the evidence of her escapade and faced Justine. "It will all work. There will be no duel."

"Certainly not *this* day," Justine said severely, but her pretty mouth began to twitch. "I cannot believe I have involved myself in this. It is not at all like me."

Pippa tossed her head. "On the contrary, I think it is prob-

ably exactly like the real you. The you that you were meant
to be.''

"We will not discuss that notion further." Justine slipped
her hand beneath Pippa's arm and limped beside her into the
salon. "We must be careful getting you to your rooms. The
entire house is in an uproar, people rushing hither and thither.
The physician has been here for several hours."

"They will live," Pippa said, but she did feel a little
ashamed. "What of the dowager?"

"Grandmama has also taken to her bed. She says she will
not come down until all this nonsense is over."

"Very wise. Perhaps we should follow her example."

A careful reconnaissance of the vestibule outside the salon
confirmed the confusion that reigned in Franchot House.
"They will never notice us," Pippa said, thinking aloud.
"Come, we will go to my rooms together."

She was right. Servants dashed up and down staircases.
Folded linens or steaming jugs of water filled their hands and
arms and they scarcely spared a glance for the two women.

They gained Pippa's lofty chambers and Justine immediately turned upon her future sister-in-law. She plunked her fists
on her slim hips. "Now," she said. "I thought you said you
intended to use some *mild* device to accomplish our ends. I
want you to tell me exactly what you did to my brother and
his friends."

Pippa gestured airily. "Very little, really. I merely employed one or two remedies my nanny found cause to admin-
ister to me when I was a small girl. Senna was for those times
when everything that went into me did not seem anxious to
leave me in an acceptable period of time."

Justine's cheeks turned fiery red and she whispered,
"*Pippa.*"

"And then there was ipecac. My nanny found that necessary when—through my own headstrong nature—certain
things went into me that should not have done so and which
she wished to retrieve."

"*Pippa.*"

"Mmm. One doesn't tend to forget such moments. Anyway, in order to ensure that my fiancé and his friends were
completely—er—*emptied* of anything undesirable they might

have partaken of last evening, I added the appropriate substances to their final four bottles of hock. And to the two bottles of cognac with which they completed their revelry. How fortunate for them that I had the foresight to save them from the dreadful headaches they would have suffered today."

"Oh, Pippa. Oh, my, they are so . . . *unwell*."

"I should imagine they *are* unwell," Pippa said matter-of-factly. "I should imagine they hardly know which end is up, so to speak."

❧ Nine

"*If this* don't beat all," Struan said in a low tone. He elbowed Calum, who sat beside him on one of the damnably uncomfortable benches in Christie's auction rooms.

"Not *now*," Calum said. London's premier auction house had never paid particular mind to the comfort of its patrons. A small fire spitting to one side of the large room did little to soften Spartan surroundings. Calum moved forward on the bench. "The Reynolds should be up next. Arran's been lusting for this piece. If we get it, he'll have to hide it. Grace will say it's a boring waste of money."

A wave of muttering arose around them, and more than a few exclamations of awe went up.

"*Calum—*"

"There it is," Calum said as one of Reynolds's distinctively rococo-style portraits was hoisted onto a high easel for the edification of the well-heeled crowd. Light from the square, glassed-in dome overhead lent a golden glow to the subject's painted face. Calum leaned forward for a better view. "I must say I'm glad Arran decided to return to Scotland—not that I don't enjoy his company, of course."

Struan's strong fingers, digging into his arm, finally captured Calum's attention. "Don't look now," Struan whispered, "but London's most celebrated coward is, as we speak, approaching. And the *boy* in green is on his arm."

111

"*Don't* mention that," Calum said through barely parted lips. "*Ever.*"

"Damn me," Struan said. "If I didn't know better, I'd say he's actually hunting you down, old chap."

"Can't be." Not turning to look at Pippa—and Franchot—tested Calum's will beyond endurance. He had been unable to keep those intelligent, dark blue eyes, or the touch of full, tremblingly soft lips, from his mind for anything but brief periods in the four days that had passed since the "duel."

"He *is*, I tell you. He's coming this way. He must have gone to Hanover Square and been told you were here. Boy—sorry—*lady*-in-green is on his arm, with La Hoarville bringing up the rear in the company of one Henri St. Luc, if memory serves."

"Face the auctioneer," Calum commanded. "For my sake."

Dutifully, Struan did as he was asked and said, "As you will," in a tone that left no doubt as to his reluctance. "This is a good time to mention that I returned to Whitechapel last night."

"You what?" Calum turned sharply sideways on the bench—and looked into the troubled, dark blue eyes of Lady Philipa Chauncey. Instantly he leaped to his feet. "Good afternoon, my lady," he said, avoiding acknowledging Franchot.

The memory of their last meeting was instantly between them—and the knowledge that he had asked her to leave Franchot for him but that she had refused. She lowered her eyes and allowed him to take her hand. He bent to touch his lips to her fingers and felt her tremble. Surely Franchot must feel that quaking in the woman on his arm.

"You're a difficult man to confront, Innes," Franchot said. "I've been sending messages for days."

This time Calum looked the man in the face. "*I* am a difficult man to confront, Your Grace?" He heard the offering for the Reynolds begin.

"It is absolutely imperative that we speak," the duke said. His face was not quite as Calum remembered. He appeared haggard, with purple smudges beneath his eyes, and his clothes might almost have been intended for a slightly larger person. "It was not . . . I was too incapacitated to come myself before today. Please, Mr. Innes. This is a very delicate matter. Would you do me the honor of accompanying me fiancée and meself—and our companions—for a short promenade along the Mall?''

"Viscount Hunsingore and I are engaged in a piece of business for his brother, the Marquess of Stonehaven." Even as he spoke, Calum heard the auctioneer finish his impassioned description of the portrait and open the floor for bids.

Lady Hoarville clung to a cadaverously thin and definitely demonic-looking man whose French blood showed through his skin. She dimpled at Calum and drew her companion forward. "Have you met Henri St. Luc, Mr. Innes?" To her companions she said, "Mr. Innes and I have made a prior acquaintance, haven't we, Mr. Innes?"

"Good day to you, Lady Hoarville," Calum said stiffly. "And to you, Monsieur St. Luc."

"A pleasure," St. Luc said in flawless English.

"Henri is a *connoisseur*," Lady Hoarville warbled with apparent rich appreciation for her companion. "He has the most exquisite taste in everything. Furnishings, paintings, sculpture, garden arrangements—and dress. Henri's taste in the matter of dress is incomparable." Today the lady's own taste was revealed in the cunningly situated circle, cut from the bodice of her garnet-colored pelisse, that allowed her white breasts to press into view.

"Really?" Calum spared the most fleeting glance for La Hoarville's *connoisseur* and summarily dismissed him as a self-consciously affected man bent on proving his discriminating flair by wearing outlandish garb and a bored expression.

"I'm delighted to make your acquaintance," St. Luc said with the merest downward flicker of heavy eyelids. A purple velvet cravat drooped in a manner that matched its owner's apparent ennui, and the man's deep green coat sagged at pockets from which large, lace-trimmed kerchiefs trailed.

Calum decided that Byron had yet another slavish imitator and returned his attention to Pippa—who stared back at him with anxious eyes that made him want to take her into his arms and kiss away her fears.

From behind Calum, the auctioneer shouted, "You *insult* us all, sir! The bidding opened at a thousand guineas."

"I must ask your leave," Calum said to Franchot. He cast

another look at Pippa. She was more *striking* than merely
pretty, more *memorable* than simply beautiful, and the insipid
spring green of her muslin gown and silk spencer annoyed
Calum. Her drama would be well served by brilliant hues and
daring designs. With difficulty, he shifted his attention from
Pippa to Franchot. "Arran—the marquess desperately wants
this painting, Your Grace. So if you will excuse me . . ."

Franchot, visibly hunching, glanced toward the offering and
made a sign.

"Now that's more like it," the auctioneer roared. "His
Grace the Duke of Franchot bids five thousand guineas."

Calum swung around and met Struan's questioning gaze. A
hush had fallen on the crowd.

The hush stretched on and on, broken only by the occasional tutting of florid Lady Ernestine Sebbel, who was famous
for her magnificent disapproval of most things.

Struan, suddenly furiously intent upon the proceedings,
made a discreet motion.

"*Six* thousand guineas," the auctioneer announced with relish. "Do I hear seven?"

"*Seven*!" he roared a moment later as another bid came
from somewhere on the floor. Then: "*Nine* from the gentleman in puce."

"Gad," Calum muttered. Arran would never forgive them
if he didn't get his wretched portrait. Calum raised his program
a fraction.

"I have *ten*." The auctioneer rocked on his podium as if
about to be transported to a higher plane.

The bidding from other interested parties heated in earnest,
and within minutes the plump, smiling face of an undoubtedly
dead lady commanded a promise of twelve thousand guineas.

"This is unheard of," Struan said to Calum. "I don't even
like the thing."

"You are not the one who has to like it."

"Grace will have Arran's ears if we pay this kind of sum
for something she will undoubtedly consider worthless."

Calum smiled. "Grace is very singular in her tastes, but she
would not do other than see Arran happy."

"Nevertheless, she will not fail to mention how much good

such a little fortune could accomplish for the tenants of Kirkcaldy," Struan reminded him.

"The tenants of Kirkcaldy want for nothing," Calum said truthfully.

"We are at *thirteen thousand guineas.*" The man on the podium seemed close to swooning from joy. "Thirteen, once. Thirteen, twice. Thirteen—"

"I have *twenty thousand guineas*!" Absolute silence descended in the big room. "The Duke of Franchot bids twenty thousand guineas. This is indeed a most singular day."

After a few seconds of observing the faintly shocked faces of the assembly, the auctioneer pronounced, "Twenty thousand, once . . . twenty thousand, twice . . . "

Calum barely heard the man announce, "Sold!" before facing Franchot again, the full force of his own hatred so powerful he feared he might take the wretch by the throat here and now.

The duke signaled an auction boy to come close. "My man will deal with the details," he told the runner. "Kindly arrange for the painting to be transported to the Marquess of Stonehaven. At . . . ?" He raised a brow at Struan.

"Castle Kirkcaldy." Struan responded like a man whose mouth was operated by strings. "Scotland."

"Just so," the duke said.

Calum glanced about him and slowly the uproar that had followed Franchot's outrageous exhibition came to life for him. "What was that for?" he asked Franchot. "Why in God's name would you do such a thing?"

"A gesture of friendship." Franchot, whose face now shone slightly with perspiration, shrugged weakly. "It seemed appropriate. You had a mission you had to dispatch. *I* need to talk to you at once. I bought something to show my esteem for you and your close friends, and dispatched your mission at the same time. Now I assume you will accompany me, sir."

"Oh, do come along, Mr. Innes," Lady Hoarville cajoled. "Etienne has come to throw himself upon your mercy, haven't you, darling Etienne?"

Darling Etienne cast Lady Hoarville a stare that would have destroyed a less self-absorbed creature.

"I'd be much obliged, Innes," Franchot said.

Struan moved forward suddenly. "My brother will not accept a gift from you, Franchot. Kindly arrange for the painting to be delivered to your own accommodations."

Franchot waved carelessly. "That is a matter for a later moment." He concentrated on Calum and said in low, urgent tones, "In God's name, man, I'm pleading with you. They're all watching us. *All* of Society's agog. Walk out with me now and show some sign of comradeship, I beg you."

A moment made in heaven—for a man bent on throwing another into hell—shimmered before Calum. Blessedly, reason was fast upon the heels of revenge's lure. "As you will," he said, smiling thinly and ushering the duke ahead of him toward the doors. "Keep me company, if you will, Struan. Never let it be said that *I* am a man without sufficient honor to be merciful."

Struan gave the appearance of a man on the verge of apoplexy, but he did as Calum asked and walked beside him as they followed Pippa, the duke, Lady Hoarville and St. Luc out into a sunny afternoon on Pall Mall.

"We are perhaps among the last to enjoy the auction here, since they intend to move their location," St. Luc said pleasantly enough, his native French audible only in his unusual choice of construction. "I have long admired the quality of what is presented at Christie's."

No sooner had they progressed a few yards than Franchot turned abruptly on Calum and thrust an envelope at him. "I cannot accept this," he said, visibly pained. "For the sake of my good name, I implore you to assist me in a fabrication that will do you no harm, yet will *save* me."

Calum stared at Pippa until she slowly raised her face. They both knew that the envelope he held had been the one she pressed upon Saber Avenall almost a week before. "Am I to open this?" he said to Franchot.

"Of course. But you already know what it contains." The duke nodded graciously to passersby on their way to waiting carriages and as he did so, recited: " '*I, Your Grace, am a gentleman. As such, I shall endeavor to forget that you failed to appear for our appointment this morning. Let us put this event behind us.*' It is signed C.I."

Calum removed the paper from the envelope and read what

a hand other than his own had written in his name. "This would seem generous enough, Your Grace," he said. "Intended to ensure no repeat of the unpleasant event." He felt Pippa watching him.

"I cannot be thought to have begged off," Franchot said.

"But you did."

Franchot's shoulders heaved and it was Lady Hoarville who stepped forward to slip a steadying hand under his arm. St. Luc, wiping perspiration from his own brow, looked on with a fixed smile.

"I was not able to appear," Franchot said. "I was . . . *ill*."

"So you say," Calum commented.

"It is so. There was . . . it would seem that we ate something tainted. And I ask you to help me in this difficulty by saying that I *did*, in fact, appear in Hyde Park at the appointed time."

"Damn me," Struan muttered. "Incredible."

"Incredible indeed," Calum said.

"It could do you no harm to say that your aim was faulty and my pistol discharged prematurely."

Calum laughed in disbelief. "No harm?"

"You do not have to consider your reputation as I must mine."

Such arrogance defied understanding. "No," Calum said shortly. "No. What you suggest will not be possible."

Franchot said, "I will make it worth your while."

What I want, you will not readily pay me, imposter. "No," he repeated.

"Look, I am yet ill. I came today because you had ignored all my efforts to get you to come to me."

"True enough." Messengers had been sent a dozen times a day, imploring Calum to attend the duke in Pall Mall.

"Very well. Let us try a new tale. *Both* of our weapons discharged prematurely. *There*. What more can I offer?"

Hah! Slowly, an idea took shape. Calum looked to Struan as if searching for approval, then at Pippa, who stared back, her dear face a study in utter misery. "Should I perhaps consider that you are offering me something in the way of a friendship, Your Grace?" This cur had paraded her forth today as part of his spurious public display of personal bliss. "I do not put myself well. Am I to collect that you have had a change of heart toward me? That you wish me to join you in this deception so that we may draw closer as two men of character with the good of our respective reputations in mind?''

Struan coughed.

Franchot blinked, slowly—repeatedly.

Pippa could be seen to hold her breath.

The foolish Hoarville creature grinned and bobbed, for all the world as if she bore witness to the forging of a treaty between two nations she regarded as equally her own.

''Perhaps I have misunderstood—''

''No, no,'' Franchot said quickly, before Calum could finish. ''You are exactly correct. That is *exactly* what I had in mind. From the moment I set eyes upon you . . . Well, certainly, shortly after that, I said to myself, 'Now there is a man whose friendship I should regard as a great boon.' Only ill fate set us upon the wrong path. Yes, indeed, I should regard your friendship a treasure, sir.''

''And our weapons discharged prematurely on the morning of our intended duel?''

''Yes, yes, yes.'' Relief brought Franchot's short breaths spurting forth. ''Praise God you are a man of reason. Premature discharge, and we are both determined to show our gratitude at our good fortune. Good fortune that we were not deprived of the opportunity to spend many satisfying hours together.''

La Hoarville clapped her plump white hands.

Struan pushed forward his lower lip and rocked up onto his toes.

''You are very gracious, Mr. Innes,'' Pippa said in her charming, softly clear voice. ''And now, we must not detain you further.''

Instantly, she won a scowl from Franchot. ''We must not be perfunctory, m'dear. Not the done thing under the circumstances.''

''What would you suggest?'' Struan asked him, much too pleasantly. ''Tea, perhaps? A game of croquet on the lawn?''

''Those and more,'' Lady Hoarville caroled, and then bowed her head coyly. ''Oh, dear, I have overstepped myself as usual. Dear Etienne and I are old friends, but I must never forget my place, must I? I only thought that it would be so perfect if he invited you down to Franchot Castle for the lovely house party that starts there next month. That's when we celebrate Etienne's birthday, you know."

Had lightning cleaved the flagway before him, Franchot could not have looked more undone. Calum stared at the man who slept in the beds that should have been Calum's own and realized that they must share virtually the same birthday.

Lady Hoarville continued unabashed. "Don't you think it would be lovely, Lady Philipa? There will be Henri and Saber and Etienne and me. The dowager, of course. And Lady Justine, although one doesn't exactly count Lady Justine, does one?"

Calum regarded the woman and felt, for one of the few times in his life, a desperate need to shake a member of the weaker sex until she could no longer speak at all.

"Mr. Innes would be such a marvelous addition." She turned to Struan and said, "And you, too, of course, Lord Hunsingore. And there would be you," she said to Pippa without looking at her again.

"Incredible," Struan murmured once more.

"Marvelous idea," Franchot said hollowly.

Struan was shaking his head.

"What a charming suggestion," Calum said before Struan could deliver a flat refusal. "Don't you think so, Struan? Charming and generous. Only this morning we were speaking of needing a respite from the Season. We discussed spending some time in the country. Of course, Cornwall hadn't been our intended destination, but—"

"I insist," Franchot put in, clearly warming to the hope of absolute victory in the cause of restored honor. "You shall come to Franchot Castle as my guests and stay for as long as possible."

Struan's dark, narrowed eyes flashed his virulent disapproval.

"The viscount does not look convinced," Lady Hoarville said, her blue eyes round and innocent. "*You* convince him, Lady Philipa. Tell him how much it will mean to you to have his company and that of Mr. Innes at this time when the celebrations for your upcoming marriage are to begin.''

Pippa swallowed visibly and color swept her cheeks. "If it would please everyone else, then of course it will please me."

She did not want him to come. Calum clasped his hands behind his back. *She did not want him to come because she feared what might happen if he did.* "Thank you, Lady Philipa," he said formally. *You do not trust me, and you do not trust yourself if you are with me.*

"It will be very jolly, I assure you," Lady Hoarville babbled. "Why, we shall have continual entertainments. If you are very good, Mr. Innes, I shall insist upon escorting you to the fair myself. What do you say to that?"

He shifted his regard from Pippa's face to Lady Hoarville. Her words came to him slowly, much more slowly than they had been spoken. "The fair?"

"Of course, the fair," she said, shaking a finger. "*Everyone* knows the duke leaves the Season early and returns to Franchot for his birthday and for the fair. It is to be held next month. It is in the same week every year, and has been for absolutely *ever*."

"The Franchot Fair," Struan said indistinctly.

"Yes," Lady Hoarville said, obviously delighted. "This year, the fair shall have a new reveler. *Our* dear new friend, Mr. Calum Innes."

❧ *Ten*

"*This mystery* of yours wears my patience," Calum said.

Pretending to doze, Struan jounced against the squabs of the Stonehaven town coach that bore them through the night. Since their return to Hanover Square during the late afternoon, he had kept to his rooms—until he appeared and announced this insane outing. He had refused to explain his visit to Mrs. Lushbottam's establishment the previous evening in other than general terms.

"Struan," Calum said sharply, "if you do not give me the courtesy of your attention, I shall have the coach turn around."

"*My* coach," Struan said without opening his eyes.

"How true." Such comments were unlike his friend, and Calum frowned the deeper for it. "In that case, I think I've decided it's a fair night for a walk."

He raised his cane to rap the trap, but Struan was instantly above him, capturing his hand and standing where he could glare down into Calum's face. "We are going to Whitechapel," he said.

"So you've already told me," Calum responded. "What I don't understand is why we are going in this conveyance that announces our presence, and *why* I am to engage in this elaborate charade you say is imperative."

"I told you plainly," Struan said, visibly angry as he sank back onto his own seat. "And I cannot understand why, when I have gone to such lengths to assist you in a foolish quest of

121

yours, *you* should become hostile when I ask you for something.''

"I didn't ask you to go to Whitechapel on your own and interfere."

"You should be damnably grateful I'm trying to do something useful."

Calum bristled. "You've probably sent them running for a fresh blind. I had things well in hand."

"Well in hand?" Struan snorted. "So well in hand you've now got us parading down to the bounder's castle, for God's sake. And for *his* pleasure, I might add."

"The better to keep a close eye on him," Calum remarked evenly enough. "And the better to look for clues that may lead me to proof of my identity."

"And the better to keep you within easy reach of the fair Lady Philipa," Struan commented, sniffing.

"Lady Philipa may become my greatest dilemma." Calum knew he was voicing his own growing fears.

"How so?"

"She is gentle, with a generous heart. I feel that. I would like to spare her pain, but that may not be possible."

Struan braced his weight on his arms. "You mean you would sacrifice the charming Philipa if she were to interfere with your plans?"

Calum looked out into the darkness. "Let us hope it won't be necessary. But I cannot pretend that she will not—if all goes my way—discover that I have, to some extent, used her. At that point . . . well, then I shall have to see." He must not be diverted from the matter at hand. "Why does it have to be me who creates the diversion at Lushbottam's?"

Struan looked pained. "As I've told you—several times—after last night I doubt the woman would let me back into the place. I really do think Milo and Miranda have paid her to make certain neither of us gets anywhere near them."

They drew closer to their destination and Calum huddled lower into his cloak. "There's nothing to be gained by my engaging that creature in an altercation. All I'll do is give her an excuse to refuse me admittance in future."

"The man's *deaf*." Struan spread his hands as if in defeat. "He doesn't understand that while *he's* diverting Lushbottam,

I will be using that diversion to make my way upstairs and find out if our witch doctors have really left—as Lushbottam insisted they had when I called last night. I ask you,'' he asked no one in particular, ''is this such a difficult concept?''

Calum was not entirely diverted. ''Why in a family coach?''

''To capture attention.''

''*Why*?''

''To accomplish our mission as quickly as possible. The women in the windows will alert Lushbottam. She will be awaiting you. The commotion will commence at once and I can accomplish our business at once.'' Slapping his knees, Struan smiled engagingly. ''And we are already at our destination.''

''I believe you came here last night to see the fair Ella.''

''You are a suspicious man.''

''I am a man,'' Calum said, unblinking.

The carriage door opened and the coachman, his face showing nothing of his thoughts, placed the steps.

''Go,'' Struan whispered urgently. ''Tell her you want something better than she has shown you so far.''

Calum glanced around. ''Why are you whispering? I see no one.''

''I'm whispering because I must be certain no one overhears,'' Struan said. ''When you suggest dissatisfaction with what she's already offered, she'll be determined to prove she's got the best in London. Then she'll have someone take you into a room where you'll be offered a few things you're not supposed to be able to refuse.''

''This sounds abominable.''

''You are a man of the world. Enjoy for a while—just a little while—then raise a fuss to make sure Lushbottam comes running. When she does, detain her for as long as you can. Leave the rest to me.''

''The *rest*?'' Calum scoffed. ''Sounds to me as if all but the simplest part will be my task.''

''The entire affair is for *you*, you ungrateful rattlebrain.'' Struan caught Calum's arm. ''Hurry, man. And if the brother and sister raise an alarm, be prepared to join me. We shall barricade the door and force them to speak honestly.''

''I cannot understand this change of heart,'' Calum said,

shaking his head. "Only yesterday you insisted—"

"That was yesterday. I *have* had a change of heart. Do what must be done."

Still shaking his head, Calum left the coach and approached the front door of Mrs. Lushbottam's establishment. In the windows on either side of him, fluttering eyelashes and sly winks were the only signs that he'd been seen by the industrious lady "tailors" at work with their needles.

Concentrating on the bronzed cat to his left, he knocked and braced for Mrs. Lushbottam's tongue-lashing.

There was a creak. A slice of light widened across his polished boots. The moment had arrived.

"Well, now," the familiar voice of Mrs. Lushbottam said. "If it isn't one of our *real* gentlemen customers. And I thought as how you'd not been pleased with the quality of our work the last time you came."

Calum looked up into the woman's hollow, lipless face. "Good evening." He stepped over the threshold. "I'd like"— he swallowed —"that is, I wondered if you might not have something of . . . a *most* exceptional variety."

From the direction of the room where he and Struan had witnessed the "performance" came the sound of music played on a wooden pipe.

Mrs. Lushbottam inclined her head toward the noise. "We really don't like interruptions once a production is in progress, but I *could* make an exception for—"

"No," Calum said quickly. "I am a man who prefers to take his pleasures more privately, thank you."

Teeth appeared in the gash of the woman's mouth. "No requests denied," she said before calling out, "Veronique! Come 'ere, if you please." She pushed the front door shut.

Within moments a female stepped from one of the bay windows. She was small and dark-haired, her painted face pretty, and Calum could not guess her age.

"*Oui, madame?*" she said to Mrs. Lushbottam.

"This is a gentleman who's thinking of availing himself of our most individual products. I think he wants to go upstairs. All the way up, I think it'll have to be."

"That won't be necessary," Calum said, trying to glance

behind him without appearing to glance behind him. "Isn't there somewhere right here?"

Mrs. Lushbottam's laugh was a truly fearful thing. "Oh, sir," she said, tugging on the points of lace at her thin hips, "we do have to remember that not everyone understands the finest things in life. Right here? Oh, my, no. Although the idea does appeal. Someone might come through that front door by mistake, and *then* where would we be?"

He'd like to be done with this gruesome masquerade.

"Will you show him the way upstairs, Veronique?" Mrs. Lushbottam asked. "Top floor. Your favorite room."

"I know the way," Calum said.

"You don't know Veronique's way with *your* way, sir. Take him up, dear, and make sure he gets exactly what he's come for."

With a desperate sense of having made a hash of things, and casting about for a way to rescue the situation, Calum followed Veronique up the ten flights of stairs to the top floor.

In the narrow, dimly lit passageway leading to the bedrooms—and to Milo and Miranda's room—she stopped and leaned against the wall. "Yer wanted something really special, then?" she said, sounding purely cockney. "Sometimes Lushy don't get the little hints what Veronique gets. What yer want is an audience what's not an audience, right? Yer want to be watched while we do our business."

"Right." Calum peered at her. "No, I'm afraid I don't understand. But then, I don't suppose you understand, either. Not that it matters."

She giggled. "You're an odd one, and no mistake. I do understand, y'know. Yer want to *pretend* like we're bein' watched, only yer don't *really* want to be watched. Right?"

"Right. I mean—"

"Well, that's what I want, too," Veronique said, pushing her bright red lips into a pout. "We'll stay right 'ere. Spread yer legs and wave to the crowd, ducky."

He stared at her, trying to decide how to get them both—and Mrs. Lushbottam—away from this passage.

"Oh, all right, then," the girl said. " 'Ave it your way, but I'm not a bleedin' mind reader, y'know. *I'll* wave."

She smiled to the right and the left, held a hand aloft in the manner of the old queen acknowledging adoring crowds from her carriage and began undoing the tapes on her modest gray gown.

"Look 'ow jealous they are," she said, indicating the empty passageway. "And can we blame 'em, ducky?"

She let the dress fall to her feet. What lay beneath was anything but modest.

Calum glanced at toes shod in purple satin, surveyed purple silk stockings secured above dimpled knees with gold ribbons and passed rapidly on to well-rounded thighs . . . and purple stays.

Veronique was a study in a little purple and absolutely nothing else.

"Come on, then," she said, moving in to open his cloak and reach for his trousers. "We can't disappoint the audience, can we? Best get on with it."

With one hand Calum caught both of her wrists together and held her away. If he shoved her into the nearest room, she'd probably raise enough fuss to bring Mrs. Lushbottam upstairs.

"Yer just want to look?" Veronique asked. Her brown eyes held no particular interest. "Is that it? It's all right with me, ducky."

He felt suddenly, unaccountably, weary. "That's all I want," he told her. The empty, pathetic creature deserved more pity than disgust.

Clearly his response pleased her. "That's all right, then." She thrust forth her naked breasts. "Look all yer want. Are they still there, then?" She indicated the empty places where the "audience" he supposedly desired hovered.

"They are indeed," he assured her. There was nothing for it but to work this out on his own. "Scream," he told the woman. "I want you to scream."

Veronique opened her small mouth and shrieked. Her expression didn't change.

"Scream for Mrs. Lushbottam," Calum ordered desperately. "Shout for her to come here at once."

That brought doubt to vacant eyes. "Lushy? Yer want Lushy to come? Yer want 'er to watch?"

"*Do* it," he told her, and when she hesitated, he gave her

a small shake of encouragement. "Get the woman here *now*."

If Veronique had taken to the boards with Mrs. Siddons, the latter might never have known fame. Veronique's chilling wails and shouts for "Lushy" to come and save 'er were real enough to strike cold to Calum's bones.

But he got what he'd wanted. The floor beneath his feet shook with the approach of heavy footsteps. He waited long enough to see Mrs. Lushbottam appear at the top of the stairs before he opened the nearest door and shoved the struggling, shrieking Veronique inside.

Within moments the head tailor arrived.

The instant she entered the room, Calum slammed the door shut and threw himself against it with the flailing Veronique clasped to his chest. "We've got a live one 'ere," the girl panted between yells. "Wants yer to watch 'im watch me. 'Ave yer ever 'eard the like?"

"Anything for the gentleman prepared to pay for custom orders," Mrs. Lushbottam said, crossing her arms. "His money is our time, Veronique."

Calum prayed that some miracle had told Struan that now was the moment to pay his visit to Milo and Miranda.

At the gruff sound of a throat being cleared, Calum tightened his grip on Veronique and looked around the room for the first time.

On a large, tumbled bed reclined an elderly, sandy-haired man who was not alone. "Be a good chap and remind the lady of our presence, would you?" he said to Calum, indicating Mrs. Lushbottam. When she turned around he said, "Forgotten about the *time* we get for *our* money, have we, Lushy?"

Struan's was the name Calum silently cursed as he closed his eyes, shutting out the vision of the big man's stubby fingers playing with the curly black hair on Henri St. Luc's chest.

There were times when Anabel wondered why she'd been so patient with Etienne for so long.

Summer it might be, and her fur throw certainly kept out any unpleasant night drafts, but she was bored with sitting in her post chaise and doing what Etienne should have the wit to do for himself.

She held a window blind open just enough to allow her a

view of the front door of Lushy's—and of the carriage that had borne Calum Innes there.

Really, if she had not had the sense to decide to make quite sure of Innes's activities, silly Etienne would not have discovered he might be in danger until it was too late.

If Etienne was in danger, so was Anabel—only she did have a great deal of sense, enough to turn this development to her own advantage.

"Is Lord Hunsingore inside?" Calum shouted to the waiting coachman.

"He is, sir, he—"

"Praise be! Hanover Square, man. Make haste." Calum hurled himself inside the carriage, collapsed onto a seat and let his eyes close.

"I almost left without you," Struan said. "What in God's name took you so long?"

Calum rested his head back. "We will not discuss that. Were they there?"

The only reply was the grind of carriage wheels and the creak of springs.

Calum opened his eyes. "Were they—" His attention went immediately to a huddled figure that occupied the opposite end of Struan's seat.

Struan regarded the back of one hand, then the other. His signet ring required a rub, first with a finger, then on his sleeve.

A hooded cloak completely hid the identity of their companion.

"Well?" Calum said when he could contain himself no longer.

"Ooh—" Struan frowned deeply and wrinkled his nose. "Hard to explain, really. Better wait till we're at Hanover Square and alone."

"The hell you say," Calum exploded. "Who is *that*?"

"I'm afraid you aren't going to be happy."

"Who? . . ." An inkling pierced its way into an absolute conviction. "Struan, please tell me I'm wrong. That isn't . . ." He pointed to the cloaked form.

"Afraid so," Struan said.

"No."

"Mmm. Seemed the only thing to do."

"This is what this whole frightful affair was about from the beginning?"

"It is."

Calum narrowed his eyes on their latest dilemma. "Did you attempt to see Milo and Miranda?"

"They aren't there."

"You didn't even check, did you?"

"Didn't have to," Struan said. "Saw them leaving yesterday—bag and baggage."

Calum grew utterly still. "Did you speak to them then?"

"Look," Struan said, shifting forward, "there isn't any way to make this a less scurrilous act than it was from your point of view. But I had no other choice. In time you'll agree."

"I doubt it. Did you speak to Milo and Miranda?"

"I heard Lushbottam tell them their room would be otherwise occupied until their return. She said they'd better not forget that their rent would be higher then, because . . . because it would be winter and there'd be extra money needed for coal," he finished in a rush.

Calum blinked. They'd gone. His last chance to get whatever proof Miranda might have been persuaded to produce had disappeared—until winter.

"Struan," he said, fighting for patience, "why didn't you try to talk to Miranda? Surely you could have followed them."

"I was otherwise occupied."

Calum glanced at the third passenger.

"No," Struan said. "You make assumptions you'd do well *not* to make, my friend. I secured the company of one of Mrs. Lushbottam's ladies. I knew I took a huge chance, but I thought that if I paid her enough, she might be persuaded to take a note to—" He inclined his head. "In the note, I wrote that a Stonehaven coach—I described the coat of arms—would be waiting outside this evening and that Mrs. Lushbottam would be distracted for long enough to allow an escape, should an escape be desired."

"You took a chance indeed," Calum said, considering Struan's story with only part of his whirling mind. "Your messenger might have told Lushbottam, or merely kept the money.''

"If she told Lushbottam, she'd not have been assured of keeping the money—or not all of it. And I suggested that if she did keep the money without delivering the note, I would return. She assured me she would be delighted to be of service. It was a great deal of money.''

"You have abused our friendship," Calum said.

"Utterly.''

"I shall not easily forget this night.''

"Neither should you," Struan agreed. "I am a wretch.''

"What is this creature's tongue?" Calum asked, casting about for what his next move must be to reestablish his acquaintance with Milo and Miranda.

"Don't know," Struan said. "But either she reads English or she got someone to read the note to her. She came to the coach direct and in clothing designed to draw no attention, just as I instructed.''

"I speaks English, too," the girl said clearly. She pushed off her hood and brushed tousled black hair away from her hauntingly beautiful face. She turned her attention entirely upon Struan. "Whatever it is you want, I'll do it. You're a good man, you are—real good and kind." With that, she lodged a shoulder into the corner and closed her great, slanted dark eyes.

Calum leaned across the coach, drew Struan's ear close to his mouth and whispered, "And what, you madman, do you intend to do with her?''

Struan drew in a deep, audible breath and said, "God will provide. At least she speaks English—more or less.''

Anabel's trusty postilions urged their horses to travel as fast as they dared. The sumptuous little post chaise sped forth through London's streets toward Hanover Square.

Anabel could not be certain, but she thought she'd seen a figure slip from Lushy's and enter the Stonehaven carriage only moments before Calum Innes—in a great tear—exploded from the front door. Rather than wait and follow again, she had decided to arrive at the Stonehaven house first and position herself where she might have another opportunity to see exactly who traveled in Innes's company.

As the chaise approached Hanover Square, a light rain began to fall. Droplets scattered the windows, and Anabel had to put her face near the glass to obtain a better view. She had instructed the postilions to draw up before a house to the right of the Stonehavens' and stand as if awaiting their employer's departure from that house.

The riders did as they'd been told, but all was not exactly as Anabel had anticipated. Another coach—one that she had no difficulty in identifying as belonging to the Duke of Franchot—had just arrived. While she watched, a coachman hopped down and opened the door.

Anabel held her breath. What would Etienne be doing here? And what would it mean that he'd come without telling her of his intentions?

Her questions were quickly proven unnecessary. Not a man, but a woman, alighted and spoke to the driver. He nodded and watched her run up the steps to knock on the front door. It opened and Anabel saw a butler peer out. As Lady Philipa Chauncey was admitted, the Franchot coach pulled away from Calum Innes's lodgings.

Anabel smiled. She could scarcely believe her good fortune. Now she had the damning weapon she needed to use against "pure" Philipa.

Tapping the window, Anabel signaled her desire to drive on.

❧ Eleven

𝒫*ippa jumped* when the butler closed the salon door behind him—closed her inside a room that did not look at all as she might have imagined one of Calum Innes's rooms to look.

Not that it was his room.

Or his house.

Not that she had any particular reason to know what manner of rooms Calum Innes would choose . . . if he *were* choosing rooms.

Backing slowly away from the door, she bumped into a tiny japanned table and barely caught the grinning china dog that tipped from its top. "Oh." She sighed aloud, softly, replacing the ornament. She should not have come, yet she could not stay away. Coming had been a responsibility.

Vividly painted panels lined the walls of this little salon, panels edged with gilt moldings above gilt wainscot. Each panel glowed with riotous flowers, and similar bouquets cavorted over a pretty little tapestry couch and several chairs in formal French style.

Pippa looked into a gilt-framed mirror above a fireplace plastered in turquoise blue and saw the reflection of dozens of candles in an ornate bronze chandelier.

The Franchot coachman would find a place from which he could see the front door. As soon as she appeared, he was to carry her back to Pall Mall. And Justine—once persuaded that Pippa was not to be dissuaded from her mission—had given assurance that the coachman would hold his tongue about this night's venture.

Why would Justine—quiet, refined, *careful* Justine—show such obvious sympathy for Pippa's interest in Calum Innes when she was betrothed to Justine's own brother?

This was inappropriate and it simply would not do.

Pippa settled her blue crepe cloak more firmly upon her shoulders, took in a determined breath and contemplated how to depart the house without encountering the formidable Stonehaven butler again.

The sound of the front door opening, followed by male voices, set her in a complete and fluttering panic.

She spun to regard the windows—and stubbed her toe against a brass dolphin at the base of a chair leg. Wincing, she resisted the temptation to sit down and rub the offended part. Even if she could open one of the windows and scramble out before someone came to find her, she would have to drop to the paving stones in front of the kitchens a story below.

But a broken leg—*two* broken legs—might be preferable to what was about to happen.

The voices had stopped a while. Now they came in a fresh spurt; then there was a pause.

Then the door opened and Calum Innes stood there, framed by light.

"Oh!" Pippa wrung her hands together in front of her, winding the strings of her reticule so that the little bag swung back and forth. "Oh, *bother*. This really is *too* bad of me, Calum—I mean, Mr. Innes." She must not forget her vow to return to formality in this situation.

"Pippa?" He came in and closed the door. "Pippa, my dear, what can have happened?"

He was so . . . His was the face she would never forget. In that moment, Pippa knew that wherever she went and whatever her life became, the sharply defined lines of Calum Innes's handsome face—and the way light caught his dark eyes and the red in his hair—would be a picture that entered her mind without bidding. And she would see his mouth . . .

His lips parted and he jutted his chin, just a little, when he said, "Pippa?"

"Er, *nothing* has happened. Absolutely nothing. I was . . . that is, I decided to take a drive . . ."

Calum shook his head and one darkly arched brow rose. "No, Pippa, you did not simply decide to take a drive."

Oh, fie, this was not by way of being a reflection of her usual nature. "I am a very reasonable, calm female. I am not given to rash decisions. Certainly not rash actions. In fact, if one had a dilemma in which a cool head might be of use, one might do well to come to me."

"One might?"

"Oh, yes. I expect I get these traits from my father. He has them, too, you know, and I've always—"

"Admired him for it?"

"Quite."

"Sit down, Pippa."

"Well . . . thank you, no. I must leave."

Calum approached her. "Springer admitted you only a few minutes ago."

Pippa reached for her hood and dropped her reticule. "Oh, *bother*!" Really, being clumsy was such a trial.

Before she could retrieve her bag, Calum bent to swoop it up and slip it back on her wrist. She thought he might be smiling—just a little. Let him smile at her awkwardness. Everyone else did.

"As I was saying," Calum continued, "Springer has only just admitted you to the house."

"True." She managed to arrange the soft hood over her hair without further mishap.

"The hour is exceedingly late. Some might even say it is exceedingly *early*. A young female doesn't venture abroad— alone—at such an hour for no reason. I cannot allow you to leave without telling me why you came."

Telling him quickly—pleading with him to understand quickly and do what she was certain was imperative for his safety—was the only way. "I had to wait until I was certain— or as certain as I could be—that no one was likely to notice. That meant it had to be rather late, don't y'see."

"I see that you are a young female in dire distress." Frowning, he stood before her. "You do know how incautious you are to place yourself in the company of a man, in the privacy of his lodgings, without a chaperon?"

"It is more than incautious: it is outrageous and could well result in my ruin." Now he knew that she was no foolish green girl who did not know the way of things.

"But you have come," he said more softly. "So we must do everything we can to ensure that no harm comes either to you or to your reputation, mustn't we?"

"It will not," she responded with certainty. *Tell him and leave!*

"So certain?"

"Naturally." How could he doubt that she had thought everything through with great care? "You are a gentleman."

"And, therefore, you trust me?"

Pippa found she could not breathe quite properly. "Of course."

"There is no part of you that suggests you might do well to be even a little afraid of me? Particularly in light of what has passed between us on—let me see—" He squinted and pretended to count. "*Three* occasions? That's correct. Three."

"I . . . no." Was there? Uncertainty hovered in tiny places within her, but she would not allow it to grow. "You are far more likely to have reason to be afraid of me." She clapped her fingers over her mouth, horrified at what she had implied.

"Really?" He smiled then, really smiled, and rested his fists on his lean hips. "How so, Pippa? Are you also in the way of tossing out challenges? Have you come armed with a pistol?"

She laughed. "I would never need a pistol to guard myself against you, Calum."

He turned his back on her so abruptly that she flinched.

"I think you are in much greater danger than you know, Lady Philipa."

Something had entered his voice, something strange and still. And now she was Lady Philipa again, but perhaps that was as well. "The events of recent days lead me to believe you are in need of my advice, Mr. Innes." It was only appropriate that she follow his example and address him formally.

He wore a black coat, and when he crossed his arms, as his movements suggested he had, the material stretched tight across large shoulders and a straight, powerful-looking back. Pippa stared at his back. Then she stared at his dark hair with its hint of red where it curled against the stark white of his linen collar.

"The matter of the duel was a very close call, sir," she said, not liking the wobble in her voice. "If events had not gone exactly right, I am not at all certain we would be having this conversation tonight."

"Because I would be dead? Dead at the hands of a superior opponent?"

She wished he would face her. She also wished she didn't wish so terribly strongly to flatten her hands on his back, to rest her cheek there against his strong muscles, to close her eyes and simply *feel* him.

Pippa straightened her own spine. It was happening again, this unforgivable desire for evil, carnal things with a man who would doubtless be horrified if he could see inside her head. He would probably have her ejected from this house at once!

"I should not be discouraging you from leaving this house at once," he said. "In fact, at this precise moment, I should open the door of this salon and order that you be dispatched forthwith."

"Yes," she said. "I expect you are right."

"You do?"

"I certainly do, Mr. Innes."

"I don't intend to do so."

"Oh." Pippa fiddled with the gloves she held in one hand. She took a step toward him, and another, until all she could see was the expanse of his black-clad back—and his hair on his collar. "I have angered you, haven't I?"

He didn't respond.

Pippa raised a hand. She could touch him, very lightly, as if to draw his attention—or make a point. Carefully, she settled her fingertips on smooth kerseymere.

He did not move, did not say a word.

"There was a reason why I came this evening—Calum." What point was there in pretending they had never taken a single step toward the small intimacy of first names? Why, they had kissed! More than once! Many more times than once! And they had done considerably more than kiss!

That heavy, hot sensation began inside Pippa, the one that burned low inside and pressed between her legs.

She flattened her palm on him and smoothed—just a very little. "I don't believe I am foolish to trust you." Her action would be construed as forward. She removed her hand.

"Don't," he said sharply. "Please touch me, Pippa. Just as you were doing."

With only the slightest hesitation, she did as he asked. He was warm—and tense. Pippa rubbed a ridge of muscle. If she could, she would ease whatever made his body so tight. She would soothe him, muscle by muscle, inch by inch of skin drawn tight over flesh and bone by whatever force she felt within the man.

"I should send you away," he murmured.

"I know."

"I am too weak, Pippa."

Her second hand joined the first. And she rested her cheek, very carefully, between.

"You were right," he said quietly. "I should definitely be afraid of you."

She did not understand him. "If I could, and if you would allow it, I should like to look after you, Calum Innes."

He laughed again, that short, sharp, amazed laugh that, again, she did not understand.

"I believe," she told him, "that strong people often are more deeply in need of care than weak ones. You see, everyone knows weak people need to be looked after and so they are. The strong are supposed to be beyond the needs of mere mortals. They can be so alone in all that strength. At least that's what I've often thought."

He bowed his head and she ran her hands up to touch his hair. She found it thick and soft.

"Have you always been thought to be strong, Pippa? Is that where you come by so much wisdom for someone so young?"

She considered. "Perhaps. My mother died when I was still a child. My father has been exceedingly busy about important matters and he expected me to make him proud by accomplishing my own personal affairs. So I did." Stroking, she gauged the texture of his shoulders, and then of his arms.

His hands found and covered hers. "And so you did. But

how sad it would be if there were never to be anyone who
found and cherished the real Pippa.''

What the intention of his words might be, Pippa could not
be certain, but she felt a warmth and softness inside that was
both incredibly sweet and achingly sad. ''I think you are telling me that you wish . . . You do not know me, Calum.'' She
tried to pull away.

He held her fast. ''What I wish is of no moment for now.
But I do know you, sweet one.'' He turned around and settled
his hands loosely around her neck. ''Only dire concern over
something other than your own safety would bring you here
tonight. The girl who risked herself to stop a duel the other
morning thinks of others before herself.''

She thought of *him*—only him. ''My life is not my own,''
she told him, without intending to tell him any such thing.
Squeezing her eyes tightly shut, she let him know the rest. ''I
am a simple woman, with simple needs and dreams. I do have
dreams, of course. But they are that I shall be useful . . . and
loved. I do want to be loved. I should like to have children of
my own to teach, but until then, I should very much like to
continue to teach children who would not otherwise learn.''
She paused for breath.

''And why should you not be able to have these things?''
His gaze traveled over her face to her hair, and he lifted down
her hood. ''Surely the duke intends for you to bear his children.''

The trembling she could not control began deep inside
Pippa. ''Yes. He has told me so.'' If she locked her knees,
perhaps she would not shake so noticeably that Calum would
feel it.

''There. So all is well,'' he said. With light behind him, he
was all shadows.

There was nothing more she could tell him. She had already
said far too much. ''Quite so.'' Pippa smiled and straightened.
''But none of this has anything to do with this visit that must
seem so strange to you. It *is* strange. I'm afraid I am occasionally given to impulsive actions.''

''I had noticed.''

''Yes, well, this has been a most difficult day. A most difficult evening.''

His expression hardened. "I doubt if your evening was more difficult than mine."

Pippa resolved to end the conversation and be on her way. "I wish to make a request, Calum. Do not come to Cornwall."

He stared at her.

"Heed me, please, and remain in London. Or go elsewhere. But do *not* come to Franchot Castle."

His eyes narrowed. "Why?"

"Trust me. I have a very good reason."

"Then by all means, share this very good reason with me."

Pippa attempted to draw away, only to discover that Calum's hands, resting upon her shoulders, were exceedingly strong.

"Do not play with me further, my lady. Explain yourself."

"I do not know *how* to explain." Each word rose higher. "I am . . . I am bemused by myself. Afraid for you and afraid for . . . I know it would be disastrous for you to make this journey to Cornwall. Please, accept what I say and ask no more."

He shook his head slowly.

Surely . . . surely she was mistaken in thinking his eyes had lost focus. "Oh—" when he pulled the tie on her cloak undone, she clutched at his wrist. "*No.* I am definitely leaving."

The cloak slipped from her shoulders to the floor.

"I do not approve of the colors you wear," he said, and yes, he looked at her *differently*. "They are too muted. And your clothes are—"

"Too boring," she said breathlessly. "I know. I dislike them also, but the dowager considers them appropriate and I must do as I am told. I have always done as—"

"As you are told?" Calum finished for her. "Because your father is a man who adheres to the proper order of things and you have always admired him for that?"

"Quite so."

"And does the dowager instruct you in all things, Pippa? Does she speak to you of what will be required of you as the duke's wife, perhaps?"

Heat flooded Pippa's face and she knew she must be unbecomingly red. "She has bravely made my instruction in those unpleasant necessities her responsibility."

He lifted her chin. "The dowager told you that marriage is an unpleasant thing?"

"Oh, yes. And I am truly reconciled to accept what must be."

"Must be?" he repeated, as if musing. "The duke himself has shown you no sign of a gentler side of this arrangement?"

"There cannot be a gentler side!" What could Calum be thinking? That she was an addlepated girl who believed the stuff of fiction? "It is not intended to be so. Oh, no, I am aware that it is my responsibility to submit . . . to . . . That is . . . I am aware of the way of things, Calum."

"Fools," he muttered. "Criminal, wasteful fools."

"I beg your pardon?"

Rather than answer, he framed her face and studied her with such concentration that she could not be certain he remembered she was there at all.

"Calum?"

"Franchot tried to kiss you. You said as much."

"Yes."

"That suggests he did not actually kiss you."

To her disgust, she felt her eyes fill with tears. "His Grace probably did not particularly want to kiss me at all." She swallowed. "In fact, I'm not certain he knew it was me he had encountered."

Calum brushed the backs of his fingers over her cheek. "How could he not know? How could any man who ever saw you not feel his heart stop simply at the sight of you?"

He was telling her . . . She must not misconstrue. She must not, out of her need to feel loved, imagine what did not exist. "It was dark," she told him. "He had returned very late and I happened to be standing in the red salon. I like it there, particularly at night if I cannot sleep. My mind is very active, you see—too active, so I've been told. I often cannot sleep."

His short, sharp laugh sounded again before he said, "My life seems well fated to encounter brave spirits too busy about their imaginings to stay in their beds at night. Tell me more about your encounter with your betrothed—unless I am being too inquisitive."

She would tell him anything—gladly. "There is little more, really. He had, I think, partaken of rather too much . . . well, he was not entirely himself. He stumbled upon me and tried to . . . I moved my face and . . . This is embarrassing.''

"Then do not make yourself repeat it, sweet one.'' Calum brushed her cheek and brushed and brushed again, and tilted his head to smile into her eyes.

"He bit my ear!'' She announced it so loudly she startled herself. "It was somewhat painful, and I'm afraid I failed badly in what the dowager told me is so imperative.''

"Which is?'' he asked very ominously.

"That whatever is required by one's husband must be endured in silence. But I screamed. Oh, dear, I should not be talking about this!''

His gaze centered on her mouth. "You did not scream when I kissed you.''

"You did not bite me.'' Pippa looked at Calum's mouth. "In fact, I have found your kisses . . .''

"You found them pleasant?''

"Mmm. Yes.'' Much more than pleasant.

She was not aware of leaning against him, or of raising her face and closing her eyes—until Calum's lips settled upon hers. His breath was fresh and clean, his mouth faintly salty in the way she'd remembered. And his tongue, when it touched the soft inside of her lips, tickled, just as she'd remembered. And this time when he reached his tongue a little further into her mouth, past her teeth, to flicker across the tip of her own tongue, her body became softly warm and intensely aware of every sensation.

When his mouth left hers and slipped across her cheek, she turned her face, following it, but he took her earlobe between his teeth and nibbled—and little muscles in Pippa's stomach tightened with pure pleasure.

"There,'' he said, breathing delicately on sensitive skin. "You see. Nothing *has* to be unpleasant, sweet.''

"No.'' She arched her neck. "Oh, no.''

Calum spread his fingers over the soft rise of her breasts above the neckline of her bodice, and her eyes flew open.

He smiled down at her and kissed her lips again, more insistently this time. With his free hand he surrounded her waist and drew her against him.

That part of him was easily felt. Most interesting, Pippa

decided through senses that seemed determined to float away on ripples of hot wanting. Really, her fascination with That did grow stronger with every encounter.

Again the wanting. *What* did she want?

His little finger slipped beneath her neckline and Pippa froze. She clutched at Calum's shirtfront and stared at him with wide open eyes.

"What is it, sweeting?" His gaze was fervent. "You don't want me to touch you—here?" A little further beneath the neckline went his stroking fingertips.

Pippa braced. "It—hurts." Once more a fiery blush suffused her cheeks.

Calum's eyes regained hard focus. "Did your good fiancé hurt you in that way also?"

She tried to hide her face, but he would not let her.

"He did? Well, it seems to me that I will be doing His Grace a favor if I prove to his future wife that she should not have to fear his touch."

Pippa shook steadily. Calum swept his hand entirely inside her gown to surround and lift her breast.

"You *should* not," she told him.

"I think I should," he said through his teeth. White lines formed beside his mouth. "I should do this and a great deal more."

He could be such a puzzle.

For an instant he released her, but only so that he could slip her small sleeves from her shoulders and push them down her arms. With them went her bodice and shift. She felt cool air on her bared breasts and turned her head sharply away in shame.

What she felt next was her final undoing. Calum's mouth, fastening on a nipple while he tugged lightly on the other with his fingertips, rendered her legs useless.

"Oh, my sweet, untried one," he murmured, catching her as she started to fall. Sweeping her up, he went with her to the little tapestry couch and set her down. He knelt before her and took the dress all the way to her waist.

"No," Pippa said indistinctly. She fell against the back of the couch. "I want . . . I *want*."

"Tell me what you want." He pushed her skirts up, parted

her legs and moved between her thighs so that he could kiss
and suckle her breasts until she wanted to scream—this time
with unbearable ecstasy.

Calum straightened long enough to work off his coat and
throw it aside. He tore away his neckcloth and shirt and Pippa
gasped afresh. His body was as powerfully muscled as she'd
imagined—and she *did* want to touch all of it.

Before he could return to his lavish attention upon her, she
released her arms from the constraining sleeves and began
feeling him. He was rough where dark hair covered his chest
and narrowed to a thin line that disappeared inside his trousers.
Where skin shone over strongly muscled shoulders and arms,
he was hard and toned. Skin at his sides felt softly firm and
taut. Around his neck hung a talisman fashioned of worn
leather with a gold inscription so faint she could not read it.

Pippa touched the leather. "What is this?"

"Just something I have always worn," he said, reaching for
her. "My good-luck charm."

Her eyes flew up to his and she found him smiling at her
with the faintest hint of a question.

"You touch me as if it gives you pleasure, Pippa."

"It does. Such great pleasure. I have never seen a man
without his shirt before. I have never seen a man other than
entirely dressed before."

He cupped her breasts and she glanced down, blushing yet
again. Against his tanned skin, her small breasts, pointed and
uptilted to pale crowns, were white. While she watched, he
slowly suckled first one, then the other. A strong pulsing began
between her legs. This pulsing was something else she had
never felt before.

"You and your good-luck charm must have cast a spell on
me," she said at last as her hips slid forward on the couch.
"And I want to feel it forever."

"Forever would be the end of both of us," he said, dragging harder on her breasts with his mouth.

"No. Oh!" Just when she thought he could make her feel
no more undone, he found that pulsing place between her legs
and eased a thumb back and forth over a small bud of flesh.
"I don't think . . ." She *couldn't* think. The bud became a
throbbing thing that blazed with each burst of fire. Pippa

grabbed Calum's wrist—to keep him, not to thrust him away.

The fire broke over her and welled brighter and hotter. And then, slowly, it faded, flickering away in spreading ripples. And when it was gone and the man with hot black eyes stroked her breasts once more, kissed her lips once more, spoke to her of her beauty once more, she knew that if it was possible, she would come to him again and again.

"I do not think this is what the dowager meant," she told him when she could speak.

"No?"

"Is it possible that allowing one's husband to do what he will could mean this . . . what has just been between us?"

"Oh, yes. Between us it will . . ." He closed his mouth before continuing. "If you and I were husband and wife, it would be this and more."

"There is more?" It seemed amazing, except for that other—That. She would very much like an opportunity to explore That.

"Will you try to make me understand why I should not go to Franchot Castle, Pippa?" Even as he spoke, he caressed her breasts, traced her ribs, bent to quickly dip his tongue into her navel. "Surely you want me to after all."

"No," she said with certainty. Now, more than ever, she was convinced he must not do so.

"You must do better with your explanation than that."

"I know, even better than I did before I arrived here this night, that you must on no account travel to Cornwall with the duke and his entourage."

"Not convincing. It is an order, not an explanation." He seemed intent upon drawing an entire breast into his mouth, and Pippa began to pant. "Do better," he instructed.

"If you come, His Grace will find cause to engage you in a duel. You are a stronger man, but *he* is experienced in the matter of these dreadful, deathly encounters."

"And you do not want me to die?"

Helplessly, she arched into him. "If you die, I shall also die."

"Do *not* speak of such things."

"Stay in London."

"What will give the duke an excuse to kill me?"

"This," she said simply, slipping to the floor, to kneel between his thighs this time. Before he could guess her intention,
she surrounded and kneaded *That* part of him.

Calum groaned aloud and his chest rose in a great pant.
"You must not, sweet." He did not try to stop her. "If you
do, I may not manage to let you leave at all."

"As to that, of course you will not stop me. I will leave, and
very soon. But I am merely trying to explain myself. The duke
would never tolerate finding me doing such things to you."

A deep, amazed frown puckered Calum's brow. "*Finding*
you doing such things?"

"Indeed," she said, looking down while she judged the
length and form of That part and found it considerable in all
respects. Promptly she released it, ran her hands up his thighs
and leaned until she could reach around and cup his buttocks.
"All of these things."

He chuckled, but was almost immediately serious again.
"Are you suggesting you are likely to ... you mean you
might, at any time, *touch* me intimately?"

"Most definitely." She ensured that her expression con-
veyed the seriousness of the situation. "I am most fascinated
by That." With one finger she touched the part of him that
instantly leaped. "I find myself looking at it, and at all of you,
and wanting to touch. To touch and taste and hold. And I want
you to be naked when I do so."

"Really?" He sounded strangled.

"Oh, *really*. And I am certain that if the duke discovered
me so engaged, he would call you out on the spot and that
would be that."

"That would be that?"

He seemed to be having difficulty understanding the clearest
of explanations. "The end," Pippa said seriously. With great
reluctance, she stood up and began replacing her dress. "The
duke would be very unlikely to understand that I have these
yearnings to do as I will with you."

At that, Calum seemed incapable of speaking at all.

Good, she had made him see the seriousness of the situation.

"There," she said when she was finally clothed properly again. "So we are in agreement."

"We are?"

"Yes. To safeguard you from my . . . *unnatural* preoccupations, you will write and decline Franchot's invitation." She looked away. "I shall think of you, Calum. Very often. But I cannot allow you to suffer the embarrassment—and the inevitable danger my nature represents when I am with you. Will you accept my apologies."

"You are unique."

She still throbbed where the fiery sensation had so recently burned. "I shall certainly have difficulty forgetting you."

"You have never had these—*urges*—before? With any other man?"

It was Pippa's turn to frown. "Of course not."

He shrugged and stood up, but made no attempt to cover himself. "I only ask because it seems possible that a passionate woman such as you might be likely to have such *difficult* longings whenever she was faced with a—er—man who appealed to her."

Amazed at such ignorance in a man of the world, Pippa waited for him to place her cape around her shoulders and retrieve her reticule before she explained the situation to him as clearly as she could. "If you consider the matter carefully, Calum, you will realize that such a thing could not happen— that one could not experience such urges for more than one man."

He drew her hood over her hair and stood there, his thumbs pressed together beneath her chin.

"There is in the world one man for each woman."

"For every man and woman?" Calum asked. His beautiful mouth did not smile at all anymore.

"Oh, yes. The sadness lies in the fact that, most often, they do not meet each other."

"But we are such a man and a woman?"

"You know we are."

He looked toward the ceiling. "Pippa, if you believe this— and I believe this—perhaps you should not leave me. Perhaps you should remain with me and never return to Franchot."

She let her hands fall to her sides. Surely he toyed with her.

"I am not a wealthy man," he continued. "But I have a reasonable living left me by my guardian—and my expertise in estate matters always assures me of a position."

"You are asking me to . . . You *would* not."

"I would and I am." He held a hand toward her. "I have already asked you. Walk away from him, Pippa. Reject Franchot."

Pippa felt she might die—from a desperate longing to say, *Yes, yes!* And from fear so intense it threatened to choke her. "Oh, Calum," she said. "Thank you."

He watched her in silence.

"I cannot." Just as she could not bring herself to say that she feared her fiancé might be a madman, and that if she left him—shunned him—publicly dishonored him—he would hunt Calum down and kill him. Franchot would, she had no doubt, kill them both.

"Why?" Calum asked at last.

"Because sometimes even when the right man and woman actually meet each other, there are other responsibilities that intervene."

"And they should not be abandoned?"

Pippa frowned at him. "You know they should not. That they cannot. I am promised to the Duke of Franchot and I will become his wife. From the day of my birth, it has been known that one day I would be the Duchess of Franchot."

"And that matters above . . . above all else?"

He had not grown up as she had, with the strict understanding of what could and could not be done. "It isn't what matters to me that counts, Calum."

"No? It could not be of greater importance to me."

"You make this so difficult." Difficult because she felt, for the first time in her life, that she—Philipa Chauncey—was a prize in herself. "This is a matter of what is expected."

"Then *change* what is expected," he said, his face strained with emotion. "Change the future by grasping what the present offers you."

She shook her head. "My father has always let me know what is expected of me." Every word felt torn from her throat. "It is a matter between the Franchots and the Chaunceys. It involves property. The property is of far greater importance than anything I may want.''

''I cannot bear to think of you denying your own needs.''

Pippa knew she must not stop now. If she did, she would be lost. ''Papa never let me doubt my responsibilities, and I admire him for that.''

Calum uttered what sounded like, but could not possibly be, an oath. He extended a hand, then slowly dropped it. ''Very well,'' he said quietly. ''I must bow to your wishes. I bid you a good night, then, my lady.''

Pippa found that her mouth was too dry for her to form words. And her eyes smarted—from tiredness, no doubt. Calum had turned away.

She approached the door, caught a foot in a ruck in the rug, but managed to regain her balance without mishap. ''I am not sorry we shared . . . I do not regret holding and kissing you, Calum Innes. If you do think of me again, I pray it will be kindly.''

''I'll think of you again.''

''And I shall think of you.'' She would think of him all the time. ''My coachman will be watching for me. I'll find my own way out.''

''Good night,'' he said, still with his back to her.

Pippa said, ''Good-bye,'' opened the salon doors and hurried from the house.

When she was finally inside the Franchot coach once more, she looked back at the Stonehaven house and waved, although no one would see her.

And she would never see Calum Innes again.

She began to cry quietly.

ℰ Twelve

"*There you* are, Etienne. I've been waiting simply ages for you."

He stopped on the threshold to his bedroom and peered through gloom alleviated only by the red-gold glow from the fire. "Anabel? How the hell did you get in here?"

"I paid your valet."

"I'll have his ballocks."

"I already did. That was part of the bargain."

"Bitch."

From somewhere in the region of his great tapestry-draped bed, she giggled. "I know. And don't you love every minute of it?"

"I haven't been getting many minutes of it of late." He stumbled to fall into a chair. "Which is a matter I'd intended to discuss when next we met."

"Don't sound testy, Etienne, darling. Just tell me what would make you happy with Anabel, and she'll do it right now."

"First, you can promise to keep your hands—and other parts—off my servants' cocks."

"Only my hands," she assured him. "The rest is entirely yours, dear one."

"Fair enough." He really had drunk a few too many at his club, but not so many that he wasn't already growing hard. "Then you can get over here and use other parts on *my* cock."

149

She laughed uproariously and he heard the bed creak as she left it. "I do love it when you're completely naughty, Etienne. We are so absolutely suited to each other."

Dimly, he was aware that he must be prepared to fend off her demands—yet again—but first he had some very pressing needs. "Come here, my pet," he wheedled. "Come and show me some new titillations. I am a man who requires a constant supply of fresh entertainments."

"No more so than I, Etienne," she said, appearing at one heavily carved bedpost.

"Why're you still dressed?" The fact that she wasn't already naked surprised him. Anabel took great pleasure in reminding him, preferably within the hearing of some other interested male, that she was a woman who would never wear clothes at all if such a habit could only gain acceptance.

Rather than answer Etienne's question, she promenaded by, her cream satin gown swishing, and sank with studied grace into a chair facing his own.

Etienne blinked. "Asked you a question, Annie," he told her. She was a bit fuzzy 'round the edges. The last bottle of hock might have been overly excessive after all.

"I don't like it when you call me Annie," she said. "Did you have a pleasant evening?"

He burped loudly and wiped the back of a hand across his mouth. "Pleasant enough until now. You never used to mind my calling you Annie."

"We are no longer children. Things have changed between us."

Her hauteur amused him and he grinned. "Things *changed* between us when we were about sixteen, if memory serves."

Anabel pulled up her skirts and hooked one rounded leg over the arm of her chair. "*You* were sixteen. I was considerably younger." She swung her foot, swept the skirt higher and regarded her thigh all the way up to a thicket of hair of a much darker shade than her shiny, pale coiffure.

Etienne squirmed in his chair and began releasing his trousers. "Come here." His breathing was already becoming more labored. "Come here, *now*."

"I don't believe I shall." A twitch of the skirt, and that part of her that most interested him was again covered. She sighed hugely. "I was in Regent Street this afternoon. At Howell and James."

Etienne leaned forward to divest himself of his coat. He said, "No doubt you saw something you cannot live without."

"I *did*. A perfectly delightful little pendant that would sit so beautifully . . ." She slid a finger over one breast and into the deep vale of her cleavage. "Just beautifully. Right here. A blue diamond, Etienne. Surrounded by amethysts. Think how wonderfully such a work of art would complement my eyes."

Etienne's attention was on the way Anabel's finger stroked down, deep into the vale he so enjoyed exploring himself. "Buy the thing," he said, his tongue thick. "Put it on my account. But there's a condition, my love."

"Condition?" she said innocently.

He sniggered. "Have it delivered to me. *I* shall give it to you. And I shall choose the manner and the place in which the presentation is to take place." He was remembering a little piece he'd read in a titillating underground rag for gentlemen. If his memory served, little gold bells, or strings of pearls, were found to heighten certain sensations . . . why not a diamond-and-amethyst pendant?

"I want it *now*," Anabel announced with sudden petulance.

Etienne tore at his neckcloth and pulled his shirt open. "You'll get it soon enough. Help me, Annie. I'm deuced foxed."

"Mmm. Probably too foxed to even notice."

He peered up at her. "Notice what?"

"If I took you in my mouth."

"*Damn!*" Somehow he slipped off the edge of the chair and landed on the carpet. "Come here, Annie."

"I think you should come to me," she retorted.

"Don't tell me what to do. I don't like it."

"*You* don't like it," she said, throwing her arms over her head with the desired effect that her rouged nipples rose above the neck of her gown. "What *do* you like? Truly like? What do you want, Etienne? You tell me: then I'll tell you what I do and don't like."

He did not particularly care for her tone. "I truly like inspired rutting. But then, I truly like uninspired rutting." He giggled at his own brilliance. "I think perhaps I'd also like to go to me bed and have you use your lovely little mouth on me."

"While you rest, you mean, Your Grace?"

Rest. "Now I think of it, I believe I shall rest right here. Going to me bed would take entirely too much effort." The carpet, when he lay upon it, was warm from the fire. He pushed his trousers down. "There. I helped."

Her laughter brought his head off the floor. He narrowed his eyes to bring her into focus. "Glad the prospect of servicin' me brings such mirth."

Anabel got up and approached to walk a circle around him. "No," she said and choked. When she recovered, she studied a certain part of him from several angles and announced, "My dearest Etienne, in its present condition, *nothing* could help *that.*"

He frowned and concentrated. He closed his eyes and thought about what he was feeling. Cautiously, he reached down to touch himself.

Anabel howled. When Etienne looked at her, she pressed her hands over her mouth and pranced about in an enraging manner. Tears coursed her cheeks.

He wasn't . . . "It's *your* fault," he roared, covering himself. "Hardly expect a man to perform when a woman treats him the way you do."

"Marry me."

"Forever flauntin' yourself with other men. Makin' a fool of me. Shouldn't wonder if you were ruttin' with me own servants. Caught that jackanapes Dickson sneerin' at me just this morning."

"Etienne!"

"Henri told me you're forever stoppin' by his rooms."

"*Etienne!*"

"You'd best never meddle with Saber, I'll warn you of that. Some things can't be tolerated."

Anabel snorted. "Why? Are you saving him for yourself, or for Henri?"

He attempted to rise onto his elbows but fell back. "Saber is . . . Saber is in my care. We'll not discuss him further."

"Your deluded sense of responsibility is no affair of mine. You will make me your duchess."

"I will do what—"

"*Etienne*."

"What, damn you?"

"*Marry* me."

His head had begun to ache, but his vision was definitely clearer. "Don't be difficult."

"You will marry me. I have waited quite long enough."

"You married Hoarville. Didn't worry about *me* then, did you?"

She poked his thigh with a sharp toe. "That, dear one, was a necessity. My mother had no choice but to agree to the match my father arranged."

"Your mother was a whore."

"True." She appeared entirely unruffled. "A highly successful whore in the manner of most prime courtesans. At least I know who my father was, and he looked after Mama."

Pain smote him between the eyes. "Damn you," he muttered. "You've gone too far."

"Because, when you insult me, I remind you that you and I have very similar beginnings? Except in the matter of paternity. My parents might not have been married, but their relationship was no secret. Lord Wallister took good care of Mama and he never shirked his duty to me. Mama always intended that I should become your duchess, but she had to be clever about it."

Etienne grunted. "She had to marry you off to Hoarville because that's what Wallister had arranged. But you didn't object, did you?"

"You are being so difficult. I didn't *know* the truth about you then."

"You mean you didn't know the truth and so you didn't know it was time to start trying to blackmail me into making you my duchess."

"I think," Anabel said, raising her skirts and pointing a toe while she admired the rounded shapeliness of her leg, "I think that you should be grateful I am prepared to put aside the knowledge that you haven't chosen to accept me gracefully. When the time was right, Mama told me the circumstances of

STELLA CAMERON

your birth. Your mama was not in a position to bring about a friendship between us, Etienne. My mama was, and she did so from when we were children.''

''Because she intended to get her claws into the Franchot fortunes.''

''Because she intended that her daughter should eventually marry her best friend's son.''

He covered his eyes with a forearm and muttered, ''Blackmail.''

''Posh!'' Anabel said. ''True, I have placed certain letters with my solicitors. But I did so because it is businesslike to make provisions. It would seem only professional to ensure one's safety.''

He felt incredibly morose. ''In case I decide to have you killed in your sleep, you mean?''

''Of course not.'' Anabel's laugh tinkled. ''Why would you? We both know I have no intention of telling the world that you are not the Duke of Franchot.''

''*Enough.* I have warned you never to speak of that.''

''So you have,'' she said. Her smile became cunning. ''I would merely caution you not to forget that you and I are bound together now, and that we always will be.''

Even while his head pounded and his flesh felt numb, he knew the curl of fear in his belly. ''What was arranged at the time of Lady Philipa's birth cannot be put aside,'' he said. ''She will become my wife.'' Anabel appeared to be the only one in their set who didn't understand the true importance of his marriage to Lady Philipa.

Anabel lifted a leg and stood with one foot on either side of his hips. Gradually, she raised her skirts until he was presented with an unimpeded view of her woman's parts. ''Any hope of an improvement in your present condition, my love?'' she asked, spreading her legs wider.

The numbness lifted—as did other aspects of his being. ''Get down here,'' he hissed, grabbing her ankle. He could *see* her moist readiness. He could *smell* her lust.

Dropping the skirt, she undid the tapes on her bodice, her pointed tongue clasped between her teeth as she did so. ''You are bound to me,'' she said, hunching her shoulders forward to slip off the bodice. ''We will always be bound together.''

Her breasts spilled forth, large and white and red-tipped. Planting her hands on her hips, she bent her knees and leaned forward to sway above him until he felt his flesh leap so solid he gasped.

"I'm what you want, Etienne," she said. "What you have to have."

With the sound of his own low growl in his ears, he reached up to squeeze and fondle her. "Sit on me," he begged. "Please, Annie."

"Get rid of the Chauncey girl."

He rocked his head from side to side. "I *can't*. You know I can't. She was betrothed to me on the day of her birth."

"She was betrothed to the man whose place you took."

He grew still.

"You, my dear Etienne, are like me. You are a bastard."

His mind became oddly, coldly, clear. She had never exactly called him that before. The fact that he did not know his father had been stated in many different ways, but never so baldly as for her to call him a *bastard*. Distractedly, he resumed fondling her breasts. Something was afoot here—something different.

"Am I wrong?" she asked.

"We know you are right," he told her. "We also know that it is exceedingly dangerous to speak of such matters."

"I'm glad I have your attention." With that, and with unerring accuracy, she dropped to her knees and impaled herself upon his rod. Steadily, slowly, rhythmically, she raised and lowered herself, drawing him off the ground to meet her with each withdrawal.

"You are a bastard and so am I." She levered herself up, inch by inch. "The difference between us lies in the fact that, whilst both of our mothers started their careers as common whores, *my* father was a nobleman—*yours* was—"

"Enough."

With hidden, well-developed little muscles, Anabel squeezed him tight. "Your father was someone your mother could not even name." She started her next descent. Raw drive to join her in the dance almost crazed him. "Your mother hatched a very clever plot. True, a plot based on fury at being abandoned by a lover is a weak motive for replacing his son with her own—but she pulled it off.''

Sweat bathed his body. He needed to throw her aside—to banish her. Possibly he needed to *kill* her to silence her forever . . . although there were the letters she frequently reminded him of . . .

Most importantly at this moment, he needed to empty himself into her.

"Funny to think of our mamas as struggling little prostitutes at Lushbottam's."

"*Don't.*"

"You really ought to visit there sometime. I do think you'd enjoy that crone's lady *tailors*. Quite entertaining, I assure you."

"I will never go there," he said through his teeth.

"But so much of your history is there," Anabel persisted. "It was there that you were born. And it was there that your mama met the woman who made sure you got where you are today."

"For the love of God!" Etienne said. "Do not continue to say these things aloud."

"It was at Lushy's that your mama told my mama about how she'd arranged to have the real duke stolen and murdered."

His body was drenched. He couldn't summon the energy to do what he desperately wanted to do—to take her by the throat and squeeze.

"Enough of the past," she said in a crooning tone. "The present is far more important to us. Let us think about Calum Innes."

Etienne closed his eyes.

"Calum Innes was at Lushy's tonight."

His arms dropped to his sides.

"He went in a Stonehaven carriage, stayed for some time, then left in a great hurry."

Sweat began to cool on his skin. "Why would he be there?"

Anabel shifted her hips and he shuddered. "Who can be sure why he was there?" she said. "Perhaps everything did not die with the child and with our mothers."

"*Enough!*" He shoved her off, sending her sprawling, and struggled to stand and straighten his trousers at the same time. "*Never* speak of this subject again. Do you hear me? *Never* mention it again."

"You are not the Duke of Franchot." She parted her lips in a snarl and scrambled away from his grabbing hands. "You are a bastard who was placed in the rightful Duke of Franchot's cradle while his family was distraught over the death of his mother."

"Stop it!"

"*Your* mother was a whore spurned by the real duke's father. He spurned her when he discovered she had many men and that you had been conceived while he was on the Continent. She did what she did intending to eventually use you to get everything she thought should have been hers as that man's paramour."

"But she died," Etienne said, reeling, following Anabel but hampered by the effects of the drink. "She died and no one should ever have been any the wiser."

"But they were," she shrieked. "She bragged to my mother, and in time, my mother told me."

"We had been childhood friends," he reminded her, desperate now. "Before old Lord Wallister died, he made certain you and your mother wanted for nothing and that you married Hoarville."

"But then I learned about you, and you had *so* much more to offer than that sickening, grabbing old fool Hoarville." As if she sensed that his strength had failed, she stood up and faced him. "So I decided it was only right that you and I should have the pleasure of living your lie together."

He frowned at her. "But . . ."

"But I was married. Yes. *Was.* As I have already told you, I had to marry the man my father chose for me or risk raising suspicions about my motives for trying to refuse. But I poisoned Hoarville for you. I have *paid* for you, Your Grace."

He eyed her with wary disbelief. "You *poisoned* your husband?"

She tossed her head. "He was old. It was time for him to set me free for the role I was intended to play—as the Duchess of Franchot."

"No," he said stubbornly. "My marriage is arranged and must go forward. Why won't you understand that I *have* to have access to the port on Chauncey's Cornish lands, and the only way to secure that access—and the actual use of the port—is by marrying the girl?"

"You are a fool. Listen to me well." She had not bothered to replace her bodice and advanced upon him, her naked breasts quivering from the power of her emotion. "You *must* listen or you are finished. Think. Innes all but forced his way into your life."

He squeezed his eyes shut and tried to concentrate.

"Now he turns up at Lushy's," Anabel continued. "Doesn't that seem a coincidence to you?"

"I don't know," he said, utterly miserable.

"Thanks to the former Duke of Franchot—your esteemed mother's one time protector—Lushy's establishment became the sought-after diversion it is today. Lest you may have forgotten the details, it was at Lushy's that the duke first encountered your mama, the fair Florence Hawkins."

"So help me, if—"

"I am helping you. Does it not seem possible that the reason Mr. Innes was at Lushy's—in light of his having deliberately placed himself in your way—is because he is, in fact, attempting to check out your pedigree?"

Horror weakened Etienne's knees. He backed up and collapsed into the nearest chair. "You're mad," he whispered. "Why would anyone do such a thing? There is no evidence against my claim. There never was any evidence."

Anabel bent over him, her hands supporting her weight on the arms of his chair. "*Never* was? What of the real duke? What of the baby who was taken from his cradle at Franchot Castle?"

He was in danger of casting up his accounts. "Dead," he murmured. "Murdered. My . . . She paid for it to be done."

"She paid." Anabel's smile was a sickening, suggestive thing. "Who saw proof that what she paid for was accomplished?"

"It was accomplished," he whispered.

"What if Chauncey's gotten wind of something?"

He breathed through his mouth and rested his head back. "Chauncey?"

"The fair Lady Philipa's papa. What if someone went to him and suggested he ought to question the man to whom he'd promised his daughter? What if it's been suggested that you have no more claim to the Franchot lands than any whore's son, and that marrying his daughter to you will not guarantee the safe harmony of the Chauncey Cornish lands with yours?"

"I want Cloudsmoor," Etienne said, breathing hard. "And I mean to have it, damn it. It was part of the agreement. Old Chauncey's feet—when he *is* in England—are buried in Yorkshire. I cannot risk some upstart worming his way into that pallid little female's affections and gaining control of her dowry. By God, it would mean being held to ransom every time a load of Franchot tin went on its way. No. No, I tell you. With my marriage to Lady Philipa, her father's Cornish lands become mine. They are worth a fortune for that port alone and they will be mine."

Anabel drove her fingers into his hair and gripped tight until his eyes flew open. "Wanting the Chauncey property may lose you everything. Do you understand?"

"I do not believe he has wind of anything. There is nothing left to trace what—to trace any of it."

"What I have witnessed tonight means you can no longer be certain of that."

"I *am* certain," he insisted. "The woman Rachel, the snake man's assistant, is dead. Florence Hawkins assured me of it."

"But we have always known that the snake man's assistant could have had help in disposing of the child."

"No." He would not think of this.

"You cannot hide any longer. If the child was indeed killed, Rachel may not have acted alone, and it is more than possible the mountebanks, Milo and Miranda, assisted her."

"Pure speculation."

Anabel tightened her painful grip on his hair. "You should have questioned the presence of those two at Lushy's years ago."

"There was always a connection between Lushy and the people who followed the fairs." He detested to as much as mention that place.

"True," she agreed. "And I put it to you that the only way Milo and Miranda could afford to take up a valuable room at Lushy's is because they gave her something she thinks will be worth a great deal. I think they told her that Florence Hawkins arranged the murder of the former Duke of Franchot's heir and left her own bastard in his place."

Etienne finally tore her hand away. "My *God*, why must you continue with this absurdity?"

"Because I must. We both have too much to lose. Cry off with Lady Philipa and Chauncey will have no reason to persist. If he does so, it will be assumed that he seeks vengeance for the spurning of his daughter, and none will take him seriously."

Etienne thought then, thought hard. After Florence Hawkins had approached him when the man he'd grown up thinking of as his father had died, there had always been the faint, sickening possibility that he could somehow be removed from the only life he had known.

"We could be married at once," Anabel said.

"If you *are* right," he said thoughtfully, "and I say *if* you are right, then on no account must I do anything other than go ahead with plans exactly as expected."

"If you do, Chauncey will continue to look for evidence against you."

"*We have no proof he is looking at all.*"

"*I* know that someone is, and it can only be Chauncey. Someone sent Innes with the instruction that he was to draw close to you by means of engaging Lady Philipa's interest. He is looking for information on you."

"Philipa would not lead him to Lushy's."

Anabel was red with emotion. "I tell you, they *already* knew of Lushy's. Very possibly they were sent there by someone who knew what Rachel had done.

"Do not forget that it was at Lushy's that your charming mother met Rachel, and that it was because of that meeting that the arrangement to place you at Franchot Castle came about. *I* believe the snake man's assistant confided in Milo and Miranda. Now I believe that those two see a chance to reap great rewards by unmasking you to Chauncey. He would be likely to pay them well for saving his daughter from marriage to a bastard *pretender*."

Etienne could not believe it—could not allow himself to believe it. "No. No, you are wrong."

"I think Innes was chosen for this mission because he is attractive to women, and I am convinced Lady Philipa has already been ensnared by him."

Etienne laughed shortly. "You mean that her plain and foolish head has been turned by his attention."

"For whatever reason, she is besotted with him."

His head had almost completely cleared. Only an annoying pain remained behind his eyes. "*You*, dearest Annie, are trying to incite me. You want to turn me against Philipa simply so that you may get what you want."

"Have it your own way," she said, turning her attention to refastening her gown. "I had not intended to mention this, but even as we speak, your betrothed is with that man."

He stared at her for a long time before the import of her words became apparent. "You jest," he said and guffawed. "And your jesting makes you ridiculous. Such a thing would not be possible."

"Of course not." She started for the door. "But since I am a little tired, I will lie down in her empty chamber until I find energy enough to return home."

In a trice he was out of his chair and rushing after her into the hallway. "Stop this," he whispered hoarsely, half-expecting some servant or relative to appear and start asking questions. "Stop at once."

Ignoring him, Anabel led the way around the balcony above the vestibule and went directly to Philipa's door. This she threw open, and before Etienne could stop her, she marched inside.

With Etienne in her wake, she crossed the sitting room to the bedroom and pushed its door open. She didn't pause until she stood at the foot of Lady Philipa's bed.

Etienne gaped.

"Do you see any slumbering virgin?" Anabel asked.

"Damn me."

"She is at the Stonehaven house in Hanover Square. She is there, alone, with Innes."

"I will *kill* him."

Anabel appeared to think. "Mmm. No, I don't think that
would be at all the thing just yet. I think we have set matters
up tolerably well. As long as we are agreed that we are working together for the common goal of achieving our marriage,
I will help you make decisions that will ensure our permanent
happiness."

How he hated everything about this woman except the eager, welcoming place between her thighs and the abundant soft
flesh he used to pillow himself while he availed himself of
her. "Very well," he said, suitably meek. "Guide me, Anabel."

She all but ran to him and wound her arms about his neck.
"Kiss me first, dearest."

He did so, joining in the titillatingly coarse play of tongues
that was one of her beloved sexual parodies. Before they were
done, she had his hands inside her bodice and her hands inside
his trousers and they both sank onto Lady Philipa's pristine
bed.

Within minutes he lay sated, his spent cock shriveling inside
Anabel's wet passage.

"That's a good boy," she crooned over him. "Always so
good when you listen to your Anabel. This is the way it's
going to be."

"Mmm?"

"We are going to be too clever for Lord Chauncey and Mr.
Innes. We shall have both Mr. Innes and Lady Philipa at Franchot Castle, where we can watch them. Let us pretend we
know nothing, but keep them very close."

"I shall walk so close I may well step on their heels,"
Etienne murmured.

"Caution, dearest, in all things," Anabel said. Her recovery
after sex was invariably enviable. "There is always the possibility that Innes may be drawing her into a flirtation simply
to see how he can turn such a situation to his own ends. After
all, she is an heiress worth catching."

"In which case I shall kill him," Etienne said sleepily.

"With my blessing," Anabel agreed. "There is also the
possibility that he is working for Chauncey but has learned
nothing at all about you."

"He will still die for what he's done."

"Exactly." Anabel moved Etienne to a spot where he could rest his open mouth over a nipple. "But it is more likely he has found out something, yet does not have enough proof."

"Can't follow that," he said, using the end of his tongue and enjoying her wriggling.

"If he already had enough proof," Anabel said impatiently, "we would not be having this conversation."

Etienne thought about that. " 'Spose not. Makes it all hopeful in that case, don't it?"

"Hopeful indeed."

"Dashed fellow's overstepped the mark regardless."

"He certainly has."

Etienne slipped out of Anabel. "He's got to die. Nothing else for it. Honor and all that."

"Yours and mine, my love. All that remains is to time his death appropriately. And hers."

Etienne rolled away until he could see her face. "*Hers*?"

"Of course hers. Only way to make certain you get her dowry."

"Don't follow you." In fact, he was getting remarkably sleepy.

"If it becomes necessary, we'll make it look as if you killed Innes while he was in the act of stealing your fiancée and she died by accident at the same time." Anabel steered his face back to her breast. "Do you get my meaning?"

"No," he mumbled around a mouthful.

"It's simple," Anabel said, sounding irritable. "Naturally, Chauncey would never draw further attention to his daughter's infamous ruin by an adventurer. At our suggestion to Chauncey, the world will learn that Lady Philipa died at the hands of her kidnapper—Calum Innes—and that you were wounded while attempting to save her. Chauncey will insist you keep what's rightfully yours."

She was clever, he'd grant her that. "It might work."

"It will," she said happily. "You'll get Cloudsmoor—and me!"

❧ Thirteen

There were times, Struan thought, when Calum Innes could be a remarkably sanctimonious devil. "This is no easier on me than it is on you," he told Calum now. "I could never have foreseen having to flee London in such a manner."

They had instructed their coachman to stand ready while they took a walk. In truth, Calum had demanded that they walk and talk.

Calum marched ahead. Without looking back, he said, "Of late, I've seen no evidence that you see anything particularly clearly."

Arguing was almost useless while Calum was in this mood. "You do agree that we had no choice but to leave London when we did?"

"After what you did?" Calum raised his arms and let them fall. "I have no doubt that if we'd stayed longer we might already be dead men. Set upon and killed by Mrs. Lushbottam's tailors or whatever. Chopped up and scattered upon the waters of the Thames to be gobbled up by gulls."

Struan gritted his teeth. For days, since they'd left London in the middle of the night, Calum had raged about his friend's idiocy. "Look," Struan said to him now, attempting to sound reasonable, "I had hoped that long before we arrived in Cornwall, you'd have helped me think of a serviceable solution."

Calum waited until they were out of earshot of the coach before turning upon Struan. "You abducted a fifteen-year-old

164

girl from a brothel," he said, his nostrils flaring. "And, not satisfied with *that* debacle, you agreed to add her revolting little brother to our menagerie."

"How could I have *known* she was but fifteen?"

Glancing at the coach where Ella and her spindly, red-haired brother, Max, sat with noses pressed to the windows, Calum shook his head. "When you did discover how old she was, *how* could you have promised to find a place for her *and* her brother?" He paced back and forth beside a crumbling stone wall.

"I *will* find a place for them, I tell you," Struan insisted. With every passing mile on the journey from London, he'd felt more desperate and more convinced that they might *not* come upon some childless farmer, or innkeeper, or—

"A childless farmer or innkeeper," Calum said, as if he'd heard Struan's thoughts. "And I allowed you to make me believe it might be possible for such a saint to exist."

How could he have guessed Ella was only fifteen—or that she would be a charmingly determined miss for whom he would quickly develop fatherly feelings?

What in God's name had possessed him to champion the girl? How had she managed to persuade him to help her rescue her brother from the squalid circumstances she'd been forced to accept from Mrs. Lushbottam?

"It isn't as if I did not *feel* for them," Calum said. "But we're here, by God. We're in Cornwall, and Franchot Castle lies over that ridge." He indicated a steep, heavily wooded rise behind him.

"Surely the Franchots might know someone who could—"

"Oh, my *God*!" Calum said explosively. "Of course, I am not already faced with an overwhelming task. No, no. It will be a simple matter to approach the Franchots and ask them to help us with two ill-bred, *homeless children*." Every time he emphasized a point, his dark eyes blazed and the lines of his handsome face grew sharper.

"Quite so," Struan said, feeling sheepish yet again. "Naturally, that would be difficult. Anyway, the family will not be here for some days."

"And dashed awkward that's going to be to explain,"

Calum said, frowning deeply. "Turning up at the castle before Franchot and his party."

"There was nothing for it but to make our getaway at once." Struan smiled, reassuringly, he hoped. "It's a matter easily enough dispatched. We tell the castle servants we had business elsewhere that took us out of London a little early. Then—so we'll tell them—the business was more easily attended to than expected, so we came here direct."

"Very plausible." Calum's frown had become a scowl. "But it does not deal with the real problem, does it?"

"No."

"This is a disaster," Calum said.

"Yes."

"Poor little devils."

A chink had appeared in the opposition's armor. Struan's spirits lifted, but he made certain that condition didn't show. "What makes you call the children that?"

"I was lucky," Calum said morosely. "I got dropped on your father's doorstep before I became old enough to know hopelessness. Unless I miss my mark, those two have already been to hell and back, and they still belong nowhere and to no one."

Struan glanced away. He should have known Calum would eventually relent.

"I want to climb the ridge," Calum said. "Franchot Castle will be visible from here. I'd like to see it from a distance."

Struan made no comment. He followed Calum through a gap in the wall and over rough grassland toward the trees. Although the summer day smelled sweet, a bite sharpened the wind, and gray-edged clouds had begun to pile high in a pale sky.

Marching onward, Calum began to talk again. "I should never have allowed you to persuade me to bring them. How in God's name shall we explain the presence of a fifteen-year-old girl with a cockney accent who resembles an exotic goddess—*and* a ten-year-old boy who is supposedly her brother and who should have been drowned at birth?"

Struan tripped on a rock and cursed. "Ella needed my help," he said, drawing in a hissing breath. "I felt that from the moment I saw her."

Calum made a snorting sound. "She is a beautiful creature and you wanted her."

"As I have said, *many* times, I did not *know* she was only fifteen. Now that I do, I have one concern—her safety."

"Fortunately for her, you are a man of honor and high sensibilities," Calum said grudgingly. "But this is a disaster, man. We should never have traveled this far with them."

Struan turned around to look in the direction of the coach. Max, the brother Ella had produced, now leaned out the door.

"We must think of something." Calum shook his head and struck off through rowan trees heavy with clusters of white blossoms. "A *ten*-year-old child—a *monster*. And you could not have chosen a more ill-fated time to visit these disasters upon us."

Struan strode behind him, batting aside branches that swung back in Calum's furious wake. "We should not leave them alone in the carriage." The fact that he understood Calum's ire made it no easier to tolerate. "They have both suffered enough without adding the fear of yet another desertion in a strange place."

"The girl is not afraid," Calum said without looking back. "And if she is not afraid, neither is the boy."

"How can you be certain?" Struan hurried to catch up.

Calum eyed him sideways. "Unlike the black thing that beats within my breast, your heart's goodness is easily felt, my friend. Ella knows you for the gentle man you are, and her brother trusts her judgment implicitly."

"I believe there is much she has not told us."

"Indeed," Calum agreed. "The story of how she came to be in Lushbottam's clutches is vague. Which market did the old hag find her in, one wonders? And how exactly did Ella and Max come to be alone and at the mercy of this nefarious band to which she refers?"

"Questions I have asked myself more than once," Struan said.

The uphill path was exceedingly steep, and soon all their breath was required for the effort. The crest of the ridge slashed southward, toward the sea, and when they reached the top, Struan instantly crouched and stared about in wonder. "Magnificent," he said, filled with awe by the sweep of meadowland that rolled away into a wide valley beneath them. "And so is that." He pointed to a castle somewhat more south of them, clearly silhouetted against the sky.

"Aye," Calum said, and Struan saw the flicker of muscle in the other man's cheek and the narrowing of his eyes against the wind. "Franchot Castle is wondrous, isn't it? What man would possibly consider needing so much?"

Struan eyed him curiously. "Men—powerful men—have always aspired to building great homes, Calum. And you would like to claim that Gothic marvel as your own."

"It *is* my own," Calum murmured. "But I'm not certain I want it."

Struan wasn't sure what to say. Surrounded by high walls, the castle stood on an elevated mound and seemed poised in the air with the steel-blue English Channel beyond.

"A fine fortress," he finally commented. "The cliffs would make it impenetrable from the sea, and no army could have approached its walls without coming under attack from within."

Calum nodded. "True enough. It is overwhelming. Overwhelming to me."

Struan realized that this man who had grown up in a great castle had never viewed it with the assessing eyes he now set upon Franchot Castle. "It puts me in mind of a clever child's creation," he told Calum. "All towers and turrets and grand elevated terraces. What is it that catches the light? White marble, d'you think? A sugar castle. How it must glitter by moonlight."

Calum said nothing.

"Such gardens," Struan remarked, deliberately filling the silence. "Flowers everywhere. Even from here I see their brilliance. Symmetry. See the flights of steps? They would not be visible from lower land. Some former Franchot must have been in Italy and fallen in love with the gardens there."

Still Calum did not reply.

"Would you like me to leave you alone?" Struan asked.

Calum started and looked at him, his eyes slowly lightening. "No. Forgive me. I was preoccupied. There is so much to consider here, so much I am not certain of. I feel drawn to this place and I know it is only right that I claim justice for the wrong done to me. But it would all change . . . My life would change so, Struan, and I'm not certain I should like it overmuch.''

Calum had always had a clear mind. Even when they'd been boys together—Arran included—Calum had been the quickest to see the way of things and the way things would best be accomplished.

"Do you understand?" Calum asked, watching Struan's face intently.

"Yes," Struan said, putting an arm around his friend's shoulders. "Yes, I understand. Much lies ahead of you, Calum. But with each day's events, you'll make the right decisions."

"I hope—" Calum stiffened and took several steps forward to peer down the hillside. "Do you see that?"

Struan followed the direction of Calum's pointing finger. "What? No . . . The cart, d'you mean?" Below them, on a narrow track running parallel to the ridge, a fat nag hauled a cart on its bumpy way.

"There was a lane through the trees to the highway not long before we stopped the carriage," Calum said, turning to look back in the direction from which they'd come. His old boyish grin widened. "I'd not say no to a ride rather than a steep downhill climb. What say you? I'll wager that cart goes the way that will save our boots."

Struan found no argument with that notion. "And perhaps the man who drives the cart will have an answer to our dilemma."

"*Your* dilemma," Calum retorted, starting downhill, running and sliding and using his arms to keep his balance.

They misjudged the distance to the track, and by the time they arrived on the narrow, stony path, there was no sign of the cart.

"Damn," Calum said. "Hurry, man. If we have to walk the way now, we'll be lucky to find the carriage before nightfall."

Side by side, they set off at a rapid clip, and it was Struan who saw how they could shorten the distance between them and the cart by using a narrow switchback around a bush-covered hillock.

"Hurry!" Calum called, breaking into the full run that had so often proved a boon in his early days. "I hear it."

Winded, Struan arrived back on the cart track a second behind Calum and several seconds behind the cart, which swayed along, its hunched, roughly cloaked driver oblivious to his pursuers.

"We'd best call out," Calum said, closing the distance with a loping stride now. "Wouldn't want to cause the poor old chap to have apoplexy."

"No," Struan agreed, and shouted, "You there—wait!"

The cart slowed and Calum approached ahead of Struan. "Nothing to fear, man," he said. "My friend and I would appreciate a ride back to the road."

There was no answering greeting. The carter hesitated, drawing almost to a stop. Then he clucked and jerked the reins, urging his horse onward.

"I'll be damned," Struan said, momentarily nonplussed. "Surly fellow. Cabbage-headed, too. Obviously thinks we intend to set upon him and doesn't think we can outrun him."

"We've surprised him," Calum said, lengthening his stride again. Within moments he caught up with the cart and hauled himself onto its open back. He motioned for Struan to join him.

Once they shared the back end of the ancient, apparently junk-laden conveyance, they raised eyebrows at each other and Struan inclined his head questioningly to the carter, who must have felt them climb aboard.

Calum nodded.

"I say," Struan said loudly, "this is very good of you. We left our carriage on the road and climbed the ridge. Rather farther to the top than we'd expected. We appreciate your hospitality."

Very gradually, the cart slowed until it merely crawled forward.

Then it stopped.

Calum had been studying the contents of a rickety chest. A faded green satin cushion concealed ugly pieces of china, a cook pot and assorted kitchen implements. He dropped the cushion, got to his feet and climbed over the chest to kneel behind the driver. "We mean you no harm," he said kindly.

"If you'd prefer, we can most certainly walk, and—" Calum broke off abruptly.

"What is it?" Struan asked, sensing the other man's tension. He scrambled forward in the cart.

Calum gripped Struan's arm as if restraining him. Struan looked from Calum's still face to the driver, who had turned sideways on the seat.

"And what," Calum said, his fingers digging into Struan's arm, "do you suppose this could possibly mean, my lord?"

Struan dropped to his knees beside Calum and studied the cloaked driver's profile. "It means that yet another outrageous complication has been added to this ill-fated journey."

That remark brought a searing flash from dark blue eyes before Lady Philipa Chauncey said, "I assure you, my lord, that the complication here is the arrival of yourself and Mr. Innes—and the inconvenient coincidence of your finding me in this cart."

He stopped her heart.

Simply to look upon him was to feel all breath leave her body, all blood leave her veins—all will to move desert her limbs.

"And from the look of you," she said, startled by the sound of her own voice, "you are in no better condition. Though doubtless for a quite different reason." Calum's presence here was unbelievable.

He visibly collected himself and said, "I beg your pardon," in the voice she had been hearing in every conscious moment since she'd fled Hanover Square on that fateful night that had made her insist upon coming to Cornwall directly.

"I said," she told him as calmly as she could, "that you appear as shocked as I. What are you doing here? I thought we had agreed it would be wiser for you to decline the duke's offer to come to Cornwall."

His dark, slightly tilted eyes stared so steadily, she wanted to look away yet could not.

"We agreed to nothing, my lady," he said at last. "In fact, I would say that there is a very great deal upon which we *ought* to seek agreement and understanding. What are *you* doing here today? This cannot be a safe venture for a young female—to be abroad alone where any rogue might come upon you."

How he muddled her usually clear mind. And she had a certain mission to complete, a mission made impossible by the presence of her two passengers.

"Why are you not in London?" Calum asked.

She ignored his question. "I am perfectly safe here, I assure you," she said briskly, turning back to the swaybacked gray mare Nelly had miraculously procured. "This hill and this path are on Chauncey land. It belongs to our Cloudsmoor estates. I've known the area well since childhood. I'll drive you to the road. Then I'll be on my way."

Pippa urged the mare onward and wooden wheels began churning through rocky, deeply indented ruts. She braced herself for the questions that must come.

"I don't suppose, my lady"—Viscount Hunsingore spoke for the first time —"that you know of any farmer or such—"

"*Struan*," Calum Innes said in a tone resembling thunder.

"Quite," Viscount Hunsingore said gruffly.

"A farmer?" Pippa asked, grateful for any respite from trying to explain what she was doing in a peasant's cloak and driving an ancient cart loaded with household castoffs.

"You cannot help, Pippa," Calum said, and despite the enormity of the situation, she smiled at the sound of her name on his lips.

"It would appear," Viscount Hunsingore said, "that we are not alone in having a small matter that might require, shall we say, *extraordinary* tact?"

Pippa stared grimly ahead.

"The lady's affairs are her own," Calum Innes said. "Just as yours are *your* own."

"Gallant of you," Hunsingore said in dulcet tones. "But hardly practical, old man. I'd say the lady will be asking for our—er—*discretion* about activities that call upon her to move about in disguise. Am I correct, Lady Philipa?"

"*Struan*—"

"Quite correct, my lord," Pippa said, interrupting Calum. She drove around a wide, arching bend and began the descent to the road. "My situation is not particularly interesting to anyone but me. However, I should prefer that no attention be drawn to a little diversion that brings me pleasure.''

"What kind of diversion?" Calum asked promptly.

Pippa frowned. "Really, you are very direct, sir. And you are very inappropriate . . ." She closed her mouth. If she made too much of this, the result might be exactly what she did not want. "Very well, I will tell you. At my home in Yorkshire—Dowanhill—I was always accustomed to spending time in solitude. My father expected me to entertain myself. I always—"

"Admired him for that?" Calum suggested.

"Oh, yes," Pippa said. "What a bother it would have been to be fussed over. Anyway, I developed a fondness for nature and was fortunate enough to have the use of a small place on a distant corner of the estate where I could enjoy my surroundings and . . ." How silly it sounded.

Neither of the men commented.

"There is a similar situation here at Cloudsmoor. A hunting cabin. I do think it's important for every soul to have time to reflect peaceably, don't you?"

After a pause, both men mumbled unintelligibly.

"I knew you would agree. The cabin was abandoned many years ago. I found it during a summer holiday here. Today I took a few things there to make it more—*habitable*." Ooh, she sounded light-brained.

"Good idea, I should think," Calum said. "Shouldn't you, Struan?"

"Indubitably," Struan agreed. "So why are you bringing the jun—Why are you bringing the things back?" He'd been about to call the things she'd assembled "junk."

"I am returning what I don't need," she told him, tilting her nose up a little. "There are others who will find good use for them. I abhor waste. My father taught me to do so and I always—"

"Admired him for it," Calum finished for her in a monotone.

"Yes." Really, it seemed that Calum frequently finished sentences she'd begun. A potentially annoying habit. She kept her eyes on the path and said, "It would be very inconvenient if you were to mention seeing me today. Here, that is. In these circumstances . . . that is . . ."

"Consider the episode forgotten," Calum said promptly.

"Thank you. I—"

"We also have a delicate situation on our hands," the viscount said rapidly. "One you might possibly—"

"Lady Philipa cannot have been in the area more than a few days," Calum interrupted.

"You've just heard her say she knows the area well," Struan argued. "Surely she might—"

"She cannot possibly help us. And you need never fear that we will mention our meeting today, Pippa."

"There are two young people in our coach," Viscount Hunsingore said, rushing out the words. "A fifteen-year-old girl and her ten-year-old brother."

"Oh, my *God*!" Calum said.

Pippa glanced down at the top of his thick dark hair where he rested his head in his hands. She said, "Do go on, my lord." This promised to be a fascinating story.

"Ella—that is the girl—was in a—"

"No!" Calum roared, raising a face slashed with red across high cheekbones. "Do not say *that* word in front of this lady."

"In a *what*?" Pippa kept her attention on the track with difficulty.

"A, er"— the viscount cleared his throat —"an inappropriate establishment for one so young. For *anyone*, in fact. But particularly for a gentle young female such as Ella."

Pippa could not imagine what kind of establishment Viscount Hunsingore referred to, but from Calum's tone, it would appear to be quite terrible and unmentionable.

"I'll deal with this," Calum said. "Do you know of a childless family who might consider taking in two young people?"

How could she? Despite the fact that she knew the countryside quite well, she was all but a stranger to the tenants of both the Franchot and the Chauncey estates. "No," she said slowly. "There is a housekeeper at Cloudsmoor. And some casual staff. And the gardeners, of course. But we haven't actually stayed there in some years, and I don't really *know* anyone. But—"

"Of course you don't," Calum cut in, sounding almost relieved. "That's that, then. Don't give it another thought."

"Someone had bloody well better give it some thought."

At the viscount's profanity, Pippa sat very straight and hid a smile.

"Watch your tongue, man," Calum said predictably.

"Look," Viscount Hunsingore said, "this is *my* affair, but I'm in a fix and I'd appreciate any help I can get. I rescued Ella because—"

Pippa was almost certain Calum muttered something about lust. Certainly he'd said something to interrupt his friend.

"As I was saying," the viscount continued, "I rescued Ella and her brother, Max—and due to certain circumstances, we were forced to get them away from London."

"This is *not* Lady Philipa's affair," Calum declared.

"Normally I would agree," his friend said, obviously agitated. "But the situation is desperate. I *have* to find a place for them."

Pippa considered. She had not missed the suggestion that the viscount's silence could be bought with her assistance in the matter of the children. "Do they have any skills?" she asked.

"Dancing in veils and picking pockets," Calum replied darkly.

She almost pulled up the horse. "I beg your pardon?"

"Calum is in high humor, my lady," the viscount told her, sounding anything but amused. "No, Ella and Max do not have any . . . any usual skills."

"What of their parents?" She realized the question was belated.

"None," Hunsingore said flatly.

"Orphans?"

"Yes."

"Sad, but I believe I can think of a solution."

The viscount loomed over her left shoulder. "You can?"

"Absolutely. I shall return you to your carriage and make haste back to Franchot Castle myself. You will arrive considerably before me, but Justine—Lady Justine—is there. The dowager duchess has taken to her bed. She frequently takes to her bed." And Pippa wished she did not feel so very relieved by that fact.

"I do not understand what the solution to our problem is to be, Pippa," Calum said.

"Have you heard of illegitimate children?" she asked.

The total silence that followed went on for a long time.

"I can tell that you have. Of course you have. You are men of the world. I refer, of course, to children who are born to a mother who is not married to their father. I have never been entirely clear as to the manner by which this is accomplished, but I have definitely heard such arrangements discussed. At gatherings." She wrinkled her nose. "Among ladies who whispered about it," she finished.

"No doubt," Hunsingore said, sounding oddly distant.

"Yes, well, there we have our answer, then," Pippa said.

Calum's face was rather close to the side of hers. Suddenly he lifted down the hood of her cloak. "There, now I shall be certain not to miss a word of this wondrous solution. What answer do we have, my lady?"

"It's so obvious," she told them, smiling at her own ingenuity. "When you arrive at the castle, tell Justine you will require care for two children during your stay. After all, although I have heard illegitimate children referred to only as *fatherless*, why should they not be *motherless* instead?"

She turned on the seat and looked into Viscount Hunsingore's frowning face. "People make explanations entirely too complicated, my lord. Tell Justine you are accompanied by your two illegitimate children."

Fourteen

"*I can't,*" Struan said.

"You can and you will," Calum told him, watching Pippa and the dreadful old cart sway out of sight.

Damn, but he could hardly believe encountering her under such circumstances.

And damn, but he wished he were not drawn to her like a hawk to a glint amid Scottish heather.

Somehow he must learn to be colder in the matter of Lady Philipa Chauncey. He said, "We should have thought of pleading your relationship to the little starvelings ourselves, only we do not have Pippa's wit."

"Wit?" Struan sat heavily on the wall beside the road. At their request, Pippa had set them down on the highway, but out of sight of the carriage. "She is one of—no, she is the most addlepated female I have ever encountered."

"I should prefer that you not refer to her as such."

"Innocence can be charming," Struan said, evidently oblivious to the protective ire rising within Calum's bosom. "Innocence is to be *expected* in a young female. But for such a creature to invent a fantastic solution to a serious problem *and* to behave as if we shall, of course, be glad to implement that solution—it's maddening!

"I do believe the silly chit has some notion that a man may somehow produce offspring entirely without the assistance of a female."

177

Calum looked at his feet and willed himself not to explode. "You may be correct. On the other hand, I think it far more likely that Pippa knows more than you think. She may even see a certain humor in this." In fact, he was almost certain he'd seen a sparkle of enjoyment in her eyes after Struan's horrified reaction to her suggestion.

"*I* do not see any humor," Struan said truculently.

"Nonetheless, we are going to do as she has suggested." Calum offered Struan a hand and, when he reluctantly took it, hauled his friend to stand beside him. "You have no better plan."

"I will not do it."

"We might, of course, try suggesting you were secretly married and now are left a widower with two children."

Struan stared at Calum for a long time before saying, "You would do well not to push me further in this."

"Quite so," Calum said. "That would be going too far, since most people know your history. So Pippa's story must stand as it is."

"I will not do it," Struan declared again.

"You most certainly will."

"Absolutely not." Struan's firm mouth turned sharply downward at the corners. "How could you expect me to be believed if I told such an astonishing story?"

"You are not the only man who has two bastards to his credit," Calum replied, evil glee in his heart and an angelic expression on his face.

Struan turned on him. "You . . . I do *not* have two bastards to my name."

"No," Calum agreed, puckering his brow. "No. Not that I am aware of."

"You try my patience, Calum."

"Not too difficult a task to accomplish," Calum responded with absolute sincerity. "At least not on this day. Come, we will go on to the castle."

Struan hung back. "We must think of another plan."

"There is no time."

"Then we should go back to the nearest village and find lodgings. I need more time. Perhaps we could cast about more carefully for an appropriate solution."

"Too late," Calum said.

"We are early yet for our invitation to Franchot Castle."

Calum took a deep breath. "You forget that we are already committed to this course."

"How so?"

Calum shook his head. "You are not thinking well, my friend. The *addlepated* female we recently encountered will not simply forget that she saw us. She will return to the castle and if we have not arrived, she may announce that she has seen us on the road with your two illegitimate children."

"Do *not* say that again," Struan fumed. "We can stop her. She also has a secret—"

"Pippa will *not* be used to further our ends," Calum said shortly, and felt the twisting of unwanted premonition within him. Since their last meeting in London, the conviction had grown in him that he might eventually cause Pippa, at the very least, deep humiliation. He glanced at Struan and said, "What she has proposed makes absolute sense."

"That I have two illegitimate children? One of them *fifteen*?"

"You were perfectly capable of fathering a child at eighteen. And Pippa is correct, y'know. This *is* the only answer."

Struan paced back and forth. "How shall I explain it all?"

"Leave it to me."

"Good God, no!"

Calum's patience grew thinner. "We are going on to the castle. At the very least, *I* am going on to the castle. You have two charges now and I do not think you will easily relinquish them. I know you, Struan. You will not be lured away from this path you have chosen. And the *only* solution rests with a complete *lie*. Come, let us return to the carriage."

"I will not allow you to tell my *lies* for me," Struan said, matching Struan's stride toward the bend that would put them in sight of the carriage.

"You will get no argument from me," Calum said, deliberately training his eyes ahead. "When we gain the castle, you may go in ahead of me. Ask for Lady Justine and throw yourself upon her mercy."

"Throw myself . . ." Struan's voice trailed off.

Calum schooled himself not to look at his friend. "Precisely. Appeal to her finer feelings. I assure you that Lady Justine has very fine feelings.''

"How do you know?'' Struan's feet beat hard on the road now.

"I know,'' Calum said, mildly enough. "My sister is a truly gentle woman. She is also exceedingly intelligent.''

"What has intelligence to do with—''

"If I am not mistaken, Lady Justine may grasp that your story does not have a totally true ring, yet she will—since I also know she is a good judge of character—she will decide to champion you and your children.''

"They are *not* my children,'' Struan said through his teeth.

"Oh, but I rather think they are. You have made them so.''

"I am appalled at the prospect of telling such an outright lie to this woman who has every right to expect my good faith.''

"At the moment, you have a more pressing dilemma at which to be appalled.'' Calum stopped and indicated the road ahead. "Here comes one of your inconvenient offspring.''

Before Struan could react, Max—with the coachman hot on his heels—shot around the bend toward them. Seeing Calum and Struan, the boy threw wide his arms and flailed like a mad windmill. "Save me!'' he yelled. " 'E wants t'kill me! 'E wants t'kill a poor, abandoned boy. 'E says 'e's going to cut off me fingers and toes and string 'em on a braid made of me 'air. 'E's a monster, that's what 'e is!''

Max, his red hair glowing, flew into Struan's arms.

"Working at unhitching the carriage, 'e was, your lordship,'' said William, the Stonehaven's London coachman. "Caught 'im at it. If the 'orses 'adn't agitated, gawd knows what would 'ave 'appened.''

"I do believe this is where we must begin what we intend to continue,'' Calum said, clasping his hands behind his back and rocking onto his toes. "William, there is something you need to be made aware of.''

"Oh, my God!'' Struan, with Max still attached to his body like a morning-glory vine to a stalwart tree, shook his head adamantly. "Do not do this, Calum.''

"William,'' Calum said, not to be dissuaded, "how long have you been with the family now?''

"Seven years," William said promptly and with evident satisfaction. "Seven good years, and the marquess 'as made it clear 'e considers me a man worth trusting."

"And so do we, William, so do we," Calum said, beginning to enjoy himself far more than he knew he ought to. "We trust you so much that we are going to take you into our confidence in a most delicate matter."

"Calum, *please.*"

"William is most trustworthy, Struan. You know that as well as I do. These children—Ella and Max—they have suffered greatly, William. They have been abandoned to the whims of evil men."

"You don't say." William sounded bored.

"Yes," Calum said. "But that has all changed. Now that Viscount Hunsingore has decided to assume responsibility for their fate, their futures will be forever changed, and for the better. He could not have guessed how desperate their need for him to come forward and face this obligation had become."

William, short, muscular and ruddy, met Calum's eyes squarely. Calum saw the other man slowly form conclusions about what he'd just been told before muttering, "You *don't* say," in a voice heavy with understanding. "Well, now, in that case, I can only congratulate you on your devotion to duty, my lord. And if I can assist in any way, you have only to say the word."

Trying to pry Max loose, Struan groaned.

"Well," Calum said, "there is something you can do, William."

"Only ask, Mr. Innes."

"Very simply, we would appreciate your learning to refer to Miss Ella and Master Max as his lordship's children. Do you think you could do that?"

A grin slowly split William's round face. He swept off his hat and pushed sandy hair out of his eyes. "Consider it done," he said.

"What are you grinning at?" Struan asked suddenly, loudly.

William was instantly sober. "Me, my lord? Grinning? Never. I expect I was just thinking about 'ow 'appy the marquess was when 'e found out you lied—I mean, pretended about being a priest. I reckon as 'ow 'e and 'er ladyship will be beside 'emselves with joy when they meets their new nephew and niece for the first time.''

The woman who confronted Struan made him entirely forget his reason for being in a marvelous Gothic drawing room at Franchot Castle.

"Lord Hunsingore?" she said, her voice the kind that broke a little, as if with secret laughter. "I understand you and Mr. Innes are to be our guests here."

Struan stared at her.

"We had not expected you so soon. In fact, had we waited to leave London until the appointed day, you would have arrived here before any of us."

"We would?"

"Oh, yes," she said seriously, averting her eyes each time she met his, as if she were afraid direct contact might wound her. "As it is, my brother and the rest of his party will not arrive for several days."

"I see." He saw a tall, slender, straight-backed woman with thick dark hair shot through with red lights. She was no longer a girl, but she was lovely in a refined manner, with dark eyes, arched brows, a straight nose and a mouth that was beautifully cut—a mouth cut, in fact, like a more restrained version of the one belonging to Struan's very best friend.

Good God, Calum could very well be right. He could be related to this woman.

"Where is Mr. Innes?"

Where he had no right to be, meddling wretch that he was. "The long journey made him restless." The villain had ducked out in Struan's hour of most desperate need. "Mr. Innes is a man who delights in a great deal of exercise. He is walking about. Admiring this marvelous castle, no doubt. But I'm certain he will join us soon." Without uttering a word, Calum had left the coach at the top of the final rise to Franchot Castle and had disappeared into a nearby thicket. At this moment, William was in charge of the surprise Struan had no choice but to visit upon Lady Justine.

"The dowager duchess will not be able to greet you, I

fear," Lady Justine said, coloring slightly. "She, er, feels somewhat indisposed and may decide not to leave her rooms for some time."

"Yes," Struan said, intending to convey understanding but fearing Lady Justine would hear what he truly thought, which was that the Dowager Duchess of Franchot had little interest in minor nobles and their untitled friends. "Even less in inconvenient offspring," he muttered.

"I beg your pardon?"

Struan blinked and centered his gaze on Lady Justine's striking face. "Less inconvenience," he said, casting about for either help or an escape. "Less inconvenience might offer the lady some . . . *spring* . . . to her being, that is."

"Inconvenience?"

"We . . . that is to say, I fear I may present you with a dilemma for which you cannot possibly be prepared."

"How could you, my lord?"

As if to answer her question, the door was opened by a footman, accompanied by Ella and Max.

"These two young people said they wished to be with Viscount Hunsingore," the footman announced, clearly disapproving. "They were most insistent that he would want them with him because of their previous experiences while residing with a Mrs.—"

"*Thank* you," Struan interrupted quickly. "Thank you very much. Come in, you two." He tried, probably without success, to sound and appear jovial and delighted at the sight of the pair. Whatever happened, he must make some sort of excuse—other than the unthinkable one Lady Philipa had proposed—find a distant place in this castle in which to hide his two charges and place them elsewhere as quickly, and quietly, as possible.

Ella, her exotically angular face set in as demure a mold as such a face could accomplish, approached Struan across the expanse of silken green carpet. A girlish, pale pink pelisse over a muslin gown of a like shade did not at all suit her, Struan decided, but it was a definite improvement over the transparent red creation in which he'd first seen her.

When she stood before him, her head tilted, he saw anxiety in her great dark eyes. She looked over her shoulder and beckoned for Max to join her. He came, head hanging in a manner so uncharacteristic that Struan was filled with alarm.

"Mr. Innes told us to come in 'ere," Ella said in her clear voice. "'E said you'd want us to meet a lady."

Lady Justine had not moved since the children had entered the room. Now she came toward Struan and he vaguely noted that she limped quite markedly.

"Lady Justine, er—" Struan looked into the woman's warm brown eyes.

"Girvin," she said, giving what must be her family name.

He would have Calum's interfering hide for this. "These young people are—"

"There you are!" Calum's voice, booming through the room, emptied Struan's brain of any coherent thought. "Meant to come in with these two rascals. Had the good fortune to run into Lady Philipa."

Struan scowled.

Calum smiled and walked over to ruffle Max's hair. Amazingly, the boy grinned with pleasure.

"Have you explained our small *contretemps* to Lady Justine?" Calum asked.

"Well, I—"

"I thought not," Calum said with a resigned expression. "Never mind. Struan is a shy fellow, Lady Justine. The children and I will deal with the matter at hand, won't we, children?"

"Oh, yes," Ella said and smiled sweetly from Struan to Lady Justine and back again. "Mr. Innes is right. I can feel it. The lady won't think nothing of finding a place for two children what 'ave learned to manage with very little. Am I right, lady?"

"*My* lady," Struan murmured with quiet desperation.

"*My* lady," Ella said obligingly.

"But of course," Lady Justine said, smiling for all the world as if there were nothing she relished more than the intrusion of two uncultured, unexpected guests.

"There," Ella said triumphantly, and threaded an arm through one of Struan's. She gazed up at him adoringly. "I told you everythin' would be perfect soon as we got 'ere, Papa."

❧ Fifteen

Franchot Castle was beautiful. Fearsome in its massive grandeur—particularly as evening slid into night—yet definitely beautiful. Pippa left the cover of a vast stone urn overflowing with ivy and fragrant sweet Williams and slipped along the terrace to which she'd secretly followed Calum Innes.

He'd spoken very little at dinner and excused himself immediately afterward. Pippa had wanted to follow him at once. Decorum and good sense had forced her to wait a few minutes, and when she had finally made fatigue a reason to leave, she'd feared there would be no hope of finding out where Calum had gone—if he'd gone anywhere other than to his rooms.

Miraculously, the moment she'd quit the dining room for the adjoining elegant blue-and-gold salon, Calum had been standing in one of the doorways to the echoing stone passageway beyond.

If he'd seen her, he had given no sign. Instead, he had chosen that instant to turn and walk away, and Pippa had sped across the salon, annoyed at the rustle of her gray gros des Indes gown. She need not have worried. Calum's progress from the castle had held single-minded purpose, and he certainly had not appeared to hear the faint sound she'd been helpless to mask.

Now he moved into the clear moonlight that bathed a wide flight of steps leading from this terrace to the one below. He

185

strode swiftly, silently, downward—and continued descending past the second and third terraces to heavily shadowed lawns dotted with topiary and hemmed in by high, meticulously clipped privet hedges.

She should go back and make her way to her rooms before she would be missed.

Pippa clamped a hand over her heart and felt its wild beating.

Going back was out of the question. All her life she had pursued what interested her most with steadfast determination.

A wild one. And you'll come to no good, mark my words.

Pippa checked her step, startled by the clearly recalled admonition of Binns, the woman who had been Pippa's indifferent nanny until she'd left, when Pippa was twelve, to *take up a post where children know how children are supposed to behave and won't keep a body forever in fear of a terrible misfortune befalling them in their wild doings.*

Binns might have been right. Perhaps Pippa was wild, but she could not change her nature.

If she delayed, even for a few moments, he would disappear. Swiftly, she gained the lawn and flew to the cover of a bush carefully shaped into a large and perfect cone.

Calum was now strolling at a leisurely pace, meandering among bushes molded by the castle's legion of gardeners into bears and birds and all manner of fanciful shapes.

At last, without putting more than a few additional yards between himself and Pippa, he halted at a spot where a white marble statue guarded an exit from the garden. He stood there, apparently gazing at the moon's glittering stripe upon a night-black sea. He rested a booted foot on the statue's elevated base and placed a forearm on his thigh.

Pippa hovered between high, almost overwhelming excitement and some abjectly unhappy realization that seemed poised to grab and swallow her.

Calum was the excitement.

The horrible certainty that every moment spent in his company—even when he did know of her presence—brought her closer to never seeing him again was the unhappy realization.

She stayed in the blackness created by a hedge. From there she could see his profile clearly where it caught the silver of moonlight. He seemed transfixed by what he saw, or perhaps by what he thought about whilst he stared into the darkness.

A soul who enjoyed solitude.

Like her, Calum thirsted for quiet moments alone with his imaginings. Pippa was certain he did.

She swallowed and felt pain in her throat. Soon she would be a married woman, and the demands of that state would doubtless keep her from dwelling on those simple pleasures that had, since childhood, brought her so much joy.

Married. Married to Etienne Loring Girvin, Duke of Franchot, the autocratic, indifferent man to whom she must submit in all things. Pippa recalled the foul smell of stale drink upon his breath when he'd tried to kiss her. Shuddering, she involuntarily wiped at her mouth.

Within her sight stood a man quite different from the one to whom she must, in the dowager's words, "relinquish herself entirely," and for whom she must "put aside the nonsense of maidenly dreams and maidenly modesty for the purpose of accommodating his needs." The dowager had, with her eyes averted from Pippa's, added that there would be much that caused Pippa discomfort—even pain on occasion—but no sign of disgust must ever be visible to the man who would then be her lord.

For a woman to find any pleasure in the marriage bed was unthinkable. Women of refinement and good breeding must be passive and gladly accept inevitable unpleasantness. In the unlikely event that such a woman might find any enjoyment in the marriage act, then she must, at all costs, never tell this sin to her husband. An immediate confession to her minister, followed by firm resolve never to err again, would be her only salvation.

When the time had come for her to join the Franchots in London, Pippa had tried to talk to her father, to tell him she wished she might be released from this marriage. Her pleas for him to give Franchot a guarantee of perpetual free passage across Chauncey land had resulted in a sharp reprimand for her foolishness. A man did not simply give away part of one of his estates. Papa had not seemed to notice the depth of her agitation and had left for the Continent on business for the

King, saying that he would endeavor to be present for her wedding.

Her wedding.

Weddings, so she'd thought when she'd been a foolish little girl, were beginnings. When she'd become older, sixteen or seventeen, she'd started trying to remember what Etienne—whom she'd seen only once or twice when she was very young—looked like. And she'd tried to spin a magical story around her marriage to him, making of it a fairy tale like those she'd read of knights and ladies, when the knight came for his lady and carried her off on his horse and they were both so very happy as they galloped off into their future.

The first instruction Pippa had received from her "knight" was that he'd prefer that she call him Franchot—so much more suitable, he'd said—rather than Etienne.

And Franchot did not particularly care to ride. He'd told her as much when she'd unwisely tried to engage him in conversation and had mentioned her own fondness for horses.

Franchot did not like horses or riding, but biting the ear of a female far too insubstantial to defend herself made him laugh. Forcing his hand inside her gown and . . . She closed her eyes, trying to push away the memory but failing. He had taken her breast into his hot hand and squeezed until tears sprang into her eyes. That had made him laugh a great deal. And he'd swayed against her and said, "Nothing more than a little apple here. What a disappointment. Much prefer large fruit meself. But no doubt I shall enjoy taking many bites from this little apple—until you have discharged your duty to me."

She knew what he meant. More or less. Without absolute understanding of exactly how it should be accomplished, Pippa was certain Franchot referred to the bringing forth of his heirs.

One of the benefits of very little supervision, since Binns left, had been Pippa's freedom to explore the library at Dowanhill. In that library were some unusual texts—hidden where they were probably never supposed to be found—that spoke of how a man, when he wished a woman to produce his heirs, must be tireless in the planting of his seed. Unselfishly taking that seed into herself—as often as might be needed—and nurturing it until it brought forth the essential fruit was the wife's duty.

The equation between Franchot's taking bites out of her breasts and the planting of his seed for her to nurture was not at all clear. However, there had been a certain small volume, written in a language Pippa had never seen before and containing sketches of male and female parts, that had given her a fair idea—fantastic as it seemed—of where the seed came from. It came from That—the part she had felt against her when Calum Innes had held her close—and although she was certain she must be unnatural, she would very much like to *see* exactly what That looked like—other than in a picture.

There had been several sketches that had sent Pippa scrambling to replace the volume. She'd tried, unsuccessfully, to close what she'd seen from her mind. Could it be that a woman must *swallow* a man's seed to produce his heirs? Oh, dear, she did hope not. The thought of having to . . . with Franchot? Oh, surely not.

Calum had kissed her so very gently at first. And then his kisses had done wonderful things to her, made her feel—yes, charmed, as spun about by a charm as if he'd been her knight bearing her away on his horse, she was certain. He'd told her he knew the feelings he caused in her and that those should be the feelings that came to her with her husband.

And he had *touched* her. He'd touched her in places and in ways she was certain were most unsuitable.

But she did not care.

And he'd kissed her in places where she was certain he should not have kissed her.

And she did *not* care.

Then he had caused that burning, heaving, flaring sensation that turned her legs weak and made her body throb and suggested, outrageously, that there was much more she wanted to experience with him.

She did not care.

If he wanted to and there was an appropriate opportunity, she would choose to experience it all again.

An evil, carnal creature. She knew herself to be just such a one because the dowager had assured her, most seriously, that only evil, carnal women experienced any pleasure when touched by a man. Of course, she'd been referring to a woman's husband, so perhaps if the man in question was not the woman's husband . . .

Despite the absolute knowledge that she was as wild as Binns had suggested, Pippa hugged herself and reveled in the memory of Calum's touches.

She wanted to feel his arms around her again, and his mouth on hers—and his mouth on her neck and her shoulders and her breasts. *Oh, she was beyond help.* She wanted to feel his mouth on every part of her and to taste every part of him.

Something was very definitely wrong with her.

She leaned a little farther from the shadows to see him more clearly.

Calum appeared transfixed by whatever he was thinking.

There had been times, many of them, when Pippa had been glad of her solitary life at Dowanhill. As her father had always mentioned, not with approval, Pippa was a person who seemed to require inordinate amounts of time in which to do nothing but think.

But then there had been times, just as many, when she ached for another with whom to share all the wonderful things that kept her so absorbed. For as long as she could remember, Pippa had been certain that somewhere there was a person— only one, of course—who would find equal pleasure in observing a small animal that thought itself unobserved; in sitting, with his eyes closed, listening to rain upon the roof and the windows; or in watching the wind send ripples across a lake.

What bliss it would be to sit, with her eyes closed, listening to rain on a roof with Calum and to be certain they could stay forever if they chose.

On the previous day, with the unwitting help of one of the friends Nelly Bumstead had quickly made among the castle staff, Pippa had relocated the small, abandoned hunting cabin in the hills just beyond the Franchot estate—on Cloudsmoor land. When Calum and Viscount Hunsingore had put in their amazing appearance this afternoon, she'd been returning from making the cabin into her own special nest.

Pippa could scarcely wait to return there. Rain would undoubtedly make a marvelous noise on the slightly buckled slate roof. Yes, the cabin would be lovely with Calum in it . . .

And then there were children.

Surely there was, somewhere, a person who would feel about children as she did. They were the embodiment of all she loved: free, unpredictable, sometimes wildly loving, sometimes sad, sometimes naughty—but usually naughty only because they needed to be shown how important they were.

Justine felt very close to children, too. Pippa was certain of this now that she'd seen how Justine had instantly accepted Ella and Max and how she'd taken so active a part in getting them settled at the castle.

Viscount Hunsingore had looked completely horrified at Pippa's suggestion that he say the children were his. She smiled to herself in the darkness. The viscount had thought her entirely ignorant of the manner in which children came into the world. How surprised he would be if he knew the truth about her education in such matters. That Ella and Max were, indeed, his children was beyond doubt. After all, why would he agree to champion them under any other circumstances? The mystery, given their evident lack of culture, was the identity of their mother and how Struan had come to be in sole possession of them.

Would Calum, Pippa wondered, understand how much she yearned for the company of children? Would he fail to find it strange that she worried about being forced to follow the prescribed rules among people of her class and put her babies into the care of nurses from the moment of their birth? Would he find it in his heart to sympathize with her belief that no small boy should be separated from his parents and sent far away to a school where he was supposed to learn, through the example of bullies, how to become a better man?

"All such a bother," she murmured. But that was the way of it, and she would have a fight on her hands to change what was considered inalienable tradition.

"Fie," she exclaimed suddenly and much more loudly than she'd intended. Her attention had wandered, and Calum no longer stood beside the statue in the opening in the tall hedges.

Pippa sped toward the gap and passed through. On the other side, the downward slope became steeper, and since clouds drifted like India-blue scarves across the moon, she had to divide her attention between searching for her quarry and watching where she set her feet.

She reached a place where white marble slabs formed a terrace around an oblong pool. The surface of the water, driven by a breeze, gleamed like crumpled black satin.

Pippa stopped and looked around. There was no sign of Calum now.

Papa would tell her she was making a poor choice in seeking out a man who could only cause her inconvenience. Yes, Papa would call it *inconvenience*. Not danger. No, Papa would not tell her that at this moment, she was trembling on the brink of throwing the careful order of her life into chaos, chaos that could leave her ruined.

She wanted this danger.

Pippa began walking along the edge of the water toward an elevated fountain that chattered like a sharp rainfall over marble statuary at the end of the pool. The only thing she could do was the only sensible thing *to* do—return to the castle and her bed. She'd have absolutely no notion of what to say to him if she did encounter him anyway.

"Oh, how surprising," she said softly in the kind of coy voice she'd heard so many young ladies of the *ton* employ. "I happened to decide to take a walk in the dark and you happened to decide to do the same thing." *Widgeon.*

Sighing, she turned around, stumbled on a crack—and walked into a very solid chest.

"How surprising," Calum said, settling his hands loosely around her neck. "We both happened to decide to take a walk."

Her face flamed and she blessed the darkness. "I thought you were ahead . . . I mean . . ."

"I know what you mean. I was ahead of you. Then you became distracted and gave me a chance to get behind you."

Her heart beat so hard she was certain he could hear it. "How did you know where I was? How did you know I was outside?"

"Because you did exactly what I intended you to do," he said. "I made certain you saw where I was going. Then I set off, hoping you'd follow. And you did."

Pippa drew in a huge breath but still felt light-headed. "You were very sure of me."

"No." He settled his thumbs on the point of her chin and eased her face up. "I wasn't completely sure."

"I am not good at word games, Calum."

"I believe you are good at whatever you decide worthy of the effort. You are not a coquette. Thank God."

"It was a mistake for me to come after you."

"Was it?" In the darkness, his teeth flashed white. "Do let me help you change your mind, sweet lady. If you had not come to find me, I should surely have come looking for you."

Her stomach clenched. The subject must be changed. "What do you think of the castle?"

"I think the castle is magnificent with you in it."

He *was* dangerous. "You will enjoy seeing more of the inside. It's sumptuous. No expense was spared."

"I shall enjoy exploring—with you."

"Why do you pursue me?" Her lips remained parted. How could she have been so plainspoken? "I mean—"

"You mean exactly what you said, my lady. I am pursuing you. What I do not understand is your reason for asking me why."

"I begged you not to come here."

"You begged because you knew you wanted me to come more than you wanted anything else."

"No." She stepped away and he immediately dropped his hands. "I *meant* that you should not accept the duke's invitation."

He laughed and half-turned away from her. "What lies beyond this terrace?"

"Nothing really," she told him promptly. "The outer walls are not far away. Below them lie a rocky beach and the sea."

"Ah." He sought around and gathered up a handful of stones. "The edge of the world. I find I very much enjoy the thought of standing on the edge of the world with you."

There were no words with which she could answer. Beneath her skin, nerves quivered. She should not remain, yet she could not seem to make her feet move away from him.

Calum faced the sea and shied a rock high into the air. He

cocked his head to listen and said, "Nothing," after what felt like a very long time.

Another white rock soared heavenward and fell without a sound. "We are a very long way above your rocky beach," Calum said and commenced to hurl rocks, first with one arm and then with the other, with equal strength and accuracy. "Do you know if that rocky beach is the one on which Lady Justine suffered her childhood accident?"

"I believe so."

"Hmm. She is delightful, isn't she?"

"I already love her like a sister."

"You have good taste."

He puzzled her.

"Come, let us take a turn around the pool."

There seemed nothing for it but to stroll at his side.

"What would you say if I took your hand?" he asked.

"You must not try to do so. A member of the staff could appear at any moment."

"I doubt it," he assured her, turning and walking backward, smiling at her, his black eyes catching moonlight. "Indeed, I doubt it very much. I think everyone thinks I have gone to my rooms because I am tired from my journey. What excuse did you give for leaving the table?"

"That I was tired."

"There you have it. I am tired from my journey and already slumbering in my bed. You are tired and already slumbering in your bed. Gardeners do not work in the darkness, my sweet. We are quite alone."

"Do not call me your sweet." As petulant as she sounded, the attempt at establishing appropriate behavior was essential.

"We can stay here as long as we please—*Pippa*. Do you know why I think this is so?"

"No doubt you will enlighten me." They had arrived at the fountain.

"Lady Justine likes me as much as I like her."

"Conceit becomes no man."

"I am not conceited, merely honest." He offered her his hand. "Lady Justine has noted, correctly, that you and I are drawn to each other. If she should discover your absence, she will assume you are with me and say nothing. Take my hand."

"My maid may well announce my absence." Pippa pressed her hands into the folds of her skirts. "You should leave Franchot in the morning."

"Not possible." He continued to offer her his hand. "Your maid is a romantic. She sees us as a man and a woman intended to be lovers."

"You *must* not say so," Pippa said. "I was afraid you would make trouble. That is why I asked you to remain in London. The duke is not a man who will tolerate another's attention to his future duchess."

"You said I should not come, yet you look at me constantly."

She blessed the darkness that hid her blush. "That is an outrageous, unchivalrous suggestion."

"It is the truth. At dinner, your eyes rarely left my face."

Mortification froze Pippa in place. For moment after moment she listened to the cascading water, then said, "I have looked at you this evening because I am afraid."

Calum faced the fountain. At its base was a large bowl that filled with water before overflowing to the rocks below. "This is beautiful," he told her. "Come and see how oddly serene the surface in the bowl is before it rushes away."

Cautiously, she walked to look, making certain not to stand too close to him.

"Why are you afraid?" he asked softly.

She could not tell him.

Calum sank the fingers of his left hand into the water. "Strange, it's almost warm. Feel."

Slowly, Pippa dipped in her very fingertips.

Calum's hand moved, just beneath the surface, until he barely touched her. "Water is sensual," he murmured. "I have always loved water. Even as a small boy, I swam in Scottish lakes where others were afraid to go for fear of dying of the cold."

"But it did you no harm?"

He chuckled. "It invigorated me. Sometimes I think the water was my mother. Just being close to it brings me utter peace. Do you feel the peace?"

What she felt, he could not possibly imagine. She was all

turning and twisting—except for the skin that touched his skin beneath the shimmering surface of the bowl.

"I will ask you again," Calum said. "Why are you afraid for me to be here?"

"Please do not press me."

His fingers slipped between hers, lacing them together in the clean warmth of silken water. Slowly, he all but withdrew his touch, only to return it again and lock his grip upon her.

"Can you swim, Pippa?"

"I don't know."

"You mean you have never tried?"

"I was never allowed to try."

"Then I shall teach you. The Channel is most pleasant at this time of year. We'll locate a suitable spot and you will learn."

She felt herself blush again. "I could not possibly allow any such thing. Calum, His Grace will be here very shortly and you must be gone before he arrives."

"I shall not be gone," he said, sounding entirely unperturbed. "And I am determined to teach you to swim. I cannot have you so close to the sea and unable to do so. I should not rest for a moment."

She ducked her face and closed her eyes. He sounded as if he *cared*. So much confusion.

"Surely there is a hollow where children swim. You must have encountered such a place when you spent holidays here."

"There is, but *I* shall not go there," she said with finality. "And now it is time to return to the castle."

"Not a bit of it." He continued to clasp their hands together. "When I teach you to swim, you shall wear a chemise. It will be heaven to be with you, to hold you and watch you. Your hair will spread upon the surface and I shall kiss your wet lips until you turn into my arms and forget your maidenly modesty."

Pippa tried to pull her hand away, a hopeless task.

"But that is for another day," he said. "You are afraid because you watched me at dinner and thought about the last time we were together."

"Stop, I beg you."

"You remembered, darling Pippa. You remembered how it

felt to be in my arms, to touch and be touched by me. You remembered how you confessed that you were certain you could not stop yourself from touching me again, *intimately*, if we were close.''

She held a breath, then let it out slowly. ''Yes,'' she said simply. ''Yes, I was remembering. I'm remembering now.''

''And you would like to repeat what we have shared.''

Although he still held her hand, she turned away from him. ''I came after you tonight because I could not stay away.''

She expected him to make a flippant retort. Instead he said, ''And I'm here because I cannot stay away.''

Pippa closed her eyes. She had begun to throb in all the places that had surely not even existed before Calum Innes came into her life.

''The difference between us is that you fear what you feel for me. *I* embrace what I feel for you, sweet Pippa.'' He cleared his throat. ''If you had truly wanted me not to come here, you wouldn't have been so hasty to find a place for . . . for the children.''

''Children are dear to me.'' Any caution about what she said seemed to have fled. ''I told you as much once before. For a moment—after the viscount spoke of his dilemma—I forgot that I was being rash. I thought only of the plight of his dear children.''

The odd noise Calum made could have been a cough or a laugh. ''You are too kind, my lady.''

''Children are the best of what we ever are,'' she told him, turning back to look seriously into his face. ''They are laughter and light. They are promise. They are clean slates upon which to write great things, or simply good and kind things. We must guard our children well, for they are our future.''

His face was clear in the moonlight. Pippa saw his slanting brows draw together, and an unfathomable expression in his eyes.

''You disagree?'' she asked, aware that his answer meant much more than it should.

''You take my breath away,'' he told her and, as if to make sure she believed him, brought her dripping hand to his chest and clasped it against him. ''Where did you come from, magical one? And where have you been for so long?''

"I have been . . . I have been," was the only response she could make.

"You have been." He nodded. "Yes. And I have been, but when I think that I might never have known you, *I* am afraid."

"Ella and Max *are* Struan's children, aren't they?"

He frowned. "No."

Pippa smiled. "Of course they are. Why else would he go to such lengths for them? Was he married?"

"No."

"Their mother died."

"Very probably.

"So the viscount is a widower?"

"No."

"Fie!" He was vexing her with his mystery. "Tell me the truth of it, then."

He jutted his face closer to hers and, before she could try to evade, kissed the tip of her nose. "You, my dear, are very persistent. Listen carefully. I shall tell this once and you may accept or not. That is your choice. But I shall not make any other excuse. Do you agree to those conditions?"

She considered before saying, "I agree."

"Very well. Ella and Max were in very serious trouble in London, through no fault of their own. Struan made a hasty decision. He saw that if they were not rescued from their unsuitable condition, their lives would be ruined. He rescued them. That is all."

It was Pippa's turn to frown. "I . . . I do believe you. But now I want you to agree to something for me. Justine believes they are the viscount's children by some . . . *unusual* union, and she is perfectly at peace with that deduction. I suggest you do not trouble her with stories that would upset her. She is not a happy woman, and I would not willingly cause her more unhappiness."

"Very well," he said, almost too quickly. "We shall leave that as it is for now. What makes Lady Justine unhappy?"

It was not her place to discuss her future sister-in-law's unhappy life. Pippa shrugged. "She should have married and had children of her own. Like me, she was born to be a comfort to a husband and a loving guide to little ones, yet her lot appears to be that of a spinster. Please, I should prefer not to discuss this further.''

He was quiet for a long time.

"You will not mention what I have said?" Pippa asked at last.

"I will not," he said. The stillness that was so much a part of him had descended once more. Thoughtfully, he raised her damp hand to his lips and kissed each knuckle with slow deliberateness.

She could not have stopped him—even if she completely remembered that she should. His touch was drugging. Pippa felt her lips part and could not close them. She rose to her toes and could not make her heels seek the ground again.

Keeping her hands against his mouth, he bowed his head until she could not see his face,

Pippa wanted to stroke his hair.

She wanted to caress his face, his strong neck, his wide shoulders.

His back had felt so good when she'd rested her cheek there.

Pippa *needed* to press her cheek to his back again—his naked back!

She gasped aloud.

Calum didn't raise his face.

He was distant now, and . . . angry?

"You are angry?" It was as much a statement as a question.

Once, twice, he brought his brow down upon her fists; then he released her. He released her and put her, very deliberately, from him. "I am not angry, Pippa."

He sounded angry. "You would like me to leave now," she said, backing away.

"Do *not* leave me."

The still fury in his voice took her breath away. "What is it, Calum? What *is* all this? What is happening to us?" She took a step toward him, but he retreated. "Please, tell me how I may comfort you."

"No one can comfort me," he told her. There was ice in his voice now.

"But you are in pain."

"What would you know of pain?" His harsh laugh hurt

her. "You have never known confusion. You have never known a moment of doubt. Not about who you are or what your life is bound to become."

"No," she said slowly. "That is true."

"Well, I . . ." He pinched the bridge of his nose and she saw muscles flicker in his jaw. "I have been deeply troubled about a friend of mine. I have known him a long time, and of late, he has changed. That causes me grave concern."

"Do I know this man?"

"He has moved in circles entirely removed from your own. Mostly in Scotland."

"Ah, I see." Her one visit to Scotland had been some years since. "Why do you think this friend has changed?"

His ragged breath seared her heart. Pippa reached for him, but he held up his arms, warning her off.

"Tell me about him," she said gently.

"He is a man adrift," Calum said. "Are you cold?"

"Not really," she lied.

Calum removed his coat and slipped it around her shoulders.

"Now you are cold," she told him, but she breathed in his marvelous masculine scent and held the garment close.

"I shall like that coat the better for knowing it has kept you warm."

Tears sprang into her eyes and she blinked them away. His simple words could reduce her to trembling vulnerability.

And she adored that vulnerability—with him. "Your friend?" she prompted, praying he would not hear the depth of emotion he aroused in her.

Bowing his head again, he rested his fists on narrow hips. "He doesn't know what he should do next in his life. He has encountered such tragedy. Such wasteful, useless tragedy."

His full-sleeved white shirt billowed. Moonlight shone through the fine fabric, casting his powerful body in dark silhouette.

She wanted to put her hands inside his shirt and feel his warm flesh.

An evil, carnal creature.

Beyond help.

Pippa averted her eyes. "What was . . . If you would like to tell me. What was this tragedy?"

"He has confronted the fact," Calum said, his voice so low she had to strain to hear it, "that he lost something very dear before he ever had it."

"I don't understand."

"How could you? He has discovered that his parents died before he could meet them."

"Oh." Pippa stepped involuntarily toward Calum and this time he didn't retreat. She slipped her arms around his waist and looked up at him. "How could such a terrible thing be?"

"There was a mistake. He was lost to his parents, and when he returned they were no longer there."

"Poor man."

"Poor man, indeed. Poor, confused man. He feels a great sense of loss, as if he is grieving, yet he had never expected to grieve."

"This is so sad. We must help him."

He looked at her then. "We?" He brushed the backs of his fingers over her cheek and tilted his head sideways to study her.

Pippa swallowed hard. "I am not a stranger to adversity. At Dowanhill, I was the one our people came to with their problems."

"And you dispensed a little food and instructions for exercising greater thrift in future, no doubt."

She should be angry, but she couldn't be. "You are suffering for your friend," she said. "That suffering is making you unkind. I am a good listener, Calum. Sometimes people most need to be listened to."

"You are wise beyond your age and sex," he said. "My friend is lost, Pippa. He is a man who has never really known himself. A man always playing roles and trying to be what he thought he was supposed to be without ever finding true comfort."

A coldness stole about Pippa's heart and she felt again the welling of tears.

Calum tucked back curls that had fallen forward from her chignon. "I have upset you," he said gently. "I did not intend to do so. I would never willingly do so."

"I think this friend of yours knows my heart," she said in a voice that shook.

He appeared bemused. "How so?"

"Like your friend, I have never been entirely certain of my place. Or rather, I have known what I yearned for, but at the same time I have understood that it could never be."

"It is not at all the same thing," he told her curtly.

Pippa stiffened and tried to blink back the tears.

"Damn!" He swept an arm around her waist and drove the fingers of his other hand into the hair at her temple. "I have made you cry. I never want to cause you pain, sweet one."

She shook her head, laughing through the tears that were overflowing despite her best efforts to stem them.

"Yes, I have hurt you when you sought to understand . . . You wanted to find a way to comfort my friend."

"I would very much like to comfort him."

"Would you?"

She would like to help this friend because she wanted to help Calum.

She would like at this very moment to be kissed by Calum.

"I would help him," she said, her lashes flickering downward. "Tell me how I can do that."

"He is very close to me. My happiness invariably makes him a great deal happier."

"It does?"

"Most certainly."

"And you are not happy?"

"I think I could be. And you could help me in this."

"Tell me how."

The scent of sweet Williams reached her on a breeze. Water from the fountain scattered upon marble, like crystal chips on ice-coated glass. From below the cliffs came the sound of waves shushing over rock and sand.

"How can I help you, Calum?"

His lips were parted when they descended to hers. Firm and commanding, his mouth slanted over hers. Pliant, clever, practiced, his lips and tongue sought and found, delved and tasted and stole what they sought. And Pippa began to crumple in his arms. Her legs wobbled and Calum brought her firmly against his body.

He was hard and honed and warm and strong.

And he was pulsing and pushing and huge and hot where That leaped at her belly through his breeches and through the gown that was too insubstantial to disguise the length and thickness of him.

"Yes," she said on a sigh. "Yes, that is exactly it."

"What is it?" he asked. His hands sought and covered her breasts beneath his coat. With his palms he made circles over her nipples and she began to melt. "Tell me, Pippa."

She must not tell him. Inexperienced she might be. A fool she most definitely was not.

"Tell me."

He eased her bodice the tiniest bit and cool air stroked her bared nipples.

"*Tell* me."

Gently, with fingers and thumbs, he tugged her nipples.

Pippa's knees became nonexistent.

He bent his head and, with the greatest of care, sucked a nipple into his mouth.

"Don't . . . stop," she gasped. "I wanted to tell you not . . . to . . . stop. And I want to . . . I want to . . . touch you."

She heard the *plop* as he pulled with his lips and let go before moving to her other breast. Working with the tip of his tongue, he paused just long enough to say, "You are touching me," before he continued to roll her nipple back and forth and to swirl his tongue around it in a manner that blotted all conscious thought from Pippa.

"I should like to do whatever you would like me to do," she told Calum, clinging to him by handfuls of his hair.

"Whatever?"

"I am in your hands."

"And in my mouth," he murmured, pulling hard enough to make her cry out with exquisite ecstasy. "I want you for my own, Pippa, and I intend to have you."

"We can be together like this for a long time, I think." She fumbled with his stock. "You are undoubtedly right. No one-will come looking for us."

"That will not be enough."

"No."

"You agree?"

"Yes. Only I don't know what I'm agreeing to."

"You're agreeing to swim naked with me. And sleep naked with me. And share everything there is to share between a man and a woman."

"I should like that awfully much."

Fastening his mouth to her breast again, he pressed a massive thigh between her legs and braced his foot on something Pippa couldn't see.

"Oh," was all she could say. The rest of her wits were required for her to cling to his shoulders.

She heard a tearing sound and realized her bodice had given way. "Oh, Calum, my dress."

"Forget the dress." He hadn't finished talking before he held her to him with one arm and lifted her skirts up around her waist with his other hand. "I want to give you pleasure, Pippa. You are a passionate man's dream and I want to be the passionate man you need. Give yourself up to me."

Rocking her, he caused her to ride his thigh as if she were astride a bareback stallion.

"Calum—"

"Hush." His big hands covered her breasts and his fingers beneath her arms anchored her.

Helpless in the grip of sensations that ripped from her slick center to parts deep within her for which she knew no name, Pippa filled her hands with Calum's shirt and let her head fall back.

"So beautiful," he said. "My God, I will have you, Pippa. I will make you mine, and no other man will ever be able to satisfy you but me."

"I am not supposed to fe—el this." Throbbing, pulsing waves of fire began to break. "It can only be because you are not my hu—usband."

He kissed her throat and manipulated his fingers between her legs.

"Oh, Ca-lum." She could not bear it. And she could not bear it to be over. "*Please*."

When she felt his finger press inside her, she tried, without success, to stiffen. "We must not do this," she told him.

His finger was inside her and his thumb stroked back and forth over the small bud of flesh that felt swollen and slippery.

He stroked her inside and he stroked her outside and the fiery waves crashed.

Pippa jerked; she bowed forward and found something with her teeth, something that gave just a little but afforded a means to stop her from falling through space and time forever.

Waves of fire became rings of fire, spreading outward as if her body were molten liquid heat into which Calum had thrust a silver arrow fresh from the smith's oven.

Pippa could not guess how much time had passed with the fading ripples before Calum caught her up into his arms and held her so fiercely it hurt. She didn't care.

Then she realized it had been his shoulder into which she had sunk her teeth, and she cried out, ''I have wounded you''

''You have branded my shoulder,'' he said. ''I'll wear your brand with pride, my sweet.''

''I do not understand myself,'' she said when she could speak again.

Calum nuzzled her cheek and kissed her closed eyes. ''I know you don't. You amaze me. You are a treasure. My treasure. When I think I might never have found you, I am sick to my soul.''

She was weak. And her gown was in tatters. And there were many things to be said. Many things to be dealt with. She had been incapable of stopping what had just happened, but she knew it should not have happened.

''It must not happen again,'' she said, knowing that she wanted, more than anything else, for it to happen again.

''You'll not be hurt, Pippa. That I promise you.''

''Neither will you,'' she told him. ''This thing that happens between us is entirely my fault.''

She heard him draw in a breath and hold it.

''Yes, Calum. You are disturbed now that you consider the truth. I have tempted you into this behavior. I followed you because I cannot stay away from you. I am beyond help in this unless you go away where I cannot find you.''

''You tell me to go with your lips. Your heart tells me otherwise.''

''You are dangerous—the devil—tempting me, charming me, until I do not know myself. If I do not find a way to keep you from me, you are doomed . . . and I am doomed.''

"You really think Franchot would—"

"He would kill you, and if he spared my life, I would soon wish he had not done so."

"Oh, my dear. I shall never let anything happen to you. Such a thing is unthinkable. I have known other women. You must know that without my telling you. But none could ever compare with you. You do things no fine brandy could do. You are golden sunrise and crimson sunset. You are ice patterns on winter windowpanes and sun scintillating through summer leaves. You enchant me."

Tears again. "You take my breath away, Calum."

"You have entirely stolen mine."

"Please put me down."

"I don't ever want to put you down."

"Put me down now. Please, Calum."

Carefully, sliding her down his length, he did as she asked.

Pippa surveyed the wreckage of her gown and set to work pulling and patching and smoothing. "Hopeless," she said. "I must find a way inside without being seen."

"We cannot act too quickly," Calum said. "There are others to be considered now."

"I will make certain we see as little as possible of each other," she told him. It was the only answer.

"You will make certain of no such thing."

"I most certainly shall."

"This is no longer in your hands. It never was."

Pippa's face shot up. "No, it was never in my hands. Neither was it in yours."

In the darkness, his smile was harshly determined. "It may not have been in my hands once. It certainly is now."

She had done this. She had created a ghastly disaster.

A crashing sounded from somewhere above them.

Pippa stood still, holding Calum's coat around her. "What is that?"

He raised his chin and listened.

"They're coming!" a young voice shouted. "They're coming. They're coming. They're 'ere!"

Calum made a growling noise and muttered, "Little ruffian."

"Max?" Pippa frowned. "That's the boy, isn't it?"

Calum had no opportunity to respond before the thin little boy with red hair leaped down the steps leading to the pool area. "I'm the advance party," he shrieked, flinging his arms in circles. "Come to warn you of an attack."

"Max," Calum said—rather reasonably, Pippa thought. "Kindly return to the castle and your bed at once."

Pippa turned her back on the boy and hoped he would not see the condition of her clothing and report, possibly in screeching tones, that she appeared to be wandering the grounds almost naked.

"I'm returnin'," Max yelled. "Got to go to ground. Saw you and the lady leave and thought you might want to arm yourselves. It's terrible. *Terrible*, I tells you."

"Max—"

"They're after me ears," the boy shouted. "And me nose and me tongue."

Pippa flinched and shivered at the same time. "Ask him what he's talking about, Calum."

"A lord 'as arrived," Max announced firmly. "A lord with an angry face and a loud voice and flashing eyes that cut right through you. Me bones bleed, I tells you."

"Oh, no," Pippa whispered. "Oh, *bother*."

"Bother seems a trifle mild for the occasion," Calum remarked. "I think we'd best get you to your rooms."

"Good idea, sir," Max said, jumping up and down. "Then you'd best make haste to the battle. That other lord—I mean Papa—Papa is sitting on the angry lord's chest."

Pippa looked anxiously at Calum. He pulled her against him and started hurrying uphill.

"That's it," Max yelled. "Go and rescue the angry lord from me papa. Or don't rescue him. Don't make much difference now."

Calum halted so abruptly, Pippa clung to him to stop herself from falling.

"Why wouldn't it make a difference?" Calum asked.

"Oh, well"— Max capered around them —"Lady Justine was screaming and the visc—Papa—got furious and killed the angry lord. 'E asked me t'sit on the corpse while 'e went out and killed all the others what come. The army."

"Calum," Pippa said, horrified, "Etienne has somehow discovered my . . . He has discovered what's happened and he's come with an army.''

"An army. An army," Max chanted, leaping and whirling. "An army come and we killed 'em all."

"Oh, *my God*," Calum said. He lifted Pippa into his arms and ran uphill with her all the way back to the castle.

⚘ Sixteen

"*Psst!*" Calum bent over, one index finger to his lips, and crept toward a flunky stationed outside the salon where he would have expected to find Lady Justine and Struan enjoying a companionable after-dinner conversation.

The flunky, his face almost as pale as his powdered wig, ducked his head and peered suspiciously at Calum.

Calum crooked his finger and uttered another loud "Psst!"

Copying Calum's crouch, the man came toward him on the balls of his shiny-slippered feet. His little calf muscles popped out like partridge eggs inside his white silk stockings. "Sir?" he whispered, his exaggerated steps creating a picture reminiscent of an albino cockerel scratching in a farmyard.

"Good man for staying at your post," Calum said into the man's ear when he drew close enough. "Not a sound, now. I've got to get in there without being seen."

The man reared up somewhat and his Adam's apple bobbed. He nodded, but Calum saw no comprehension in his bright brown eyes.

"Carnage, I understand," Calum said.

The man brought his face very close to Calum's and said, "You'll be all right, sir. Happens to all gentlemen now and again."

"Not to me," Calum informed him. "And I'm not going to stand by and allow it to happen here without putting up a fight."

"You do that, sir," the man said, walking a circle around Calum. "It'll make you feel a lot better just knowing you've—er—dealt with it, so to speak."

The instant the man finished speaking, he backed away for several yards, then turned and broke into an ungainly, flapping run.

"Bloody amazing," Calum said aloud. "This whole *place* is bloody amazing." And he loved it. He loved every turret and tower, every worn stone staircase and passageway and every nook and cranny filled with the unseen, unremembered memories of centuries of Franchots before him. For an instant he closed his eyes. What would Pippa say if she knew his "friend" was none other than himself?

He stood tall, flattened his back to the wall and edged closer to the nearest of the salon's closed doors.

"Hell and damnation!" reached him in muffled tones from inside the room. Didn't sound like Franchot, though. "I'm through with it, I tell you," the voice announced. "I have taken all I will take, and now the time has come to seize matters with my own hands."

A murmur followed, a placating female murmur, unless Calum was much mistaken. Bloody hell, Justine was trapped in there with some marauding maniac.

He should have armed himself, but now it was too late. Casting about, he fixed his eye on a pair of ancient steel battle-axes displayed on the wall.

Tiptoeing close enough to reach the axes was a simple matter and they were easily enough lifted from their brackets.

Calum returned to his place beside the door and held both axes in his right hand. Stretching out his left arm, he made contact with a door handle, turned it stealthily and flung the door open with all the power in the fingers of his very strong left hand. And he praised God for giving him the gift that had brought such disapproval in his schoolroom days—equal dexterity with either hand.

Quickly, hoping it would not be seen by anyone inside the room, he dropped his arm to his side and held his breath. The element of surprise could be his most valuable ally here.

Carefully securing a firm grip on an axe in each hand, Calum waited.

What he waited for was unclear to him.

"Come in! Or stay out!" a loud male voice demanded. "Or shut the bloody door!"

Justine would be beside herself with fear.

Bracing himself, Calum lifted the axes aloft and charged, praying as he went that his opponents would not be armed with pistols or, in fact, armed at all. "Back!" he roared, rushing to the center of the dramatically proportioned chamber. Holding his arms above his head, he brandished his evil-looking weapons and glared. "Leave us, Lady Justine. The rest of you—against the wall or I'll have your heads!"

Moments passed—and more moments. Nobody moved.

"What is it, Calum?" Lady Justine asked at last. "Are you unwell, dear sir? Something you ate, perhaps?"

Calum looked around the room. The thudding of rapid footfalls made him spin toward the door—just in time to see Max, his freckled face crimson, his green eyes avid, leap into sight and come to a panting stop a few feet from him.

"In God's name," Struan said in a voice that held complete disbelief, "what *are* you about, Calum?"

"You were a marvel, sir," Max said. "An absolute marvel. Wasn't 'e . . . Papa?"

Struan wrinkled his nose. "Hmm. A marvel."

Calum looked from Lady Justine to Struan to Max and back to the one newcomer in the salon. The young man was disheveled, his clothes splattered with mud as if from a long, hard ride.

"I thought . . ." Calum spun in one direction, then in the other. There was no one else in the room. "I understood some dangerous altercation was in progress here."

"Well," Struan said, "it isn't. Put down those ridiculous axes."

Calum realized his arms had begun to ache and lowered them awkwardly. "There is no corpse?"

Lady Justine gasped audibly.

"No," Struan said, clearly annoyed. "Kindly avoid frightening Lady Justine with your wild talk. Are you in your cups, man?"

"No, I am not in my cups." Calum felt dangerous.

Calum felt a fool.

"Sabers," Max said darkly. "I think they're 'iding somewhere about. I 'eard the lady shout about sabers. An army is 'ere somewhere, I tell you. They've said they'll kill everyone if they're given away."

Calum stared at the boy.

"Max," Lady Justine said, "do come and sit with me. You are oversetting yourself. What you heard me say was *Saber*. Saber is this gentleman's name." She indicated the dejected-looking fellow sprawled on a chaise with no apparent care for the boots that were muddying blue brocade upholstery.

"You shouted it," Max said stubbornly, walking slowly toward Lady Justine.

"I said it excitedly," she told him. "Saber is one of my favorite people—my only cousin, in fact, and I was delighted to see him."

" 'E looks the ruffian to me," Max insisted. The flush had left his face and his carrot-colored freckles stood out sharply.

"Brat," the man on the chaise said disgustedly. To Calum he said, "We meet again, Mr. Innes. You remember me?"

"Lord Avenall?" Damn the axes that made him look like an ass. "We seem doomed to meet in less than tranquil circumstances."

"Life is less than tranquil," Avenall said. "Please call me Saber. Justine has told me she thinks highly of you. Anyone trusted by Justine is trusted by me."

Calum could not be certain, but it seemed probable that young Avenall was a little the worse for drink. "Thank you, Saber. You seem in ill humor. Has some ill befallen you?"

Saber gave a barking laugh. "Divest yourself of the war tools, Innes. And get one of the damn flunkies around here to bring more cognac. I find myself in need of a great deal more cognac tonight. You must all join me."

"A drunkard," Max said suddenly and too clearly. "Beware the drunkard, Fast Freddy always told us. And 'e ought to know. 'E *was* a drunkard."

"You should be in bed," Calum and Struan said in unison. Calum wasn't certain who Fast Freddy might be, but he had a good idea that discovering that person's identity in this company might not be at all the thing.

Saber pushed himself to his feet, walked unsteadily to the

soaring plaster fireplace emblazoned with the Franchot coat of arms and began to tug on a satin pull.

"I believe there's port in the decanter," Lady Justine said.

Saber tugged and tugged and tugged. "Don't want port. Mewling female swill. Cognac!" he said with full lung support. "Come along, Innes—and you, Hunsingore. You'll join a man in finding the courage to do what he must do."

"The boy," Lady Justine said in a small voice. "Have a care what you say in front of the child, Saber."

Max, as if suddenly realizing he might miss a show, shot to sit beside Lady Justine on a stiff little couch. He crossed his bony knees inside the green velvet breeches that were part of the clothing Struan had rapidly supplied before leaving London.

Lady Justine leaned over to look into the child's face and smiled. She brushed back the straight hair that drooped over his eyes and kissed his brow.

Calum waited for an outcry of disgust. None came. Instead, Max nestled into Lady Justine's side and seemed satisfied to sit thus indefinitely.

"Can *you* get hold of a flunky, Innes?" Saber asked, sounding desolate. "I shall die if I don't get some brandy."

"Calum," Innes told him. "Call me Calum. Do you think you've had enough brandy, Saber?"

"*Never*," Saber announced, just as Figerall, the castle steward, made a surprising appearance. Evidently he'd been informed of conditions requiring the attention of a servant of great authority. "Finally," Saber said, bunching up his lips. "I should damn well think so. Cognac, man. And be quick about it."

Figerall, short, bald and ruddy, looked at Lady Justine. There could be no mistaking the respect in his manner toward her, or the fact that he seemed to expect her to tell him the right thing to do.

"Kindly bring cognac," she said. "And I think some coffee would be nice, Figerall. I know the hour grows a little late, but could you perhaps persuade Mrs. Biston to send up some sandwiches? Substantial sandwiches?"

The steward's smile was for Lady Justine alone. He bowed calmly, said, "As you wish, my lady," and withdrew.

"Sometimes you have to be firm with these people," Saber said, his words slurring. "Show them their place. Good enough. A good start. From now on, I'm taking control of the things that matter in my life. No more acting the flunky to that cousin of mine."

The effect of his announcement was electric. Struan looked hard at Calum, who raised a brow before checking Lady Justine's reaction. Pink had spread over her rounded cheekbones and there was a brilliance in her dark eyes.

His sister was a lovely woman, Calum thought, and found that simply thinking about her as his sister brought a rush of pride.

"Franchot being hard on you?" Struan asked in a tone that encouraged trust.

"I'm three and twenty," Saber said, spreading his booted feet. "No longer a child, in God's name. I want control of what's mine, I tell you. I want Shillingdown and all that goes with it, and I want it *now*."

Lady Justine cleared her throat. "You should sleep, Saber, dear. You'll think more clearly in the morning and then you can start to decide how best to present your case to Etienne—and to Grandmama."

Calum's interest was sharply piqued. "What does the duke have to do with control of your estate?" he asked before realizing his interest would appear inappropriate.

"He's my guardian, damn his eyes," Saber said, with no sign of reticence on the subject. "My father and the previous duke were brothers. My pater, God rest his soul, died at sea. Intelligence for the Crown. Highly secret stuff. Attacked by pirates, and all aboard murdered."

Justine's hands went to her cheeks. "Do not torment yourself with these memories, Saber. It was so sad."

"Yes," Saber agreed. "My father was a great man and I've missed him terribly. But he'd made arrangements for your father to oversee things for me if anything happened—with Mama already gone and no one else to ask."

"I know," Justine said. She had grown pale and her face was strained. "So much sadness. You are very important to us, Saber. You always will be. Never think of yourself as alone or without a family. We are your family."

"*You* are my family," he said darkly.

"Let me get you a little port, Lady Justine," Struan said suddenly, rising to his feet and going to a tray on which a single crystal decanter stood surrounded by glasses. "You have had far too much excitement for one evening."

Struan poured the port and brought it to Lady Justine. He bent over her and waited until she took a taste and smiled up at him. "Thank you," she said. "You are very kind."

"I've 'ad too much excitement for one night, too," Max said in his piping voice. "A little port would probably put me to rights."

Struan eyed him narrowly and walked away. While his back was turned, Lady Justine put her glass to Max's lips and tipped a sip of port into his mouth. By the time Struan had sat down once more, Max was smiling up into Lady Justine's face with open adoration.

"I am a man," Saber declared as Figerall arrived to deliver the cognac himself. The white cockerel Calum had encountered outside the salon scuttled in his superior's wake with a food-laden tray.

"I am a man," Sable repeated, signaling for Figerall to pour drinks. "And I expect to be treated as one. The time for some wet nurse to wipe my nose and tell me when I should and shouldn't do things is past."

He accepted a shimmering bubble glass half-filled with glowing amber brandy, promptly emptied it and held it out for more.

Plates of sandwiches and substantial slabs of fruit cake were placed upon a low table. Sugar-coated fruits were mounded on a three-tiered silver dish, and an array of sweetmeats had also been included, together with a variety of little tarts.

Before the servant backed away, Max slipped to the floor and sat with his feet under the table, eyeing the food with the avid concentration of any healthy ten-year-old boy.

At last the servants left, and Saber went to appropriate the entire decanter of brandy. This he set upon the mantel, above a fire that crackled in the grate.

"This is what I'm going to do," he said expansively, re-filling his glass yet again and waving the bottle around. When everyone else had declined, he set the decanter down and said, "Eat, boy. You look like a scarecrow."

"Saber," Lady Justine said crossly, "do not be unkind."

"Why not? I've suffered enough unkindness for an army of boys—and men."

A clear voice from the doorway captured everyone's attention. "You 'ave not suffered it for my brother, sir," Ella said. Dressed in a demure, high-necked white muslin gown and white satin slippers, she ventured a few steps into the room. Her black hair was drawn smoothly up at the crown and cascaded in loose curls around her shoulders. She blinked her dark, almond-shaped eyes slowly, and her heavy lashes made shifting shadows on high cheekbones. Calum decided he had never seen more perfect skin than Ella's golden skin. He wondered, not for the first time, at the exact nature of her parentage.

"Ella," Lady Justine said, "I thought you were long since in your bed, child. You must be exhausted."

The unexpected crash of glass on granite made Calum start violently. He heard both Struan and Lady Justine exclaim.

Saber, his intensely blue eyes fixed on Ella, had let his brandy glass slip through his fingers to the hearth.

"I couldn't sleep," Ella said, as if nothing had happened, "so I looked for Max and found 'e wasn't in 'is bed. It frightened me, so I dressed and came looking for 'im."

There were, Calum decided, and not for the first time, far too many secrets about Ella and Max. To date they had even managed to avoid giving a family name.

"Didn't mean to frighten you, Ellie," Max said around a large mouthful of strawberry tart. "There was a fracas 'ere. 'Ad to go in search of reinforcements."

Calum glowered at the boy. "You came to me with a pile of untruths, my boy. A more rigid man would suggest you be horsewhipped."

"But you are not more rigid," Lady Justine said, twinkling at him. "Obviously Max misunderstood what he heard and became agitated."

"Max tells stories," Ella informed them calmly. "You'd think it was on account of 'is very active imagination. It's a great trial and a nuisance sometimes. But once you understands, learning to ignore 'im is a simple matter.''

Struan coughed, and Calum saw that he smiled at the girl like a proud . . . *father*? Dear heaven, Struan was beginning to persuade himself he really was parent to these two mysterious and very possibly hazardous creatures.

"Who is she?"

For an instant Calum wasn't certain who had spoken. Then he turned to look at Saber—and felt his own gut suck in as if he'd been struck there. The Earl of Avenall stared at fifteen-year-old Ella as if he'd been brought into the presence of Venus.

Struan was the first to recover. "Ella, kindly take Max and ensure that he goes to his bed and stays there. Then retire yourself, please."

"What right have you to send her from me?" Saber said to Struan without ever taking his eyes from the girl. "Your name is Ella?"

"Yes," she said simply. To Max she directed a stern frown and told him, "You oughtn't to stuff yourself so late, Max. You know 'ow delicate your stomach is."

"Hah," the boy scoffed. "*You* don't know 'ow often my stomach 'as 'ad no reason at all to be delicate. You was lucky. While you were at Lu—"

"Enough!" Calum and Struan bellowed together.

"Don't you dare shout at him," Lady Justine said, getting to her feet and going to stand beside Max. "You stay where you are until you've had your fill. Boys' stomachs can take a great deal. Boys require large amounts of food to sustain their considerable energy."

Saber scoffed. "When did you become an expert on boys, Justine?" he said, although his attention still centered on Ella. "Should have thought the sewing of fine seams was more in your line of expertise."

"Something tells me Lady Justine has made an acute study of the human condition," Calum said swiftly, unnerved by his own rush of protectiveness toward the lady. "Unless I am much mistaken, she could well advise us all in matters relating to the care of children."

A small, awkward silence followed—broken only by the sound of Max's loud chomping.

"You flatter me undeservedly," Lady Justine said, but she smiled gratefully at Calum.

"I don't think he flatters you," Struan said. "I think he speaks the truth, and I, for one, am certainly grateful for your help in the matter of—er—these children."

"Do you ride?" Saber asked Ella, evidently oblivious to the discomfort he might have caused others in the salon.

Ella raised her pointed chin. "I ride very well, sir."

" 'E's a lord," Max said, using both hands to pop several sweetmeats into his mouth at once.

"I beg your pardon, my lord," Ella said, and Calum thought she was considerably more responsive to handsome young Saber than a fifteen-year-old girl should be.

"Not much of a lord," Max continued with bulging cheeks while lifting a piece of bread to examine the contents of a sandwich. " 'E's got an estate, but 'is cousin's in charge of it, not 'im. Makes 'im testy, Ellie. A nasty temper 'e's got. Threatening sort. The sort who creeps up on a body and pushes thistles down 'is back."

"I *beg* your pardon," Saber said, his mouth falling open.

"Stories, you see," Ella said, as if that explained everything about her incorrigible brother. "Escapes into 'em."

" 'Is estate's called Shillingdown," Max said, studying a piece of fruit cake from all sides. "Don't know where it is, but 'e's going to try to get control of it. 'Is cousin's—"

"*Go* to your bed," Struan thundered. "At once!"

That got through Max's dramatic muse. He brought his pale red brows down, regarded Struan anxiously and got to his feet. "I don't think I can find me way to me bed," he said, sounding querulous. "This is the biggest place I was ever in and—"

"Take him, please, Ella," Struan interrupted. "Or are you also lost?"

"I'll take them," Saber said quickly, detaching himself from the mantel and going to stand over Ella. "Should you care to ride in the morning, Ella?"

"Saber," Lady Justine said gently, rising to her feet, "we will pursue the question of riding when tomorrow comes. For now, I should like to take Ella and Max to their rooms myself. You stay and talk with Calum and Viscount Hunsingore."

Lady Justine's announcement brooked no argument, and the three men bade their good-nights to Ella and Max as the lady shepherded them from the room.

"I like my cousin," Saber said after the little group had departed. "Justine, that is. She has always been very civil to me."

"Charming lady," Struan agreed. "Lovely, too. One wonders why so lovely a woman did not marry and have children of her own."

"Don't think the lame leg helped much," Saber commented.

"If that was the only impediment, then the world is full of foolish men," Calum said with enough vehemence to draw a warning stare from Struan. Taking his friend's meaning, Calum forced a laugh. "But then, we know the world is full of foolish men, don't we?"

Saber, apparently already disinterested in the subject of Lady Justine, turned to Struan and asked, "What is your relationship to the girl Ella, my lord?"

"Please, call me Struan. It seems we may be destined to know each other moderately well."

"Struan," Saber said agreeably, and waited expectantly for an answer to his question.

Struan cleared his throat and the clean-cut lines of his face became tinged with red. "The nature of the relationship between Ella and Max and me is somewhat delicate. May we simply agree to accept that I am responsible for them at present?"

"Responsible?" Saber's handsome young face folded into a study in puzzlement. "What exactly does . . ." He paused, looking past Calum, and said, "Lady Philipa. Good evening to you."

Calum turned in time to see Pippa, the tattered gray gown discarded in favor of a lavender silk, standing uncertainly on the threshold.

She said, "Good evening, gentlemen," but looked at Calum.

He felt everything within him grow still. Overhead, candles flickered in a great chandelier, but the flickering felt distant, its light a gilded glow that hovered about the edges of the space he shared with Pippa, and only with Pippa.

Struan said something.

Calum could not make out the words.

Pippa's dark blue eyes were luminous, her pale skin even paler than it had seemed before.

Her lips parted and she passed her tongue over their pink fullness.

His insides fell away. Where had the air gone? No air. No way to fill his aching lungs.

Saber said something.

Calum could not make out the words.

He walked toward Pippa, smiling. He knew he smiled because looking at her made him want to smile with everything that he was.

"Calum?"

He heard *her* voice. "Pippa," he said. "Your eyes make the lavender silk a pale thing." He knew he was indiscreet. And he did not care.

He was near enough to look down into her upturned face.

She reached up and pressed a finger to his lips, and he realized he screened her from Saber and Struan—and that she was warning him to be careful of what he said.

"I understand Max created a stir," she said. The words were meant to allay suspicion of any bond between them, but her voice shook. "I passed Justine on my way here."

They could not see his face. "You are beautiful," he whispered.

Pink washed her cheeks. "I understand Max has a very large imagination for so small a boy."

"He is ten," Struan said loudly from behind Calum. "Not so small."

"Beautiful," Calum said, so very softly. "Your face is an angel's face and your body makes my body ache with longing."

Her lips remained parted and her small breasts rose and fell rapidly with the shallow breaths she took.

"Sure you won't have cognac, Calum?" Saber said. When Calum didn't respond, he repeated his offer to Struan, who accepted this time.

"I only came to be certain everyone was well cared for,"

Pippa said. She attempted to move away from Calum, but he stayed her with a single finger upon the shadowy place between her breasts. "I . . . I see that you are comfortable. And since I find I'm tired, I'll bid you a good-night."

"Good night," Struan said.

"Later I shall come to you," Calum murmured.

"What did you say?" Saber inquired.

Calum regarded Pippa's mouth and held his tongue between his teeth.

"Calum said it's late and he's tired, too," Pippa said, shaking her head slightly.

When she tried to take a step back from him, Calum quickly tucked his finger into the neck of her gown. "I believe I shall walk with Lady Philipa, gentlemen. She knows this labyrinthine monument better than I." The warm flesh that rose against his skin brought his manhood to throbbing awareness.

The desire in her eyes was not a thing of his imagining. She was, as always, afraid of herself with him—but she wanted him nevertheless.

Would she still want him if she ever had reason to believe he had claimed her to thwart another man? *Would* he claim her to thwart another man? Was he, even now, drawn to her as much by what she represented as by . . . My God, what price would he pay to claim what had been stolen from him at birth—his soul?

"Thank you, Calum," Pippa said. "I'll be glad to make sure you don't lose your way."

He drew a deep breath. Oh, regardless of her efforts, the way would be lost here—very lost—and they would both find joy in the losing. Might they be spared pain in the wake of the joy? "Thank you," he told her. "You will guide me. And for my part, I shall be your protector in the night, my lady."

"She'll not be needing your protection on the way to her chamber for long, Calum," Saber said.

Slowly, Calum raised his gaze from Pippa's. He looked over his shoulder at the young earl. "What do you mean by that, Saber?"

"*He* sent me on to start the proceedings. His lackey, that's what I am. And such a thing was never my father's intention."

Calum saw Struan frown but ignored the warning not to interfere. "He. You speak of the duke?"

"Aye. My beloved cousin Etienne. I have to be free of him, I tell you. You have no idea how he weighs upon my spirit. He and that lewd woman he parades—"

"Saber!" Struan all but shouted.

"She would bed any animal with the—"

"Saber!" Calum and Struan roared in unison.

"And Henri St. Luc follows me with his eyes like a man follows a girl he desires—"

"My lord," Calum said, turning to face Saber, "May I remind you that there is a lady present."

Had Saber not been the worse for drinking too much brandy, he would doubtless have been suitably chastised. The drink made him careless and daring. "She might as well know what she's about to buy with her dowry," he said, swaying a little. "My grandmama will be no prize as an in-law, either. She cares only for the damn *family*. And by that, she means the title my degenerate cousin holds. She'd toss everything to the wind to preserve the damnable honor of the Duke of Franchot."

"You are not yourself," Pippa said, her voice thin but steady. "Please rest. I'm certain the duke will want to listen to your concerns if you'll only inform him of them."

"Inform him of them?" Saber slapped a thigh and slopped brandy on the blue-and-gold silk rug. He curled the fingers of one hand into his palm and held it toward her. "Until my twenty-eighth year, my cousin holds my life like this, my lady. A word from him to the effect that I am not worthy of what my father left in trust for me, and the good duke may cast me out to toil in some far-flung family venture and take what is mine for himself."

Pippa drew herself up. "He would *not* do so, Saber. He would not, I tell you. I refuse to believe the duke to be a man entirely without . . . entirely without . . ."

"Honor? Charity? Loyalty? Courage? Integrity? Take your pick, my lady. And then be assured that he is equally deficient in all these and many more qualities." Saber uncurled his fingers and pointed at her. "And he will grind your gentle little spirit into *dust*."

Struan was on his feet. "Enough, Saber. You are beyond being foxed, sir. You are a disgrace."

"He is young," Pippa said.

Calum grinned. "Not as young as you, Pippa. You must not heed anything he says in this condition." Even though Calum knew every word to be true. Even though Calum yearned to tell Pippa that the man she thought of as her fiancé was an imposter who would be removed, or Calum would die in the attempt.

He would become Duke of Franchot or die in the attempt.

"Go to bed, Saber," Pippa said kindly.

He would do whatever he had to do to claim the dukedom and everything that went with it—including Lady Philipa Chauncey. And when she discovered his reason for pursuing her, she would hate him . . .

Saber pulled himself up straight and tall and yanked at the bottom of his waistcoat. "I'm going to bed," he mumbled. "Not myself. Sorry."

"It's all right," Pippa said, smiling. The corners of her mouth quivered with the effort.

"Certainly it's all right," Saber agreed. He looked at her direct. "I'm to inform you that the duke has made certain decisions of interest to you."

Pippa ducked her head. "Decisions?"

"Decisions. Etienne will be on his way here from London sooner than expected. He said to inform you of this. He also wishes you to ready yourself."

Calum clenched his teeth and waited.

"My cousin has decided the matter of dealing with the tedious preparations for marriage are an annoyance to him. He told me to inform you that he intends to dispense with those preparations."

Caution no longer interested Calum. He went to Pippa's side and pried apart her clenched hands. One of her hands he held in his, and he felt the weight of her anxiety in the iron grip of her fingers.

"I do not understand you," she said to Saber. "My father returns from the Continent by September. The marriage is planned to take place after his arrival."

''Not anymore,'' Saber said, avoiding her eyes. ''In my dear cousin's words: 'Tell the lady I am bored with the niceties. Our bond is for reasons of business alone. I intend this marriage to be over and done with at once.' ''

❧ Seventeen

The gown was for him.

Pippa smiled at Justine and knew they shared the knowledge that this morning Pippa had dressed to please Calum Innes.

What they did not share was Pippa's wild and sinful disappointment that Calum had not kept his promise—or had it been a threat?—to come to her last night.

"I should not wear this," she said.

Justine, her brow puckered in concentration, twitched at the gold lace trim stitched beneath tucks in the bodice. "Wearing this is exactly what you should do today. Your spirits need all the help they can get. Besides, it is entirely appropriate for strolling among my ancestors. They were a flamboyant lot."

Pippa was not at all sure what to make of that comment. "But what would the dowager say?" she asked, standing quite still in the middle of Justine's daffodil-yellow sitting room while the other woman walked in a circle to survey the gown she had designed herself and supervised in its construction. Pippa bobbed a little.

"Be still," Justine ordered. "How can I tell if the hem is straight if you wiggle?"

"Oh, *bother*," Pippa said. She caught the lace at one cuff on a bodice button and struggled to free herself. "Oh, *bother*. Why am I so clumsy?"

"You are not often clumsy, Pippa." Justine carefully disentangled the lace. "It is only agitation that makes you awkward."

Pippa sighed. "The dowager would say this gown is entirely *inappropriate*."

"Grandmama is determined to plead a decline. We shall not see her. And she is an old lady with an old lady's ideas." You are a young woman. Young and lovely and alive, and your gowns should show you off."

"But poppy, Justine. *Poppy*."

"Yes, *poppy*. Who better to wear a gown of poppy-red muslin and gold lace trim than a girl with black hair and white skin and eyes as blue as the ring around a winter's moon? Anyway, you said you loved the gown on the fashion doll I gave you. Surely you were not funning me?"

"Of course not." Pippa felt herself blush, but as much with happiness as with embarrassment. "You are so good to me, Justine."

"That is because I love you." The other woman spoke as matter-of-factly as if she were pronouncing the weather fine. "You are like the sister I never had. Yes, I like this gown. I may even make myself one—in a different color, of course."

"Good! Then I shall take even more pleasure in looking forward to shocking the dowager in *your* company."

Justine's own dress was of russet-brown watered silk with hints of red in its depths. Her eyes caught the shifting colors perfectly. Around her neck hung the only ornament she ever wore, a plain gold locket inscribed with a discreet, apparently religious emblem and suspended on a heavy gold chain. The entire effect of Justine's toilette was dramatically simple, and Pippa thought her future sister-in-law made a delightful picture.

Sister-in-law.

Pippa's stomach twisted. "What am I to do, Justine?"

Their eyes met, and there was no need to repeat the story Pippa had already told, about Saber's announcement of the previous evening.

"Should I speak with the dowager?" she asked.

Justine considered. "I think not. Although Saber's message does trouble me a little."

Pippa tilted her face until Justine raised her eyes again. "Do not try to spare my feelings,'' Pippa said, walking to view her new dress in Justine's baroque-framed pier glass. ''You are deeply concerned and so am I. But I must be honest with you. That is only fair, when you have been so kind to me. I am not . . . am not certain I want to . . .'' She could not finish.

Justine came to stand beside her. She smoothed the back of Pippa's bodice and rested her hands on her shoulders. ''You do not want to marry Etienne,'' she said, looking at Pippa in the mirror. ''I know this. And I don't know what to say, except that I believe you are truly good and that your goodness has been perceived by another who is good and true and strong.''

It was Pippa's turn to frown. ''You speak in pretty verse, but I don't understand.''

''Perhaps Grandmama will not allow Etienne to jeopardize your reputation by starting the tongues of the *ton* wagging. You may think you have seen my grandmother at her imperious best. My dear, you have seen nothing compared with the storm that would descend upon this castle if Etienne did anything to bring notoriety upon the Franchot name.''

Pippa stared at her.

''You are not entirely without knowledge,'' Justine said, lowering her lashes. ''You know that a woman starts increasing after she has known her husband in the biblical sense. That, naturally, must not take place until after marriage. If there is any suggestion of this marriage being hastily arranged, there might be the rumor that you were not an innocent on your wedding day.''

Pippa's face flamed. She had the vision that had haunted her in recent days, a vision of herself with That part of the Duke of Franchot between her lips.

One must have to *swallow* the seeds.

Rather like the earth swallowed seeds for marrows.

Pippa's hands went to her waist. She'd seen ladies in voluminous and horribly heavy-looking gowns intended to conceal things that appeared quite like marrows ready for Harvest Festival.

Young Mrs. Tremilant, wife of a rather elderly clergyman near Dowanhill, had been increasing before Pippa left. The picture of slender, pale little Mrs. Tremilant on her knees before her corpulent cleric husband made Pippa shudder and close her eyes.

When she opened them again, she looked into Justine's and saw anxiety there.

"Please try not to worry so," Justine said. She caught Pippa's hair and pulled it back behind her neck. Taking a length of the gold lace she'd used on the gown, she began to braid it through Pippa's black tresses.

As Pippa watched, Justine created heavy gold-threaded braids and bound them around Pippa's head until she resembled an exotic creature she did not know at all. "Justine, don't you want me to marry the duke?"

"Do not press me in this."

"I must. You have encouraged me to spend time with Calum Innes. Even now you are preparing me to see him in the gallery. You came to me while I was yet in bed and told me you had issued him the invitation to join us there. You are pushing me at the man. Why?"

"Don't ask these questions."

Pippa crossed her arms tightly. "You do not want me as your brother's wife. I can think of no other reason."

"*No!*" Justine rested her brow on Pippa's shoulder and said faintly, "I am not certain I know my brother at all. I have known him all his life, yet he is a stranger to me. You came to us only weeks since, and already I feel I could not bear to part with you."

"Then *explain* yourself."

Justine lifted her face. She put the finishing touches to Pippa's hair and stepped away. "I cannot express in words what I cannot think clearly. I can only tell you that I *feel* that Calum Innes is . . . He is not what he appears. That should frighten me, but it doesn't."

"Nor me," Pippa whispered. "But I do not know *what* he is, or why he is here."

"Don't you?" Justine smiled over her shoulder at Pippa. "*Don't* you know why?"

Fear, deep, burning fear, tore through Pippa. "It cannot be. The duke would kill him."

"He might try."

"I cannot allow it."

"You cannot change fate."

Pippa went to the window seat and pushed open diamond-paned windows. Sun warmed the morning air, and on the highest branches of a tulip tree a speckle-breasted mistle thrush uttered its runs of fluty notes toward a pale blue sky.

When she had filled her lungs with crystal air, Pippa said, "Tell me what to do. Tell me how to send him away and accept my duty to the Franchots and my father without distaste."

"None of this is in my power," Justine responded. "And it is not in yours. You must not try to change what is meant to be."

"We already know what is meant to be."

"I suppose we do." Justine's uneven steps were more noticeable since she'd knelt on the floor to examine the hem of the poppy-colored dress. She limped to the window and sat on the padded velvet seat. "The viscount is a handsome man, don't you think?"

Pippa hid a smile. "Very handsome." She had dared to hope that Justine might take more than a polite interest in Struan.

"I wonder how his wife died."

These were the questions Pippa had expected and dreaded. "He did not say," she told Justine, grateful it was the truth.

Justine looked thoughtful. "From the sound of those two dear children, she must have been beneath his station, yet I'll be bound he would never say as much."

"I could not say."

"Ella and Max do not mention her."

"No."

"I do believe he is trying very hard to be both father and mother to them. Not an easy task."

"No," Pippa agreed. "Not at all an easy task."

"Do you like the viscount?"

"I like him very much."

Justine rested an arm beneath the open window and raised her face to sniff summer scents. "I have always counted honesty and courage the most important of all virtues."

Pippa stared hard at the tulip tree's trembling leaves. "Have you?"

"Oh, yes. The viscount is obviously most honest in confronting the world and he has the courage to do what honesty tells him is right. Many men would have parceled their motherless offspring off with relatives or left them in the hands of paid servants. Instead, his true heart accepts that he and only he can give his children the guidance they need.

"I have guessed that possibly the viscount had not spent much time with them before they were left without their mother. When he realized how sadly neglected they were—in their education, that is—he remonstrated with himself and determined to make amends. A most unusual man. Most unusual."

"Indeed," Pippa said, trying not to squirm in her discomfort.

Justine squinted into the sun and smiled. "I saw Max this morning. He was following Mr. Innes around the grounds." She laughed aloud. "I declare, the boy was trying to match his very steps to the man's. Yes, Mr. Innes has a great admirer. I pray he does not come to rue the fact."

"Calum will be careful of the child's heart," Pippa said and marveled at her own careless tongue.

"Most probably," Justine said, evidently unaware of the longing that had been in Pippa's voice when she spoke of Calum.

"How old do you suppose the viscount is, Pippa?"

This was another expected question. "I am not certain. Probably about your age."

"I think I am older," said Justine. "Imagine, I am thirty-four and have never even had a beau. The viscount is probably several years younger and has been married, widowed and left with two children. How different lives can be, one from another."

"Yes." It was a start. There was the matter of how Justine would feel toward the viscount when she discovered the lie about the children, but at least she was beginning to consider the question of herself in relation to a man. Pippa dared not push for more than that as yet.

"I have no doubt Viscount Hunsingore will find himself a pretty young thing who will accept responsibility for Ella and Max and make him a fine wife," Justine went on with no apparent trace of envy. "I certainly hope it happens soon. He is obviously somewhat overwhelmed by his task as a parent and he speaks of needing to deal with his affairs in Dorset."

"Really?" Pippa studied Justine's face and decided that there were definitely no traces of longing there. Apparently it would be necessary to look farther for a husband for Justine. Pippa was determined to make that search just as soon as an opportunity presented itself—say at the festivities for her own nuptials.

She tried not to shudder.

"Thank you for inviting me, my lady," Calum said to Lady Justine, walking between her and Pippa along stone-floored, oak-paneled corridors in the west wing, which was farthest from the sea.

"I'm delighted for an excuse to visit with old friends I've known all my life," Lady Justine said. "I come here alone frequently, but I often wish I could share what I know of my family with others."

Calum made a polite sound and looked at Pippa.

Pippa looked ahead.

"I'm certain Lady Justine will agree with me that you are a vision in red and gold, Pippa," he said.

Still she did not look at him.

"Isn't she?" Lady Justine said. "Do encourage her to be more daring in her choice of wardrobe, Mr. Innes. I fear she is overly concerned with taste at the expense of style."

"Justine!" Pippa's eyes blazed. "You know those dreadful dresses are not—" She closed her mouth with a snap and marched on, causing Lady Justine and Calum to walk faster.

"Forgive me," Lady Justine said, and Calum wondered what Pippa would think if she could see her future sister-in-law's wicked smile. "Of course those dreadful dresses are not any fault of yours. But I think the time has come for you to exert yourself. After all, soon you are destined to be the lady of this household. Surely you will not allow an irritable old despot of a woman to intimidate you then?"

Such spirit his sister had. Calum had to work hard not to laugh.

Pippa didn't respond. She moved rapidly ahead of them.

The way led along what felt like miles of corridors, down several flights of stairs, through a chamber open at either end and lined with leather-bound books, down deeper yet to a gallery packed with relics of ancient armor and, finally, to a sharp right turn where an ascent began.

On the fourth upward flight, Calum put an arm beneath Lady Justine's elbow. She gave him a small, grateful smile and leaned on him. "The leg does tire, I'm afraid," she said. "But it is good not to favor it too much. Of that I'm convinced."

Pippa, whom Calum had thought entirely closed off in her own cross world, stopped instantly and returned to hold Justine's other elbow.

He smiled at Pippa and saw her swallow before she smiled back.

A madman he might be, but he would almost swear that tears had sprung into her eyes.

Lady Philipa Chauncey was a woman under siege and he played a part in the dilemma she faced, yet he could not withdraw, not now—not *ever*.

"I'm not a cripple," Lady Justine said lightly. "But thank you both for helping me."

"Helping you brings us pleasure, doesn't it, Pippa?"

She held her bottom lip in her teeth, and now there was no mistaking the tears. They hovered against her lower lashes and shimmered in her eyes. "You bring everyone pleasure, Justine," she said softly.

"Thank you. And here we are."

A short hall and three final steps brought them to the castle long-room. From where Calum stood, he could see the portraits that studded the walls.

Rush matting divided the considerable length of glowing wooden floors, worn to a silken finish by the feet of generations of Franchots, their friends and guests.

"I confess that my leg complains of my disregard," Lady Justine remarked wryly. "Pippa, be a dear and start Mr. Innes with whatever pleases you. I think I'll sit with Great-great-grandpapa Franchot until I am rested."

Without awaiting a response, Lady Justine turned from them and went to sit on a bench in a nearby alcove.

Calum gestured for Pippa to lead him.

She raised her elaborately coiffed head a fraction, seemed about to say something, then walked determinedly ahead of Calum instead.

Graceful, Calum thought, enjoying a leisurely opportunity to observe the way she swayed when she moved.

Sensually graceful. Last night, when he'd longed to go to her and, for once, had forced good sense to keep him in his bed, he had known sexual frustration of the kind that had not plagued him so strong since his adolescent years.

Lying in that wretched, hot, tangled bed, he'd visualized the woman before him now, visualized her naked and beckoning. She'd beckoned and he'd come, and she'd run from him, her hips flaring invitingly below a tiny waist, her breasts rising and falling as she turned to laugh back at him. And her black hair had flown free, lifted on a warm wind, the same warm wind that caressed and excited his own aroused body.

Now Pippa's slippered feet thudded on coarse matting. They thudded with her determination not to enter into any intimacy with him in this lofty room filled with the faces of men and women who were his ancestors. *His* ancestors, not those of that prancing, debauched creature set upon getting his marriage "over and done with at once."

Calum set his teeth and found that, despite his curiosity about the painted faces, he could not concentrate on even one of them unless he did so with Pippa at his side.

She reached the far end of the gallery, where a single window stretched from floor to lofty, stone-arched ceiling. Facing him, she placed her fists upon her hips and tapped a toe.

"Anger becomes you," he told her, approaching and walking a slow circle around her. "Aye, it becomes you very well."

"You have toyed with me enough, Calum Innes."

He held a forefinger aloft. "No, no, no, lady. I have not toyed with you nearly enough. In fact, I have barely begun to toy with you. Look at me."

He stood before her, his booted feet planted apart, his own fists on his hips—and raised his chin. "Look well. And tell me what you see."

She found great interest in the painted panels of the vaulted ceiling.

"Well," Calum said, "until you are ready with your report, I shall give you mine. You are exquisite in that . . . that whatever red it is, and gold. You are a jewel. But you are a jewel in wrappings I should take great pleasure in removing."

She gasped, but quickly pressed her lips together and continued her study of the ceiling.

"Obviously this is not an appropriate time to completely unwrap you, but might I at least take your breasts from their safe hiding place for a little while?"

"Don't!" Her face turned the marvelous pink he'd come to find delightful and she glared at him. "Think of *Justine*."

"Justine will not come too soon."

"How do you know?"

"I know." He took a step toward her. "The little gold buttons on your bodice are so clever. I could undo them with ease and hold your breasts in my hands—"

"Stop!"

"Hold them in my hands and test their tips with my tongue, and kiss them, and—"

"If you do not stop this, I shall leave at once."

"And make a terrible scene that would need explanation?"

"Why do you torment me?" She crossed her arms over her chest. "Why do you persist in . . . In whatever this is when you know it can only bring disaster?"

Calum no longer felt any humor in the situation. "I persist because I must," he told her. "I asked you to tell me what you see when you look at me."

"A man."

"Brilliant. What manner of man?"

"An impudent . . . a man skilled in the torture of a young woman who . . . who . . ."

"A young woman who?" He found his heart had begun to beat faster. "What is it that you are, Pippa? When you're with me?"

She clasped her hands together and brought them to her brow. "I am *beset*." Her voice broke. "When I am with you I am beset. I am confused. I am undone by my own wrong longing. I—am—*desperate*."

For once, words deserted him.

Pippa slowly opened her hands and drew her fingers down her face. "This is no game to me, Calum. There is so much I do not understand, yet I want to."

"You told me," he reminded her, "that when you were with me, you were driven to touch me. You told me you were afraid that you might not be able to do other than touch me *intimately.* I was flattered, but I thought you dramatic and I did not really think you sincere."

"I was sincere."

If he touched her, they would both be lost. "It is not possible for me to go away from you, Pippa."

"It is not possible for you to stay."

"Because if I do, you will come to me? Is that what terrifies you, that you will come to me and become completely mine?"

Her soft lips worked before she said, "I seem to know a great deal of life, yet I know such a very little. I do not even understand all of what it would mean to come to you completely."

Calum turned from her. "Why could you not have been that other creature?" he cried before caution could close his lips. A woman such as Anabel Hoarville would have been easily dismissed.

Her hand on his shoulder made him start. "I don't understand you," she said. "What other creature? You would have me be someone else?"

Think, he ordered his errant mind. *Think before you say even more that should never be spoken.* "I mean," he told her, "that I wish you did not belong to another man." That, at least, was true. If they'd met under different circumstances, when all that he must do was accomplished, there would be no impediment to their— *Was it love*?

He truly was losing his mind.

"When I put on this dress, I imagined you seeing me in it. I hoped it would please you."

Calum closed his eyes. "It pleases me."

"You please me, Calum."

"My God, too much restraint is expected of me."

"If things were other than they are, I would wish to feel your body beneath my hands. Without this fine coat and without the linen I would like to rest my cheek upon before I pushed it from your shoulders.'' Her fingers pressed into his muscle.

His thighs flexed. "There cannot be another girl like you," he told her. "And you cannot understand what you do to me."

"I understand that I am inept in this matter of telling you how you appear to me. And how you make me feel."

And what of how you make me feel? He was full and hard and heavy, yet the greatest ache of all curled inward from every part of him. The ache needed salve and she was that salve.

"I should like to lie naked with you beneath soft summer trees and say nothing at all," she told him. "I should like to listen to the birds and the breeze and to feel warm rain upon my skin whilst I watched it turn your skin to shimmering."

"*Pippa*," he said, pleading for mercy he did not really want.

"I should like to rest my body on yours while you held me. I think that if I could do that, just once, I would truly understand what it means for a man and a woman to be as one."

Calum prayed. He prayed nonsense, yet there seemed nothing else to do.

"I'm certain I am an evil, carnal creature," Pippa said softly, touching his neck, running her fingers into his hair. "But even so, I should also like to feel all of *That*."

He opened his eyes and said, "Pippa, you and I are meant . . ." He coughed loudly. "We are meant to greet Justine, who is leaving her great-great grandfather and walking toward us in this gallery."

Her hand curled into a fist on his back and fell away.

"I'm sorry I took so long," Justine called, her smile visible even at a distance. "Have you shown Calum everyone, Pippa? No, of course you haven't, and you don't really know them very well yet, do you?"

"Not too well," Pippa said, stepping beside him and pointing to a picture of a strapping, dark-haired man in military dress. "I did remember your uncle Francis. The one who died when the Spanish captured Minorca in '82."

"He would have been your father's brother?" Calum asked Lady Justine as she drew close. "Or your mother's?"

"My father's youngest brother. My mother was an only child. The Franchots have been better known as philosophers and men of letters than as soldiers."

Calum thought of his own interests and found no fault in Lady Justine's description. She started away again and he dared to glance at Pippa. When she returned his look, a tendril of hair wafted across her lips and he lifted it free. For a moment they stood, her face raised to his, his fingertips resting on her cheek.

"Come and see Papa," Justine said. "You will understand what I mean about the Franchot men then."

The spell that had surrounded Calum and Pippa slipped away. The deep breath he took matched hers, and side by side, they followed Lady Justine.

"Here he is," she said, stopping in front of a rather small painting of a man seated at a desk. Depicted in profile, he sat with his right hand spread on his thigh and he stared ahead whilst his quill point rested on a sheet of paper.

For the second time in the same unforgettable morning, Calum felt an overwhelming blow. "You would appear to be right," he said carefully. "A man of letters." A man with dark, curling hair tied at his nape. A man with flashes of red in that dark hair and a set to his face that was so familiar to Calum that he felt as if he were looking at a painting of himself.

Lady Justine's father.

His father.

"And next to Papa is Grandpapa," Justine said. "They might almost be the same man. Except for the clothes, of course."

Calum studied the second, much larger portrait and scarcely knew how to contain all that he felt. It was as if the artist for the smaller painting had copied the pose from this second, older work.

"Handsome men," Pippa said, and her voice sounded as if it hadn't been used in a long time. "So dark and lean."

"Mmm." Lady Justine smiled—a smile more of contentment than of pride. "I wish you could have met them."

"You look like them," Pippa said. "The duke must resemble his mother."

"Not really," Lady Justine said. "She— Oh, my goodness! *Grandmama*! She's here. And she's using the *cane*."

Wondering at the great significance of the *cane*, Calum stood in a cluster with his companions and observed the slow progress along the rush matting of a diminutive, white-haired woman dressed in black. Her back was rod-straight, but she used a cane and punctuated each step with a hard *thwack* on the wooden floor beside the matting.

"Oh," Lady Justine said, as if remembering herself. "Grandmama, let me help you."

"Stay where you are, gel," the woman said. "You are the lame one who needs help. I am quite capable of walking alone."

And this, Calum thought, was his beloved grandmother.

"I'm glad to see you are improved, Duchess," Pippa said.

"I am *not* improved," the dowager responded. "I am simply forced to attend to my duties despite my indisposition. Duty comes first in all things. That is a rule you would do well to learn quickly, gel."

The Dowager Duchess of Franchot came to a halt a few yards in front of Calum and his companions. Her nostrils narrowed when she looked at Pippa. Lady Justine received no attention at all.

"*What* do you think you're wearing?" the dowager said to Pippa. "An opera dancer's vulgar garb?"

"Grandmama—"

"Silence!" the old lady snapped, cutting off Lady Justine. Then she raised her eyes to Calum's and he saw her withered lips slacken.

"Good morning, Duchess," he said, offering her a formal bow. "I'm delighted to make your acquaintance at last."

"I was not aware that you had been waiting a long time to do so," she said in a voice that rose with each word. "You are that young man who caused Lady Philipa to disgrace herself at the Esterhazys', aren't you?"

"I am—"

"Mr. Innes danced with me, Your Grace," Pippa said. "As I remember, neither of us was disgraced. The duke invited Mr. Innes and his friend, Viscount Hunsingore, to—"

"I know all that," the woman said, waving Pippa to silence.

"And I do not understand a bit of it. I also do not understand what he is doing here."

"I brought him, Grandmama," Lady Justine said tightly. "I thought he would enjoy meeting some members of our family."

"Don't talk *posh*, girl," the dowager said. She had sharp eyes that glittered out from draping folds of papery wrinkles. "This is *my* gallery. And these are *my* relations. I do not choose to have strangers *gawping* at them."

All the time she spoke, she stared at Calum. Her hands rested, one atop the other, on the ivory head of her cane and he noted how her fingers wound tightly together.

"Please forgive me," Calum said. "I wouldn't wish to disturb you in any way, Your Grace. Please excuse me."

Before he could take his leave, the old woman shot out a bony hand to grasp one of his. "I shall excuse you when it pleases me."

Her action shocked him. The slightest move on his part would free him from her, yet he found himself rooted in place.

"Who are your people?" she asked him.

He schooled himself to breathe slowly and deeply. "None that you would know, Your Grace."

"Explain yourself."

"I was a foundling."

She narrowed her eyes. "How old are you?"

"I believe I am thirty-four. Possibly almost thirty-five."

"Where are you from?"

"Scotland," he told her automatically.

"You were born there?"

"No."

"Where then?"

This was no idle curiosity. "In Cornwall," he said. "I believe."

She flinched and looked at the painting of her husband.

"He appears to have been a thoughtful man," Calum said, needing, without wanting to admit why, to reach out to this brittle creature.

The dowager turned back and moved closer to Calum, peered more closely into his face. "Leave me!" she said abruptly. "Get away, I tell you. All of you."

Lady Justine touched her grandmother's arm but was flung aside. "Take him away from here," the dowager told her. "He does not belong among my loved ones."

"Grandmama—"

"Go *now*. And make certain I never see him again."

"Do not overset yourself, Your Grace," Calum said, while the sound of his heart thundered in his ears. "I can find my own way, ladies. Good day to you."

He strode away, certain Lady Justine and Pippa would be circumspect enough to let him go without further comment.

Once out of earshot of the long-room, he broke into a run, seeking a way outside.

At last he found a door that opened into a courtyard facing the northern hills on Chauncey land.

Calum leaned against the castle's cold stone and allowed himself to accept what had just happened.

He did not believe he was merely inventing some source of proof for the claim he intended to make.

He believed he had shaken the Dowager Duchess of Franchot to her frail old bones.

He believed she had seen her husband and her son in his face and that she was afraid he might have the power to sully her precious family name.

Calum bowed his head. Either the woman thought him a bastard son of her dead offspring come to demand his portion in return for discretion, or she had been part of the plot that stole his heritage.

❧ Eighteen

"*For two* nights and two days I have listened to you tell this tale," Struan told Calum.

"But it's true." He trotted his bay hack a little ahead of Struan's gelding. "It happened that way." They had ridden out from Franchot after breakfast and put in an hour on the cliffs before turning for home once more.

Struan caught up and passed Calum on the final approach to the castle. "Have I suggested it didn't happen that way?"

"As God is my witness, that woman knows I am her grandson."

"I believe she reacted strangely to seeing you."

Calum reined in his horse and sat at ease with his hand resting on one thigh. "She said she never wanted to see me again," he said, to himself rather than to Struan. "Why would she say such a thing to a stranger unless she felt threatened by him? And now Pippa doesn't come out of her rooms."

With a clatter of hoofs, Struan returned. "Lady Justine has said that Pippa is indisposed."

"I don't believe a word of it and neither do you."

"Give it up, Calum. For God's sake, *give it up*."

"I can't."

Struan leaned to clasp Calum's arm. "You mean you *won't*."

"I do mean that. There can be no going back now. I don't

241

expect you to understand. How can you? But I do ask you to accept and support my wishes."

Struan sighed gustily. "I support you in all things, my friend. And although I'd rather not, I accept your wishes in this matter. So with that established, what do you propose to do next?"

"Prove it." Calum looked at the broad approach to the castle, at the noble oaks and giant sycamores that flanked the way, and on to the white fortress that shimmered even on an overcast afternoon. "I shall prove it. And I shall have Pippa as my wife."

"Would you want her if she were not already destined to become the next Duchess of Franchot?"

Calum eyed Struan sharply. "What are you asking me?"

"Simply, what drives you in this business with the girl. Think, man. Why do you want her so?"

Calum wheeled his horse past Struan's mount and said, "She was meant to be mine," as he urged the hack into a trot.

"Is that all?" Struan asked, catching up. "The ownership? The drive to possess everything you believe is yours?"

"I don't think I care for your tone," Calum told him. The air he breathed, air fresh from the English Channel, was cold in his throat.

"If you do not care for my tone," Struan responded, "it's because you do not care for truth in this matter. Answer me. Is Lady Philipa no more to you than the stones in that castle— than the crops in the fields around us? Than the *tin* in Franchot mines?"

"If I choose to claim her, she will be mine. She will have to be."

"I don't follow you," Struan said.

They drew close to the great stone gates in the wall around the base of Franchot Castle's mound. Peregrines atop each massive gatepost, their wings spread, aimed their carved eyes at the sky.

"Explain yourself," Struan persisted.

Calum returned the wave of the man who swung open the gates. "The task of claiming Pippa would not be difficult," he said, narrowing his eyes. "She is an innocent, but there is passion in her—passion for me."

"You would not force her."

"I would not have to force her . . . overmuch."

Struan snorted. "I know you. This thing would not make you happy."

Calum looked sideways at his friend. "I believe you may be wrong. This thing might be all my soul needs. If nothing else, my marriage to Pippa would give me a way to bleed that man of a great deal that should be mine."

They rode beneath the arch that joined the gateposts, and the gates were swung heavily shut behind them.

"The man who speaks isn't the man I've known all my life," Struan said tonelessly. "That man would never use another to gain his own ends."

"Perhaps," Calum said, "you never really knew the man."

"You are not yourself. But we'll not waste what time we have together in argument."

The anger he felt in Struan hung heavily upon Calum. "We have all the time we need together," he said. "But I agree— we mustn't waste any of it in disagreement."

Struan cleared his throat. Calum studied him and noted that he resembled Arran more with each year. The profile was as uncompromising, the bearing straight yet easy, the body less massive than Arran's but no less imposing. The two brothers were handsome, commanding devils.

"Am I forgiven?" Calum said, cajoling.

"You haven't done anything that needs forgiveness—yet. I must leave you for a while, Calum. I'm needed in Dorset."

"*Leave*?" Calum pulled up his horse so abruptly the animal reared. "You cannot be serious. You cannot possibly consider leaving me now."

The wind whipped Struan's curly black hair. He passed a sleeve over his brow and turned his face away. "I've no choice. Surely you know I wouldn't choose to go when things are so unsettled with you."

"*Unsettled*? My life is a chaos, man."

"You'll manage till I can return."

"Why? Why must you go?"

"I told you. My affairs in Dorset require attention."

"You told us you'd acquired a small holding there while you were playing at priestly poverty. You said you would retain it because it brought a pleasant income which, although you do not need it, is more than should be easily let go.''

"I'm glad you remind me of my explanation," Struan said shortly. "All true—except for the fact that I did not acquire Heathsend until after I left the priesthood."

Calum frowned. "But I understood—"

"Evidently you understood very little. I will return just as soon as possible. I have a good man managing the estate there. He has sent for me and that means I am needed."

"But—"

"No," Struan said, inclining his head toward a small, red-haired figure seated on an upturned iron urn not fifty yards from where the two men's horses stood. "Not now, Calum. I think we must continue our discussion later."

Calum regarded Max. "I swear he is everywhere," he said, although he was coming to enjoy the boy. "It will be hard on Ella and Max to have to make another journey to a new place so soon."

"I intended to speak to you about that."

Max had popped up from his urn. He ran toward them, his red hair flying as usual.

"What did you mean to speak about?" Calum asked.

"The children. I shall talk to Lady Justine also, of course, but I'd be much obliged if I could leave them in your care while I'm gone."

"What?"

"Lady Philipa and Lady Justine seem to get along famously with both children. But naturally, you would be the one to take my place in my absence."

The boy drew near. "And what exactly *is* your place? They're no relations of yours, Struan. You appropriated them."

"I'll not argue that point. But what's done is done. I can't send them back."

"And *I* cannot become a nursemaid to children who are nothing to do with me. What can you be thinking of? To bring them here, then abandon them to me?"

"Quite. Don't blame you for thinking me outrageous. There doesn't seem to be another alternative. Helloo, Max! And now it is up to us to help set them safely on their way."

"What if I find it necessary to leave at short notice? I never—" Calum stopped when he found himself looking down into a freckled face. "Hello, Max. What are you doing so far from whoever's looking after you?"

Max shrugged thin shoulders inside a loose brown wool coat. "Waitin' for you, sir. And, um, Papa, o'course."

"How nice."

"It's a long way back up that 'ill to the castle," Max said, frowning toward the massive building. "What a very big place it is."

"A very big place," Calum echoed, raising a brow at Struan, who appeared not to notice. "Well, I suppose we'd all better make our way there. We'll need to . . . we'll all need to do whatever it is that's needed next, shan't we?"

"Right," Max said. "Long walk for a little lad. I'd best get started, I s'pose."

Calum pursed his lips for a moment before saying, "Should you like to ride with me? Probably easier on your feet."

Instantly a grin split Max's face, and little effort was needed to haul him in front of Calum on the horse. Calum sent Struan a "why must I take charge?" look and set off again.

"Lady Justine tells me you and Ella are doing some lessons," Struan said. "I don't suppose you particularly like that."

"I likes it well enough," Max said. He held the horse's mane with both fists. "So does Ella. 'Course, we don't like everythin' about it. I'd as soon not do so many sums."

"Sums are very important to a lad," Calum informed him.

"Well, it probably wouldn't be so 'ard if the dog didn't keep bumpin' me and makin' me lose my place."

Struan looked at Calum. "What dog would that be?"

"Ooh"—Max waved an arm airily—"the big black dog what Lady Philipa brings in."

"Lady Philipa comes in during your lessons? With a big black dog?"

"Well . . . I talks to everyone 'ere, y'know."

"I'm sure you do."

"Everyone thinks Lady Justine's a real gent."

"A real *what*?" Struan and Calum laughed together.

"Well." Max hunched his shoulders. "With the lord—

that's the duke—not being around much and the old—that's the older lady, the duchess—being old, they all looks to Lady Justine, and she does for them real nice.''

Calum winced at the boy's massacre of the language. ''I take it you speak of the servants?'' he asked.

''And them what lives around the castle. I've met all sorts, I can tell you.''

''Do they say the duke is a careless landlord to his estates?'' he asked, feeling Struan's hard stare upon him.

''They say 'e's pleasant enough as long as you don't cross 'im. Funny, you askin' about 'im. Lady Philipa wonders what 'e's like, too.''

''Does she?''

''Yeah. Funny, ain't it? She's marryin' the cove and askin' me what people 'ere say 'e's like. Funny.''

''I suppose she asks you when she brings the big black dog to make you lose your place in your sums,'' Struan said, grinning at Calum. ''No doubt the tutor Lady Justine secured becomes quite irate about all this.''

''Lady Philipa's our tutor,'' Max said, as if nothing could possibly be unusual about such a situation. ''She's taught lots of children. She said so. In that Dowanhill in Yorkshire where she come from. And that's no lie. She even showed us where it was on a map. She's ever so interestin'. Reads stories to us. Comes every mornin'. You can ask 'er about it.''

Calum thought about what the boy had said and didn't find the notion at all surprising. After all, Pippa had made it plain that she enjoyed the company of children.

''Shall we ask her about the big black dog, too?'' Struan inquired.

Max's shoulders came up another notch. ''I wouldn't bother if I was you. She's always so busy thinkin', I shouldn't wonder she ain't even noticed no dog. It probably just lays in wait, like, till she opens the schoolroom door. Then 'e slips in and gets up to all sorts of mischief. Oh, lor, look what's comin'.''

From around a bend in the drive, a rushing figure approached. ''Lady Philipa's maid,'' Struan commented. ''One Nelly Bumstead, I believe.''

She bore down on them until they all converged, and she glared up at Max. ''You're a naughty boy, young Max.

You've had us all searchin' for you. You were told t'go direct from the schoolroom to the nurseries and stay there.''

"He's all right, Nelly," Struan said kindly. "We'll deliver him."

"Y'don't understand, your lordship. Lady Justine gave strict orders that Ella and Max weren't t'be runnin around until the duke's settled in."

Calum stiffened.

"Come on down here, you ungrateful boy," Nelly said. Her pretty face was flushed and she seemed even more disheveled than usual—not an easy feat.

"Just a minute, Nelly," Calum said. "Are you telling us the duke has arrived?"

"*Arrived*?" The girl all but pulled Max from the horse. "I should say he's arrived. Shoutin' at everyone. And with that fancy woman of his flouncin' all over the place. And that nasty Mr. St. Luc demandin' this and that. And then there's poor, dear Lady Justine, tryin' to keep everybody 'appy."

"When did the duke arrive?"

Nelly tried to straighten her soot-smudged apron. "An hour or more ago."

"No doubt the dowager duchess has greeted him?" Calum suggested.

Nelly tutted. "And that's the worst of it. So far she's re- fused to see 'im at all. She's thumping about in her rooms with that nasty stick she uses when she's angry. And he's thumping about in the library, shouting for my mistress. And she won't see him."

Calum gripped his reins tightly and faced straight ahead.

"Oh, sirs, I know it's not my place, but I wish someone could do something for my mistress."

"Why?" Calum swung in the saddle to stare down on the girl. "What's the matter with her?"

"Oh, dear." Nelly sighed hugely while she kept a firm hold on Max's hand. "It's been going on more than two days. She doesn't sleep at all. And whenever she thinks she's alone, she cries. Or she just sits and stares. D'you know what I think?"

"What do you think, Nelly?" Calum asked, not daring to look in Struan's direction.

"Well, I shouldn't say."

"Oh, but I think you absolutely should."

Struan cleared his throat.

"Come along, Nelly," Calum prompted. "It's your duty to tell me if something's wrong with Lady Philipa."

"That's what I thought," she said. "I think she's pining, that's what I think. I think she's in love and doesn't know how the other party feels, if you know what I mean."

Calum swallowed before saying, "I believe I know exactly what you mean."

"I thought you would. The trouble is, that man she's supposed to marry has arrived, and he sounds for all the world as if he intends to drag my poor mistress down the aisle the day after tomorrow. He's rantin' about how it's all arranged. And d'you know what I think about that?"

"What do you think about that?" Calum and Struan asked in unison.

"I think she'll run away . . . or *kill* herself first."

What should she do?

What *could* she do?

Surely if Papa could hear the duke, hear the way he roared and raved and ordered, he would see that this marriage should never take place.

But Papa was somewhere on the Continent and she was under the protection of the Franchots.

And the duke had sent word—as if he needed to send word when she could hear him plainly from the little minstrel's gallery above the lofty vestibule—but he'd sent word that she was to present herself before him immediately. *Present yourself at once. I wish to inform you of my marriage plans.*

His marriage plans. And he would inform her, not consult with her. Really, it was a complete bother. It was not to be borne. She was not a simple-minded widgeon.

She would not stand for it!

Pippa spun away from the open windows in her pretty blue bedchamber and promptly snagged a ruffle in her skirt on a splinter in a little lacquered chest.

"I *hate* being clumsy," she wailed.

As if she'd rung a bell, the door opened and Nelly slipped into the room. The girl raised her chin and frowned fero-

ciously. "You're not to overset yourself, my lady," she said,
advancing with a determination and seriousness quite unlike
herself. "There won't be a wedding nearly as soon as that
duke thinks there will be. You mark my words."

Still attached to the splinter, Pippa struggled to free herself
and look at Nelly at the same time. "What are you talking
about?"

"I've had a few words with some people, that's what I'm
talking about."

"*Help* me, will you? I am beside myself, and now I'm all
tied up in this wretched chest. I am *so* clumsy."

"You are not clumsy," Nelly said, setting her mouth in a
grim line. "You are put upon, that's what you are. And it's
going to stop or my name's not Nelly Bumstead."

In a trice Nelly had freed Pippa's skirt.

"Thank you," Pippa said, contrite. "I'm sorry to be such
a bother."

"You are not a bother. And if you hadn't spent so much
of your life trying not to be a bother for that thoughtless . . .
Oh, forgive me, my lady. I've overstepped myself."

"Thoughtless who?" Pippa asked.

"I'm sure I don't know what I was saying, my lady, and
that's a fact. I was babbling because I'm overset myself. I'm
worried about you. But I've got us some help and you're not
to worry anymore."

"But—"

"I wish you weren't wearing that dress. Beige just isn't my
favorite color on you. Not that my favorite color matters. Me
not being of any account, that—"

"*Nelly*! What have you done? Who is to help me?"

"Lady Justine," Nelly said, raising her chin. "And Mr.
Innes."

Pippa's legs were instantly watery. "Mr. Innes," she whispered. "Oh, Nelly, you haven't gone to him. Not after what
happened . . ."

Nelly waited expectantly, but Pippa wasn't about to explain
that she and Calum seemed unable to spend more than a few
moments together without longing to fall upon each other. At
least she wanted to fall upon him and had even *told* him so!
She had told him she wanted to feel That. Oh, the shocking

embarrassment of it all. And then there had been the dowager's extraordinary behavior toward Calum.

"What happened, my lady?" Nelly asked quietly.

"It doesn't matter." It mattered a very great deal.

"Oh, well, that's all right, then. You're to come with me to Lady Justine."

Pippa began to tremble. "What is to happen?"

"Lady Justine wouldn't tell me exactly. She said I was to bring you to her."

"Nelly—"

"She told me to tell you to wait and see what happens."

𝒏 Nineteen

𝓕*inding a* way to speak privately with Lady Justine was the surest way of arranging to see Pippa. Now that Lady Justine had sent a message for him to await her here, Calum was certain his wish would soon be granted.

He hovered in the corridor that led to Lady Justine's apartments. He knew he was in the right place because helpful Nelly had given him careful instructions.

He also knew that Pippa's rooms were in this same wing of the castle, on the same floor, but on the other side of a minstrel's gallery from where he now stood.

Going to her would be easy enough.

And it could prove disastrous.

At the sound of a door opening, he swung around—in time to see Lady Justine step into the corridor.

He hurried toward her, a forefinger on his lips.

"Mr. Innes—"

"Calum. Call me Calum, please. I know you said you wanted to see me, but I must speak to you quickly. Please, just listen to me before you ask any questions."

She nervously fingered a locket at her neck, but she nodded briefly and pulled him farther into the shadowy corridor.

"Nelly told me about your brother's arrival," he said. "She said . . . please forgive me for being blunt, but I have no choice and I believe you have a special fondness for Pippa."

"I love Pippa."

251

"I . . . I am concerned for her health. I understand the duke is demanding an early marriage and I do not believe Pippa is ready to marry him yet." He did not believe she would ever be ready to marry him.

Lady Justine turned her face from Calum, displaying a neat, heavy chignon from her crown to her nape.

"My lady," Calum whispered urgently, "help me. Please help me to see Pippa. To talk to her."

She faced him again, her dark gaze speculative.

Calum smiled at her; even in his anxiety he had to smile at her. So lovely was fair Justine. His sister. Didn't she see herself in him? Him in herself?

She smiled back. "Our minds work as one. You may be the final ingredient I need," she said, and when he would have questioned her, she touched his lips and shook her head. "Don't ask. Just pray that I'm not making a greater muddle than already exists."

Her future husband behaved as if she were not in the room.

"She is betrothed to me," he said to his grandmother, pointing a blunt, beringed finger at Pippa. "She was betrothed to me at her birth. And I have decided the time is right to marry her."

Ensconced on a rose-colored chaise, the dowager wore a black lace cap on her white hair, and her small body seemed not to exist at all inside a voluminous black silk robe. Black silk slippers, placed precisely side by side, showed beneath the robe. She held an ebony-handled lorgnette to her brilliant eyes.

And the ivory-headed cane was firmly grasped in her other hand.

"I agreed to see you," the dowager said, "because Justine asked me to do so. If she had not insisted that I hear what you propose, I would not have granted this interview."

And if Justine had not insisted that Pippa present herself, she certainly wouldn't be here. What Justine had in mind, Pippa could not begin to guess.

The duchess studied her grandson intently and said, "Continue."

"I have brought a minister with me from London," the

duke said. "He assures me there is no impediment to performing the ceremony the day after tomorrow."

"And how does he intend to discharge the necessary formalities?" The dowager's voice cracked. "The license? The banns? Small details such as these?"

"Potter says he can arrange three services for the purpose of calling the banns. We've already got the license."

"What is the purpose of this haste?"

The duke, resplendent in a kerseymere coat of a deep plum shade, spread wide a hand, opened his mouth to speak, then closed it again.

"Yes?" the dowager prompted.

"The purpose is the accomplishment of what pleases me," he blustered, his handsome but too-florid face growing even redder. "I'm a busy man. A man of weighty affairs, Grandmama. I cannot spend more time on the matter of this marriage. I want it discharged promptly."

"Do you?"

"Yes." He nodded fiercely. "And so it shall be."

"And what of you, gel?" Pippa became the subject of close inspection. "Is this hasty wedding your wish also?"

"Well—"

"I say," the duke interrupted. "I hardly think it appropriate to ask her opinion."

"Perhaps not, but I'm asking it anyway. What have you to say for yourself, Lady Philipa?"

"I had hoped my father would be at my wedding," Pippa replied, her throat aching.

"I'm not marryin' her father," the duke retorted.

No, he wasn't marrying her father, he was marrying her father's land.

"Grandmama, I truly think this is the best course." The duke's smile transformed him into a boyishly charming creature. "Come along, dear thing. You've long complained that I am wild. *Have* been wild. It's my wish to change my ways. I want to be married. I want to have children."

The old lady pursed her lips and shifted her frail shoulders beneath their burden of rich silk. "Hmm. It's time for heirs. I won't argue that."

Pippa felt light-headed. Why had Justine insisted she come

here? Had she thought Pippa might somehow be able to plead with the dowager and the duke to await her pleasure in this marriage?

"You see," Franchot said, dipping a knee engagingly to his grandmother, "I am not the scapegrace you once knew. I am changed, I assure you. I shall do nothing but bring our fortunes into even more favorable condition."

"The autumn was to have been the date. Everyone expects this wedding to be the affair of the year—very possibly of the decade."

"But why wait?" Franchot asked. Flipping out his coat tails, he sat beside his grandmother on her chaise. "The sooner there are little Franchots in our nurseries, the better."

"Hmm." The dowager resettled her bones once more. "There may be some truth to what you say. But I would like to hear more from Lady Philipa."

"I—"

A rap at the door brought Pippa a blessed reprieve in which to consider how to answer.

The dowager motioned to the maid, who stood silently by. The woman went to open the door.

With the entrance of Calum Innes, Pippa's concentration shattered. She felt her mouth open but was helpless to close it again.

"Good afternoon, Duchess," he said, walking confidently toward the woman. "We meet again, Franchot. I didn't want to waste any time in coming to thank you for inviting us to join you in Cornwall."

"Innes," Franchot said, making no attempt to rise, "glad you could come. Understand you've been here some days."

"Yes." Calum told the tale he and Struan had presented about prior business easily concluded.

"Ah," Franchot said. "My sister and my fiancée been looking after you, have they?"

"Viscount Hunsingore and I are very much enjoying our stay," Calum said, catching Pippa's eye.

She noted the hard set of her fiancé's features and pressed a hand into her middle. He did not wish Calum well, and if there had not been the issue of endangered honor, Calum would not be standing in this room.

A rustle caught Pippa's attention and that of the men. The dowager duchess got to her feet and stood with both hands atop her cane.

Franchot scrambled up and tried to hold his grandmother's arm. She promptly batted him away as if he were an annoying insect.

"I find I am tired," she said. "I shall retire."

Pippa couldn't fail to notice how the old lady stared at Calum, to whom she had said not a word.

"Of course," Franchot said. "We'll proceed with things as I've planned them, then."

Pippa's eyelids drooped. She felt faint and sick. They were going to marry her off to Franchot without even hearing what she really wanted.

"I understand Lady Philipa is tutoring Viscount Hunsingore's children."

At the dowager's abrupt statement, Pippa rallied. She crossed her arms tightly and willed herself to be strong.

"Indeed she is," Calum said. "Most kind of her." He smiled at her and she smiled back—she couldn't stop herself from smiling back.

And she couldn't change the fact that Franchot saw the smile. His fair brows drew down over the bridge of his haughty nose.

"Motherless, I understand," the dowager continued. "Most unusual for a man to be travelin' around with his motherless offspring. Better off at home with appropriate staff, I say."

"Daresay you're right, Your Grace," Calum said.

What, Pippa wondered, would the dowager say if she actually saw Ella and Max? What if she *heard* them? Despite herself, she shuddered at the thought. Her pupils were intelligent and quick to learn. She was trying her best to teach them some of the things in which they were sadly lacking polish. Ella possessed great natural grace and a clear and pretty voice that already showed signs of improvement, but much more time would be needed to complete the task.

Pippa very much wanted to complete the task.

"Grandmama," Franchot said. Veins stood out at his temples. "I'll take my leave of you and start the necessary preparations."

"Preparations for what?" Calum asked, his voice so innocent that Pippa turned her full, startled attention upon him.

"My weddin'," Franchot said, his nostrils flared and white. "I've decided to move the event forward."

"But I thought the happy festivities were set for autumn," Calum said, frowning as if perplexed. "Surely that's when Lord Chauncey expects to return for the affair?"

Franchot's chin jutted. "And what business is that of yours?"

Calum fell back a step. "Absolutely none, Duke. I hold you in high regard, you know that. Only your best interests at heart, I assure you."

The dowager's lorgnette was firmly anchored against her nose. She appeared to study first Franchot, then Calum, then Franchot again.

"I've stated my best interests," Franchot said, glaring now.

"No doubt," Calum said, his eyes wide and worried. "Don't suppose the *ton* will, er . . . Well, you know how that can go."

"I'll thank you to keep your opinions to yourself, Innes."

"Oh, sorry. Of course. Presumptuous of me. Consider it unsaid. I was hoping you'd show me some of your favorite haunts around the estate—if you've any time, that is."

"Mr. Innes," the dowager duchess said, "what exactly do you think the *ton's* reaction would be to an early marriage between my grandson and Lady Philipa?"

Calum blew up his cheeks and stuffed his hands behind him. "Shouldn't have spoken out of turn," he said, rolling onto the soles of his feet. "Man like the duke doesn't have to give a pig's— He doesn't have to give a fig for what people think or say. Go to it, man. And I wish you the best of luck."

"Thank you," Franchot said grudgingly. "Good of you."

"Mr. Innes is from Scotland," the dowager said, and Pippa began to wonder if the old lady's faculties were slipping. Her train of thought certainly was.

"I know where he's from," Franchot said.

"I think we should ensure that he has a very satisfying visit with us before he returns to Scotland."

Franchot's frown deepened even further. "I'm sure he'll be well enough treated."

"I know he will," the dowager said, and repeated her scrutiny of first one and then the other man—and repeated it again. "And you can send your minister back to wherever he came from, Etienne. We've a perfectly good minister of our own here at Franchot."

"But—"

"Our arrangements are already in progress. I see no point in risking any wagging tongues, hmm?"

"But—"

"Do *you*, Etienne?"

"Of course not, but—"

"Good. I knew we should agree. Entertain yourselves and stay out of my way. Remember that *my* signature is also required on the marriage documents, won't you? September it shall be."

The Dowager Duchess of Franchot, her cane borne before her like a baton, signaled for the door to the rest of her apartments to be opened, and swept out.

Franchot rushed in her wake and closed the door behind him.

Calum cast a glance at the maid, who had remained, and said only, "Lady Justine has extraordinarily good judgment."

Etienne longed to hurl something through every window in the summerhouse. "If that oaf hadn't arrived, the old bat would have agreed, I tell you. I had her in the palm of my hand, and he had to remind her of the threat to her precious family reputation."

"The threat to our precious family reputation," Anabel said sweetly. "If only you would listen to me, my darling. Thank goodness you didn't manage to get your grandmother to agree. What could you have been thinking of?"

Really, this woman was becoming a strain from which he longed to be freed. "Shut up, you stupid bitch. You don't know what you're saying."

"I know that to go into a hasty marriage while Chauncey has a spy sniffing around could bring all our plans crashing around our ears," Anabel said, turning red. "I'll thank you to have more care how you speak to me."

"I'll speak to you any way I damn well please, madam. You exist by my pleasure."

She whirled about, flipping the full back of her violet velvet pelisse-robe behind her. "*Don't* suggest that you have any power over me. One word and you are *finished*. Do you understand, Etienne? One word from me—or rather, the *failure* for me to give a certain word when it is expected—and you are a dead man."

"You will not give me my orders, madam."

"If my solicitors should ever fail to receive word from me on dates already appointed between us, they will instantly open letters sealed in their vaults. Do I make myself clear?"

God. How he was oppressed by damnable females.

"Etienne," she crooned, positioning herself between him and the nearest window. She spread her arms, bracing them against the frames. "My own dearest one. When will you learn to trust Anabel? When will you learn to stop being frightened and let me take care of everything for us?"

When would he be free of her?

"My plan is perfect, sweetest. You need do nothing. *Nothing*. I shall ensure that Innes slips neatly into our hands."

"This story of yours is exactly that, a story. You have no proof that the man is anything other than an opportunist looking for a patron"— he compressed his mouth and stared at the full flare of Anabel's hips beneath the pelisse —"or a damnable seducer set on snaring himself a rich bride."

"You need me, Etienne," Anabel said, swaying. The motion showed how her high-collared robe opened daringly to reveal a hint of a very low-cut black gown and a great deal of the woman's big breasts.

He narrowed his eyes, bent his head to one of those breasts and sucked in a soft, scented mouthful of white flesh.

"Ouch!" Anabel pulled him away by his hair, but she was laughing and her tongue made a slow progress around her lips. "I shall make you pay for that."

"How?" He enjoyed her, dammit. And he'd use her until he could find a way to get his hands on her precious letters— if they existed.

"How shall I make you pay for hurting Anabel?" she

mused. "First, you must promise to allow me to deal with the annoyance of your little *fiancée*."

"You will do—"

"I will do what must be done. And we shall have her dowry. Fear not. As I have already explained, Innes will die in the act of kidnapping dear Philipa. Philipa will die at his hand and Chauncey will give the grieving groom the only suitable price for his silence—*Cloudsmoor*. Delicious."

Etienne looked into Anabel's blue eyes. Clever blue eyes. If her plan could work, he might be free. And he need never marry this conniving jade. This time she'd be permanently silenced by her own crime.

"You are an inventive gel," he told her, pulling undone the satin bows that closed the front of the pelisse. "Why shouldn't I give you a chance to see if you can accomplish this thing?" One by one, he undid the bows.

"I can accomplish it, I tell you," she said, slipping away from him to sit on the back of a cane couch. "You have been very preoccupied of late, Etienne."

He followed until he stood between her splayed thighs. "Can you wonder at my preoccupation? My future is at stake."

"The viscount is leaving," she told him. "That will make my task easier. I don't like that man. He sees too much."

"Do not underestimate Innes. His innocent prattle is all an act. I swear he has put himself in my way to interfere with the marriage."

"He has," she agreed. "I've told you as much. But do not worry, my pet. Entertain me instead. To inspire me."

He fumbled inside the robe and hefted her breasts free. For a while she was content to mewl and pant and writhe whilst he suckled her distended nipples, but then she plucked at his shoulders and pushed him away and said, "Imagine how the mouse, Philipa, would please you, Etienne. Imagine how *she* would attend to your needs."

Smiling, he took off his coat. "Regardless, I do believe I shall make sure I take that particular pallid flower before that thief, Innes, can have her." With one hand he began loosing his trousers; with the other, he sought to tear the remaining

bows away. "If you are very good, I may arrange for you to
watch. Should you like that?"

"We shall see—later," Anabel said, laughing and staying
his hands. "Not so quickly, Etienne. There is something I have
come by recently. I could use it selfishly, but I'd much rather
share my pleasure with you. Stand quietly. Be *good.*"

Already his shaft sprang free of his clothes.

"Ooh," Anabel said, her mouth remaining in a moist pout.
"How *lovely.* I'm going to have such a lot of fun tonight."

He fumbled with her clothes, only to be pushed away again.

Anabel opened the robe and revealed, not a gown, but black
satin stays edged with lace below her breasts. Black satin
drawers, of the kind he'd seen on Frenchwomen, parted beneath her fingers. "Now you can feel," she told him.

He felt. She was wet. "I like these new possessions of
yours," he told her, applying the heel of his hand in the way
he knew drove her to a frenzy, and anticipating watching his
rod enter her between the black satin folds of the garment.

"Not these," she said, her voice as satiny as the drawers.
"What I have is not satin. It is this." Leaning back, she retrieved something long and shining from the couch—a golden
tube that glittered in the weak shafts of late sun through dusty
windows.

Etienne frowned, then narrowed his eyes once more.
"Where did you come by that?"

"From . . . It is said to have belonged to Nefertiti."

He made a grab for the elegant toy, but she held it aloft.
"I asked where you came by it," he said and saw her breath
quicken. She had good reason to be afraid of his anger. She'd
tasted it before—and suffered before enjoying it, he thought
darkly.

"A good friend gave it to me, Etienne. You aren't jealous,
are you?"

"Jealous?" He snorted and thrust his engorged rod toward
the enticing gap in those black satin drawers. "What need
have I of an Egyptian queen's dildo?"

"Wait," she told him. "And watch."

Where he would have found his pleasure, she slowly in-
serted her cold, golden substitute. So very slowly, the shim-

mering thing passed inside her and she dropped her head back, panting aloud, her breasts heaving.

Fascinated, sweating, he watched her body easily take in the massive plaything until her fingers rested in the thicket of golden hair between her legs.

Ah, yes, she was inventive, his little nemesis. His penis throbbed and the ache was exquisite. "Finish your game, Annie," he gasped, his eyes squeezing shut. Another moment and he'd have little need of her.

A cool hand surrounded him and he sagged forward.

"You are so beautiful," a familiar and hated voice said.

Etienne opened his eyes and looked into the saturnine face of Henri St. Luc. He summoned enough alarm to mutter, "How long have you been here?"

"All the time, darling," Anabel said with a bubbling chuckle. "Henri is our friend. And he is my insurance. He will look after my interests. Just as he will look after yours."

"But of course," Henri said, pressing his lips to the other man's while his strong, clever fingers did their work. "It has been too long since you and I were together, *mon ami*."

Even while some shred of him clung to loathing, Etienne's body betrayed its voracious appetite for what Henri St. Luc offered.

"See?" Anabel said, withdrawing the golden rod and driving it in once more. "See?" Her voice rose and she fell to her knees.

Etienne felt Henri slip down the length of his body, felt his knees surrounded and held in a strong arm—felt himself drawn in, and milked.

"We will have it all!" Anabel shrieked, and collapsed, writhing in the throes of her self-made satisfaction.

They would have it all here, Etienne thought. They might have it all again and again—before *he* had it all for himself.

Then he fell through pulsing blackness, gave himself up to that which the world forbade yet he craved.

The evening's entertainment had truly begun.

ॐ Twenty

"*Repeat after* me," Pippa said to Ella. "I am not happy to hear this."

Ella settled herself gracefully in her straight-backed chair, pleated the skin between her brows in concentration and said, "I am not happy to 'ear this."

"*Hear* this," Pippa said, walking to the schoolroom windows to look down upon the stable yard far below.

"Hear this," Ella said, her voice pleasing. "I am not happy to hear this. I'm gettin' better, ain't—am I not?"

Pippa smiled at the girl. "You are getting better so quickly, I can hardly believe it. Your mother will be so pleased," she added before she could contain the urge to find out more about her mysterious pupils.

Ella's dark eyes assumed their familiar shuttered expression. "How old is Saber?" she asked, the tilt of her chin declaring her determination to keep her secrets to herself.

"The earl is twenty-three," Pippa said, pressing closer to the window to look down on top of two dark-haired men beside a single horse. "Lord Avenall is a man of the world, Ella."

"I don't think so," Ella said.

Calum and Struan were in the stable yard. Pippa watched Struan mount the horse, wave and spur the animal into a gallop. Through the open window she heard the distant clank of metal tack and the clatter of hoofs on cobbles.

262

"Hmm?" She glanced back at Ella. "What did you say?"

"I said that I don't think Saber's a man of the world. Not like some anyway."

"Has he told you to call him by his given name?"

"Of course."

Pippa frowned, not knowing exactly how to answer. "He is a great deal older than you, miss, and you'd do well not to entertain any romantical notions about him."

"She is, y'know," Max said, breaking the silence that invariably accompanied his labored efforts at penmanship.

"Shut your mouth, Max," Ella snapped.

"Hush," Pippa said. "She is what?"

"What you said. Soppy about that young lord."

"I ain't—am not," Ella argued.

"Of course you aren't," Pippa said, smiling a little at the faint flush that showed on Ella's honey-colored skin. The feeling of protectiveness and empathy she felt with the girl brought Pippa a secret joy. "Max, you are doing extremely well with your *D*'s. Clearly you are going to be a remarkable man of letters one day."

Max, his tongue between his teeth, finished his latest letter with a cramped flourish. "Like Mr. Innes," he said. "I think I'm going to do lots of things like him. Papa's had to go to, er, Dorset. 'E'll be back, though. 'E said so, didn't 'e, Ella?"

"*He*," Ella said. "Of course he did."

"Yes," Max said. "I 'spect Mr. Innes would rescue us again if we 'ad t'be rescued, but—"

"*Max*," Ella said ominously.

Pippa stopped herself, not for the first time, from telling the children that she was well aware of their peculiar position. As long as she hadn't been given permission to reveal that she knew their secret, her silence was a trust.

She returned to the window. Calum stood in the stable yard, staring into the empty spaces where Viscount Hunsingore had disappeared. Even at a distance, she felt a need in the man left behind.

Oh, what was to happen? None of this was as it should be. Surely Franchot would not suffer the presence of a man he despised much longer. Already a week had passed since the duke's arrival, and tension sprang from him every time he as much as looked at Calum. Franchot didn't look at Pippa at all, thank goodness.

"Ella," Pippa said, "would you kindly attend to Max's lessons until it's time for your luncheon? That will be quite soon. And I'll see you here tomorrow morning."

Without waiting to hear more than Ella's assent, Pippa left the schoolroom in its lofty tower perch and ran swiftly down the spiral stone staircase, past a succession of floors to the stark, undecorated hall at its base.

By the time she'd made her way through a corridor bordered on one side by storage used by the castle steward and on the other by the laundry, she was out of breath and convinced Calum would be long gone when she finally reached the stable yard.

A kitchen garden and a big herb patch, hemmed in by a high stone wall, led to the stables, and Pippa was fully running by the time her slippers hit the cobbles.

She'd been almost right. Calum, mounted on a bay hack, cantered from the yard and began to drop from sight even as she watched.

If she waited to find a mount, she'd never know which way he'd gone. Her feet flying, trying to ignore the stares of stableboys and grooms, she held her skirts above her ankles and dashed from the yard to the stony pathway that wound downward toward the castle's great drive.

He was below her already. Heedless of who might hear, she called, "Calum! Wait! *Calum*!"

The bay continued to pick a path on slipping shale and Calum didn't look back.

"Fie," Pippa said. "Everything is such a *bother*." And she launched herself in a reckless downhill flight, stumbling, catching her balance, only to slide again.

"Calum!" Her voice rose to a squeak and she began to fall.

Pippa hit the ground with a thud that knocked out all her wind. She thumped, twisted sideways and slid—and heard a hard, rapid thrumming she knew were returning hoofbeats.

Ooh, she *hated* to be humiliated.

"Stay," Calum called. "Do not move, Pippa. Stay exactly where you are."

She shut her eyes tightly, then opened them a crack and saw the legs of a bay horse.

Then she saw the legs of a man.

The long, powerfully muscled legs of a man who wore doeskin breeches and top boots that clasped tight to strong calves.

"My dear," Calum said. "My dear one." He went to his knees beside her.

Pippa held her breath.

Gently, he stroked her freed hair back from her face. "Can you hear me, Pippa?"

She nodded a little.

"Thank God." His sigh was audible. With careful hands, he felt first one of her arms, then the other. "Where do you hurt?"

"I don't know," she said honestly.

After a small hesitation, he began to test her ankles, then her calves. When he reached her knees, Pippa could no longer bear to trick him.

"I am *so* clumsy," she said. "Really, it is *such* a trial. My father always said so and—and—"

"And you did *not* admire him for it," he suggested with such an odd note in his voice that Pippa opened her eyes and looked up into his. "Poor Pippa. You did not hear nearly enough praise for your virtues when you were a child, did you?"

She could not criticize Papa. "I did very well, thank you. I was a most fortunate child."

He smiled down at her, slid one arm around her back and the other beneath her knees and lifted her easily into his arms. Back on his feet, he studied her face as if she were both interesting and a stranger.

"Did I hear you call my name just now?" he asked.

Pippa chewed the inside of her lip. A lady was not supposed to chase after a gentleman, particularly when the lady was already engaged, and not to the man after whom she chased.

"Did you?"

"Yes. And you can put me down. I am quite unhurt, except for my pride."

He threw back his head and laughed. He laughed and

showed marvelous, strong teeth and made his chest rumble against Pippa's side.

"I cannot find any humor in my damaged pride, sir."

"No," he said, struggling for control. "But I find true wonder in your lack of coquetry and guile. I've never met another woman who would willingly point out her faults—even faults she does not have."

"Where are you going?" she asked, unwilling to continue this examination of her character.

He studied her for a moment longer, then hoisted her sideways onto his saddle and leaped up behind. Settling her, he held her safe against his big body and urged the hack back on the path he'd been taking before Pippa had managed to make herself the fool.

Her hair had completely slipped its bonds and whipped madly about her face. The air was warm, the wind gusty. Pippa felt the warm, sweet wind. She thought only of the man who held her, of his strong, gentle arms—of the comfort he offered, if only for a little while.

They avoided the drive, going instead by way of a path through towering trees where sun wands pointed earthward through rare gaps in the dense growth. In those bright wands, sparkling fairy motes spun.

Pippa would have curled into Calum's embrace, but the comfort she found with him, the sweet yearning to forget that there was any world outside the forest, was tinged with an ache in her heart. This could not be—not for more than a few stolen moments.

At last they were within sight of the edge of the trees. In the distance Pippa could see a meadow sweeping down to the castle walls, and the glitter of the sea beyond.

Calum drew his horse to a halt.

Pippa sat quite still, leaning against him, waiting.

His hands on the reins were long and tanned and capable. The hands of a poet or a farmer, a painter or a smith. Hands that had been used. They made her want to be touched by and to touch them.

As if he heard her thoughts, he crossed his arms around her and chafed her arms, rested his cheek atop her head and held her so tight she could scarcely breathe.

The silence stretched on and on.

Pippa could not bear it to end, yet she could not bear for it to continue. The time for confrontation had arrived.

"I wanted to talk to you," she said.

"Where is your private place?"

At first she didn't understand; then she nodded. "I told you. At Cloudsmoor."

"Will you show it to me?"

"Perhaps." Somehow she must keep her head.

"When?"

"I only said perhaps. Even being together like this is a dangerous thing."

"I am not afraid of Franchot."

"I am. I'm afraid for you. He is a dangerous man."

He found her face and felt its contours like a blind man. "Do not be afraid of him, Pippa. Trust and let me lead the way for both of us."

Suddenly she could no longer contain the questions. Turning, sitting half on the saddle, half in his lap, she caught his coat with both hands and looked into his face.

Before she could speak, Calum bent to touch his parted lips to hers. She saw his eyes shut tightly and her own lids drifted down. The touch of his mouth was tough silk, commanding surrender.

Her grip moved to his shirt, where the heat of his body beat into her hands and coursed through her veins.

"No!" Pushing herself as far away from him as her position allowed, she held back her hair with one hand and turned aside her face when he would have kissed her again. "Stop."

"Why? We both want to be together."

"Why do you want to be with me?"

His hands traveled up and down her spine. When the horse shifted restlessly, Calum calmed him without taking his touch from her neck beneath her tumbled hair.

"Calum," she said, and forced herself to stare into his serious eyes. "*What* do you want with me?"

"Time," he said simply.

Again she avoided his kiss. "Time for what?"

"There are things I cannot tell you."

"Yet you pursue me."

He laughed softly and forced her face up to his. After he had kissed her soundly, he said, "I believe it was you who pursued me this time, my love. And you found me. I'm glad and you're glad. Need we waste precious time on questions I will not answer today?"

"When will you answer them?" she asked, and gasped when he caressed her breast: "Don't. Please, don't."

"You have told me how difficult you find it not to touch me intimately. I have the same dilemma." His fingertips slipped inside her bodice to find a nipple. "Ah, my dearest. I must complete what I have to do here, and then . . . Are you not desperate for some of those intimate touches of yours?"

She covered his hand on her breast and bit her lip against the sweet, exquisite surge that swelled from the place his fingers had found and pooled, hot, low, in her belly.

Her gown was light and soft and offered a flimsy barrier between them.

That part of Calum was heavy and hard.

Pippa flattened a palm on his lean middle, pressed downward over breeches that hid nothing of the man's swollen proportions.

She cupped him and leaned up to kiss his neck.

"Aah." He raised his sharp jaw and she saw his teeth clench. "Not here," he said suddenly, catching her wrist and pulling her hand to rest on his chest. "Not now, but very, very soon. Otherwise, I shall die of wanting you."

Pippa's skin was a raw thing, and the flesh beneath trembled. When she could speak, she said, "I ask you again, Calum Innes from Scotland, who stays in a castle where the lord does not want him, and cares for children who are not his own, and angers an old lady who has no reason to be angered by him, and pursues a woman who is promised to another . . . *what* do you want with me?"

"And I tell you again," he said, firmly turning her to face forward once more, "that I want time from you. *Can* you give me that? *Will* you give me that?"

The hack trotted onward and Pippa did not answer Calum.

From the trees they passed onto the sloping meadow where shy yellow pimpernels arched their coy flowers from shiny vines among wild grasses. Blue forget-me-nots and magenta

Hottentot fig flowers flipped to and fro. All around was peace. Inside Pippa, confusion and dread raged. She dreaded the thought of a life lived where she would see this man everywhere, *feel* him everywhere, yet where he would no longer be.

Once past the wall, Calum guided the horse toward a narrow track that led to an overlook above the village of Franchot. He rested his chin on her shoulder and blew softly against her cheek.

"You are not here because of me, are you?" She'd known she must eventually ask him this. "It was not by chance that we met in London?"

His lips found sensitive skin on the side of her neck. "Let it be for now," he said into her ear. "Let it be, Pippa."

"There is something you intend to do here. And it is dangerous."

"I will never do anything to hurt you."

They crested the hill and a valley opened before them, a valley with the village at its center. "Oh, look." She sat up. "See?" Wagons piled high with colorful burdens ranged around the common ground outside the village. Figures made small by distance scurried in every direction.

Behind Pippa, Calum straightened and grew still.

"I had forgotten all about the fair," she told him. "But, of course, it is time. Justine says it is great fun. I wonder if we shall be able to go tonight."

Calum made a sound deep in his throat. "I shall go," he said in a tone she had not heard him use before. "Oh, yes. I shall go to the fair tonight."

Pippa looked down at his hands once more. His knuckles shone white. "Is something wrong?" she asked him.

"Something was always wrong," Calum said. "To hope for a miracle is to risk despair. I have lived to take this risk."

🍃 Twenty-One

A purple glow folded into a moonless night sky over the fairgrounds.

Laughter and music, shrieking and the bellow of animals, reduced everything about them to turmoil.

"I'm t'see everythin'," Max shouted to Calum over the din. "And t'do everythin'."

"Are you indeed?" Calum kept an eye on the rest of his party and searched in every direction for Milo and Miranda's wagon.

"Lady Justine give me this," the boy announced, holding out a palm filled with coins. "Ellie's a silly one."

Calum looked sharply at Max. "Why is Ella silly?" He curled the child's thin fingers over the money. "And keep this out of sight or you'll soon be parted from it."

Max laughed and capered about. "They'd 'ave t'be quick t'pick from a—" He halted abruptly and hunched his shoulders. "I'll watch my pockets."

"Yes," Calum said thoughtfully. "What's this about Ella?"

"She slipped away and went back. Said she didn't like it here."

Calum hadn't noticed the girl's absence. "She's wiser than some of us," he said. "Tired, no doubt. Make certain you don't go far from me."

"I'm off t'see the bear." With that, Max dashed away, stopping every few steps to twirl back and wave.

The purple glaze upon the skies came from open fires that sent sparks spiraling upward. About those fires rollicked clownish fellows intent on cadging prizes for their foolishness. A band brandishing tambourines made noise by which to dance. Skirts and voluminous trousers of brightly striped gauze whirled together, and a crowd gathered to clap in time.

Nowhere was there any sign of the painted message promising cures from all ills. His belly clenched. He hadn't really expected to find Miranda here, but he'd hoped.

"For all the world, Calum, one would think you were at your very first fair."

He had no need to look at the face of the woman who pressed close to his side to know who she was. "I am a man interested in everything he sees," he told Lady Hoarville. "What of you, my lady? Do you find things to interest you here?"

"Oh, yes. Some very interesting things."

Under the cover of the jostling throng, she contrived to stand where her skirts hid her actions and slipped a hand between his thighs.

Calum, his arms crossed, remained still and pretended to be engrossed in a pair of white dogs with red ruffs around their necks. They minced on their hind legs and leaped, still upright, over sticks their owner placed repeatedly before them.

"A great thing of interest," Lady Anabel said, and there was an annoyed edge to her voice now. "I think you need some assistance."

"Not from you, my lady."

She closed her hand hard on his shaft. "Are you certain?"

"Quite certain."

Her hand dropped away. "We shall have to find an opportunity to test your resolve, sir. Listen to me, please. There is something you must do."

Calum was tired of this creature and he had a great deal to do. The sooner he was rid of her—and of the rest of the company from the castle—the better.

"Do you hear me?" she demanded.

"I hear you."

"I believe you told me the truth when you said you were not retained by Philipa to make Etienne jealous."

"Wise of you," he said, searching around for Franchot and his odious friend, St. Luc. They appeared inseparable, except when St. Luc could be seen dogging the steps of Saber Avenall. St. Luc clearly assumed Calum would keep a "gentleman's" silence regarding their encounter at the brothel in Whitechapel.

Calum wondered about the closeness between Franchot and St. Luc and thought about Franchot's intention to marry Pippa. The idea sickened his very soul.

"She's over there," Lady Hoarville said with angry intensity. "With Saber. At the farthing toss."

Calum turned and saw Pippa. She and Saber were laughing together while he tossed farthings at painted numbers in squares upon a board.

"Have you had her yet?"

Calum frowned and gave Lady Hoarville his attention. "I beg your pardon, my lady?"

"Pippa. Have you bedded her yet?" She shrugged eloquently in her unsuitably extravagant, swansdown-trimmed blue cloak. "It doesn't matter. What does matter is that I am a generous woman and I know when I'm looking at a man and a woman in love."

Anabel was a viper. A grasping, unscrupulous harridan who hadn't the wit to as much as attempt to cover her meddling. "I'll take my leave of you," he told her.

"No, you won't." Her fingers curled into his arm. "I'm going to help you."

"*Help* me?"

"I knew that would make you pay attention."

Calum collected himself. "Please excuse me."

"If you marry Lady Philipa, you'll get her dowry," Lady Hoarville said, appearing for all the world to be fascinated by the little white dogs. "Is that interesting to you?"

She must be acting for Franchot, asking questions to find out how Calum would react. "Lady Philipa is betrothed to the Duke of Franchot and will marry him in a few weeks. That, my lady, makes your suggestion a joke."

"I never joke about things that are of the utmost importance," she said.

"Of the utmost importance to you," he responded.

"With my help, you will leave Franchot and take Lady Philipa with you."

"Leaving you to take her place as the Duchess of Franchot?"

"All that should concern you are your own affairs."

"And they do concern me. Enjoy the fair."

Her sharp fingertips stayed him long enough for her to tell him, "Think about what I have said. You will change your mind and be glad of my help. Think of it, Calum. Take her away and you will have Cloudsmoor and all that goes with it."

"Good night, madam."

"You and I could enjoy each other, Calum."

He looked at her.

"You saw some of what I have to offer at the Esterhazys'," she said, smiling with confident satisfaction. "And you wanted me. Then it was not convenient. Now it can be."

"Why should that be?"

"Because I believe in paying for what I want. Many men would pay a great deal for what I will do for you—"

"Thank you, but no."

Her eyes widened, then narrowed. "I am offering to buy what *you* should pay me for. With my favors, I will buy your departure from here with Pippa. I will pleasure you to persuade you to grab a fortune, you fool."

"Thank you," he said. "But no."

"Damn you. Money, then. I will *pay* you to take her away."

He had neither the time nor the stomach for this. Forcing a smile, he offered her a bow. "You are generous, madam. And I will consider your offer."

She swayed with agitation. "You will consider money rather than . . . Very well. But do not consider too long. Soon it will be too late."

"I will inform you of my decision soon enough," he said. "I believe I see the duke over there. We'll speak again."

Sidestepping a chain of village youths singing and winding

through the throng, Calum joined Saber and Pippa. "Has he won you a pretty trinket yet?" Calum asked, smiling into Pippa's flushed face.

"There is some trick to it," Saber protested to the grinning and toothless woman who gathered up fallen coins into pockets in her grimy apron.

He leaned as far forward as the barrier would allow and tried a delicate flick of the wrist. The small coin reached the end of the game board and plopped into sawdust scattered beneath.

"Hopeless!" Calum announced. "Let me show you how."

"You are unkind, sir," Pippa told him. "Do not tease us, please."

Saber did not look like a man who took teasing seriously. He peered past Calum. "Where's Ella? They said she would come with you."

Calum caught Pippa's eye and quickly looked away. "She went back."

The smile left Saber's face. "Surely you're mistaken. Max said they were all agog about—" He replaced his smile and made a passable attempt to appear unconcerned. "I think I'll leave you two to the clutches of this impossible feat. Young Max will be up to no good if he's left alone. I'll make sure he's in no trouble."

"Ella is only fifteen," Pippa said when the young man had disappeared into the crowd.

"Saber knows that." Calum found he wanted to plead that, despite his youth, his cousin was honorable. This longing to acknowledge and be acknowledged by his rightful family was becoming a thing that almost choked him.

"I've seen the way she gazes at him," Pippa said, frowning. "And you know how a woman looks when she's in love?"

Pippa met his eyes directly. "Yes, I know how she looks. And I know how she feels. There can be no future for those two. You know as much. They are from different, irreconcilable worlds. I dislike that such unimportant things are made insurmountable, but they are."

"Saber knows what he's about."

Pippa took a farthing from Calum's hand and turned it over in her palm. "Saber is good. But he is a man. Ella is not . . .

How can I say it? In some ways she seems older than her years and she certainly looks older. In the viscount's absence, you must ensure her safety."

"I think you are coming to believe our little deception," he told her quietly.

"It is all we have," she said tartly. "Ella and Max are special children and I am glad of them. I am glad that, for whatever reason, they were rescued from circumstances I'm certain were unsuitable. *I* shall champion them, if you will not."

He shook his head. "*I* shall champion them, Pippa. You know I shall." Her fiercely protective nature ensnared his heart.

Pippa fingered the farthing, then turned to toss it at the board.

"No luck, yer ladyship," said the rosy-cheeked woman who quickly pocketed the coin. "Try again."

"I suppose I shall simply have to forget that pretty little prize I wanted," Pippa said, sighing hugely.

"What little prize?" Calum asked.

"Why, the fan of purple feathers, of course."

Squinting, Calum scanned the prizes arrayed behind the board and located the frightful piece Pippa described. When he opened his mouth to say what he thought of it, she contrived to dig him hard in the ribs and shake her head.

"Her ladyship's got fine taste," the attendant said. "Prize of prizes, that is. Calls for four farthings on the twenty, it do. Try yer luck, yer lordship."

"Don't trouble yourself, Calum," Pippa said. "I shall simply have to—"

"Stand back," Calum said, pushing his coat sleeves above his shirt cuffs and flourishing his elbows.

Pippa's laugh delighted him. "You are impossible," she said.

"You won't say that when you hold the pretty purple fan in your delicate hands."

She leaned against the booth and covered her face.

"Watch this, my lady," Calum said. He held the coin as he would a rock for skimming on the lake at Kirkcaldy. With a flick of the wrist he sent it gently skimming up the sloping board to land—just barely—inside the necessary square. "*One* farthing," he announced.

"Ooh," the toothless one said admiringly. "A fine 'and you've got, yer lordship."

"You've seen little yet." A second farthing found its mark.

Pippa clapped. "You are a marvel. I had no idea your talents were so advanced."

He spared her a grin and said, "I assure you, lady, my talents are *very* advanced."

The third farthing landed in the top left-hand corner of the square.

"I don't believe it," Pippa said. "And you use both hands."

"I forget sometimes," he said, pursing his lips. "I frequently forget the lessons of my schoolroom days."

"They tried to stop you from using the left hand?"

"Naturally. Not quite the thing. Now, to finish this."

"You cannot do it," she warned him. "You are inflated with your success like a drunken pigeon. Give it up, and we'll take the green clockwork mouse for three on the twenty."

Calum took his coat off entirely and handed it to Pippa. He tugged at the hem of his waistcoat and assumed a pugilist's stance. Amid bursts of the laughter he loved more than any in life, he shied a fourth farthing.

"Oh," Pippa said, standing still, her hands pressed together. "Oh, oh, oh!"

The coin hit the board too low and slid slowly, slowly upward.

"Oh!" Pippa cried. She jumped up and down, clapping wildly. "You did it, Calum. Oh, you did it."

Her eyes, her clenched hands, the forward incline of her body, held her pent-up longing to throw her arms around him. He took the fan from the crone and bowed. "For you, my dear one," he murmured, outlining Pippa's face with purple feathers made beautiful by the skin they touched. "Do not cry, love. Please, or I shall be undone, and *we* shall be undone."

She shook her head and smiled—and the unshed tears glittered in her dark blue eyes. "Thank you, sir. I shall treasure this gift." She took the fan and gave him his coat in exchange. "I wish we were . . . I wish things were different."

"As do I. Come, let us see what else this madness has to offer." He could not bear to part from her now. If an opportunity presented itself, he could be subtle in his questions.

They strolled from stall to stall. Pippa did not like to see the animals perform. She did not like to see children pressed into service as beggars and cajolers. He watched expressions pass over her clever, lovely face and began to feel he would surely die if he could not make her his own.

"Look," Pippa said, engrossed in the scene. "Such a small child to be about at this hour and in this company."

Calum looked. At first he saw nothing but the weaving people. Then he knew what she'd spoken of.

A child, apparently a boy of four or five, in a concoction of colored rags, made his way around one of the fires. In his hands he carried an iron pan by its handle.

"Begging," Pippa said. "How does such a little one survive?"

"He survives," Calum said automatically and went closer, reaching into a pocket for change.

"Fine show, ladies and gen'lemen," the child said in a high voice. "Help the fine show." He shook the pan and Calum saw that it was too heavy for the thin wrists that bore it.

He no longer heard Pippa's words. Moving forward, he tossed a gold coin into the pan.

The little urchin bent over the pan in an almost comical manner. Slowly, his black-eyed face came up. "Thank-ee," he whispered. "I never seed one o' them in me pan."

Calum smiled silently.

Nearby, the fire crackled.

Voices rose and fell.

"A fine show," the child caroled.

Colored cloth. Stars in dark skies. Fires.

Pictures from the past mingled with pictures from this night.

The scent of smoke and the crackle of sparks. Costumes that swirled, red and yellow and gold.

Clinking sounds came from close by. A girl danced in a costume sprinkled with glass beads, her hands weaving above her head, the beads tapping together.

Coins on headdresses. And coins that clinked against metal in the pan he held. "You are young to be so sure of yourself, my boy."

"See the show," the child in front of Calum said.

"See how he holds himself? Like a prince strutting among his subjects rather than a beggar-boy among his betters."

"Calum," Pippa said, startling him, "are you unwell?"

"No, no." He managed to smile at her.

"Fine show, sir," the little boy said, clearly still amazed by his golden prize. "See the snake man and his lovely lady assistant."

The beating of Calum's heart ceased.

"Come," Pippa insisted. "We should not care for such a display."

He took her hand and tucked it through the crook of his elbow. "A small look and we'll move on. Experiences are broadening."

The sound of silver bells had eluded him until now. Making a path for himself and Pippa, he found a place where they could watch as a weathered, brown-skinned man shook little bells attached to his fingers and marched in a commanding circle around the spectacle that held the onlookers in thrall.

"Calum," Pippa whispered urgently, "surely this is dangerous."

"No," he told her. "Not dangerous at all."

He did not explain that the snakes winding their way about the lovely body of a scantily dressed woman could no longer deliver poison to an enemy.

"Be still!" the brown man commanded, his jutting brows shooting up. The bells at his fingertips made a sound that was at odds with the threatening glide of the vipers' sinuous bodies over their human host.

"She is not afraid," Calum said of the woman whose mouth gaped with apparent horror as a snake drew back its head only inches from her face. "She has no reason to be afraid. It is all an act."

"A horrible act."

"I can't do this again. I can't, I tell you. You'll have to find someone else."

The new voice, female and tired, had not come to Calum's memory before.

"We've got no choice. You didn't ask enough gold for your efforts. Thanks to your foolishness, we've got another mouth to feed."

A man's voice now. Familiar. More familiar than the woman's. And they'd been speaking about him.

"Please, can we go now? It's over."

Calum glanced down at Pippa. "Please be patient. There is something I must do here."

She nodded and stood close beside him as the act ended and the crowd drifted on in search of fresh entertainment.

The snakes were peeled from the woman and dropped into baskets. Calum looked hard at the snake man's assistant and silently cursed himself for his own stupidity. For a few moments he'd expected to recognize someone from his childhood. The snake man's assistant was young, not more than eighteen. The Rachel he sought would be . . . she would be approaching at least her fiftieth year. Not that he had any recollection of her features or form.

"Calum."

"Be patient, I beg you," he told Pippa, waiting, although he knew not for what.

The snake man divested himself of his bells, tucking them into trouser pockets. Then he looked up, looked at Calum and frowned. "Another show in an hour, your lordship," he said, bending his head a little to peer through darting light from the fire.

"May I speak with you?" Calum asked.

Pippa's hand gripped his arm tightly.

Smoothing his hands on his full-sleeved yellow shirt, the brown man came cautiously nearer. "What do you want with me?"

The assistant called to the boy with the pan and they departed between two wagons.

"I must go," the man said.

Calum looked into the face that had seen many winters and summers on the land, many travels by cart through weather most would hide from, and saw the features as they had once been.

"Calum?"

"Be patient." He covered Pippa's hand on his arm. "Do

you remember me?'' he asked the snake man. ''Am I familiar?''

''Why should you be?'' Another step brought them within feet of each other. ''Why . . .'' The man's dark eyes grew unblinking and piercing.

''Your name, sir?'' Calum asked.

''Yours?'' was the response.

''Calum.'' He breathed in with difficulty. ''Calum Innes.''

If it were possible, skin as brown as saddle leather grew paler. ''I am Guido. We have never met.''

''Guido?'' Was the name familiar? ''*Do* you know me?''

''Why should the likes of me know the likes of you?'' Guido backed slowly away, but Calum followed. ''What is your business with me?''

''I need your help,'' Calum said. ''Please. You have no need to fear me. Only tell me if you see something in me that reminds you of a child you once knew.''

Guido stood still and his lips parted. Suddenly he looked right and left. ''Your mind is unbalanced, sir. You are not yourself.''

''Am I not? That is not your concern, is it? I asked you a question and I think I have my answer. We met before, didn't we? You knew a small boy, much like the one who works for you now. That other boy was brought to you by Rachel.''

Alarm flashed so instantly in Guido's eyes, and in the tense set of his body, that Calum felt a rush of triumph. ''Help me. I came to you first in this place. Many years since. I could not help myself then and you would not help me. Change that now.''

''Get away,'' the man hissed. ''You are wrong, I tell you. Wrong.''

''I am *right*, and I will follow you until you admit as much.''

''I told her we would suffer,'' Guido moaned. Then he seemed to collect himself. ''I don't know what you're talking about.''

''You do. You've admitted as much.''

''I've admitted nothing. If you had proof, you wouldn't be here this night.''

''I shall not cease to persecute you until I have my proof,''

Calum said. "I shall follow you for the rest of your life if I have to."

The man swept his arms wide in a gesture of defeat. "I am innocent, I tell you. Ask *her*."

Triumph became a burning thing in Calum's breast. "Only tell me where I may find her, and I'll gladly ask."

Guido wiped a sleeve over his sweating face. "She's gone," he said.

Calum's gut curled sickeningly. "You just said I should ask her."

"I am muddled. The one you seek is no more. Go to the fortune teller." He pointed an unexpectedly elegant hand into an aisle lined with tents and stalls. "Go to Sybel and ask what she can tell you. Tell her I sent you."

Calum snorted and shook his head. "It is not my future I seek here, friend."

"Go to her, I tell you," Guido said, backing away. "She who tells the future must also know the past. First she must determine where you came from, or she cannot tell you where you are going."

Pippa was frightened. For Calum and for herself. The man who stood beside her, his face stark, was a man suffering in some place where she could not reach him.

She shook him gently. "The fortune teller must be this way," she said, trying to pull him along.

"You should not be here," he said, sounding as if he were barely aware of her. "Where I have to go you cannot come. I will return you to the castle."

"But I will not go," she told him, planting her feet apart on the sawdust-strewn ground. "You are not ready to tell me what this is all about and I shall not ask. But I will go to that fortune teller and you will come with me."

"No."

"You want to."

"My God!" He turned his face up to the night sky and shut his eyes. "You cannot know what I want or do not want. I want *peace*."

She felt full to bursting with a desire to press him for explanations. "Humor me, Calum, and in return, I shall ask you nothing. Come to the fortune teller. Now."

Like a man exhausted from hard labor, he let his head fall forward. He said not a word, but set off in the direction the snake man had indicated. On the way they were often stopped by capering revelers who made lewd gibes and demands. Calum seemed to notice none of them.

Once, Pippa caught sight of the duke, but he appeared drunk and absorbed on the one hand with Lady Hoarville and on the other by Henri St. Luc. Of Sable or Max there was no sign.

"Here," a husky voice said from the shadowy entrance to a small tent. "Here, Calum Innes. Guido has told me you need my services."

Pippa looked at him. "This is the place."

"You cannot come with me," he said.

"I cannot remain out here alone," she reminded him.

He appeared to give up the argument. Holding her around the waist, he entered the tent.

A woman dressed from head to foot in dark green silk seated herself behind a small table. She raised her veiled face and indicated for Calum to sit in a chair facing her.

When Calum paused, Pippa urged him forward, waited for him to sit down and stood at his shoulder.

"You may call me Sybel," the woman said. From the narrow space between the draping shawl over her head and the veil stared eyes as black as any Pippa had ever seen. Eyes that were both young and incredibly old. "Move closer where I can see you," Sybel instructed Calum.

He hesitated, but did as she asked. "I am looking for Rachel," he told her. "Do you know of her?"

Rather than answer, Sybel leaned across her table with its litter of cards and stones and crystal beads. She placed her hands flat upon the surface and stared at Calum. "You are a handsome man," she said. "Life has treated you well. You are not at peace, but you have accomplished much. That is as it should be."

"Rachel?" he repeated.

"There is no point in concerning yourself with Rachel." So quickly that Pippa didn't have time to flinch, the fortune teller touched Calum's face, smoothed his high cheekbones and sharp jaw, ran a single finger the length of his straight nose. Then she drew his head toward her and rested her brow against his. She stroked his hair and said, very low, "Let go of the past."

His sigh made Pippa hold her throat.

"I cannot let go," he said. "You do not understand what is at stake. I must find Rachel. I thought I had found help with Milo and Miranda, who sold remedies, but they have disappeared."

Sybel's hands stilled in Calum's hair. "What you seek is dangerous."

He raised his face, pulling away from her. "If you know that, you can help me."

She lowered her lashes and took both of his hands in hers. "I am assuming things I do *not* know. Let me see your palms."

He turned his hands over.

Sybel supported them in her own and Pippa heard the woman moan, very low. "You use both of your hands as most men use only one," she said.

"Yes."

With a single finger she traced a wide, shiny scar on his left palm. "This destroys the lines."

"It does not destroy my fortune," he said. "I do not know how it happened."

"When you were very young," she said tonelessly.

"It was always there. I was abandoned in Scotland. I was very sick and needed care and I was left at Kirkcaldy Castle. They cared for me there. They have always cared for me."

"Fire," Sybel said under her breath.

Pippa put her hand on Calum's shoulder and felt tension coiled in his rigid muscles.

"*Fire*," Sybel repeated.

"Fire!" Calum leaped up, all but overturning the table. "The handle of the pot had been heated by the fire and I picked it up."

"I must go," Sybel said. "What you know, you know. Do not press for more. There can be no changing what has happened."

"It must be changed, I tell you," Calum said, advancing on the woman.

Sybel held up a warning hand. "I am tired. I must sleep. Leave me now and do not return."

"Tell me what happened," he said. "Tell me how I came to the fair and why. Tell me who commanded that my life be stolen and given to another. I will not rest until I know."

"What you want, you cannot have," Sybel said. "Accept the life you have, Calum Innes. If you will not let the past die, it will kill you."

The revelers at the fair had grown fewer in number. When Calum escorted Pippa to the place where the carriages had been left, he found that the duke's had already returned to the castle. The remaining coachman, showing signs of having enjoyed a jug or two of the strong ale offered from leather bladders at the fair, gave a rambling account of his master's departure "with his fine friends."

The man, bleary-eyed and focusing with difficulty on Calum and Pippa, recalled that Lord Avenall had left much earlier with the boy.

"Stay here," Calum told the coachman. "It's a fine night and we find we are not tired. We'll walk a while. Await our return."

Pippa didn't wait long before swinging to face him. "I cannot be silent any longer," she said, her face white in the thin moonlight. "There is so much you have not told me, I am afraid to know it all."

"You need know none of it," he said, sidestepping her and going to lean on a fence overlooking a dark field.

She came behind him and rested against his back.

At the soft pressure of her body, he closed his eyes. "I should never have allowed you to be with me tonight."

"It was for this that you came to Cornwall," she said, rubbing his arms. "You made my acquaintance, then Franchot's. You made certain there was reason for him to call you out. How did you intend to make certain he asked you here? What if he had killed you?"

"I did not plan for him to call me out. I did not plan to go this . . . I did not plan all this."

"You did not plan to go this *far*? Was that what you almost said? But you have gone far, Calum. And now you do not wish to turn back. Am I right?"

She was too clever, his little betrothed who did not know she was rightfully his. "You are right. But I cannot explain further."

"You must."

"No. I must not." He caught her hand and took it to his lips. "If you've a mind, you can reveal what you've witnessed tonight."

"To the duke?"

"Who else?"

"I would tell him nothing. But why . . . Calum, please tell me what is happening."

"When I can, I will." If only he could truly believe that day would come.

"You are not the man you present yourself to be."

He held his breath.

"How could I not guess as much after what I have heard and seen tonight?"

Calum turned to face her. "Would you help me if you could?"

"You know I would. I will," she said without hesitation.

"Then help me by trusting me and asking me no more questions." She knew too much. "Will you show me the way to your hideaway as soon as possible?"

"Why? I have not even been able to return there since that first day."

"You believe it is truly secret? No one knows it is there?"

"No one does."

"I may need a place to hide. A place where I can still watch what goes on at the castle. If that time comes, I will ask you to be my eyes, Pippa."

"Calum—"

"Please, my love. Say you will do this, and then I will pray we need never resort to such measures."

She went into his arms and held him. "I will help you in anything. Only please tell me what is happening."

He must appease her and make certain she would remain silent, for the sake of her safety—and for his own.

"Pippa," he said, lifting her chin, "you are right. I am not who you thought I was. But I cannot tell you more now and I may never be able to tell you."

"Did someone here do something to you when you were a child? You've said you were born in Cornwall."

"We will return to the castle," he told her. "Remember only what the fortune teller said. If I do not let go of the past, it may kill me."

"She said," Pippa whispered, "that it *would* kill you."

❧ Twenty-Two

Saber strained to hear any sound of footsteps on the stairs. He'd been wrong to tell Max to send Ella to him. He should pray she had the sense not to come. And if she did come, he must remember she was scarcely more than a child.

The space beneath the stairs in the wing that housed the nurseries was dark, and he could not see to read his watch. Surely an hour or more had passed since Max ran upward with Saber's message.

There was something in Ella, something he felt, that made him want to protect her. In the blackness, he pressed a fist into a rough stone wall and swore a silent pledge that he would do no more than offer her his friendship—and he felt with his heart that she needed that more than anything else he might offer.

And he would wait until she was of an age for him to pursue her in quite another manner.

A year, two?

A lifetime.

Soft scratchings sounded, then stopped, then came again.

Saber leaned out from his hiding place and narrowed his eyes to see.

A blue-white shape drifted down the staircase, stopping from time to time until it hovered just above him.

"Ella?" he whispered, knowing his own indiscretion.

"Yes."

He didn't know what to say.

"Max told me you wanted to see me."

"I was wrong to ask you to take this risk."

She descended further and with her came the scent of meadow flowers that seemed part of her. "I wanted to come," she said, stepping to the floor in the small hallway. "I 'ad—I had looked forward to seeing you at the fair."

"Then why did you come back to the castle?"

Rather than answer, she touched his arm.

Saber stood quite still. That simple touch was as if she had smote at something deep within him.

Her fingers felt their way until she could slip them into his hand.

She held onto him like a trusting child. She *was* a child. And he could be trusted with her.

"Who watches over you here?" he asked.

"The maids take turns," Ella said. "But they sleep in a room separated from mine by a cupboard where clothes 'ang—hang. They never come to check on me before morning."

He would not think of how many hours there might be until morning. "I wanted only to know that you are well and safe."

"I am," she told him.

Saber found that he held her hand very tightly, but could not make himself release her. "Should you care to come into the air outside? I have my cloak and it is pleasant enough."

"I'd like that."

And he should not take her from safety in the middle of the night.

He swung his cloak around her shoulders—and held her hand once more.

The nearby door opened into a small, walled courtyard where roses grew in heady, flamboyant profusion. Saber led Ella to a stone bench and seated her. The moon afforded him a shaded view of her astonishing face.

She was a child and he must wait.

"Why didn't you stay at the fair?"

"Thank you for caring about me. I'm . . . Lady Philipa is teaching me to speak like a lady."

He bowed his head. "To me you are a lady. You will al-

ways be a lady. Do not concern yourself with silly conven-
tions. Soon no one will ever know you were not born a
princess, at the very least.''

She giggled a little at that.

A child. "Think of me as the older brother you do not
have,'' he said, trying not to clench his teeth. Less than eight
years separated them, but they were years that made him a
man with a man's urges. "I do not know the exact nature of
what your childhood has been, but I have felt sadness in you.
Your father isn't here, and in his absence I would like to help
if I can.''

"I trust you!'' Her voice caught.

"Hush,'' he warned. "We must not be discovered.''

"I wish I could tell someone all about us—Max and me.
And I wish I wouldn't have to worry that if I did, we'd be
sent packing from 'ere—here—at once.''

"Whether you tell me or not, I shall protect you. If anyone
troubles you, you are to come to me directly. Do you understand?''

"Yes,'' she said quietly.

With her head bowed, her hair shone blue-black. Hair restrained in childish braids.

Saber braced a foot beside her on the bench and rested his
hand on top of her head. "There. I've said what I came to
say. I'll watch while you return to your chamber.''

"My mother was not married to my father.''

Saber frowned. "Viscount Hunsingore—''

"He's not our father. He took us away from London when
we were in terrible trouble.''

"I see.'' He did not see at all.

"Max and me—we're bastards.''

Saber smiled wryly in the darkness. "That is not so shocking, little one.''

"I don't know who my father is. When Max and I were
younger, we were kept by a family with a provisioner's business. Our mother paid them and we worked. But they were
kind enough and we were safe.''

He opened his mouth to say she did not need to tell him
this, but decided he must be the listener she craved. "I'm glad
they treated you well,'' he said.

"Then our mother got sick. She didn't have the money to pay for our keep, so she took me to live with her. Max was sent somewhere else. I didn't know where he was for a long time. First we traveled around a lot, till my mother was too sick to travel anymore. Then we went to London, and . . ." She made a noise that was a muffled sob.

Saber stroked her hair and the back of her slender neck. "It's all right now. You'll never have to be unhappy again."

"In London I was kept with my mother to help pay for what we needed. I found out poor Max was with an 'orri—a horrible man in Covent Garden who sent boys and girls out to pick pockets. If the viscount hadn't been a kind man, Max would still be there, and I don't know what would have happened to him."

"Then I'm grateful to the viscount," Saber said. "But what of you? How did you live?"

He felt her shudder beneath his hand. "In a house," she muttered, so softly he had to strain to hear. "In a house with my mother."

"Your mother's house?"

Ella wrapped the cloak tightly about her. "No. It belongs to someone else what—who runs—who runs a business there. I had to do what I was told."

With an effort, Saber stopped himself from taking his hand from the girl's neck. "I see," he said. God, he was so cold. He was cold to his bones—to his heart.

"I wanted to get away. Every night I 'oped—hoped I'd find a way to escape. Then the viscount came, and now there's a chance for Max and me."

A chance to turn from a life of prostitution and crime.

She was only a child, Saber intoned within his soul. A wronged child. He had offered to be a brother and he would not turn back from that. "Come, little one," he told her. "Let's return you to your bed before someone misses you."

Shivering, she went with him back inside the castle. At the bottom of the stairs, she removed his cloak and gave it to him. "Thank you," she said. "I thought all men were monsters. Now I know the viscount . . . You mustn't let on that he's not our papa!"

"I'll never—*let on*."

"I know you won't. I know the viscount and Calum and now there's *you*. There are good men, aren't there?"

"Yes, there are good men."

"My mother always said there weren't—except for her brother. He was all right, but he only cared about my mother. They've stayed together forever. When I traveled with them, they taught me to help them."

"Help them do what?" Saber couldn't stop himself from asking.

"Make potions that cure people's ills."

When he'd finally secured Cloudsmoor and dispatched his dear sister and grandmother to live in the house there, he'd be free to carry on the activities that satisfied him most in the comfort of his own rooms.

Etienne staggered a little as he approached his apartments and paused, leaning against the wall, while he waited for his head to clear.

Creeping around, visiting Henri and Anabel in places where they would not be discovered, was becoming a bloody bore.

He rolled to rest his back against the wall. He felt weak, drained. Grinning, swaying, he let himself into the small sitting room off his bedchamber. He *was* drained. Anabel and Henri had taken every ounce of the juices he'd poured forth for them for hours.

And they'd enjoyed the taking.

And he'd relished the giving.

And they would play again on the morrow, when they would devise fresh entertainments. At the fair, a young girl from the village had been offered to him by her father. Yes, he'd have to consider that offer very seriously and soon—by the morrow.

Damn these people who meddled in his pleasures. He should be in his bed with his faithful friends, not falling about, awaiting the ministrations of his damnable man who was nowhere around.

Etienne screwed up his eyes.

No. Nowhere about.

"Belcher!"

Not a sign of the lazy bounder.

"*Belcher*!"

"Belcher is not here, Etienne." A tall, dark-haired man rose from a wing chair near the fire. The back of the chair faced Etienne, which accounted for his not having noted that he had a visitor. Perhaps he was about to be offered another little virgin.

"I say," he said. "Bit late for visitors, ain't it? Or is it a bit early?" He giggled at his own jest.

"There would never be a good time for this visit," the man said. His voice scratched and Etienne decided he did not like it at all. Not at all. This was not a fellow of any culture.

"You'd best seat yourself," the man said. "You'll soon find your legs a deal less strong. Not that they're strong now, by the looks of things."

"The devil you say." Etienne made careful steps across the Aubusson carpets and fell into the leather chair behind his writing table. Position of authority. Table between the nobleman and the serf. Impertinent, vulgar peasant. "State your business here and get out. Where's Belcher?"

"Belcher was told you would not need him tonight," the man said. "You wouldn't want him to be here for our little talk."

"Don't wish to talk with you."

The man was exceedingly tall. His black hair was straight, overlong and dull, and his sharp silvery eyes hid beneath the hairless, jutting bones of his brow. "It's time for you to pay your accounts, *Your Grace*," he said, resting big-knuckled hands on the writing table.

A shred of clearheadedness threatened Etienne's warm haze. "Accounts?" He sat straighter. "I don't know what you're talking about. Who sent you?"

"Someone who knew you'd be willing to pay handsomely for the information I can give you. And for my silence."

Etienne gripped the edge of the table. Sweat broke out on his brow. He must keep calm. This could be any sort of foolery. Nonchalance would win out over this oaf. "Get out," he said, as imperiously as his thick tongue allowed.

"Get out?" The man's thin lips parted in a grin that sent deep lines into his sunken cheeks. "You wouldn't want me to do that. I might tell someone else what I know about you.

There's someone else as would pay a great deal for the information, and then *you'd* have nothing left to pay anything with.''

Etienne blinked to clear his vision. There was something about the man . . . Yes, he'd seen this creature before. "Where do I know you from?" he demanded.

"You don't know me at all. But then, maybe you know me very well. Who can tell? The answer depends on what you mean by knowing."

"I'm in no mood for riddles." Etienne swallowed bile, but the drink's effect was waning. "Speak your piece."

"I want half of everything you own," the man said. "I've chosen an estate north of Cloudsmoor. From there I can be certain you never forget to provide my portion."

Etienne stiffened, then collapsed back in his chair. He laughed, wiped the back of a hand over his mouth and laughed again. "A madman. *Belcher*! By God, I'll have his hide for sleeping when I need him."

"Miranda is ill," the man said. He stood and walked around to sit on the edge of the table—close to Etienne. "You do remember Miranda? Milo's sister?"

Etienne swallowed. He was sober now. "No," he said. "I have no idea what you're talking about."

"I thought you would remember," the man said. "Miranda can't work. I'm going to have to look after her. Make sure she's in a safe place where she won't be tempted to tell what she knows in order to get the money she and Milo need to live."

The horror that had haunted him since his wretched . . . This horror had haunted him since the appearance of the wretched woman who had told him she was his mother. He had never ceased to fear that someone, somehow, knew about him and would come to torture him.

"Miranda knows all about you, but that doesn't surprise Your Grace too much, does it?"

Etienne stared unseeingly ahead.

"You did guess it could be true. Cora Bains, Lady Hoarville's mother, knew, and she was friendly with Miranda."

He could try to reach a weapon.

"Your own dear mother told Cora, and Cora told Miranda.

Such a pity. Florence always was such a chatterer.''

"*Don't* mention that woman's name!''

"Florence Hawkins,'' the man said casually. "A beautiful creature when she was young. So sad the way she died. And right after you'd been so kind as to arrange another meeting with her. A fever, the doctor said. Cora said it was poison and so did Miranda, but who would listen to them? Must have been a shock, finding out you were a whore's bastard son.''

"No!'' Etienne clawed at the nearest drawer, where a slim steel knife lay. He found the drawer handle and pulled.

A big, hard hand closed over his and clamped it atop the table. "A whore's bastard son, placed in an infant duke's cradle because the whore hated the infant duke's father and intended to get her hands on what was his. Through you. Clever of her, wasn't it?''

Etienne panted and felt spittle bubble from the corner of his mouth.

"Too bad she told you everyone who'd known was dead—except her. Silly, that. Thinking that when she told you she was your mother, you'd keep her safe. You killed her for it. But the snake man's assistant wasn't the only one who knew she had taken the duke's rightful heir and left you in his place. She was gone, all right, but not Cora and not Miranda.''

"Cora's dead now.'' Etienne whimpered.

"We'll not speak about that. Miranda's not dead and neither am I, and you'll pay for our silence.''

"I'll kill you both.''

The man laughed, and it was a sound that made Etienne cast up his accounts.

When he'd finished soiling his clothes and the polished desk and the Aubusson carpets, he peered up into the impassive face above him. "I'll kill you both.''

"No, you won't,'' the man said. "Because we have taken precautions. *I* have taken precautions. You'd do well to watch the Hoarville bitch. She may become a problem.''

Anabel? Anabel must never know what had happened here tonight. "I can deal with Anabel,'' he said, scarcely able to draw a breath. He fumbled for a kerchief and pressed it to his bitter-tasting lips.

"Listen to me and listen well. You have something else to

deal with. When it is done, I'll return to make the rest of our arrangements.''

The man stood and Etienne's burning eyes followed the unfolding of the tall, thin body.

"Innes," the man said. "You must dispose of him. And of his friend if he knows."

"Knows what?" Etienne asked. "Chauncey? Is Innes Chauncey's man?"

For a moment there was question in the man's small, light-colored eyes. "Chauncey? Forget Chauncey, you fool. There's no problem there. Innes is your problem."

"Because he's sniffing around after my fiancée? He'll never manage—''

"Shut up! And listen to me. You will deal with Innes before he deals with you."

"I'll tell him to leave and that'll be an end of it."

The lipless mouth pressed briefly shut. "You will kill him, and *that* will be an end of it. You will kill the rightful Duke of Franchot."

"The . . ." Etienne's tongue refused to make any more words.

"He is the man who should sit where you sit, *bastard*. Move carefully. Take enough time to ensure there is no other witness against us; then *do* it."

Etienne could only nod.

"I'll leave you now. But I'll never be far away."

"Your name?" Etienne choked out, tearing at his already loosened shirt. "Tell me your name and where I may find you."

"I shall find you. My name is of no interest. Think of me simply as your *father*.''

❧ Twenty-Three

Autumn. Pippa felt its impatient sting at the edge of the morning's scant warmth.

Her imagination only. August was yet with them.

Mist rose from the lawns like a drifting sheet of muslin. Pippa was glad of the light cloak she'd thrown on before coming in search of Calum. She felt autumn. And with autumn would come her wedding.

He had not eaten breakfast, so the dour servant in attendance revealed. And Max, who always knew where Calum was, did not know this morning.

There he came, head down, walking slowly up flights of steps between the castle's terraced gardens.

Pippa hugged the cloak of fine gray wool closer. Anyone looking from this side of the castle would see them clearly. No sign of the urgency she felt must be visible.

But her feet moved as if she could not stop them. Down, down, down.

Calum raised his face, saw her and stopped climbing.

And she was close enough to see desolation in his eyes.

"*She said it would kill you.*" Her own words of the previous night echoed.

He smiled, but it was a poor attempt.

"Good morning, Calum," she said, taking the final steps that brought her to his side. "I should like to hold you very close in my arms, dear friend."

296

His expression changed slowly, as if her words were not immediately clear to him. "You would do well not to risk sentiments like those where they may be heard, my lady."

Anger flared in her breast. "Who will hear?" She looked around. "I should like to kiss you and have you kiss me. I should like to lie with you on the mist upon this very grass."

"We can be clearly seen from the castle."

"We cannot be clearly *heard* from the castle. I wish I need never again leave your arms. Without you, I am not even half of myself."

"My God, Pippa." He turned his face from her. "You do not know what you're saying. Go back."

"Go back!" Her eyes stung, but the tears that threatened were born as much of fury as of hurt. "What can you be saying? Go *back*?"

He faced her once more, the lines of his face stark, his dark eyes glittering. "Yes, go back. I want to hold you, too, you little fool. I want to lie with you here on this grass and never let you go from me again. Without you, *I* am not even half of myself."

The tears overflowed and she reached for him.

Calum stepped back. "Don't. We can be seen, I tell you."

"Let them see us. Let them all see us. Calum, you sought me out. For whatever reason, you followed me here and *you have* pursued me. Yet now you try to hold me at a distance."

"Yes!" he cried, hanging back his head. He drove his hands into his pockets and stared at the sky. "I hold you at a distance because I'm afraid I may destroy you."

"I don't—"

"You don't have to understand more than you do." He looked at her and the passion in his eyes tore at her. "I want it *all*. And no, you do not understand me. I want everything. And in taking everything, I might consume your very body, your spirit. Stay away from me before I destroy you."

Etienne stood close to green damask draperies drawn back from the windows in a tiny salon beneath the bell tower. From here he had an excellent view of the terraced gardens.

"What are they doing now?" Anabel asked.

"They are mooning over each other," he told her, careful to keep himself in the cover of the draperies.

Anabel, in rustling peach-colored satin, paced green silk carpets before a fire in the exquisite little Italian-tiled fireplace.

Etienne looked at the woman from whom there might be no escape—ever—and felt rage at his plight.

He'd told her of the night's travesty. There had seemed no choice. He needed an accomplice, someone to advise and assist him, and there was no one else. She had promised that his confidence would remain between them, that even Henri would never hear the horrible truth.

"Now?" she demanded, twining her fingers together. "What are they doing now?"

"Parting, I believe," he told her. "What shall we do?"

"We shall make certain they do not succeed in their plot against us," Anabel said. "They are in it together. I had always suspected as much. I don't care what your—what that man said. Chauncey is somewhere behind this. He discovered there was some doubt about your identity and came up with this Innes. Innes persuaded Miranda he is the duke, and she told *him*."

"They are certain. If you are right, that means Chauncey is also certain and will expose me. He—that man said I must dispose of Innes before he tells the world I am an imposter."

Anabel took up a delicate crystal dish and squeezed its pedestal in one fist. "If Calum Innes had enough proof to make his claim, he would already have made it. He does not have that proof."

"What if he gets it?"

"Are they parting?"

"Yes. She is returning to the castle. He is walking downward once more."

"Good. Lady Philipa has misused you. Now *we* shall use her. It must be as I have always told you. The two of them will die together."

The idea found new merit with Etienne. He had already made a private pact to marry Philipa rapidly and in secret to ensure there could be no impediment to his gaining Cloudsmoor. Perhaps Anabel's plan would be preferable after all.

"Do you understand me?" she asked.

He nodded slowly.

"Answer me," she shouted.

He detested her common, strident voice—a legacy from her coarse mother. "Yes," he agreed. "We must be cautious."

"We must do what I say we must do." With that she smashed the priceless Ravenscroft dish against the hearth. "Listen well. And do as you are told."

Pippa, her throat so raw she felt she might never swallow again, entered the castle by a little-used door in the west wing. Almost no one came this way, and she had learned how to come and go to her apartments in relative privacy.

He had told her to leave him—to leave him forever.

Calum did not want them to part, she was certain he did not. But he was afraid of something and he would not let her help him. She smiled bitterly. He was a man. It would never occur to him that she *could* help him.

"Pippa." She heard her name and saw the duke at the same moment. "I have been desperately searching for you, my dear. Please, we must talk."

She opened her mouth to tell him she never, ever wanted to talk to him about anything. Some shred of prudence stilled her tongue. "Good morning, Franchot. I trust you enjoyed the fair last night."

Some odd expression . . . *sadness*? . . . entered his face. "I have been very remiss in my treatment of you. I see that now and I hope you will allow me to make amends before we become husband and wife."

Pippa felt her eyes widen.

"I can see you are not moved to take my declaration seriously," he continued. "And I cannot blame you. But I throw myself upon your charitable spirit—and my dear sister has told me how very charitable you are. Please, may we be friends, my dearest?"

Pippa's stomach rolled unpleasantly. "Friendship is always so much more agreeable than the alternative," she told him, making to pass by. "It is a pleasant morning, Your Grace. I'm certain you would enjoy a stroll."

"I do not want a stroll," he snapped, before his smile spread once more. "Forgive me. This is not easy, this confession. I am a proud man and it has been a fault that has not served me well. Will you come and sit with me on the window seat here? We can look out at your pleasant morning while I tell you what concerns me.''

There seemed no choice but to do as he asked. The window he indicated made a half circle. Worn tapestry covered the seat cushions.

When she was settled, Franchot sat also—facing her and closer than made her comfortable. In the harsh light of morning, she saw the web of red veins that held the whites of his eyes and she could not help but smell stale drink on his breath.

He cleared his throat and smiled engagingly. ''We have not at all had a good beginning. Perhaps it did not help that so much was assumed from the very time of your birth. A man needs something to conquer, and you were already mine. No chase, don't you see?''

She breathed in slowly through her nose.

''My loss, of course. Should have noticed what a prize you were. I'd like to make amends, er, Philipa. Could we begin by having you call me Etienne?''

Something was wrong here. She was not such a fool as to believe he'd had so great a change of heart.

''Want to apologize for that little . . . Well, there was the time I pushed you somewhat. Poor form. Regret it. Can we put it behind us?''

''We can try,'' she said, longing to escape.

''Good, good!'' He positively grinned and reached to pat her hands in her lap. ''Now to the part that's not so pleasant. I've heard something very troublesome about our friend Innes.''

Pippa swallowed.

''I can see that troubles you. You like him. Don't blame you for that. I do myself. Or I did. He's a bounder, Philipa. Word has it he boasted in London about hating me and intending to cripple me financially.''

She found her tongue. ''That's outrageous. How would he do such a thing?''

Franchot pursed his lips and spread his hands on his thighs. ''At first it was thought he intended to trick you into marriage to get his hands on Cloudsmoor. Would mean he'd be able to charge me anything he liked to get Franchot tin to market. Did he suggest anything like that? Trust me now and be honest. I shan't hold it against you."

"No," she said automatically. "Of course not." That Franchot needed her dowry was no mystery. He'd be bound to feel threatened by any competition for her hand.

He sighed and shook his head. "Almost wish you'd said yes."

She frowned at him. "Why?"

"Because that would make the worse charge less likely."

"The worse charge?"

"Fantastic, my dear," Franchot said. "Absolutely fantastic, but I fear it's true. Innes is deluded. He plans to have you because he thinks you belong to him by right."

"But—" No, she must not be tricked. "That is more ridiculous than fantastic, Franchot."

"Call me Etienne, I beg you. It is absolutely factual. I'm now convinced that what I've been told is the truth."

Pippa edged away a little. "Then please don't keep me in suspense a moment longer. Share this truth with me."

"He believes that he is the rightful Duke of Franchot."

❧ Twenty-Four

*W*omen *were* contrary.

They were a damnable nuisance.

A man should avoid, at all costs, allowing a woman to ensnare any part of his body or mind.

"Damn it all," Calum said, hovering in the entrance to the minstrel's gallery Pippa would have to pass when she left her apartments. "Did she have to take me so literally?"

A door opened and he drew back into the gallery. Holding his breath, he waited for the sound of footsteps. They came and he timed his appearance with their approach to the gallery.

"Good afternoon . . ." Nelly Bumstead came to a halt, a heavy water jug in her hands, a startled expression in her open face. "Good afternoon, Nelly," Calum said, smiling and clasping his hands behind him as he turned to walk further into the gallery and look down over the elegantly proportioned vestibule below.

He heard Nelly's muttered "Good afternoon, sir" before she bustled away.

That female who had wormed a way into his brain was making a damn fool of him. And he needed her. He needed her at once. Well, Justine was playing the piano in one of the rooms on the floor below. Pippa would be alone now, so he'd just play her silly game and go groveling to her. Well . . . not that, exactly.

He left the gallery and clamped a hand over his heart. Pippa, dressed in a russet-colored riding habit and a beguiling brown velvet bonnet, was closing her door. She saw him and for an instant seemed about to return to her apartments.

"Pippa," he whispered urgently. "I must talk to you."

She let her hand fall from the door handle and walked slowly toward him. "I thought you told me to stay away from you. Wasn't the word 'destroy' used? Or did I imagine that?"

"Please. This is no time for recriminations. I was deeply troubled."

"And you aren't deeply troubled anymore."

"I've been deeply troubled for five days," he said before caution could stop him. "That is the length of time during which you have avoided me."

"As I've just told you, I felt I had to abide by your wishes."

"Well, I've changed my mind. Remember I told you I might need your hideaway?"

She grimaced. "My hideaway where I get no chance to hide?"

"The same. How far is it?"

"Not so far. An hour on a good horse."

Relief made him sag. "Exactly what I need. Will you come with me to meet Struan? I believe it's important that I have help near at hand, but not too near. I should like you to allow me to take him to your cabin. Will you agree?"

"Why?"

"There is no time to explain. Only believe that I would never do anything to harm you."

She caught her lower lip between her teeth and he saw her struggle with her decision before she said, "I do believe you cast some spell over me, Calum Innes. You keep casting that spell. Come, you say, and I come. Go, and I go. And now it is come again. And, *yes*—I will come."

They left the stables separately and by the back path Calum had used on the morning the fair had arrived. Once past the castle walls, the route agreed upon took them north, toward the highway winding between Chauncey and Franchot lands.

Pippa, after managing to gather some food, had left last but easily found Calum in the appointed copse of birches on a knoll where they could see the highway without being seen from any direction.

Already the light had begun to fail.

"You will have to stay close behind me," Pippa told Calum, who held a second horse by a leading rein. "I know the way well, but it is narrow in places."

"We'll follow well enough," he said.

Hatless and minus a neckcloth, he wore the collar of his shirt open beneath a dark coat. Pippa found herself fascinated by the black hair that showed on his chest.

"What holds your attention?" Calum asked. "Are you shocked that I'd come to you without a neckcloth?"

"I wish you need never wear a neckcloth."

Silence swelled between them.

"You are impetuous, lady."

"I know."

"Your mama should have taught you not to say the first thing you think."

"I had no mama to teach me anything."

"Forgive me. I'd forgotten."

"Yes." She did find his chest ... spellbinding. "Men are so differently made from women. But I expect you'd noticed that."

"Possibly." He shifted in his saddle.

His legs were powerfully elegant. Lithe. The long, large muscles shifted beneath buff-colored breeches in a manner that mesmerized Pippa.

"Is there now something remarkable about my breeches, my lady?"

"Only because *you* are wearing them."

He laughed shortly. "You are incorrigible. Beyond help where propriety is concerned."

"I shouldn't be at all surprised. Probably long past any help at all. I should like to touch your legs. They are very hard, I imagine. They would feel—"

"God, give me strength!"

"Oh, He always does if we ask."

"Watch for the carriage, Pippa."

"We shall hear it. I would rather watch you."

Calum brought his mount closer and leaned over its neck

to narrow his eyes at Pippa. "If I did not know better, I would think you were trying to woo me, my lady."

"Would you? Well, in that case, I should consider you a most perceptive man. Generally, I do not find men perceptive, and it's a quality I admire." Fie, she was beyond discretion. Ever since Franchot's mad suggestion about Calum, she'd struggled to decide what she thought of it. The answer, when she'd settled upon it, was obvious. Franchot was a desperate man trying to rid himself of a potential rival. Calum no more considered himself the Duke of Franchot than did Nelly Bumstead.

Calum still regarded her as if she were an interesting butterfly.

"I *am* wooing you," she said, lest he'd missed her meaning. "Mad I may be. Possibly a wanton. I have been investigating that word and I find it appears quite appropriate to—"

"Young ladies would do well to keep their noses out of books."

"Piffle. I have a mind, as do most young ladies—most people of all kinds, in fact. And as I was saying, wanton seems—"

"You are *not* wanton."

"How do you know?"

Calum pounded his brow. "You torture me. I *know* you are no wanton. Do not pester the subject further."

"Very well. Do you suppose you could manage to kiss me without our dismounting?"

His face assumed the intensely dark quality she'd seen before and found so very exciting. "I should find kissing you whilst mounted the most desirable thing in life," he said.

"Oh." How odd he could sound sometimes. And how he could make ordinary comments sound quite uncommon. "Thank you." She closed her eyes and put her face as far forward as her seat would allow.

Calum muttered something that sounded like, "Damnation," and contrived to pull her from her sidesaddle and into his lap.

Pippa threaded her gloved fingers into his thick hair and smiled at him. "I love looking at your face. You're far too handsome, you know."

"They say love makes a face dear."

Her heart turned and didn't feel in quite the right place afterward. "And love makes my face dear to you?"

He kissed her softly, teasingly, and looked at her again. "It was you who said you found my face pleasing."

"*Men.*"

"*Women*," he responded, bending to kiss her once more and with unmistakable ardor. "I find your face the dearest I have ever seen."

"Oh," she murmured. Had he just told her he loved her?

His hand was on her breast and Pippa was digging her fingertips into a steel-tough thigh when she heard the sound of carriage wheels—and the sound of Calum's soft curse.

Watching Calum and Struan together, Pippa saw how each man knew the other's mind without need of words.

Calum had left Pippa in the beeches while he rode out to intercept Struan's hired carriage. With hardly an exchange of words, Struan had mounted the horse Calum provided and dispatched the carriage back the way it had come.

The old friends had not hovered on the highway to talk out of her hearing. Instead, they joined her at once and, after Struan nodded a greeting and kissed her hand, Pippa knew she was to lead the way to the cabin without further delay.

The abandoned hunters' cabin lay deep in heavily forested land well south of Cloudsmoor Hall itself. Once beside the tiny yellow stone building, Calum quickly dismounted and helped Pippa down. Struan had already leaped from his gray, a single piece of baggage in hand. He'd taken very little with him when he departed Franchot and must have expected to use again what he'd left behind.

"Quickly," Calum said, his voice almost toneless. "It will be best if we return separately and there's scarce any light. I'll settle Struan and follow you in a few minutes."

She looked at him fearfully. "But you do not know the way."

He smiled and opened the cabin door. "Tell her that I have a hound's nose for the way, Struan."

"He doesn't lie," Struan agreed, following them into the building's single room.

A chimney faced with pebbles climbed to the roof. The fire was the only means of heat or cooking. Water came from a pump outside. When she'd visited earlier, Pippa had brushed the earthen floor and set down a colorful rug made of rags. The table and two trestles had remained from the cabin's days as a hunters' refuge. A red cloth added cheer, as did red cushions piled on a couch made of woven and leather-tied tree wands.

Calum glanced around. "So this is your hideaway, Pippa. I like it well."

"It is nothing," she said. "And it will offer Struan little comfort." From a chest beneath the single window she removed a patchwork quilt, a woolen blanket and a pillow.

Struan grinned. "All the comforts necessary, my lady. No wonder you find it so pleasant."

She wondered if she would ever have a chance to enjoy it as she had planned. "There is wood near the door. Light a fire and keep it alight. When I was a girl I used to come here even on cool evenings, and I was never cold once there was a fire."

"*Evenings*? When you were a girl?"

She inclined her head. "My father thought me capable of looking after myself. I always—"

"She always admired him for that," Calum said, sounding grim. "I do not like to do this, but I must send you on your way, Pippa. Go directly to your apartments. I shall make certain you are safe as soon as I return."

Outside, he lifted her to her horse, hesitated, then drew her face down to receive his kiss. "Go with care, sweet lady. You take my heart."

Hastily dispatched, her head filled with whisperings and yearnings, she set off on the trail she knew so well.

She had scarce reached the first fork when she realized what she had forgotten. The food she had slipped from the pantry while no one was looking was still in a bag hanging from her saddle.

Quickly, she turned around and trotted back, dismounting before she reached the cabin and running swiftly over the soft bed of fallen needles that swallowed her footsteps.

Men did tarry so. They had not begun to light the fire.

Carrying the bag, she approached the door Calum had failed to close behind him.

"How could you be certain it was the same snake man?" she heard Struan ask distinctly. "So many years would have passed. Surely it would be someone else now."

"His name is Guido. He is the one. And I remembered more. I remembered how I burned my hand as a small child."

Pippa set the bag down quietly and made to leave without letting them know she'd returned.

"You *think* you remembered."

Calum told Struan about the visit to Sybel. "She knew about Rachel. She told me Rachel was dead and that if I continued to seek out my past, the result could be deadly."

Pippa closed her eyes.

"Then take heed," Struan said. "Yet again, I say let us leave this place now. There is no reason to think you will ever get what you want."

"I am begging you to do as I ask you, Struan. I have waited for your return because if there is trouble, I may need your help. That is why I decided to ask you to remain here in secret. I could send word, and you could do what might be necessary without anyone anticipating your arrival."

"What of Pippa?"

"Pippa is mine."

"Ah, yes. Of course. I'd forgotten for a moment."

"Accept what has to be," Calum said urgently. "I shall return to the fair and press the fortune teller again. I believe she almost told me what I wanted to know. The fair will move on within a few days, so there is little time."

"I am deeply troubled," Struan said. "Even if she tells you what you want to hear, how do you propose to make her testimony bear on the matter?"

"She will tell me," Calum said. "Now I must go in case Pippa may have encountered difficulty."

"Yes, you must safeguard your possessions, mustn't you?"

There was a silence, and Pippa found she could not move.

"I shall try to forget your tone, my friend," Calum said. "I hope that when I send for you, it will be because I have proved my right to claim the title of Duke of Franchot and *all* that goes with it."

*   *   *

When Pippa burst into Justine's yellow sitting room, Justine was dressed in a night-robe and seated before the fire with an embroidery hoop in her hand.

"Please forgive me," Pippa said, tearing her bonnet strings undone and pulling off her gloves. "I beg you to forgive me for intruding upon you so rudely."

Justine dropped the hoop and rose to limp rapidly toward Pippa. "You could not be rude," she told her. "Shut the door and come here at once. Whatever can have happened to you? My dear, is it Ella? Max?" She pressed her lips together and frowned before saying, "Has . . . has my brother done something . . . ?"

"The children are well," Pippa said. "And Franchot . . . I have not seen Franchot of late." *Thank goodness.*

"What then?"

"I do not know how to start. Or where to start."

"Sit down." Justine pushed her gently into a chair facing her own. "And I shall not annoy you by suggesting you start at the beginning."

Pippa managed to smile at that. "Calum Innes and I . . . that is . . ."

"That is, you think you care for him and that he cares for you," Justine said as if asking for a second cake at tea.

"Yes," Pippa said simply. "But that is the simple part. That could be . . . well, not *so* simple, I suppose. But there is more, much more."

She told Justine what had happened at Franchot Fair and how strange and desperate Calum had been the following day. Then she explained how Calum had come to her earlier that afternoon and begged her to go with him to meet Struan and then allow them to use the hunting cabin as a hiding place.

Justine listened without interruption, but she did pace slowly before the fire.

"And tonight I discovered what he seeks to prove," Pippa said. "He believes he, not your . . . not . . . He believes that he is the rightful Duke of Franchot."

Justine stood still, her brows furrowed.

"And I think he wants me because if he is the rightful duke, then I am rightfully betrothed to him. Franchot has already said as much.''

Justine swung around. "You told Etienne?"

"No! He came to me several mornings ago and suggested just such a theory as I have told you. I don't know where he got the idea, but first he asked if Calum had tried to marry me to get Cloudsmoor—so that he could make great sums of money from Franchot for the transportation of his tin across Chauncey lands. I told him Calum had suggested no such thing.''

"Then Etienne made the other suggestion?"

"Yes."

Justine shook her head. "An uncanny coincidence," she said. "I'm convinced of it. When you did not support the one theory, he concocted the second from nothing but air. Under no circumstances must he know what you have told me.''

Relief overwhelmed Pippa and she pressed her temples. "I came to you because I think you like Calum and that you will help me decide how best to ensure that no harm comes to him.''

"No harm must come to him," Justine said, returning to her chair. "We will not allow it.''

The fervor in the other woman's voice startled Pippa. "No," she said automatically. "Although I should not blame you if you felt your loyalty to Franchot demanded that you tell him what I have told you and corroborate his suspicions.''

"I feel no loyalty to Etienne," Justine said, her face like marble. "He would have let me drown, you know. On the beach when my leg was trapped. He stood and laughed while the sea overtook me.''

Pippa drew back in horror. "Surely he was just a child. He must have been overset.''

"Etienne bears no affection for me. I have never known why. He was fourteen and a big boy. If he had helped me, I might not have been so badly hurt. But, of course, the sea would not let me die. At last it tore me from the rocks and bore me to the beach and safety.''

"Of course?" Pippa was bemused. "Why of course?"

Justine started. "Ignore me. Sometimes I become fanciful. It was no more than chance, of course. But I have often felt that Etienne is not like me, or like our father or grandfather. Grandmama is a bitter old woman who is disappointed in life and has nothing except her family name to cling to. But the Franchots have been known as generous men. Etienne is not generous."

Pippa smoothed her gloves on her lap. "What has this to do with Calum?"

"Perhaps nothing. Perhaps a great deal. I have felt a powerful affinity for him, Pippa."

Pippa looked questioningly into Justine's eyes.

"Yes, I have felt there is something different about him. Something different and yet familiar. As if there is some special thing I should know about him but do not, not consciously."

Pippa drew a shuddering breath. "I am deeply troubled. I feel . . . I do not know if what I thought he felt for me is true."

"I think he cares for you deeply," Justine said. "But that will come to light in time. For now, we will say nothing."

"But how can we remain silent when—?"

"We can, because if we don't, we may never know the truth. I assure you that the man who is supposedly my brother would be delighted to hear your story. Calum Innes would promptly be disposed of. And the rest of your life would be a torment while you paid the price of having loved your husband's enemy."

❧ Twenty-Five

After leaving Justine, Pippa walked around the gallery overlooking the great vestibule and stood, looking down. Calum had said he would make certain she'd arrived back at the castle safely.

Who was he? Had Franchot—accidentally, if Justine's theory was correct, stumbled upon Calum's reason for wanting her?

Did he want her merely because she was part of all he thought was his by right?

A shadow lengthened across the vestibule, and before Pippa could draw back, she found her eyes locked with Franchot's. The urge to flee was quickly squashed.

Slowly, deliberately, he climbed the stairs and strolled around the gallery to join her. "Late for riding, isn't it, m'dear?" he said, surveying her habit.

"I returned some time ago," she said vaguely, noting that, for once, he was neither drunk nor disheveled, an unusual event for the time of night. "I stopped to speak with Justine, but I'm afraid I'm very tired now. So I'll bid—"

"I was coming to see you, Philipa."

Coming to see her. "Were you?" In her rooms?

Franchot took her elbow and steered her firmly in that very direction. "Ever since our little talk the other morning, I've been unable to get you out of my mind."

She fought not to let him feel her revulsion. "Indeed?" she said.

"Indeed, yes."

Too soon they arrived at her apartments, and he opened the door with a familiar authority that chilled Pippa to her bones.

"It is very late," she said.

He placed a hand at her waist and ushered her into the sitting room, where Nelly nodded in a chair near the windows.

"You there!" Franchot said roughly, and when Nelly jumped to her feet, he flipped a hand. "Leave us, if you please."

Nelly bobbed a curtsy and sidled by, all the while looking at Pippa questioningly.

"Your mistress and I are betrothed," Franchot said, as if that were a perfectly adequate explanation for impropriety. "We are soon to be married and we have a great deal to discuss."

"Yes, Your Grace," Nelly said. "I'll return later, then."

"You won't be needed again tonight," Franchot said.

Pippa had never felt closer to screaming.

As soon as the door closed behind Nelly, Franchot paced about the room, examining its contents with the eye of a man who had apparently never seen them before. "You've been comfortable here?" he asked abruptly.

"Very, thank you, Franchot."

"*Etienne*!" He raised his brows. "Etienne, if you please, Philipa. Is that so great a familiarity to ask from the woman who is to be my wife?"

"Etienne," she said, praying for some means of ridding herself of him. Still holding her bonnet and gloves, she sat on the very edge of the tulipwood chair Nelly had vacated.

"You will be considerably more comfortable in my duchess's quarters."

The windows were open a crack and cold air slipped in. Pippa raised her face and blessed the refreshing current.

"Did you hear what I said?"

"Of course. You are too kind."

"I am not *kind*, dammit, madam. I have come here tonight, hat in hand, so to speak, because I am determined that we shall make a fresh start. And soon."

"September is quite soon, isn't it? A mere three weeks?"

Franchot strode toward her and, to Pippa's horror, went to his knees before her. "My dearest," he said, passionate sincerity hanging from his words. "You deserve a formal proposal. I have given the matter much thought and know how remiss I have been."

Pippa held her breath.

"I shall put this error right and we shall go forward afresh. My lady, it gives me great pleasure to know that you are to be my wife. You are a woman truly worthy of the honor."

He was . . . he was a boor even when he thought he was scattering charm. "Thank you," she said, inwardly rejoicing in not having been called upon to verbally accept him.

On his feet again, Franchot began taking off his coat. "Oh, I am a happy man. I don't want you to be afraid. Leave everything to me, and we shall get along more than tolerably."

Pippa drew as far back into the chair as possible.

Franchot smiled expansively. "Shy little thing. Only to be expected of virgins, m'dear. We'll dispense with that small inconvenience easily enough." The coat was tossed aside and he pulled off his neckcloth, smiling all the while. "Come, let me help you undress. I assure you that this will make our wedding night so much more pleasant for you."

Desperation drove Pippa to her feet. "May I tell you something, Fran—I mean Etienne?"

"Anything, my little bird."

"You may not know this of me—in fact, of course you do not. But I am most interested in having as many of your children as possible. I intend to make myself a . . . a *vessel* for your seed. I shall be tireless in the receiving of that seed until I have born your fruit . . ." Her nerve failed and she ran her tongue over the dry roof of her mouth.

Franchot's mouth hung open. "The devil you say," he muttered. "Dashed good of you. That is, you take my breath away, dear gel. I'm of the same mind meself."

He reached for her but Pippa evaded him.

"Oh, I'm certain you are," she told him. "And because that is the case, it seems symbolic to me that our union be blessed before I avail myself of the pleasure of serving you."

Franchot appeared, finally, to have lost the power of speech, but at least he'd ceased removing his shirt.

"Don't you agree—Etienne—that there is something very beautiful about the thought of our dealing with the seed-and-fruit issue on the day of our marriage?"

"I . . . well, I . . . yes, of course. Very beautiful."

"Oh, good." She almost sank to the carpet with relief. "I'm extremely glad we've had this conversation. I feel I know you so much better and that you know me so much better."

"Well . . . yes."

She picked up his coat and handed it to him. "I'm hoping your grandmama may soon be well enough to continue my instruction in what will be required of me as your wife. And my papa must surely be on his way back from the Continent by now. Really, it is all *too* exciting."

"Too exciting," Franchot echoed. "I'd rather hoped you might consider putting aside all this waiting nonsense . . . as we discussed the other day?"

"The invitations have gone out." Pippa contrived to appear sadly torn. "It would not be fair. Not to the dear dowager or to my father. And not to *you*, Etienne. This will mark a new triumph in your life, the time when you are about to ensure the continuation of your line. You will want the whole Polite World to mark that triumph with you."

"S'pose you have a point."

She shepherded him to the door, trotting beside him, peeping up into his face and smiling. "Why have we taken so long to arrive at this agreeable condition, Etienne?" Her face would split, and what little she'd eaten this day would part company with her stomach. The order of those events was in doubt.

For one dreadful moment, as he stood in the open doorway, she was afraid he would attempt to kiss her. Instead, he frowned as if trying to decide exactly what had just occurred and left, shaking his head.

Calum watched Franchot leave Pippa's rooms. The man's coat was over his arm and his shirt was disheveled. He appeared stunned.

Surely he hadn't . . .

He wouldn't force himself upon Pippa on the same floor

where his sister slept and where any scream might be heard. Would he?

Franchot went slowly down the curving staircase and then his boots rang on the stone floors below as he headed toward his study.

Calum began to shift himself from his hiding place in the passageway leading to Lady Justine's apartments, but the sight of Nelly Bumstead stopped him. Nelly Bumstead, all the while darting fearful looks in the direction Franchot had taken, scurried upstairs and into Pippa's rooms.

More than an hour passed before Nelly, moving slowly and on tiptoe this time, left. Calum, his neck stiff from his repeated peering out of the passage, waited until silence drifted in, then made his own way to Pippa's sitting room door.

He let himself into the dark room without knocking. In the wall facing the fireplace, what he knew must be the door to the bedchamber stood open a crack. Faint light showed there. Moonlight through windows where draperies had not been closed.

"Pippa?" he whispered. Frightening her was his last aim.

She did not answer.

Reaching behind, he turned the key in the lock and the action tightened every muscle in his body. There was no longer any doubt in his mind about what he would do this night.

Moving cautiously, silently, Calum crossed to open the bedchamber door a little wider. "Pippa?"

Moonlight shone through the casement to wash silver over the bed and the shape of the woman curled on her side there. Softly came the sound of her even breathing. She was asleep. Calum did not spare a glance for the rest of the room.

He approached, holding his own breath now, unwilling to startle her awake . . . and unwilling to deny himself the pleasure of looking at her while she slept.

Pippa lay with one arm stretched up beneath her head, the other flung behind her. Black hair flowed over the white pillows and over one white-clad shoulder. The room was warm and she'd thrown back the covers. Her full lawn shift draped her body, the thin stuff clinging, somehow revealing more than if she had been naked.

Calum stood looking down at this woman he had not chosen yet would have chosen had the choice been his.

What had passed between her and Franchot earlier in the evening?

He thinned his lips. If she'd been ravished, she'd hardly be sleeping peacefully now.

If he did not touch her, he would die—or, at the very least, explode from needing her.

He turned his head to see her face—all shadows painted with light over fine bones and closed lids and the sweet bow of her lips. Her lashes were dark upon her cheeks. Her vulnerability made him long to gather her into his arms and bear her away where she would be safe forever.

The satin tapes that closed the front of the shift had been carelessly tied. A slight move, this way or that, and they would part. Calum rubbed a hand over his eyes. Looking at her was not enough. He must *touch* her.

He gained the other side of the bed and very carefully lowered himself to lie behind her. Propping his head, he studied the roundness of her cheek, the slender line of her neck and shoulder, the curve of her small, pointed breast. The nipple pressed against cobweb cotton.

He could take that nipple into his mouth through that cotton and hear her cry out with the pleasure he brought her.

Pippa sighed and wriggled, turning half onto her back.

And the tapes parted at her neck.

When she settled again, it was with one perfect breast exposed.

Calum tightened his thighs. His shaft sprang hard and urgent against his breeches. This was what he'd been made for, for this woman's body. And she had been made for his.

With the backs of his fingers he stroked her cheek and whispered, "Pippa, do not be afraid."

"Mmm." She smiled a little in her sleep and turned her face up to his.

The tapes were open to her waist.

Mesmerized, he settled his hand on her throat. She was cool. Gently, he fondled her breast, then simply savored its soft, satiny weight.

Pippa arched her back.

Riding and tension had exhausted her. But her sleeping smile made him smile. She was ready to come to him. In her quiet, secret moments she had dreamed of being with him, and now she was in another such dream.

Carefully, Calum slipped his hand over her ribs, over her flat stomach, and felt the dips in front of her delicate hipbones. She was small. He frowned. She would need great care in the matter of childbirth.

His rod reminded him of what must come before any thought of a child, and he stroked on to find the soft hair between her thighs.

Curling his fingers over her mound, he sought the warm folds of her womanhood and found them already moist.

Ah, yes, she was so ready for him.

Bending over her, he took the nipple that was still covered by her shift into his mouth and flipped his tongue over the instantly hardened bud.

"What?" She writhed and he knew she had awakened.

The instant her scream began, Calum covered her mouth firmly and brought his lips close to her ear. "It is I, sweetest. Calum."

She struggled.

"I know, I know." He grimaced. "I have shocked you, but I am only a man. I came to find you and you were . . . You did not awaken when I called you."

She grew still and he took his hand from her mouth.

"Do you have any idea how you looked to me? Lying here in the moonlight. So lovely, Pippa."

"What are you doing?"

He almost grinned. "I wanted to hold you and to bring you pleasure."

"You frightened me."

"I'm sorry. But before you awakened, you were happy."

"How do you know?" She sounded suspicious.

"Your body told me," he explained simply.

This time he pulled her into the crook of his shoulder and smoothed the shift upward to bare her legs.

"I just know you should not," she said in a panicky little voice. "No. You absolutely should not do this."

"Why?"

"Because . . . because . . ."

"There, you see? You have no reason, do you?" And while he spoke, he found that warm, wet hiding place of soft dark hair and parted folds grown plump with desire. "You are ready to become fully a woman, Pippa. I want you to become a woman with me tonight."

"I . . . Oh!" Her back arched off the bed and he fastened his lips over hers in a demanding, driving kiss. She plucked ineffectually at his shirt, but he could not make himself release her long enough to remove it.

She was at the brink of her release. Abandoning her lips, Calum drew a circle around her revealed nipple, moving close, but not taking that crown she rolled to try to press into his mouth.

This was an innocent, he reminded himself. He must not allow his own drive to obliterate her need for his restraint. Again he circled her nipple.

"Calum!" His name was high and thin on her lips. "Please."

He made yet another circle, growing closer, and her body bathed his fingers with her woman's hot, slick essence.

Writhing afresh, she found his rod and tested its steely length and weight. Reaching, she supported all of his manhood and kneaded desperately. She did not know what she did and he was glad. He would not want her to be afraid now.

Almost beyond control himself, he gave her relief and drew the center of her breast deep into his mouth. The sound of his own suckling drove him to near insanity. Her hips came off the bed and soft sounds escaped her throat.

Summoning all restraint, Calum withdrew his hand and listened to their panting in the darkness.

She was waiting, yet he knew she was not sure what it was she waited for.

He could take her now, and so simply. But he found he wanted to wait and breach her on their wedding night. Tonight he would do what he must to find peace—after he'd taken her to a place she would never forget.

Rapidly, he pulled enough away to flip her onto her back entirely. Pushing up her knees, he knelt between them and buried his face in her sweetness.

He made love to her with his darting tongue and felt himself pulled into the dark, boiling space where she hung. His manhood pulsed and he held back only with a force of will he would not have dared hope he possessed.

"Calum," she moaned. "No. Oh, *Calum.*"

His tongue darted again and he took the small, thrusting nub at her center between his teeth.

And he felt her fly into pieces.

Her release was long and shuddering and impossibly joyful to Calum. When at last he drew her damp body into his embrace, he felt as he had never felt before with a woman. Her pleasure made him more of a man than had he lain sated himself.

Minutes slipped by, many minutes, before she raised her face to seek his. "You came for this?"

She knew so little for one who undoubtedly thought she knew so much. "I came because it is time," he told her.

"Time?"

"I am going to take you away. Now. Before morning."

With a forearm, she pushed the riotous mass of her hair. "Away? We cannot. Where would we go?"

"To get married."

He felt her grow still. "Then that is why you came. To urge me to go with you."

"Is that so bad? It is as it should be."

"As it should be. That I should marry you, you mean?"

He frowned. "Of course." This was not the reaction he expected. "Franchot was here earlier. He didn't try to touch you, did he?"

She was silent a moment before saying, "He did not touch me, no."

Her honesty was something he accepted without question. "My darling, let me help you gather a few things. Then we must make our escape carefully."

"Why now?"

"Because it has to be. You are meant to be with me and there must be no more delay."

"Because you believe you are the Duke of Franchot?"

He did not think he had heard her correctly. "You said—"

But he had heard correctly. "How do you know? It was not said at the fair."

"You said it to Struan at the cabin. After you thought I had gone. I forgot to leave the food and returned."

"Why did you not come in."

"You would not have wanted it. You had no intention of telling me. Even now, when we have just been together like this, you would not have told me."

He wetted his lips.

"Would you?"

"Not until the time was right. The less you know, the better."

"Really? I should come blindly to you, believing you want me only because you have formed a *tendre* for me? When would you inform me that you sought me because you believe I already belong to you?"

He grew chilled. "You did not mind what just happened between us."

"I . . . I loved what happened between us. Why couldn't you have told me what you believe and why? And then asked me to come with you? Why didn't you tell me the night of the fair?"

"Some knowledge is dangerous."

"Dangerous because I might tell your rival, you mean? Dangerous because if I knew the real reason for your ardor, I would not be such a simpleton?"

Anger swelled within Calum. "I do not regard you as a simpleton."

"Dangerous because I might become an impediment to your claim on the Franchot titles and lands, then? And to the alliance with the Chaunceys?"

"Damn you, woman. You time your protests to your own convenience."

"You came to me whilst I slept. I did not ask you to come."

"I want you as my wife. I want you to leave with me now."

"You want me because you believe I am yours by right. Franchot wants me as his wife because he wants my dowry. He came here tonight to ask for a speedy marriage also."

"Bounder," Calum said under his breath.

"Is he more of a bounder than you, I wonder? Franchot . . .

I suppose I should not call him Franchot. Or perhaps I should call you both Franchot. That would be the fairest thing." She flung herself from the bed and cast a robe about her shoulders. "Please leave me, Calum. *Please*."

"Not unless you come with me."

"Oh, I cannot bear it." She turned away and went to the windows.

He was behind her in seconds, chafing her cold arms through the robe. "I . . . Believe that I want you, dearest."

"*You* want me. *He* wants me. How am I to know if your reason is any different from his? I am a *pawn*. Wanted by two men for what I can bring them."

Her words hit Calum like a blow. He dropped his hands. "You believe that?"

"*Yes*." He could hear that her teeth were clenched.

The pain in his throat would fade. The pain in his heart and the throbbing in his loins would take longer. "Very well. If you believe this invention of yours, then you have a simple task. Either decide to have neither of us or choose which one you prefer."

"You torture me."

"*You* torture *me*, Pippa. I trust you will not repeat what you heard at the cabin."

"I . . . How can you even suggest such a thing?"

"I have made many mistakes with you, my lady. Good night."

He left her whilst he felt he could still control himself. The urge to sweep her up and take her with him bowed him down.

In the dark passageway with its flickering wall sconces, he stood still, his back to the wall, and tried to gather his breath.

The slightest noise made him alert and he looked to the right and the left.

A flicker of something pale wafted in a distant corner and was gone.

Walking with careful steps, he approached that corner and turned.

Nothing.

He was a man besieged on all sides, and his imagination, like the rest of his mind, showed signs of bending.

Calum left the house at once, went to the stables and took

the bay hack. The rest of this night he would spend riding the hills, perhaps in the company of the one friend who might judge his sanity but who would never doubt his honor.

Pippa stood where she was by the window. How should she bear it? The loving him, yet knowing that even if he cared for her at all, that caring was second to his need to claim her as a rightful possession.

She could not bear it any longer.

Quickly, before she could change her mind, she found paper and ink and wrote a note to Justine, telling her that she had decided to leave. She asked that no one search for her because she needed to be alone for a while. When she was ready, she would let Justine know where she'd gone.

With the note finished and propped beneath a Venetian paperweight, Pippa hurried to dress in her most serviceable riding habit. She would set out for Cloudsmoor but could not stay at the Hall because they would look for her there first. There were several empty tenant cottages where she could find a refuge for a day or two whilst she thought.

When all was done and a few possessions were tied inside a shawl, she doused the lights once more and went to stand where she'd stood with Calum before he'd left her. By the window.

Why should loving hurt so much?

From the sitting room came the sound of the door being softly opened.

Pippa closed her eyes. She was wrong, but joy flooded her. He had returned to make her understand what he had not been able to explain before.

She stood quite still, waiting.

His footsteps approached, and when she knew he was close behind her, she began to turn.

Strong arms surrounded her.

Strong arms trapped her while someone else, someone smaller, pressed a hard goblet to her lips.

"No!" She choked and coughed, and bitter wine flowed down her throat.

Pippa tossed her head from side to side, but hard hands

clamped her skull, and more and more wine was forced down her throat.

Almost at once, sick faintness burst upon her like a black, red-tinged blossom.

"Drink," she heard a voice say. "Drink."

The blossom swelled and Pippa slipped into its dark center.

🌿 Twenty-Six

"Come along, now. We both know you're awake, don't we, ducky?"

Pippa heard the rough male voice and struggled to raise her eyelids. They felt heavy and damp, as if she'd cried for hours and fallen asleep still crying.

"Hey! You can hear me. Turn your head this way and let's have a look at you."

She lay facedown on splintered boards. When she did get her eyes to open a fraction, she saw a crude stone wall illuminated by flickering candlelight. From somewhere came a high, wailing sound.

Something—a foot, she thought—dug into the small of her back. "Don't you want to know how long you've been here, ducky? Don't you want to know who it is 'as paid to have you brought here?"

Her head would break open if she lifted it. "Where am I?" she asked, but the words sounded like a burble in her brain.

"Come again, ducky?" the man asked. His hand descended upon her aching head. "Let me sit you up. No point lying in the dirt any longer than you have to, right?"

"Where am I?" Pippa repeated, and was relieved that she sounded clearer.

"That's for me to know and you to find out, as they say." His laugh was a braying noise. "Up you come."

He turned and lifted her to sit in one motion. Her back

thudded against the wall. She cried out and held her head.

"Ache, does it? Well, I said as how you probably didn't need so much. Being a little thing, that is. But—as usual—I wasn't listened to. Never mind. My turn will come."

Pippa cupped her hands beside her eyes and looked up into a thin, long-nosed face framed with lank black hair. "Who are you?" she whispered. Even though he was on one knee before her, she could tell he was exceedingly tall.

"I'm no one you have to worry about. No one you'll ever have to think about again once this little lot's over."

He had no lips. His long teeth appeared and disappeared in a rolled slit in his face, and his eyes shone like gray agate.

She would not panic. "Why was I brought here?" If she asked what he intended to do with her, she might precipitate his awful plans.

"I think we should talk about where you are, after all," he said expansively, peering at her more closely. "Pale thing you are. And thin. Shouldn't choose you myself. But no accounting for tastes, I suppose."

Pippa decided his disapproval of her was the best news she'd heard thus far.

"You've been here two nights and a day. That is, this is the second night."

She gasped and clutched her middle. Every muscle and bone in her body hurt. "I cannot have been here that long." *Wine poured into her mouth. Blackness. She'd been drugged.*

"Have it your own way. What'll really surprise you is where you are."

Thumping. Thumping and jostling and the clink of a horse's hoofs on rocks.

"You're within spitting distance of Franchot Castle, you are. What d'you think about that?"

"I want to go," she said, unable to hold back the desperation any longer. "I want to go now."

"No, no, no. You'll have to stay, ducky. Can't disobey my orders. This is the abandoned lighthouse. The one on the head to the west of the castle. Remember it?"

She cast about in her fuzzy mind. "No. Yes, yes." The lighthouse had been there, but she'd never paid it any attention. A new one had been built farther inland. She seemed to remember being told that this one was abandoned because it was too often endangered by high seas.

Pippa edged away from the man and he showed no sign of following her. Slowly, she started to push herself up until she stood, her head on a level with the gaping openings around the top of the lighthouse. She gulped in sea air and all but gagged on its heavy salt tang.

"Don't you go casting up your accounts again," the man said. "Had enough of that, I have. Might decide I couldn't wait any longer."

"You don't have to wait," Pippa said quickly. "Really, I'm very good at being on my own."

His awful mouth opened in a guffaw. "Really, I'm very good at being on my own," he mimicked. "And I've been sitting here wasting my time with you for nigh on two days only because I like looking at dirty, skinny little women snoring and snuffling. You're here until he sends word."

"He?"

The man merely grinned.

Oh, dear Lord, *Franchot*. Franchot had arranged to have her kidnapped so he could take her away to marry her instantly and put his fears to rest. She tried to compose herself. "I left a note, you know. If I were you, I'd make my getaway while I could. They'll be bound to be looking for me already, and this isn't very far at all, is it?"

"No, it isn't," he said, still in a parody of her accents. "And it was so nice of you to leave the note. I understand the lady who received it has arranged for parties to scour the countryside. They've gone particularly wide, so I'm told. Following your horse's tracks. Got in someone specially for the job."

"But I never got my horse . . ."

He grinned afresh. "*You* didn't, but someone did. And they rode fast and far. So far your little band of rescuers will be busy a nice long time. And when they do give up, the last place they'll look is so close to home as this, right?"

Pippa's legs would not hold her. She slid back down the wall and hit the wooden boards hard enough to jar her spine. "Why?" she asked. "What could it possibly . . . You will ask for a ransom. Of course. Why didn't I think of that? My father will pay you, but he . . ." No, she *must* not say that Papa might not return for two or three more weeks.

"I won't need your father's ransom, my lady," her captor said. "I'll be paid handsomely enough by the gentleman who arranged this little holiday for you. He told me to tell you not to worry. And—as you can see—I haven't hurt you, have I? No, not too much, anyways."

"There were two of you," Pippa said suddenly. "I remember. One of you held me and one of you forced me to drink."

"Don't go straining your mind. Save yourself. You're going to need all your strength."

He came closer, grinning his horrible grin, and she shrank away. "You could try saying your prayers. I've heard some females do find a lot of comfort in their prayers."

Sniffing, he pulled a flask from his pocket and took a swallow. "Need something to keep me going. Cold up here."

"Let me go!" Pippa cried. The wailing came again. Gulls. Seagulls. She was so close to Cloudsmoor and familiar places. *Calum.* Calum would be searching, too. "Please, let me go!"

"Can't do it," he said, shaking his head. "Not till I get orders. And then it won't be orders to let you go. Not exactly."

She pushed her hair from her eyes. "What's happening to me?"

"Simple," he said. "You're waiting here with me until I get word that it's time for you to go to sleep again. Should have come by now. Can't imagine what's keeping him."

Pippa opened her mouth, but no sound came.

"That's a clever, quiet girl. Not that it matters if you scream. Even if someone heard you, they'd think it was the seabirds. When he sends word, you'll go to sleep. I'll make sure you don't know any more than you did the last time. Only this time you won't have the worry about all this nasty waking up."

She did scream—and clamp her hands over her mouth to try to hold it back. Gasping, coughing, she drew her legs beneath her and said, "You're going to kill me. Why?"

"Don't go on. It'll only make things worse. And Mr. Innes said I was to try to keep you happy till it was time."

❧ Twenty-Seven

*C*alum *met* Struan's eyes and between them passed the understanding that the wisdom of this return to the castle would not be questioned again.

Side by side, they rode beneath storm-laden clouds, up the great drive to the peregrine-flanked gates.

Beneath the stone escutcheon bearing the Franchot arms, those gates stood open.

"Odd," Struan said.

Calum drew up the bay hack, twisted in his saddle and searched for the gatekeeper. The door to his quarters also stood open. "Probably means nothing." He looked at Struan again. Unspoken was the thought that they did not know what awaited them at Franchot Castle.

"Pippa will not have told him," Struan said.

"No."

"We will hold to the tale that you rode out to meet me and I'd had difficulty on my travels from Dorset."

Calum knew how Struan detested falsehood. "Thank you," he told him. "I cannot give her up, Struan. I cannot."

"And I must make certain all goes well for Ella and Max. So we both have reasons to return." Struan urged his mount onward.

Calum fell in with his friend. "Franchot is innocent in whatever plot took place here."

"He is a bad man."

"Yes, but he is guilty of no crime against me other than having been used."

"So"—Struan looked sideways, and in the gray, early morning light, his lean face was starkly somber—"you have decided to leave him with everything you believe is yours?"

The day and two nights since Calum had left this place had been the longest in his life, and they had taught him a great deal. He said, "Everything but Pippa."

Struan smiled. "I do believe you shall have her. What woman could resist a man prepared to give up his claim to so much in exchange for her hand?"

Calum faced the castle. "*If* I can persuade her to believe I want only her. And if she does want me."

They broke from the avenue of trees to the rise before the great entrance.

Struan pulled up once more and wheeled. "Who is that?" He referred to a figure dashing down wide steps from open double doors. "All is not well here."

"Nelly," Calum said. "And Justine behind her." And after Justine came Max.

Nelly and Max reached them at the same time. "Oh, Mr. Innes," Nelly said, catching at his arm as he dismounted. "Oh, sir."

"I saw 'em go," Max said, jumping up and down. "I saw 'em."

"Hush, Max," Justine said, arriving slightly out of breath. All three appeared disheveled and the rising wind tossed their hair. Justine looked to Struan. "I would have sent for you had I known where Pippa's cabin was. That is where you were?"

"Yes—"

"I wished I'd known, too, your lordship," Nelly said, rolling her apron around her hands. "There's none here but womenfolk and children. The rest are all out searching."

"For me?" Struan said, rumpling his brow.

"I saw 'em," Max said. "The black-haired man and a big 'orse. Breathing fire, the 'orse was—and smoke. And there were black dogs the size of bears with ghosts holding their chains. And the billowy lady went in the carriage with the other 'orse behind."

"*Hush*, Max," Justine said. "He is severely agitated and

must be forgiven. This is a terrible strain and far too much for children. Grandmama refuses to leave her rooms.''

Calum restrained himself from mentioning that the dowager frequently refused to leave her rooms.

''Poor little Ella's beside herself,'' Nelly said. To Struan she spoke very earnestly. ''She's taken on terrible about her mam, your lordship. I think with what's happened here, it's brought it all back. She keeps talking about her mam dying like it just happened.''

''Did,'' Max said. ''You've got to go after 'em, Mr. Innes. Before it's too late.''

''Go after whom?'' Calum caught the boy by the shoulders.

''He's not slept in two days,'' Justine said, shivering and folding her arms tightly. ''You know how he makes up stories, but forgive him, please.'' She pulled a note from her pocket and gave it to Calum. ''Read that. Everyone's been out searching ever since.''

With Struan looking over his shoulder, Calum read.

''When Nelly went to her yesterday morning, she was gone,'' Justine said. ''We think she left in the night. Her favorite horse is missing. But so far no one's come to say they've seen any sign of her.''

''Where's . . . where's your brother?'' Calum asked.

''Searching with the rest. They took every able man from the estate. Villagers volunteered, too, and a host from Cloudsmoor.''

''I saw 'em go,'' Max shouted. ''I saw 'em. Cacklin' and whisperin'. Fearsome, it was.''

Nelly shook her head and tried to take the boy into her arms. ''He's been telling his stories ever since it happened. Poor little motherless boy.''

''Poor Pippa,'' Justine said. Dark smudges underscored her tired eyes. ''I'm afraid for her. There's going to be a terrible storm and she's alone out there.''

This was his fault. Calum glanced at Struan. ''Let us get them inside. Then I'll set off.''

''Not until someone returns,'' Justine said. ''What point is there in going where others have already been?''

''I have to do something. I'll go to Cloudsmoor Hall.''

''We already know she didn't go there.''

"My *God*," Calum said. "I blame myself for this."

"No," Struan said simply, casting Calum a warning stare before taking Justine's hand and tucking it beneath his arm. "Come, dear lady. I'll see you safely inside and we'll think what will be best. Come, Nelly, and you, too, Max."

"I'll deal with the horses," Calum said, gathering the reins of both beasts.

"The billowy lady helped the tall man put 'er on the 'orse," Max said when the others had disappeared inside the castle. "*No one will listen to me.*"

Buffeted by the wind, Calum started for the stables. "Come and help me," he said to the boy. "The viscount and I will need fresh mounts."

"No, you won't." Max capered at Calum's side. "I'd go on my own. Honest, I would. Only I'm afraid of that big man and I don't mind sayin' as much."

"Billowy ladies and tall, black-haired men," Calum said. *His fault. He'd driven her out into the night alone.* "And fire-breathing horses and giant dogs led by ghosts."

"*One* billowy lady. You know the one. 'Er. I don't know 'er name, but she was at the fair with the nasty duke what owns this place and that other man—the one what pinched my cheek."

Calum paused. "Henri St. Luc? He pinched your face?"

"Yes, yes. That's the one. That's 'is name. 'E wanted me to go with 'im to 'is rooms one day, but I wouldn't. 'E was drivin' the carriage when the billowy lady left."

"Lady Hoarville?"

"I don't know 'er name. The one with silver hair, and—"

"Anabel," Calum said, dropping to his haunches in front of Max. "What does she have to do with Lady Philipa?"

Max spread his arms. "I've been tryin' to tell you. Nobody will listen to me."

"I'm listening now."

"It's because I've told too many tales, and I won't never do it again."

Calum made fists on his thighs. "*Tell* me."

"I wanted someone to 'elp Ellie 'cause she wouldn't stop cryin'. I tried to get you, but you was gone. So I went to find Lady Philipa, because Ellie'd sneaked away to the fair and

found out our mum's died. When Ellie come back, she
wouldn't stop cryin'. I didn't know our mum much.''

Calum was speechless.

"Anyway, I went to get Lady Philipa to 'elp. And I saw
'em.''

"Yes?'' Calum's heart hammered.

"A big man what I ain't never seen before carried Lady
Philipa out of her room. That lady was there, the one what
you said. I followed 'em and they put Lady Philipa on a 'orse.
She was asleep. The man rode away with 'er and the other
lady left with that Henry.''

Calum schooled himself to speak calmly. "And you told
this to the duke?''

Max shook his head. "Nobody would listen to—''

"No, no. I understand.'' He stood up. God help him, he
didn't know which direction to follow.

"I'll come with you, Mr. Innes. I can be brave if you're
there.''

Calum tried to smile. "Thank you, my friend. But first I'll
have to decide where to start looking for them.''

"But I know. I saw 'em.''

Focusing on the boy's green eyes, Calum tilted his head.
"You saw them? You mean you saw them ride away?''

"Yes. And then I followed. I didn't think I'd find 'em. But
with Lady Philipa slipping about in her sleep, they went
slow—and they didn't go far, see. The 'orse is tied up outside,
so I knew I was right. Only nobody would—''

"I'm listening,'' Calum said.

Pippa could scarcely make out the newcomer's face in the
gloom.

"Get out,'' he told her captor curtly. "Go wherever it is
you go and wait there.''

"But you aren't supposed to be here. She—''

"Hold your tongue or you'll wish you had. You have made
a great error. The party to whom you refer has just revealed
the nature of this disastrous venture to me. I was searching
the countryside when she—when I was told.''

"Now you listen to me—''

"No. You listen to me. If you hold to silence for one month, you can expect to benefit. Do I make myself clear?"

"Very clear, *Your Grace*," the man said. "But I think you'll have trouble with—"

"*You* deal with that problem. Make certain no further approach is made to me at the castle. *Leave* us at once."

After the briefest of hesitations, the man turned and left the beacon room, thudding down the steps at a great rate.

"My dear Philipa." The Duke of Franchot came toward her, his arms outstretched. "Thank God I found out this evil plan before it was too late. I can scarcely believe you have been here through two terrible nights. I was searching for you. But you are safe now, my dear."

She closed her eyes and hadn't the strength to resist when he pulled her into a tight embrace.

"Innes was going to kill us both," Franchot said. "Then he was going to say I'd murdered you because you believed he is the rightful duke."

Shuddering rattled her teeth together. A rising gale sent an icy blast into the chamber, but it was not the cold wind that chilled her.

"My poor, dear creature," Franchot said. "He has not accomplished his scheme. I have my own ways of ensuring that my interests are preserved. And your interests are also my interests. We shall leave this frightful place now."

"What has happened?" she asked, trying to draw away.

Franchot lifted her into his arms. "He is not apprehended, but he will be. Meanwhile, I must take you—and myself— somewhere safe. We must preserve your honor at all costs. Fear not, dearest, that will be easily done. I have a boat in the cove below. We shall put in farther down the coast and marry immediately. Everything is arranged."

"But I don't understand. Why don't we go back and confront him?"

Franchot strode with her from the lighthouse and set off down a rocky trail to the shore. "Save your strength," he said, breathing hard. "The tide is high and we'll have a harsh pull ahead of us."

Calum could not have done what Franchot had said. "Please," she urged. "I do not think this is wise."

"It is the way it will be," he responded, muscles contracting in his jaw. "That man will not get the better of me, and neither will anyone else. What is mine is mine, and it shall not be taken from me."

Pippa closed her mouth and felt a scream rise in her throat. He appeared quite mad.

The boat Franchot referred to was a crabber's rowboat, one of several drawn up on the narrow strip of rough beach. Depositing her inside, he shoved the broad-beamed little vessel to the water's edge and pushed off into foaming waves.

"It's too rough," she said as he jumped in and took the oars. "Surely we would be wise to return to the castle and deal with this matter."

If he heard her, he gave no sign. A glossy sheen filmed his pale eyes and sweat stood out on his brow. His fine clothes were already sodden.

Slowly, he began to row away from shore.

"There will be a storm," Pippa cried, pointing to leaden skies. Heavy drops of rain spattered the seas around the boat and wetted her upturned face. "We will go back and ensure all is done appropriately."

"I shall beat them all," Franchot said, while the rain soaked his hair. "Any that get in my way shall die." Laughing, his face streaming with water, he pulled farther and farther into the roiling sea.

Depositing Max inside the castle with firm instructions not to follow had taken too much time. Calum had ordered the boy to explain his story to Struan. Pray Struan would listen and follow without delay.

In front of the lighthouse, Calum leaped from his horse before the beast came to a complete stop. An untethered horse, one he recognized as coming from the Franchot stables, raised his head as Calum ran past.

He took the steps inside the lighthouse by twos and burst into the room at the top, his legs bent, his stance braced for battle.

Empty.

Desperately, he cast about. A candle lay on its side beside remnants of bread and cheese upon a grimy kerchief.

Rain beat through the openings into the tower and Calum

strode to stare out. The horse must have been the one Max saw, but where were the man and Pippa? They couldn't have left without a mount.

He scoured the countryside and saw nothing move.

Below lay only the beach with several small boats pulled up high. They'd need to be brought higher shortly or their owners would lose them. No doubt those owners were busy searching for Pippa.

The storm had fully broken and waves roared onto the shore.

With desolation in his soul, Calum glanced at the rising seas and grew still. A boat, like the ones on the shore, headed out from the beach. Two people were in that boat, a man and a woman.

The woman's long black hair whipped like a dark flag.

Pippa.

The blackguard who'd taken her must have seen Calum coming and was bent on escaping with her—even if he killed them both. Evidently Lady Hoarville had offered a great prize to rid herself of her rival.

Calum thudded into walls in his mad descent from the lighthouse, and his boots slid on shale as he dashed to the beach. Looking to sea, he saw that the boat containing Pippa was tossing, rising on the brow of each wave only to plummet into the trough in its wake.

Shutting out thought, Calum dragged another boat to the water's boiling edge. From early childhood he'd rowed on the Scottish lochs, but never on the high seas.

With his back to his quarry, he pulled with all the desperate strength of his fury and desire.

Minutes passed—or were they hours? Calum rowed, leaning forward until his chest crowded his knees and heaving a path through walls of steel-gray wrath.

A sheet of water hit the boat broadsides and rose like wavering pewter-colored glass. As it fell, Calum was drenched.

And, not a hundred yards distant, the laboring boat that carried Pippa was still afloat.

She had not seen him.

Franchot had.

Calum noted nothing but the way Pippa hunched over and the other man's sudden release of his oars.

And Calum prayed. He felt the strength of a hundred men but knew he needed more.

Franchot wrestled a while with something Calum could not see, then abruptly stood up. In one hand he held an oar—the other had slipped into the ocean.

Frantically, Calum sculled, turning his boat about and hauling on his own oars to draw closer.

"Careful . . ." Franchot's shout was lost in the tempest.

Clutching the gunwales, Pippa stared toward Calum.

"Not too close . . ." Franchot called.

Calum understood. If he drew too close, they'd likely ram and go down together.

Sitting again, Franchot extended his remaining oar in Calum's direction. In turn, Calum positioned himself as best he could, shipped his own oars and, after four pawing misses, snagged a hold on Franchot's lifeline.

The two boats rose and fell. Calum knelt in water gathering in the bottom of his boat and reached, using Franchot's oar as an anchor, until he grasped the gunwale of the other boat.

He had no warning of the mighty yank that toppled him into the roaring deep.

Franchot had used the oar to overbalance Calum. The thought was the only one he had as he fell downward into suffocating cold.

A miracle brought him up beneath a hull. He didn't care that his enemy might be waiting to club him from above. Bracing himself for blows, Calum clawed his way over the side of the boat and hung on.

Huddled on a seat, soaked and wild-eyed was Pippa. There was no sign of Franchot.

Her lips moved, but he heard nothing she said. She clutched at his hands and wrists and tried to pull him aboard.

"No!" Desperate that she not throw herself into the sea, he managed to push her back and drag himself up to lean over the side.

Water reached the seats, and Calum realized what Franchot had been groping for. The bung. He'd removed the bung to swamp the craft and sink Pippa.

The boat wallowed and rolled over.

Through the gray wall that separated them, Calum saw her skirts billow. Black hair streaked across her face, and her arms flailed.

She'd told him she could not swim.

Jackknifing his legs, Calum cut through the distance between them, twisted her so that her back was to his body, and gained the surface.

The sea will bear you to shore.

A voice he'd never heard before whispered in his shattered mind.

Bear you, bear you, bear you.

On the crest of a wave, with Pippa clasped to his breast, he rose. And then they fell again. He searched around him but saw no boat at all.

Then he saw an arm rise, not ten yards distant. A man's arm with fingers clawing.

Franchot deserved to drown.

The arm rose again, then a head. And Calum stretched until he could catch hold of the clawing hand.

Bear you, bear you. The sea will bear you up.

Pippa lay atop Calum. Franchot's head was clamped to his right shoulder. He worked with legs that had long since ceased to feel pain and drew breath into lungs that were beyond aching.

I will bear you home! The voice had the hushed quality of tranquil waters.

His back met something hard and shifting.

Pippa was lifted from him and Franchot was pried from his right arm.

Strong hands drew him backward on the rocky shore, and unbelievably, he staggered to stand and fall against Struan.

"A miracle," his friend shouted against the wind. "You are all alive, yet we thought you would all be dead."

Calum drifted up through shades of darkness. Beneath him was warmth, and on top of him, and when he opened his eyes, it was to the flickering of firelight over walls and furniture in his bedchamber at the castle.

A door opened and closed softly.

"That maid says the gel is still resting," the dowager said in her brittle voice, none too softly.

"Hush." It was Justine who answered her grandmother. "Calum must sleep on."

"He's slept all day."

"So has Etienne."

"Etienne has had a terrible experience."

"He would be dead if it were not for Calum Innes."

Calum let his eyes close again. His body was weighted and aching.

"Etienne would not have drowned," the dowager said.

When Justine didn't respond, the old lady tutted. "You know he *could* not. Any more than you yourself drowned when the sea would have had you all those years ago."

"Because of the caul," Justine said softly.

"Because of the caul, indeed," the dowager said. "You and your brother were both born without the breaking of your mother's waters. Such infants come swimming into the world and are forever protected from death by drowning. I notice you never fail to wear your own caul."

"You gave it to me in the locket, Grandmama."

"And you were wearing it when you were trapped by the rocks. You wear it always because you believe you would have drowned without it."

"Etienne was not wearing his caul today. He never has. He will never even discuss it."

The dowager coughed. "He keeps it safe. And today he was proven right in that the circumstances of his birth would always save him regardless of whether he had the caul in his presence."

"Perhaps," Justine said. "Calum saved him, Grandmama. What is it about Calum that causes you discomfort?"

"Do not be impertinent, Justine. I have no interest in Innes beyond the human kindness of wishing to see him safely recovered and sent on his way."

"He belongs here."

Calum held his breath.

"Hold your tongue," the dowager said. "And never say such a thing again. It isn't seemly for you to be here with him. Leave us at once."

"But I—"

"*Leave.* You may have a point in that he did Etienne some service. I will ensure that he does not awaken alone."

"Grandmama, I should like to remain."

"And I should prefer you to leave. Allow me the respect I deserve, if you please."

Without another word, Justine left, and Calum heard the rustle of black silk as the dowager approached the bed and stood over him.

The lamp beside him flared and he looked into the woman's seamed face.

"How long have you been awake?" she asked.

"Long enough."

"Can you get up?"

"I am a strong man." He pushed back the covers and swung his feet from the bed, grateful for the covering of a nightshirt in which someone had clothed him.

"Come by the fire," the old lady told him. "There are things that must be said and forgotten."

On legs that shook, Calum followed her and sank into a chair.

The dowager sat opposite him. From the folds of her skirts she produced a dark velvet bag tied at the top. This she undid and then slipped a small portrait from inside.

She set the painting facedown on her lap and took a pen from the bag also. The pen she offered to Calum. He took it automatically.

"Did they try to break you of the habit when you were a boy?" she asked.

He frowned and followed her gaze to the pen in his left hand. "Ah. Yes, they tried and failed, I fear."

"You use both hands equally well?"

"I do. Sometimes a very useful fault." As in when called upon to carry two drowning people from the sea. "I prefer the left."

"An affliction," the dowager pronounced, turning over the portrait and putting it onto Calum's lap. "My husband."

He picked up the piece and saw yet another depiction of a dark-haired man at a writing table with a pen in his left hand. "A man one wouldn't easily forget," he said. The woman was admitting that she knew who Calum was, wasn't she?

"I shall never forget him. Like all Franchots, he was dedicated to the honor of this family's impeccable name."

Their eyes met.

"He had the affliction of wrong-handedness, but never allowed any to suggest he was other than sane, as is so often said of such people. His father before him held the same order of things, and my own son. How fortunate it is that Etienne has no need to defend himself in such a manner. The first in generations. A great blessing."

"Perhaps the time has come for plain speaking, Your Grace," Calum said.

She took back the portrait and returned it to its pouch. "My boy," she said, sounding weary, "sometimes there are things that cannot be changed—despite a longing that it might be otherwise. Too much would be lost."

"You know who I am, don't you?" He watched her closely.

The dowager avoided his eyes. "I'm certain you understand that family honor is inviolate," she said. "And some scandals could never be overcome."

"How could such a travesty have happened? How could I have been—"

"No!" She raised a hand. "Do not say it. Be certain that if such a thing truly occurred, it was without the knowledge of anyone who might have changed it." She looked at him fully now. "But also be certain that there are those who have wondered at certain things. I don't suppose you . . . Is there anything you feel you might show me? Anything you have been able to obtain?"

Even though she was telling him she would not acknowledge his claim, she wanted to be certain he had no proof, the kind of proof he'd hoped to get from Miranda. "I have nothing to show you."

There could be no mistaking the relief that softened her features. She smiled a little. "I thought not."

"And you will not recognize me?"

"You are no one I recognize," she said. "But I wish you well."

"You can do this thing?"

"I must do this or see my family made a laughingstock."

She leaned toward him. "I will say just this to you. If you were who you think you are, you would do anything to avoid the scandal such a revelation would represent."

Calum turned the pen in his hands. "So I am to sacrifice myself for the honor of a family that will not recognize me?"

"We understand each other. I wish I might have known you." She rose. "I shall find a way to compensate you to some extent."

"I want none of your money," he said through his teeth. "But I want Lady Philipa Chauncey."

The woman hesitated and drew herself up very straight. "Lady Philipa and my grandson will marry shortly—just as soon as she is recovered. That was agreed on the day of her birth. Do not try to see her. She is very weak and is to be protected from all excitement. Sleep. We will arrange for you to leave as soon as you are strong enough."

Calum remained by the fire after the dowager duchess had departed. Strength poured through him again. Strength, anger and determination. For the sake of his family's pride, he was to pretend he was not one of them. He could do that. He could *not* leave Pippa to the murderous devil who wanted her only for what her dowry would bring him.

The door, opening again, and hurriedly this time, brought Calum to his feet. He put the chair between him and his visitor.

Confronted with Franchot in a dressing robe, Calum had to ball his fists on the back of his chair to stop himself from taking the other man by the throat.

"I came to thank you," Franchot said. His lips curled. "To thank you and to warn you. I have been informed of your dangerous plot against my family. I had feared you had some designs here, but nothing could have prepared me for anything so fantastic."

"Fantastic?" Calum returned the other man's stare without blinking. "You think so?"

"Enough of this. We helped each other from the sea, and for that, we owe each other a debt of thanks. I am discharging mine."

"*Helped each other*?" Calum laughed with bitter disbelief. "You tried to drown me. *I* should have allowed *you* to drown."

"You will leave now," Franchot said. "Hunsingore and his brats will go with you. And unless you wish to be held to public ridicule, you will never speak of this again."

"I want Pippa," Calum said shortly. "And I intend to have her."

Franchot's expression changed from anger to pity. "Ah, I should have thought of this. Do not think of her further, Innes. She is not meant for you."

"She was always meant for me."

"She will *never* be yours."

Calum started around the chair and Franchot's hand went to the doorknob. "Philipa was glad to see me at the light-house," Franchot said. "She had been terrified to learn that it had been at your command that she was taken there and that you intended for her to die there."

"What are you saying, man?"

"Poor Philipa. Such a shock to discover that the man who had declared his affection for her would sacrifice her. When I told her that it had been your plan to make it appear that I killed her because she believed you bore the right to my title and lands—and that I was also supposed to die so that you could claim that prize, she came to me willingly and with gratitude."

Calum pushed the chair from him and it fell to its side. "I don't believe you."

Franchot laughed. "Of course not. I'm probably lying. But I was at the lighthouse for some hours before you came looking for my passionate little fiancée. Ah, yes, a delightful surprise indeed. If the seas had cooperated, we would be far from here and already married. That situation will soon be remedied."

"She would not," Calum said. "Not willingly."

"Willingly?" Franchot opened the door. "Don't tell me you have not noted that the lady is *spirited*. In her relief at being rescued from your designs, she was *most* generous with her gratitude toward me."

Calum rushed at him.

"Do not try to touch her," Franchot said. "She is probably already carrying my child. The *next* Duke of Franchot."

The door slammed in Calum's face.

🌺 Twenty-Eight

Within the hour Calum was ready to leave. He went in search of Struan and found him in the nursery wing with Max.

"You should be sleeping," Struan said when he saw Calum.

Calum nodded at Max. "So should he. But no doubt you've been informed we're to *disappear*."

Struan, sitting beside Max on the lad's bed, propped his elbows and steepled his fingers. "Justine was the messenger," he said. "She is as good as a prisoner in this great house, yet sees no way out."

"She told you . . ."

"Everything. The story of the cauls. About the portraits. Her grandmother's insistence that there be no more discussion of your claims."

"Justine believes me, doesn't she?"

"Possibly," Struan said. "Franchot was with Pippa at the lighthouse, then?"

Calum glanced at the boy. "Justine *told* you that?"

"She said the dowager intimated that Franchot rescued Pippa and that they are now close. She said the old woman spoke of your having been discredited to Pippa and that a hasty marriage to Franchot had become imperative for the sake of her honor."

"So it is to end this way," Calum said.

345

"Perhaps not entirely. Max has been telling me about his mother."

Calum went to sprawl in a lumpy armchair. "I'm sorry about your mother, Max. Where is Ella?"

"With Saber," Max said promptly.

Calum narrowed his eyes. "It's night. In God's name, what can you be thinking of, Struan?"

"I'm assured by Saber that he thinks of Ella as the sister he never had. He is also answerable to me for her safety. He has returned with her to the fair, where there is someone she has said she must see again. I gave my permission. I'd have gone myself, but I knew you would need me when you awoke."

"I must get away from this place," Calum said, resting his head against the chair back. "Perhaps I may come with you to Dorset for a while. Surely there we can find a place for these children."

"Ella blames herself for her mother's death," Struan told him. "She is convinced that if she had not run away from Mrs. Lushbottam's, she might have found a way to help Miranda."

Calum sat up abruptly. "Help Miranda?"

"Miranda. She died of a fever shortly after leaving that house. Ella discovered this at the fair."

"Miranda died?" Calum was beyond emptiness. "Poor woman. What had she to do with Ella—or her mother?"

"*Think*, man."

Calum's vision slowly, acutely, focused. "*Miranda* was Ella's mother?"

"And mine," Max said. "But I was sent away when I was a little 'un. They couldn't afford me. What's goin' to 'appen to us now?"

"First you will learn to speak like a gentleman," Struan said severely. "And then we shall decide your fate. Something with black dogs chained to ghosts might be in order."

Calum couldn't smile.

Footsteps clamored on the stairs outside and Saber Avenall burst into the room. At the sight of Calum, he stopped and took a pace backward.

"Saber," Calum said, nodding.

Avenall appeared speechless.

"Where is Ella?" Struan asked.

"In the green drawing room," Saber said. "There's someone with her. Ella told her how she came to be here at the castle . . . and the rest of the story you shared with us tonight." He approached Calum, but still didn't address him.

"We'd best join Ella in the green drawing room, hadn't we?" Struan asked.

"Yes."

"Very well. Remain here until I send for you, Max."

"But—"

"*Remain* here."

Calum got to his feet and his eyes locked with Saber's. He made to pass, but the other man caught his arm.

"What is it?" Calum asked.

"I can't believe it," Saber said. "But I want to. Come. Servants have gone for the rest of them. They may be curious enough to be timely."

Pippa leaned on Nelly's arm and made her way to the green drawing room as steadily as her weakened limbs allowed. Saber had sent for her on a matter of great importance. And, so Nelly said, Lady Justine was also to be there.

"Why could Justine not come to me herself?" Pippa asked. And why could she not simply close her eyes and die—and be finished with all of this?

"I wasn't told the reasons, my lady. But the dowager's been summoned, too. And the duke, I shouldn't wonder."

Pippa swayed. "I cannot face him. I cannot." Not when she suspected that he was a villain more black than any she could have imagined.

"Here we are," Nelly said in hushed tones. "Now, you lift up your pretty chin and don't let any of them see you're anything but your own self."

"I shall never again be my own self," Pippa said, but she raised her chin and took her hand from Nelly's arm before walking into the drawing room.

Justine hovered near Ella, but neither the dowager nor the duke was present. Pippa stared at the only other occupant of the room, a veiled woman in flowing blue robes.

"What's all this?" Franchot, wrapped in a red dressing robe, joined them. "I'm a sick man and I've suffered enough for one day. There had better be a good explanation for this intrusion."

He did not acknowledge Pippa.

"Sit down, Etienne," Justine said tartly, then guided Pippa to a chair near the fire. "Sit quietly, my dear Philipa. I believe you will be glad."

Pippa could not take her eyes from the veiled woman.

Grumbling, attended by two harried maids, the dowager arrived and refused to be seated. "What do you have to say for yourself, Justine?" she inquired, planting her ebony cane firmly on the carpet. "How dare you create a stir on a day such as this."

Ella, her eyes swollen, retreated to a corner, but at the sight of Saber, who strode in with Struan at his right hand, her eyes brightened.

"You are Sybel," Pippa said to the woman in blue. "You are the fortune teller from the fair."

"Fortune teller?" the dowager repeated in disbelieving tones. "My own home is become a fairground."

"We visited you. Calum and I visited you at the fair."

The woman rose slowly, looking not at Pippa, but at the last man to enter the room.

Calum. But the dowager had told her he was dead!

"Stop this!" The dowager duchess trembled visibly. "Who is to blame for this masquerade? *You*?" she said to Calum.

"*I* was responsible," the woman Sybel said. She pointed at Calum. "He was an infant and his mother's body was not yet cold. I took him from his cradle in this castle and left the other one in his place."

Franchot groped for a hold on a nearby chair. "Get this madwoman out of here."

Sybel shook her head and approached him. "Your mother's name was Florence Hawkins. We knew each other in a certain house in London. It was there that some of us were forced to go from time to time when there was no other way to live.

"Florence caught the eye of the former Duke of Franchot. But Florence caught many eyes. When she was increasing with you, she thought that if you were a boy, the duke could be

made to accept you as his own. At that time he had a baby
daughter and no son and heir. She became obsessed with the
idea that the duke should force his wife to pretend you were
her own child. Florence was convinced that, out of his gratitude, the duke would then install her in great splendor somewhere.''

"Heresy," Franchot said. "Remove her."

"The duke laughed at Florence," Sybel continued. "He
said, correctly, that you were most definitely not his child—
that he had not known Florence for such a time that no unborn
offspring of hers could possibly be his. And then he revealed
that his wife would bear her second child at much the same
time as you were to be born. And that is how all this came
about. The duke had a son of his own, and so did Florence.
She would not give up her rage at him. But in the end, the
fault is entirely mine, and I have suffered greatly for it. I took
gold for the crime Florence asked me to commit. It was her
intention to reap her reward when her son assumed the title.''

The woman looked at Calum. "The only thing I did not do
for the gold I was paid was to kill you. Guido said I should
never be able to do that and he was right. I took you with me
and we traveled with the fairs. Until you got so sick. Then I
had to leave you where you might be cared for.'' She removed
the veil and smiled. "I am glad you grew so strong and fair
and that the people of Kirkcaldy were so good to you.''

"You are Rachel," Calum said. "The snake man's assistant!''

"I *was* Rachel. Now I am Sybel, or I am if you will allow
me to remain so.''

"My God!" Franchot moved suddenly, approaching Pippa
with horror in his light eyes. He touched her face, took her
hands in his and sank to his knees beside her chair. "This is
even more desperate a plot than I had imagined, my love. This
woman has been paid to come forward with this amazing nonsense.''

Pippa tried to remove her hands, but he held her too tightly.

"Grandmama," he said, "we cannot allow this in our
home. This female is a fortune teller who used to be a snake
man's assistant!'' He cast his eyes dramatically upward, and
his lips moved as if in silent prayer.

Pippa looked at Calum, who stared back as if she were unknown to him.

A furor arose outside the drawing room and the doors burst open to admit the steward, Figerall. "Your Grace," he said to the dowager, his eyes popping, "I could not stop . . . them." The steward's voice trailed off.

"They" were Lady Hoarville, the pink satin of her swans-down-trimmed traveling costume splattered with mud, and an exceedingly tall, plain woman dressed entirely in black and wearing a quantity of unbecoming rouge.

"Bloody hell," Viscount Hunsingore muttered.

The rest were silent, except for a moan from Ella and the loud, umbrage-filled breathing of the dowager.

"So it is true," Lady Hoarville said, glaring at Franchot. "You thought you could abandon me and that I should leave without a whimper."

Franchot's hands became as cold stone on Pippa's. She noted what she had not seen at first. Lady Hoarville held a pistol to the other woman's side.

"*Who* is *that*?" the dowager finally asked, pointing her cane at the stranger.

When no one answered, Viscount Hunsingore said, "A lady, er, tailor, Your Grace. She runs the establishment where I assume Rachel and Florence Hawkins met."

"And Cora Bains," Rachel said. "Anabel's mother."

Lady Hoarville, her hair tangled in her swansdown collar, glared around before returning her venomous gaze to Franchot. "Now you shall pay. *All* of you shall pay me for what I know, because, unless you do, the world will learn the aberration that is the family of Franchot."

Franchot jerked to his feet, releasing Pippa as he did so. "Anabel, my dear friend. Thank goodness you have returned. I was so concerned—"

"I helped my poor old husband leave his world of pain a little early so that I might stand at your side as your duchess," Lady Hoarville said. "Just as you *helped* Florence Hawkins to a more peaceful place to make certain she could not interfere with—"

"My dear"—the woman in black spoke for the first time—"I do advise you not to do this."

Lady Hoarville's response was to jab the pistol with enough force to produce a noisy groan.

"My mother told me all I know," Lady Hoarville said. "Unfortunately, she also had to go to a better place because she insisted upon interfering. A great deal of effort has been expended, and *now I want what I've worked for*."

"Anabel, I beg you to be circumspect," Franchot said. His step in the furious woman's direction earned him a momentary view down her pistol barrel. He promptly subsided beside Pippa once more.

"This—" Lady Hoarville poked her unfortunate prisoner again. "This traitor was preparing to sneak away, having left me a note. A *note*, mark you. Informing me that I was to remove myself permanently from your life unless you chose to contact me. Etienne, how could you?"

"I . . ." Franchot swallowed audibly.

"You do not even try to defend yourself, so I have no alternative, do I?"

Standing on tiptoe, she tore out the black comb that secured an ugly lace mantilla to a chignon atop the other woman's head. The chignon came away with the comb, and a sparse quantity of rather long hair, obviously dyed black, fell around the cadaverously thin face. Lady Hoarville used the lace headpiece to wipe away rouge from sunken cheeks, and blacked eyebrows applied to ponderous, hairless bones.

"No, no," Franchot whimpered, covering his face.

Pippa shrank back in her chair and felt a deep shudder. It was *him*.

"Tell them who you are," Lady Hoarville instructed. "Then we shall discuss an appropriate settlement for the indignities and inconveniences I have suffered at the hands of *some. Tell them*!"

"I'm Lushbottam," the man said sullenly, flinching with each fresh assault of Lady Hoarville's weapon. "And I'm his father." He pointed at Franchot.

"No," Franchot murmured. "Grandmama, please."

"He's my son by Florence Hawkins, and if you nobs don't give this lady what she wants, I'll tell anyone who wants to listen."

The dowager turned her back on Lady Hoarville. Pippa saw

Calum widen his stance and flex his hands. Viscount Hunsingore shifted slightly, never taking his eyes off the woman with the pistol.

"I think you have done quite enough, my gel," the dowager said, swinging around with remarkable agility. In one hand she held a wickedly pointed blade, and this she applied with a very steady hand to Lady Hoarville's neck. "Take the pistol, one of you. Not you, Etienne. Calum, do it."

He moved quickly to do as the old lady asked.

"You wouldn't dare," Lady Hoarville said, and squeezed her eyes shut when the tip of the blade made a tiny cut on her white neck.

Laughter threatened to bubble from Pippa. The dowager had produced her blade from the ivory-handled ebony cane she carried whenever she was displeased. And she now displayed the calm of a seasoned soldier faced with just one more battle.

"St. Luc," the dowager said, her lip curling. "Where is that creature?"

"Left me," Lady Hoarville whined. "We were waiting for Etienne at an inn—only he never came. And Henri caught the eye of a prince traveling from some Eastern place. *And* he took the emeralds dear old Hoarville gave me."

At a command from the dowager, Figerall was dispatched to round up the burliest of the castle staff. When these arrived, they were charged with placing Lady Hoarville and Lushbottam in a safe place until "a suitable destination" could be found for them. They were to be closeted together—with Franchot.

He went silently, and for that Pippa was grateful. Lady Hoarville could be heard shrieking threats for some time.

"Grief," Saber said when peace finally settled. "What a pickle." He draped a protective arm around Ella's shoulders.

"*Pickle*?" the dowager said, and addressed Rachel. "You have wronged us—but you have now done us a great service and I believe you have suffered enough. There would appear to be no reason to involve you further. Etienne . . . He and that woman will implicate each other without you. You may go."

Rachel inclined her head and swept from the room without another word.

"Well, now." The Dowager Duchess of Franchot sheathed

her blade and gave the closest thing to a smile Pippa had ever seen. "We must deal with this little *contretemps* with the least fuss possible. Obviously there will have to be a trial. These criminal charges must be addressed—but swiftly and finally. The sooner any gossip can be put to rest, the better."

Saber gave a barking laugh. "There'll be enough gossip for a lifetime in this lot."

That earned him a raised brow from the dowager. "We must arrange a small but selectively well-attended wedding. I will inform certain people at once." She considered. "It shall take place—hmm—a week from next Tuesday morning. That should give time for a few important witnesses to arrive. We must make certain the world sees how united we Franchots are in all this."

"Marriage?" Pippa said faintly.

"Of course. I'm so happy for you my dear. And for . . . for you, Grandson." For the first time there was the vaguest waver in the woman's eyes as she looked at Calum.

He shook his head. "I hardly think you will find it so easy to arrange such a marriage, Your Grace." Still he avoided meeting Pippa's gaze. "Certainly not until there has been an official investigation and some ruling by the Lords."

The dowager gave a haughty shrug. "Nonsense. My influence goes beyond the Lords. This will be accomplished handily and you'll be married with *royal* blessing."

For the first time in many hours, Pippa found the energy to be truly angry. She pushed to her feet and, disdaining the hand Justine rushed to offer, marched toward the door. "Royal blessing or no," she said, "I shall *never* marry that oaf."

"For the sake of your honor, my dear, I think you will," Calum said, his harsh voice drawing her to a halt. When she faced him, he said, "I should prefer a more faithful, tender bride, but no doubt we shall manage tolerably well."

Viscount Hunsingore swept up a crystal decanter of brandy and began pouring generous measures into glass after glass. "A toast would seem in order." He raised a goblet and drank deeply without waiting for any to join him. "To my eternal gratitude that *I* was born a younger son!"

❧ Twenty-Nine

From a distance came the sounds of revelry. Music—the strains of violin and harp—soared.

The celebration of a wedding. His own and his new wife's.

Calum tried not to look at Pippa.

They sat—he and Pippa; Arran, Marquess of Stonehaven, and his blond wife, Grace—beneath the domed ceiling of a small jewel of a salon on the floor above the ballroom where, presided over by the dowager, the "select" festivities were now in progress.

Playful Italianate *putti* frolicked across the salon's gilt-and-painted ceiling. Furnishings that had once belonged to a Dauphin echoed the art's opulence.

All his.

He was in hell.

"Too bad of Struan to leave like that," Arran said when the silence had stretched to an agony. "Seems to have a habit of popping out at inconvenient moments."

"He remained as long as he could, Arran," Grace said, sounding exceedingly worried. Her lovely brown eyes were clouded as she addressed her husband. "He assured me he could not wait another moment to leave for Dorset with those dear children."

"Struan is angry with me," Calum said, "although I cannot imagine why."

Arran grunted.

Calum did look at Pippa then.

From the frightful night after they'd almost drowned together until this morning in the castle chapel, they had not encountered each other. Calum had seen his bride approach him as if through a Scottish highland mist—all softness and dew, a veil upon her loveliness. And then their vows, which should have made him the happiest man in the world, had become distant mouthings.

Her gown was simple. Stark white tulle over satin, square at the neck and with long, tight sleeves. Pearls and rosebuds caught the tulle hem into puffs that revealed satin beneath, and strands of the same pearls were threaded through her black hair. Calum wondered that she had not chosen to wear the fabulous Chauncey diamonds on such an occasion. But then, she was not a woman concerned with public display.

"Does something about me trouble you, Your Grace?" she asked.

Calum started and gazed into her magnificent blue eyes. "Nothing more than we are already aware of, *Your Grace*."

"God give me patience," Arran muttered.

"He will, He will," Grace said, slipping her small hand into his huge one.

"Nice of my *grandmama* to arrange this charmingly intimate little respite from the revelry," Calum said.

Grace made a humming sound. "She is being thoughtful, Calum. We all know what a trying time you and Pippa have had."

Arran and Grace had arrived with baby Elizabeth two days previous and had tirelessly—and without success—attempted to bring about a reconciliation between Pippa and Calum.

"Should you like a little champagne, Pippa?" Grace asked, getting up and taking a glass from a silver tray. "And a small cake, perhaps. I declare, you have eaten absolutely nothing and you will need your strength for . . . Oh." She blushed madly.

"Nothing, thank you," Pippa said.

She was so lovely. Calum pressed down the urge to take her in his arms. But she had allowed her faith in him to be shaken. And God knew what else she had allowed. "Did that man make love to you?'' he blurted out, unable to hold back the question an instant longer.

Grace plopped down beside Arran, who directed a glare at Calum that should have frozen his heart and anything else that lived within him.

"Well," Calum persisted, "did he?"

"How could you?" Pippa whispered, and he saw the sheen of tears in her eyes.

He bowed his head. "On that night, the night when you were taken, you had told me you thought I only wanted you for selfish reasons. You doubted me. And you believed *him* when he said I had arranged for your abduction."

"I didn't know what to believe."

"Truly a marriage made in heaven," Arran remarked. "It grows late. Perhaps it's time for you to retire to wedded bliss."

"*Arran*," Grace hissed.

A discreet knock announced the dowager's arrival. Dark mauve had replaced black for the occasion of the wedding, and she smiled benevolently upon the four in the room. "I hope you are enjoying yourselves. Justine is assuming command quite nicely below so that I can come and read you two messages I've received."

Pippa brought a white-gloved hand to her face and Calum saw that her fingers shook. How would they ever overcome this disaster?

"Philipa," the dowager said, holding a piece of paper in one hand, "I know you will be relieved to know that my letter—actually, the letter I wrote some weeks ago—reached your father. Good fortune brought his reply on this very day. Dear Lord Chauncey sends you his felicitations and says that since the wedding formalities would be complete before he could make the return journey from the Continent, he wishes to be informed of the birth of your first child. He will definitely be present then."

Calum noted that the white-clad fingers covered Pippa's mouth now, but she gave no other sign of emotion.

"Well," Grace said with a puff, "*I* think that's perfectly dreadful."

"Grace," Arran said mildly.

"Well, I do. I know how it can be to have a less-than-supportive parent. Never mind, Pippa. *I* shall do my very best to help you in any way I can, and I know Lady Justine is equally devoted.''

"Thank you," Pippa said.

There were tears on her lashes now. They sparkled like those damnable diamonds.

"Yes, well," the dowager said. "And this is the really important letter. It came by special messenger not half an hour since. I am *so* excited, and I know you will be, too.''

He needed to hold Pippa.

"This"—the dowager duchess flourished a piece of creamy parchment—"is from the King himself. Stand up, both of you. It is only fitting.''

Pippa got up immediately and Calum followed. He noted that Arran and Grace also rose.

"Take your husband's arm, Philipa. This is the appropriate note to send you forth to bear fruit.''

Calum winced at the woman's insensitivity. Then he straightened his spine and offered Pippa his arm. She placed a hand upon it. Standing close, he could not help but gaze, as he had in the chapel, upon his bride's skin, so soft and almost as white as her gown against the lustrous darkness of her hair. Her damp black lashes were lowered now, and her full lips trembled before she set them firmly.

In a sudden burst of motion, Arran went around the dowager and opened the door.

"In time you shall be privy to your family's long history of faithful service to your country," the Dowager Duchess of Franchot said. "Those years of service are justly rewarded now.''

Calum was not ready for his first family history lesson. "I'm glad," he said politely.

"All matters of legality are discharged," the old lady said, reading. "That is what he says. You, Calum, are to assume your rightful title." She beamed. "In time you will become comfortable with the name with which you were baptized. Until then, of course, you must use whatever name pleases you.''

"Thank you," he said, glancing at Arran. "I shall always choose to be called Calum by those who are close to me.''

"Perhaps." Clearly the dowager was not in the mood to be

less than generous. "But here are the words that you must take with you to your marriage bed. 'The King bestows a royal blessing upon your wedding and upon your marriage.' *There*." She stood at her full, diminutive height and held the missive to her bosom.

Calum finally made his feet move and approached the door.

"A blessing from the King!" Grace said, and he heard desperation in her voice.

He looked at Pippa and said, "A blessing from the King? It seems I shall need it."

The full force of her blue gaze blazed upon him and she snatched her hand away. "It will do you no good."

Whatever Arran did, he must not remind Calum that he himself had been a fool who needed a thrashing even before the day of his marriage to Grace.

"I behaved like a fool on my wedding day," Arran said and smiled secretly. There were special moments when pride must be sacrificed for the greater good.

"Are you suggesting that *I* am behaving like a fool?" Calum asked. Minus his wedding coat and neckcloth and with his back to Arran, he stood with his arms braced on the windowsill in the small study that was part of the quarters he'd chosen over the existing ducal apartments.

"I'm suggesting you are not seeing things quite clearly. Through there"—he pointed toward Calum's bedchamber, toward the door that led to Pippa's rooms—"through there lies your wife, man. Use your head and claim her."

"She does not trust me."

"I believe she does."

"You do not understand all that has taken place here."

"I understand enough. *Claim* her, man."

"I do not need to be told when to take my own wife. It shall be in good time."

"Good time is now."

Calum swung to face him and picked up a glass of champagne, one that Arran had poured from a bottle left for the bridal couple. "There is no haste in this thing," Calum said, and drained the glass before pouring another. "I am assuming this place that is rightfully mine under the suffrage of my family. There will be a great deal of adjustment to be made.''

"Lady Justine and young Lord Avenall could not be more delighted than to claim you,'' Arran reminded Calum. "And that old—the dowager is a narrow woman who has made her family's pride the reason for her existence. She will give you what affection she is capable of giving anyone. Your bride will give you enough affection for all—enough for you to drown in, friend.''

"You heard her last words to me,'' Calum said. "She told me I should need more than the King's blessing this night. Very well. I find I've not the stomach for disdain from my wife just now. And things that are a matter of duty must only be accomplished as the need arises.''

Arran smiled. "Are you telling me the need doesn't *arise* every time you look at that lovely creature?''

"I am telling you nothing.'' The glass descended sharply to its tray and Calum proceeded to all but tear off his sash, waistcoat and shirt. "I am tired. I'm going to bed.''

"Tell me one thing, and I'll leave.''

"Anything. Just give me peace.''

"Do you love her?''

His childhood friend was not quick enough in assuming his mask. Before Calum's expression faded, Arran saw naked longing in those familiar dark eyes.

Sighing, he pushed himself away from the mantel and picked up his own coat. "Say no more,'' he told Calum. "Unrequited love makes a tormenting bed partner. I wish you joy in it.''

Grace would regard this as practice for when she was called upon to instruct Elizabeth in matters of the world. "He is a bridegroom,'' she said to Pippa. "That is all this is about.''

"He hates me.''

Oh, dear. "He does not hate you. Quite the reverse. I have certain otherworldly instincts and I *know* these things.''

Some mild interest flickered in the other woman's eyes. "You do?''

"Oh, yes. Arran—the marquess—had absolutely no faith in my gifts until they were proven several times. I would tell you about some of them—and I will, when there is time.''

"There is time."

"Not now. We have more important matters to attend to. Calum loves you deeply. And you love him deeply."

"*Bother*."

"I beg your pardon?"

To Grace's discomfort, Pippa began to cry quietly. "I said, bother. It is *all* such a bother. You are right. I do love him. But he believed that I believed ill of him, and that shows no trust. He also thought I might have ... Well, he thought I might have allowed some intimate behavior with Franchot— the man we thought was Franchot. How can I forgive him for as much as considering such a thing?"

"You can forgive him. You are both the victims of such extraordinary circumstances, but now they are over. It is time to share the gift of your love."

"*Posh*."

"I beg your pardon?"

"The dowager says it. I've never liked the word, but it does seem to fit the moment."

Grace removed the chocolate pot she'd been heating on a trivet by the fire in Pippa's bedchamber and poured two small cups. One she handed to Pippa. "Warm yourself. We have a deal of discussing to get through, and it must be accomplished quickly. You need the restorative properties chocolate offers. My husband has had to learn to use chocolate in such circumstances. Fortunately, it is something he has loved since childhood, so he is always pleased when I insist he turn from his work a while. He's a composer, you know. He writes the most marvelous music ... Oh, I am such a chatterer—everybody says so. Forgive me."

"You are the sweetest creature," Pippa said.

Grace flushed a little with pleasure. "I feel a charge is upon me that I assist you and Calum through this difficult situation."

"I expect your own wedding was purely a fairy tale. I am certain the marquess showed his adoration for you then as he does with every look now."

Grace's heart squeezed with joy. Then she remembered and said, "Arran used to be a blockhead. An arrogant, self-important noddycock in need of learning a good lesson."

Pippa's mouth dropped open a little. "Really?"

"Yes, and . . ." Grace had to be absolutely truthful. "And I was more than a little silly myself, but that is all another story. I will tell you, very briefly, that our wedding began as a dream and very nearly ended in disaster. Yet you see how we have overcome."

"You adore each other. That is evident."

"And it is true. Just as you and Calum adore each other."

Pippa's lower lip trembled and Grace feared the tears would flow again. "You see how his adoration has brought him to me this night?" Pippa said. "Obviously he is already taking his rest and has entirely forgotten me."

Grace took an invigorating sip of her own chocolate and regarded Pippa. "I am going to be your mother tonight. That is, I am going to do what your mother would have done had she been here."

Still dressed in her exquisite gown, Pippa resembled a beautiful, forlorn child and showed no confidence in the assistance Grace offered.

"Yes, well," Grace said, setting aside her cup and getting up to examine the night rail and robe that had been spread upon the bed in preparation for the wedding night. "This is a magical thing. A gown meant for dancing in the moonlight. Calum has always had a great eye for beauty and he will love the very sight of you in this."

A glance at Pippa's pink and averted face warned Grace to be more cautious. "Let us speak plainly of the problems at hand."

"You must be tired," Pippa said. "I've detained you far too long already."

"*Posh.* No, I don't care for that word, either. I take it the dowager has been responsible for your instructions in wifely behavior?"

"Oh, bother," Pippa said softly.

"Exactly," Grace said. "I imagine she did make it all sound quite a bother. You are not to believe a word of it."

"I don't."

Startled, Grace returned to take another sip of chocolate. "You don't believe the dowager's instructions?"

"That wifely duties are frightful and to be borne without

complaint despite inevitable suffering? No. Of course not.''

"I see.'' Grace puffed up her cheeks and exhaled slowly.
"Well, that is certainly a very splendid beginning. Because
they certainly are not. As to the matter of Calum's behavior . . .
Becoming a bridegroom has provoked an attack of nervous
sickness. That is it, pure and simple. I shall always believe
some of Arran's strange behavior was the result of nervous
sickness.''

Pippa's brow furrowed. "Nervous? Calum?''

"Why, certainly! He has a great responsibility. It is his task
to ensure that all goes smoothly between the two of you. After
all, he is the man. He is the one who thinks he must lead in
all things.'' Grace wrinkled her nose. "Men can be such perfect cabbage heads.''

"Can't they just?'' Pippa said, shaking her head. "Calum
is the most cabbage-headed of all.''

"Will you allow me to guide you?''

"I really don't think—''

"Good. That is just as it should be. You will not think, and
I will think for you. Let us get you into your beautiful, gos-
samer night rail.''

"Why?''

"Because you are going to go to him.''

"I cannot!''

"You most definitely can. Up with you. Begin as you mean
to continue. All that is necessary in the management of these
things is to allow men to *think* they lead us. Allow them to
stride about assuming they are the heads of their households.
We are the true leaders, my dear friend. And with my help,
you will begin exactly as you will be happy to continue with
this new husband of yours.''

Pippa rose silently and suffered through Grace's ministrations until she was dressed in a gown and robe that together
were still as transparent as cobwebs. Grace turned discreetly
aside so as not to embarrass the young bride.

"Now we are ready to proceed. I imagine Calum will have
partaken of a measure or two of strong drink. One hopes not
too much, because I understand that can have most undesirable
effects.''

"What undesirable effects?'' Pippa asked anxiously.

"That discussion is entirely too advanced as yet. Let us pass on. Calum will be in his bed—or so I imagine—and he may most likely have fallen asleep. You will learn that men have another facility most women do not seem to possess. Whilst we remain awake and desolate over our troubles, they manage to set their troubles aside and fall into a deep slumber almost at once."

"So what purpose would be served by my going to him?"

Grace braced herself to be strong. "You will . . . hmm. You will *arouse* him."

Pippa's lips pursed.

"There are certain ways by which a male may—without exception, almost—be caused to want his wife. *Want* is what a husband feels toward his wife in such moments when his body, and sometimes his mind, wish to be . . . hmm. When he wishes to *join* with you."

Pippa's face cleared and she nodded. "Ah, yes. Of course."

Grace frowned. "There are *touches* which are guaranteed to produce a response in these—"

"Yes. Yes, quite." Pippa looked toward the door that led to the dressing room and Calum's room beyond. "And you think I should . . . you think I *should*?"

"I think you *absolutely* should. And I think I can promise that Calum will be a most considerate husband. Of course, men have . . . *appetites*. The odd thing is that they think their appetites are not necessarily matched by their wives. Fortunately, Arran and I have passed that . . . *Oh, dear.*"

"I expect they think this matter of appetites is closely related to the matter of the giving of their seed," Pippa remarked.

Grace stared.

"You have been most helpful," Pippa said. She picked up her chocolate cup, drained it and faced the dressing room. "I shall follow your instructions."

"But I did not finish—"

"I assure you I am well informed—via my studies." Ethereal in her lovely gown, Pippa approached the dressing room. "Thank you for giving me the courage to do what must be done. I shall go to him now. And I am prepared to receive

Calum's seed as often and for as long as is required to bring forth fruit.''

When the dressing room door closed behind Pippa, Grace found she must sit a moment before going in search of Arran. And when she did return to him, she would definitely need more chocolate.

❦ Thirty

$\mathcal{C}$*alum's bed* sheets had become twisted ropes that bound his blazing body. A small breeze through the open casement did no more than grow warm on his hot skin.

Sleep began to claim him, a fitful, drowning sleep. Darkness slipped upward past his seething brain and he grew still at last.

Faint sounds came to him, the settlings of a strange room in an ancient castle.

A soft hand rested on his ankle.

Now there were to be tormenting spirits in his unkind dreams.

The hand smoothed upward to his knee, then slipped behind and passed over his calf to return to his ankle once more.

Somewhere deep within him, Calum shuddered. He rolled his face toward the windows and willed his nerves to release him from this torment. Sweet torment.

From ankle to knee went the fingers once more. And a second hand began a similar ministration to his other leg.

The outsides of his thighs stiffened under this feathery touch.

And the insides of his thighs.

He was not asleep.

Carefully, he turned back just far enough to look down upon a figure in white that stood beside his bed.

She had come to him.

Slowly, she straightened, and he saw how the moonlight

turned her tall, slight body to a tender, shapely silhouette inside some garment of wispy white.

She did not know he watched her.

She did not know, because *she* watched *him* . . . part of him.

His shaft, already erect, leaped beneath her intent scrutiny.

When she touched it, lightly, with a single fingertip, he clamped his jaw closed and felt sweat bead on his brow.

Then he heard her sigh—a sigh that was not at all unhappy.

Her fingertip passed along the length of him, from stretched tip, over distended veins, to the dense hair at the base.

And then she retraced her path.

Calum held his breath and prayed for guidance.

Another small sigh reached him. Pippa surrounded and stroked him downward until she met hair again, and this time she extended her explorations further, weighing and testing every male contour as if memorizing him for some future purpose.

He shut his eyes, tried and failed to contain a grimace that was pure, ecstatic excitement, and forced himself not to reach for her.

The next sensation he felt brought his eyes wide open. Pippa's silken hair spread across his belly, slithered over his thighs, and she drew his shaft between her lips and deep into her mouth.

Calum groaned aloud.

Such things did not happen—except in the maddened minds of men about to die of frustration on their wedding nights. Wedding nights when they were denied the presence of their brides.

He was dreaming.

Her cool hands grasped his hips. She withdrew her mouth—and within only a moment buried him once more in the moist magic beyond her marvelous lips.

Not a dream.

"Pippa," he groaned. "In God's name, woman, what are you trying to do to me?"

He pushed himself to his elbows and she lifted her head. Her face was all shadows, but her eyes caught the moonlight. "You are the head of this household," she said breathlessly. "And it is my duty to ensure that your needs are met."

"But how," he scarcely dared ask, "how do you know these things? The things you do?" Surely there was only one way.

"You find this unpleasant?" Her anxiousness might have made him laugh—at some other time.

"I find it most *pleasant*."

"Oh, good. I could only guess you might."

He could no longer stop himself from touching her hair, from stroking her face, her neck—from dropping his hand to cup her breast. She gasped and he smiled a little. "You are such a puzzle, my lady. Why would you be guessing at such a thing?"

"I was blessed with so much time alone at Dowanhill," she said. "That is how I was fortunate enough to find the books. I didn't realize then just how fortunate, but I do now."

"Books?"

"In my father's library. Not intended for me, of course, but perhaps fate did plan that I should see them, since I had no other source of instruction in such things."

"No." If she continued to fondle him, he would surely disgrace himself.

"Unfortunately, the book with the most useful drawings was written in a language with which I am not familiar. But the drawings were very well done. I am doing this correctly, am I not?"

"So very correctly." He could well imagine the kind of texts her young eyes had happened upon.

"Good. You are most beautifully made. But that is what I had surmised from my studies of you." Promptly, she began to take him into her mouth once more.

"Studies of *me*?" His voice broke.

Pippa couldn't answer him.

"Stop!" With one fluid motion, he sat up, caught her beneath the arms and lifted her to the bed. Depositing her against the pillows beside him, he stared down into her face. "What made you come to me tonight?"

"Someone had to help you through your attack of nervous sickness."

He shook his head in quiet disbelief. "My nervous sickness?"

"Bridegrooms invariably suffer the condition. Probably because they are so anxious about their brides having the fortitude to accept their seed often enough to bear fruit in a timely fashion. I assure you I am stronger than I appear. I shall accept and accept. I shall swallow all night if necessary. And then I expect we should wait and pray."

Calum dropped flat onto his back and covered his face. His rod ached, and his gut. His thighs strained. His brain struggled with the wonder of the woman who waited beside him.

At last he trusted himself to turn back to her, to draw her into his arms and kiss her with a tenderness that cost him dearly in restraint before her pure sweetness tempered his lust.

He caressed her hair, stroked her long, straight spine past the curve of her waist to the firm roundness of her hips. "Pippa," he murmured, "forgive me for being the fool."

She framed his face with hands that trembled. "We are blessed that we have been given to each other. And I am grateful my early instruction will help us so."

Calum smiled against her neck. "You are indeed well informed on some things, dearest. On others I fear you are hopelessly ignorant. However, because I love you to distraction, I shall spend the rest of this night, and tomorrow and possibly the next night and the next day—and who knows how many more—attending to your education."

I love you, I love you, I love you. "I love you," she told him.

"I know. And I thank you."

He stripped away her robe and her gown, and she felt no shame. He touched her in all the ways he had touched her before, and in so many more—and she felt awe.

And then there was *That*. It was absolutely as magical as she'd expected. Calum could even use it to make her feel the white-hot throbbing, the slipping away, that he'd created with his fingers and with his mouth.

So much to learn.

"Now," he whispered, his lips on her neck, "we shall see to the planting of the seed, my dearest love."

When she made to find his shaft with her mouth, he eased

her down upon the bed once more and rose over her. "No, sweetest. Not that way. *This* way."

He pressed himself against the hidden place that led into her body. He pressed and entered and stretched her. "Aah," she moaned, could not help moaning. There was a sheer, scalding shock of sensation, and a small pain, as if something within her had torn.

Calum grew still. "Can you bear it, sweet?"

"I cannot bear for it to stop," she told him.

He moved again, slowly, driving deep within her and pulling all but entirely away again, only to return, harder and harder each time.

Pippa arched her back, arched her breasts to Calum's hair-rough chest and dug her fingers into the iron muscles of his neck.

A wave of sensation broke. It broke and broke and rolled, rippling over her skin and through her flesh with a force that bore her along to a place where she was formless and one with the man above her.

He knelt beside her on the bed and soaked a soft linen cloth in warm water that had been discreetly left in his sitting room at some time during the night and day they had spent together here.

Many bowls of water had been left and removed. And tempting food and drink. Yet never had Pippa or Calum seen those who waited upon them.

"It's growing dark again," Pippa said drowsily.

Calum slowly bathed her face, her neck, and smoothed the cloth between her breasts. "We have not discussed our honeymoon," he said, smiling when her back arched beneath his ministrations. He did not kiss her breasts. That way led in one inevitable direction, and he would make himself wait just a little longer this time. "Honeymoon?" he said, settling a thumb on her lips.

"They usually last several months, don't they?" she said, whipping the linen from him before he could resist.

"Certainly," Calum said, gasping when the cooled cloth met his shoulder. "Yes, certainly several months would not be unreasonable."

"Oh, good. I've always thought a honeymoon should be memorable. Several months spent alone with you in this room should be entirely memorable, thank you."

"Pippa, I am serious."

"And so am I. You will need your time here to become accustomed to the very great demands your new life will place upon you."

He allowed her to sit up, rinse the linen and proceed to gently wash his body. "I shall be very capable of dealing with the matters of this estate, madam wife," he told her. "True, I have not been solely responsible for anything as extensive as is now my lot, but I'm considerably experienced."

"It was not the estate I had in mind, Your Grace. Mine are the demands you may find most taxing."

When Calum laughed, her whole world smiled. "I'm glad I amuse you so thoroughly," she said. "I am also glad you are to take your rightful place. But I confess I should not have cared at all what manner of life destiny gave us as long as we were allowed to share it."

He only smiled and smiled, and contrived to plant small, nipping kisses on every spot he could reach without tumbling them both from the bed.

"What is this thing?" She set the cloth aside and lifted the square of worn leather he wore on a thong about his neck.

"Something I was given to wear as a child. Our nurse at Kirkcaldy said it was a scapula that would keep me holy."

"Hah!" Pippa turned it over and looked closer. "Clearly it has not worked."

"You are disrespectful to me, wife."

She reached for the lamp and brought it near to see the faint inscription on the leather. "You must have replaced the thong many times."

"Boys grow into men. Many times."

"But the scapula is the one from your childhood?"

"I have already told you so."

"Calum, I think Justine's locket bears the same inscription. A bird, perhaps, with spread wings."

He grew still. "I had not studied Justine's locket." Slipping the leather from his neck, he put it into Pippa's hands. "It was tooled in gold once, I think. That faded long ago.''

She turned it over and examined the fine stitching that joined back to front. It was Calum who took a small knife from a tray bearing fruit and carefully slit the talisman in two.

Into his palm fell a small, pale thing, dried to papery whiteness. When Pippa touched it, she found the folds soft. ''What is it?'' she asked, and when she looked at his face, she knew he fought to speak.

''It is a caul,'' he said. ''I was born inside this. All the time I wore the proof of who I am.''

He glanced into her eyes. ''I will explain, but it will take a long time. For now, we will call it a gift from my mother, given to make certain I should one day come home.''

Calum took her hand and pressed it to his breast. ''What do you feel?''

''The beating of your heart,'' she whispered.

He rested his brow on hers. ''Do you hear it? Do you hear what I hear, Pippa?''

With her eyes closed, she listened. ''Yes.'' Her breathing speeded. ''Yes. A soft voice, like the sea?''

''Like the sea. My mother's voice.''

With their arms entwined, they listened.

''*I will bear you home!*''

THE MOST SENSUOUS VOICE
IN ROMANTIC FICTION
BRENDA JOYCE

"Brenda Joyce has a distinctive style
that captures and doesn't let go."
Johanna Lindsey